Nick Ashton-Jones has been a planter and a project manager; he remains an environmentalist, a writer who cannot help himself, and a psycho geographer and historian to the point of obsession. He has spent most of his working life in the tropics: in the South Pacific and in Southeast Asia, but mostly in Nigeria which is his second home, if not his first.

Nick was born in Sheffield, and educated in the West Country and by Newcastle and London universities. He has a son who is Swiss, he is based in Derby, and although he thinks the best bit of Britain is the Isle of Arran, he admits to being unavoidably English, from the top of his head to the soles of his boots. He now shares most of his life with David, an artist and illustrator.

Dedication

To Ken Wiwa, to others who know who they are, and to forgotten ideas.

Nick Ashton-Jones

ANNU

A novel about a journey

AUSTIN MACAULEY
PUBLISHERS LTD.

A CIP catalogue record for this title is available from the British Library.

ISBN 978 184963 689 6

www.austinmacauley.com

First Published (2014)
Austin Macauley Publishers Ltd.
25 Canada Square
Canary Wharf
London
E14 5LB

Printed and bound in Great Britain

APOLOGY

Some readers may think they recognise New Sudan and Van Island. However, these places are countries of my mind, although their literal geography is an amalgam of locations I know in the South Pacific and in West Africa. The same readers may also think that the Van Island Palm Oil Development Company refers to a company with a similar name that thrived on a large island (not the largest) in the South Pacific in the 1970s and 1980s. But while my memories of the company undoubtedly make it a useful setting, or should I say container, for the action of the novel, the same readers will agree that the company was a model of its kind, notable more for the humanity of its policies than otherwise. The general manager of the day was one of the few men I have known in my life whom I would describe as 'great'. What he taught me shaped my life. 'Whatever you do,' he told me, 30 years ago, 'be yourself. If you try to be something else, you'll have trouble'. He was right, and he was the antithesis of the GM in the novel here. The human condition I describe in Annu indeed comes in part from my twelve years in the South Pacific but my driving desire to write about man's inhumanity (and about his more rare humanity) to man mostly comes from my experience of the Niger Delta in the 1990s. The 'Andrew' of the novel bears no particular resemblance to the three Andrews who have played roles in my life: like all my characters, he came to me with a name attached that I was powerless to change.

Contents

Part I

Awake thou that sleepest, and arise from the dead

Ephesians 5, 14

Prologue

A grey, chill dawn. A rocky plateau, empty except for a single skeleton tree overhanging a ravine.

A black fruit bat hangs in the tree. Unusual because the place is lifeless and uninviting compared with the heaving forest below, early morning sounds of which invade the silence.

The morning passes.

About midday, the bat shits.

The sun blasts the rocky plateau from a white sky.

Despite the dead land, a life is begun.

[][][][][]

Single seed falls into ravine.

Lodges between two granite rocks.

A gamble: risky, one might say.

Dormant, destitute.

Maintaining, nonetheless, its chosen point in space and time.

[][][][][]

The scent of moisture comes up from the forest below.

Who tastes it?

The scent is made by the tasting of it.

Afternoon rain clears the horizon to a band of gold beneath retreating fury.

Who sees it?

The view is made by the seeing of it.

[][][][][]

Morning mists from the forest reach up into the ravine until they touch the seed. For a few hours each day the granite rocks are damp. The water and the dissolved minerals from the rocks nourish the seed which swells with life.

Sheltered from the afternoon sun, the ravine is dark and humid. The place smells of green life. The tiniest of spores, borne by the wind, settle here and grow. Now, the drip, drip, drip of water echoes, echoes, echoes across the dense, living space.

Who hears it?

The sound is made by the hearing of it.

[][][][][]

Seed case splits.
Root tip emerges.
Searches for hold.
Finds suggestion of primitive soil amongst rocks.
Cotyledon leaves.
Shoots up.
Roots down.
Spiral of elongating life.
To light above.
To safety below.
The beginning.
Two leaves, four leaves, eight leaves.
Ever upwards, it seems.
Risky world above.
Ever downwards, also, drawing up earth to bloom above.
Speed at which this life force... lives... is... astonishing.
Yet.
As common as dirt, transformed into beauty.
Rush is halted by furious darkness of pouring, crashing, thrashing war between air and water.
Rain comes to the plateau.
With it, life.
Two, four, eight.
The tree branches above.
Below, roots explore the earth, anchoring tree to subterranean rocks.
Wonderful!
Our being creates this reality. The gamble of life pays off. Blimey! A tree is born. Stunning are its glistening leaves after the storm.
You'd think he'd never seen a tree before.
He hadn't. He hadn't tasted it and watched it in this way. I can tell you. Neither did he again. Once is enough for any life. This is something remembered on the deathbed.
Above the top of the ravine by even an inch, the tree is scorched and blasted to pieces in the blasted dry season. Can't get away from the fact. It's a risky business this life but the tree is a tough one. Down there in the temporariness of life in the ravine, it thrives, becoming the centre, the home of all life for miles around.
A miracle if one has the sense to recognise it.

[][][][][]

The biological clock and all that. No life can resist it. The tree shrinks back into itself and into the earth it has helped to create. Two small rocks there somewhere; a little smaller; a little more broken up but enduring nonetheless a little longer than the tree.

Bits break off, fall and degrade. Another storm. It reaches into the ravine. Once in a hundred years stuff. The old tree is felled. Who sees it? Is the destruction in the watching?

A good piece of wood falls down the ravine. It is small but it is strong. One might say it is, it is, the heart of the tree. The storm waters carry it down to the river that runs through the forest.

The piece of wood floats down the oily river, of which, in its dark wetness, it is a part. If there is light, in this silent tunnel of dark trees, then it is reflected in the wetness of the piece of wood. From time to time, disturbed, the water throws out a piece of light which connects with the canopy above through a shaft of golden sunlight.

[][][][][]

Wood makes canoe.

Canoe moves down river.

Canoe moves down river, easily. Small, compact man guides it with paddle. In his tough, naked blackness, he is one with the canoe. Man, paddle, canoe, water, darkness and essential light. A single thing in the glory of creation.

Indeed, you might say, the very essence of Bune-ness.

Fisherman he is, this essential Bune.

A simple fisherman: flesh, fibre and an idea.

From whence sprang he?

Knowledge of him created him.

This man of the river.

Forest dweller?

No.

Bune dwelt on the edge of the forest. That is the nature of man and no less Bune.

Bune dwelt in the river.

He looks – in his shining blackness, in his beauty – as if he might dive from his canoe to catch a shining fish in his jaws. Even, white teeth snap shut, a trace of blood. It is gone, to become a part of Bune. Quite right.

Self-containment the essential Bune. He survives on no artificial, external force. He is an efficient part of the environment in which he dwells.

He is innocent, acting by instinct. It is the world of man acting upon Bune that creates his soul, his suffering, and, therefore, his thoughts. Bune the beast becomes Bune the man.

[][][][][]

Travelling further than usual down the river swollen by the rains, Bune, the man, meets a woman, whom he recognises as being more than a mere man. The woman is washing clothes on the edge of the river.

Bune acts by instinct and thus within the bounds of total innocence. He takes the woman who yields but as an act of revenge she gives Bune a wrapper. From now on he is clothed. Each has given the other knowledge.

14

Thus, Bune stays with the woman. A son is born. Soon after another son is born. Other children follow until there are five. Bune considers the two boys, as his sons, a development of himself. The others, girls, are dear to him but he does not watch them as he watches his sons grow. His wife and his three daughters he lumps together as women. He loves them as an undistinguishable lump of femininity he mistrusts a little as something mysterious. He understands the boys. He sees them as individual creations, created by his understanding of them. One boy is a fisherman, like his father; the other, more like his mother, hunts on the land. The two boys fight each other and are destined to separate; you know the story.

Another day comes. Bune is taken even further down the river in his fishing. Why?

He knew that morning it would happen. He had glanced back at the family home knowing it was the last time. The family – his family it had once been – ignored him. They had their own lives now. He was no longer necessary. The river took your father. He was a good man. Without him you would not be here.

For the first time, Bune sees the sky unencumbered by the canopy of trees. The river opens to a wide swamp. The space, limitless, is intoxicating to the self-contained man free within it. He looks up; he watches the birds flying out to sea. He smiles, screwing up his eyes at the unfamiliar sun.

1

Nalin's Daughter

The breeze rouses the sleeper who hears the first crash of thunder. Heavy drops of rain touch tin roof. Midday storm hits, thrashing the building with a black energy that takes his breath away. An exhilarating confusion of water and terrified vegetation. Lightning cuts through dark chaos, throwing agonised trees into relief. Thunder made small by wind and water. The smell of the living earth refreshed is intoxicating.

In those days Andrew could not describe such things. He felt them all the same: the wonderful isolation up there in the house on the hill, lost in a furious sea. No more than a mass of positive ions in the air perhaps but the feeling contrasted starkly with the lonely separateness which usually hung on him when he came out of a sticky afternoon sleep longing for something, he knew not what, feeling weak and afraid. Then the men down in the compound were a mystery to him and indeed only the idea of Tarlie could restore his confidence.

But the storm makes him feel powerful; able to do anything. He is the boss, the Master, the whole landscape out there is his, hundreds of men are in his power. Tarlie is right: Andrew is stupid at times. Those hundreds of men could kill him if provoked. It had happened before. It might happen now. Safer to be afraid.

Storm draws breath. Uneven tread on wooden, creaking stairs.

"What do you want, Tarlie? It's Sunday." Andrew shouts with mock, loving impatience because he is pleased to see the man with whom he would connect if only he knew the trick.

Another wave of thunderous rain stops the answer. Tarlie sits heavily on the floor, the fly wire door leaning incidentally on his massive shoulder. He looks down uncharacteristically, scratching a pattern four square upon the floor. He will not meet Andrew's eyes.

If Andrew could know Tarlie intimately by looking, then looking would be enough. He cannot get enough looking. Tarlie's deformed stance, his pronounced limp, arose from childhood polio which had wasted one leg. But his body was by contrast and compensation immensely powerful. He had no trouble turning the generator, the maintenance of which was one of his jobs. His naked torso, twisted as he sat, could have been that of a world-class, heavyweight boxer. The enamoured Andrew is a weed beside him.

Encouraged by their isolation, Andrew wants to make an intimate gesture. Instead he shouts, again, as if perversely he wants to keep his distance: "So Tarlie? Why've you come to disturb me?"

The question is lost in another crash of thunder. Andrew has to move closer, sitting down on the floor beside Tarlie. He smells the warm, smoky smell of the man and is about to bellow into his ear when Tarlie turns to face him.

16

"Andrew," he calls through the storm, "help me."

Andrew looks into the face which has attracted him from the very beginning and which he has come to know as the essence of the man. He told me this later when he had learned to talk. Tarlie's expression summed up the man and remains forever in our memories now he has gone. His broad open features were split by a huge mouth that was always, it seemed, grinning, creasing his eyes into a smile and exposing large, white teeth, the gap between the front two almost wide enough for a third. He could not but grin even when his mood was tragic, as it was on that Sunday afternoon. To the receptive and loving, Tarlie's grin was brightly infectious, like a flash of sunshine. To the self-corrupted turned-in man, holding on at all costs to a small idea of himself, it was insolent with jovial superiority, even threatening. But Tarlie was a good man. One of the best.

Lost in admiration, Andrew hears not the message, but is nonetheless dragged halfway down the garden until blasted by a sudden gust of cold rain – or by something more uncertain – he shakes himself free and retreats back onto the veranda. Why should he follow Tarlie into the rain? Damn him. But seeing again Tarlie's desperate expression, Andrew is dragged out of his white man act. The grin that split Tarlie's face, squeezing his black eyes almost shut, is forced with anguish, his forehead furrowed with an unbearable impatience. And recognising the pain, Andrew is filled with such an unusual compassion for his brother that he forgets his damned self for once and follows Tarlie like a lamb, running a little to catch him up.

They take a steep, narrow path out of the garden through long, bent, sodden grass which whips their legs. Tarlie negotiates the stream of mud with ease despite the uneven swing of his body, elegant in any event to the eyes of Andrew who slips and skids behind the man upon whose back the raindrops join to flow as rivulets of pure gold.

[][][][][]

On the level ground, Andrew's smart jeans and tee-shirt are a clinging muddy skin. The saturated air suffocates him. Tarlie heaves with contained impatience. They walk through curtains of rain and Madiak's garden out onto the main plantation road. The labour lines run off it at right angles, the first looking onto the sodden football pitch, the last backing onto the dripping oil palms.

Sullen eyes watch. A tinny transistor radio blasts a manic song of high-pitched voices.

Jumping the streaming ditches and padding the mud, soaked but hot as the rain eases, Andrew follows Tarlie to Nalin's house. They push through a crowd of people around the door, mostly young men. A few women also, their arms folded. They're not surprised by what has happened.

No one dares go into the dark little room where the girl lies on a mat on the floor. Andrew pushes impatiently through the crowd. He has to do something. In the shadows, he senses Nalin himself, sitting and scowling out at the world, silent and dejected, while his daughter suffers separately a few feet away.

17

Tarlie is already squatting beside the girl's head. He looks up at Andrew, who looks down at them both. The girl is covered with what most of them wear: cheap trade-cloth, once brash, now mud coloured, wet where flies play. Shoulders and one leg exposed: young limbs, rounded, and shiny with apparent health. But her head, turned towards the wall – rough wooden planks – and partly lost in shadow, shows dull cheek and childlike nose, both streaked with blood.

Andrew assumes she is dead and that all Tarlie requires, as the compound supervisor, is help in getting the body to the morgue in Akaranda quickly. An annoying but unbreakable company rule. He would have to make inquiries and write a report before Monday morning. He wants to blame Tarlie but catching the man's eye and looking therefore back to the girl he sees that she is breathing, just perceptibly moving the filthy cloth. Seeing this, Andrew is suddenly furious for some reason he does not understand. He wants to fight someone. He wants to fight Tarlie because he loves him so much. He kneels down beside the girl as Tarlie watches.

The dampness of the cloth is blood, fresh, glistening in a narrow slice of grey light.

"What's wrong, Tarlie?" He is desperate for an explanation. "Has she had a baby? Where is it?"

"Masta, we must get her to hospital. She will die." Tarlie's huge, gentle hands clasp the girl's head. He is in agony.

"Stay here," says Andrew, "I'll fetch the car."

The rain has stopped. Andrew paces impatiently over hot-smelling mud. He sweats under the bastard sun. He wants to run but so slippery is the ground, he cannot and this infuriates him.

They watch his tall, slightly hunched figure leave them. They do not expect the white man to return. He'll send someone else to deal with us.

[][][][][]

But Andrew does return, driving his little utility truck himself. He stops where they have carried her, on the mat, to the road-side. A larger crowd has gathered, colourful, under the vicious sun.

Andrew does not get out as they lay her, Tarlie shouting orders, in the back. As usual, too many men climb on board. "I am not going," Andrew shouts to no one in particular, "til some of you get out."

Someone gets in quietly beside him.

Andrew cannot express his anger enough: "Who are you?"

"Petrus, Masta," answers a small man, dressed neatly in shabby jacket and big shorts. He is the carpenter. Andrew knows him well. He has paid him to make bits of furniture, simple, strong and unassuming like the man himself. Andrew feels awkward beside him.

"How many men in the back, Petrus?"

"Not many, Masta."

Andrew sighs: "How many? Go count them."

Petrus is soon back, shutting the door so gently that Andrew knows it is not closed properly: "Eight, Masta."

"Tell two to get out."

"It's alright, Masta."

"It's not alright, fuck you. What are you doing here anyway? What's all this got to do with you?"

No answer.

"Well, Petrus? Perhaps you'd better get out then."

"I'm helping Tarlie, Masta."

"Are you? Well you can help him by getting some of those men out. Otherwise I'm not moving."

Petrus sits in silence. He badly wants Andrew to do the right thing.

Andrew knows this but the very idea that Petrus wants him to be good makes him obstinate. He wants to smash Petrus's simple faith. He is about to get out himself when Tarlie appears at the window, the great smile an ironic mask.

"Please Masta. Go."

Andrew ignores him: "What are all these people doing in the back?"

"They have to hold her."

"Tell some of them to get out." Andrew grips the steering wheel, hunching his back, staring ahead stubbornly. He hates himself.

Tarlie's large hand grips Andrew's wrist, pathetic in his grasp. He wants to hurt Andrew: "You're selfish, Andrew," he says. "Yu mangal man, Andrew. Yu gat savi long yu tasol, yu no gat savi long arapela man. If I had a car I wouldn't have to know people like you."

Andrew is stung, or at any rate his idea of himself is stung. "OK, Tarlie," he whispers, feeling small beside Petrus.

"Thank you Masta. Please drive carefully while we hold her. She's in pain."

Andrew wants to say "Yes Sir" but instead he says, "Pull the door to, Petrus, please."

[][][][][]

The empty hospital forecourt is a pitted expanse of drying mud. A trio of vultures shift lazily in the stifling air. The men who care stand around useless while alone in the back of the truck, Tarlie holds the girl's head on his lap. Childlike it is, closely cropped hair and delicate, doll-like features. The body lies awkwardly, immature breasts exposed. Legs stick out at odd angles, incidental to the body they had once supported.

Andrew grips the side of the truck. He looks at Tarlie's great hands. How could the little body have produced so much blood? The grass mat is black with it, the cloth drenched with the stuff. Yet still it flows. It flows along the drainage channels on the floor, and drips onto the mud below. He remembers the girl now: Nalin's daughter. At Tarlie's request he had given her a job, helping keep the compound clean. She had done so, her proud, quiet and easy little figure disdainfully collecting and burning the litter, sweeping around the houses, cleaning the drains and helping Tarlie cut the grass. Together they had done more: planting flowers – crotons and flaming canna lilies – to soften the hard outlines of the houses and adorn the ragged clumps of plantains. She had been a flower herself, delicate and untouchable amongst the ruffians all around. She had kept her distance, coming out of the house only after they had gone to work. In the evenings, sometimes, she had sat with Tarlie on the rough plank bench beneath the old mango tree. Here they would chat softly into the night, their voices floating up to the house above, to Andrew on his veranda.

Andrew remembers all this. He looks at Tarlie's face, broken like the body he holds.

"Oh shit, Tarlie, I'm sorry."

2
They'll Believe Your Lies

"One less kanaka, Andrew – actually two in this case – is neither 'ere nor there but you'll 'ave less trouble if you get in a couple of prostitutes. That'll relieve their sexual tensions, less..." He searched for a word, "less inconveniently. Mind you, they'll fuck anything that moves, but the advantage of a woman is that she 'as to be bought. You'll learn that yourself one day." Jim grinned at Andrew: "That means, Andrew, that they'll have to earn some money. An' earning money means doing work an' working keeps people out of mischief. See?"

Andrew saw.

"An' what we want is work an' no trouble. Joseph!" Jim shouted at the bar-boy: "Bring this pommie baby another beer." He knew how to deal with these pommie boys who fell in love with the labour and thought their job was a bloomin' social service. He knew how to make them into men. Lucky he'd found Andrew at the club this evening, otherwise he'd have missed the chance and the poor bastard would've gone on moping for days, getting more and more sentimental over these buggers and messing up everything. "Things'd go up the spout if I wasn't here," he said to no one in particular. Joseph looked at the ceiling.

"Look Andrew," Jim wanted to be serious, "I've seen it all before. Trust me, you 'ave to stand up strong or they'll get you. And then who wins? They've got no work and we produce no palm oil. So you're not helping anyone. Are you?"

Andrew supposed not, thinking of Tarlie.

"Listen, I love these buggers too. Don't I love you, Joseph? Don't I?"

"Yesa."

"See? I got Joseph this job. Didn't I, Joseph?"

"Yesa."

"An' he still wears that filthy lap-lap full of pox just to spite me. Don't you, Joseph?"

"Yesa."

"You see, Andrew, the labour en masse is an animal. It's not human and once you treat it as human... Well, you're fucked."

Andrew thought of Tarlie again, of the uncharacteristic tears, of the broken body: "But as individuals, Jim..."

Jim cut him short: "Forget that twaddle, Andrew; forget it. It'll git yer nowhere."

Andrew looked into his glass.

"What man-management's all about," Jim went on, boring in his little drunkenness, "is forgetting the 'uman side of things. You keep a man fit not because 'e's 'uman but because you want 'im to work. These people," he looked in Joseph's direction, "'ave to be led. It's easy because all 'umans is greedy and lazy. They want someone else to think for them. And come to think of it, it's a pity we haven't got television. That'd do the trick. They wouldn't think of sex while they're watching cartoons." Jim's body jogged a little to indicate his amusement.

Andrew didn't laugh but Jim knew he'd go along with it; they all did in the end. It was easier to manage people by not considering individuals. That way, Andrew's anger would be deflected away from the company and towards the kanakas who had done the thing. Eventually he'd blame the girl herself because, let's face it, she must have encouraged them. These gins are all the same.

"Got me, Andrew?"

Andrew got him.

"You can do it," said Jim, almost but not quite touching Andrew. "Go back, get some sleep and start first thing Monday morning." He stuck out his lumpy, alcoholic chin, making a deliberate effort to look Andrew in the eye.

Andrew saw two yellow, bloodshot eyes, the black pupils his mirror, summing him up. He looked towards Joseph but saw only darkness behind the bar. "I will, Jim," he said weakly, "thanks for your advice." Then, a little more certainly: "I'll do it." He thumped the bar unconvincingly and left immediately. Joseph watched him go.

"An' Andrew. . ." Jim shouted, a little desperately, into the dark.

"Yes?"

"Write up a report. Say the right things. They'll believe you."

[][][][][]

The night takes Andrew.

Jim pours himself another whisky.

Joseph moves from his station behind the bar. He has the audacity to cross the room without deference to Jim who is astonished momentarily until he reminds himself that the ways of kanakas are unaccountable and trying to account for them only leads to trouble.

Joseph goes out onto the veranda.

The club sits on the side of a hill which is barely a pimple upon the coastal plain. Nonetheless, from where he stands, apparently suspended above the night, Joseph can look down into the night. As he looks, the clouds part, enabling moonlight to drench the pathetic little golf course which the white men have laid out at the foot of the hill. For a moment or two he watches the insect thing that is Andrew crossing the moonlit space. Then he turns back into the club.

[][][][][]

Crossing the golf course and encouraged by the beer inside him, Andrew wonders if he ought to learn to play the game. He imagines himself talking about handicaps in the club with Jim, the others listening. This makes him think of Joseph behind the bar also listening or, more likely, not listening, to the unnecessary chatter of the white men.

He looks up into the night sky, seeing the glorious moon blacked out the moment he catches it. Thinking he is going to faint he hurries for the protection of the dark plantation ahead where he remembers Nalin's daughter, and Tarlie. The organic earthy smell, the pungent aniseed scent of the male oil palm flowers, the rotten stink of a dead snake and the thick insistent roar of the night-time insects bring him round. The moon emerges from the clouds, a breeze ever so lightly moves the warm air, shifting the palm fronds above his head. The earth beneath his feet begins to push up at him so that catching the almost imperceptible decline of the ground he takes off his boots to pad the footpath barefoot. He wades through a narrow stream feeling the sand gritty between his toes.

On other nights, walking through the plantation had been merely the pleasure of moving through the night air, allowing easy thoughts to fill his head. An intense pleasure where hard physical exertion was the thing, defeating the space and time between the club and his house. But tonight is different. Like the insect roar, the memory of Tarlie's tears and her damaged body fill his head to bursting. Tonight he has an urgent desire to get to somewhere more than his house and his bed.

And the thing I could barely think about and which felt like a knife in my stomach was the idea of Tarlie dismissing me. Calling me a selfish man, a mangal man, a man he did not want to know. For the first time I did not look forward to going back to my little house on top of the little hill in the plantation. It would be easy enough getting things going in the morning – even writing up something to satisfy Jim – but what I was going to miss, was Tarlie.

You and your self-pity, Andrew. It makes me laugh.

[][][][][]

Chan's store was the centre of the white man's world to us. I had seen places like it in Markham, although nothing so crude. It was the magic that made the men work. As Petrus once said, in an unusual expression of sudden anger which stunned us, it stole men's souls.

Here is the Highlands man who has owned nothing material in his life beyond a few cowry shells, the bilum[1] his mother made him and an axe-head – which would have been a stone axe-head in his father's day. He is enchanted by the sight of so much cargo. Cargo that until the very minute he entered the doors of the store for the first time had been the sole preserve of the white man, favoured as he undoubtedly was by the strange god he worshipped. Suddenly all these things are in his grasp and immediately he is a convert to materialism, the most seductive of all the religions. He is drunk and he wants it all now. Now! The dyed cloth and the coloured tee-shirts, oil lamps, gleaming pots and pans, enamelled plates and mugs, transistor radios and tape players, scissors, cigarettes, matches, torches, plastic sleeping mats and spoons. Such wonders not known before and in colours never seen in the Highlands, where beneath misty

---

[1] A sort of apron worn by men from parts of the Highlands. It is loosely woven from string made from bark.

skies the brief fresh green of new grass after fire is the only memorable colour he has known. So much! To own all these things is surely to be happy beyond all knowledge of happiness. First, a plastic belt or wallet for the cash – those magic bits of paper – he has earned, then perhaps a bright piece of Indian cotton for a lap-lap – the colours soon fade – or even a pair of shorts like the white man wears to show off his insect legs. Little things, but he is caught and soon all his money has gone on the trash.

Chan is clever: he gets to know the man and he points out something expensive, say a radio which costs a fortnight's wages or more. 'Don't worry, My Friend' – Chan is a cute little fellow with wrinkly eyes behind glasses below a shiny bald head – 'give me a little each pay day and I'll put it on one side for you; when you've paid for it, it's yours.' Nice one, eh? He has bought the sucker, who is grateful at first for having been caught. He thinks the man who is eating him alive is his friend. But despite his old sun-bleached shirt, his grubby shorts and cheap sandals, Chan is rich; his children are being educated down south.

Bit by bit, our innocent from the Highlands is taken in until he feels that all his work is for the enrichment of Chan. He barely has enough to eat and is grateful for the badly paid overtime you give him, Andrew. He cannot run away; the forest behind the plantation is treacherous and no place for a man of the open, airy Highlands; and he cannot go home because the cost of a ticket will be forever beyond his means. His dreams of a new life have been dashed. He is angry and his anger is compounded by his ignorance of the system which is devouring him. A raging frustration overtakes his senses. Angry and ignorant he may be but he is not stupid. Neither is he on his own; his friends are suffering the same pain, and they talk about it. Chan's store, that crude warehouse full of cargo, with its earth floor beaten flat by their naked feet, becomes the focus of discontent. And it's lucky for the company that it is, otherwise it'd be the oil mill or the expatriate houses. Their time will come, I can assure you, but for now the trade store is the thing. Destroy it and destroy the pain within me. It happened, you remember, one Friday night, after pay day. Just like that, they marched, drunk – we all get our courage from that – and they tore it down, tin sheet by tin sheet, opening the boxes and throwing out the goods, unravelling the bales of cloth and treading the trash into the mud. It was methodical, lacking in any sense of joy but there was – as you would say, Andrew – a grim satisfaction in the doing of it. I remember that more than anything else and as I trampled the cheap, colourful cloth into the dirt, I thought of you. I did! You had spoken to me by then, but carelessly, over the store counter, not bothering to look at me, because some spare part you wanted for the tractor was more important than the man who would give it you. I remember emptying packets of biscuits onto the ground and then feeling them break and squash into dust beneath my naked feet. That was good.

No one stopped us, although had we gone further they might have. I remember thinking of how their women might be trembling and holding their children, thinking the worst thoughts of us. And I wanted them to be afraid. I wanted them to fear us for inspiring that fear and for exposing their nakedness. Those women. They like to look at us. They compare our strong blackness to the weedy whiteness of their husbands, and they hate us all the more for those thoughts. Did you know, Andrew, that at one time we were forbidden to wear shorts for fear of exposing our strong thighs to those women? More than our thighs. The bulges in the fronts of our trousers as well – the big dicks they imagined we had. The white men didn't like that so we were not allowed to wear trousers at all; instead we had to wear lap-laps to cover up our manhood.

We were back at work on Monday morning as if nothing had happened. Chan re-built the trade store but he put up a high fence around it, topped with barbed wire. You people love that stuff.

This happened before we knew Annu. Annu had nothing to do with it. Tell them that, Andrew. Tell them what you know. They'll believe you.

[][][][]

He passes Chan's store, which is beside the football pitch, a dustbowl at this time of year. Beyond, beside the sluggish stream carrying away the oily filth of the mill, below the hill upon which sits the club where Joseph serves, there is a tight grid of lanes containing small bungalows. These houses are, each one, a parody of the more spacious affairs in which the white men live – who may, for all we know, indeed deserve something better. At any rate these smaller houses, apparently dropped carelessly upon the low-lying land, have little verandas upon which the tenants more or less live, in addition to messing around in the traditional huts they have built at the back for cooking. The gardens, originally landscaped with lawns and tastefully placed shrubs, have been planted up with bananas and fruit trees. What with the old cars, the huts and so forth, the whole place much more resembles a settlement on the edge of town than the obedient suburb intended.

In the leafy shadows parents chat quietly, soothing their children to sleep. A tinny radio hints at Puccini or Cliff Richard; the cough and the expressive spitting of the betel-nut chewers, the flapping together of the banana leaves in the breeze – all these cosy sounds push the noise of the mill into the background.

Andrew is the intruder, brushing the bananas; too awkward by half: "Excuse me."

A man's talking stops suddenly, as if he has been caught.

"Do you know where Alloy lives?"

"Wass at?"

"Alloy, Alloy the stores clerk."

"Down there." The man, visible only as bits of light caught upon his beautiful skin, thumbs a gesture somewhere behind and continues his conversation.

Andrew pushes on down another lane, tripping over the dry ruts. He dares not arouse the sleepers.

A young man, astride a motorbike, smokes dangerously. He is looking up out into the stars, his naked torso shiny in the moonlight, the concave curve of his belly so beautiful Andrew wants to touch it.

"Alloy, the stores clerk." He whispers urgently. "Where is he?"

25

The boy is startled, gazing at Andrew open-mouthed. The cigarette drops as a tiny glow on the hard earth and dies.

"Alloy," more brutally now, "where does he live?"

No response. The boy, much younger now that Andrew has time to study him – a teenager – stares like an idiot.

Andrew enunciates his words slowly, using the local pidgin in the European way: "Alloy, Alloy. Em i stap where?"

The boy is suspicious. Why should a white man want Alloy? Why should he want any of them at night? It means trouble. He avoids Andrew's eyes: "Mi no savi em."

Andrew is the impatient Masta: "No gat yer. Bulsit. Yu savi em. Em i man husat i wok long woksop. Em i kuskus bilong woksop." He spits it out but he draws a blank, frightened stare.

"Luk, mi sori tumas." Andrew tries to stem his rising impatience: "Dispela man em i fren bilong mi. Mi laik toktok long em bilong givim sampela moni," he lies.

The boy wants to bolt but is, no doubt about it, stuck on the bike.

Andrew's turn now to stare back stupidly. He is exhausted and empty of ideas, too tired to walk back home but lost here with nowhere to go.

Why has he bothered to seek out this man Alloy in his, in his lair, in his hole? A man whom he has only confronted across a counter; a man whose eyes he has avoided; a man whose eyes he has sought; a man who has dismissed him as worthless. Why does he want to apologise? Why should he, a plantation manager, apologise to a clerk? Why on earth, for God's sake, should he have walked all this way in the middle of the night to apologise to a, to a . . .

The raw, rancid palm-oil smell rushes in at him; filth, floating on the stream. He wants to sit down. There is nowhere to sit.

The door of the house behind the motorbike opens, blasting yellow light at them. The boy makes a dash, trips, and is gone. The bike falls with a crash that would raise the dead, but does not. The silhouette of a man comes onto the little veranda:

"Husat i stap?"

It is Alloy, skinny-looking in shorts, his head, with its mass of hair, is much too big.

3
Angelina Cut Down the Trees

The screaming came from beyond the tall, fleshy plantain trees amongst which they lived. But as his head cleared and as he recognised the sound, he recognised her anger. He began to laugh. He always did when she was angry, encouraged by his mother, his Ma, sitting on her little stool outside the door, peeling the sweet potatoes. Her great big body, over which he loved to play, shook as she laughed: Listen to her, listen to her; she's screaming like a pig because she's lost the little paper she wipes her arse with.[2]

And she would press him to laugh, pick him up and tickle him until he giggled and they would both laugh in a fit of giggles until they forgot the screaming woman and did not have to hear her. But once, his mother could not laugh, and the big tears rolled down her face. Then he cried too, holding on to Ma's big fat knees for support, his little naked body lost in the folds of her dress. They did not laugh either when his father came home: the silent intruder into their world who made them think of things beyond the comforting plantains.

So laughing to himself and hearing the usual noise, the child scrambled off his mat to go find Ma and play the game. It was dark in the little house but outside, the dusty yard and his mother's vegetable garden glowed in the last light of the setting sun. There was Ma's little stool, pushed into the ground by her bulk. But where was Ma? There was the tin bath hanging beside the doorway, the ragged, flapping leaves of the plantains that surrounded his world, the little hedges of crotons that divided it up into his spaces and the line of assorted washing that defined the sky. But where was Ma? For the first time in his life, he sensed loneliness. On the shiny red stems of the plantains the little sun lizards nodded their heads at him, ready to dart away should he approach. He was on his own.

The noise from outside this world – the screaming – confirmed the existence of the universe beyond. But without Ma the screaming was not funny. He did not want to laugh. He did not want to cry either because the very thought of Ma, with her great big presence, reassured him: she was out there somewhere and all he had undoubtedly to do was to go out, grab her hand and drag her back to safety.

So the naked little boy entered the narrow path that led him through the plantain grove towards he knew not where. He had always imagined that the universe was filled with plantains and that his father spent most of his time with the screaming woman, amongst the plantains. He imagined that other people –

---

[2] Harim em, harim em. Em i singaut olsem long pig. Em i lusim liklik pepa bilong wasim as bilong em.

he knew there were others from the stories Ma had told him – lived like they did in a small, snug space amongst the plantains.

The path out of this world was easy to follow and he was sure he would bump into Ma any minute. Then she would pick him up, laughing and smelling of Ma, and carry him back home. But before he had time to enjoy the thought, he was out of the plantains and lost in a space so vast and limitless that he felt dizzy. Looking for the safety of the washing line he saw not the little velvet sky of home, with its scattered lights surrounded by a fringe of black, waving plantain leaves, but the great crushing dome of the coming night with its terrifying number of countless stars, multiplying as he watched.

He gagged, staggered out of the narrow border of kana lilies and was sick on the lawn. As he turned to find the path back home, it was gone and he sat with a childish thump upon the prickly grass. He took one gulp and was about to yell Ma, when his attention was caught by the screaming again. He stood up and set off towards the noise.

Hope you can manage it Alloy! You're on your own now.

Alloy's memories of that shattering childhood experience are confused. In retrospect, he sees it with all the experience of later life and not through his childhood eyes. Before he woke up that afternoon to discover his mother's absence, he had been entirely conditioned by her and by his life in the little servants' quarters surrounded by the plantains, where he had grown up. From the moment he started his search for Ma, everything he experienced was new except – when he found them – his parents but even they were in an unfamiliar situation that made it necessary for him to reassess his idea of them. I mean, for instance, he had never seen a lawn before, let alone the sort of grand, unworldly space that this one occupied. Certainly he had never seen a white woman and the one whom he was about to encounter – Angelina was her name – set firmly his idea of white women for the next twenty-five years or so.

The little naked boy made small but confident steps up the slope of the lawn. The house up above sent forth a sickly yellow light which in its local intensity dimmed the glorious stars above, suggesting an imbalance that even the ignorant little boy sensed and remembered acutely years after. All this to the accompaniment of Angelina's shrieks, discordant against the symphonic background of night-time insects. Such a piercing sound did Angelina make as Alloy approached the house – now picking up recognisable words, and words whose meaning he would soon come to learn well enough – that for the first time since leaving his home, he was aware of the insect song which fills the tropical nights with such solid and harmonious music. It sounded good, Angelina's screams did not.

The house sunk from view, no more than a noisy glow. When it rose again it was shockingly large and real, its windows tall slits of heavy yellow light oozing thick across the lawn to where Alloy stood.

In the bland light of day, the house was and remains a cheap affair behind a mean and narrow veranda. It staggered on short concrete plinths allowing just enough space for Angelina's dogs to crawl out of the midday sun and scratch themselves, shaking the whole house and Angelina in it.

Oh, but to Alloy then, and to Alloy now as he sees it in his mind's eye, in that other night reality, the house is a monstrous thing ready to eat him up just as it had so obviously eaten up his mother. Oh, and it did – still does to Alloy in his dreams – actually seem to be alive, the slow throbbing of the generator – the giver of the ghastly light – its evil, pulsating heart; Angelina its rasping tongue.

Angelina would not have appeared to us cynical adults, now, to have been the devil incarnate Alloy pictures. But, but she was bad enough and there is no doubt that she was, then, Alloy's. . . What? His devil or his angel? He is not always sure. Now, in his own adulthood, Angelina is a shrunken old lady: selfish, sharp-tongued and stubborn in her opinions but not wicked. It might do Alloy good to see her, although he'd probably strangle her.

The shrieking stopped; but there was Angelina herself, framed in the light of the centre window, open, like the others, onto the veranda. A quick sketch of the woman? Just to give you an idea of her embodiment, as it were? Not as Alloy saw her then, of course, but as we would have seen her had we been standing behind him, knowing her a little.

Angelina was way on the wrong side of forty and could never again have pretended otherwise even with the light – evil or otherwise – behind her. Nothing wrong with that – but Angelina was convinced she was still what she had been until, about, her thirty-seventh year. That is, or was, a neat, tanned, beach blonde who looked good in shorts and something brief on top. Neatly shaped with small, neat features, although her mouth tended to shut tight and live an existence quite separate from her eyes. Her eyes smiled only when a dog was around. Angelina got on well with dogs.

As a child, Angelina's nose had been described as a button. But who, in later life, wants a button for a nose? As a youngster her body had been slim and she'd never had trouble keeping it that way. She fed on the hot air in which she lived and no one had ever seen her eat a proper meal. When she was very young, a bragging lover – a lover? Of Angelina? – had described Angelina's body as boyish, as he caressed her sharp shoulder blades. Sharp little elbows had the young Angelina too, they said, but she'll get better when she has babies. She never did have any babies, couldn't, can't, stand kids, preferring the dogs any day. She still has those sharp elbows. Watch out!

Angelina was not tall – so she could not see beyond her button nose – but she looked tall because of her slimness, and being an outdoor type she had always looked fit and healthy, ready to jump up and bark. Rangy, they called her in her thirties, something less flattering thereafter. Anyway that was Angelina up to thirty-seven and even a little after, with the light behind.

So you can guess what Alloy, the child, saw, although he was not, obviously, judgmental about her looks. What he saw was merely the manifestation – the flesh and bones (bony, bony Angelina, wash yer face and make it cleaner) of the shrieks and of she at whom he and Ma had laughed: the white woman, all white women.

See her? She is wearing shorts and a tight, white cotton shirt, knotted at her navel. Her navel! She did have one, I can assure you. But is her mother to blame for Angelina? 'My Little Angel', she called her. It started in the North End Road market, Fulham, London, about 1915. Fruit, which ought to have been forbidden. It was not only what Angelina's dad did to her but the others too.

Exposing her navel – a woman past forty. I ask you? Is it right? Better a voluminous smock and her hair tied back in a bun. But then it would not have been Angelina. This woman, dressed as she was, showed to advantage her scrawny, sun-dried, tanned-leather body, her long, bony legs, her waist, as small as it had ever been but somehow like the waist of a dead thing. The face – Alloy did not see the face at the time, so fascinated was he by the mass of sun-dried, dry-grass and crinkled hair – the face was what happens to the mirthless, shrieking sort of face that Angelina had, has: the nose has gone, somewhere, the eyes dead and hung over – no laugh lines there, you can bet, but the narrow slit of a mouth, the mouth, tries hard to live with a smudge of bright red lipstick to suggest lips. That mouth stretches the skin across the hard jaw and pulls taut the scraggy neck as it makes a dead grin. The teeth are good and pearly white. Cor blimey Angelina: your boyish slimness was once desirable but now you're, you're skeletal, as if you don't have enough to eat. Too rich to eat, I suppose, like the Duchess of Windsor.

This was what Alloy saw. But he did not judge. This was merely, at last, what a white woman looked like. Another woman but a lot different from Ma, all the same, with her big generosity. Angelina! You really were a bitch. And it's a pity. Because you only just missed the mark of being a tolerably decent woman. What made you so dried up inside that it showed? What had turned you in on yourself only to find something there which frightened you? And yet you were fascinated by yourself, by yourself as the centre of your bitter world. Only your dogs gave you, give you, what you wanted: dumb, unquestioning and uncritical love. Only they would rise up to defend you. No human being had ever loved and cherished you or held you tightly for yourself and valued you, though as a child you had been loaded with every material need by guilty parents. But that does not excuse – not even what your dad did to you that time – that does not excuse you, Angelina, for not respecting Alloy's dad, with his own demons. He might have loved you like a dog. God help you, Angelina. God help us all.

To Alloy then, in retrospect, Angelina looked like the very devil (poor Angelina), bony legs planted apart and hands on hips, spitting hot anger (poor, poor Angelina). But little Alloy approached nonetheless, brave and determined to find his Ma, curious also about the strange animal before him.

As he approached, the world outside the house diminished while the room itself grew larger and became the whole world. The noise was terrific: the insect chorus, the generator and Angelina herself no longer shrieking but making a squawking noise, the result of too much cigarette smoke on the larynx. But Alloy noticed nothing now except his mother, kneeling before something that had, apparently, to be appeased. Alloy's father was somewhere in the background, looking on silently; but Alloy did not see him, his eyes were for Ma.

Ma! Nothing else existed and with a cry of joy, Alloy ran towards her and climbed upon her. That was it and all well settled. Surely? An immediate return to normality and all would be right with the world. So easy and so natural for a little child to teach us. Perfect balance and harmony. Perfect Love. The child is on his mother's lap; the father, so long absent, comes forward, his dead heart quickened with love. He stands beside his kneeling wife touching, daring to touch, her shoulder as he watches his son, now sleeping; soon he too is on his knees beside them, encircling the beloved pair in his arms.

And Angelina watches. Her bitter heart is sweetened by the sight, truly now able to fulfil her roll of sponsor, if not mother, of this materially poor but spiritually rich family. She watches, her hard face softening as a tear escapes her eye: a jewel of rare joy. She too kneels, leaning her head against Dad's shoulder, the man whom she has abused and de-manned for so long in her frustrated need for him. At last he too now fulfils his role and meets his destiny face to face: he can now easily and joyfully support these two women who need him as he needs them.

Heaven's gate opens and this family of joy walks into paradise.

Not likely. This is real life: not some arty-farty fairy tale.

Angelina is appalled. She stands utterly gob-smacked, as her father would have said (North End Road market, Fulham and then the Narangburn harbour side – fruit was his first trade, the other came later). She stands aghast, speechless for a moment. Horrified by the entry of this dirty infant. Naked, too, and therefore shocking and reminding her of the carnal. She cannot look. Alloy's father shrinks, hating his wife for witnessing the life of which he is unbearably ashamed.

Only for a fleeting moment do mother and child experience bliss before all Hell is let loose.

"Aaaah," shouts Angelina, her voice breaking into the usual shriek as it fills the diseased larynx, "help me. Get away, get away, get away!"

She bats at Alloy and his mother with the back of the hand, fundamentally unable to bear the sight. She does not know what she is doing and is actually blind with rage.

Ma would have got away if she could. Quietly rising, her large, generous body indifferent to Angelina's batting and with Alloy shielded in her arms she would have left the room, descended the lawn and returned to the calm sanity of the world within the plantains. Then, perhaps, little Alloy's father would have given Angelina the wink and found the courage to strangle her.

Chance would have been a fine thing: Ma was cornered and Angelina in a fighting mood. (When, as the pain gnawed away at her heart, was she not?) The devil had got hold of her. She attacked Ma, screaming obscenities that echoed down the years to Alloy as he learned what each one meant. Angelina fought Ma as her opposite and as her adversary, as everything she hated in herself because Ma was good. She hit, she slapped, she spat, she tore at Ma who turned to the wall to protect Alloy. Her back and head and buttocks took the force of Angelina's anger until she was naked and bloody. The child took it all in, too terrified to utter a sound, his breathing troubled, his eyes dry as he lay paralysed, tight in Ma's arms.

Alloy's father ceased to be a solid body at all. He watched. He never had been a man of words, in any event; even his courtship of Ma had been a silent, shadowy, uncertain thing that had nonetheless filled her with pity and a sort of love. After all this he never spoke another word although he stayed with Angelina, her dumb and absolutely faithful servant, until he crawled under the house with the other dogs to lick his sores and scratch at his fleas. He is still there, for all I know.

Angelina could make no impression on Ma's solidity, for all that she danced in anger and tore her hair. So she turned to the dog in the corner and stuck out her chest at it, ripping off the skimpy blouse as she did so. It was a joke: this skeletal thing projecting its ribcage at nothing. The breasts were lifeless, the sharp elbows sticking out behind had more life.

"The panga, the panga," she babbled at him, "I want the panga."

He was dumb, but her eyes darted around the room for the panga until she found it, the bush knife, lying on the little table by the window. Old and rusty but as sharp as a wetted stone could make that cheap Birmingham steel.

She grabbed it, turned towards Ma, and flew out of the window, a half-naked angel of vengeance. Angelina ran down the lawn on her bare, bony, devilish feet. She crashed through the bed of kana lilies and started at the plantains, hacking away for all she was worth, the sweat flying from her as she hacked until not a single plantain stood. Until Alloy's world stood exposed and worthless, the pathetic little house naked in the raw universe. Then, exhausted, her skin etched by the splashes of acid plantain sap, Angelina flung herself on the dusty floor beside Ma's stool and wept. Scratching and scrawling at the ground until her mouth was full of dirt and she wet herself. Then she slept.

Damn you, Angelina. Leave her there and forget her.

Angelina pees, Angelina cut down the trees, Angelina can go to Hell.

So sang Ma later. So sang Alloy with his friends in the camp of shacks near the airport in Markham where they lived for a while. But there was no laughter in the song.

4
Ples

Assuming no insurmountable drainage problems, and that the land is flat, then clearing and planting is a straightforward job. This is especially the case where an existing plantation is being extended. First, parallel harvesting roads are surveyed, cutting the land up into a series of blocks. Each block is a hundred and fifty metres wide. This is because seventy-five metres is the furthest a harvesting labourer can reasonably be expected to carry oil palm fruit to a pick-up point on the roadside. A new road starts off as a surveyed line, cut through secondary or primary bush. Chainsaws follow, cutting down and chopping up any large trees or logs in the way. This enables the bulldozers to open up the road behind. The bush between the new roads is cut down and the dry trash is burned. By the time the rains come, the roads have been graded and ditched and culverts put in as required. At ground level this new country looks a mess: an atomic bomb might have been dropped; but from the air, no doubt, the land has been organised properly and tamed, broken if you like. Oil palm seedlings are planted between the new roads. Within a few years, another layer of magic is laid upon the land. No one said it was good magic!

[][][][][]

Monday started well. At about seven-thirty, a gang of men under Madiak started marking out the new road and clearing a path through the bush. Andrew laid out the first thirty metres or so then left them to it. He might have stayed longer but he was unbearably restless and only wanted to get away.

At first he thought he might go to the beach, but the idea of clear blue sky and distant horizons depressed him. The club, then? But it'd be empty except for Joseph cleaning up; except for Joseph working around him and pretending he was not there, wishing he'd go away; wishing he'd come back at the correct time, when it was dark behind the bar and the light on the other side was a false light.

He drove into the workshop yard and came to a halt beside the spare parts store. The moment he caught sight of the daunting figure of the stores clerk, he thought of Tarlie, and suddenly, quite badly, he wanted to explain how he felt, and to explain to the stores clerk in particular, a man whom he knew only as the essence of barely disguised hostility behind the counter. A man with whom he felt he had to do battle every time he wanted a spark plug, a fuel filter or a can of engine oil. Often he sent Bune. Yet here he was today of all days facing the man he wanted to avoid. I don't even know his name.

He avoided the possibility of the man's eyes, hidden in any event under overhanging brows. Instead he focused on the massive halo of black hair above, into which a ballpoint pen had been stuck for safekeeping. His voice gave way as he tried to bark an order. The man pushed forward the requisition book: "You can fill out one of these, please," he said, "it's the usual process." He looked beyond Andrew who filled out the form. The man took it and returned with the part – a spark plug in a small yellow box – which he placed on the counter just out of Andrew's reach. It was all done, so it seemed, as one carefully choreographed movement. Poetry in motion, and as he stretched across to get the box, Andrew wanted to feel the man's eyes – wherever they were – burning the top of his head. He glanced at a broad and bony hand resting on the edge of the counter before turning to leave; unable to utter a word.

"Fuck you," the man muttered.

Andrew swung round angry but for only a second. "What?" he said, the word dying in his mouth as he searched for eyes he could not find. He wanted to say something, anything, to apologise if necessary. The man, the same age as himself, perhaps a little older, had not moved. The great mass of black hair, the halo of hair, seemed to have grown larger. The head was too big for the body belittled by the dull warehouse coat beneath which Andrew imagined emaciated, vulnerable nakedness. He felt another unusual surge of compassion. But why for this bastard? He wanted to touch the man somehow, to make him react, but still he could not find the eyes lost in the mysterious caverns that penetrated the man's skull. "Listen," he managed to force out, "I'm…"

But he was cut off. The man did at last look at him, although Andrew could still not catch the spark. "Fuck off, white man" he heard, or rather felt, as if he had been punched. The man turned and walked away no less beautifully than before.

I thought I was going to cry but by the time I got outside, I was singing.

Andrew wasted the rest of the morning and slept through the afternoon.

[][][][][]

They sat either side of a small table on Andrew's veranda which together with the filing cabinet made up the office.

"I can't believe you've finished it, Madiak. It ought to have taken much longer. Perhaps we picked the wrong place. Did you measure it?"

"Yes, Andrew. I did," replied the man who was old enough to be Andrew's father and who spoke to Andrew as if one part of him was sucking up and the other merely humouring someone who was not very bright. It was maddening.

Andrew said: "So how long is it?"

"Six hundred and eighty-three metres, Andrew."

"Exactly?"

"No, Andrew, approximately."

"Well then. . ." Andrew didn't know what to say.

Madiak stared at him with a flat smile on his face: "What, Andrew?"

"Nothing. I mean, how come you did it so quickly? What's at the other end?"

"The river, Andrew."

"I know that, for God's sake. Anything else?"

"Sweet potato gardens and cassava, and some houses."

"Houses?" Andrew was surprised. "Are you sure?"

"Yes, Andrew," Madiak sniffed. Is not a house a house?

"What sort of houses?"

Madiak looked at Andrew silently.

"I mean whose houses, Madiak?"

"Some of our men, Andrew."

"Are you sure?"

"Yes, Andrew. I saw them."

"Well I'd better go and see for myself then, hadn't I?"

"I'll come with you, Andrew."

"No thanks, I'll go on my own, when it's cooler." He pretended to get on with some work: "Thank you, Madiak."

Madiak did not move. He wanted to say something. Andrew knew, with a hollow feeling in his stomach, that it would be about the weekend he'd almost forgotten. During his siesta, as he drifted in and out of sleep, he had thought only of the incredible meeting of the morning. He wanted to see the man again. He could not get him out of his head. He looked up at Madiak seeing eyes that needed, he thought fleetingly, a good cry. "Sorry, Madiak," he said, "what did you say?"

"What are you going to do, Andrew?" Pushing him as he had done in the early days when Andrew was new and bewildered. But although it was in his nature to be pushed, this time Andrew resisted.

"I'm not going to do anything," he said, thinking he'd play Madiak's game, but the infuriating man only stared at him impassively. Andrew's inability to understand the simple realities of life baffled Madiak. Was he not a white man? What was the point of white men if they didn't know the answers? Madiak wanted Andrew to know everything and be strong. He wanted to help Andrew but Andrew wouldn't be helped, he only lost his temper and shouted. This time, however, he quietly asked another question:

"Where's Nalin?"

Which surprised Madiak. "He's gone," he answered and then added, "he's taken all his things with him."

Andrew saw Nalin's skinny old body shuffling barefooted down the road. A refugee under the hot morning sun, carrying his few rags wrapped up in a towel in one hand and his harvesting hook in the other. "Where's he gone?" he asked.

"I don't know." Madiak looked beyond Andrew's shoulder.

Andrew did not push the point. Bune would supply the answer later. And afraid of what he might hear, he didn't want to ask Madiak about Tarlie, either. Instead, he thought of the stores clerk, seeing a face creased with anger. He wanted to see it again, urgently. He heard Madiak calling to him.

"Andrew?"

"Yes, Madiak?"

"Are you alright?" Madiak was worried. It was alright for white men to lose their tempers but it was not alright for them to disappear into a sort of trance. Then things really might fall apart.

Andrew pulled himself together. He didn't want Madiak to see him stark naked. "So what actually did happen, Madiak?"

Madiak looked straight back: "They were drunk, Andrew."

"Who?"

"The Kanga men."

Andrew wasn't surprised, although there would have been others involved as well. "But they were at muster this morning." He saw the little huddle of Highland men, pathetic in their rags and bare feet despite their bodies, made muscular by strenuous work.

"Not all of them, Andrew. Some have gone."

"The men who did it. They've run away, I suppose?" He hoped they had, but Tarlie was a Kangaman.

"Yes, they've gone, Andrew."

Madiak would not look at him. Andrew was relieved. He studied the table top, he said: "There won't be any more trouble. Will there, Madiak?"

"No Sir. Andrew." Madiak was as relieved as Andrew and he would let everyone know that the blame would be pinned on those who had run away. He knew that the company would not press the issue any further and Andrew knew that Jim would square it with the authorities and with London. One or two others would disappear over the coming days and things would settle down, which was what everyone wanted. She had asked for it, after all.

Andrew began to work in earnest. "Thanks, Madiak," he said, as he looked through the daily harvesting records Bune had brought up earlier, the small, tight writing precisely like the man himself. He was relieved to hear Madiak's big, flat feet flap down the hollow veranda steps. "Madiak!" he shouted.

"Yes?" From the garden.

"Tell Bune to put on the generator at six. I've checked it myself."

"Yes, Andrew."

Andrew trusted Bune. He trusted Madiak too for that matter, but in a less sure way, and it occurred to him that if he was going to set up a trade store in the compound, Madiak would run it rather well. Jim would think it a good idea, at any rate.

□□□□□

A dead tree stretches up into the burning sky. A large carrion bird lifts up into the heavy air, a dead lizard hanging from its beak. Nothing else stirs in the lazy heat. The dusty road runs straight over the undulating land, tall ranks of gloomy oil palms on the one side, and on the other a thick tangle of vines and vigorous young trees through which a path has been marked by a neat line of sticks. Andrew follows the path, taking in the scent of freshly cut vegetation, assuming he will eventually reach the river and perhaps have a swim. He is therefore surprised – despite what Madiak had said – to find himself in a wide clearing which stretches to a distant line of dark trees above which rise steep green cliffs gilded by the setting sun. He stands amongst gardens of sweet potato – neat, rectangular patches, highland fashion – leggy cassava and stands of maize, taller than himself, rising from cushions of fresh green groundnut. A footpath leads to a group of grass houses, clean and square, which seem to embrace some sort of meeting place, shaded in one corner by a great clump of plantains. The empty quiet dignity of the place is enhanced by distant laughter and splashing from beneath the cliffs.

The doorway of a larger building opens out of the little square. A white cross stands up from the roof.

[][][][][]

Darkness shot with speckled light. Bare earth floor, rows of low benches, an altar covered with brightly coloured trade cloth, a plain wooden cross and a pair of candles in tin cans painted bright primitive colours. Behind, a painting of the Crucifixion on warped, splintered plywood: Christ in his agony, stretched naked, vulnerable and emaciated upon the cross rising from the mud, the background an angry sky. Despite the torture of His body, He looks out: it's OK, it doesn't last. A Melanesian Christ, the crown of thorns set upon a great halo of black hair. Large feet protrude, waiting to be placed firmly on the earth again.

[][][][][]

Andrew sat on one of the benches and rested his head in his hands. The restlessness of the last twenty-four hours drained away. Someone sat beside him. He knew it was Petrus. They sat in the silence, together. Beyond his closed eyes, Andrew imagined candles flickering in the dark and the man on the cross looking down onto the top of his head, burning him with His eyes.

"What is this place?" He mumbled through his hands.

"We call it Ples."

Andrew sat up, opened his eyes and looked towards the altar: "Who lives here?"

"We do," said Petrus, baldly, adding after a pause: "We have our food gardens and on Sundays we have the church as well."

"Are you Christians?" Andrew sounded incredulous although he was not.

"Some are, but anyway it helps to have a place where we can come together outside the company."

"A sanctuary?" Andrew asked.

"Yes. That's why we call it Ples, ples bilong mipela."

Andrew said: "Is Tarlie here?" He wanted Tarlie to be in this place of safety.

"Yes, he's in my house."

"He is OK, isn't he, Petrus?"

"No. He's a bit mad. He's Samson after his hair was cut off and they had blinded him." Petrus paused, then: "I don't want him to die. We need him." And after another pause: "But don't you worry, Masta, he'll get better."

And you'll mend him if anyone can, Andrew thought; surprised therefore when Petrus answered him: "No, Andrew, he has to heal himself."

"Does he?" Again Andrew sounded incredulous.

"Yes. And you too."

Andrew wanted to be offended. Instead he laughed: "Do I need mending?"

"Oh yes, Andrew. We all do."

Andrew knew that Petrus saw him stark naked. He said: "And Nalin? Is he here?"

"No. He's staying with his family in the mill compound. He's not like Tarlie, he was mad before it happened. When he looks into the future he sees nothing. He's frightened. If he was here we could look after him." It was the longest speech Andrew had ever heard Petrus make.

They looked at the Crucifixion together. The emaciated Christ with his halo of black hair, which ought, Andrew thought, to have a ballpoint pen stuck into it.

"Is He enough, Petrus?"

"He's enough."

"Why?"

"Because He's real. Because He is unconditional love, Andrew. That's stronger than anybody."

"Is it?"

"Yes, Andrew. Do you believe it, Andrew?"

"I'm not sure. What is it?"

"I can't tell it to you, Andrew. You have to know it."

Andrew didn't know what he knew. He looked away from the picture, seeing a blackboard on an easel standing in the corner. On it was written the words: 'Love Your Neighbour'.

"Is this where you have your school, Petrus?" He had heard about it from Bune who had asked once for some kerosene lamps for night classes.

"It is." Petrus whispered, as if ashamed that the secret had been discovered.

"What do you teach?" And for a moment Andrew saw himself joining in, the hearty teacher commanding the rapt attention of the class.

"Just reading and writing. People want to learn your magic."

"Is it magic?"

"No," Petrus laughed, "they soon learn that."

"Where do you get the books and things?"

"We buy them, and Missis Margaret gives us things."

Andrew was surprised. Margaret was Jim's wife. He couldn't imagine her getting involved in anything so specific. Yet just as the calm and giving Petrus naturally belonged here, so did she. Maybe it was the only place where she did belong, because she certainly didn't belong with Jim. In fact, now he thought of it, the very idea of Margaret being associated with Jim at all was outrageous. This place is also Margaret's place, he thought. It made nice and tidy sense. He was pleased with the deduction and was about to ask Petrus what he thought, when the little man checked him:

"Master?"

"Yes?"

"Are you going to plant up this land? We've seen the sticks."

"No Petrus, don't worry. We won't plant any of it. Ples is safe." He seemed to thump the bar again. Joseph laughed.

5

Bune Shoves Andrew

Across the level spread of the plantation, Andrew could see the distant chimneys of the oil mill dribbling thin smoke into a bleached sky. Miles away, a trail of dust was raised by a motorbike which buzzed irritably in the dead afternoon. He hated this weather when even the mornings were warm and cloying. He groaned in selfish agony: "Ohhh," as if in real physical pain.

"Sir?"

It was Bune. In the hierarchy of the plantation division run by Andrew, Bune was not supposed to approach him directly. He was supposed to work under Madiak. But Bune ignored this artificiality, insisting, by his existence – which was enough – upon direct contact with those of whom he, Bune, took account. His purpose, at this point, was to take account of Andrew the white man, whose own purpose – Bune had no doubt – was to ensure that the plantation functioned, at least for a little longer, as a part of the greater scheme. Yes, Andrew would have agreed despite his lethargy, we have to be efficient cogs in the great machine. It is what we are here for.

He was glad to see Bune, not only for the diversion but also for the man himself. "Bune," he said, turning to face the man but feeling he had something to hide. His hand automatically reached for his flies.

"Sir," replied Bune, his wide mouth and broad nose, his whole expression, a picture of cooperation. His eyes shone.

There was an insistence in Bune's attitude, a fact of his Bune-ness, which meant he was always and inevitably a part of Andrew's consideration of things, but, unlike Tarlie, in a way that made no emotional demands. Bune was like an automaton: never had he let Andrew down and never had his work been other than exactly what was required. He existed for his work, it seemed, and Andrew pictured him at night climbing back into his little box like a toy soldier, waiting to pop up for work again as soon as he heard the muster bell in the morning. It was impossible to imagine a life for Bune beyond the plantation. Bune was small and strong, no more than muscle and bone. His receding hair line and slightly protruding navel only enhanced his photogenic perfection. He had been, Andrew was sure, born in the prime of life, and would die in it. Sometimes Andrew wondered if Bune was actually a human being, so perfect did he appear to be. Far too perfect to excite the sort of carnal thoughts which often stirred his uneasy mind when Tarlie was around.

All the same, Andrew was not blind to Bune's charms. Bune knew it and therefore he faced Andrew easily, naked except for the neat cotton shorts that were ever his only covering.

Thus they amused one another. Looking at Bune's navel, Andrew said: "Yes, Bune?"

"Yes Sir?" retorted Bune, putting on a face of concerned interest, the hint of a frown creasing his forehead as he watched Andrew's face.

Andrew did not know what to say, but it was good to have someone with whom to get back to ordinary things. Forget the growling man in the stores whose eyes were so deeply set in their sockets that they were invisible, making Andrew want to explore the interior of the man to discover them. Forget, for God's sake, the beautiful and heart-breaking departure, the back of the dull warehouse coat beneath which... Andrew glanced up at Bune's face that looked at him as if his thoughts were being read. Again he blushed. He put his hands in his pockets and sat on one of Petrus's chairs. "Um... Won't you sit down?" he said.

Bune perched on the edge of the chair opposite. It was as an incidental action. He did not take his eyes off Andrew's face and Andrew could not avoid them. The black pupils held him, at first against his will, but as he was held, his unease subsided. He felt that if he moved an inch or two nearer, he'd touch Bune's forehead with his own. The depression of the last few days lifted. "Bune," he said, unable to stop himself, "do you know the name of the stores clerk, at the workshop?"

Bune looked not a bit surprised, as if it was the very question he had expected. He raised his eyes ever so slightly, seeming to look out at the world over the top of Andrew's head. "Alloy, Sir," he said, as if it was incomprehensible that Andrew did not know the man's name.

But Andrew felt that he did know. He said: "Do you know anything about him? About this person who is Alloy?"

"He's from Markham. He was born there."

Which was enough, because Markham, Port Markham, was the capital on the mainland. People born in Port Markham were different from everyone else in New Sudan. They were the first generation to be born away from home, homes to which their parents and grandparents said they intended to return, while knowing in their hearts that they never would. They were stuck in the place made by the white men even though the white men themselves lived separately with their cargo, which they guarded with a passion. Touch a white man's cargo and you were in trouble, everyone knew that.

All the same, only in Port Markham did people come to know themselves as New Sudanians. So this is the name of the animal which has devoured us, is it? Which has, it seems, shat us out as servants of the white man. We are, therefore, and are determined to be, wild, uncontrolled and rootless, our ties with the land, our home, having been severed. Our senses are blunted in an unknown landscape that is ever changing, noisy and filled with traps and surprises, our help-mates as helpless as ourselves. Confused, we are bound to define ourselves by the churches, secret societies and gangs to which we belong, fiercely protective of our new identity and violently resentful of any challenge to it.

"What else do you know about him?" Andrew was eager for information. As if Port Markham was not enough.

"He's the workshop store's clerk," said Bune baldly. No further enlightenment came, but he looked back into Andrew's eyes intently.

Andrew was not in the least disconcerted or annoyed by Bune's apparent obtuseness because Bune, unlike Madiak, was indisputable. If Bune had said Come, follow me, Andrew would have followed. He tried to outstare Bune but the man did not flinch, although the frown was gone and he seemed to smile. Eventually Andrew returned the smile: "So what did you want me for, Bune?" and he was sure Bune answered: Was it me who wanted you? So that Andrew replied:

"I didn't call for you, did I?" And again Bune seemed to reply, although his lips did not move: Not in so many words. But then he burst out loudly presenting his prepared speech, surprising them both:

"It's the new planting, Sir. What do you want me to do? Should we start clearing the road line tomorrow? We could bring in the D5 at the weekend to make up the roads."

"No Bune, don't do anything yet," said Andrew, "for God's sake," and he thought of the man who was Alloy, who surely belonged to Ples and not to Port Markham.

But Bune persisted: "But we are going to plant it, aren't we, Sir? It's in the plan."

"I don't know, I don't know Bune," said Andrew, laughing. What does it matter? He wanted to wrestle Bune, knowing that he could only win if Bune would let him. If Bune wanted him flat on his back then that's where he'd have to be.

Bune pretended surprise and with a familiar leer looked past Andrew's shoulder and said what Andrew had expected him to say all along: "But Madiak says. . ." He stopped, waiting for Andrew's expected reply.

"Fuck Madiak!" Anger that quickly turned into laughter: "I'm in charge. Am I not?"

They both considered the idea until Bune said out loud and with even more emphasis than usual: "Yes Andrew, Sir." He looked pleased.

Madiak's purpose for being had been defined to their mutual satisfaction, and for what he was, they liked him and needed him.

Bune got up to go but at the top of the steps he turned to look back at Andrew, who was watching him descend.

"Andrew?" It was unusual for him to use Andrew's name on its own.

"Yes, Bune?"

"Tarlie has gone. He won't come back."

"I know; he's at Ples."

"I'll manage the generator now. I can turn it. You don't have to worry." He descended a few more steps then stopped again, twisting his neck to look up at Andrew. His face lit up as if the idea – the reason for his visit – had only just occurred to him: "I want to show you block fourteen," he said. This was about as far away from Andrew's house as they could walk; it was a good hour. He added: "The palms are sick."

Andrew sprang forward, eager for the excuse to exert his body: "I'll go now."

He pulled on his boots before a delighted Bune. Down the veranda steps he ran, two at a time, striding into the dark palms at the back of the house, Bune at

41

his side. "It's OK, Bune," he said, "I'll check this out on my own," and he was off, walking hard, Bune happily watching him disappear down the avenue of palms that eventually swallowed him up.

[][][][][]

The hard, fast walking was what Andrew needed. He took well-known paths between over-arching palms, crossing the narrow roads without a glance left or right, leaping obstacles careless of injury. His eyes directed him but he saw not the view, focusing only on defeating the enemy, the distance between here and there.

He reached the gloomy gothic aisles of the so distant fourteenth block in the late afternoon. He stopped in his tracks, searching for the sickness of which there was not a hint. He was nowhere and he knew it. Time to move on. He pressed forward.

[][][][][]

That Andrew should have done something so emotionally focused and committed, so apparently reckless, was and always would be amazing to him. The very idea of himself doing it stopped him dead in his tracks years and years afterwards, making him wonder at the fantastic possibilities of life, the tragic lost opportunities. "Phew," he said later, "thank God I did it."

'Rubbish', you say, 'it's typical of the man, it just shows his erratic and over-charged nature. What's so amazing about that?'

Nothing now, I agree. But back then Andrew being what he was, given his narrow, comfortable origins, given the nature of the company for which he worked apparently so well, given his self-centred and defensive personality, defensive for the very reason that he felt at such odds with the world in which he found himself and unaware, then, of any alternative: well, in the circumstances, I insist that it was wonderful. Wonderful that Andrew grasped the nettle, so to speak, and did it.

No less wonderful, in fact more so, that Alloy, then and now, took it in the way he did and responded so positively. Andrew's defensiveness and the cool arrogance of his connection – or rather non-connection – with the world, arose from ignorance. He was bound to change once a splinter of light got into him, illuminating his soul and thus forcing him to acknowledge the facts. But Alloy, Alloy was the opposite: his aggressive arrogance, his cynicism, his dark view of the universe arose not from ignorance but from an excess of knowledge. He was corrupted by his acute knowledge of the pain of existence. Early in his life he had learnt to defend himself by fighting the world and winning. He had to win or else he would have gone under, would have fallen into the abyss, joining the dispossessed of the world, their numbers beyond counting. As Alloy matured into a man – while Andrew was still a boy – he learnt the world for what it is. For him all beauty, all goodness was tainted and corrupted by the reality of what men were, of what they had done to the world. When Alloy inhaled, he smelled the rotten stink of mankind. Alloy was the Man with the X-ray eyes, driven mad by the vision.

Yet Alloy knew the good things of life, like tenderness, joy, affection. He knew them to be possible because he had once had a mother who had loved him. How else could he have hung on to his beliefs? How else, come to think of it, could he have so vividly sensed the evil of the world if he had not had something good with which to juxtapose it? How else to explain the good things in Alloy: his loyalty, his tenacity, his sudden spurts of compassion and humour and, above all, his lack of greed? Clarence, Alloy's boss, recognised the good in Alloy from the very beginning.

"At the end of the day," said Clarence, born in the sugar-producing regions of Queensland, "at the end of the day," and it always was the end of Clarence's day, "he's good at his job, he makes a good stores supervisor, the books is always spot on, the place is tidy and you can trust him to do it right. He won't run away with anything, but," and Clarence looked up at the fan slowly revolving above his head, "I don't understand him. He's funny: 'smile Alloy,' I tell him but all I get is 'yes Sir,' and he goes on growling. And his temper! It'll get the better of him one of these days. Say the wrong thing and he fumes. He boils and broods inside himself. He'll burst one day. You'll see. And you won't want to be around when he does."

So, is it not a wonder that Alloy responded to Andrew the way he did?

Look, what makes us humans different from the other animals? What is it? It is the fact we can dream, consciously day-dream. We can dream of a better world. And what is our tragedy? It is that awful chasm between our dreams and the reality of our lives. Think of that too much, like Alloy did, and you're bound to be a little bit mad, if not a lot.

[][][][][]

Andrew presses forward through the darkness towards the animal bulk of the mill: a mass of pent-up anger and energy likely to explode any minute. Its parts groan in the heat, the steam escapes, the night is shot with flame. Metal hits metal, metallic vibrations, a man shouts, another screams, yet another laughs. The vibrations reach a climax, and die. Andrew presses forward, irresistibly attracted to the mass of hot and active machinery that has repelled him before, growing ever larger and more frightening in his nightmares of hard unyielding metal. But now, it grows no more; he can deal with it.

Nonetheless, as he approaches the mill, the falling night grows more dense: hotter, heavier and darker, thick also with the sound of industrial activity. The night is a solid mass in which Andrew moves as if – and he feels it acutely – as if he is integrated into it, like a stain moving through water. He is a part of the night; an idea in the solid intelligence of the night. The earth is forgotten beneath his feet.

The mill pushes up into the night, of which it too is an integral part, to catch the moonlight above on its chimneys. From them drift disconnected wisps of smoke, caught as moments of dirt on the bright disc of the moon. Around the mill – the hot centre of active night – is the small paraphernalia of the day:

disjointed, disfigured, dismantled bits and pieces of things diminished under the huge energy of the mill. Baked hard for the moment is all this stuff that men have made and broken. The men who must, it seems, be there, seek comfort in each other around little fires. Their words mean nothing and thus they are nothing in the industrial night. Not so Andrew. This is his night and he is a part of it. He presses forward. He passes by, unseen.

[][][][][]

To say that Andrew fainted on the little patch of lawn in front of Alloy's house would be untrue, but that is how it seemed.

What actually happened was that Andrew, having had enough of whatever it was just then and feeling nauseous, sat with a thump on the ground that brought him round and out of the night into which, you could have said, his soul had descended. Or, perhaps, ascended.

Alloy came to him cautiously but recognising him, picked him up and, without a word, took him into the house.

The small living room opened straight out of the front door. A single reading lamp focused on a small coffee table and the sofa and armchairs surrounding it – all cheap, imported company issue. The table was loaded with books and it seemed as if Alloy slept, had been sleeping, on the sofa, covered by a cheap and colourful piece of trade cloth.

Andrew saw nothing else as he was helped onto the sofa and made to lie down: his head resting on one of the back cushions moved to become a pillow on the hard wooden arm. His boots were removed.

"Hey, man?" Alloy's usual economical vocabulary failed him in a situation demanding . . . affection.

He sat opposite Andrew, looking at him. The same old frown – there was just too much flesh on the forehead – but it was benevolent and expressive, as always, of heightened emotion. Terrific emotion, at this particular moment in his life, for which Alloy had nowhere near enough words.

"I'm sorry." Andrew laughed, because he was embarrassed.

"Why?" (Is it not good that I am here for you?)

"No," Andrew wanted to get it right, "I mean I'm sorry. I'm . . ." He wanted to say he was sorry he was a fucking bastard, a selfish, arrogant, pampered white man, who had no right to be here at all in Alloy's house, lying on his sofa – the cloth of which smelled strongly of Alloy – with his feet up. But the words would not come. He wanted to cry although that was no doubt because of low blood sugar. Englishmen don't cry.

"That!" Alloy laughed, "Fuck that."

There, the pain exorcised forever. A small thing was now nothing.

[][][][][]

There they were: two healthy young men, not boys, each wanting and able at last to give affection; and each wanting, for once, not to rub the other up the wrong way. Alone also in the night, they were, in Alloy's house, and

44

undoubtedly attracted and fascinated by each other. What was supposed to happen?

Indeed it happened, but the consummation of their relationship was a response to pent-up frustration. A mutually astonishing realisation of the possibilities of life. Satisfying sexual gratification, confused with an idea of love: 'I love you', breathed, groaned, whispered, thought, in the literal heat of the moment. Not love, of course, but a connection all the same. A connection that liberated them from the isolation they had both until now assumed to be the norm of human existence. To use clichés, it gave them each a hand to hold in the night, waking up suddenly from a bad dream; it gave them someone to run to.

In the end, it gave them courage.

6
The English Way

"Tinklor?"

"Here, Sir."

"Balham?"

"Here, Sir."

"Whinney?" then louder, "Whinney!" and again, more gently this time, "Whinney." Coaxing him.

Mr Evans was decent, but they all held their breath and did not dare move until Whinney's tiny whisper was heard through the cold morning:

"Here, Sir," in a voice close to tears.

That was Trafalgar House finished. Mr Evans pressed a large red tick onto the page and turned it over, moving on to Waterloo. The houses were named after famous English battle victories: Agincourt, Blenheim, Trafalgar and Waterloo. The boys in Waterloo maintained that they were named after the London railway terminal. Hollands, the House wag, had suggested, in the annual essay competition – My School – that the other Houses ought similarly to be named Paddington, St Pancras and Charing Cross. The idea had not gone down well with Beaky, the headmaster, who proposed to give Hollands two for irreverence. Hollands claimed he was a pacifist, which had gone down even less well with a man who had lost both wife and leg in the war – he had to grip the back of his armchair when he beat the boys – so Hollands got three, and a fourth for continuing to argue while getting the third. The recent closure of the local railway station by Dr Beeching did not encourage Beaky to take the matter lightly.

Andrew liked Hollands, who called himself a London boy and who dedicated his life to challenging authority. He was finally expelled for asking Matron – Miss J – to instruct him in carnal knowledge on his 12th birthday. It was during bath time, when she would sit with the boys in the large room that contained three old-fashioned cast-iron baths each supported, Andrew had noticed on his first day, with animal feet; muscular and large-clawed.

"Waterloo," barked Mr Evans. Choo, choo, choo, Hollands would have whispered in reply, setting off an irresistible ripple of giggles for which he would have received the slipper from Evans afterwards in the gym. But that bright spark had departed in a chauffeur-driven car one drab Monday morning.

"Alexander?"

"Here, Sir."

"Blemish?"

"Here, Sir."

"Nwufoh?"

"Here, Sir."

"Owens-Montague?"

"Here, Sir."

Alexander the tall Head of House; Blemish, small and wriggly, the best hooker in the school; and Nwufoh. Nwufoh was huge, towering over Andrew. A gentle giant and saviour of the first fifteen. Andrew loved Nwufoh.

In his entire time at the school, Nwufoh had been beaten once, and then only as part of a mass dorm beating for talking after lights out. That whole episode had terrified Andrew – new to boarding school and lost in a system the others seemed to understand so much better – but as they trooped down to Beaky's study in their dressing-gowns, Nwufoh had flicked him on the bum as if to say it doesn't matter. And in the end, that time, it didn't.

They got two each – Beaky never gave less, there was no balance in a single stroke – stinging beneath thin pyjamas. Nwufoh was as tall as Beaky himself, who sensed the inappropriateness of beating this large black boy whose strong frame seemed capable of absorbing the strokes without feeling them. Beaky was no sadist, he did not enjoy beating children, but he did get satisfaction out of it on the assumption that it somehow did them good, preparing them for the cruel world beyond the school. He would have been hurt to learn that to boys like Andrew, the school itself was the cruel world, rendering everything beyond not quite so bad.

[][][][][]

"Nwufoh?"

"Yes, OM?" expressing the two letters of Andrew's diminutive with a deliberate exaggeration, as if highly amused by the idea of contact being made.

They walked in silence along the muddy track towards the rugby pitches that lay beyond the fields behind the school. Just the two of them, on a quiet autumn afternoon, the dank smell of rotting leaves heavy in the air. On rote, the boys were sent in threes on Wednesday afternoons – a non-games day – to re-mark the pitches. It was the turn of Blemish, Nwufoh and Andrew – OM – but Blemish had developed a large boil and was being kept in the sickbay for observation – what he needed was fresh fruit. Nwufoh and Andrew were on their own, Nwufoh carrying a rugby ball.

"Will you show me how to pass the ball, Nwufoh?" Andrew's inability to deal with the ball properly was infamous: he was Butterfingers and as a result not only a joke but a liability in the team. It made Andrew miserable. He dreaded games, when they would all throw the ball at him hoping he'd drop it. The trouble was that no one, not even Mr Evans (a professional rugby player in his youth), bothered to show you how to do it; you were supposed to know the trick. But Andrew did not know; he wondered if he had some sort of mental disability.

"Will you show me how to pass the ball, Nwufoh? Please? And how to receive it?" He would not have dared ask anyone else; certainly not Blemish, who would have laughed and thrown the ball straight at his head, screaming 'Butterfingers' as he did so.

Nwufoh also laughed, but the bigness of the laugh was aimed at them all for taking things so seriously.

"Come on," he said, "jog beside me." They jogged, their boots squelching the autumn mud.

"Not so close, OM, we'll hit each other. Move away a bit. That's better. Now run with me."

They ran, slowly.

"No, OM, I said run with me, with me, so we're running together. That's it! Well done. One, two, one, two, one, two, one, two."

They ran together in a steady rhythm, along the edge of the field, beside the raggedy hedge, beneath the sodden elm trees; one almost a man, the other still a boy, the only people in the whole wide world.

"Now," commanded Nwufoh, "fall behind me."

Andrew fell back.

"More, so you can see me at an angle. Can you see me?"

"I can see you." I'll never lose sight of you.

"Now when I pass the ball, OM, watch it coming towards you. Aim the centre of your body at it and hug it to you." Andrew hugged the ball as he would have hugged Nwufoh.

[][][][][]

Two boys run beside the hedge and pass through a gap between ash trees where the ground is churned muddy by the cows. They climb a gate into the sports field. They run up and down the pitch, in straight lines, in zigzags. They run to the centre, they run in wider and wider circles until they are beside a hedge again, under dripping trees, the leaves falling one by silent one. They pass the ball to each other in increasingly complex movements.

Nwufoh darts across the field with large strides, daring Andrew to get the ball from him. Andrew trails behind. It is enough to follow until he can throw himself at the older boy to bring them both down in the mud at the centre again. They scramble for the ball. For a second Andrew has it but Nwufoh is on top of him, hugging him, pressing him down into the ground before letting him go. The game starts again. And again. Autumn shadows make them giants.

[][][][][]

Nwufoh made a drop kick. Andrew stopped, panting, to watch in wonder as the ball rose higher and higher through the cold air to disappear into the disappearing day. They heard it land with a wet thud beyond the posts, Nwufoh running forward to disappear also until Andrew heard him shout:

"A try!" As a distant echo lost in the cold, new night.

For a moment Andrew felt alone in the universe, with Nwufoh, silent now and hiding, his only hope. So he ran for his life, his boots thrashing the wet ground, pushing through the resisting air, his controlled and heavy breathing containing him. He wanted to punish the ground beneath his feet for keeping him down when he wanted to fly.

Nwufoh lay on the ground hugging the ball, just beyond the white posts. A waiting, steaming, heaving animal. Andrew stood panting above him, hands on hips, the hunter studying the animal he has mortally wounded. But the animal sprung, grabbed his ankles and brought him to the ground with a thump that winded him. The sudden shock made him want to cry out but Nwufoh was on top of him, holding him down, grinning into his face:

"You see, it's easy isn't it? Anyone can play with the ball once they know it. You have to use your whole body." He grinned into the evening sky, and then back at Andrew, his victim. "But did you see my drop, OM? Did you see it?" His face filled the whole of Andrew's sky: "Did you see it?"

"I saw it, Nwufoh."

"And was it wonderful?"

"It was wonderfully wonderful, Nwufoh, honest."

Nwufoh stood up, a colossus. He looked down upon Andrew: "Not everyone can do that," he said, "I kicked it further than Evans."

"You did, my boy," said Evans himself. "I saw you do it. I could do it myself, once. Now it's your turn. Take the ball and run with it. It's your life." He spoke to them both, hugging his old coat around him as the only life he had left. He was pleased to see that they were friends; pleased that Andrew had learnt one or two of the tricks. They'd beat St Dunstram's next term for the first time in years. "Come on," he said, "it's time we got back. Get up, Owens-Montague. I saw those passes; they were good."

Nwufoh offered Andrew his hand and pulled him up. For the first time in his life, as they walked back, the boys each side of Evans, Andrew felt he belonged to the place. He was part of it with Mr Evans and with Nwufoh there in the real night. A cold night – a first frost promised the following morning – the hard air stings Andrew's nostrils and bruises his young chest, expanded after all the running, warm, wonderfully warm nonetheless; together with the smell of the muddy fields and the invisible cattle, all his, as were the homely lights of the school – that dilapidated old house – beyond the raggedy hedge and the naked near-winter apple trees of the old orchard that overlay what had once been the priory herb garden. For the first time in his life – as a step in his personal progression through it that was also an atomic part of the progression of everything – Andrew recognised the night as a thing of which he could be, actually was, part; not, as before, something of which he had been afraid. Now that the night welcomed him, the night was wonderful. He thought he had taken hold of the truth and held it in his hand. The silent, chewing, apparently thoughtless cows, steam gently also.

[]][[][]

Andrew's rugby improved with his confidence. He seemed – and it was noted in the staff room – to have less of a crush on Nwufoh. But each, nonetheless, was acutely aware of the other. A brief eye contact between them was enough. Sometimes, when passing, Nwufoh would shove Andrew hard with his shoulder but without any other sign of recognition, sending Andrew careering, dropping his books. Andrew loved it. They found themselves in adjacent beds at the beginning of the spring term. Evans had arranged it. The two boys pretended it was something they did not want. Making their beds in the morning they would deliberately bump into each other and make disparaging comments for the whole dormitory to hear:

"Get out of my way, OM, you tick."

"How can I make my bed with a great fat ape like you standing there, Nwufoh? Go away."

"You should sleep outside, in Matty's kennel." Matty was Beaky's dog, a stringy mongrel who adored the boys and whom they insulted remorselessly while he wagged his tail and begged for more.

"You should be in the zoo, so's we don't have to hear your snoring." But Andrew loved Nwufoh's snoring. It was not much more than heavy breathing but it was music to Andrew's ears. He lay in the big, high-windowed, naked bedroom, the moon pouring cold silver upon eight narrow iron beds, snugly listening to Nwufoh, his guardian, until he too fell into a dreamless sleep.

[][][][][]

Angela was her name. She was Beaky's daughter. She taught general science: she had a good degree in physics although she found it difficult to impart the secrets of that fascinating science to anyone else. This was because she only felt secure in the neat world of Newtonian mechanics. The less certain physical realities proposed by the likes of Einstein, Bohr and Dirac – local boy made good – disturbed her profoundly. So much so that she went around with a permanent frown of incomprehension, as if these bad boys had wilfully upset her own equilibrium as well as that of the universe.

But, despite her large glasses and the little girl's page-boy haircut, she was an attractive young woman. She behaved well; she could be polite and even entertaining; she had a well-shaped, healthy body. The trouble was, no normal man got anywhere near Angela. Those who did find their way down the mile of badly surfaced driveway to stay at the school were, of course, going to be school masters. Apart from the rare but more-or-less normal men resigned to their fate, like Evans, they were of three distinct types. First the abysmal failures, sufficiently abnormal to rule out the possibility of whatever it was – connection, companionship, security – altogether, despite, from time to time, desperate offers of marriage. Second, those who were normal in most respects but otherwise homosexual, who found a dangerous refuge of sorts, in those days, by teaching in obscure boarding schools. And lastly the young, intelligent and highly desirable types passing through between public school and university or between university and a bright future somewhere anywhere but in a small English prep school in the years of Angela's prime. These were the ones that drove her mad; their young, energetic and irresponsible manhood irresistible. That they often made up to her, either out of well-bred politeness or because of their own youthful lust, only made matters worse; as did the occasional fumbling act of coitus when she delighted in the young body but was left with a feeling of unbearable loss afterwards. An endless procession of attractive men passing through her life. They remained young and fresh, while she became older sister, young aunt and before long, she knew, mother figure.

For this reason schoolboys generally exasperated her. She saw in them the selfish young men they would become. For the older boys in particular – their crackling voices, their spots and the downy hair above their upper lips – she felt a special revulsion; they represented all the animal dirtiness of the men that she knew, in the end, she wanted desperately.

But – and it is important to understand this, in view of Andrew's brief relationship with her – Angela was not by any measure a stupid or careless woman. For a start she had a reserve of compassion which could overcome all her raging frustration, manifesting itself most fervently to those who had initially generated the strongest revulsion. In this respect she was a saint, and so saintly did she seem to be at times, with boys who were ill or homesick, that when her exasperation showed through and she was unable to control her anger she appeared, by contrast, to be more calculatingly mean than she really was. She was characterised by those who thought they knew her, including her father, as having a 'mean streak'.

Then, although Angela could not let things alone and had always to see them through to the bitter end, she was good at much that she did: bad as her physics teaching was, she taught basic biology and chemistry almost brilliantly, so that the boys went on to their public schools with a smattering of atomic theory and an understanding of photosynthesis which stood them in good stead. Moreover, and this was her glory, she taught games with a wonderful enthusiasm to the ticks who, as infants, were allowed to play the yobs' game of football. Football brought out the yob in Angela who could dribble the ball with the best of them, as she steamed around the pitch in her gumboots ignoring the finer points of the rules, the tiny men screaming after her. All parties forgot the harsher facts of life in the process. Seeing her thus enthused was what made the bright young men passing through think they might make a pass at her.

Oh Angela, Angela,
Rushing around the place,
Come to me tonight
And sit upon my face.

Thus wrote the aspiring poet in memory of red-faced Angela, laughing and puffing out steam into the cold winter afternoon of her prime.

[][][][][]

Angela also taught spelling – someone had to do it – and she had devised a method that suited normal boys well. It started the minute you arrived at the school as a tick. You learned one new word each weekday, in weekly batches of five, with a test on Saturday mornings at which you were supposed to score five. Anything less than four meant going to Beaky at break and getting one for each wrong word. Not a bad system. Most of them had no trouble learning the words and enjoyed the process, testing one another throughout the week and getting a good sense of achievement by passing the test. Even the constitutionally lazy and apparently irredeemably wicked were brought around in the end.

However, she dismally failed the few boys who could not spell however hard they tried to learn the words. Andrew was one of these. He could remember the few words necessary to pass the weekly test, but as he learned new words the old ones slipped away; his essays were littered with mistakes. In the end, he avoided certain words. The trouble arose in the middle of each term when there was a mammoth test which would cover everything learned since the middle of the preceding term. Fifty or sixty words in all, of which twenty-five would be tested. Anyone who scored less than twenty was in trouble. In the same spring term in which Andrew's bed had been placed next to Nwufoh's, Andrew got into trouble.

After the test, the boys swapped papers with their neighbours for marking. Andrew and Nwufoh were sitting together for once. They knew what the other had scored before they knew their own scores. Nwufoh scored twenty-five, Andrew fifteen; he was bottom of the class. For the first time in his life, Nwufoh doubted the rightness of things. Should he have cheated the scoring for Andrew, his friend?

Angela put the papers in order. Only Andrew had failed.

"Owens-Montague?" She stood up as she said it.

"Yes, Miss." Andrew sounded sullen, although he was abject.

"Every time you do badly. Why?" she asked rhetorically: "Because you're lazy." She spoke to the entire class which hated her for the embarrassment she caused. "You're a very stupid boy. You've had plenty of time to learn the words and you won't do it." The plum in her mouth grew larger as she ground remorselessly on. "You refuse to do it for some reason I cannot understand." She then sat down leaving Andrew standing. "Oh," she added, "you'd better go and see the headmaster now. I don't know what to do with you. Take this." She wrote something while Andrew remained standing, burning with shame. He did not want to cry but he had the tight feeling inside his chest of the child oppressed.

"Here," she held up the folded note for Andrew to take. She watched him leave, unable, though she tried, to avoid feeling revulsion for the clumsy man-boy. Only when the door had closed behind him did she relax and turn her attention to the perfection that was Nwufoh. The slight projection of his lower lip, exposing the interior pink, fascinated her. She wanted to touch him.

[][][][][]

Beaky's study was the old gun room. Andrew knocked on the door as was the custom; three delicate knocks halfway down, ear pressed to the wood to catch Beaky's weary: "What is it now?"

Andrew opened the door just wide enough to let himself into the terrifying room that was Beaky's cosy refuge. The best place in all the world, where Beaky could not conceive of being more happy. Here were his books and pictures, his chair and reading table under his standard lamp beside the fire, and best of all, his desk, a great mahogany table, which had once belonged to Admiral Nelson.

On the desk, in the window bay, overlooking a little lawn at the side of the house bounded by woodland, Beaky had written five volumes of his History of England. A neat stack of filed notes awaited his commencement of the sixth in the summer holidays. This would take him to the Glorious Revolution. He had three more planned: The Growth of Empire, World Domination and the last.

The idea of this last volume oppressed Beaky because it would have to cover the period from the First World War to the present depressing state of affairs. The Suez debacle was a personal humiliation. He could not bear to think of his England as a small country kicked around by other small countries. His life – at public school, in the navy, as Headmaster here, in his writing – had all been based upon the notion of himself as an Englishman; therefore a citizen of a Great Nation, part of a Great Idea. He could have borne the present tribulations if he could have romanticised modern England as small but plucky, able to outsmart its bigger rivals, as he had written about Alfred the Great and the Elizabethans. But he could see nothing plucky about the present condition. Having the H-bomb seemed to be an underhand sort of thing, not quite playing the game.

Ah, the Glorious Revolution! Those were the days of eternal sunshine and well-made furniture. Beaky felt better just thinking about it. Here in his study, writing about England's Wonderful Story of Adventure, he felt grand; and he went on feeling more or less grand until the end of volume seven when he died at his desk looking at the invading woodland beyond which the winter sun set on Anglo-Saxon England.

Beaky's world, his Hobbit's hole as Mr Evans described it, the place where boys were beaten. A narrow strip between door and Beaky's armchair beside which you bent down holding your ankles, looking at your shoes and the worn carpet, waiting to receive what Beaky on the spur of the moment decided to give you. It meant nothing more to Beaky than an interruption to his writing. To some of the boys he beat it added much to the burden of their lives. For what we are about to receive, Hollands would have whispered.

Andrew got four. Before he knew it, Beaky was back to his writing and he was back outside, a hot cauldron of indefinable feelings. He was truly whipped, unable to communicate even with himself. He went back to the classroom, studiously ignored by his classmates and by Angela.

To everyone around him that day Andrew seemed to be deliberately withdrawn. There was nothing deliberate in it; he was dead. At bedtime, when Hollands would have willingly pulled down his pants to show off, wiggling his bottom in defiance of Beaky and the whole world, Andrew ignored the other boys so thoroughly that he frightened them. Nwufoh watched him.

Years later, Andrew could not understand why he felt so bad about that particular beating. It was not so bad. Beaky did not give anything like the stingers he got from sadistic prefects at King's Sutton. If Alloy had given him the same four he might have found some pleasure in it.

Lying in bed, as the anaesthetic of self-pity wore off, Andrew felt worse. The pain was inside him, twisting his stomach, pressing his chest. His breathing came as short, laboured gasps. A lonely soul trapped in a body of material pain and aware of its singularity in the limitless, rushing, ever-expanding vastness of space and time. God is forgotten. Despair waits in the wings. It is the human condition. Beethoven would have written another piano sonata.

〔〕〔〕〔〕

Andrew is turned in on his side curled up. He hears his own breathing as a pulsating roar but as he quietens, relaxes into sleep, he is aware of Nwufoh's breathing too, a sound so distant that it might be Matty in his kennel guarding them through the night. Andrew opens his eyes. He is acutely aware of Nwufoh, who gives a sharp snort, is silent and then begins to breathe normally again. He turns over and looks at Andrew with wide eyes. Andrew gets out of bed and joins him.

〔〕〔〕〔〕

For Christ's sake, there is nothing extraordinary about what Nwufoh and Andrew did. Or uncommon. Or, above all, bad. It was as good as anything can be.

Unfortunately, Matron, during her early dawn round, found them in each other's arms. Matron was not stupid or insensitive; the boys liked her, and her briskness only partly masked her affection for them as a race of pigmy men. But Matron, Miss J, despite a disastrous wartime affair behind her, was as limited in her emotional imagination as were most of her contemporaries. She feared abnormality as yet another attack on the rightness of England as it faltered.

"Get up, get up," she whispered with a frightening urgency. "Get up and get dressed."

They did as they were told, fumbling half asleep for clothes that would not unfold.

"Quickly now," she said, briskly but with an urgency of love; she wanted to hold them tight, to keep them safe from the world that would corrupt them if it had not done so already. She was half afraid, half excited, in her desire to do the right thing by the school and by Beaky whom she wanted to save from something. From what, it did not matter, so long as she was the one who did it. This time she must get it right.

Asleep still, the two boys followed Miss J – disastrous wartime affair and an aborted baby all behind her – down to the famous Victorianised Jacobean high-windowed hall, mysterious and shadowy in the morning half-light. They were sat on one of the green leather upholstered benches Beaky had bought at an auction of the surviving contents of a blitzed city hall.

Matron, Miss J, entered Beaky's room to disturb the best part of the day when he quietly drank a cup of tea which had come from a wonderful contraption that did it all for you. It had been given him on his sixtieth birthday by the boys themselves – Mr Evans had driven the prefects into town to buy it. Drinking his tea, Beaky would watch the dawn breaking on Ashdown, and then give an hour or so to the History of England before breakfast.

But not this morning. Homosexuality, or rather rumour of it, was death to a boarding school in those days. Before the war it did not matter, but these days it was clearly a symptom of England's decline and ought to be stamped out. Sodomy was still, after all, illegal. All the same, Beaky was not pleased by Matron's excited, whispered description of what she guessed Nwufoh was about to do to Owens-Montague. His immediate reaction was to let sleeping dogs lie: "It is something which tends to go on in boarding schools," he said, "they grow out of it, Matron, and if we make it look too serious they'll think it is serious. I'll have a chat with them and we'll put them in separate dormitories. We don't want to lose two promising members of our first fifteen, do we, Matron?" He laughed.

But the Miss J in Matron would not let it go: "No, Headmaster, it is no laughing matter. These things don't go on in well-run boarding schools." Dear man, you are sweet, I adore you but like all men in the end you are blind and unworldly. "They must be rooted out immediately, before they spread. I've said it before and your daughter agrees with me: Nwufoh and Owens-Montague are too close for their own good, and for everyone else's. If they become heroes of the first fifteen the other boys will copy them and we'll lose control; I've seen it before." Oh God, she had, during the war. "Nwufoh is too old to be here now and Owens-Montague is not, he's not... he's not manly enough to resist." Oh God, that disastrous affair in the war, when she was working in the sickbay on the airfield and he had seemed such a nice manly boy – it was hero worship did it, in times of danger, when men are as hysterical as girls.

Beaky tried to laugh her off: "Oh Matron, really, Nwufoh is only thirteen. Just leave them alone and forget it." He went back to his tea and tried to see past her out of the window, where a critical moment had been reached in the Battle; the Danes were going down.

But Matron was determined to do the right thing: "No Headmaster, I cannot let it rest, Nwufoh is a big boy." She had seen him, unable to resist her own fascination. "You must have noticed his voice is breaking?"

"Yes, Matron, of course I have. He's just a little advanced for his age. Well-fed Africans tend to be. He's leaving at the end of term anyway. His father rang me from the High Commission. They're going back, he's been asked to help set up a new regional government apparently. He wants his son to go to an elite school there. I tell you Matron, by 1990 that place will be richer than England and a better place too if people like that boy are running it. We did a good thing there, Matron. Lugard was a great man," adding and looking askance at Miss J, "Goldie was a funny fellow though, I agree." He sighed.

[][][][][]

Matron let him have his say – Lugard had been hen pecked too, Goldie escaped. She stood tight-lipped, determined, her hand resting on the back of his chair. She stared down onto the top of his grizzled grey head while he stared down onto the top of his tea going cold until the only way he could get rid of her was to agree. Nwufoh would leave immediately and Owens-Montague would take his Common Entrance early. "I can wangle him into King's Sutton if necessary," he said, "they seem to be willing to take the odd ones."

And that was that because once Beaky had made up his mind about something, however wrongly, he stopped thinking and pressed ahead. "Doesn't do to think too much," he said to Angela that evening.

Matron was sure she'd done the right thing this time round.

Mr Evans knew when he was up against the Furies. It was a pity about the first fifteen. They were thrashed by St Dunstram's. He wanted to weep.

Nwufoh had gone by the afternoon. Mr Evans drove him into Bristol to catch the London train. His trunk was sent up later. The two boys ignored each other and themselves but just before he left, Nwufoh ran into the classroom and waved goodbye with a grin on his face. He slammed the door behind him, the old house collapsed, and when the dust had settled, the cows were trampling the debris and the monks were back on their knees.

Two boys. Do you remember? Long time ago. The pair you sometimes see running around the edge of the field on an autumn evening.

At King's Sutton, Andrew kept a low profile – his own words. You're on your own was his philosophy. You certainly do not creep into someone else's bed during an emotional crisis. His rugby was useless.

Nwufoh returned to England for Sandhurst, where he was popular. Back home his career prospered. In the civil war, as a young officer, he was sent to deal with a small and rebellious group of fishermen and night-soil carriers. The bullet that entered Nwufoh's skull, having bounced back off a remarkably small and accidental rock on his darkling plain was bad luck.

7
Joseph's Lap-lap

Dark inside the club when outside is the bright tropical midday. Dark inside the club when the sun hangs as a ball of blinding fire in the bleached sky. Darker if anything then, than on the darkest of moonless nights, for during the day the darkness within contrasts sharply with the brightness without.

[][][][][]

In the mornings the women, the younger white women, came to swim in the little pool, a couple of steps down from the veranda. It was a small affair of plastic, surrounded by wooden decking that hung precariously above the active world below. They chatted and screamed and laughed and, in their skimpy swimsuits, they would beg Joseph for coffee. Most times they carried it back themselves: the jar of Nescafé, sugar, sticky tinned milk and a thermos flask on an old plastic tray. But sometimes Joseph would bring it all himself – insisting upon the fact – his measured, leisurely step priest-like and serious, his teeth sharp and ready for business. Wonderful and wild he looked, semi-naked, dark and powerful, his flesh firm against their white, pampered bodies.

They would watch him in silence as he bent down to place the tray on a little bamboo table. The thin cloth of his lap-lap tight across his buttocks and thighs, the concave curve of his lower back glistening slightly, bronze in the sunlight, the huge, naked feet claiming the flimsy decking.

In the warm morning silence – the workday sounds of the plantation below seeming distant and unreal – their eyes never left him, not until the last glimpse of the departing heel, a flash of light, disappeared into the dark interior. Forced into their own dark thoughts, they thought of themselves until the tension broke, and they remembered each other: then, a burst of hysterical exclamation, hard laughter.

"Too sweet."

"Such a darling."

"He's a cannibal, I'm sure. Look at his teeth!"

Each needs to say something about the man, their man, whose very dark oppositeness to themselves draws them close to him as if he is their own echo, their own shadow in the vain mirror, watching them always.

A sudden conscious shift in the conversation, as if they have forgotten him. But they never do: his presence is with them always and, acknowledged, adds spice to their talk, making them daring and also disloyal, when they think of their husbands. When Joseph had gone for good, they did not come to the club for a while but visited one another in their houses, remembering something they had lost, not sure what it was.

Nonetheless, although they were aware of Joseph in the darkness, inside, they would talk about him as if he could not understand them, as if he was another species, perhaps a dog lying at their feet, snapping occasionally at their ignorant conversation. At any rate, as if Joseph was not quite human. He may have been, for all they knew, a superman, one with cloven hooves.

But Joseph is the puppet master.

"I think we should buy Joseph a new lap-lap." They did not speak as individuals in Joseph's mind, but as a single cluster of noisy chickens.

"Why? He looks too sweet in that old thing," says one, "I've never seen him in anything else."

"Except club nights," from another, "when he wears those bright colours Henry got him, funny old thing."

"Yes, I know, but usually it's that old one. It's almost worn out. I should think it's been washed a thousand times."

There was a distinct silence as they thought about Joseph's old lap-lap, worn out and stretched tight to accentuate his shapely and muscular figure that rose above his thick highland calves, all supported strongly by those great, wide feet planted firmly on the ground.

That silence, Joseph said, was even more expressive than the words that followed. He laughed when he said this, knowing that they had been thinking the most primitive of thoughts about him. He kept silent, not wanting to disturb their daydreams with the clinking of glasses behind the bar. He wanted to allow their thoughts to ferment to maturity. He knew what they were thinking. He knew what they wanted to do to him, and his cock would twitch as he imagined their mouths taking it in.

He talked to me about all of this freely and although he never stated the fact, it was clear that he was in no way angry with these women. In fact, he loved them for their sins. He pitied them also as unformed things who were unlikely, unless they got a severe shock one day, ever to realise their own humanity, let alone his or anyone else's.

After a longer silence, as the women drank their coffee, looking down across the golf course to the sea of oil palms beyond and the quiet volcano in the distance, as they apparently thought serious domestic thoughts (Was the girl doing the ironing properly? Had the boy clipped the hedge too low?), there was a giggle. They looked up, waiting for her to express her idea, their idea:

"I was thinking."

"What, Polly?" Or Dolly, or Holly, or Lolly.

"About Joseph."

"What about him?" As if they did not know.

"About his lap-lap." Were not they all thinking about just that?

"No!" Naughty! Polly is very young, just married to a very young man, the accountant, and she is showing off a bit. They treat her as a little girl, feeling that they are older and wiser, or ought to be.

"I was. I wonder what, I wonder what it smells like? I mean," she quickly adds, resisting the temptation to put her hand across her mouth, "he always looks so clean, I should think it smells nice. Even if he hasn't washed it a thousand times." Bending, stark naked, over the wash tub.

They wait for her to go on.

She does: "You see, I don't think they wash their clothes that much. Do they?"

No one answers, so she goes on as if expounding an idea which may one day become the subject of an essay: "They just seem to get wet in the rain and then throw their things on the roof of their huts to bake in the sun. That's what Dickie says, and I think it's quite a good idea, don't you?" She's thoughtful and serious, as if presenting an appropriate anthropological hypothesis. She would like to have gone to university.

"He's clean alright, darling." This from an older woman who's seen it all, or so she thinks. "I bet Henry insists on that."

"Probably helps him wash." From another. They titter, proud of their perception of Henry's queerness.

Joseph watches, his presence guiding their thoughts.

"No, seriously." Polly again who is not being serious and knows it: "I 'spect it smells nice." She sniffs the air through which Joseph has walked.

There is a pause in the conversation, eyes and mouths open wide in frozen dramatic surprise as if, as if, as if they had not all been thinking just that, and Dickie such a sweet boy too. Then on they rush eager to express their ideas, to live, a little more, their fantasies, just as the erotic memories of a sexual encounter are heightened by the recounting of it to a willing audience.

"It depends on whether he wears underpants or not," says the older woman. "He probably doesn't. Then the smell would be a bit more. . ." She pauses, pretending to think about it: "more pungent."

They sniff the air, and then rush in, more eager to yap than to listen.

"What? Sort of arm-pitty?" says another, thinking of the strapping young gardener hacking away at the hedge.

"Yes, but with a hint of urine."

"Warm and sun bleached."

"Or slightly mouldy in the rains."

"Oh yes, because he's bound to sleep in it, so's it has that nice musty smell like old apples," this from a New Zealander, "and dirty sheets." She thinks of the smell of the dark little room in which the strapping young gardener sleeps.

"You're all wrong," shouts a strident, angular, youngish woman, the wife of the mill electrician, a Queenslander, raised on a struggling outback sheep farm.

They look at her, waiting for a revelation. Perhaps she has seen Joseph without his lap-lap.

"They all wear underpants," she says, and in her mind's eye she sees the pair of yellow trunks drying on the hedge behind the garage where her less strapping but nonetheless comely gardener has his own dark little hole of a room. "Look, what happens when it rains?" she asks, "they strip off to their underpants until it stops, don't they? It keeps the other things dry, and very sensible if you ask me." You fools, she seems to suggest: I know about these things, let's for God's sake keep to the facts. "If he didn't wear pants, you'd see his thing hanging down under his lap-lap, wouldn't you?"

Indeed you would. They've all looked for it and seen no more than the tantalising bulge created by his now undoubted underpants, the thought of which creates even more ideas.

By this time Joseph is, as Andrew would put it, killing himself behind the bar in the dark, rocking to and fro, heaving with silent laughter, his head thrown back, his mouth wide open, staring at the ceiling, his eyes filling with tears. But he controls himself, with an effort. Silently he walks out onto the veranda. He stands there, a foot or two above them, looking down at the coffee table, a mockery of foolish ignorance, giving them a good view of his body, having pushed the knot of his lap-lap just low enough to expose a hip-bone and the lower part of his abdomen. A couple of curly pubic hairs show to perfection.

Polly swallows.

They see him. They stop their chattering so that they can look at him not in the least embarrassed. There stands the manifestation of their dreams. Together they adore him, but each one wants him for herself. Every pair of eyes checks the slight bulge in front, which Joseph deliberately presents by arching his back a little. Joan (or Jean, or Jane) is right: definitely underpants, and rather a pity too. Had they been Joseph's own Highlands women, they would have taken the matter into their own hands there and then, whistled en masse, chased him back into the club and stripped him stark naked. But these talkative girls are not brave. They keep their thoughts to themselves, becoming (as Andrew says) dirty-minded little sluts in the process.

Joseph stands awhile, resisting the strong desire to laugh, looking stern, every inch the cannibal of their dreams. Then slowly, as the high priest of their desire, bends down to collect the coffee things on the little tea tray. He bends so close to Polly (or Dolly, or Holly) that she smells him: sort of smoky Imperial Leather she tells Andrew much later in the club, when she is a little drunk.

8
Joseph's Tea Towel

The darkness, now, is emphasised rather than relieved by small globules of light; not strong enough here inside the club to join together as radiance.

Outside, through the open veranda doors that take up an entire wall, the globules float on the surface of the empty swimming pool. Members prefer to stay inside, where it is hotter but where the mutual company is more reassuring than the huge night outside. Ceiling fans stir the air.

Saturday night. There are better things to do than go to The Club, as is expected on a Friday – Club Nite. Nonetheless, there are those souls (lost, dear or otherwise) who, having nothing better to do, will end up there on Saturday night. Those who Happened To Be Passing By, or who Just Thought I'd Pop In and who will go on dropping into some club, pub, bar or other watering-hole until they can no longer avoid the unavoidable reckoning.

Jim showers, shaves, dresses in clean clothes and puts on after-shave lotion – Leather, Texas, Hell's Angel, or some such macho brand – and joins the other transitory souls who inhabit this limbo, The Club, where they are drawn to one or other puddle of yellow light that is My Usual Place, as inevitably as bits of driftwood will drift ashore somewhere. Sometimes they sit, Quite Happy Thank You, until someone or other drifts up beside them.

Joseph watches from the dark, an unattached, ghostly tea towel polishing a glass: the pointed knees of a pair of crossed legs, a skirt, floral pattern; a shoulder and one attached arm, long sleeve guarding against mosquitoes, hand playing with a whisky glass and managing to hold a cigarette at the same time; disembodied bits and pieces of two or three bodies mutually snug and safe with each other or, alone – Quite Happy, Really, For The Moment, Thank You. Occasionally, a face, hot and strained perhaps, forcing a laugh, detached and lost; vacantly staring inwards or over the horizon, fearful of either view; or relaxed and happy even, This Is The Life. Joseph sees all.

From a distance, below the hill on the golf course, the globules of light coalesce to form a single globe in the dark. A delicate, fragile thing of distant conversation lost in the largeness of the roaring night beneath a moonless sky. Further away, on the hill where Andrew's house stands, there may be a speck of light, or not. Beyond that, nothing.

Joseph is attentive. It is part of the job.

"Joseph, two more beers and a G and T, please."

"Joseph, clear away please will you? And bring another bucket of ice. There's a good boy." Joseph is older than Andrew.

"Where is that Boy? Joseph! Are you deaf?"

"I sometimes think we'll have to get rid of him. He's too lazy and he's getting uppity. He's a bighead."

"Don't you dare. I love him. He's too sweet."

Polly, Dolly, Molly is a little pissed: "Don't worry, Henry wouldn't let him go. Would you Henry? He's Henry's pet. He tucks him up in bed."

"No, he can stay."

Henry the old darling, Senior Planter, is also a little drunk but nowhere near as gone as Polly, whatever her name is.

"Joseph'll be here when he's a lapoon and we're all dead."

Do not talk of death, thinks Henry, I feel it out there, waiting.

"Boy!"

A tremor of, of what you might call outrage but it's not; rather, it's a sense of unease about a newcomer who is too loud and who does not know the rules. But they say nothing.

"A scotch on the rocks and vodka lime, I said. Quick!"

The visitor knows no better. Love triumphs. Joseph serves the drinks with his expected deference. Someone pats his bum in the dark.

"My usual please, Joseph; and a glass of that red wine we got in last week for the wife."

Joseph, back behind the bar, looks at Jim's torso in its own globule of light. Bulging blue shirt hanging over low-slung belt of shiny black, pulled so tight it must hurt blue jeans.

Joseph cannot see Jim's head but would not look at it if he could. He would look past it towards Margaret. Margaret does not amuse Joseph like the other women. The sight of Margaret there in the club is good, but the thought of her is enough. Joseph would not mind if Margaret touched his bum.

Your usual? What's that? Why should I remember your usual? I want to forget about you when I can, Mr Masta-Bastad. Just tell me what you want and I'll give it you but don't ask me to remember you. You can blow me.

Joseph says: "Yes'er." He pours the whisky for Jim into one of the best glasses he knows Jim likes: cut, Waterford, pattern like a thistle, someone brought a set over once for a leaving present which never got given. He pours the water over the ice the way Jim likes it, as deferentially as he pours the red wine into the warm glass for Margaret, warmed by his own hand. Watching, you might think Joseph loves both of them equally.

Jim is sober. He picks up the glasses and walks over to his wife, Margaret. Joseph does not exist. Therefore, Jim passes out of his particular puddle of light and ceases to exist also.

Joseph can see Margaret's head and shoulders now, in her piece of light. But in this case it is Margaret who provides the light. When she moves, the light moves also. Joseph watches her until Jim comes into view extinguishing the light. Joseph turns to replace the bottles on the shelf behind.

Jim and Margaret sit on matching rattan armchairs at a small, matching, glass-topped table. There are two empty chairs across the table to which no other bits of drift-wood drift. The whole set is identical to the others in the club, and to the one they have in what is called the Family Room at home. Only there is no family. It is company issue. They are in all the family rooms, in all the houses on the hill. Some of the wives have covered the seats in their own material, bought from Chan's other store in town. Chan knows what they like: soft, pastel shades. He gets the stuff from his relations in Hong Kong. Margaret would have preferred armchairs and a coffee table made by Petrus, with cushions in bright colours, but Jim would not like the idea. She would have no argument against him: you need rattan in this climate, girl, I should know. Indeed he should.

Children might have helped, some people said.

Margaret smiled her smile. The idea of Jim as a role model for children, the idea of Jim as a father was. . . the universe would not stand for it. It was the one mitigating factor of her marrying him: it stopped him reproducing.

Some people looked at Margaret and thought she was stupid. Perhaps it was the washed-out blonde hair. She's not all there. Bovine in her inactivity, she seems to be.

They drank their first drink as if they were together: the GM and his wife, my missus.

[][][][][]

"It's too bad. After all I'd done for him. He didn't even say thank you, and when I asked him if he didn't think he owed me something, he just looked at me and smiled at me as if, as if . . ."

"Yes, Daff? Go on." Her husband was laughing at her.

"As if I owed him something."

She didn't mind being laughed at because she did not take herself seriously either. Half the time she wanted not to be married; but when she was away, she wanted to be back. She thought about her husband when she played tennis in the afternoons with the other wives. Despite his laughing, she knew she was a necessary part of his life: wife, and mother of his children. Playing the part gave her some sort of substance.

What had unsettled her in the morning was that despite the man's bare feet and poor clothes, the fact that he was a head shorter than her, she had felt Annu towering above her, watching her with his understanding brown eyes and somehow pitying her. It was more than pity; it was as if he – she blushed all over – as if he loved her, and wanted her to be more than she was. Well, she wanted that for herself. But what could she be? She was what she was: Daphne, known as Daff, like the cartoon duck, married to Peter, the mill engineer, mother of Alison and Tommy.

"You did!" Peter laughed out loud.

"I did what?"

"You owed him something."

"Did I?"

"Yes silly, you forgot to give him the money. I'd left it on the table and it was there when I got back at lunch time. And that is odd, I grant you, Daff. If there's any money lying around you can bet these buggers'll have it."

"Yes." She agreed, readily. She wanted to belittle the man with his strong, brown, shiny shoulders. But she could not: "And that's what was odd: he goes off suddenly but there's nothing missing. Nothing, and he'd done his morning's work perfectly." She felt disloyal for some reason, remembering that he'd hung out the clothes, made up the beds, dusted and swept the bedrooms – even under

63

the beds – and washed up. Had she not searched out every sign of him? "He even put some flowers in a jar on the little table in the family room. It was sweet." It had made her want to cry when she saw it. She did not want to denigrate him. She wanted to praise him.

"Oh-ho." Peter laughed again, enjoying, as always, her little act: "So he's sweet now is he?"

"No, he's not. I hate him. When you think what I did for him," she said with emphasis. "I taught him to work the washing machine and how to lay the table and fold the napkins. I even taught him some elementary cooking. Martha's so useless." She had loved the intimacy with him as she taught him to make omelettes and a proper salad with vinegar and olive oil in the kitchen one snug wet morning, the rain thundering on the tin roof. She remembered the smell of him: so clean and fresh, like a baby. She remembered thinking that angels were supposed to smell like that: like babies and new bread. Him making the salad: a servant under her direction and yet so strong that she had wanted to go on her knees in front of him.

These gaps in his wife's conversation were so common that Peter had ceased to comment on them. They had started when Alison was born, and at first he had wondered if she was suffering from some sort of epileptic fit. But they were just her mind wandering; thinking of the child, he supposed, and later the children, when Tommy had come. He was quite content to accept that he would have to take second place now. It was OK by him so long as he had her. After all, he could not have wished for a better mother for his children. Now, when she disappeared to whatever planet it was she went to, he was quite happy just to watch her. After nearly twenty years of knowing her, he had never tired of watching her face: a little more lined but the same face with its laughing, mischievous eyes and turned-up nose under the curly blonde hair, more attractive to him now than ever with its hints of grey.

"Oh, it's too bad." She was off again. "Just as I'd got used to him and trained him the way I wanted, he puts down the duster – I was writing to the children – and cool as a cucumber says: 'Madam.'" It had been like a command and she had stood up. "'Madam, I'm going. Goodbye and God bless you and your children.' I was speechless. I just let him go." She expected to feel a gap in her life. Where he had been. And yet, she did not. The idea remained, claiming her. It was odd.

She could feel Peter watching her with his amused expression. She pulled herself together.

"Of course I was furious. He might have warned me. It was the weekend and there I was stuck with the ironing, your silly lunch to get and planning to play tennis in the afternoon with Molly. Oh, Annu, I could kill you."

"There's no need to shout, Darling."

Had she shouted?

"It's not that bad, you've still got Martha."

"I know, but that's the trouble, it's never going to be the same again. I'll never find anyone as good and poor Martha seems even more hopeless by comparison. I mean, after all these years, she still can't lay the table properly. I might as well do it myself."

"Get rid of her then." He was still laughing.

"I can't do that. She's old. She'd starve."

"Rubbish. You're too soft. If I ran the mill the way you run the house it'd be full of useless people by now. If someone's no good, get rid of them. That's what I say. They need to think they'll get the push. It keeps them on their toes."

"You bully."

She was teasing him, but he meant what he said. He was afraid of letting go, of being seen to be weak. He didn't want to be like Henry, who was a soft touch if ever there was one. Peter's motto was: it paid not to get too close to them. It just led to a lot of complications and you got walked all over. He had built himself a little castle, Daphne thought, to keep anything too complicated or too emotional at bay. His job was the first line of defence, so that he got into such a panic if the mill did not run like clockwork. Even when Tommy was born the mill had come first, she remembered.

Then there was his weekend routine with the boat and the fishing on Sunday, which they had to join in with. It never occurred to him that they might like to do something else. And they felt that they had to be with him: Daddy can't be all on his own, he doesn't like it. He defined himself in his especially masculine activities, she supposed, just like the writer, whatsisname, Ernest Hemmingway. A man's idea of a man. Only, of course, Peter couldn't write at all. Even his love letters had been stilted and conventional.

She was the last line of defence: the loyal wife and mother. The part she had acted from the beginning when – she had no illusions about herself – she had been out to get him, the handsome man, who was nonetheless uncertain of himself but in whom she defined herself as a woman. She had wanted him alright; she still did, which was lucky.

"I'm not a bully, Daff," he said, but pleased all the same, "but it makes sense. I can't have the mill filling up with layabouts. If they're no good, I send them on their way." He looked at her sternly.

She pouted her lips, as if about to stick out her tongue.

"And don't look at me like that; I know what I'm talking about. No one has to starve here, there's always work on the plantations. Martha could get a job weeding for Andrew, they're always short." He folded his arms.

"Really, Peter! How could she? She's old and she's been in the house for years. I couldn't send her out in all weathers at her age. It'd be cruel."

"It is not cruel. It's just..." He could not think what it was for a moment... "It's economic reality."

She opened her mouth but he stopped her:

"He who does not work does not eat." That sounded good.

"Lenin, old boy."

"What?"

"I said Lenin." It was Henry, on his way to the bar. He stood behind Daphne, who was looking up at him fondly. "You just quoted him. Are you a Marxist, Peter?"

"No, he's a Leninist-Marxist, Henry, with a Trotskyite tendency," said Daphne, "get it right. He says I have to go out into the plantation and do some weeding or else he won't feed me. Do you think I'd be any good?"

"Hopeless, my dear." And the old boy continued on to the bar, to his beloved Joseph and to his third brandy.

"Why did you say that, Daphne? I never said it."

"You quoted Lenin, and that must include me darling, because I don't work, do I? And yet I eat. Why Martha and not me?" Poor Martha, she'd miss Annu as well. He'd helped her, he'd given her time off because it was he who helped in the evenings when they had dinner parties. He had taken a special delight in waiting at table: so assured and confident in his lap-lap and clean white tee-shirt. She could relax with Annu around. Martha was no good at all, dropping things and getting everything wrong. But Annu was a saint. "What, darling?"

"I said what's given you all these liberal commie ideas anyway? You never used to have them." He was definitely cross now, sounding pompous and middle-aged.

"You mean egalitarian, old boy, there's nothing liberal about communism." It was Henry again. Carefully carrying a brandy and a jug of water. "Mind if I join you? Mine drinking chum Clarence hath joined the Kaiser and that much-put-upon woman, his wife there, to discuss matters of state in which I have not the slightest intention of . . ." He trailed off.

"Join us and shut up, Henry." But Peter was fond of the older man. It sounded in his voice, which brought his wife back to him. She said:

"I'm sorry, Peter, it's losing him so suddenly, just as I'd got used to him. I was thinking, at last a really good house-boy and then he goes off. I wish you'd never sent him up. You should have kept him at the mill. I'm spoilt for life now."

"Golly, Daff, now you tell me. I wish I had, then. No one knew how to make coffee like he did. He was the only person who knew how to operate the machine. He kept the office perfectly. Of course I sent him up as soon as you said you were desperate but I missed him. He was unique. Most of them doing a job like that, just a cleaner, are either horribly servile and mincing or they think the work's beneath them and sulk all day. They're like that bolshie bugger in the workshop stores that Clarence can't seem to live without." Peter remembered Annu as different from the others. With Annu he'd never felt he had to put on a show. "Don't think you're the only one who misses him."

"Oh, Peter, I'm surprised at you. He was probably softening you up for a loan."

He did not hear the sarcasm: "No Daff, you're wrong. Annu was different."

"Did you say Annu?" Henry woke up. "Wonderful little man."

"I did, and come to think of it, Henry, it's all your fault." Peter was not sure if he thought the matter was serious or just another joke. Again he remembered, he remembered how much he had liked the man who had so thoroughly upset his nicely constructed ideas about how New Sudanians were supposed to be.

Henry blinked above his glass: "What's my fault?" He liked to play the old fool. "And what's Annu got to do with it?"

"About two months ago, Henry, you asked if Joseph could bring some chum of his down to my office about a job. Have you forgotten?"

"Indeed I have not, Peter. I could never forget Annu: best man we ever had on the plantations. You didn't want him at first but I knew you would once you'd seen him."

"You were right for once, Henry."

Henry raised his eyebrows.

"As soon as I saw him I knew he'd be good. He was confident, without being cocky."

Henry nodded into his brandy.

"And he just answered my questions, straight. He showed respect as if he meant it. I thought straight away I'd keep him on. As soon as an opportunity arose I'd get him onto the floor and train him up as a foreman. You could see he was a Big Man, for all his being five foot nothing to look at."

Daphne had never heard Peter so fluent. She glanced at Joseph who was watching them, and she wanted to praise Annu too: "Yes, and there was something almost sexual about it. He was a charmer. And it's funny, isn't it, that a man like that was happy to be a servant. He never showed that the work was beneath him."

"I can see he charmed you, Daff. Perhaps it's a good thing he's gone; he might have carried you off to the jungle." Peter looked at his wife, who looked away from him, so he stood up straight and put his spare hand in his pocket for the comfort of some coins he could hold. He laughed. Then he frowned into his glass. "And there's Alison coming back for the holidays. Wouldn't do to have that type around then. She's turning into a pretty young woman." He looked at Henry, who was looking at Joseph, who spat something out of his mouth.

Daphne felt embarrassment and then indignation. "No, Peter, don't be so silly. You're a man so you don't know what I mean. He wouldn't have played any silly games like that, he was too. . . he was too big. Henry, you know what I mean."

"I do. Annu is not the type to play games with people, but he does have what you might call sex appeal – if you want to be flippant," which for once, Henry did not want to be. "Charisma, star quality, call it what you like. He draws people to him, and he has the self-confidence to lead them. It's what we're all looking for, isn't it? A saviour. Someone to forgive us our sins."

"Yes," said the woman who was saying new things, "but it can be dangerous in a bad man, a Hitler or a Stalin."

"Indeed it can," said Henry, beginning to pontificate a little, "or even in one of those gang leaders in Markham one reads about. But that's the thing about Annu: there's absolutely nothing bad about the man."

"I wouldn't go that far, Henry," said the man who was still repeating the same old things, "no one's that good."

"No, you're wrong. There are plenty of good people around. People who instinctively do the right thing and who can be depended upon to do it all their lives. They often seem to be simple because they're undemanding, and often not even very imaginative or educated. They're the ones who never have much to say."

He stopped but Daphne said: "Go on."

"These good people – not you and me, as I say, we're too rich, but there are many of them if you look – they have no power because money, status, political control, possessions and all that have no meaning for them." He gulped at his drink. "It's the damned bad people who take charge. And look at the mess we're in. One really bad person can mess it all up. He even makes the fairly good people – you and me, I trust to God – do bad things."

"Rubbish," Peter snorted. He'd had enough of this claptrap and of the daft expression on his wife's face. Henry talked a load of rubbish when he was drunk. "I don't see many good people around. None on this island, for a start."

"Well, there you're wrong, Mr Cynic," Henry replied rather sadly, looking around for Joseph who had disappeared under the bar for some reason. "There are millions. It's just that you – and I – don't come across many in the world we inhabit. In this rich, consuming world of ours where we think we have a right to everything, where we're excused of thinking about the consequences by so-called laws of economics. If you were poor, Peter, and you lived in some village miles from anywhere, scratching a living from the soil, or you lived in the slums of Manila or Port Markham you'd meet plenty of good people. You'd need them to survive."

"And you're an expert are you, Henry?" Peter sneered. "With your boarding-school education and your planter's life in Malay*ah*?" He mimicked Henry's old-fashioned way of clipping the word. "And your good life here on Van Island. Old boy."

"Peter!" Daphne was cross with her husband. It was so typically brutal of him to go walking all over people's ideas without thinking.

But Henry put up his hand to stop her; he did not want to be the cause of friction between husband and wife; that really was a foreign country: "No my dear, he's right. I'm part of the whole thing I pretend to despise. And maybe I'm wrong: there's not much evidence of good people if you look around objectively." He scanned the room, moving his whole body melodramatically. But he looked at Margaret as if he was afraid.

Peter knew he had gone too far, but what Henry was saying made him feel unaccountably restless and aggressive. He ignored his wife: "And Annu? What is he in your precious scheme of things?"

"Annu? Why, Peter, he is unique because he combines natural goodness with leadership. He inspires by being himself."

"Too good to be true, if you ask me. Is he Jesus then?" Peter asked crossly. "Are you in love with him?"

"I might be." Henry was not afraid of the truth any longer, even if he did not act on it. "I might have fallen in love with Jesus if I'd met him. Thousands did. But I don't know what Annu is. Think about him."

They do, and for a moment each has a view of his own soul, buried deep inside the public presentation. Had they been asked what they were thinking of they would have said Oh nothing, or An odd idea just crossed my mind, or Someone just walked over my grave.

Peter feels an intense jealousy, attributing it to the assumption that his wife is sexually attracted to the man Annu. He is glad Annu is out of the way, and is determined not to think well of him in the future. If Annu is so wonderful then what am I? He avoids the answer. Easier to think of his children: if anyone said they were not good enough, he'd biff them one. He feels he would like to pick an argument with Joseph, who is watching him again. He wants to say Piss off, Joseph, but the idea makes him ashamed of himself. Time for another drink.

Henry feels immensely sad about the tragedy of mankind: potentially so wonderfully creative and loving, actually so irredeemably wicked and damned. Annu shone like a light but only to define the darkness all around. He thinks of the whore who had been killed last weekend in some drunken brawl in Andrew's compound. Jim had told him in confidence, we must hush it up. Andrew had shown admirable qualities in dealing with the whole thing apparently. Her pointless life and inevitable death out there in the dark makes Henry feel sad. Andrew's Admirable Qualities make him feel sadder. He had hoped Andrew would be better than that. He had hoped once that he himself would have been better. The disappearance of Annu makes him feel sad. He had liked the idea of Annu being around with them. He thinks of his own past and steps back, afraid. He is glad Joseph is reassuringly there behind the bar.

Daphne has a sudden, electrifying sense of joy, of liberation and of the wonderful possibilities of life. Oh, she is so pleased her children have met Annu. She wants the idea to stay with them all their lives. She catches Joseph's eyes and he smiles at her.

But because Daphne feels good, it is she who breaks the spell: "So why was he looking for work in the mill, Henry?" She didn't like to see the poor sweet looking so sad, and she was determined to cheer him up. "Was he going to reform Peter, the wicked factory manager?"

Henry laughed: "No, but it's a simple story."

"Tell me." She wanted to hear more about Annu.

Peter got up: "Excuse me." He walked towards the toilet.

Henry watched him go, and then turned back to Daphne: "He appeared out of the blue one evening, with Joseph." He looked towards the bar where Joseph was standing, as immobile and apparently as uninterested as ever. "I took to him immediately, so I offered him a job in the garden. I was rather busy at the time. We had just decided to bring in more village out-growers, if you remember." Oh God, what he'd give to go back only to that day, and start again. Daphne watched him; Joseph had moved into the shadows. Henry continued: "My little collection of fruit trees was a mess. I thought I could teach him how to prune and mulch and all that, but he didn't need teaching. He knew exactly what to do. I marked him down as boss-boy material immediately. He was well educated but when I tackled him on the subject, he was modest. He said he had no plantation experience, but that he'd like to learn how to prune and harvest the oil palms."

Henry remembered the conversation well, sitting with Annu on the steel bench Clarence had made for him, amongst his precious collection of fruit trees. Before Annu, he had trusted no one. The orchard was dark, dank and smelt of decay. After Annu, the place was brighter and more fresh, the diseased and useless branches ruthlessly removed, each tree thereafter standing up clear and healthy. The subsequent yield of fruit had been astonishing.

"I couldn't keep him all to myself, could I? And I had an idea, even then, that he wasn't the type to stay in one place for long. So I suggested that Bill um, whatsisname, the chap before Andrew, take him on and let him learn. Within weeks he was a boss-boy and Bill said he was the best he'd ever had. It was a nice retirement present for him."

Henry banished the thought of old Bill, rotting away somewhere in his retirement.

"As soon as Bill was gone I moved Annu on because I didn't want Andrew to have anyone that good; it would have spoiled him for life. So I sent him to Bunubu Estate as a harvesting and pruning supervisor. The place was in a mess after that poor alcoholic Pearson had run it down."

Where was he rotting, for God's sake?

"I was managing it myself while we looked for a replacement. Annu did wonders. Within three months he'd made it the smartest estate we had. The oil quality went through the roof. I sent Andrew there for a few weeks to learn what a good oil-palm estate should look like. He learnt his lesson well. Annu stayed on for about a year as the senior supervisor, which suited me. I could trust him and I was quite happy to let things go on as they were. But it was funny. . ."

He broke off: "I'm not boring you, am I?"

"Not in the least." She shook her head: "I was just thinking how funny it was. Annu more or less running a plantation and then becoming a house-boy. Go on. What was funny?"

He thought for a moment. "It was Jim," Henry glanced in Jim's direction, but saw only Margaret. A spasm of panic possessed him, but he took another large gulp of his drink and it passed. Daphne seemed not to have noticed, but she was watching him intensely so he had to go on: "Jim knew what was going on, because he kept coming up with people who ought to have been able to run the place, but I rejected one after the other. Things were fine. Why shouldn't a local chap have a go?"

He stopped and glared at Daphne as if it was her fault, so she said: "Why not?"

"Why not, indeed, but Jim'd got a bee in his bonnet. Like he does. He went to have a look at the place and met Annu himself. I'll never forget his reaction because it was quite different from mine. He saw Annu as a danger and as someone who was sly, inevitably up to no good, bound to be doing something against us. 'Working behind our backs,' was the way he put it." Henry stopped.

Daphne didn't like to interrupt, so she waited. She wondered if he was ill.

What Jim had said was: "You can't put these kanakas in a position like that, Henry, bound to lead to trouble. You can't depend on 'em. They'll crack and then where'd we be? We'd be in the shit in five minutes. I should know. We got to have someone we can trust. One of our own. I'm surprised at you Henry. Thought you knew better."

"It was ridiculous," continued Henry, "when you think of how that Pearson messed up the place, and how Annu had sorted it out. But I couldn't persuade Jim and the more I tried, the worse it became for Annu. Jim assumed he was one of my favourites and became even more determined he should go. In the end, he seemed to hate the very idea of Annu. So Annu went." He looked at Joseph before going on: "Maybe he was right. We have to maintain our control, I suppose. I don't know. It was about the time Chan's store got wrecked."

"Yes? Then what happened to him?"

"To who?"

"To Annu."

"Oh, the next I heard was from Joseph who said he'd been back home and now he'd returned could I find him a job. That's when I sent him to Peter."

Daphne was fascinated by the story and by the way in which Henry, usually so distant and flippant, warmed to the telling of it. Peter, she noticed, had not come back but had joined Jim and Clarence, the three of them deep in some technical discussion about transport and ignoring Margaret, as usual, who sat motionless. Glancing at the bar Daphne saw that Joseph, back in her sight again, was staring at Margaret; not rudely, but watching her as if he was watching over her. It shocked Daphne because it made her realise how little she knew of Margaret, of the woman who could inspire what looked like adoration. She wanted to ask Margaret to join them but the distance between them was vast. And she was the one who had to make the journey, she knew that.

Henry had stopped, assuming Daphne had lost interest. He did not mind. He leaned back, his eyes closed. He'd be happy never to open them again.

"Please go on, Henry. I was just thinking about what you said. It's so funny, isn't it? When you dig down a little bit everyone seems to have come across this Annu: you, me, Andrew, Jim, old Bill. I bet Clarence knows him too, somehow. What made Annu so good at cleaning up the plantation, do you think?"

"I told you. He has charisma, animal magnetism, leadership quality. Call it what you like, but everyone wanted to work for him. They worked well for him: the old women weeding, and those strapping young harvesters who are usually so much trouble. That was his secret. But it was more than that. I remember talking to a young man once who had always been in trouble before Annu came. You know the type: they're wild with a sort of desperate and undefined anger, like caged animals. They want to fight life on all sides. They come down here and stay for a while because we offer them so much money. And what good does it do them? No good at all: they lose contact with their villages in the Highlands and become sexually diseased drunkards here." He thought again of what Jim had told him about the whore, of the way she had been carved up the previous weekend. "Anyway, he said, he said. . ."

"Henry, Darling, whatever is the matter?"

Henry was crying. "I'm sorry, Daphne, I've obviously had much too much to drink. I think I'd better go home."

She leaned across to touch his hand. "What did he say, Henry? Tell me, please." She had to know.

"Who?" Henry appeared to have recovered.

"What did the young man say about Annu? Please tell me."

"Oh, he said that Annu loved him."

[][][][][]

"'Enry, come over 'ere will you. We got a little problem."

Jim was not drunk, but he was feeling powerful and optimistic from the drink. A warm glow of benevolence had spread through his body. He loved these ordinary men sitting with him, despite their manifest inadequacies and their need for his leadership. Only he had the guts to do what had to be done. It took a brave man to run this sort of thing in this god-forsaken place, infested with kanakas who couldn't tell their arses from their elbows and who fucked everything they touched. But he was their man alright, and he knew what he was doing. Didn't he?

They acknowledged Jim's ability to direct the monster that was the Van Island Palm Oil Development Company; to bully, to cajole, to seem to beg even, so that what he wanted them to do, got done. To go out and do it himself if necessary, making a mess you had to clear up. But having done it in bluster, anger and misplaced energy, he then disarmed you by not mentioning it. He did not blame you for being a useless no-hoper who had ended up in this dump because nowhere else'd take you. You were born that way and you couldn't help it, just as others were born kanakas and therefore irredeemably incapable of anything. As he said to Margaret, in one way or another, just about every day: 'Look girl, don't teach a dog to type a letter; better do it yerself and 'ave done with it. Dogs is fer barking.'

They had to support Jim and try to give him everything he wanted, because they needed him like they needed the air they breathed. He was rough, rude and a bully but he did indeed keep things going and, in terms of the things that the directors in London wanted, he did move the project, and therefore inevitably the great human project itself, forward: number of hectares planted increased steadily; number of out-growers increased at about the same rate; yields, OK, declining to an acceptable level once the natural fertility of the soils had been exhausted; quality of the refined oil good; and numbers of gainfully employed New Sudanians more or less in line with what the government had been told was required by some economist or other. Most importantly, the loan was repaid to the bank in record time and the company made a reasonable profit, which made the shareholders happy.

Just don't ask any questions. No one dared.

But each one had something to say. Henry would say 'Any port in a storm', but he knew Jim was a rare port providing him with every comfort, even the opportunity to feel morally superior.

Peter would puff his pipe in a manly way, saying 'Jim's a rough diamond, but we all help him along when he needs it', hinting at Jim's social inferiority. When Peter reported back from leave, Jim would say ''ello Pete, never noticed you'd gone.'

Whenever Jim was criticised, Clarence would say, 'But we can't do without him, let's face it. Can we? We mustn't make a fuss.' If anyone could be said to have fond feelings for Jim, it was Clarence, his fondness being one of the few things that made an impression upon the thick hide that protected Jim's emotional whatever they were. That dog adores me, girl. I can't think why.

Henry, Peter and Clarence. They knew the worth of Jim. Jim knew his worth as well but he deceived himself sufficiently to believe the lies they told him. Not calculated lies, exactly, but by the accumulation of little bits of flattery, of the giving in to Jim's vanity for the sake of a quiet life, of never saying what ought to be said, of letting Jim always have his way, of avoiding the misgivings about the way Jim ran the show, they allowed their lives and their relationships with Jim and to each other to become one monstrous piece of white-washed infamy. As Jim said to Margaret, 'Look girl, they love me. That's what keeps me going in this dump.'

In the club, therefore, surrounded by his supporters, Jim is The Man of Action. He can look the world in the eye, or pretend to.

"'Ere, Joseph! Where is the bugger? Joseph, bring a chair for Masta Henry." Joseph brings it.

"Come on, Henry; sit down here beside Uncle Jim," he calls across the room. Margaret has shifted her chair back a little in order to make room for Henry. She moves out of the light in which parts of Jim are now the centre. She takes her light with her.

Henry walks across the room, his tall, spare figure slightly hunched as if, like Andrew, he is ducking something. The difference being that Henry has spent longer doing it, and is now fixed in the position. He clutches his glass for support but otherwise appears sober. He pretends not to have seen Margaret.

Joseph watches. He sees Daphne left alone. He sees her isolation as he removes the rattan chair upon which Henry had sat. Having placed the chair near Jim he returns to the bar where he pulls at the shark's tooth necklace which Henry had given him but he leaves it in place. He does not want to hurt Henry's feelings over a small thing.

End of Act One?

☐☐☐☐☐

Act Two?

Left is the bar. Joseph leans a little across it, into the same bit of yellow light Jim had occupied when he ordered his first drink. The long, strong profile of Joseph with its protruding lower lip is obvious. His large head is sunk into his big shoulders. He might be naked but for the shark's tooth necklace that hangs forward a little.

Right, the open wall of the club gives out to the moonless night in which the club is suspended.

Left again, but a little nearer to the centre of the stage, just discernible, is the immobile Daphne. Her legs are crossed, her chin is cupped in her hand, her elbow is on the arm of the chair; the other arm rests on her lap; a large white handbag is on the floor beside her. She is barely visible: we only see her because she is wearing a light-coloured dress, maybe white even. It catches a little of the light escaping from elsewhere in the room.

The cast is in a state of suspended animation. A pin could be heard to drop were it not for the roar of the tropical night out there, the millions of insects.

Centre Stage then draws our attention; the little group of people. Margaret to the rear left; red dress and washed-out blonde hair. On her right, Jim is in the centre of the group but he is not quite facing us. Margaret dominates although we do not always see her.

Jim is brownish and blotchy, with a thick mat of brown hair. Seeing him at a distance, walking, Jim appears to be a short man but although shorter than

Henry, he is not especially short and is in fact the same height as Margaret who, nonetheless, impresses onlookers as being a Tall Woman. Sitting, he is too big for the small chair, filling it to bursting with his well-fed body, in youth muscular and solid, now losing its definition: the lips are gone, the eyes are shrinking and the nose is a lump of incidental flesh, useful for smelling rats.

Nonetheless Jim sits above the men around him who are lower down in their chairs watching him, and because of his position Jim has a clear view of the bar and of the shark's teeth behind it. But never, during the whole episode which follows, does he appreciate that it is Joseph who watches him the most.

Although he perhaps ought to be sitting on the right of Jim, Henry sits on the left side of the table, slightly in front of it. This means he has his back to Joseph and therefore cannot see him, unless he twists his neck. Nonetheless, and unlike Jim, he is aware of Joseph watching. Also in contrast to Jim, Henry is by no means too wide for the chair in which he sits but is slumped so low that his legs stretch away forever, way out of the limelight; somewhere in the dark his ankles are crossed above his well-polished brown brogues. Slumped thus, he has to look at Jim by squinting upwards.

Clarence is too small for the little rattan chair altogether. One has the impression that his feet do not touch the ground. He almost has his back to us. We see little more than a vulnerable neck above defeated shoulders, which are nonetheless held straight when he remembers.

Peter? Well if clothes maketh the man, they make him. He looks like one of those 1950s insurance advertisements in his big-checked shirt, with his pipe and his black hair combed back.

□□□□□

"Now listen, I don't want this to go any further just yet," said Jim. He looked around to be sure of their privacy. "Listen, we got a little problem, 'Enry, as I've already told Clarence and Pete 'ere. Not one I can't deal with, but I need your cooperation. We can't 'ang around like we usually do. Action is the thing and I want to see it. OK?"

He looked at each of them in turn, screwing his eyes up as if thereby he could see them better and somehow by doing so make sure that they would do just what he told them, knowing he would 'ave to do it all myself, you see if I don't, girl? He looked at each one of them so that the others knew who he was looking at, until they each felt individually uncomfortable: Peter pulling on his pipe harder and harder for all the world as if he was hopelessly masturbating, Henry hating Jim but hating himself even more for being part of the charade, Clarence grinning amiably and rocking like a small boy who wants to go to the lavatory.

Joseph watches.

Jim was satisfied that they appreciated the seriousness of the situation. It did not warrant this conspiratorial gathering at night, but he had learnt that one way to make people listen was to give the impression that what you were saying was a secret in which they, as very special people, were being allowed to share. Gather round, friends.

"Now see 'ere, it's our lot in London," – as if the board was his own private property. "They want us to increase the rate of planting to meet the original target that those ignorant buggers from the bank set ten years ago. We got to do it." Then he added dramatically, as if they had, en masse, protested at such preposterous nonsense: "Yes, I know they're ignorant fuckers but we can't argue with 'em. We 'ave to get out there and do it."

Jim was good at this type of show. It was much easier to act Jim than to be Jim. Always, 'Them in London' were driving him. The fact was that when Jim decided he had to Do Something, because not doing something was anathema to him, it was the Doing of it that was the imperative, not the reason. If Henry's heaven was running a little tea plantation with a routine that got the best quality tea in the world, giving him plenty of time for his garden, his music, his books and his collection of blue-and-white china, that was Jim's hell. Jim would have fought his way out of it, ripping out the tea in order to plant coffee, with the cry that that was what the directors in London wanted him to do and who was he to argue.

Jim looked Henry straight in the eye, challenging him to deny it: "What's more, they say we got to push ahead with these hybrid dwarf thingies I been telling 'em about." When Henry had first launched the idea of dwarf palms, Jim had laughed at him. "So we got to increase the planting. What did we do last year? Hundred and eighty hectares. And only a bit more the year before. Not enough." He gripped the arms of the chair. "I want four hundred hectares cleared before Christmas ready to plant in the wet, and then we got to think of a thousand next year."

Was there a clamour of objections? Did Henry point out that it would take another twelve months before they had the seedlings? Did Peter say that mill capacity was already fully used up? Did Clarence protest that he had not the foggiest idea what they were talking about? No: they nodded their heads in agreement.

"Good," said Jim. He would issue a memo on Monday confirming what they had agreed, as if the subject had been thought out carefully and discussed at great length. Polly's husband, whatever his name was, the young accountant would work out some figures making quite sure that the returns justified the expenses incurred.

In the end it would look as if the decision was based on common sense and economic opportunity. So it's agreed, we'll invade Poland and then go for Moscow by Christmas. By the time anyone sees the folly of the enterprise it's too late and it's all happening. Why the fuck didn't you say something about the winter then? You'd think these Poles'd be grateful for what we've done for them!

"'Enry!"

"Yes, Jim?"

"How much could we plant now, just filling in the bits and pieces we've already got cleared?"

Henry pretended to think: "Well, Jim, if we keep to the plan, we have precisely one hundred and twenty-four hectares. That's the last sixty hectares of Bunubu, forty-five hectares of the Harrisons' place up the coast and then the balance is the old mission coconut plantation we want to convert on the Lingalinga road." He knew Jim would not be satisfied. There was of course the extension land but he did not want to mention it, otherwise before they knew where they were, Jim would have doubled his estimate.

"That all?" Jim had an idea Henry, the old dog, was pulling a fast one on him. "I was sure there was more. You sure?"

"Yes, Jim, if you remember, what with forecasted prices looking rather grim we decided at the policy meeting last year to limit the planting to not much more than a hundred hectares a year for two or three years." He coughed, feeling like a pompous old fool. "If prices do improve, which is unlikely in my view, we can push up the yields with fertiliser for a while. You agreed at the time, and . . ."

"Yes, yes, 'Enry, I may 'ave. I don't know but if they say in London we 'ave to plant, we have to plant. What we got in the nursery?"

No use giving Jim the wrong answer, he'd check the records himself: "About three hundred hectares."

"I got another seventy-five hectares' worth." He beamed at them. There ought to have been applause, but Henry was wary: "Where, Jim?"

"Blyton Bay!"

Blyton Bay was another oil-palm project.

"Blyton Bay! For God's sake, Jim." Henry sat up. "What do you mean? It's on the mainland."

"I mean, Henry, that Blyton Bay, as usual, 'as cocked it up." Jim was triumphant: "This time it's thousands of seedlings and no land. They let those stupid Blyton Bay kanakas have it back again. Sets a very bad precedent. They'll have to trash 'em if they don't let us 'ave 'em. Looks bad, that."

"But the cost, Jim. We'll have to ship them over."

"Leave that to me, 'Enry, that's my problem." Jim tapped his head. "I got it sorted. All you got to do is find the land. We got it somewhere."

"Yes, we have," said Henry, forestalling Jim. "There's about three hundred hectares in Andrew's extension." Had he betrayed something? He felt that he had.

"Good boy. I knew it. I was telling Andrew only last week 'e should get going on it. Take 'is mind off that other little problem." He winked at Henry. "But I didn't know we had that much. Well done!" As if Henry had conjured up the extra land, and Andrew's connivance, just in order to please him. "He's a good boy that one. I knew 'e'd come round. So we got enough for now. You'd better start thinking about the nursery, 'Enry, because they'll definitely want the thousand next year. We'll be up to the mountain in no time." Jim saw a vast plain of oil palms stretching all the way from the coast to the mountains, and even a little way up.

"So, no reason why Andrew shouldn't get moving. Will you tell 'im 'Enry? I think you should." He winked at Henry again, and again Henry felt he was doing something dishonourable.

[][][][][]

The light around the four men dims a little so that we notice Margaret. We can tell that she is watching Joseph who is intent on Jim, taking in every word he says. After twenty seconds or so, the light around Jim becomes brighter again, making Margaret appear to fade. Of Joseph, all we see are the shark's teeth. Except, from time to time, the sudden flash of his own teeth, whiter than Daphne's dress.

The roaring chorus of the night-time insects becomes louder, drowning any general conversation there may have been.

While everything in creation is moving ever further apart at incredible speed, they are tied ever more together, destined to become one conscious act of wickedness despite Henry's efforts to resist. The primeval gang, atomised by education and self-awareness, writing, artistic creation and all that, welded together again by its own collective, devious inventiveness.

No wonder Joseph laughs.

Another small light, further out from the centre, stage-left of the bar. We cannot but be aware of it in the general darkness all around. It is at the entrance door to the club, from the car park. The door most people use. Clearly the light comes from outside, shining into the room where the action is happening, but there is not much of it. So the two figures in the doorway are difficult to define.

Is it a trick of the optic nerves which happens when we stare at an object? The light appears to get brighter, pulsating a little. Bits of energy float off into the room, but insufficient to make a real impact on the solid darkness. The bits of energy die in here, like the boy's cigarette butt died on the grass.

Alloy's silhouette leans against the upright of the doorframe, arms folded, his great halo of hair making his head too big for his skinny body, his shoulders a coat-hanger on which his shirt hangs.

Andrew steps forward into the dark of the club. The roaring night holds its breath.

We watch Alloy standing on his own for a moment, until the clink of glass on glass draws our attention to the bar and to Andrew who now sits on a bar stool in the same puddle of light Jim had occupied earlier. Shark's teeth hang above him.

Andrew drinks on his own, in his white shirt, which is all we can recognise. His back is to Jim and co. Does Margaret watch him? We are not sure. None of them see Alloy in the doorway, but Joseph knows he is there because Andrew has told him.

"Give me half a dozen beers to take out, please, will you, Joseph?"

It is not allowed. Beer has to be consumed on the premises. If a member wants beer at home he has to make his own arrangements. Club beer is for the club, otherwise there is no knowing where it might stop. Andrew could just as easily have got the beer from the junior staff club where Alloy is a member. They break the rules there; that is what it is for. They could be drinking in Alloy's house by now, but Andrew insisted on going up the hill for some reason, dragging Alloy with him.

Anyway, Joseph does not always stick to the rules. As long as he gets the empties back. He will collect them himself if necessary from Alloy's house. Joseph will pass the beers out the window to Alloy, and Andrew will slip away, unobserved. Even if they see him, can't he go into the club without having to greet everyone he sees? Actually, Andrew, you can't: it would be odd if you did not acknowledge your clan.

Margaret watches, Joseph smiles his smile, but the limelight is on you, Andrew.

Jim moves, increasing the light around him a little, incidentally illuminating the others.

Margaret slips back into the shadows, but we do not lose sight of her altogether.

"Andrew!" Jim is pleased to see another one of the gang. "We were talking about you. Come 'ere." Come and be one of us.

What Else Can You Be? sings the male chorus.

Be yourself, Margaret might have whispered. Courage is the thing.

"What, me?" sings Daff, but more or less to herself, and it might only have been the hopeless batting of an insect against one of the light bulbs.

Andrew obeys by standing up to face them.

The light moves with him. He is illuminated from head to toe. Nonetheless, he stands irresolute. He is dressed in a sort of parody of his working clothes as if it is many years later and he is going to a fancy dress party dressed as a late-twentieth-century, European, New Sudanian Planter: white polo shirt, khaki shorts, long white socks turned down to pads around his ankles above clean boots that have nonetheless lost their polish. It is actually how he would appear on a Monday morning, but this is Saturday night. He smells of Alloy's soap.

Also, Andrew is covered in dust. It is dry. They have come up on the motorbike which, oddly, no one heard.

Jim says: "Get another chair, Pete, for this pommie bastard." He gets up, as does Peter who is shoved aside to make room for Andrew. Peter fetches a chair but has not had time to remove his pipe, which he clenches between his teeth. Deep teeth marks remain.

Clarence jumps up also, wanting to please. "I'll get some drinks." He toddles off to the bar.

No one else appears to move but once they are settled again, Andrew sits between Margaret – miles away – and Jim. He is opposite Henry. Clarence has his back to us. Peter is half in the dark. By the time he has returned with the chair there is no room for it near the table. He faces his wife out there but he resolutely does not look at her; for most of the following action, he watches Andrew.

"This is nice," says Clarence: friends sitting around a table together drinking. He loves them all, feeling that they really are his friends, who are here together because they like each other. They are his family because they are all he has. Everything he does, he does for them: organising the beer and wine supplies from town; getting bits of things made in the workshop for them – Henry's bench, a swing for Alison and Tommy when they were all younger, a trailer for Peter's boat, a funny sort of standard lamp for Andrew because he knew Andrew liked reading at night; having their cars serviced for them at the workshop although it is against the rules. A silly old man? But it is Clarence who understands Alloy, who gave him the job and who tactfully showed him how to do it. Clarence offers a lot of love. He is notoriously kind to animals: he owns a dog called Blackie and a cat called Pussy. At home he has everything ready for tea or coffee should anyone call. But they never do.

[][][][][]

"Now," said Jim, with his pudgy hand on Andrew's arm. The two men sensed the connection of the warm, damp hand on the lean and hairy arm, also warm but dry to Jim's senses because of the dust. Andrew would have run, but he was held.

They paid attention: Clarence just happy to be there, Peter thinking, unusually, what crap all this is, and Andrew feeling, as he always did in the club, that he was back at King's Sutton.

Henry watched Andrew intently, noting that he looked uneasy and weak.

"Now, Andrew, Henry says we got to start planting up the extension. Am I right, Henry?"

"Yes."

"So how're you getting on?" He did not wait for an answer. "Because Clarence is getting the D5 ready. He says it can be out by Monday."

"Tuesday, Jim," chirped Clarence, making a mental note that he had better move fast. They could service the D5 on Monday and into the night if necessary. He knew Alloy would have ordered the parts in that last batch from Markham.

Jim heard, but otherwise ignored Clarence. "Tuesday, Andrew, no later. We got to get the roads in and the burning done while it's dry. That'll keep you busy." He patted Andrew's arm and winked at Henry who almost winked back.

Andrew said nothing.

"OK, Andrew?" Jim looked at Henry, smiling like the friendly uncle he was playing.

"Andrew?"

Andrew swallowed and looked towards the way out where Alloy was waiting: "That's just the hundred hectares, isn't it Jim? Yes, we've started on that."

"Nooo," sang Jim, still smiling at Henry who smiled back like an idiot, "we're going to do the whole lot. Isn't that right Henry?"

"Yes, Jim." Up to his knees in the shit now: "Yes, that's it Andrew. We might as well do the whole lot at once. We've got the seedlings and it would be better, you must agree, to have it all the same age."

Was Andrew cool and calm? Was he sure of what he had to do? To tell them all to fuck off? No, he was not: he was panicking. Here in the club, he wanted to please Jim. He resented Alloy out there, fuck him.

Henry noticed that Andrew was beginning to sweat. The beer no doubt, after the walk in from the estate. Andrew usually walked.

Andrew said nothing, so Jim removed his hand and resisted the temptation to scratch his arse. He clapped: "Good, that's it. More drinks? Joseph," he shouted, "you bugger! Where are you?" When you're needed.

Joseph, the bugger, did not move. He watched Andrew from the dark. The shark's teeth were motionless, watched by Margaret.

Andrew gulped his beer: "I think some of our people live there," he said. The chorus looked at him and then at Jim, but it was speechless.

"What?" Jim was amused.

"There're people there. Living there."

"Well they'll have to go. Joseph! Where the fuck is he?" Jim did not look at the bar where the shark's teeth remained immobile, assuming that Joseph would materialise, as usual, out of the general hardware of the club.

What Jim said to himself at the time, or words to the effect of, was: they have no right to be there, they are lucky not to have been disturbed so far, Henry should not have let it happen, no doubt he had given someone permission to plant a garden because he was soft that way, that having been given an inch they had taken a mile as was their devious way, and he, Jim, had to sort out the mess. The manifestation of this reasoning was a dramatic sigh that ought to have been funny but was not.

"Joseph!" Why the fuck did the man not appear to divert them with more drink?

"It's not that easy," Andrew seemed to be saying to him, or perhaps it was Henry: "They've settled."

The word rattled Jim, made him wild: "Settled! What yer mean, settled? Then they'll 'ave to unsettle."

Andrew looked at Henry. Jim looked at them both and exploded: "Now listen 'ere Andrew, I've 'ad enough of this, I'm telling you. That area is got to be cleared for planting and no buts about it. Do you 'ear me? You got to start Monday like what you should 'av done last Monday." Red in the face, he glared at them all defiantly.

It was the public attack that upset Andrew, not the crude ideas. In those days he was, of course, still very conventional. He said nothing, but looked down into his glass. Had he said anything just then, his voice would have sounded unsteady. He remembered a time in the dormitory, listening to Nwufoh snoring.

But Jim had not lost control. The best thing was to be reasonable. Andrew was a sucker after all. Henry's reasonableness would be much more difficult to oppose. It was the best tool in the end for getting bad things done.

So Jim said reasonably: "You tell 'im, 'Enry."

Henry leaned towards Andrew. He wanted him to feel at ease and to be one of them. He was a good-looking boy, after all. He liked having him around: "Jim's right, Andrew, it's alienated land. The owners have had compensation and we have to fulfil our obligations to the bank and to the government." Then he added: "It's not as if they're local people."

"And what if they are?" Jim chimed in.

Henry was beginning to feel uncomfortable. "It's not as if they're local people, Andrew, who might just have some argument for being there." He saw that Jim could barely control himself. "They're from the Highlands, most of them, and they have no rights. They'll have to leave at some stage and really – you must see – the sooner the better." There was no passion in his voice. He badly wanted Andrew to resist him. But he droned on, Peter nodding his agreement, the experienced man of the world, clamping on his pipe to prove it;

Clarence not sure what they were talking about; Margaret waiting. "I mean, they've had the advantage of the gardens for a year or two. . ."

"An' that should never have been allowed," interjected Jim. Henry's prattle was unbearable to him: "All this rights nonsense! These people are brought here to work," he shouted, "they're paid and they get the best labour quarters in the country. If they don't like it then why don't they go 'ome? They can't just come here and then expect to take over the place. Jesus wept! We got a right to plant and that's all there is. Why waste yer breath, 'Enry? You pan. . ." He stopped and raged.

Henry pressed on, all the same, wanting Andrew to tell him to shut up: "They can't have expected to stay forever. Can they, Andrew?"

Andrew sat, looking not only defeated and at a loss, but also stupid, embarrassingly so, his jaw sticking out.

But Henry insisted: "What do you say, Andrew? Say something."

And Jim burst the silence, parodying Henry: "Ah say ol' boy, what do yoo think, my ol' bum buddy, lets 'ave a cup of tea. Fuck that! You pommies make me want to puke with your ol' boy this and ol' boy that. I don't care a fuck what Andrew thinks. That land will be planted, I tell you, and if they don't clear off... Well, they'll 'ave to. Or they'll 'ave to deal with me."

He might have looked at his wife, had she looked at him, but Margaret was looking past Henry towards Andrew.

All the same, Jim needed Andrew to do as he was told. To do Jim's right thing because if Andrew did not do it – and he knew that Henry could not, any longer – then he would have to do it on his own. He would have to justify himself on his own. It was not enough to have Peter and Clarence behind him. He needed more substance than that, God help him. He realised for a moment that Andrew, for all his pommie ways, was the only man amongst them whom he did want on side. The others counted for nothing, simply because they were so easy to pull along.

So Jim pulled himself together: "'S'orite 'En', you leave this to me, our Andrew 'ere's a bit muddled. It's been a 'ard week for 'im; you should know that 'En'." Again he winked. "'E'll do what 'e's told. Monday 'e'll tell 'em to go and Tuesday we'll send in the D5 won't we Clarence? OK boy?"

Andrew said nothing.

That was alright then. It was agreed. Jim was sweating.

"Good, that's done. Let's 'ave some drinks. Must be your round, Andrew. Like to fetch 'em?" He had given up on Joseph, ordering Andrew to serve as if he was now a Pete or an 'En' himself. It would be 'Andy' next.

Henry was uncomfortable. Hotter than he should have been. There was nothing he could do but wait in the dark prison he had made for himself. He felt his own cowardice. Again he had failed to meet the man he still wanted to be, the man he had exchanged for his furtive life of shadows and hidden meanings. Senior Planter indeed! Senior Shit, more like.

[][][][][]

Andrew carries the empty glasses to the bar. He is about to ask Margaret what she wants but he passes by, ashamed.

And Margaret, Margaret as if following him, gets up. Her figure is somewhat heavy but she walks, nonetheless, with an easy grace on high-heeled shoes so that her hips sway a little, swinging the light fabric of her red skirt. She walks in front of the seated men, who watch her, between the bar and where Daff sits, and then to the door where Alloy may or may not still be waiting.

She carries her own light. She moves through the door and is, apparently, swallowed up by the night, which roars back in triumph.

Daff, much more Daphne now, grabs her bag and rushes after Margaret.

The three men watch the space through which Margaret has passed. Jim's mouth is open. She has never left the club like that before.

Clarence says: "Not feeling well I 'spect, wrong time of the month, prob'ly."

Jim and Peter accept this as the best explanation. Henry thinks he has had a heart attack. He clutches his chest.

Andrew appears to be messing around with a bar-boy who is not Joseph because Joseph, the man, makes no more contact with Andrew than he does with any of the others. He serves Andrew but he looks past him. Andrew watches the shark's teeth because he dare not look at Joseph's eyes or at the door, where Alloy may or may not be waiting.

Is it over, then? The universe rushing on and out, beyond our control?

Andrew's heart is beating so fast he is surprised no one hears. So aware of himself is he, as he stands at the bar, that he believes he is alone in the universe. He does not want to go out there on his own. As if, for God's sake, Alloy and Joseph and Margaret are not waiting for him. He wants to feel that he is a part of the place as he did that night before with Nwufoh and Evans. Surely, he asks himself, asking the wrong question, the thing to which I want to belong is the management structure of this plantation company? Is it not what I have been bred for? This is what Andrew's intellectual, reasonable, responsible self asks.

The night is without end. Andrew is nothing in it. The club, the company, the country that has been named New Sudan are nothing in it. If they ever were, they have fallen apart a long time ago.

Andrew is lying in bed, on his side. He watches Nwufoh. Nwufoh is sleeping, but he breathes louder than the roaring night. Andrew wants to be with Nwufoh. He wants to be with Nwufoh more than anything.

And at that moment of wanting Nwufoh, Joseph grabs Andrew's wrist, holding on to it until it hurts. He says nothing. Andrew is red hot and his shirt sticks to his back. He feels a spasm of excitement. He looks at the door, out of the club, to where Alloy is still standing. He looks through the room at us. Or, he seems to.

Joseph lets go. The night no longer holds its breath. Andrew takes the drinks on a tray – indeed the same plastic tray – to the four remaining men, Jim, Henry, Clarence and Peter. With exaggerated dignity he places the tray on the glass top of the little rattan table and then places a drink in front of each man.

For Jim another whisky, on the rocks, in the fine Waterford glass. Jim looks at the drink, not at Andrew: Good boy, Andrew. I knew you'd do it. He is reassured in himself.

For Clarence, a beer and a glass. Clarence looks at the drink, not at Andrew: Thank you, Andrew. That's nice. He is happy.

For Peter, a beer also but no glass. Peter looks at the drink, not at Andrew: Well done, Andrew. One of us, eh? He also is reassured in himself as a man in a man's world. He is a little worried about Daff; she's not herself tonight. All that talk of Annu. He wants to pick his nose.

For Henry, a brandy in a large glass and a small jug of water. Is Henry shattered? He does not appear to be. He also looks at the drink and not at Andrew. But he says nothing. He has said more than enough and accepts what has happened with the resignation he habitually feels when another battle has been lost.

Andrew sits on the edge of his seat.

Jim takes a sip: "You not drinking mi boy? You need a drink."

"Yes Sir," says Andrew with what Henry detects as a slight sneer. Unlike Andrew. Maybe he imagined it. Oh well, that's life. Tomorrow will be the same and the following Monday. Silly to think that it would change. Silly to think that Andrew would be any different from me. We are, after all, just men at the mercy of whatever it was. He feels a sudden warmth for Andrew who reminds him so much of his young self. It reassures him. He isn't so odd. He does what all men do. In the end.

Andrew goes to fetch his own drink. He returns, carrying a beer in a cooler, a manly sort of drink. He'll be smoking a pipe next.

He sits down beside Jim and as if on cue they all begin to drink, while the night roars at them. Except Andrew. He places the cooler on the glass table top and deliberately tips it over onto its side so that the beer covers the small top, falling over the edge, beneath the thick woven rattan rim, trickling loudly onto the floor, like someone pissing himself. They watch the beer flow onto the floor. It appears, as Peter describes later to Daphne, who seems rather more established on Venus than usual, as if he'd had a sort of nervous breakdown.

No one moves, waiting for Andrew to break into uncontrollable weeping or do something equally embarrassing.

Clarence says: "Whoops. I'll get a cloth." He is, as it happens, the only one who feels a surge of sympathy for Andrew. The others are cross, but for different reasons; especially Henry who, for a moment or two, hates Andrew with a sudden spiteful dislike which shocks him.

The silence lasts a few seconds only. Peter says: "Really, Andrew, what are you playing at?"

Laughter from behind the bar.

Andrew gets up.

He walks across the room towards the door. On his way Joseph joins him, leaving the ghostly tea towel on the bar, the shark's tooth necklace Henry gave him lying beside it.

They disappear, together with the light that has followed them. Darkness prevails, out of which recognisable voices linger for a bit.

Clarence: "Poor chap, must have been something he ate."

Peter: "Poor chap, my arse. He's funny, I always said so. You had better keep an eye on him, Henry. Henry? You alive?"

Henry: "I think so."

Peter: "You'd better. He could make trouble."

Clarence: "No. He's just young," like I was once.

Their voices are lost in the night.

9
The Last Chance

Alloy has asked me to write this because he says that Master Andrew wants it. So I have to write it. Alloy says to write everything I can remember about the time when Master Jim came to Ples and frightened us. Also, Alloy says I must say who I am so that they will believe me.

I am Petrus, Grade III Carpenter. I am forty-three years old but I am not married. I was born here on Van Island but on the other side from the Company. My father worked on Lingalinga Plantation but he was killed when the Japanese came so I did not know him. I lived with my mother who worked on the plantation until she died. When she died I was fourteen. I left Lingalinga because I was sad. I went across the sea to live with my uncle in Port Markham. He worked as a house-boy for a white man who worked for the government. In Port Markham my uncle paid for me to go to school and I helped him do his work. At the school they taught me to read and write and the Bible. Also, I joined a church called the New People's Mission. I liked the church, and Master Wilfred who was the minister let me work there in the carpentry shop where I learnt to be a carpenter. Master Wilfred always wanted me to be with him and help him to take the church service. All the time he wanted to teach me the Bible in his room. He said we were like David and Jonathan but I did not like that. That is what those Highlands boys do, but not us Coastal people. The Bible says it is wrong. St Paul says so, although Andrew says it is St Paul who is wrong. I don't know any more. I liked Master Wilfred because he was a white man and white men know everything. All the same, I did not like that he wanted to fuck my arse, so when I read in the newspaper for artisans for the Van Island Palm Oil Development Project I wrote an application and I prayed to God to give me a job back home. God heard my prayers and I was given a job. That was twelve years ago. I worked in the workshop stores making the shelves for Master Clarence. He was good to me. When the big compound was cleared and they built the small compounds on the plantation I asked Master Clarence to ask Master Jonson to give me a job on the plantation because I wanted to be with the plantation workers. I wanted to help them find God instead of drinking and fighting. Master Jonson was alright. He treated us all like kanakas so we knew where we were and we were all the same. I made the furniture in his house and when other white people saw the furniture they wanted me to make things for them. I made a lot of furniture. It is God's will. Master Jonson took some of the furniture home with him so I made some more for Andrew. He said I was Master Sipanel. I do not know who is this Master Sipanel but Master Andrew said he makes furniture for the Queen of England. When Andrew took over the plantation from Master Jonson he was different from Master Jonson because he is younger. Some of the older men said he was a pikinini so they called him

Liklik Masta. But Andrew is a funny man who laughs sometimes but is very angry sometimes when the work is not right. So we all began to respect Andrew because we did not know if he would laugh or be angry from one day to the next. And we liked him because things did not fall down like they did with Master Jonson and also, when he was angry, all the same Andrew would still listen to Tarlie about our problems and do things for us. Master Jonson would not listen to anybody. Andrew would shout a lot in those days and sometimes the young men said they would fight him, but although he shouted we knew that he saw us as men, not as children. He did not shout at the older men or at the women. We liked that. But we knew that when Andrew was married he would stop talking to us and be like the other white men and treat us as kanakas. That is the way it is.

But it is different now. In time, when I saw that Andrew was friends with Alloy, I was surprised for a white man to be friends with a kanaka. Andrew is another kind of man now. He is a man. That is all, like us. Because of Andrew, I am not afraid of white men. Some are good and some are bad. They are just like us. I will still make furniture for them if they ask me. I will say I am like Master Sipanel who makes furniture for the Queen of England.

Yes, I built the church at Ples. I did most of the work myself but Tarlie helped me, and some of the others. Bune and the other Optik boys helped and sometimes Joseph came, bringing nails and things like that. But, except for Tarlie and for Joseph who works in the Masters' club, the Highlands men did not want to help. When it was finished some of them came into the church. They were quiet and I taught them the story of Moses. I said that Moses was special to God and that through Moses God helped the people of Israel. They liked it and asked me to tell more stories. That was good. One day I told them the story of Jesus. I said that Jesus was special as well. He is the son of God. They asked me why Jesus did not come to help them. I said it was because they were bad.

One day Joseph brought a white woman. We were surprised to see her. Joseph said she was his friend. That is Joseph's fashion; to make up a story that a white woman is his friend. Sometimes he is a bighead because he works in their club and he says he knows the white man's ways. But it was true because she followed Joseph but Joseph was very kind to her and we could see that he loved her. She was not a young woman but she was not an old woman. She wore trousers like a man but she walked like a woman and she had a big arse like the women from New Bristol and she was very quiet so we liked her. Also, she wore a big hat because she had very white skin and strange yellow hair. Joseph said if the sun burnt her skin she would be ill. She was strange to our eyes, even for a white woman, but she was so quiet and kind that we began to love her, especially the children. We saw then that she was very beautiful. When we asked Joseph where she came from, he said he did not know. He said he thought she had been sent to help us and so that we would know her. Then the children started to call her Our White Missus, so we all called her that. That is 'Waitpela Missus Bilong Mipela', in the way we talk to each other.

I have to tell you about this woman because she helped us later. Also, later we learnt that she was the wife of Master Jim. This surprised us when we learnt she was the wife of Master Jim because she was not like other white women.

She liked the church and sat inside it for a long time. She asked us if she could come again and we said yes, you can come when you like, this is God's house not ours. She came many times. Often she came in the middle of the day when it is hot. That surprised us because white people do not like to walk in the hot time of the day. We asked ourselves why she did this. Also she came in the rain. She told us she liked the rain. She did not talk a lot like other white people do, so we liked her.

She brought us things for the church and when we started the school, she brought things for that as well. She brought books and paper and pencils. One day she brought another white woman to Ples. The other white woman looked afraid at first, I could see that. But by the time she left us she was happy and I liked her. She asked me if I knew Annu. Then I remembered Annu and I was surprised that I had forgotten Annu. Annu worked with us in the time of Master Jonson. He came for about two months and very quickly he was a boss-boy because he was a hard worker. He was boss-boy of the harvesting and pruning gang. He was the only one all those Giluwe boys would listen to. I think if Annu had stayed, there would not have been any trouble because he was a good man and he did not want people to fight. When he was with us then, he told the Giluwe boys not to drink and they listened to him. He would tell stories and they would laugh. In this way he was like Joseph. When he went away we were sad, so we forgot him. But when this other white woman said Annu's name, I remembered him again and I was sad. I thought if this white woman knows the name of Annu, then he must be a great man.

So we were happy at Ples and we thought God had blessed us. Then Master Jim came, that day when Andrew was away. Jim brought his security boys with him. Those boys are bad because they smoke grass all the time and do not know what they are doing. The one we called Tudak will kill a man for nothing.

Master Jim was mad. He shouted at us to get away. Also, he brought the big bulldozer with him and it smashed the church and other buildings so that we were frightened too much. I did not understand, because Andrew had said that Ples was OK. I thought that Andrew would not let this happen. We were afraid of Master Jim because he was mad and he had a gun. We knew he would kill us with those stupid boys of his.

I myself, I was frightened. I could not move and I was shaking and crying. I thought that God had forsaken me and I did not know why. I thought of my mother at Lingalinga and of my uncle in Port Markham. I thought it is better just to be a kanaka and to work and to die. I thought it is better not to think about things. I thought I understood the Bible but I did not understand the world.

I was waiting for Jim to kill me.

I prayed to God for strength.

[][][][][]

The GM's office was at the back, beyond the toilets. To get there you had to go through the general office, which was ruled over by Mrs Livingston, the dragon, who also guarded the GM's office. Jim generally ignored the pen-pushing, bottom-polishing poofters who were the male staff and also the bits of fluff who were the girls. Mrs Livingston helped the girls to fathom the strange rituals of a European office. She did not have time for fluff either. It was the boys who needed to be taken in hand but Mrs Livingston didn't mind that. She liked men. Mrs Livingston kept the office going.

The presence of Jim was manifested by the ringing of an electric bell or by his raised voice when he was shouting. The shrill electric bell would silence the office for what seemed like minutes. That is, except for Mrs Livingston's typewriter; she would not stop for anyone in mid-sentence, or for that matter in mid-paragraph. Least of all for the General Manager. She would finish her paragraph and after a dignified pause, rise to her magnificent height: nearly six feet of her, emphasised by the white blouse and long, mid-calf skirt she always wore for the office. Slowly, majestically, she would open Jim's door and enter. She would not knock. She would leave the door wide open. When she put things in his in tray or emptied the out tray, she made sure he was not in the office. Mrs Livingston was not the sort of woman to knock on a Jim's door, for all that she was a kind woman. Her husband – who ran Public Works in town – loved her. Their children had confidently flown the nest.

Yes, Jim? Her grey eyebrows would rise as if she were humouring a patient, a lunatic patient. And Jim would squeeze out a Please for Mrs Livingston: Please do this or that for me, Mrs Livingston. Please, as if he'd like to strangle the woman.

Just let him try! I'd have him on his back in no time. I'd put my foot on his chest and shake my fists in triumph.

Mrs Livingston was brought in every morning at seven o'clock sharp by her husband's driver, Jon. At twelve noon sharp she would walk slowly around the golf course, holding an umbrella to shield herself from the sun or rain. If the rain was heavy she would sit on the veranda reading a novel. She liked Patrick White, despite his being contaminated by England. At four o'clock sharp she was picked up by Jon again. Fridays she left at twelve, because she helped at the Akaranda Yacht Club in the evening. Saturdays she would sail the little GP14 with her husband. They took turns in being crew, but she was the better sailor. She could tame the sea, control the wind.

[][][][][]

Despite Andrew having created the scene at the club the previous Saturday night, despite Andrew having walked out on them, despite Andrew having gone off with that poofter whatsisname from the stores: despite everything, Jim remained in a state of denial. He had not grasped the uncomfortable fact that Andrew was getting away from him. After all, wasn't Andrew toeing the line? And why not, for God's fucking sake? He was paid to do the job. Obviously he'd seen sense; he was bound to, in the end. Only that morning Jim had seen Madiak re-fuelling his bike at the workshop, and asked him. Never could remember the bugger's name – Goofy, probably – but he was a useful source of information about Andrew's division. Yes, the fellow had confirmed, they'd started on the extension; road lining was under way.

Jim congratulated himself. What did it matter if Andrew wanted to fuck some kanaka's arse? He wasn't the first and he wouldn't be the last. Henry was that way too, and it hadn't stopped him from becoming Senior Planter. Thing was to keep it discreet. Same if you wanted a gin: you didn't go advertising the fact. And, come to think of it, these poofters always concentrated on the job, what with no children to worry about. Given a strong hand, they'd do what you wanted. No doubt about Henry, and Andrew would come up to scratch with the right handling.

[][][][][]

After the heat outside, the air-conditioned chill of the general office came as a shock. Andrew felt as if his shirt had suddenly frozen to his back. The clerks and the secretaries who occupied the claustrophobic interior world furtively watched Andrew navigate his clumsy way around their desks to where Mrs Livingston was stationed.

Andrew liked Mrs Livingston, and she liked him. She liked outdoor men who did not mess up offices and houses. Out-of-doors was where men belonged. Andrew's sweaty, sunburned self, his dusty boots and shorts pleased her sense of how things ought to be. On Sundays her husband worked on the pickup or the boat while she cooked a heavy lunch that made them want to sleep afterwards. In the evening they would watch a video film together. Sometimes she sat on his knee. He was shorter than her, but he was a big manly man with a hairy chest and uncertain eyes.

"Is Jim in, Mrs Livingston?"

She looked at Andrew, appraising him. Yes, you will do for a man. "Go in, Andrew, he's there."

She did not expect other people to knock, either – Jim could take them or leave them for all she cared – but they did. They knocked timidly, or with a surprising show of respect. How they could respect That Man was beyond her. But they did, and that was the world for you.

Andrew knocked on the door timidly.

"Come."

Andrew came.

"Sit."

Andrew sat.

He sat on a chair placed with its side to the front of Jim's desk. Therefore he had to twist himself to look at Jim, and had nowhere to put his hands. He could smell Jim's aftershave. Jim sat with his back to the window. The blinds were down but the sunlight so strong that Andrew was blinded, seeing Jim's face as dark and as formless as it was in the light.

[][][][][]

Jim goes on writing. Then he elaborately puts cap on pen and lays it down to rest. Elbows on table, he stares at Andrew, grinning. Pleasantness emanates like greasy steam. 'I am all yours', it says. 'I know you're a poofter and I have to keep my back against the wall but I don't mind, it takes all sorts to make a world and I am an easy man, within limits. I wouldn't, for instance, want one of those kanakas using my toilet. I draw the line there.' He had said this to Mrs Livingston once, when they were discussing some repairs. She was surprised at the fussiness. She always took precautions with toilets herself but she didn't distinguish between particular men. Some men couldn't be trained whoever they were, waving their things around and forgetting to put up the seat. Why couldn't they sit down?

Andrew does not expect amiability. He expects a rude Jim. But Jim has adjusted his memory. Andrew's disappearance on Saturday night had been typical: unable to maintain his argument in the face of reason, he had run away. Margaret walking out did not register either; she was as beyond his comprehension as were the kanakas. And anyway, hadn't things gone on as usual? The man of action making things happen, dragging the others with him? Jim's image of himself is intact. The events in the club had been cast aside, as such emotional, drunken squabbles generally are.

All was well in Jim's world. He could, and would, patronise Andrew. Andrew would be useful to him. Andrew would be an obedient dog.

Jim looks at Andrew; Andrew looks at Jim.

"Jim?"

"Yes, Andrew, mi boy." He'd give whatever was asked. More money if necessary.

"It's the extension." Andrew wants to see Jim as a man with whom he can reason.

"Yes, Andrew, I hear you've started the road lining. That's good." Jim smiles and relaxes.

"There are people living there, Jim. We can't throw them out, just like that. We must. . ."

Jim cuts Andrew short: "I know, Andrew," I am a reasonable man. "Just carry on with the road lining so's they know we mean business. Give 'em . . . give 'em a couple of months to get out." He looks at Andrew, almost fondly: "About two weeks before the bulldozers go in warn 'em again and give 'em a firm date."

Andrew wants to interrupt but Jim stops him with a show of his hand: "Don't worry mi boy, I've done this before. Warn 'em every day. Then a couple of days before you start, park the 'dozer nearby. If you don't, the fuckers'll think you're bluffing. If they still don't move, start work. Mess up the gardens to start with."

Again Andrew tries to interrupt but Jim pushes on, looking away from him: "Just stop short of the 'ouses. You'll see how fast they move then. You got 'em, but don't dawdle. Get the planting started soon as you can. They can't do nothing. For Christ's sake, it's our land."

Jim grins in triumph. Looks at Andrew. Stops grinning.

Andrew sits back in chair; red face; jaw set. Looks like an idiot.

Jim is embarrassed. These queers. What is it now? I've no time for their hysterics. I'm tired of all this. Remembers Saturday evening. Fucking poofter walked out on me as if 'e, as if 'e, as if 'e thinks I'm a shit. Fuck 'im. And

Margaret, too. What's up with 'er, all of a sudden? Looks at Andrew, wants to smash him: "That's what you got to do. That's your job. That's what I pay you for." There, you fucking poofter. Stick that up your arse.

Andrew says: "No."

"No, what? You, you fucking . . . whatever you are." Jim shouts.

Andrew shouts back: "No. People live there and they have a right to. . ."

Andrew snarling in hard, staccato way, as if he mad. More frightening than Jim. Stop it Andrew. Let Jim do ugly bits. He ugly man with ugly soul.

Jim cuts off Andrew with smash on desk as if it's Andrew he hits. Hand hurts, makes him cross. Shouts at Andrew: "You pommie poofters."

Mrs Livingston hears all this. She hates Jim. She hates him because he is a crude, overbearing, ignorant man. It is a humiliation to work for such a man. He no gentleman. She cannot think straight. But she types on as if nothing happens. She does not know what she is typing but she doesn't stop. She wants to pick up typewriter and throw it across room. Staff look at her. They hear the noise. She stares them down. Get on with your work it say. Get on or I go mad. I throw typewriter at you all. I tear off my clothes. I jump naked on my desk. Stop it!

Jim shout. Jim spit. Jim cannot get words out fast enough. He wants to do violent things to Andrew. That make it easy for Andrew because Andrew has temper too.

"Do it or I will sack you, now."

"I will not do it. You do what you like. I will not do it. I will not do it for you or for anyone."

"You are sacked. Get out."

"I am not sacked. I will go back to the division. I will run it and you will have to throw me out with your own hands. And I will not plant the extension because of the people there who have rights."

"Rights! Rights. No one has rights, you stupid little arse-fucking wimp. Your type make me mad. You should be put in gas chambers."

You think I'm going to do what someone like you tells me to do? You! You must be joking. Andrew is not the least disconcerted, now that he has lost his temper and is sure of the moral – and social – high ground he is defending against the likes of Jim. Wow, is he on an angry high. "It's you should be gassed. You, you. . ." Andrew splutters to a halt, unable to find suitably crushing words.

Jim is hating Andrew. Andrew is hating Jim. They are shouting. They will fight and there will be murder. I will go mad. I will fetch Henry.

Mrs Livingston walks out of the office as cool as a cucumber as if it is four o'clock. But it is more like three-thirty. She walks onto the veranda. She looks into the bright afternoon sun. She would die for some rain. She goes to the opposite end of the veranda, to the door of Henry's office. It is locked, so she walks out onto the road, hoping to meet the car that always comes to meet her. She has forgotten her umbrella but she cannot go back for it; she is afraid of what she might do.

The driver of Mr Livingston, Jon, likes Mrs Livingston because she politely ignores him most of the time, because she never complains, and because she never does anything unexpected. Her routines are routine. She causes him no bother and gives him useful sums of money at Christmas. So he is surprised to meet her walking along the road, in the hot sun, without her umbrella. She looks hot and exhausted, as if she has been fighting. He feels something strong for her because she is a tall woman, no longer young, who looks as if she is defeated. The car stops; Mrs Livingston gets in: "Thank you Jon, please drive slowly." She says no more. He takes her home, saying nothing because he knows she wants silence. He does not drive so fast that she cannot relax, but he does not drive so slowly that she might be exasperated by the time it takes. He watches her go into the house and lock the door behind her. It is a white bungalow in a tight cul-de-sac of similar bungalows that have been built for senior civil servants. Jon drives back to Mr Livingston's office. When Mr Livingston gets home later it is dark outside. He does not notice his wife has been to hell and back. She has made the curry he likes. She learned to make it properly when they lived in Kerala. Dragon's food, he calls it. It is his joke. She laughs as if she has not heard it a hundred times before.

□□□□□

Andrew pushes at the door. The catch breaks. He wants to commit a violent act. He wants to hurt himself.

"Fuck your arse," he shouts. Red and stupid looking because his legs are long in his shorts. He does not shout at Jim but at the whole world. He might shout at the whole office in a manic way, singing it as a tuneless song but roughly to the nursery rhyme: This is the way we fuck your arse, fuck your arse, fuck your arse, this is the way we fuck your arse on a cold and frosty morning.

He doesn't but it goes through his head. It would have amused Henry.

The tops of the desks are studied like mad. The ground moves a little. But not so much.

By the time he reaches the outer door, Andrew has sufficiently calmed down to merely leave it open. "Go on," he shouts back at it, "you can air condition the whole fucking, fucking, fucking universe."

For a second he knows not where to go. Then he is off in the same direction as Mrs Livingston.

Jim stands outside his office and glares at the office staff. Fuck you, too, he wants to say. Instead, he slams the door. It bounces back at him. He slams it again, so hard that a pane of frosted glass cracks.

"Mrs Livingston. . ." She's not there. Where is that woman he could've strangled? Lucky for her she's not there. Lucky? Better she had been and that he had tried to strangle her. Cor blimey, much better, for then she might have killed him. Got him on his back and smashed his head in with the typewriter. Ooooooh, that would've been a good show: Mrs Livingston killing Jim with her typewriter. Cheers from the onlookers and Jim dead in his tracks; stopped from going on to Ples.

But Mrs Livingston has gone. Her typewriter sitting there innocent-like, as if it wouldn't harm a soul. This is despite the paper with her crazy words on it that Jim doesn't see. He picks up the typewriter as if he divines their meaning, and throws it with all his might into his own office. It smashes onto the surface of the desk, breaking more glass. Last thing he thought just then was he'd 'ave to get 'er a new one; electric this time, quieter. The old bitch. And just then, he thought of his wife, Margaret. The old bastard himself.

Jim storms out the outer door, just like Andrew. I'll get that bastard, for sure. I'll fuck him.

Jim's driver, Sammy, is waiting, having heard the commotion; ready, the engine running. Jim ignores him, walks instead onto the road, around and into the workshop compound. He walks like a drunkard as if he would fall down any minute. Sammy follows at a discreet distance. Jim catches him.

"Get the boys, Sammy," he yells.

The boys are the security guards known as the SS; Special Security. Half a dozen pathological cases Jim got out of the Togulo Farm penal colony. Early release if they work for him. And they do. They are his most obedient dogs, willing to tear out the throat of anything.

In the workshop compound, Jim shouts and screams. Clarence the nominal superintendent is irrelevant. He stands back for the storm to pass through.

At four o'clock the bulldozer sets off. It's not far, and at five miles an hour Jim is at Ples by five. By six, the fire has started.

Jim thought of Andrew all the time. Got 'im well and proper the little poofter: 'e can fuck off.

And Andrew has, but with his temper spent he does not know what to do. He walks for miles along the main road, feeling sorry for himself. At first his heart beats fit to explode, but he calms down. He takes long strides, his jaw is set. He looks funny.

In the dark he stops at a roadside bar, drinks beer, gets drunk; wants pity from the other drinkers but instead gets their embarrassment and silent resentment. They push him out into the night. He sits by the door; they ignore him. Then he walks home through the plantation. It takes about two hours. He thinks of Alloy, a little, in a pornographic way. He smells the burning in the night, but he doesn't associate it with himself.

[][][][][]

Letter from Alloy to Andrew:

Hope you get this Andrew, where ever you are. You have to take a lot of the blame for what happened. You are responsible, Andrew. Do not try to hide from yourself or from me, because eventually we shall both find you. Then there will be trouble.

You know, they taught us at mission school, where they tried to teach us to be good house-boys, that the sin of omission is as bad as, if not worse than, the sin of commission. Do you know what that means, Andrew? It means that when you are in a position to stop a sin, or relieve its consequences, you have to do it. If you don't, it counts against you. You see what I'm getting at Andrew, don't you? I don't have to rub it in, but I'd like to. Andrew, you shit. I thought you were different. When I saw Jim at Ples, I was sure you'd be there to stand up to him. I was sure you'd stand up for what you had said you believed in. But you're just words, Andrew. I want to hit you and see your blood flow. I hope you get chopped up one of these days with a panga knife.

You could have stopped what Jim did. If you had been there and stayed there and held your ground. That's all you had to do, be the witness.

I'm sitting at your table, Andrew, on the veranda, to write this. I can see the smoke from Jim's fire. It was a great black pillar of smoke earlier, casting a shadow across your house, Andrew. Under the setting sun it was beautiful.

I came to find you. I wanted to fight you. I've smashed some of your things and eaten some of your food and taken some of your clothes. I'm still angry but not violently now. Don't be afraid. But I wanted to kill you. I wanted to kill you because you are one of them – you Master Bastard. I've waited for you for hours but you haven't come, you coward. I'm writing this to tell you. I'm going now because you are one of them, Andrew.

Alloy had intended to stop here but after pausing he had continued.

Andrew, where are you? I could not believe that my people would do what Jim told them to do. He couldn't have done it on his own. He couldn't have driven the dozer in on his own. The operators and some of your workers were with him. Following orders, they said. They think the company is a god. They think the company is the government. They must do what it tells them and it makes them bad. They wanted to go in and cause trouble for their own people. To hurt them as if they had to do it to prove that they existed at all. That's where Jim is clever, when he's not stupid. He's clever and dangerous. The Ples people were all outsiders, all Highlanders except for Petrus, so Jim used local people and Coastals. He took the divide in our people and used it against us. It's the way of the world, isn't it? Driving people apart rather than uniting them. Driving people apart with ignorance and suspicion and hatred. I was born in that divide. I wanted you to pull me out of it.

Again Alloy had paused here. He wanted to write the letter carefully.

But what has Jim got? He's got the land but only by causing hatred and resentment that will smoulder for months, maybe years. What does he expect people to do? Lie down and die? He probably does.

You must know what happened, where ever it is you're hiding. I was there.

He brought the dozer over. The biggest monster they've got, taking it straight in down the road line you had set out for him. We heard the noise. The slow, vibrating, crushing noise that shakes the ground like a guria. But we did not think it was coming our way until we heard it smashing the vegetation and smelt the sweet, sickening smell of wounded and broken plants. Then we saw it coming for us. It was not a human thing. How can men make something so terrible? But they have and it was coming for us.

We knew it would push through the gardens. Your line of sticks went marching through, so that was obvious wasn't it? People had been harvesting their crops along the line since morning, but no one thought it would go for the houses. But it did. It never stopped, and there was Jim hanging on to the side of

94

the monster shouting at us. A gang of his men was running behind waving pangas. We could see Jim's face distorted with red anger but we couldn't hear him. I saw him point to Petrus's church and tell the driver to go straight for it. It was smashed. What if someone had been in it? Some of the old women stay there all day, Andrew. But it saved the houses for a time and the women ran to get their children and their things, screaming above all the noise. In the rush, people were hurt.

Jim's men chased us down to the river. I tried to stop them but it was pointless. They were so crazy they would have chopped me up. We watched the village being flattened. There was nothing we could do. Tarlie was with us and I never saw anything so pathetic as he limped with us. His helplessness and hopelessness represented our condition. I thought of what he used to be.

I thought they would go away but when the dozer had stopped and it was quiet, with only the noise of the river and some women crying, they walked down to us, a threatening mob with Jim in front waving a pistol. For all his swagger I thought he would be conciliatory as you people are when you've got us and you've done something wrong. I thought he would defend his actions and tell us to go back to the compound and settle down to work. You crazy kanakas. But he was the crazy one. He'd lost control of himself and called us all the terrible names we know you use for us. And more. Words we hadn't heard but that were spat out at us nonetheless like snake poison. He waved his pistol around and we cowered beneath it. We were dumb with fright but what hit me, Andrew, what hit me was the thought that the crazy hatred was for himself and he had to convince himself that we were hateful and worthless in order for him to bear the reality of his own agony. But I feel no pity for him. He will have to suffer until he knows himself well enough to die. I want him to suffer. I want him to die, but not before he has the full knowledge of what he is. The bastard. I tell you, I'll get him one day.

He went on and on screaming at us until I was sure someone would get shot. Even his men looked uneasy, no longer grinning. Some had dropped their panga knives. What upset me as well then was the thought that we, I, could be the focus of so much wrong emotion. I doubted my own humanity. I felt we were all of us damned: Jim, his men and ourselves. I felt sad. I was sad, Andrew, you were not there with us.

You know what, Andrew? Petrus is a brave man. If anyone could persuade me that there is a beneficent god, then Petrus could do it. He walked towards Jim and he would have allowed himself to be shot. But Jim stared at him as if, as if he was looking at something funny. What do you want? he bellows at Petrus, pointing the gun at him. And Petrus is afraid, he loses his nerve. Jim sees it and laughs all the more, wanting to strip Petrus naked in front of us all. But we love Petrus, Andrew, because he IS brave, which you are not. Jim shouts at Petrus for us all to hear: What you want, you prick? Jim is shaking with laughter and Petrus mutters something we cannot hear. But whatever it is, it sends Jim into a senseless rage. My wife, my wife, he shouts. What the fuck's she got to do with this? With you lot! And he takes a swipe at Petrus, who runs. He runs for all he's worth, expecting a bullet in his back any minute. When I saw him running, I thought I'm a coward, and I thought of you, Andrew. Where were you?

Another pause.

But then the miracle happened. Tarlie stands up. He'd been sitting and looking into the water with his back to the drama. He stood up and grew before our eyes as he walked slowly to Jim. You know how he walks. It's a heavy limp that twists his body with every step. But it is slow and dignified, the way he walks, as if he owns the ground under his feet. He pushes the air aside as he moves through it. You can feel the space behind, which seems to suck you in. You are a skinny nothing beside him, Andrew, with your chicken legs.

Tarlie stopped in front of Jim, daring him to shoot. He said nothing while the other man ranted. Tarlie looked at Jim with his head cocked and his big hands hanging beside him as if he could not understand what he was looking at. I shall never forget the sight of his great big black back, the shoulders as strong as the sky. His skin was dusty, with glistening streaks of sweat which flowed down to the small dark hollow of his back. I felt safe behind him. We all did.

Jim was silent, although he still held his gun out in front of him. He was frightened now, I could see. His little eyes shifted around, looking for some excuse. There was none. No noise, except for the rippling of the river and the odd crack of a broken stem springing up again. The women had stopped crying.

Then Tarlie shouted. It was wonderful to hear. So strong that it echoed back from the mountain. It tore through the afternoon. 'Shut up', you know how we say it:

'Sut up.'

He kept shouting it.

'Sut up.'

'Sut up.'

'Sut up.'

Then we joined him, until there was a great chorus pushing at Jim and his men, making them look as helpless and stupid as they were:

'Sut up.'

'Sut up.'

'Sut up.'

It was a relief. It felt good.

We did not stop until Jim put his gun in his pocket, turned round and walked back along the strip of torn land.

He has a bad walk, that Jim. He walks in on himself like a soft ball with his head down. He does not roll along like one of those fit and fat happy people, he scrapes along the ground unnaturally as if he is not happy with his condition and only bearing it. His hair looks unnatural on the top of his head.

His men followed in silence. They did not know what to do with themselves. The dozer started up with an explosion of hot, stinking gas, slowly grinding around to follow like a stupid dog.

But Jim and co were frightened, not chastised, and on the way out, when they felt safe, they started the fire. Easy to put a light to one of the broken houses. The bastards. You bastard.

Pause.

Tarlie came back to us as calm as if he'd been walking home after a good day's work. He was our Tarlie. Like he had been before. We trusted him. We were happy, despite what had happened. But I felt suddenly winded and drained of my blood. Had I not been working at that end of things? Had I not maintained the parts for that dozer? That morning I had issued parts for it. And I thought of you, Andrew. If you were irredeemable then so was I. We are keeping each other company on the way to hell. I hated you even more at that moment as I sweated.

Tarlie talked quietly to us. He said we had nothing to fear, that we must wash ourselves in the river, salvage what we could and go up into the mountain where we could settle for a while until things got better. Petrus was standing apart from us, ashamed, until Tarlie broke away. He went up to him and took him in his arms, hugging him. He said Petrus was his brother and that he couldn't have done what he'd done without Petrus. He said Petrus had nursed him and Petrus had given him the courage to live when he had wanted to die. He said this out loud. So we cheered Petrus and loved him like Tarlie loved him. Then Tarlie said to Petrus, but still out loud for us all to hear, he said You're the one Petrus who will take the weight. Will you do that? Petrus said Yes, and I knew that Tarlie was also telling us that we must help Petrus. I don't quite know what he meant, Andrew, but I knew that we would be with Petrus whatever he is going to do, because he is a good man who knows fear. Will you be there with us, Andrew?

Then Tarlie told us what we must do. Petrus was to take some of the stronger women and men to collect as much cassava and corn as possible before the fire got to it. He, Tarlie, would come back for them later when he had settled the others. I watched him go into the mountain with the children and the older people. He carried a child on his shoulder. I wanted to be that child, with all its innocence. The mountain had never looked more friendly but I stayed with Petrus. Then I thought of you, Andrew, and I wanted to tell you what had happened. So I left Petrus to find you, but you were not at home and that made me angry. You see, Andrew, I was there. You had run away.

I have put this letter inside the book you are reading beside your bed. I hope you find it. I'm sorry I messed up your things.

Find me if you want me,

Your Alloy Momus.

Having put the letter in Andrew's book, Alloy lay down on the bed and slept. When he awoke, it was still dark so he decided to stay until morning.

[][][][][]

He walks up the gentle incline, through the palms to the back of his house. The roaring night is moonless and dense, but he knows the way.

The house sits up high on stilts to catch the breeze. It is a comfortable place with a cemented space beneath for parking the car and for doing the washing.

In front, the ground falls precipitously to the mango tree beneath which Tarlie used to sit with Nalin's daughter, and to Madiak's back garden with its fruit trees and washing line.

There is no light, because the generator is cut off at nine; by Bune now, in the absence of Tarlie.

The compound below is invisible. The plantation beyond is a void. Yet the little house appears to be unassailably secure, a sure refuge from a threatening world. Andrew assumes that the smell of burning has nothing to do with him. What he thinks is: This is my life, but where am I going? An image of Alloy passes through his mind. Or is it Nwufoh, or Tarlie? Someone to hang on to, at any rate.

On the veranda he kicks off his boots and enters the house.

"Shit!"

In the dark, the furniture is not in its usual place. He knocks against the overturned table. His books are on the floor. He walks on things that ought not to be there.

He thinks of Jim dancing around the room breaking things, his hair jumping on the top of his head. Laughter expands in Andrew's belly rising up as bubbles of delight and alcoholic gas. He belches. To have driven Jim to such silliness is a triumph he did not expect. He cannot be sacked by a lunatic. The Board would not stand for it.

Indeed, Andrew, they would stand for it. The Board needs Jim to do its dirty work a lot more than it needs you. Jim has destroyed Ples, so the damage to your living room does not count. Tarlie and the people of Ples are hiding in the mountains at this moment, as you laugh. The Board will stand for that, and for all sorts of things. Your standing, Andrew, is nothing.

Nonetheless, Andrew smiles. The events of the day seem small. He will sleep, pretending illness in the morning. Madiak and Bune will get things going. One of the boys will help him clear up. Petrus will repair the damage.

It does not occur to Andrew that there may have been a break-in, that someone might be waiting for him in the dark with a panga knife.

What does occur to him is that it is nice to find Alloy in his bed. The warm smell of the sleeping man, turned on his side facing the window, excites him. The open window takes up most of the wall; he feels as much outside as inside the room. He sits on the side of the bed, preparing to curl up behind Alloy, to take him in his arms and to push his face into the mass of gritty hair.

"Fuck you."

It has been said before, expressing the violent, unpredictable Alloy that Andrew likes, confident in what he thinks is their love. He wants to tell Alloy about his row with Jim. He is proud, in front of Alloy, of having taken on Jim.

"Wow! You should have seen Jim. . ."

He is cut off: "Fuck you . . . white man."

Alloy is motionless, staring through the window. He is outside, moving away from Andrew who takes his shoulder.

Andrew is not shaken off but he is repulsed and he feels it. He tries to pull Alloy around. He is shaken off. Tentatively he moves his hand to Alloy's hair to push his fingers into it as he has done before.

A roar of anger escapes: "Leave me, white man." The agony shakes the dense night that holds them together.

□□□□□

The two spectators sit on opposite sides of the auditorium. They watch the romance in which two self-styled revolutionaries are pitted against an unsympathetic establishment determined to crush them. Wow, each thinks separately, that is me down there. Am I not something significant in the universe?

No, comes the celestial reply, that they mistake for a burst of applause, you are not especially significant. The hostile world you imagine is against you and against which you press your pointless struggle, is at its worst indifferent and at its best willing to love you, if only you will let it.

If, continues the celestial pontificator, you two were to bump into each other in the street outside this theatre, in your present state of mind, the chances are that you'd not recognise one another. I'd like to knock your silly heads together. You've had the sex (and you might have some more), you've sympathised with each other thereby recognising that you have something in common. Well done! But it's not enough. I made you and I know what you must be. You two will not be content to live your lives amongst strangers. You two are meant to be part of humanity, not separate from it. But before you make the greater connection you must first make the lesser. You must connect properly with each other. Have I not given you freedom? Distant thunder rumbles. You may ignore My design, but you do so at your peril. Thwart Me and you thwart yourselves: because I know that if you do not express your youthful selves by love, you will go on to express yourselves by other means: by sexual perversion, by acts of violence or by a rejection of the world – suicide or the sterile withdrawal of the mad medieval anchorites who had the audacity to cop out in My name. More distant thunder as the Mighty One clears its throat.

Listen to Me! Did I not make you by traumatising you? Are you not the sum of your traumas? Without them you are only a couple of blank pages of the many millions upon which the stories of lives are yet to be written, and written, and written. I didn't stop you loving the angels I sent you. As day followed day you refused to forgive. As you grew up to know better you disobeyed My command and to make matters worse you turned your backs on the world I created for you. You, Andrew, you made detachment a design for your life: you avoided love and affection. Alloy, you were no better: you deliberately expressed yourself by aggression towards anyone who tried to get near you – love and affection were your enemy not to be avoided but to be attacked, "Fuck You, Fuck You All" was your war cry.

Wilfully disobedient, both of you, so does that not make your providential collision – yes, that was by My design – does that not make your providential collision all the more wonderful? Think of what happened! First, Andrew, in response to Tarlie's desperate cry for help, your own no-less-desperate realisation that your humanity could only be proved by making sympathetic human connections. Then, your subsequent lurch towards Alloy for reasons indeed that may have been perverse but that were, nonetheless, tinged with a sort of pity veering towards the compassion that Tarlie himself had taught you to recognise. Indeed initiated by you, Andrew, but made successful by Alloy's innate compassion (did I not create it?) expressed as compassion for the struggling man who I caused to be dumped (Bune, My agent, no less) in front of his house.

The divine presence sits back to contemplate its own pomposity. It takes a deep breath and sighs. An ominous breeze disturbs the night. Embers glow in the dark and become a lively flame. The divine presence continues:

Sexual attraction fuelled by sexual starvation also, I grant you. And it did indeed do you both some good. But also, it gave you the wrong idea (I sometimes regret giving you the freedom to think for yourselves). It gave you the idea that it was the sex that made you compatible. But, actually, the sex got in the way. It was no more than mutual masturbation, Andrew. You could have as easily done it with Nwufoh or Tarlie or even with Bune for that matter. Walking out the club was indeed a first step forward but fighting Jim was an act of self-centred self-destruction on the way back to easy detachment. Running away and getting drunk. I ask you. I ask you! You know as well as I do you should have immediately returned – stone cold sober – to Alloy. Was he not always waiting for you (first outside the club and then at Ples)? Yes, Alloy, you were right to suspect Andrew's lack of courage. But you were wrong to define it as a wilful betrayal of Ples and therefore of yourself. You were wrong to define it as something a white man was bound to do, thereby, Alloy, giving you the silly excuse to retreat to your old hostile habits. Remember My command, Alloy. Remember it!

Listen to Me. Listen To Me! An earth tremor ever so slightly shifts the firmament a couple of inches. Listen to Me you two: this is your last chance. If you do not connect properly then you might as well be apart. But it's not what you want. I know that because I created you. I know that in this essential moment you both feel the loss of the old romantic boyhood adventure like a knife in the guts: But Us Two Against The World and all that baloney won't do. It never has done and now you know it: a return to the past is impossible for two young men such as you. You have to express yourselves loudly or not at all. You're not going to accept defeat and collect china like Henry. Not this time round, Andrew. You'll connect, you two, if not living, then dead.

Silence.

A divine cough.

I mean, just do the right thing.

[][][][][]

Alloy is distilled to a pure resentment of Andrew who is now no different from Angelina; both white devils. He is back on the battleground where he must fight alone. The world is a hostile place which will destroy him if he shows any weakness. He is ashamed of having been taken in by Andrew; of having betrayed something of his essential self to a white man. He wants to see Andrew dead because a dead Andrew is easier to deal with than a living memory.

And Andrew? He feels abandoned in a hopeless wasteland of pain. Was not Alloy supposed to be Nwufoh? Was not the black skin, the male body, as far away as he could get from England and from Angela? Therefore, the idea of a rejection by this black man is unbearable. He doubts his own Andrew-ness but recognises, as a response, the Alloy-ness of Alloy which he has not recognised until now. Just at the point where Alloy is unobtainable, he wants Alloy to know him as Andrew; even to reject him as Andrew; but not to reject him as a white man, as an abstract idea: that frightens him.

Andrew looks at what he can see of Alloy in the dark. He sees something immobile and unforgiving. He gets on his knees beside the bed. He wants to raise Alloy from the dead:

"Alloy," he whispers.

No response.

"Kill me, then." It is a silly, melodramatic thing to say, and he knows it, but he means it because he wants a contact of some sort that is real. Otherwise what is there for him? Back into the cage of isolation. The man in the iron mask, again. That is how it seems in the roaring night. Andrew is quite sincere in his emotion, no less than is Alloy.

"Alloy," he begs, "what's happened?"

"You know."

"Is it Jim?"

"You know. You are Jim. You are Jim's man."

"No, I am your man, Alloy."

"Never."

Alloy is talking out of the window, at the night. Andrew is on his knees. Both are in pain: Alloy believes what he says; Andrew feels only loss and bewilderment. Both feel they are at the end of the road that ends in the ever-expanding universe.

"Well kill me then for God's sake, Alloy, if you mean that."

"Fuck off, stupid white man. You're a joke."

"I'll kill you then."

Alloy moves his body almost imperceptibly, expressing his contempt.

Andrew stands over him and hits the naked black back as hard as he can. It's pathetic but he wants to damage the blackness, to affect it, to hurt it physically.

The responding laughter is miles away.

But Andrew is determined to make an impression. He sits astride Alloy and tries to turn him onto his back but he is not strong enough for the man smaller than himself, who is, nonetheless, coiled wire. He puts his hands around Alloy's neck and finds it is not easy to strangle a man lying on his side. Alloy's laughter is derisive but it suggests a man who might be sobbing. Andrew is mad for a few seconds. He sees red. He will kill if he can.

Alloy's response is instinctive. He uncoils suddenly, this lean, black man with his mass of combed-out hair in which you can lose things. He springs up and around with a yell pushing Andrew's shoulders with such a force that Andrew is thrown against the tacky wardrobe, smashing through the doors to sit amongst the remnants of his clothes. Alloy pulls him out roughly, tearing his shirt which he then rips off entirely, bit by bit, tugging at the tough stitching.

101

Andrew takes it, dumb, unable to move, his own bloodlust turned to an almost erotic death wish. But his immobility only disgusts and enrages Alloy further. Close to tears, he throws the rags that were the shirt aside, and slaps Andrew's face so hard that Andrew falls back to sit in the bottom of the wardrobe again, his nose bleeding. He sits up for a moment, blinks once, then falls back, the blood running slowly down his face. He is breathing but he keeps his eyes shut deliberately. He wants to smile because he knows that this is the end or, more likely, the beginning, of something.

The demon Alloy sits opposite, cross-legged on the bed, watching. "Fuck you, Andrew," he says gently. He is Alloy again, remembering Andrew seated on the grass in front of his house, remembering Andrew leaving the club for him, remembering sitting with Andrew on Jim's veranda with Margaret and Joseph. He remembers Joseph sitting at Margaret's feet, holding her hand until her breathing is steadied. He remembers holding Andrew's hand, talking to him with his thumb pressing the palm of his hand. "Fuck you, white man. Why do you fuck yourself?" The tears run down his face as the blood runs down Andrew's in the darkness they share.

Alloy sits motionless, waiting for Andrew.

Does time stop? It might well have done.

"Alloy?"

"I'm here."

"Why?"

"Ples."

"What about Ples?"

"You don't know, do you?"

"Know what?"

"Wait."

Alloy, nimble around the furniture he has broken, the books he has upset, the crockery he has smashed, fetches the kero lamp and matches. Returning, he sets the lamp alight on the bedside table. He throws Andrew's book at him.

"Read the letter I wrote you. It's inside."

Andrew reads, seated inside the broken wardrobe, sniffing up his bloodied and bruised nose.

Alloy lies stretched out on the bed, his arms behind his head. He feels better, a lot better.

They sit in a snug cocoon of light.

When Andrew has finished reading, Alloy pulls him up. He pulls off what is left of his clothes, takes him to the shower, sits on the toilet watching him and then joins him. Afterwards they lie naked together in the sticky heat. They lie together in that good darkness in which they are both black. Or, for that matter, both white.

Do they sleep?

If they do, it is not for long.

Do they dream?

If they do, then surely it is of fire.

Smoke fills the night air. Smell it!

The fire rages. Hear it!

For God's sake, are you dead to the world?
Yes.
For a while.
For a little bit of eternity.
But they are woken by the clanging of the muster bell.
"It will stop," whispers Andrew.
It does not: it is urgent.
Wake up.
Fire! Fire!

10
The Raid

Petrus Remembers

Tarlie came to Ples at the time when the daughter of Nalin was killed by the Giluwe boys when they were drunk and they had been smoking grass. They are violent men but it is the plantation that makes them blind. When they come to Van they are like children. Everything is new to them and they are afraid. At home in the Highlands they are men, but here they are treated like children and that makes them mad sometimes. Often they said they would kill Andrew but Tarlie said they could not do that as it would make a lot of trouble for us all. So they did not kill Andrew.

Tarlie was brought to us by Joseph on Sunday night when we were having the church service. Some people said there had been a fight in Andrew's compound, but there were often fights. Joseph told us that the daughter of Nalin had been killed. Tarlie stayed in the little house I had built beside the church. At first I did not understand why Tarlie was unhappy because Nalin's daughter was only a girl who was not even a woman. The children die all the time and God takes them for himself. The Bible says so. But Joseph said that Nalin's daughter was going to be Tarlie's wife. Nalin was going to sell her to Tarlie so that she could have his child. Then I understood and I prayed to God to make Tarlie forget. It is the only way in this life.

At first I thought Tarlie would die because he did not eat or wash. He lay on the floor of my house for three days and three nights. Joseph came to visit him every night when he had finished his work. He brought food. Alloy came as well to sit with him but they did not talk. I read the Bible to Tarlie. I read him the story of Jesus coming to us.

One day, Tarlie walked to the river. He stood in the river for a long time looking at the mountain. The children who were playing told us this. Every morning he walked to the river. In the evening he would come back to the house to eat the food we made for him. But he did not talk. He was thinking. Later he told me he was praying to God to send Jesus to us.

This was before Annu came back to us. In those days, as I have said, we had forgotten Annu. Some of the people did not know even Annu's name, because they had been recruited by Andrew. We did not know that Annu was a friend of Joseph. We did not know that Annu knew about our suffering. But I remembered his name because the friend of Our White Missis had told me. But Annu was not with us then.

When Jim came, Tarlie was at the river. I prayed to God for strength and I spoke to Jim but he was mad. He waved his gun at me so I ran away in my fear. I prayed to God not to forsake us. Then Tarlie stood up and shouted at Jim, so I knew my prayers were answered. Tarlie shouted very loud because he is a big man. As well, he is a brave man because Jim was mad and he had the gun. But Tarlie showed us then that the white man can also be afraid. Afterwards, Tarlie said that Jim was afraid because he could not kill us all with his gun. When I saw Tarlie in front of me, big like a mountain, I stopped crying. I knew God had not forsaken us. Tarlie did not move. He stood up to Jim, waiting for Jim to fight him. But Jim turned around and walked away. The bulldozer and his boys followed him.

Despite the broken church and houses, the people of Ples were happy that Jim had gone. But Tarlie did not laugh. He had a serious face. He said that Jim would come back with more men and bulldozers to chase us away. Jim would bring the police with him. If the police caught us they would beat us and lock us up. The police are that way. They are stupid because when they put on the white man's uniforms they think they are white men so they can be our masters. It does not take much to make a man stupid.

So again fear overcame the people because they had nowhere else to go.

I watched all this from afar, because I was ashamed of my fear before God. But that was my pride. God gave me my fear so that Tarlie might be strong again. So I thank God for that. And Tarlie came to me and he held me like his brother and he comforted me. Then I knew that Tarlie would indeed bring Annu to us.

Alloy also, yes you, Alloy. You, who are reading this. You comforted me also. Then I knew that you were a man blessed by God, although you are a strange and angry man who forgets he is blessed. We talked of Andrew then, and you were angry with him. Your eyes burnt with your anger. You asked me, where was Andrew? You said this man Andrew has betrayed us. You ran off before I could stop you. I was afraid that you might kill Andrew.

After you had gone, we saw the fire coming. Jim and his men started the fire on their way out of Ples. Already the fire was big and rushing towards us with black smoke reaching up into the sky. It was like a cloud that threw a shadow over us and we were cast asunder. Tarlie said we must collect what we wanted quick and go down to the river. We sent the children ahead and we collected our things. We were afraid and we were running about like children, but Tarlie shouted at us to behave like men.

Yes, those were hard days on the mountain, but Tarlie looked after us.

But I was afraid because I understood that we were lost, like the children of Israel who had forsaken God, and God's wrath was upon them.

I prayed very hard and then I thought of Annu.

Why had I forgotten Annu?

Yes, Annu came into my mind at that time when things were hard for us. I talked to Tarlie about Annu. I said that if we could find Annu, Annu would help us.

Tarlie said, yes, it was the thought of Annu which made him strong to stand up against Jim. He said it was his forgetting of Annu that had made him weak.

So Tarlie said yes, he had been thinking of Annu. He said it was no good going to Andrew for help because Andrew would be under Jim again. Andrew had nowhere else to go. We could not trust Andrew because he was a white man. The only man we could trust was Annu. Then Tarlie said that Annu would return to us.

Petrus Remembers

Alloy does not let me rest, but it is God's will. He says I must write what happened when we went to Master Chan's store that time with Tarlie and with Keramugl.

Now, after Tarlie had taken us across the river after Jim had destroyed Ples, we walked up the mountain on the hunters' path. The mountain is very steep beside the river, like a wall, and the path is hidden, but we knew the way. Higher up, it is not so steep and the walking is not so hard but olsem we were tired with our fear of Jim and afraid for the night in the bush. We settled beside a big tree that we Van people call a Nulu tree because it has big roots like the feet of a giant man. Because there was no rain we did not make a shelter. We were not worried for water because of the river below us, but we were hungry.

We had a woman with us whom I loved as I had loved my mother. She was old and bent, but strong. Her name was Nakini. Now, Nakini was born many years before the company came to Van Island. She was born near to where Andrew's house is now. In those days Nakini's father gave some land to the mission for a farm. Nakini said they planted coconut trees and fruit trees. When the company came to Van Island, they paid the mission big money for the land but they did not know that the land belonged to Nakini's father who had given it to the mission. Nakini said that the mission farm was in the forest. It was one day's walk to the coast. Today the time is one hour in the truck. Nakini has been all her life here. She told us she was afraid when the white men came to cut down the trees, but she thought they must be doing a good thing because they themselves were only bush-kanakas in the forest and the white men would make them civilised. Nakini worked in the plantation weeding when Mr Jonson was the boss, but when Andrew came she was old. She came to live in Ples, where she made a garden for her food while she waited to die. Nakini's children have gone away. One is living in Port Markham, one has died, and one she does not know. It is wrong that Nakini has no children to take care of her, but at Ples we could watch her.

So Nakini knew the forest. She showed us what leaves and what roots we could eat. This helped us. Now, one of the Giluwe men was Deni. He could shoot birds like the highlands men do with an arrow like a fork, so we ate the red parrots that live on the steep mountain side above the river. So God provided for us, and I thanked Him.

At night, Tarlie and Keramugl and some of the other men went to our old gardens near to the river to dig out the kaukau, but we were afraid. Also, we were afraid to go back to the compound to see Andrew. If we had been able to trust Andrew, things would have been better.

Yes, we thought of Annu but we did not have him with us. Yes, also we thought of the white woman, Our White Missis, but we thought Jim would stop her now and she would be afraid. God had abandoned us to our enemies. I thought we must have done some wicked thing in the eyes of God, but I did not know what it was.

By this time Tarlie was more like a madman than the Tarlie we knew before. He was still our big man but he inhabited strange ways. He said he would not clean himself until Annu had come to us. He talked very little. He talked only when it was necessary. To me he said he would not pray to God until Annu came to us. Only then, Tarlie said, would he believe that God was not a white man's God. This made me sad because I thought yes, why do the ways of evil men prosper? Even myself, I was losing my belief in God.

Then Tarlie told us that we must go at night to Master Chan's store where we could buy things, because Master Chan did not shut the door until the last men had come out of the mill at nine o'clock. Tarlie said we would go when it was dark so no one would see us.

Now it was Keramugl and Burara and Weno and myself, Petrus, who went with Tarlie to Master Chan's store.

We did not have bows and arrows. Why should we want those things? We had no thoughts of fighting. We wanted to buy some things with the little money we had. Why would we think of fighting? We are kanakas but we are not stupid.

We passed through Ples. We saw that it was nothing. The earth had been scraped up to make a new wide road. We were surprised because we had not heard the bulldozer. I thought that Satan had taken over the earth and I was afraid.

We walked along the new road and we found ourselves on the old plantation road. Jonson's Road, we call it, because Mr Jonson made it. It is a narrow road, because in those days we did not have a bulldozer. The Highlands boys built it with shovels that Mr Jonson gave them.

But as I walked along the road I met fear and I have forgotten many things.

Keramugl Remembers

Yes we are afraid. We are afraid of Tarlie himself because he is wild. But when we look at Tarlie we see he is strong also. He is strong like our grandfathers were strong, in the time before the white men. So with Tarlie beside us our fear is not a big thing.

We walk near the oil palms so that we are in the dark. Then we come to the big road and to the mill where there are always people, night and day.

We are not afraid, because we are black in the night. Who can see us? In the white man's eyes we are all the same. They do not see that I am Keramugl but they see I am a kanaka. That is all.

Now Weno thinks he is a brave man and he says that he alone will go into Master Chan's store to buy the things. He says that Tarlie cannot go inside the store because everyone knows that the big man with a limp is Tarlie. This is true so we, that is me, Petrus, Burara and Tarlie, we stay outside in the dark. We stand beside a tree. Now, it is true, Weno is my good friend. But Weno is proud, and his pride is his undoing. This is what happened.

Weno does not take the money with him because the money is in the pocket of Petrus. And Petrus is afraid so he forgets he has the money.

We watch Weno go to the store. There is a bright light from the big door of the store, and also a big light that lights up some of the ground outside. The security men are old men who have worked for Mr Chan for many years. They carry bows and arrows. They wear yellow raincoats to keep themselves warm. The store has a high fence all around, with a big gate. On top of the fence is the barbed wire.

Now, we are waiting and waiting but Weno is still inside. So, we walk to the gate. That was myself, Petrus, and Burara. Tarlie himself is not afraid to come, but they will know him because of his limp. I say to Tarlie you wait outside for us. We will bring Weno.

The store is a big shed. Other people are in the store, but not many. The light is very bright inside.

Weno is at the counter. He is talking to Vincent who is the clerk of Mr Chan. Vincent is from Van Island, like Petrus. He is Mr Chan's man, but he is alright. He does not like to confuse the minds of the Highlands men but, all the same, he is proud. Vincent thinks all of us Highlands men are true bush-kanakas.

All the things Weno wants to buy are on the counter. Weno is arguing with Vincent. Vincent wants the money. But Weno is proud. He thinks Vincent is a child while he, Weno, is a man. Weno does not think straight all the time. He says he is not a thief and he will take the goods and that Petrus will bring the money. We see Vincent is laughing. He says he is not a child. He says he will not give the things to Weno before he has the money.

Now, because Weno is proud he does not want to walk out of the store without the goods. We know he is angry because he does not move. I, Keramugl, tell Petrus to give Weno the money. Petrus does not hear because he is afraid. Then Weno takes the goods. He tells Vincent he is a stupid man and he runs out of the store carrying the things and we are following because we are afraid and the security men are already shutting the big gate. The electric bell is ringing.

The big gate is shut and the old security man is putting on the chain. So we fight the guards with our hands because that is all we have. We have no panga knives. What else can we do? We cannot stay inside because they will not believe us. Jim will say we are thieves, and they will believe him because he is a white man. The police will take us and they will beat us and call us bush-kanakas and other bad names. They will take us to the court in Akaranda. They will send us to the Togulo Farm where we will be fucked by the bad men there. So we fight the security men. That is easy, because they are old men. We are not afraid of their bows and arrows because they cannot shoot straight and we are close to them.

So they run away. We open the gate and we run across the sports field. But there are many people around, brought by the electric bell, so we are confused.

We do not know where to run. The people stand around us, looking at us. I, Keramugl, see people I know, like Domus from the mill, and Pecto from the transport. But they do not know me, because they think I am a thief. They do not say there is Keramugl, we know him, and he is alright. No, because Jim says he will give plenty of money to the man who catches the thief, they see only the money. So they do not see that it is the good Keramugl. They want a thief, so I am the thief. They are not thinking I am a kanaka like them. They want the money. It is the money that makes people think badly. So I think I cannot fight all these men.

I think of Annu as I knew him in the Highlands, in the time before we come to the coast. Where is he now? I think of Ples. I ask, what has brought me to the company to die? But I have no answer, so I am sad.

Keramugl Remembers

I am pleased that I can tell my story, because then a good thing comes to us. We hear Tarlie crying out loud. Tarlie is shouting out loud. He is waving his arms around. He comes through the crowd of people to us. The people make way for him because they are afraid of him. They can see it is Tarlie, although he is wild with dirt on him. He comes into the middle of the crowd with us and he cries out, telling the people that it is himself, Tarlie. He says:

Do you not recognise me, with Keramugl and Weno and Burara and Petrus?

And they are quiet as they listen to Tarlie. Then one man calls out. It is the man we call Diwai because he is the head carpenter in the workshop. He says:

Yes it is Tarlie, because of the limp, but he should wash himself then we can recognise him.

Some people laugh, but Tarlie says nothing. Then it is Alloy who talks. He is in the crowd. Alloy says listen to Tarlie. He says we know Tarlie well. He says Tarlie is a good man. He is not a thief. How is it we want to fight him? Some people call out to agree. Other people are quiet because they are ashamed.

I am afraid before, but now I am strong with Tarlie. I feel Tarlie with me. Tarlie moves to the crowd and the crowd moves away. But it is not with fear that it moves away. It is the strength of Tarlie like a fire that makes the crowd move. The people are silent. I can hear the mill hissing like an animal. When I look at the crowd I see that the people are lit up by the red light from the mill. I see that some are ashamed so that they look at the ground. I can see that some men want to go, but they cannot because of the others behind them. I, Keramugl, feel I am a brother to Tarlie and to Petrus and to all my friends. Now I know what it is to be a man. I am no longer sad for the time before, because I know this is why I am born. I know why I am come to the company. I am come to see Tarlie. I am come to hear him.

Then Tarlie talks to the crowd. He does not shout like he shouts at Jim in Ples. He talks loud so that all can hear him talk. He tells the story of Jim coming to Ples to destroy Ples. He tells the story of us going onto the mountain because we are afraid of Jim. He says how Jim destroys Ples and chases us onto the mountain as if we are animals. He says all of us here are like animals, stolen from our homes to be children working for the white men. He says that the parents of children love them but that the white men do not love us although we do the hard work. He says we are black because we work hard under the sun and then we are chased from our homes into the mountains. People are saying, yes, Tarlie is right, we are like animals.

Tarlie tells them we have come to the store to find food and medicine. He says we are not thieves, we have money to pay. He tells Petrus to show them the money, and Petrus shows the money. Tarlie takes the money from Petrus. He says to the people:

Suppose you want the money, we will give it to you.

Then he throws the money at the people. It falls to the ground but they do not pick it up. They look at the money, but they do not pick it up.

Then Tarlie is angry but he does not shout. He says to them:

Pick up the money. It is the money you want. Take the money and sell us to Jim. Sell us to the police. Send your brothers to the Togulo Farm for them to die. Pick it up and buy beer in Master Chan's store so that you can forget.

And they are ashamed.

I, Keramugl, am saying this because this is what I saw.

Then Tarlie shouts louder:

Pick up the money, I say. Jim's men, where are they? The men who come to Ples? Where are you? Pick up the money.

But Tarlie is not angry now. Tarlie is stern and I see that some of them are afraid. I see them in the light of the mill. I hear the crying of the mill. I see Tarlie walk towards the people. They want to move away from his eyes but they cannot.

Then Tati comes forward. Tati is an old and silly man. He is mad in his own way. It is good. He is like a child and he lives on what we give him. At night he sleeps in the doorway of the big office. He is always there. I think when he is not there, people will be sorry. Our masters give him clothes and soap because they like to see he is clean. Tati is always clean. He is happy all the time and when the rain comes he stands on the grass and looks up into the sky and thanks God for the rain. Yes, Tati is a good man but he does not think about his food or his clothes or of a place to sleep. All the same, he eats, he has a clean lap-lap and he sleeps in the doorway of the big office.

When Tarlie sees Tati, he laughs and he says to Tati:

Yes, pick up the money.

Then Tarlie looks at the people again and he says:

If the money belongs to Tati it is good, like Tati himself.

Tati is smiling at Tarlie and he picks up the money. When the people see Tati pick up the money they laugh also. We all laugh because we are happy. I see the people who are ashamed. They look at Tarlie then and they are no longer ashamed.

Then Tarlie speaks again. He says, yes, he, Tarlie, is afraid before. He says he is no longer afraid. It is his limp that makes him strong because he cannot run away. But, he says, he is not strong enough because he does not have education. As he says this I see that some people are sad, because they want Tarlie to be strong. They want him to be stronger than all other men. Like me, they want Tarlie to be their man. But Tarlie says no. He says he is not our man. He says he is not enough. Then Tarlie raises his arms and he looks up into the night. All the same, he says there is one man who can lead us, his name is Annu.

When I hear the name of Annu I am happy. I want to shout out the name of Annu but Tarlie takes my arm and I shut my mouth. He says he, Tarlie, comes to tell all the people that Annu will come soon to help them. He says Annu is a better man than himself. He says he, Tarlie, is here with all of them to tell us to be ready for Annu. That is all.

Some men in the crowd know of Annu as well. I can see them nodding their heads, because they know Tarlie speaks the truth.

I am thinking then that I want Annu to be with us, now. I want him so much that my stomach is hurting. I can see Annu. He is a great man who is taller than the trees. I, Keramugl, I know that when Annu comes, the white men will shake like the leaves on the trees before the rain comes. They will run away before Annu. I am happy. Tarlie is strong but he says he is not strong enough. I, Keramugl, I know Annu will be enough.

Then Alloy shouts out the name of Annu. Then I shout out his name. Then everybody is calling: Annu, Annu, Annu.

Tarlie is throwing up his arms so we follow him, shouting: Annu, Annu, Annu!

Tarlie walks forward and the crowd opens up for him to pass through. Myself Keramugl, Petrus who is writing this for me, Weno and Burara, we all walk behind Tarlie. I am the last, so I can see that Weno and Burara are happy. Also Petrus himself, who, as we know, is a man who does not shout out but who talks carefully and who tells only the truth, even he is calling out the name of Annu.

Keramugl Remembers

Later, when we think about these things, we know that Mr Chan is afraid that we will go to his store again to destroy it. He goes to Jim. Also there is the electric bell and our shouting of the name of Annu. We walk through the people behind Tarlie's back. I can remember it is like the rows of oil palms, but the trees are people that make a path. The shouting at the end of the path stops. Then all the shouting stops. We see Jim at the end of the path. He is standing in the light of the Landrover that makes him look big, but there are many of us, we are not afraid. I Keramugl, I am behind Tarlie. I think Jim is a brave man, or he is a stupid man. But Jim has his gun.

Jim holds his gun above his head and he fires into the night. It is a noise like the rock breaking in the fire. There is no noise from the crowd and I hear the mill again, hissing like a snake. The lights from Jim's Landrover are lighting up the path made by the people so I cannot see his face, only his shadow. I am not afraid for myself, but I know that Jim does not forget that he hates Tarlie. I think Jim will kill Tarlie.

Tarlie is brave. He does not stop walking. I do not stop walking either, but when Burara stops in front of me, I push him to walk. So we are all close to Tarlie. I think if Jim kills Tarlie, I will kill him in turn with my hands. I think this is why I am here, to kill Jim.

But Jim does not kill Tarlie that time.

Now, when Tarlie reaches Jim he stops and looks at him. I think he wants to stand there for all time until Jim moves. I am not afraid of Jim; although he has his security men with him, I know we are more than all of them. But Jim has his gun.

I am close to him, but it is not easy to see his face because of the lights from the Landrover. Also because his hair is like a hat that covers his eyes. But it is Jim alright. I can see the way he stands. Not strong but like a tree that shakes in the wind.

Jim laughs at Tarlie and he puts his face close to Tarlie's face. Then we see his face. It is red. He talks like a drunkard. He shouts, but his voice is not strong. It is the gun making Jim strong then, that is all. He says he knows Tarlie. He says Tarlie is a trouble-maker who tells lies to us so that we do not like to work. He says bad things to Tarlie. I do not want to say these words because I am ashamed, but Petrus says I must tell the story straight because I am the witness of Tarlie. Jim says Tarlie is stupid. He says that Tarlie is a true bush-kanaka who does not know how to shit properly. He says that Tarlie shits on the side of the road like an animal. This is a bad thing to say to a man. We know the words stupid and bush-kanaka and bloodyfuckingbastard. We are used to hearing these words, but to say a man is an animal is bad. I do not forget that. Jim says that Tarlie is a dirty man. He says he does not know how to wash. He says that Tarlie has run away to the mountain because he is afraid of him, Jim. He says that Tarlie is like a woman because he runs away.

But all the time, Jim does not say the name Tarlie. He says You, or This Man. He does not use the name Tarlie. He is afraid of the name.

When I hear these things I am angry. I want to kill Jim. I am not afraid of the gun. Myself, Keramugl, I am mad. I am like Tati who does not think. I push Burara to one side and I walk to Jim.

But as I pass by Tarlie, he takes my wrist. He holds it tight. He pulls me towards him. I remember this well. As he holds my wrist, he uses his thumb to talk to me. His thumb is stroking the inside of my hand and pressing it. It is telling me not to be angry. It is saying to me to be still. I hear it and I stop feeling angry. I am hearing Tarlie, not Jim.

Then Jim comes very close to Tarlie. His face is ugly. He tells Tarlie to run away again. He says he is the boss and he does not want to see Tarlie's face around. Then he shouts to us all. He does not call Tarlie by his name but he calls him This Man. He says This Man is not to be seen anywhere. He says that if This Man is seen then the police will take him away. He says that This Man will not be sent to the Togulo Farm where he will become fat, but instead he will be sent to the prison in Port Markham. He says that men go into the Port Markham prison but that they do not come out again. He says This Man is a very bad man who holds up progress and who wants us to be bush-kanakas all our lives. He says that he, Jim, is helping us to become civilised people, to read and write. He says we do not thank him.

Yes, when I, Keramugl, hear Jim say this and as I feel Tarlie holding me, I hear Tarlie laugh and I am filled with laughter myself. I say to Jim:

Thank you, Master.

Then Jim looks at me, Keramugl. He says he will not forget my face. He says to me in a low voice so that only I, Keramugl, can hear:

So you are Annu's boy, are you? He fucks your arse, does he?

I remember this well, because then I know he thinks that Tarlie is the man Annu. I say to Jim:

Yes, Master.

Then I feel Tarlie's thumb in my hand again and I laugh but I know Jim wants to kill me also.

Jim says fuck you too, like Andrew says in the time before. Then he walks away. He falls down a little but he stands up and climbs into the Landrover.

When he has gone the people want to shout out the name of Annu again but Tarlie puts up his hand and they are silent. He tells them to go to their houses quietly and sleep. They obey him.

Then I remember Annu again in the time before and because Annu is not with us I am sad. I look at Tarlie and I can see that he is sad also. So I think I will watch over this man and I follow him back to the mountains.

I have said enough for now, Petrus. You can give this to Alloy.

11
The Jungle Law

If black is black, then from whence comes the differentiation? This is the night, so there is no light, and yet there is brightness. There is a wonderful variety of shades, shadows and glittering movement. There is a glorious silence and yet a clamour of sounds that envelops me, such that I feel I am held up and lifted.

Your existence changes everything and your death alters nothing.

Tarlie, a shadow in the night, stands in the water that breaks the moon into shimmering, shifting shafts of silver. Quicksilver runs between Tarlie's legs, the one strong and as straight as the Nulu tree, the other shorter and weaker so that his hips, his buttocks, are twisted beneath the loin cloth wrapped around his determined strength. His shoulders carry the heavens above.

Tarlie stands. He faces the mountain, the plantation behind him. The mountain is a void in the sky. He raises his eyes to the roaring universe of which he is the centre. The same pattern of stars, the same pattern of clouds releasing the same moon. Who has not watched and wondered?

Before, Tarlie's life had been a simple pattern of inevitable events that had led him, step by certain step, on his life's journey: leaving the Highlands because the men he grew up with needed his help here on Van; the early days on the plantation when he had done the hard, tedious and unfamiliar work because he had to be, wanted to be, with those same men through their times of trouble; finding himself especially favoured by the white men – those strange, dream-like, half-people – wondering, at first, where his loyalties lay; then accepting his place as a useful intermediary, but never quite losing the feeling that he had betrayed some part of himself.

His life moved onwards, through days nonetheless filled with a definite sense of being Tarlie. Here is Tarlie, he said, as if he stood outside himself and watched Tarlie as the others did.

Andrew's arrival had been a change from Master Jonson. Despite the fact that he acted in the same white, detached way as if part of him was elsewhere; as if they, the labour, were no more a human part of the plantation than the tractors or the palms themselves; despite all this, Andrew was different. Tarlie had felt this the moment Andrew had arrived. Andrew had looked at him and talked to him as a man in whom he was interested. If he hung about, Andrew did not ignore him or tell him to fuck off, as Master Jonson would have done. Rather, Andrew's manner showed that he was happy to have Tarlie nearby. It was for Tarlie to decide when to go, and Tarlie knew he could have pushed Andrew and Andrew would have fallen. It was about the same time Master Andrew arrived that Tarlie found himself watching Nalin's daughter, wanting her; so that looking back, it was as if Master Andrew's interest in him and his interest in Nalin's daughter were the same thing.

Now, here, as the water ran between his legs as if he belonged to the water, Tarlie felt a surge of happiness as he thought of Andrew's love for him and of his own love for Nalin's daughter.

But that was in the time before.

Tarlie drew the night air into his chest. Before! His sigh, at the centre, shook the mountain and shifted the stars beyond and made the universe shudder. Nalin's daughter: working with her in the compound, whispering to her in the evenings beneath the old mango tree, holding her small hand in his hands, holding her head, feeling its weight in his hands and feeling her warmth grow cold.

His love had killed her. He, Tarlie, he who had solved their problems, he who had felt able to control and temper Andrew. He, Tarlie, he who had acted as their leader, happy to put himself in front, certain of his Tarlie-ness and of his place in his life, and in theirs, and in the universe. He had brought them to a place of greater uncertainty.

So, as if newly made, Tarlie cried out into the roaring night, his anguish expanding the universe:

Annu,

Annu,

Annu.

He fell to his knees on the sand. The water tore away the cloth that was his humanity. A madman, who used to be Tarlie, is this man with the wild and matted hair. He covered his face with his hands, afraid to see his universe.

He is found by the good Petrus who leads him back to sleep. Petrus will save Tarlie for the future.

□□□□□

All this was many years ago, so I have forgotten many things. Those days made me old. Andrew, why do you ask me to remember these things? It is better for us to forget Tarlie. Let him sleep. Tarlie was before Annu. Now it is the time after Annu.

But Andrew says I must write these things for Annu. He says Annu was brought to us by Tarlie. Yes, that is true, Tarlie prepared us for Annu. I remember, one day Tarlie was angry with us. He told us we were not fit to have Annu with us. He said that if we did not believe in Annu, then Annu would not come. He said that when we were strong, then that was the time he would fetch Annu. So we were ashamed and we prayed to God to make us strong for Annu.

It was night time. We were living in the forest, in the small huts we had made. I remember it well now. The moon was bright, so bright that it woke me up. I looked for Tarlie. He was not there. I knew he had gone down to the river again. I climbed down to the river on the hidden path we used. It was bright under the moon but there were no colours. I was afraid, but I thought of Tarlie. As I came to the river I could hear him calling. He was calling Annu, Annu, Annu. I saw him kneeling in the water. He was naked and he was very black. Yes, Andrew, he was acting mad. He was not our Tarlie like before. But I do not want to spoil his name. I say he was acting mad but he was not mad. His mind was confused, that is all. This was because he was angry with himself because he could not solve our problems. But he was not mad because he had faced up to Jim two times and beaten him two times.

But I am only Petrus the carpenter. I do not know about these things. I only know that Tarlie acted mad, but was not mad. Not mad like Tati was mad. Tati had lost his mind. Tarlie had not lost his mind. But Tarlie was like all of us in those days. He was confused. When I saw Tarlie kneeling naked in the water, I knew this and I was afraid. If Tarlie could not help us, then who could? I was afraid like the children of Israel in the wilderness. I, Petrus, also prayed to God to send us Annu.

As I came to Tarlie I heard the water and I thought that the water was carrying Tarlie away. I remember these things now as I write them down. Then I went to Tarlie and I led him out of the water.

[][][][][]

That is how it was. It is.

Tarlie limps up the hill to the club. Nonetheless strong and confident, on that night.

He is invisible in the dark, which is as thick and substantial as his own determined body.

The small and pointless lights coming from the crouching bungalows barely touch him.

A footfall as light as it is uneven, in the night. Tarlie is as much of the night as, later, the stain is of the water. Separate at first, an oily film floating, dissolving, a part of the water, changing it. His days are over; he will never see the day's sky again, be it dulled by clouds or bright in the hopeful morning.

That is how it was. It is.

Tarlie, part of the night.

Through which he unevenly pads.

[][][][][]

The biggest bungalow of all is set above the club, on top of the hill, behind a domed and threadbare lawn.

The house itself is dark because when she is on her own, Margaret prefers to sit quietly on the veranda and listen to the night. For her, the night's song, the tropical symphony of the insects, is a comfort. While her husband prowls in the night, she sits above it.

Her silence is magnificent. It is not a calculated pose, attempting a petty sort of negative impact to display displeasure. It is not the manifestation of a Dolly-like vacancy. It is not by any means an acknowledged superiority. The fact is, Margaret has nothing to say to the club crowd around her that would make any difference.

Is that Margaret then? A divine indifference? Looks like it! Looks like the placidity of a domestic cow. One wonders – Daphne again – if Jim notices her at all? Other, that is, than as the woman whom he owns. The competent

116

housekeeper, with whom, incidentally, he sleeps? The loyal partner at functions, standing or sitting beside him quietly as if, had Jim noticed, in respect for him and all he stands for. A quietness appearing as dumbness, according to Peter. Or, whispered by Dolly as if defining a profound truth, I think she's a little simple; Jim is so wonderful with her.

When the large-boned Margaret was younger and a pale, attractive blonde, willing to go along with the crowd around her, she was indeed said to be a little beyond this world, a little slow, difficult to reach. Said to be an easy lay. She wasn't, but she looked it and she didn't bother to correct the impression. Others would say she'll be a wonderful mother, seeing her tired, washed-out and exhausted by a gang of demanding children but infinitely patient. Nice to know she's down there doing all that, and happily doing it, while we sit up here painting our fingernails, watching the sun set. But it was, it is, true: Margaret is a motherly type, despite her silence and apparent distance; a child will run to her and climb upon her lap.

No children of her own. Tragic. Is it? Why? Margaret has never thought of it. Her love, as Joseph is bound to understand, is not the usual focused, calculating, selfish, consuming thing we call love. She is love. Her love is not counted out in slices to be consumed until there is nothing left! Fuck that, Alloy says. Her love is the sun in the morning, the bright and warm dawn after the chill night. All who want it can stand in Margaret's love and be warmed.

How on earth, how in Heaven's name, did Margaret get hitched to Jim? We might imagine God thumping the celestial table, making the celestial pots jump but, of course, He knows the answer for He did it.

Therefore, in that same night, and not far from where Tarlie oddly pads his way, Margaret sits relaxed, listening to the night in which, she is perfectly aware, Jim also prowls like something rotten.

[][][][][]

This night is as solidly black and impenetrable as . . . as Tarlie's eyes. Yet its solidity is an illusion for it has its fractures, its jagged openings. Do we not have a knowledge, at any rate an intuition, of fragments of warm, busy light that contain those sweating bodies, or parts of them – as Joseph sees them in the club – that are absorbed into the night the minute we focus our attention on them? No less the sounds that are lost the minute we listen: a cry, a sigh, an anguished sob. Or is it laughter and dancing feet? Perhaps the death throes of a rat as it is swallowed by the unfeeling python. The sound of a falling leaf.

[][][][][]

Tarlie turns off the dark road – its surface smooth and warm – onto the sharp, crushed-rock floor of the club car park. This small, rectangular space, cut harshly into the side of the hill, is lit by two strip lights mounted onto the back wall of the club. It is a tank of cold light, bright in itself but having no impact upon the roaring thickness of the hot tropical night all around. Stark is this place, isolated and colourless, marked only by the fixed shadow of Joseph's washing line with its solid shapes of hanging dish-cloths and tea towels.

A shadow moves quickly, in the blinking of an eye. It grows huge and is gone. Tarlie slips through a side door.

He sits inside the cramped room behind the bar. It is part store (for a night's worth of heavy boozing), part kitchen (the girls' coffee) and part Joseph's hole, where he has been known to sleep on a mat on the floor while Jim and co have drunk through the night towards the blinding dawn. Fuck me, is that the time? Later, of course, the place will be used for less innocent purposes.

Oh yes, you're right, security was slack. Jim would tighten it up later but in those days, before Annu, the kanakas never went up the hill. Not until things got really out of hand. Then, even the car park had a special purpose.

Tarlie sits on Joseph's little stool. The bar-boy doesn't need a chair: the cement floor or an impoverished stool is good enough for him. He can sit on a box for God's sake, if he has to sit at all. Anyway, he's paid to work, which means not sitting.

Tarlie waits. He doesn't mind for how long. It is his night and it will wait for him if necessary. The room is warm; it smells of beer, and the only light comes from the empty car park. From the bar, nothing; a couple of yellow globules in the thick dark make no impression upon the dozing barman. Who is not Joseph.

Tarlie is ignorant of this fact, but he waits for Joseph in Joseph's room with all its marks and memories of Joseph; even, above the stink of the beer, the smell of Joseph himself, Tarlie's comforting friend.

Joseph's absence will present a small problem but for the moment, in retrospect, an eternal moment, Tarlie sits in wonderful ignorance. Happy he feels as if Joseph is there near him and in due time – it does not matter how long – Joseph will join him and take him to Annu.

Annu: very soon, Tarlie will find his Annu and bring him back to Ples, and Annu will lead them somewhere, as he, Tarlie, has so manifestly failed to do. This act will justify Tarlie's life, and he will live thereafter as Annu's servant and messenger. Tarlie is ecstatic, on an adrenaline high, in a state of euphoria. As happy as a man can be as he sits in the dark and stuffy little room behind the bar.

Nearby, in this night of nights, Margaret sits quietly, up there behind the domed and threadbare lawn.

The night is as thick and dark as a tropical night can be. Perhaps a few drops of second-rate light are squeezed out here and there. But there is no other illumination, except for the contained, clean, cold and still white light of the car park that works for nothing but itself.

Watch out, Tarlie!

Watch out?

No, there is nothing you can do. Enjoy it for now and go with a smile on your face, your Tarlie grin.

[][][][][]

It starts. The countdown begins. But you don't know it, Tarlie.

A movement from the bar.

A shape fills the door. It is not Joseph.

A smaller, older, more shrunken and defeated man. A sort of Clarence. It is indeed Clarence's man, put there because Joseph has gone.

Joseph left with Andrew in such a manner that any chance of returning was clearly out of the question. A bar-boy does not abandon his post, let alone on a Saturday night – or, more precisely, on a Sunday morning – and survive to tell the tale. Clarence had been shocked to the core. The foundation of one of the carefully constructed certainties of his life had been shaken, perhaps irrevocably damaged. He may even have suffered a minor heart attack – only the formation of scar tissue but contributing, no doubt, to that massive and fatal expression of his mortality a few weeks later. I can't understand it. Nothing seems to be missing, so why would he run away like this? It's not like him. He'll be back, I wasn't born 'ere for nothing etc, etc. He'll be back for the money box. Then we'll catch the fucker. These kanakas are all the same.

Well in the end he didn't, they hadn't, and they had to agree he'd gone off with that arsehole of the highest order, motherfucker, cocksucker, traitor-to-his-race, Andrew. Andrew is at the bottom of all this, and when I find that commie wanker. . .

Small, rather drab moths flutter helplessly around the last spluttering candle of their certainty.

Anyway, Joseph has gone. That part of Joseph's life, the bar-boy part, is over.

▯▯▯▯▯

Tarlie calls out: "Joseph?"

Nalin is surprised to see Tarlie whom, of course, he recognises as the man who was going to buy his daughter. He is afraid because having heard the stories of madness he assumes Tarlie wants to commit a theft for which he will be blamed. He says nothing, but blinks dumbly. Life for him is a series of barely comprehensible pictures and dismissive orders. He lives on the edge of things, but he is not entirely stupid and can be trusted to do things when he is not afraid. But now he wants to run away. Again. Yes, this is a man who cannot give love but who would respond well to receiving it with simple loyalty.

But Tarlie smiles – he is happy, remember – and Nalin relaxes, seeing the strong man who confronted them all and who stood up to Master Jim outside Chan's store that other night. He is happy to have a companion in this strange building where the white men meet to drink and talk in a language he cannot understand.

He wants to keep Tarlie with him as a comfort, as he once wanted his daughter until her monetary worth became more important to him. Tarlie knows all this. He does not forgive Nalin, because the desire to forgive is a vanity he does not know. Later Nalin will remember Tarlie as Annu.

Tarlie says: "Josep? Em i stap we?"

"Josep? Husat?"

"Em i man husat i wok long hea long taim bipo."

119

"Em i go pinis."

"Long we?"

"Tasol mi nogat gudpela tinting. Me savi em i go long haus bilong Alloy."

So Tarlie moves on, happy.

He leaves Nalin behind in the club, alone.

[][][][][]

Jim is the creature of the night.

But unlike Tarlie, Jim is not part of the night. He moves around by driving his Landrover; one of the superior models with comfortable seats. He drives around with the window open, his elbow on the sill, his hand lightly resting on the steering wheel. In Jim's younger days (when he was not yet possessed with this sense of himself as the actual manifestation of the company), he would often clamp a stubby between his thick, tanned thighs and take a swig from time to time as he drove, not because he was thirsty but as an act of defiance. This was in the days when he ran copra and cattle on Lingalinga Plantation: that sporadically fertile plain behind Cape Hereford where the rocks have worn through the thin soil and the palms grow crooked. There were fat fish in the sea and it was pleasant enough on a sunny, windy day but Jim never saw that as he drove around in his beat-up old truck, bumping over the rocks and frightening the cattle as an act of defiance.

In those days, those who laboured for Jim called him longlong – mad – and laughed at him because he was young. But they did what needed to be done and more or less what he told them to do, because he was the master. In those days Jim was even amusing in a bombastic way; in Chan's little bar beside the old airstrip he could be good company. For a while, at any rate, because after a few drinks he would get maudlin and start looking for a fight. Odd for one so young. Chan knew how to deal with him, and would get him to bed in one of the little rooms above. Those days! In those days Chan was fond of Jim, treating him like a little lost brother, making sure he had enough to eat, getting him out of trouble. Until the trouble was something even the practical Chan could not deal with. Then Jim was on his own for a while. Until he picked up Margaret, that is. Margaret. In God's name, how did she get into the picture? Later, but assuredly she is part of the picture.

At night Sammy, the driver, is not required. At night, Jim drives himself.

The gun – a pistol of some sort – is in the glove compartment.

At night Jim's three special security men, silent also, sit in the back. They have been especially chosen by Jim because they are big and menacing to look at. Polished as an ebony carving, beautiful to look at, they are nonetheless stupid: the type who have been trained to act when shouted at. Tudak, in the middle, is on his way to becoming a pathological killer.

The headlights of Jim's Landrover pick out the ferny stems of the palms but cannot, for all their strength, penetrate the plantation. They pick out the men and women of the night, the night workers, the security men, the shift workers of the sleepless mill, that necessary mass, the labour.

But across the silent dead centre of the night the uneasy, discordant hum of Jim's vehicle does penetrate the dream of the unconscious sleeper. And standing on my veranda, I have seen that odd-looking bubble of light moving, miles away, across the flat black table top of the palms. As singular as the plume of dust from Madiak's motorcycle in the dry days. But whereas the dust lingers, hangs and gradually becomes part of the plantation again, merely a shifting of its resources, the bubble of light dies, just like that. As does the uneasy, discordant humming. A menacing silence remains, fretting the sleeper for a while until the night roars back and takes him.

No, do not think of Margaret up there alone in the house. Do not think that this matters to her in the way that you might think it does. She is by no means a woman abandoned by her man. It is nothing like that. The two are, in a way, together in the night, this night, Tarlie's night.

Jim's Landrover comes up the hill, passing Tarlie on his way down.

Jim's Landrover enters the tank of light that is the car park. The strong rubber tyres press the sharp, crushed rocks that therefore become a little more part of the earth beneath. The Landrover is still. Jim gets out. He slams the door into the night, as a very positive and habitual act of defiance. You might think he is doing it for Margaret up there above, but definitely he is not. His defiance was there before Margaret entered the scene. You could almost say he took up with her as another act of defiance against the others, whoever they may have been.

Margaret hears the noise and she knows what it is. She knows what he is doing. But that is all. She knows it as one hears a leaf fall or as one hears the python swallowing the helpless rat. It is a process. That is all. Margaret cannot interfere.

◻◻◻◻◻

Jim enters the club. Through the back door that brings the members in past the store in which, until a few minutes ago, Tarlie sat. Past the bar behind which Nalin waits. The same door through which Margaret and Joseph and Andrew left on that Saturday night. We know all this and the club is not much different from that other night when Jim sat with Andrew on the evening of the murder of Nalin's daughter. Nalin, perhaps fortunately, is ignorant of this temporal relationship and does not think back. He is happy to have a customer. Jim, however, is not happy: he is displeased with something, brusquely asking for My Usual. Nalin is ignorant of this also, staring dumbly at Jim for enlightenment. Jim, waiting, as if the defiant act of waiting would actually produce the drink, finally notices that this is another kanaka behind the bar, who is – and even Jim can see this – not Joseph. Even starved almost to death, Joseph would never shrink to the hollow, lost-looking object confronting Jim just then, the mouth and eyes hanging open for want of anything better to do.

Nalin is, at first, an affront to Jim. What is Jim if there is only Nalin left to serve him?

"Oo're you?"

"Nalin, Sir?" He appears to doubt the fact.

"An' where's the other one?"

"Gone, Sir?"

"'E must 'ave, fuck 'im."

"Yes, Sir."

"Give me the bottle." Jim points to a whisky bottle and upon receiving it pours a large shot. He waits, deliberately angry, enforcing his presence – and one wonders why, for God's sake, he needs to impress Nalin. Indeed the python and the rat. But why?

Nalin, like the boy on the bike, wants to bolt but he is caught.

Eventually, Jim releases him: "Ice, you stupid ka. . . bugger."

[][][][][]

Outside, Jim's men have calculated his absence and evacuated the Landrover for a smoke. They have left the illuminated car park – their heavy boots crunching the crushed-rock – for the darker comfort of the road where they smoke, red dots glowing in the dark, regaining their insecure humanity a little.

Tarlie is walking across the golf course. He takes his time, enjoying the stretching of his legs. His feet on the grass. He knows what he's searching for and the chances are he'll get it.

One small thing leads to another: the leaf will fall; the python will swallow the rat. But who is the python? Who the rat?

Jim has yet to suffer the verdict of Nemesis but he is moving towards it in his search for the man who seems to confront him at every turn these days. Whatsisname? Annu. The name came like that, from nowhere. But that was it alright: Annu, damn him. The damned bugger everyone was talking about. Other things too: they must have been started by Annu. Wrecking Chan's store that time before, that had Annu's stamp all over it. How else could it have happened? These fucking kanakas can't do anything without some sort of leadership. Those things before too, no doubt about it: the riot in the cinema, years ago when we showed 'em Zulu for Christmas; the compound fights in the early days, when things got out of hand for no apparent reason; the strikes over the years that were never about pay when you got down to it. There had to be some sort of leader an' prob'ly in the pay of the Russians who'd 'ave trained 'im to overthrow the system. An' it was this fellow Annu. 'ad to be and I got to get him. It's my duty. Duty to everyone. Ol' Jim to the rescue.

"Annu, Annu, Annu; fuck him." Jim mutters in the dark.

And in his love of himself, Jim almost loved – well, felt affection for – this Annu. Having him to deal with, Jim enlarged himself, solidified himself and made himself fit for purpose. A clear target. Get Annu and he'd got everything.

Deliver us from evil, Petrus would say.

[][][][][]

Jim and Nalin then, no less than Jim and Tarlie.

Jim as Man of Action. We know that. He must make his presence felt and dominate every situation, in order to prove his existence to himself.

Nalin, on the other hand, like Alloy's father, is inclined to slink into the shadows or beneath the house where he can scratch himself in peace. Nalin can even dematerialise himself, becoming perhaps that bottle there on the shelf, the cockroach scuttling behind it or the billiard cue there in the corner. He's almost done it when Jim catches him, pulls him back for his purpose, terrifies him back into his humanity, for all as if he is Nalin's saviour.

"Gimme the ice you bugger. Oo are you, anyway?"

"Nalin, Sir?" With a cringing desire to ensure that Jim is satisfied with the fact. The rat to Jim's oily python?

"Where d'you come from? Oo put you 'ere?"

"Master Clarence, Sir?" Will it do, oh Lord of the earth and skies, that I, Nalin, am merely a boy of Master Clarence?

Jim laughs because he is indeed happy to know that Nalin is one of Clarence's boys. They tend to be reliable. Within the bounds of a kanaka's stupidity, that is.

Jim smiles at Nalin.

Nalin's mouth makes the movements that it learnt once.

The process moves on. Jim settles: he has his rat. He settles himself onto the bar-stool to enjoy the whisky. It will be followed by a smaller shot, thrown back fast. It is pleasant to know that having drained the first glass, there is more to come. That is what he thinks. Jim's needs are paramount to him and like the unformed baby that he is, who has his responses to the world of which he is the centre, they are instinctive.

But Jim is not a baby. This is the problem. He is a grown man without a soul. Instinct and intelligence are all there is and therefore tonight, on this night in particular, Jim is a manifestation of power in a moral void, plus a wild bad temper that he uses when he needs it. This bad temper of Jim's, incidentally, is not a lack of control but rather the instinctive use of a tool he has, like Tudak, at his disposal. Jim is In Charge. Jim is The Boss. And Jim wants to get Annu.

As he sits savouring his whisky, the idea comes to Jim that Nalin is another tool he can use as part of the process of getting Annu. Annu! Joseph, fuck him, walked out on me, taking that other fucker, Andrew, with him. And who was that waiting for them at the door? That kanaka of Clarence's: skinny guy with all that hair and a frown on his black face, fuck you, like thunder. What you got to frown about? Want a fight do you? You fucking fucker. Seen you around a lot, come to think of it. Aren't you the one who brings the new tyres every three months for the Landrover? Helps the driver fit them, the two of you chatting together as if my driver, Jesus fucking Christ, is human (and despite himself, Jim laughs at this with a tiny, almost imperceptible jogging of his upper body). Aren't you the one who brought those fluorescent tubes to the house one Saturday morning and fitted them, chatting all the while to my wife as if she . . ? Jim saw a picture of Margaret as an animated thing, separate from him, and then dismissed the idea. Aren't you the one, come to fucking think of it, who comes to my office every month to service the air-con? Jesus wept, you are! The insolent bugger who actually came in the first time without knocking and who done the job as if I, me, Jim, was not there. I told Clarence to sack you, didn't I? So how come you're still around, smarmy cunt?

This last fact struck Jim as the peak of unforgivable audacity. The fucker! And something like an emotional reaction appeared on Jim's face: he held the whisky in his mouth and seemed to chew it slightly. No need to be angry because he knew what he must do. No audience – he had forgotten Nalin for the minute – no audience in front of whom to enact his anger, anyway.

And, come to think of it, so that it was almost funny because the fucker really was asking for it now, was he not the same arsehole who'd messed up Andrew? Actually, even more audacious; Jim cocked his head ever so slightly to express his fundamental amazement at a state of affairs where kanaka influenced white man. Even more amazing, come to think of it, that a white man allowed himself to be influenced. Don't make sense . . . to a Jim.

It was coming to Annu. If these things were happening then this Annu had got his hands on the place and would have to be stopped. Jim had no doubt, savouring his whisky, that Annu would have to be got rid of and the whole deck swept clean of all these useless tools. Not only useless, but dangerous. Their very existence a threat to him and to everything. How had he allowed such a thing to go on under his nose for so long? Phew! Good thing he had seen it, and no time like the present. Was he not a man of action? When things needed to be done, was he not the one to do them? Hadn't he told Margaret that very morning, and hadn't she agreed with him? Hadn't she? She must have done. He constructed the memory of her agreeing with him. There, and he moved on, justified. "No one else has the guts I've got. I'll 'ave to git it done. That's me: Man of Action." He said it aloud for anyone – as it happened, only Nalin – to hear.

The process moves on. Jim gulped the whisky and poured another, capping the bottle and handing it back to Nalin, who, wonder of wonders, put it back on the shelf. This act in itself drew him to Jim's attention. Could be useful, this kanaka; certainly doesn't have the arrogance of that bugger Joseph – Jim saw the stately Joseph, his handsome face the usual mask of efficient indifference that Jim hated, and he hated Annu all the more for Joseph's defection.

Some real bodily reaction now that might well be called emotion – or perhaps it was the whisky – showed on Jim's face as his blood heated up. A shiny patina of sweat appeared on his oddly muscular, yet apparently over-fleshy, face.

Joseph, Andrew, the fellow with the frown, and Annu. There was a connection, obviously. This new bar-boy as well, whatsyername, Nalin, "Nalin," said Jim, the friendly man of goodwill. "So where's Joseph, Nalin? He been here tonight?" Jim relaxed, having decided what to do: "'e been 'ere tonight? Maybe 'e came to git 'is things?"

Nalin melts. He is Jim's man. He is Jim's dog and wants to lie on his back as an act of submission, showing his genitals. What can he give him? What can he bring his master? Nalin wanted to give him something badly: "Yesa," he says.

"Oo? Joseph?"

"Nosa."

This apparent inconsistency did not surprise Jim. It was the tortuous way you had conversations with kanakas: "Oo then?"

"Pren bilong em."

Nalin was easier in Pidgin but Jim ignored the language he could speak, as he said to Margaret, like a native: "What's yer name, again?"

"Nalin Sir."

"So oo is this 'Pren', Nalin?" Jim is a sweetie.

"Tarlie Sir. Em i gut pren bilong em."

Jim did not know the name of Tarlie but he immediately assumed Tarlie was one of the Gang of Russian-Inspired Saboteurs – Commies – who would as likely lead him to Annu as would Joseph. Or anyone else for that matter. He stood up: "So oo's this Tarlie?"

What could Nalin say about Tarlie? He could not say that Tarlie was the man who was going to buy his daughter. Jim wouldn't be interested in that. Neither, Nalin assumed, would Jim be interested in what had happened. His instinct told him to stay clear of that topic, for all sorts of reasons. But there was one obvious thing you could say about Tarlie: "Em i man husat i gat wanpela lek skruilus. Em i wokabaut ol kranki." There was a lot you could say, after all, and Nalin said it all, so strong was his desire to serve his new master.

Jim shifted a little on his legs and his heartbeat increased minutely: "'As 'e? An' what else? When did you see this Tarlie last?"

Nalin was pure eagerness, his tail wagging for all it was worth: "Ah Masta, yu lukim em olsem. Em i longlong man husat laik paitim yu long taim bipo. Long taim bai ol boi bilong em i laik stilim ol samting long stua bilong masta Tan."

"Annu! You mean Annu. That's 'is name. Annu. Well, 'ere's a turn up for the books."

"Yesa!" Nalin will give him anything he wants. He will give him Annu, if he wants.

"OK," Jim said calmly, truly the python, "so Annu's been 'ere. When was that?"

"Em i klostu long taim long yu kamkamup."

"Just now, eh? An' where did 'e go?"

"Ah, masta, mi tok stret, em i go long luklukim pren bilong em, Josep."

Jim ignored the familiarity. He did not want to lose this rat: "Where is Joseph, then, Nalin?"

"Em i stap long haus bilong Alloy."

Alloy? Who was he? Another kanaka: "Where's that?"

"Long junya manisman kompaun. Olgeta man em i savi."

"Thank you, Nalin, keep the change." Jim handed him more money than was needed to pay for the drinks, and left.

Nalin blinked hard. It was a lot of money, it seemed, for a small bit of information. That's how treachery works.

[][][][][]

No anger or acting now. Jim carried forward the process, through the night, in a state of deadly earnestness. In the end, the python does not mess around.

He climbed into his empty Landrover, started the engine – Margaret heard it – and turned into the road where he put on the side lights, switched off the engine and cruised down the hill. He braked at the foot of the hill so that his panting men could clamber quickly in, falling over one another as he started the engine again, moving slowly and quietly along the flat.

The side lights made no impression on the night but they lit the road sufficiently for Jim to see where he was going.

[][][][][]

Something looms up in the night; hard, dense and implacable. We feed and serve it but it is wonderfully indifferent in its cruelty. Spasmodically it will crush a man, tear away a limb or scald off skin. But with such impartiality that we accept it as beyond appeal. But some men worship it.

Jim then, in the night. A small thing indeed in the universe. Yet he draws together all the action as he trails his idea of Annu, the blissfully ignorant Tarlie doggedly trailing his own idea. Both men trailing the same idea. And that idea, maybe, no more than the electrical thingummyjigs in a man's brain, his senses, his over-evolved ganglia, over-stimulated by the man-made, infuriating mill.

Jim then, ploughing on with a singularity of purpose, his men behind him. The night itself, providing cover perhaps, but all the same it is too dark and too thick with heat. You trips over things and feels clumsy. Can't think straight, for God's sake. Maddening, confusing and incomprehensible it is, but we follow Jim. What else to do? We follow orders. That's what we do.

Jim leading his men? No, he is as much driven as they are.

[][][][][]

Alloy's house is one of a dozen or so, set out beneath the cliff on top of which Henry lives. Cheap, fibreboard affairs, three rooms and a little veranda. Like the labourers' houses, they perch on short steel tubes off the wet ground, just above the flood waters. They are the type mining companies put up by the hundreds, cheap enough to abandon when the mine goes bust.

The cliff face is a tangle of vegetation. When the parrots fly in the sunny morning, they ignore the little houses down there. Sometimes, boys catapult stones at the parrots. Sometimes, very rarely, a parrot falls to the ground with a lifeless thud of colourful feathers onto the thick paspalum grass.

The river runs at the foot of the cliff. The water is polluted by the waste from the mill and by the run-off from the workshop. Rancid in the dry season. Once, memorably, it caught fire. The women and children, at home, were surprised to see flames coming from the water, flowing out to sea; but they were not afraid. They laughed when they told the men later: So you see, the white men can set fire to the water. You'd better be careful with all your talk of fighting them.

The polluted water nourishes the ground that is never completely dry, even after weeks without rain. A cancerous growth of vegetation pushes out, demanding its place in the light. But the trees are poor things, their roots discouraged by the high water table. Fruit trees grow well here – for a year or two. Then they keel over, slowly but without hesitation, as if pre-determined to do so there in front of our eyes. They stop, as if equally pre-determined, remaining at some impossible angle for years, producing prodigious amounts of leaves but no fruit. Henry trees if you like. At last the leaves fall off and they die.

Even during the dry season, the houses sit as if in a green pool of stagnant water. In the wet, the water is opaque in its movement, the ground mud where it's not inundated, the motorbikes spluttering and splattering through.

Either way, wet or dry, the darkness here is more tangible. It is thicker, moister and more grasping in its terrors than up on the hill, on the golf course or outside Chan's store. The small lights of the houses penetrate it not at all, the rank vegetation is a cover for all sorts of nocturnal activity, the vapours from the river are solid enough to chew and gag upon.

So it seemed, at any rate, in my recollection of that moonless night. But indeed, the memory plays tricks.

⬜⬜⬜⬜⬜

As Jim's vehicle came around the golf course Tarlie had just passed the back of Chan's store. He passed the security fence topped with barbed wire, and he passed under the security lights. There would be no security for him but he approached Alloy's house, nonetheless, in a state of happy expectation, expecting to meet his friends and Joseph. The place held no terrors for Tarlie that night: the air smelt sweet to him, the thick paspalum grass beneath his feet, comforting and cool, the little houses, wrapped in the night, cosy and friendly.

Joseph was most on Tarlie's mind. Joseph's proud face and noble body. Joseph's laugh, his wide mouth and his big teeth when he was laughing, when he was telling stories about the stupid white men in the club, whom he nonetheless loved. Preoccupied, therefore, Tarlie did not hear Jim's vehicle come to a stop outside Chan's store.

Jim got out. His men followed, ignorant, as yet, of their mission. Jim liked to keep things to himself until the last minute.

The little gang unwittingly followed in Tarlie's footsteps, but on the edge of the dark, Jim stopped, the pack gathering around for orders. Rabis and Pen, and Tudak; Tudak not much different from the others at this point, a handsome man but repulsive, not quite human.

"You know this Annu fellow?" said Jim, "the mad bugger with the limp. You know 'im. The trouble-maker."

They knew him; and if Jim called him Annu then Annu he was, and would be forevermore.

"'E's in there." Jim cocked his head in the direction of the houses.

They looked into the dark as if expecting to see Tarlie waiting for them.

"'E's one of them communists I told you about."

He had: they knew all about Commies. Of all the scum of the earth these Commies were the worst. They had to be rooted out, all of them. Commies were like the crabs in your pubic hairs, you had to pick them off one by one and crunch them between your teeth. Like a crab in your pubes, a commie could not be allowed to survive.

The deed was as good as done, Tudak now straining at the leash, Rabis and Pen eager to go in. Tooth, Talon and Claw.

"Wait!" Jim commanded, the 't' barely audible.

"You know the 'ouse of the workshop kuskus? The one Master Andrew fucks?"

Rabis and Pen knew every house in the compound. It was their job. They nodded. They felt important. They were in the know. They were doing important deeds. No messing around. You know the type.

"'E's goin' there. You got to git there first an' wait for 'im. You got to move fast cos 'e's on 'is way. But 'e's slow cos of 'is crook leg. Go roun' by the river an' you'll git there first. When you finished, go 'ome."

Jim walked back to the car, and drove back to Margaret.

□□□□□

Dark.

The furious darkness of moonless night. A fruitless waiting for shifting clouds to reveal . . . nothing. What light exists is manmade, artificial, slight and yellow. Stained is the night by the involvement of men.

An unflattering illumination of the sweating, startled faces of men. Captured in agony or in earnest animation, surprised as a photographic memory, in grim satisfaction, startled joy or hopeless loss.

The shifting shadows of distorted shapes thrown up as the monster of our childish dreams or, as often, more than we know, diminished to nothing.

And it is oppressively hot and restless in this humid, tropical night, where liquids move and shift themselves, thick and slow. Water oily, blood like treacle, upon the water floats a darker stain that catches no light.

Stained.

Stained is the water in which floats that thing we prefer not to know. Let it float downstream, forgotten. But we cannot forget. It sits like a piece of under-cooked, fatty pork in our stomach. There, for all our drunken laughter.

Restless.

Restless is the night of no sleep. Rapid action, thoughtless, then sudden dead inanimation, bodies flopped as rag dolls in the corner. Truly the Hollow Men. Expressions of painted stupidity, pained mirth and nightmare horror. Manic grins, simpering smiles and dead lips.

Wake up! Wake up!

Never again.

Exhausted in the infuriating dark of a moonless night.

Tarlie is dead.

Long live . . . Annu?

12
The Limitless Bright Country Beyond

Consciousness is acknowledged by a pinprick of light.

Light moves, throbs and dances with a life force.

Yet, remains stationary; remains distant.

Safely distant, yet attainable at will, waiting for me to desire it.

Loving is that light, but not demanding.

Patient is that light, and, for this eternal moment, indifferent to me in its universal love.

Loveable is that light, also.

But, it is out There.

[][][][][]

Here, inside, where I am, the life force is an enveloping warmth.

All around me but separate from me at the same time.

Comforting, infinitely giving.

But, like the sun, it is indifferent to me in terms of the in Here and the out There.

I am contained within myself; it is enough in itself yet the world waits for me.

The world will welcome me like it welcomes the dawn; its warm earth will respond to my naked feet.

But, I am not required to enter the world.

The decision is mine.

[][][][][]

The warm and loving arms of God envelop me.

I sit on His lap, as it were, as if once upon that cold and frosty morning, He warms my socks by the fire and then pulls them onto my feet.

He will give me my shoes upon request.

My feet in my shoes and socks then, are me in my life.

My warm feet on the cold ground, outside, will remind me of Him, of His lap from which I have wilfully slipped.

My feet, warm in the shoes He gave me, remind me of His warm arms to which I will return.

I may take off my shoes and make contact with the earth beneath my feet, and He will smile for my confidence, and foolishness.

He waits for me.

I know this.

So I do not join in the world at first.

I watch it, thinking of Him.

Later, when I am ready, and with the memory of Him, I will join in.

[][][][][]

The light now is all. I am the light; a part of it. The blue sky is infinite and not separate from the light but a part of it. So I am a part of the sky, which drenches me to my naked feet standing firm on the ground.

On this warm morning, a path leads up the hillside, winding around small rocks. It leads to the largest rock of them all, up There.

From where I walked, from that perspective, that rock on the top of the hill is drenched also by the blue sky in which the larks sing higher and higher.

Now that I have found the right path and have laboriously walked it, my hand touches the warm, lichen-covered rock. I rest my life upon it. As I do this, I see the view.

The view is not astonishing or breathtaking or, as they said in those days, mind-blowing. It is not any of these superlative things because it is known and expected. It is wonderful, all the same, because it is no less than expected. There is no anti-climax to this journey's end.

A broad valley, yellow and brown with touches of purple in the solid, clear light. Beyond, low hills like the one upon which I stand, rock strewn because the soil is thin up here, on top of the world.

Below, the valley is greener as the soil is deeper towards the river, meandering and sluggish, lazily wandering through swamps and reed beds. Later, it will catch the light, and purple butterflies will hover above it.

[][][][][]

It is there. She knows. And to know it is enough. To reach it is another matter.

[][][][][]

She reminds me of a story from Dostoyevsky.[3] The old woman has been a wicked, selfish old creature all her life. She dies and is condemned to Hell. But her angel pleads with God for the old woman. God tells the angel that if she can recall one good thing the old lady did in her life then she will be saved. The angel reminds God of the time when the old lady was weeding her garden. A starving beggar passes by and the old woman, moved as she has not been for years, pulls up a little onion and gives it to the beggar (I was once that beggar, the angel reminds God). OK, says God, take that onion and pull the old lady out of hell with it. The angel obeys God. She flies over hell and sees the old lady struggling with all the other lost souls. Catch hold of the onion, calls the angel, and I'll pull you out. For an instant the old woman is filled with a warm

---

[3] The Brothers Karamazov

gratitude that gives her an idea of God's boundless love. But, she cries, is the onion strong enough? Of course, says the angel. Is it not an act of pure love? So the old woman catches the onion and is drawn out of hell by the angel. Up she goes, on her way to heaven. She is saved! But just as she is leaving hell, one of the other souls holds on to the old woman's foot. Take me with you, it cries, I want to see God as well. The old woman looks down and sees the other soul hanging on to her. No, she says, the onion is not strong enough for two. She tries to kick the soul away. All this time they are flying up to heaven but the old woman becomes more and more concerned about the other soul which she is sure is impeding her journey. She kicks and kicks at the soul that, nonetheless, holds on for all it is worth. Finally the old woman forgets about God's boundless love and heaven altogether. She is intent, only, on getting rid of the damned soul hanging on to her foot. She gives one last great kick and dislodges the soul. With her heart full of triumph, she looks up towards her angel grinning, only to discover that the onion has broken, the angel a tiny thing way up there, irredeemable and more so by the second. The old woman doesn't know it but the onion broke at the very moment her heart filled with triumph.

When the old lady gets back to hell she looks for the other lost soul to blame. On finding it she vents her anger. Look what you did; you pulled me back to hell. Oh no, says the other lost soul – having had a few thousand years to get wise – if you had just concentrated on getting me to heaven, we'd both be there by now. The old woman didn't get it at first and went off muttering.

God and the beggar-angel are looking down into hell, sadly. Sorry, my little angel, she wasn't ready for heaven, says God. She'd only have gone around telling everyone how she'd got it over that other soul. She doesn't get it and until she does we can't have her up here. The angel shed a tear, thinking how grateful she'd been for that onion. Don't worry, says God, she'll get it one day: you could pull out all the lost souls with a single onion, if they sincerely want to be pulled out of their hell.

Are you beginning to get the picture?

Is this Margaret?

Our Angel?

[][][][][]

"Come to me Jojo, my sweet little darlin'. Come to Mama."

He walked steadily, the naked man-boy, for all that he was as drunk as he could be without actually falling down.

The girls would feed him the drinks, one small shot at a time, which he obediently swallowed as they undressed him. It amused them but it made no difference to his willingness to please. He would have done whatever they asked.

"Don't be shy mi dear. Ain't 'e beautiful! Look at 'im, not a mark on 'im."

He was indeed beautiful. White, he would have been like an alabaster effigy, had it not been for the hot, flickering lights that spun him gold as honey. Edible nectar he was to the women in the upstairs room. Smooth skinned, his thick hair silver or, where it caught the light, a rainbow of colours. But his pale blue eyes so distant, they might have been dead.

What were his thoughts? Theirs so obviously lustful. No one cared.

No one cared? No, because caring about Jojo was not the issue. The issue was Jojo's physical beauty. That and his willingness to be. To be played with, like a doll. The only sounds he made were low-toned, breathy mutterings of, of delight, I suppose. Certainly he offered no resistance.

Jojo's physical beauty was all there was, or rather all there seemed to be, to him, as far as the girls were concerned. No one thought about his thoughts because he had none, or rather, seemed to have none. Jojo was a mute and had, or, again, seemed to have, no desire to communicate ideas other than the instinctive. He might also have been deaf but then again, no one, there in that upstairs room, above the noise below, of the outside world, observed his responses in a scientific way. He responded to their playfulness and that was enough. They were not scientists, they were girls, good girls, Adele's girls. They gave you a good time and – Adele had taught them – they did not ask questions or think about their customers. They gave you a good time, they made you feel like a man, they stopped you feeling lonely, they stopped each other feeling lonely. They gave Jojo a good time and he generously gave them a good time in return. He was the giving type, like they were. His square, compact, clean body was a feast to their hungry eyes.

Thoughts are not good things to have in this life. Avoid them, like the plague, and focus on physical things. Thoughts are luxuries.

Later – years later, as she watched Margaret grow –Adele herself did have thoughts about Jojo. She wondered, a little, what he was, what he had been. She thought too much sometimes, until it hurt her. Then she stopped. But even back in those far-off days, being older – old enough, at any rate biologically, to have been Jojo's mother – she might, come to think of it, have been called a scientist. She was, as one is bound to say of those types of women, and one does, an expert on human nature. She had seen, over the years, the worst and the best of us. She started her trade young, behind the trenches of the First World War. She knew it all, by the end of that.

"Come to me Jojo, my puppy."

He came; on sturdy naked legs, short, broad feet upon the worn boards, a childish grin on his open face that showed his perfect teeth. He came to Adele like the baby he was.

"You git comfy on Adele's lap. There's plenty of room for you."

There was too. Her lap was as broad as her experience. She knew every trick in the book, and she'd done it. She knew how to defend herself and how to deal with the Animals, as they called the difficult and violent ones. She could tell who was going to be trouble before it started. She steered them away from the younger girls. And as often, straight down the staircase and out the back door. "An' you can go back where you came from, you sod. Go to 'ell." She believed it too and it saddened her because most of them were big babies, lonely. They just wanted a bit of affection and reassurance. They were, after all, mostly no trouble: pathetic at worst, most of them, and jolly mates at best, with money to splash around until they spent it all and had to get back to their ships. All sizes and shapes she'd seen, from the little wizened chinks to the big, black nigs. She couldn't understand what most of them said but they were all the same: just men. Sad, if you thought about it too much. Best not to.

"I'll give you whatever you want darlin'."

She did. With her own big, simple, generous heart she gave all she had. As she had given it to all those blubbing English boys years ago, making them feel like men before they died their pointless deaths on those bloody Flanders Fields. She would watch each one go, like a mother, with an aching heart. Would it never stop aching? Only when she was giving did it stop.

He was beautiful then. His entire Jojo-ness was as beautiful as Tarlie's Tarlie-ness would be beautiful to Andrew later, as Joseph's Joseph-ness was to Alloy, as Annu's Annu-ness – and oh God, forgive us – was and is to us all.

Beautiful, Jojo was to Adele. Radiantly beautiful as are only those who are truly loved and worthy of love. Few wear the halo and few can see it. Jojo: muscular and compact, clean and perfect, beautiful. As beautiful in his body as in his innocent brain. He was as innocent and as good as a human could be. Incorruptible. You might say born to please but he was innocent even of that innocent vanity.

Was Jojo an angel? Perhaps, but by the time Margaret was born he had disappeared, to be, no doubt, angelic elsewhere. Adele called their child Margaret after the English princess, Margaret Rose, born about the same time. Rosy the little girl was called for a time but the quiet and thoughtful child was, unquestionably, a Margaret.

Margaret is beginning.

[] [] [] [] []

Here she is, it seems.

But how can we know her? She inherited herself, from her parents. That was the raw material, upon which the world worked until, until her soul evolved to that critical point where she begins to be, to be Margaret? At any rate to that point where she becomes aware of herself and the world in which she lives. Will she fear the world, crouching and hiding from it within herself? Or will she meet it with joy, arms wide open in the sunshine? That depends on many things, but for a start, her mother expresses herself to the child as a secure, non-negotiable yet indifferent, loving reality. This cannot be bad.

Genes, genetic inheritance, then, must have something to do with it. On the surface, at any rate. Adele was as warmly dark as Jojo was warmly fair. Winter fireside mixed with summer sunshine, one might sentimentally say. Adele was not called the gypsy for nothing but Margaret inherited her father's colouring. From her mother came the large loosely built frame although for all her immobility at times, Margaret never did become as fat. Her easy, swinging walk arose from the fact that she rarely wore shoes until she was twelve years old. Until that time her feet were most used to the city pavements.

Then, her life changed. Adele, fifty, retired, as she had always planned, to a small outback town. With thirty years of savings, she was able to buy a guest house with a wide veranda overlooking the wide main street, empty and sun-bleached for most of the day. The ferocious midday heat would stretch the country around to breaking point: the other side of the street an exhausting journey, the surrounding hills impossible light-years away. But with the first stars the landscape contracted, shrinking to the humane by morning. That was the time Margaret loved best, before the dawn so that she could watch the stars fade and the sun rise, when, she could see the creation of light.

Shoes had been bought for the train journey. Also a modest, easy-fitting, cream-coloured frock with a tight waist and a matching hat, gloves too, in those days. The outfit made the child, tall for her age, look like a demure sixteen-year-old, the raised heels of her shoes causing her hips to swing in a way that turned heads at the big, smoky railway station on the sunny day of their departure. Adele had an instinct for dressing girls to their advantage.

The train journey described a new world to Margaret as the city dissolved into the limitless bright country beyond. Buildings might fly past the window but the transition from the secure domesticity of the coastal settlement to the less hospitable and parched landscape of the interior was slow and subtle, suggesting to the child the creation of a new world of which she was to be a part.

In the city, the world of which Margaret was tangibly a part was her mother, with whom she slept, whose bulk was always between her and the out There. It was the building, or rather the jumbled conglomeration of badly lit rooms, in which they lived and sometimes, it appeared to Margaret in retrospect, merely acted out their lives. It was the noisy street outside, and the buildings that hemmed them in all around. It was the people, usually friendly and willing to make contact, if approached, the people who made up the more fluid part of the world in the house, in the street, in the school. This was the world, or at any rate the setting, for Margaret's bodily, physical existence, the part of her existence that washed and dressed and fed her and which, from time to time, was required to supply a lap upon which to sit and arms within which to lie. This was the world that Margaret, the child, accepted as what being alive was about. Jesus, Queen Elizabeth I and the Prime Minister lived similar lives. The places for dreams, for that something else that Margaret, the child, assumed was God (the Father), were those infinite spaces of light that could be looked at and thought about but not physically inhabited: the sea and the sky.

Yet here, from the train window, before her eyes, there was spread out a new world of light that invited her to become part of it. To plant her feet upon it.

As a city child, she might have been disconcerted by the sight of so much possible space, of an apparent lack of definition to its physical boundaries, of the very solid quality of its light that nonetheless defied definition, all the more so as the mind concentrated on it. But Margaret was not disconcerted by its unfamiliarity. She was not, either, as she might contrarily have been, excited by the realistic offer of adventure. What Margaret experienced was a revelation. The revealing to her by, by the train, at any rate as the instrument, of the truth that she recognised as reality. Never seen before by her and yet entirely recognisable. She felt that she was part of the space, the limitless space, and also, the light that filled it. She no longer felt that she inhabited her body as a body moving through the world but rather, she recognised as a fact irrefutable, that she was an integrated part of the light that was itself the space. Integrated as a dye is integrated into a body of water.

Margaret's feelings were not egotistical because Margaret did not, does not, feel she is different from anyone else. She is merely Margaret in Margaret's world as you are you in yours. Maybe the difference is that Margaret recognised the fact.

[][][][][]

I see two women in my mind's eye.

It is simple: I watch them walk down the wide street that is empty, quiet in the velvet dawn. They walk towards the hills beyond, which seem grander than they are in the first light.

The scene has a cartoon simplicity but it is real enough. The sky is less dark by the second, all but the brightest stars extinguished. The rising sun is hidden behind the hills, the tops of which are touched with silver.

The larger bulk of the older woman moves to the side, leaving the other in possession of the centre of the street. Thus the distance between the two is specific but they are nonetheless close enough for conversation, if required. They remain intimate, it seems, but from mutual desire, not from mutual need. They are not hanging on to one another, these two.

The girl appears to appreciate her freedom as her mother moves away. Her arms swing, her body sways, as if to a melody, she looks up into the sky, stretching her young body as she does so.

Her mother stops. She says something. The girl moves on, doing her own bidding or her mother's, I cannot tell. She kicks off her shoes and immediately the rhythm of her movements change, her body seeming a little heavier as her feet claim the dusty street that is, after all, only beaten earth. Her strides lengthen as she takes possession of the morning, leaving her mother behind.

She moves towards the hills.

Her mother waits awhile, watching her daughter walk into the day. She picks up the shoes and then turns towards a large, plain, old-fashioned house, her house, which faces the street. A little wearily, she lifts her bulk up the wooden steps and disappears into the shadows of the veranda. I imagine that once inside the house, she wipes the dust off the nearly new, cream-coloured shoes, with their slightly raised heels and little bows in front. She places them on the windowsill of her bedroom that overlooks the street with a fine view of the hills. The shoes sit there for years until Margaret herself removes them when she returns to clear out the house.

[][][][][]

She is thirteen, or a little more, and she spends the next three years at school in the town. She helps her mother in the little guest house, she walks the surrounding country in the mornings, in the rain and sometimes, even, under the hot sun, she makes friends or, at any rate, local people get to know her, about her. They appropriate her. People of her own age come to the house, sitting on the deep, lazy veranda, overlooking the wide, empty street. They chatter amongst themselves for a while, falling silent as they fall, one could say, under Margaret's spell.

At seventeen Margaret went back to the city for a year or two, to commercial college, to learn the womanly office skills of typing, filing, of how to reply to business letters and of how to be responsive to the men around whom, undoubtedly, the city revolved. The college was selective, turning out ladylike girls by the dozen. It took Margaret because she was quiet, dressed modestly and had good manners. She arrived at nine sharp each morning, attended to her lessons, had lunch with the other girls in a genteel café nearby that was run along English lines, and left at four, catching the tram to her lodgings before the rush. To the other girls she seemed distant, but liking her nonetheless they assumed she was simple and they could feel superior. Yet, despite Margaret's apparent simplicity, she was solid, very soon gaining a reputation for dependability. It was she who most often put the other girls on their trams or trains or taxis, as delicate flowers require at certain times. Sometimes, Margaret took a girl all the way home, delivering her to an anxious mother who would recall her later when another crisis came.

She lodged with a widow in a declining suburb where the jacaranda trees, lining the streets, made it glorious for a few weeks each year. Otherwise it was dry and dusty with an air of having been abandoned by the city as a failure, its houses, in tight lots, too small for the rich, and too difficult, with their cheap Victorian flourish, for the poor to manage. A region, therefore, of private hotels and lodging houses.

Asked years later what she thought of Moraine – the name given to the place by a released convict who had squatted there a hundred years earlier – Margaret said she remembered the jacaranda trees.

The widow's son, a little older than Margaret, wild to get away, had kissed her under one of the jacaranda trees in the dusk of a Sunday evening. He had asked her to walk with him, anywheres, just so's I get out of this place.

He talked: Margaret listened. Her listening quietened his rage so that he thought he loved her. The kiss was clumsy but tender. Margaret taught him how to do it properly without him realising she was doing it. That little knowledge was good for him; it made him feel like a man.

Margaret passed out of the college with distinction. It was assumed – by whom? – that she would get a job in the city and perhaps become a Mrs Livingston, of sorts. Her mother had once had a fleeting picture of Margaret having a better start in life than herself, marrying and having children, living in a quiet suburb and. . . and what? It was never defined, clearly, in the mind of either woman.

Margaret did not stay in the city; she came home at the age of nineteen.

There was in Margaret an ability to do nothing. But she was not lazy. Despite not seeming likely to be married in the usual idea of that state of affairs, she nonetheless, would have, and did in a way, become a mother. An indifferent, yet dependable mother.

Because she was dependable, efficient at her work and quiet, Margaret was asked to sort out the books of some of the local farmers. She improved the business efficiency quite remarkably in one or two cases. She soon had a good reputation but work was limited by the scarcity of farmers in the area: each year the farms got bigger and the number of farmers smaller. In the nineteenth century the town had been a thriving market centre but increasingly big trucks linked the big farms directly with the big city: there was no need for a market town.

However, because of the hills the town attracted a few retired folk who liked the quiet, and a few tourists, for the same reason. In particular, the place attracted single men at the tail-end of their leave from New Sudan. The men who ran the plantations, the logging camps, the mines and the trading operations. Odd sods, loners and misfits. They would come south every two or three years because they were supposed to get out of New Sudan from time to time for the sake of their health. They had two or three months and time on their hands. They would start off in the city doing all the things that they had promised themselves they would do while they had been stuck up in the north, as likely to include the opera as the bay-side brothels. But by the last few weeks they had run through their money and were aching to get back to where they fitted in. Thus the little outback town in which Margaret and her mother had settled was a sort of staging post for the last lost souls of European empire.

There were four spare bedrooms, and a couple more out the back above the old stables, let on short terms with three good meals thrown in and cups of tea or coffee whenever you felt like it. The house was comfortable and like the two women themselves, unpretentious and a little untidy. An easy place in which to put up your feet, read a book and feel that you were not in anyone's way. It was recognised by its regulars as a home away from . . . at any rate, away from where they had come and to where they would return. For many it was the only place they thought of as home, returning year after year.

There was love in that house. Margaret helped her mother run it.

[][][][][]

The Henrys of the world would not be found in Adele's place but the Clarences and the Jonsons came for a week or two before returning to New Sudan. And knowing how to deal with such things, Adele could arrange women for them if that was required. Not girls but women whom she knew from the old days. Women who knew how to handle the sort of lonely men who frequented the place.

As often as not then, one of the bedrooms was occupied by a lady also on holiday from the city. Nicely but not over dressed, she would sit quietly on the veranda reading or sewing. She might take a stroll down the street in the morning or in the evening. Sometimes she would help with the lighter household chores: clearing the table, dusting, vacuuming, tidying the books and magazines. She was a lady but not the sort who expected to be waited on hand and foot. If a male guest spoke to her she would answer politely at first, encouraging conversation but not demanding it. If things developed, they did and if not, it was pleasant to chat so that the meals became a more social event, Margaret piling the potatoes on your plate. A Clarence might even ask, sending his picture postcard of some city landmark, and is Mrs So and So going to be there? It could be arranged that she was. A few marriages had resulted – you needn't call me Mrs, I'm still a single lady – the happy couple sent off from the house for a few more years in New Sudan before returning to retire in the town.

Married couples didn't stay in Adele's house but Margaret arranged for them to rent one of the holiday homes. She would prepare the house for them and clean it up afterwards. She was the dependable type.

This was Margaret's life before she went up to New Sudan with Jim.

Young men did not stay in Adele's house. They would have been as welcome as anyone had they come but its reputation was limited to the generation of men who had gone to New Sudan straight after the war. The young men of those days were a different breed; there was no communication.

Young Jim was the exception.

He got there because having just arrived in the country from New Sudan he developed a tropical disease, easily treatable but debilitating for a while. He was quite ill and some Clarence or other recommended Adele's house as a place where They Will Look After You.

They did. He needed it because he was alright lying down, but any effort made him nauseous and dizzy, his flesh becoming the yellow he finally established as his own true colour. Even as a young man, it suited him.

Margaret, naturally, was his nurse. She did everything for him. He let her do it, encouraging her when he could quite easily have done it himself. The bed bath became a daily routine to which he looked forward with erotic fervour. All the more because of Margaret's indifference. The efficiency with which this cool, blonde, athletic and apparently bovine – even he recognised that it was not stupidity – girl handled his body made Jim believe she knew nothing about the opposite sex. She was, he seriously believed, a woman in total ignorance of worldly things. Jim believed with the conviction that was one of his most stupid characteristics that this girl will be putty in my hands. Her docility excited him. It made him sort of angry; he wanted to slap her into response. The thought of hurting Margaret excited Jim.

What is rape? There are legal definitions. It is easier to say what is not rape. Helen's friends were not raped, as Margaret made them realise after. It was Bune's gang after all, hardly the marauding barbarians described in the magazine. They took those children into safe custody.

Jim did nothing violent but what he did to Margaret was rape despite the fact that she could easily have resisted him. Margaret knew how to deal with men. She was Adele's daughter, she had grown up in a well-run brothel.

For a start, in his late twenties, Jim was not an unattractive male. Recognisably Jim but attractive to look at in his healthy youth. Born on the plantation and allowed to run wild, he was sturdy and muscular: his shortness, compared with other European boys of his age, accentuating his muscles, exaggerated a little already by a thick layer of subcutaneous fat. His face, Jim's face, less fleshy than it became, was round and sun-tanned, his hair thick and wiry. He could affect a cheeky grin. It seemed friendly and open but on closer inspection the eyes did not match the mouth. Some girls found the air of menace attractive.

Generally Jim got what he wanted from girls who afterwards felt they had asked for it. He was brutal in his ardent youth. Later, as Margaret noted with good humour, he seemed merely to be re-asserting his manhood to himself, on his own. As Dolly actually remarked, you could have read a book and Jim probably would not have minded, even if he'd noticed you doing it. In one sense, Jim was just a masturbator but he needed another body to master; that, to put it crudely, is what got it up.

So the bed bathing etc of Jim by Margaret and what Jim thought was Margaret led the young Jim to determine to have Margaret. It was rape because he assumed that he could manipulate her body into doing what he wanted without her realising what was going on. It was rape because he felt a desire to hurt her. It was rape because he wanted to satisfy himself by doing these things to her. It was rape because he couldn't care a fuck what she thought, the idea itself a further excitement. Jim had often thought about fucking a mentally defective girl and here was his chance.

When she bathed him that afternoon, while the rest of the house was sleeping, Jim believed his fantasy. It was so easy, he was sure she did not know what was going on. She was not surprised by his erection and she seemed unsurprised by anything else which happened. She was indeed putty in his hands.

At any rate, Jim enjoyed it, realising the erotic ideas of weeks with a surge of physical release which proved he was well again. Margaret also, to his amazement, appeared to enjoy it. Afterwards, she lay beside him while he pretended to sleep. She did not slink away, as others had done, bruised, but turned towards him, pushing herself up on her elbow. She looked down into the face she knew was lying.

"You silly boy. You know nothing."

It might have been a put down but it was not. She stroked his forehead and ruffled his hair as a mother might do.

"You want your Mummy."

[][][][][]

They did not do it again because Jim was better and could bathe himself.

He got up and began to act like a reasonably ordinary man, one as able to give love as he is to take it. He acted the part of a young man wooing a young woman. Adele was taken in: Margaret, not for one minute. Nonetheless, she went along with it because it was what Jim wanted and because while she recognised his waywardness she believed, and she always did, that Jim could recognise goodness if only he would look at it.

Jim was an opportunist, living his life from one event to another, and making of each something to his advantage. Therefore, he needed a wife in the way all men – he supposed – needed a wife: not as something, someone, upon whom to depend and who could depend upon him but as something to enhance his own sense of himself. Jim as Mr McDonald, husband and father.

Thus, on his last night, Jim put on the best act of all. Not entirely an act, either, because a little bit of him responded to Margaret's indifferent love; he was warmed by it. He sat beside Margaret on the old sofa Adele had picked up in a sale somewhere. There, he made her promise to marry him one day when we're ready. Margaret was twenty-five, Jim a little older and Adele, well, sixty.

He left the next day and Margaret waited. She waited for three years until Jim reappeared to exact a renewed promise. Margaret reassured him she would wait and that he would not have to ask her again. He said they would marry when she was thirty so that they could still have children, yet still it was put off. It was put off until Margaret was thirty-five, when Jim was doing well in the company and needed a sensible wife, on Van, oo can entertain an' things like that. Also, he noted, about this time, that Adele was getting old an' if I don't get 'er away now, the old bird'll 'ang on like a vulture. You see if she don't. Jim did not understand that relationship either.

So Margaret was pushing thirty-seven when she arrived on Van. Jim was forty and his marriage clinched him the appointment as General Manager a year later. There was no bitterness on Henry's part: the job needed a tough man, he reasoned, and anyway he had other things with which to fill his life. He liked Margaret, at first, because she was not one of those egotistical women who reminded him of himself. A bit thick , I reckon, Jim's wife. Do you think she's all there? These were his first outspoken views. Later he wondered to himself if she was not profoundly deep. A little worrying, that idea. Margaret saw through Henry, all the way to the vacant space behind, the minute she met him.

There was a pregnancy but it aborted. Nothing thereafter.

So Jim messed up Margaret's life? No, for all his wickedness, he did not do that. Margaret made her life for herself. Before Jim, she had been happy, very happy, running the guest house with her mother and helping the local farmers. She would have been happy doing that for the rest of her life: a good life, it would have been, because everyone whom Margaret touched benefited. Her goodness was merely transferred to Van Island.

13

The Beginning of Annu

"Annu, Annu, Annu," his mother calls, because she knows the child is playing a game.

"Annu, Annu, Annu," she reassures, like the cooing of the afternoon doves.

So she gets on with her work, squatting behind the embers of the fire, in the morning sunshine.

"Annu, Annu, Annu," she sings to herself and to the giggling child in the tree above her.

The child looks down onto his world: her brown, broad back, onto the large buttocks he knows so well. Against which he sleeps at night, appreciating their comfort in contrast to his sister's bony skinniness that, nonetheless, protects him on the other side. His sister who has inspired in him lately, as he begins to see the wider world, a new sensation. A warm desire to protect, so that sometimes, in the depth of the sharp Highland night, he will squirm around, sticking his little bum into the small of his mother's back to put his arms around his sister. He nuzzles the back of her narrow, vulnerable neck. In the morning, when the first arrow of light penetrates the little hut their father has built for them, he is awake to find his mother's large arm around them both. Then he fights her, struggling to disentangle himself, giggling at the lazy slap he receives as he rushes out to meet the day.

Oh, how much does he want to be part of the bright world. Such a beautiful thing can never hurt.

[][][][][]

Standing on the branch, hugging the warm, rough trunk of the young Casuarina tree, he looks down upon the world. Beyond, framed by the older trees, he sees the broad, grassy valley sweeping up to more hills, like this one, mere ripples against the great mountains, briefly visible, that stretch up and are part of the sky, in which, specks, the kites circle.

As insignificant as the kites but alien as well, brutal upon the soft contours of the valley floor, lie the hard lines of the ground upon which the biggest birds land. These birds fly out of the sky suddenly, invading the world with their impatient buzzing and choking, as if unaccustomed to the height. Inelegant things they are but they fascinate the boy, who upon hearing them will cease his play, running to climb this, his own tree, for a better view.

The thing, more a large, annoying insect than a bird, approaches the ground slowly, then rushes at it angrily, coming to a spluttering halt, resentful of the ground that receives it. Small indeed it is, but it fascinates the boy who watches it deposit men and all sorts of strange, unrecognisable things before swallowing up the men again to rush up into the sky and disappear.

His mother tells him stories about the birds, of how she had not known them when she was a girl, of how things have changed since they appeared, of how they are the things of the white men. A cloud passes across her face so that he stops asking. For a while, but the idea grips his fertile mind. He wants to know. He presses his mother, who is bearing the cloud until it becomes a small but significant furrow between her brows.

One day she tells a story as if the telling relieves the pain of it. She tells of how she has seen the white men up close. Once only, when she was a girl. But that was enough for her: to see them again would kill her. Their sour smell, their pale eyes, their thin lips and their sharp noses, repel her. The very idea makes her choke. Where do they come from? She does not know but from some dark place, no doubt, that is not of this world, for the sun burns their skin and makes their eyes squint. They carry a strange outer skin to protect themselves, she says; their real skin, beneath, is so white she is convinced that they are, in reality, dead. They are not men: they are ghosts.

The silver birds are more real than the men, she says. The Ghost Men are the servants of the birds, their purpose, to carry the things that the birds bring. The Ghost Men are lost; slaves to the things they carry.

The Ghost Men frightened her, as if she had seen her own death.

She ran home to the freedom of the hills. That night she had lain for the first time with the man she called her husband. She became a woman with her wisdom, desiring her husband all the more because he was not white; all the more as she clung to him that night, she wanted to be part of him and part of his blackness.

The story makes the child feel more protective towards his sister. He imagines she is the frightened girl running away from the white men. But he is fascinated by the idea of the Ghost Men. He wants to know more about them. They haunt him. He feels drawn towards the idea. He feels a sympathy for these strange men caught inside their own death; enslaved, forever, down there, by the giant, silver birds.

[][][][][]

In time, fortified by his mother's love, the child, Annu, went to live with his father and the other men of the community, in order to become a man.

At this time, also, the white men made direct contact with Annu's clan. They brought gifts – steel axe heads and boxes of matches – so all the men were happy. They were impressed by the white men's power. But Annu himself quickly learnt that white men were ordinary men. One time, with the other boys, he stealthily followed them – as if tracking birds – to the river where they washed. He saw them naked and he knew that his mother was right: they were pale and sick-looking. Without their clothes, they were vulnerable: it would be easy to kill them. This idea filled him with pity for the white men.

The white men stayed for three nights. In the end, they asked, by signs, Annu's father, who was the big man of the clan, if they could take some of the boys with them in order to teach them the white men's language. Annu's father was a wise man. He called all the men of the clan together. They said it would be useful for some of the men of the clan to know the ways of the white men, then they would know how to get the white men's things themselves. This would make them strong.

He said that only the boys who were men could go with the white men, and then only if they wanted to go. Immediately his father had said this Annu shouted that he himself would go with the white men. His father showed no surprise saying he was proud that his own son was not afraid to go with the white men. But later, when he embraced his son in farewell, he held the boy for a long time. Annu knew that his father was sad.

[][][][]

Their world was defined by the mission station. Alien, neat, regular buildings set beside the airstrip, insignificant-looking for all the evil it brought, in the rolling, grassy plains of the valley. A frightening place to men used to the snug European landscape of whitewashed stone villages and green meadows where placid brown cows munch the rich grass. A tamed landscape well defined by beech woods and pine forests, by the cowbells echoing across narrow valleys of certain, narrow ideas.

In this other, wider valley there was no such easy definition, nothing against which they could measure themselves surely, against which they could mark their lives. Here, the plains of sharp grass, that cut unprotected European legs, gave to ineffectual-seeming hills, topped, occasionally, with dense, dark groves of dripping Casuarina trees beneath which crouched huddles of low, rotting huts inhabited by the old and dying aboriginal people. The other inhabitants had either fled altogether, to even higher altitudes or else had succumbed to the mission station itself, living in a skimpy line of grass houses strung alongside the airstrip as obedient Christians. For God's sake what had it all got to do with Christ?

Beyond the uncertain hills lay the mountains, appearing occasionally as grand things beneath the high, thin-blue sky. Then, as if no more than a dream of cumulus clouds, they would retreat again beyond the mist. Often, the white men in the mission would fail to catch the grandeur altogether, or if they saw it, would feel unsettled by it, preferring to look inwards. Mist was the feature of the valley, clearing sometimes for a few hours only to drift back again as the one daily certainty.

The mist thickened from time to time to become persistent rain. It would fall for two or three days at a time as a cold and solid fact. The very bones of the Europeans would become swollen and saturated with water, the flesh around them puffy, damp and chilled. During the wet season the days of rain would become weeks, the valley floor a quagmire.

But, sometimes the skies cleared and the sun shone bright and warm. The novice rejoiced with smiling eyes and would turn his face to the sky, seeing the distant mountains as the limitless potential of his life. But the older men shook their weary-wise heads, satisfied that a lesson would soon be learnt. And it was, when day after baking day, the sun burnt out of a white sky, the grass whispering its secrets into the cracked earth. Hot winds drove fires across the valley, the air thick with smoke and ash that stung the lungs.

So the white men hated the valley because they could not break it and be master of it. To the boy it was the larger world beyond the mission station. It was beautiful under the wide, over-arching sky, its moods subtle and wonderful. When he escaped into it he felt the wind and rain caress his skin. Climbing the hills he felt the earth move wonderfully beneath his feet. He saw mountains and the clear blue sky. He saw the eagle fly.

[][][][][]

Even in his more calm and rational moments Father Hermann saw only two possibilities. Either it was indeed his own essential sin that made him do what he did; or he had become an instrument of the Prince of Darkness. If the former, then he knew that he had laid the sin upon himself, layer upon layer, until the weight of it had dragged him, unresisting, willingly even, down to the hell of his own life. If the latter, then why, he asked himself, had God, the father of all things, allowed the Devil to take his life? Was it some divine experiment? Would he, Father Hermann, in recompense for his suffering, become the Little Hermann again? Innocent once more?

The idea of regained innocence soothed Father Hermann in his agony. And why not? Is this not what Christianity promises? Regained innocence for true repentance? But Hermann was beyond true repentance: the sense of his own sin was too great. He knew, inside himself, that what he did, he did for his own gratification. He knew it was wrong and he knew he could stop himself. He knew there were lesser sins that would assuage the desire.

Beyond the Prince of Darkness, and, of course, God, Father Hermann discounted the involvement of anything else. This was something that involved his own soul: there lay the problem and there, he supposed, lay the solution. He was alone in his suffering. Had he known it, his loneliness was what barred the way to salvation. That is until the boy came to the mission.

He was the same as the other boys in many ways, but in one way he stood out. The others would never, not unless forced, look Father Hermann in the eye. But this one looked straight at Father Hermann. There was no fear in the boy. He looked right into Father Hermann's soul and Father Hermann shuddered at the thought of it. He knew he was damned.

Oh God, our Father who art in heaven, help me.

But no help came to Father Hermann who roasted in the flames of his own anguish.

Father Hermann abused the boys under his charge in the mission. Abused their minds, abused their trust, abused the Jesus Christ to whom he had promised to devote his life. Abused himself in the process so that it was a pretty terrible weight of sin he carried. Take this, he said to the boys. As, he might have said, you take the holy bread and the holy wine. Take it as an act of submission to the god, to the holy saviour, I have brought to you. Doubly confusing to the boys in the mission, new to the Christian doctrine. And this, Father Hermann knew, was

144

the greater sin: the debasement of our Lord Jesus Christ who did indeed give his body to us. But all the same, Annu and the others were not unaccustomed to the sight of a naked adult. In fact when Annu first saw Father Hermann naked, or partly so, he felt sorry for the insignificant thing that was the man.

In the end, therefore, although most of the boys carried away a confused idea of Christianity, their earlier upbringing in the hills above ensured that they accepted it as yet another manifestation of the white man's strange view of the world. Father Hermann it was who was the most hurt.

[]]]]]

That boy either won't speak or he can't. Either way I can't cope with him. He's like his mother. Simple. She didn't know what she was doing when she let Heinz take her to his rotten little farm. All he wanted was some daft idiot to keep his house and help him do the work. And to share his bed of course: he would want that. He was a man and that's all they do want in the end. Well she made her bed and she had to lie in it. Stupid, she was. I had no time for her then and I haven't now. But I've given her a decent burial, no one can say I didn't. It cost me decent money too.

I said it cost me decent money. She screeched down at him. It cost me decent money, little boy. Ooh, she wanted to kick the speechless little lump, sitting there on the stool, drinking her milk like an idiot. Idiot, like his father.

My milk! Am I going to have to spend decent money on you for the next . . . how many years? She bent down, grabbed the cup from his loose hands and threw the dregs into the little fire that hissed back at her. There! She banged the cup onto the table above his head and walked out of the room unable to bear the sight of her sister's brat. The brat and evidence of her simple sister's union with Heinz – silent Heinz they had always called him. She had despised his slow and concentrated habits, although his strong and bony body with its confident movements invaded her dreams still.

Left alone, Hermann looked at the big world around him. Later he remembered this period of his life as a shadowy ill-defined confusion: a large confusion, of big furniture, of dark legs, of thick, musty trousers and skirts, of her screeching and his heavy breathing, of a thick cold that chilled his body and of a smell so unlike anything he had smelt before that it made him feel sick even in remembrance. That smell, he came to learn later, was the smell of the moth balls, cheap furniture polish, blacking, carbolic soap and all the stuff she used to clean the stuffy, gloomy little house so thoroughly that it was scraped quite clean of all the milk of human kindness. And for all the cleaning, if the sun ever poked a finger at it, during the high summer when the narrow street was warmed for a couple of hours a day, it merely picked up dust and lumps of accumulated floor polish.

In a material sense little Hermann had what he needed. A small room at the top of the house, cold in winter, hot in summer, but adequate; clothes, bought from the second-hand dealer who trundled his cart down the street from time to time, also adequate; he was fed, plainly but, again, the diet was adequate. His aunt, despite her constant complaining, did her duty by him in a material sense.

As she told him, he had nothing to complain about – he never did – and she had made sure that, unlike his mother, he would not be a disgrace to the family. Of course, later on, he was, although she was dead and buried by then – in the material sense, at least.

But the very sight of him drove her into a frenzy. As he got older and looked more and more like his father – although he had his mother's mournful, vacant eyes – they had raw, elementary conversations that recognised each other's existence, but only in a material sense. She was aware of the desert in which they lived: he, on the other hand, accepted it as the norm. It wasted her life and filled his with an infectious poison. It left an emotional vacuum in both of them but whereas hers was the completed and sealed empty seedpod, his was an empty vessel waiting to be filled.

Little Hermann had been the apple of his parents' eyes. As round and as ripe as the apples in the orchard that surrounded the house. He was the only child and especially cherished because he had been born late in his mother's life, when his parents had given up hope of having children. Hermann's parents were simple farmers; they were too poor to spoil him with material things, but their love for him, like their love for each other, drew the little family tightly together, resisting the hostile world outside. They worked the farm, ate and slept together as a single organism.

When his parents died, in the flu epidemic of 1919, Hermann was barely five years old. In the usual course of events, Hermann would have gone to the village school and learnt normal social behaviour, safe and secure in the knowledge of his parents' love. But he had developed apart from the world, unprepared for his sudden, shocking immersion into it. Having taken his parents' love for granted, he knew not how to form a loving relationship. Worse, as it happened, he knew not how to form a relationship in which he was able to defend himself. He was unformed in this respect, understanding love as his natural right and subsequently trusting all those with whom he came into contact, assuming they would love him as his parents had done. As for the art of giving love in any calculating way, he knew nothing.

All the same, in the right, affectionate hands and surrounded by good examples, Hermann would have developed the art of human relationships. Unfortunately, he fell into the wrong hands, with the result that his natural development was stunted. He grew to hate his parents who had deserted him and, as an adult, his contact with other human beings fell into two distinct types of conduct: close contact exclusively defined by sadomasochism; or no contact beyond what was essential to get him through each day and the days of his life. Thus those who knew him, knew him either as a predator or as something cold, detached and apparently indifferent.

In his relationship with his aunt, Hermann grew up in an aura of antagonistic isolation and resentment. Not so with his uncle who appeared on the scene a few years after his parents' death. Uncle Johannes might have been an older brother. He was a merchant seaman who had continued his trade during the First World War in the Baltic doing well out of the neutral flag he flew. A strange occupation for the native of a land-locked and mountainous country, but it was a tradition going back generations, based on family trading connections in one of the Hanseatic ports. The long tedious periods at sea suited Johannes' aggressively taciturn nature. Like his nephew, he rarely spoke but his silences were an expression of his disapproval of a world that did not satisfy him. He could communicate when it suited him, and, when it suited him, he could snub anyone who tried to extend a conversation beyond the necessary. He was a good seaman.

Hermann came into his uncle's line of vision when he was eleven. His habit of limited communication had become entrenched. He kept a low profile.

Johannes, at this time, was a youngish-middle-aged man, bulky and muscular, his bright blue eyes challenging the world above a large walrus moustache. His thatch of blond hair had darkened but it was still thick. His face was a seaman's weathered face but beyond the silent anger there remained a memory of the agile youth who had once been a favourite in the rough bars and brothels of the port where he had learnt his trade.

Your trade, Johannes.

You know what I mean. Based on the iron rod of your disciplined and tortured soul. Based on perfunctory contact – we won't call it a connection, let alone a relationship – with those whom you forced or whom you paid. You poor sod, I suppose, but was it your mother or your father who engendered your strange habits? Better they had strangled you at birth. They might have done had they noted your peculiarity, your, your magnificent oddness rather than let you corrupt the others, the innocents.

Your burden. It's true, but you carried it with a sort of pride as if its weight was a good thing, making you stronger by the bearing of it, rather than making you the crippled monster that you are. But no pity will you get because you never asked for it. Not once in your miserable life. Miserable? You gloried in it. Did you pity the others? Compassion was beyond you. You forfeited your humanity. You burn.

You decided what you wanted early in your life. And that was to be the best at whatever you did. If you could not be the best then you did not do it. You were the captain of your own ship early in your life and there you stayed because, let's face it, you had not got the brains to be any more than that. You did it for twenty years. In your terms, you did it well. Very well indeed. You perfected it as an art as sharp as a Swedish knife.

For that you earned respect. No, not that: you earned confidence from all those money-grubby men who entrusted their precious cargoes to you. They knew what was good for them, in that grubby respect, and what was good for them was you.

You held on to that particular material confidence with artless determination. The fear that you inspired in your, your men, in doing so, defined you. Did it not? It proved your existence, without which you were nothing. You were a hard man – as hard as iron, you said it yourself, with pride – and you were hard on yourself, in terms of the work you did. You did not give an inch.

You bastard. It was Hermann's bad luck he fell into your hard hands. It was a small, narrow house; you shared the bed with him, the boy.

And so in this tedious human saga that goes on and on through the generations Hermann takes the poisoned chalice and passes it on too, to Annu.

And Annu forgives all. He breaks the hideous progression. He absorbs it into his strong black body. He makes it into something good, for which, for which – can you believe it? – we cut off his head and throw it into the river, for which we hang his naked body upon a tree to die. That tree. How we admire it. It stands at Warsaw, at Auschwitz, at Belzec and at Treblinka. It stands at Babi-Yar, at Katyn, on the Somme and at Wounded Knee. It stands on the Place de la Révolution, on Peter's Field in Manchester, at Botany Bay and in the Old South. It stands in Nanking and in Hiroshima. It stands at Crossroads and in Soweto. It stands in Belfast and in Sarajevo. It stands in Rwanda, Palestine, Chechnya and Guantanamo. A thick forest of trees upon which Annu hangs. And while the Prince of Darkness reigns, the trees will bear a heavy load. Every day He hangs and new trees will always be found for the hanging.

[][][][][]

Annu left the mission at sixteen. They had wanted to make a priest out of him until he laughed out loud too often.

His laugh and his big head did not show respect. So they found him a job as pay clerk on one of the coffee plantations springing up in the valley. The cheeky boy was clever, and he was good: he did not cheat the men out of their pay. But the combination of cheekiness and cleverness made him an enigma to the planter-owner, a Second World War veteran called Smudge. Smudge had limited intelligence but he was decent enough as Smudges go and only an out-and-out racist because of a confirmed knowledge that kanakas were animals. But Smudge was good to animals. In the mornings after muster he chased them into the field with a stick. He was appreciated for this bit of fun, an animal himself.

Anyway, Smudge found Annu's cheekiness too much for him in the little plantation office that was a wired-off bit of the veranda tacked onto the house that was not more than a smudgy hut. 'E acts as if 'e was 'uman, Smudge complained, afraid to consider the implications any further. So the boy found himself outside the office as boss-boy to a gang of twenty or so disparate men, outcasts of every sort.

Annu was good. A leader and an intercessor between Smudge and the men. The productivity and quality of the work improved beyond anything Smudge had even dreamed of. He was beginning to congratulate himself for a shrewd move when the 'ole fuckin' lot of 'em ups and disappears.

Smudge blamed Annu for stealing his best men but what Annu had also stolen was the old rascal's heart.

[][][][][]

From the valley floor the bald hill appears to be crowned with a grove of trees. Casuarina trees. What they call Yar.

Big raggedy old things hung with lacy-looking moss. The moss grows well in the damp, motionless air. Fungus too.

Black more than green the Yar look, in a landscape yellow when it is not black. When the sun does get at this landscape for any length of time, the fires burn it black. The sun is obscured by a white haze, the Yar trees, black in black.

Up close the great trunks are fluted, ridged like the stretched neck of a strong man. Rough they are with a peeling and flaky skin, old with memories. I have pressed my face against the skin of the Yar trees up there and smelt little more than the damp air. A hint of smoke, perhaps. But these trees are strong, all the same. Prehistoric remnants dug up out of the swamp are as hard as iron.

Friendly looking are those hills, but not so friendly if you walk to them from the insubstantial road laid upon the unreceptive valley floor. A trek through a bit of a swamp and then up the steeper ground thick with the kunai grass that cuts unprotected white legs.

But they walk it all the same, Keramugl and Margaret. She wears trousers and a big wide hat because the sun burns through the clouds at this altitude. Also, for some reason, a red blouse that can, no doubt, be seen from miles away, on the other side of the valley.

Both wear boots. They are a practical necessity for a trip that takes in places unfriendly to the unprotected foot, including the rusty floor of the hired utility truck Margaret has driven from the thriving town of Mt Giluwe. As a boy, Keramugl walked barefoot along the ridge-top paths that link one hilltop settlement to another. He had scrambled through the grass in play, hunting birds with the other boys. Now he returns as a man with this white woman. So he wears boots. Shorts also because, unlike hers, his skin is tough. His legs are tree trunks, massive above the boots.

A tiny speck of red disappears into the trees.

The trees are not a grove but form an elongated ring. Inside, the level ground looks unnatural up here in the hills. It would be big enough for a few boys to play football if not quite as large as a football pitch. The old trees around it are a solid wall in the evening. At midday they are bright apart or else separated by the silent, shifting mist.

Men made the place because it had been dry and fairly flat to start with. With wooden spades and stone-headed hoes they had broken the ground a little to make it more level. They had planted it around with the Yar trees as a boundary and stamped the soil flat and firm with their big feet to the rhythm of drums.

Men thought about themselves in relation to each other and in relation to the place and they made it. They made it raw but it was their thought of it and their use of it that defined it as the trees grew. The men fixed the place as part of the earth with their singing and stamping, as surely as did the roots of the growing Yar trees. The place became permanent first and then sacred, so that it is indeed a place of men made into gods, as memory is laid upon memory. The idea and the memories will last a thousand years and more. It is what we call a magic place.

This is a Singsing ground. A place where the clan comes together to define itself as definitely as the trees grow and as the clan's feet define the firmness of the ground inside the ring of trees. The place contains – I imagine – the soul of the clan, embodying the essence and spirit of the clan. Margaret and Keramugl are aware of the sacredness of the place the moment they enter. Here, the young men, in particular, decorate their bodies with oil and paint, plant feathers in their hair. The sounds of singing, stamping and the beating of drums echo across the valley. This is the clan.

But the sacred place is empty.

Kunai grass grows high in the patches where feet have not recently stamped.

A few squalid, broken and rotten huts squat around the edge, under the dripping trees: women's huts where the women have waited for their beautiful men to return. Waited away their lives, it seems, for they are gone themselves now.

At one end of the Singsing ground there is a tree younger than the others, planted to fill a gap, to close a view of the world beyond. The tree is older now but the child could still climb it, as he did then in the bright morning. Keramugl climbs it now. He looks down into the valley that is quiet and innocent looking. Beyond, framed by the older trees, he sees the rest of the world: the broad, grassy valley sweeping up to more hills, like this one, mere ripples against the great mountains, briefly visible, that stretch up and are part of the sky, in which, specks, the kites circle.

Below, as distant from this place as the kites, the airstrip, its lines still clear, has been planted with coffee. It is no longer needed: a road connects it to Mt Giluwe town and a new airport. Pathetic the mission station looks to Keramugl who knows enough about the world to know the fact. The road has broken its isolation, linking it to new sins.

Keramugl climbs down into the Singsing ground.

He takes two coins out of his pocket. At the foot of the tree, he squats down and with his pocket knife – so proud of his ownership, once, but he is grown up now – he digs a little hole in the earth. When it is finished, it is, perhaps, about eight inches deep and just big enough for his clenched fist to fit inside. Then he puts the coins at the bottom of the hole, replacing the soil bit by bit and gently pressing it down as he does so. When he has finished he brushes the detritus from the tree over the place so that there is no sign of his work.

Another memory has been added to the Singsing ground.

Then Keramugl walks to Margaret who is sitting beneath a tree, leaning her back on it, her hat on her knees. She is looking into the centre.

He stands beside her, looking down on to her head. Her hair is as much grey as it is blonde.

"This is his place," he says.

"I know," she smiles.

They return to the valley. They do not look back.

[][][][][]

15th August 1987.

A woman came to see me today. She was a white woman. Tall and fair with blue eyes.

She was with a man from around these parts who was acting as her guide, it seems.

She did not say much. She looked down at me, as I sat here at my desk. She had such a nice smile. I liked her smile, looking at me from a great height.

She greeted me and asked if she might look around the station. I told her she was welcome. Who am I to refuse a simple request like that? I asked Brother Peter to show her the new classrooms.

The man, her guide, stayed with me. They did not seem to need each other. He was a nice man. He did not say much but he said they had flown up from Van Island by way of Port Markham. He said the woman had lived on Van Island for some years. He said he worked for her on a plantation she had bought at the Cape Hereford end of the island.

We sat in silence for most of the time but I could feel he was aware of me. He was one of those people who do not have the need to talk all the time, although I felt he had things to say.

I wanted to ask him questions about Van Island. But I have no right to ask questions. I await God's pleasure.

I offered him some coffee but he said he would prefer tea. I do not have tea here in my office. It is an English habit.

He said he learnt to drink tea when he worked on the plantation of Mr Smith before he went to Van Island. That would be Smudge Smith who used to have Narangburn Plantation. I told the man that Mr Smith had died many years ago and the plantation was part of a company that had bought all the European plantations. He did not seem to be interested in this but he said he was sorry that Mr Smith had died. He said he was a good man who loved his labourers. I was surprised to hear this because Smith was a rough sort with little education. They say he used to chase his men out to work with a stick in the mornings and use foul language. But it is something that he is remembered as a good man who loved his labourers. I would have liked to discuss this further but the man did not seem inclined to talk any more.

I would have liked to have asked him why he went to Van Island and what happened there. But it is not my place to ask a man like that questions. A man who remembers Smudge Smith as a good man who loved his labourers. It is not for me to manipulate his answers with my questions. I await God's pleasure.

I could tell he was from this area by his looks. I could tell he was one of those who for some good reason had not lost themselves. He was confident, sitting straight in the chair. He told me the things he wanted to say. He did not ask me questions, so I could not tell him things.

He sat sideways to me, looking out of the window. When he spoke he did not look at me. He spoke to the world in general. I heard him, as it were, only by accident. It is right that he should approach me in this way because I am one who must hide in shame.

Yet, each time before he spoke, he would look at me as if to be sure of my attention. His way of looking at me demanded my attention. He seemed to be demanding a connection before he made his banal statements. I felt he was holding my hand. His eyes looked at my eyes for a moment or two before he turned aside to speak into the air. I saw myself briefly reflected in his brown eyes.

His eyes are Annu's eyes. I want to see this man again.

He is a handsome man. Handsome as his race is. His thick brow, his Semitic nose, his strong chin and throat are noble in his speaking. He has Annu's profile but his face is round where Annu's was long. The eyes are the same eyes. I want to see this man again.

He is short and strong looking, like a boxer. His legs are strong Highland legs. He looks fine in his clothes, for all they are of European style. He looks proud, this short, strong man so that his body holds the chair upon which he sits and his boots claim the floor and connect with the earth below.

I feel this man's strength and confidence but his voice, as he talks to the world outside the window, is gentle and soft, humble almost as if surprised by his own ability to speak.

Why do I write like this? Am I thinking of Annu or of this man who has visited me today with the white woman from Van?

I had a class to take so I left him in my office. He did not look round to watch me go. He forgot me the moment I left.

Later, from the classroom window, I watched the two of them walk away across the grass to their utility truck parked under the Yar trees we planted thirty-five years ago.

They were miles away.

They walked as if they were strangers to each other. Far apart, it looked. But there was a connection between them. I could see that. A good connection. I knew that the man held the woman's hand although they did not touch.

They walked differently yet each held the ground confidently, connected to it. They looked up into the sky as if laughing. The sun shone out of the grey sky. I saw her spring as if she would fly. The ground shook as he trod it.

I want to see his eyes again.

I have forgotten their names.

I must ask Brother Peter.

I want to ask them about Van but I am afraid.

[][][][][]

20th November 1986.

We get the newspapers when Brother Peter drives in to Mt Giluwe for supplies. We did not get them so often at first, when I came to the valley. Then, they came once a fortnight with the plane from Port Markham or Karandawa. Less often in the bad weather. I liked it then. We were isolated. It was a three- or four-day hike to Karandawa which was the staging post between the Highlands and the coast. All the indentured labour went through Karandawa. It was not a happy place, they say.

The new road between Mt Giluwe and Karandawa has changed all that. The airstrip did not warrant the expense so we planted it with coffee. We paid a contract planter to do it. Harrington was his name. He did it well. He planted the new dwarf variety. In three years we had good yields but the prices had fallen by then.

So I do not have the habit of reading the newspapers.

But we cannot keep out the world. The new road has brought it to our door. I am told that from Karandawa one can drive to Port Markham in a day. The world is getting smaller. There is radio also and soon there will be satellite television. The airport hotel in Mt Giluwe has it, I am told.

So I have heard about what is happening on Van Island. But it meant very little to me until today. Strikes and violence are not unusual, these days.

The newspapers here do not tell you much. It must be difficult to find out what is happening outside Port Markham and the main towns. If something happens in Mt Giluwe it is reported. When Harrington killed his friend it was on the front page. It is a big story when a white man kills his homosexual lover. It made me think of Uncle Johannes. If twenty men die in the hills above here no one knows about it.

This is my diary. I have been writing it for seventeen years. I do it because it keeps me from going mad. I do not want to be a trouble to anyone. I have no right to be that.

I write in order to maintain my hold on the world around me here in the mission. I write it in order for me to feel that I have some connection with the world around. I write to reassure myself that I exist. I cannot make contact in any other way. Prayer is useless for one such as I. God punish me so that I may be forgiven. God make me innocent again. Scrape away the layers of sin which have accumulated in my seventy years. Find the little Hermann again. Oh Lord, I know you cannot do that. I have created my own hell and I burn in my own guilt. And always I ask the question, why. Why? These seventy years have passed quickly enough. They have been as nothing in all time. So why could I not have waited patiently in prayer? I saw the beauty of God once. I felt it. I could have loved that. It would have been enough for any life. I could have loved my Aunt. So easily could I have loved her. I could have learnt to love my Uncle Johannes.

If only Annu had come to us before I fell, I could have done all these things.

But they recognised my wickedness before I saw it myself. They were my just punishment. I am not fit for love. To give or to take.

I am told the boys here are afraid of me now because of my detachment. I do not look at them and I do not use their names. Brother Peter calls the roll for me and administers punishment when required. Now, the boys have to work in the coffee garden. It is better that way. Out of my hands. They learn something useful but they won't use it. They are city boys. The education we give them makes them more so. Once we have taken them from their homes they are not fit to return. We even have a computer. We bring the city to them. Our god is a city god. He dwells in stone buildings. As beautiful as stone can be made but stone it remains. Hard, cold and unforgiving.

Detached I must remain. Like the stone. I ask a question to the class by naming the row and the seat number. The personalities of the boys I see only in the books I mark. Brother Peter collects them and returns them.

Brother Peter is a good man. He has a wife and children in Mt Giluwe who make him a better man. We pretend not to know.

Better the boys fear my detachment than my poisonous contact.

This diary helps me to remain detached.

But it has no other use. The ramblings of an old man waiting for his time, which is close now. It might be worth something if I had started writing it when I first came to this valley. It would have had historic interest. A film has already been made I am told. Stone-Age to Satellite, or something like that. I was in Port Markham first, straight after the war. Then they sent me up here. They could see I was a lone wolf. The Steppenwolf. But what would I have written? Would I have described what I did? Would I have written down my sins? Listed each one of them as they were committed? The sins of a priest. Bring the little ones to me. That I may devour them.

But I cannot write them.

It is hard enough to write the name, Annu. I am confused.

The newspaper called him Annu. A man who was lynched was called Joseph Annu. It must be the same boy, the man. Why should he not have come to a bad end? Lynching is what happens to the perpetual trouble makers, the story said, in the end. Lynched by the mob in the market place. A bad end for a bad man the story said. The mob carried off the body and tore it apart. Welcome to it, the story implied. It is about time the government did something about what's going on there, the editorial said. They are sending police reinforcements from Port Markham.

So he was a bad man was he?

Not to me. He is the one I remember. The others, whom I had forgotten until today, would not look at me, for all my adoration. They would be awkward and uneasy, refusing to talk to me for all I wanted to make contact and love them. That is all I wanted. I wanted to love them. But they hated me for it. Annu was different. Annu looked at me.

Annu knew me. He did what I asked him to do. I did not have to order him with threats. I did not have to frighten him. He looked at me with a smile. It might have been insolent but it was not. It was loving. But he did it in a detached way. It was as if I had paid a man back home in the park to do it. A man who wanted the money so badly, he would do anything. He would degrade himself. When I was relieved, the wave of guilt overwhelmed me. Until the desire again came on me, wiping out the memories. He looked at me.

Annu looked at me. His eyes looked into mine so that I saw myself in his eyes. He connected with me and despite what had just happened and despite my guilt, I felt happiness for the first time in years. I remembered my first contemplation of the Lord Jesus Christ. The boy Jesus must have been like this boy Annu, with a wisdom beyond his years. The boy Jesus, teaching his elders in the temple where his parents found him.

Annu's knowledge was my shame. I was ashamed, not in front of God, but in front of this boy.

Annu stayed with us for about four years. I did not touch him again or any other boy. His eyes were enough to stop me. Not admonitory but loving. He was one of our best boys. He never caused us any trouble. He was the confident type who helped anyone weaker than himself. There are few blessed souls like that. So confident in themselves that they are no trouble to anyone. They need little and give much.

I wanted him to stay on and become a lay Brother but he said he must leave. I can remember him sitting in my office when he told me this. He did not look at me but at the world outside the window. I looked at his profile and I understood we could not keep him. He looked at me before he left and once again I saw myself reflected in his brown eyes. I recommended him to Smudge Smith further down the valley who had said he wanted one of our boys as a clerk he could trust. I knew he could trust Annu. He could trust all our boys. It was me who was not worthy of trust.

The day Annu left was unusually sunny. He did not say goodbye to me. Why should he? He owed me nothing. It was I who owed him. He spent his last few hours with the other boys, arranging when they would meet again no doubt. Excited, as boys are with their whole life in front of them, innocent. I felt an unworthy surge of envy. I watched him walk away with a heavy heart. I watched his confident stride with his head held high as if he owned the world and as if he was laughing. I watched the space through which he had walked. The morning was bright with sunshine but my life was black then without a chink of light or the slightest hope of escape from my memories. They flooded back into my head as they do today. It was as if Annu had carelessly opened the sluice gate as he left me. He had filled me with a false hope of redemption only to drown me at the last minute. Had it been any other boy, the cruel laughter would have followed me down the years. Oh yes, and I would have deserved it. I would not have complained.

But that was the devil talking to me because Annu was an angel. He was my angel. I had only to think of his laughter and the sun shone. His smile with myself reflected in his eyes as a reality. His goodness. It is the idea of Annu's goodness which has sustained me down the years.

I started writing my diary the day he left, seventeen years ago.

I have written it as if speaking to him. All the while I wrote I have had the idea of his uncompromising goodness. Not his love. I do not deserve that but his recognition of me as myself, of the child within. As if, as if those things I have done will not matter in the end.

That was my Annu. Goodness, uncompromising, which recognised me. Through which I saw the Glory of God. Annu was that love.

A small thread in all of human history but enough to save me.

Now the newspaper says that Annu was a bad man. He was lynched by the mob in the market place down there on Van. Then he must have been bad. From whence did that badness come? From me? Have I lived under a delusion for all these years? Was the goodness something I craved so much that I saw it where it was not? Was it merely a contortion of my craving for his body? Did I corrupt him also?

God forgive me.

No, I am beyond that.

I await His pleasure.

I wait.

□□□□□

20th August 1987.

They have gone now. I feel better for having seen them. It is good that they returned to say goodbye. I asked them questions and they gave me the answer I wanted to hear. The man is called Keramugl and the woman is Margaret. For what time God gives me I shall associate their names with that of Annu.

Brother Peter brought them to the office. He was smiling when he brought them in to me. He said he would take my class for me. He left the door open so that the sun shone into my dark room. It was like silver. I could see the specks of dust floating in it.

At first my heart beat fast because although I had not expected them to come, I was not surprised to see them. I wanted the answer but I did not know how to get it. I could not ask boldly: And is Annu good?

They would not know the man. On the map Cape Hereford is a long way from where Annu was supposed to have died. I thought probably they know no more than I.

As I straightened the papers on my desk it occurred to me that I did not know why they had come here. Why had they visited the mission? Why would people from Van want to visit us up here?

Later it was clear. They had come for Annu. There was no coincidence. We all sat in my office because of Annu. It is wonderful and I am ready to die now.

We sit in silence. I can see them now as I write, although the door is shut and it is dark outside.

The woman looks at me in silence, as if she knows me and likes me. That is strange to me because no one has ever liked me before. She is wearing an old, faded cotton frock which looks too big for her for all she is a large-framed woman. She sits as a lady would sit but she is very relaxed and her large mouth smiles at me from beneath watery blue eyes. She has the sort of skin which is easily damaged by the sun although she has put on a bit of make-up. It is for me, I know, because the man is not the sort of man who would care about such things although he would feel your mood and respond to it.

The man sits as before. He looks out of the window just as Annu did. He might have been impatient with the woman but I know he is not. There is a slight smile on his lips as he waits patiently. His frown is an illusion created by the thickness of his brow. He is a good-looking man. I am no longer afraid to say that.

At first I think he is waiting for the woman to say what she wants to say. I know now he is waiting for me.

The woman, this Margaret, thanks me for letting her see the mission station. She says they are driving to Karandawa in order to fly to Port Markham by the afternoon plane and then they will go back to Van the following day. She does not say goodbye. She waits as if she will wait forever, smiling. The man also, looking out of the window at the sunny hillside across the valley.

So I have to say something. I am, effectively, the senior man here. Things are expected of me.

I offer them coffee. It is accepted this time by the man. The woman also. They both take milk and sugar. I prepare it myself and they drink it as if it is a treat. They both seem to enjoy their cup of coffee as if it is their first or their last. It seems to make them immensely happy. I am surprised that such a small thing can make them so happy but I should not be.

I look at the woman again. She is not young but she has the vitality of youth. She is in love with life and the whole world. Her hair is tied back but wisps escape all over. More grey than blonde, I suppose, but in the sunlight flooding through the door it is gold and silver. I feel a love for this woman flooding through my body like the sunlight flooding through the door. I feel its warmth warming my old chilled bones.

Easy now to ask the questions.

She answers them but the man seems to nod his assent.

Her voice is beautiful. As she talks I remember the house of my parents when I was very small. Three or four years old I would have been. I am surprised to suddenly remember so far back. Her voice swings like the pendulum on the old clock in our kitchen.

She says yes they know all about the disturbances on Van Island last year. But she says it is in the past now and things are a lot better.

I ask her if they knew this man Annu. At this she laughs and the man, Keramugl, laughs as well.

They say no more. I can see that they know Annu and love him. I know that a bad man cannot inspire that sort of love.

I say that Annu was a good boy in the mission school. I say that he was one of the best and that I have never forgotten him.

The woman smiles at me and the man says yes Annu is a good man.

Then they leave.

We say goodbye like old friends united in the love of Annu.

I watch them leave again walking across the grass in the sunshine. It occurs to me that the woman walks a little like Annu himself. This time they are holding hands and they are looking up into the hills where Annu was born.

I have finished my diary now.

14
Solwara[4]

I was a boy when I went to the plantation of Masta Smit. Why did a boy like me go to the plantation? Because I heard talk of the white man there. He is growing trees and I want to know why he does such a thing. I want to see this white man. They say that men work for the white man. When the work is finished the white man gives things to them.

My father and mother are dead so I am thinking I will walk to this place of the white man and forget my home.[5] It is close to our village. When I come to the plantation I am thinking I have not seen something like this before. All the little trees are planted in lines like we make our gardens for kaukau.[6] I am very happy.[7] I am thinking I want to stop in this place. I find some men. Some of

---

[4] The original document was written in New Sudanian Pidgin (Tokpisin). It was translated by Alloy who wanted to maintain the character of the original. Those who eventually went to live on Lingalinga Plantation spoke Tokpisin or English or a combination of the two. Alloy tried to reflect this in the translation. For instance, people said solwara (salt water) for the coast whether they were speaking English or Tokpisin. A problem of translating Tokpisin to English and maintaining the idiom is the use of the past tense. Tokpisin speakers speak in the present most of the time regardless of whether they are speaking of the past or the present. The past is achieved in Tokpisin by putting the statement in the past and then talking or writing in the present. For instance: *Yesterday (asade), we go for a walk.* The future can use the same structure: *Tomorrow (Tumara), I go for a walk.* Or: *Tomorrow, I want to go for a walk (Tumara, me laik go long wokabaut).* However, in order to ease the reader's journey through what is an important story about migrant labourers, Alloy has, where appropriate, translated Keramugl's statements into the simple future tense. Thus: *I will go for a walk.* The obvious exception in Tokpisin grammar to the rules about the past, is the use of the present perfect – referring to a past event – and adjectives that describe what happened in the past. In both cases Tokpisin uses the word *pinis* (finish in English). Thus for the present perfect, Tokpisin says, for *he has died* and *he has eaten*, *em i dai pinis* and *em i kaikai pinis*. For an adjectival state that refers to the past, the rule is the same. Thus for *he is dead* and *the house has fallen down*, Tokpisin says: *em i dai pinis* (the same as *he has died*) and *haus em i pundaun pinis*. Without the word *pinis*, the statements would be in the present: *he is dying* and *the house is falling down*. When Keramugl refers to the man, Grin, whom he knew in the past and who murdered his wife, he actually says: *Grin em i man husat mekim meri bilong em i dai pinis.* That is: Grin is a man who made (past) his wife die. Alloy translates the Tokpisin as: *Grin is a man who murdered his wife.* Again, Alloy does this to make the statement flow more easily even though it is not entirely consistent with his rules of translation. But in the end what Alloy wanted to achieve is achieved. The words do sound like Keramugl, giving an impression of his simple goodness and wisdom.

[5] Home in the emotional sense in New Sudanian Tokpisin is ples bilong mi (my home), ples bilong mipela (our home), or ples bilong em (his or her home), etc.

[6] Kaukau is sweet potato, the staple diet in the Highlands of New Sudan.

[7] Literally, me happy too much. In Tokpisin: mi hamamas tumas.

them talk the same language as me so I am happy to be with my wantoks. They give me kaukau to eat. I sleep with these men in their hut. In the night the muster bell wakes me up. The sound of this bell is not a good thing to my ear. The men say it is time to work. I ask them how is it we must work in the night. They laugh at me and they say the dawn will come soon. They tell the truth. By the time we are standing in the lines beside the gate to the plantation, the dawn is coming. This is a strange thing to me because all my life it is the dawn that wakes me in the morning. To be taken from sleep by this bell with the bad sound is a bad thing. Olsem I get used to it in time.

I stand in a line with the men and some other men come up to call the names of all the men. There are many strange names that I do not know. They do not call my name because they do not know me. Then, I see the white man. I have not seen a white man so I stare at him. I cannot take my eyes off him. His skin is like the kaukau that has not been cooked. His head is bald and the few hairs he has are white also. He is short. He is no taller than me and he has a big belly. His clothes are white also. He wears short trousers and long socks. Now, at the time, I did not know all these things but on that day I think, so this man is the white man. I think if all white men are like this then it will be easy to kill all of them. I am happy with this thought. I do not want to kill him. You understand what I am staying? But at that time I think it is a good thing that if I want to kill this man it will not be hard for me to kill him. Then, in those days, I am a bighead. I think these white men are weak and we are strong. In those days I am a foolish boy. I know nothing of the world that is New Sudan.

⬜⬜⬜⬜⬜

When the muster is finished they have not called my name. This is because they do not know my name. One of my wantoks calls out that this is Keramugl who wants to work. Then the white man, Masta Smit, comes to look at me. He looks at me like I am a pig that he wants to buy. His eyes are blue. I am thinking it is strange for a man to have blue eyes. What does he see with those eyes? I have not seen blue eyes before. I, Keramugl, am not afraid because I can see that the white man is a weak man. He talks to me but I cannot understand what he says because in those days I do not know how to speak Tokpisin.[8] But my wantok tells me what he says. He says I am a pikinini and he tells me to put up my arms. This is because the law says that if a man has no hair under his arms then he is a boy and he cannot work. Masta Smit looks at my arms. He says I am a boy so I cannot work in the plantation. He laughs and he says I have no trousers. This is true I have only my belt and my as tanket and my bilum.[9] My buttocks are naked. But that is the way we are. He says I can cook for the older

---

[8] The language is Tokpisin, not Pisin.

[9] In those days the Highlands men from Keramugl's place wore only a wide bark belt. From the back there hung a bunch of leaves known as 'as tanket', and from the front a sort of apron woven from string made from another sort of bark, known as a bilum in Tokpisin. A bilum is also a bag woven from the same material.

men. He tells me to look out well because some of the men will fuck my arse. This is true.

So, I cook for the men in the hut. Quickly I learn Tokpisin and the ways of the plantation. It is a small plantation. It is not big like the oil palm plantation. It is better because we all know one another. Also, we know Masta Smit. He is a good man. He thinks we are just children but we know that it is Masta Smit who is the little child. We are about forty men. When there is plenty of coffee to pick Masta Smit brings in the women who are settled near the plantation. Everyone picks the coffee. It is a time we like because Masta Smit gives us pay for each bucket as we fill it. Then we have plenty of money to buy things at Masta Smit's store.

It is at this time that I buy my trousers. I am very proud of my trousers but after some time of wearing trousers I have boils on my arse so I wear my as tanket again. Later, when Annu comes to us, he shows me how to wash my trousers with soap, so I do not have the boils again. He says to me if you want to wear trousers you must first wear the small trousers what the white man call underpants. He says to me when I wash my body I must wash the underpants at the same time. Later, Annu says it is better not to wear trousers at all because the clothes of the white men make us sick. So afterwards I wear the lap-lap like most of us wear.

After this time, Masta Smit comes to the hut where I am cooking. He says Keramugl is a good man. All the men hear this so I am proud. He says Keramugl is a man now. This is true. I have hair under my arms and around my cock. He says I must be the gris manki.[10] This is a good job because I have to help the mechanic. I learn about the tractor and the generator. I am happy to do this work. The mechanic is Grin. He works on the plantation because he is a kilman. He has murdered his wife. For this he has been seven years in the government prison in Port Markham. He tells me that the prison is a bad place. I live with Grin in his hut. He is a good man. He teaches me how to use my cock so that now I want to fuck a woman. But there are no women on the plantation. Some old women work in the factory. They sort the coffee beans but they are old women. I do not think a boy like me can fuck an old woman. Grin says it is a good thing for me to fuck an old woman. He says the old woman will be very happy if Keramugl fucks her. I am thinking Grin is a man who tells stories, that is all. Later I understand that Grin talks the truth.

At this time I think I am a man because I know how to fuck a woman. Later I understand that I am a stupid boy, that's all. I have not become a man and it is at this time that Annu comes to the plantation. Now, the men working on the plantation are ol raskalman but Annu is the kind of man we like quickly. And why is this? It is because Annu is an honest man. Also, he is a strong man who is not afraid of any other man. No man is more of a friend to Annu than another man. Me, at that time, I want to be with Annu all the time. Yes, that is all I want. Then, in the time Annu was with us, I understand what it is like to be dog who always follows his man. But, it is not easy to say why Annu is this kind of man. There are some kind of men who are big men. They are the men we follow.

---

[10] Gris manki: grease monkey, the boy who helps the mechanic.

They are the men who speak the truth. They are the men who are brave. But Annu is more than this. The eye of Annu is straight and the breath of Annu is like the rain. Andrew says all men fall in love with Annu.[11] This is true. It is not the same as the love for a woman who we want to fuck. It is the same as the love for a woman who has given a child to a man who wants a child before he dies.

It is because of all this that I love Annu. It is not because he is a wantok.

In this way, Annu and Tarlie are the same. Sometimes I dream that these two men are the same man.

□□□□□

We do not know it at the time but the life on the plantation of Masta Smit is a good life. Why do I say this?

The plantation of Masta Smit is Narangbon Plantation because this is the name of the place where Masta Smit was born.

Now to me, Masta Smit gives a name that is Manki. He says it is because I am not a boy and I am not yet a man. I am a boy pretending to be a man. This is true. He says I am a monkey man. I do not know then what is a monkey but I am happy with the name. All the same, to myself I am Keramugl. Later, I am Keramugl to all men, when I know that I am not a boy, I am a man.

Yes, it is Annu who makes me think like this.

When Annu comes to Narangbon, first he is the kuskus.[12] We do not know how it happens but we quickly begin to know that Annu is a big man. That is a man who is born to be a leader. Many times we hear Masta Smit shouting at him, like yu bighead kanaka, yu gat tinktink long yu gat savi long olgeta samting, mi laik paitim as bilong yu.[13] Then we hear Annu laughing. It is a good laugh. It is not a bighead laugh. It is a strong laugh that says he is not afraid of any man but also it says all men are his friends. When we hear that laugh, we are very happy and we laugh with Annu. He is a good kuskus and he makes out our pay for us on the pay Saturday. The money is always straight so we like Annu tumas. Yes Andrew, it is true that we love him.

Later, Annu comes to work with us in the coffee as the boss-boy because he knows how to set out and how to record the work. Later when we are at Van Island we remember that it is a good time on Narangbon Plantation living with Annu.

□□□□□

Now one day the brother of Burara comes to Narangbon Plantation. He has all sorts of kago with him like a hanwas.[14] Like a knife that can fold. He has clothes like Masta Smit only they are not white but they have strong colours. We

---

[11] Love in Tokpisin is laik tumas (like too much). Thus I loved him (or her) is Mi laikim em tumas.

[12] Clerk. Cough is kus, so literally, kuskus means cough-cough.

[13] Literally: you bighead kanaka, you think you know everything. I'd like to beat your arse.

[14] Wristwatch.

like his clothes tumas. He has boots on his feet and a hat on his head. He has a book with pictures that show the white men and it shows their women and children. These people are beautiful to see and I understand that Masta Smit is an old man whose time is finished. I understand that the white people in the book have a special knowledge that makes them beautiful and that gives them all their kago. I understand why I am a bush-kanaka, that's all.

This brother of Burara tells us that he works with the white people at the solwara. He says the white men give him plenty of pay for his work. He says he can buy all the things with the money. The name of this man is Tematan.

I ask what is this solwara because I do not know it.

He says I do not know because I am a bush-kanaka. This makes me angry. I say I know I am a bush-kanaka. That is why I ask. This Tematan looks at me and I know that he is afraid of me.

So, this man, Tematan, tells us that the solwara is the place where the land finishes. He says it is the boundary of the land. He says that beyond the solwara it is water as far as the eye can see. He says that the name of this water is solwara because if we drink it, it is salty.

I say that this is only a dream. Tematan does not laugh this time but he says it is true. He says a young man like you must go look at this solwara. I say I cannot think about this solwara. Then Annu talks. He says he has not seen the solwara but he says the white men calls it the sea that is the same word they use for looking. Annu says that when the white man says he looks at the sea he says I see the sea. So I close my eyes but I cannot imagine this sea and I say I cannot imagine something that has no end. Now it is Annu who laughs at me but it is a good laugh that says I am his brother. He says you look at the sky. It is the same. I look at the sky and it is true what Annu says.

All of us want to hear more about the solwara. Tematan stays with us for some days but he does not work. He has plenty of money and he buys food for us.

Now I know about this solwara, I want to see it.

[][][][][]

Working for Masta Smit, all of us are happy. This is because we have food and a place to sleep but we were not happy that we are ol kalabusman.[15] At home we men can do what we want for ourselves day after day but here in the plantation we bilong to Masta Smit.

Before Annu came to us I think I am a kalabusman because I have to work. In those days I am a stupid boy because I do not understand that Annu works but also he does not belong to another man. I see that Annu is his own master but also that he is a good worker and all the masters want him to work for them.

Now the stories this man Tematan tells us make us want to see the solwara. Also we want a hanwas. We want the fine clothes. I have an idea that when I have these things, I will go back to my place so that they will see what a fine man I am and they will see that I am no longer a bush-kanaka. I am thinking all

---

[15] Kalabus is Tokpisin for prison. A kalabusman is a prisoner.

the men of Masta Smit have the same thought. We are stupid, like children, in those days.

So the time comes for Tematan to go back to the solwara. He says he is going back to his work for the white man and he will get plenty more money. All of us, we want to go to the solwara with Tematan. Tematan says no, definitely not, you cannot come with me because you are bush-kanakas, I am ashamed of you.

He walks away from us but then on that same night he comes to the hut where the men sleep. I do not sleep in this hut, I sleep in the hut of Grin but I like to sit in the other hut in the evening. Tematan says alright you can come with me and I will find you work. We are happy and we want to ask him more questions but he says it is not easy and we must do what he tells us. He says we must walk a long way to get to the solwara. Also, we must buy food that will cost plenty of money. If we do not have the money we will die before we get to the solwara. Now this talk makes us sad because we do not have money. Masta Smit gives us food and some money that we spend in the store. But Tematan says yu noken wori because I have money. I will buy the food. When you have work at the solwara you can give the money back to me. We are happy but Burara, the brother of Tematan, says where is this money? I have not seen it, this is your arse talk again and he is angry. But Tematan laughs in the way that I am beginning not to like. He says I have plenty of money and I will show it to you all. Then Tematan goes outside and comes back to us with his wallet. We crowd around him quickly to see what is inside the wallet.

When we see what is in the wallet, we think Tematan thinks we are fools and we want to fight him. Why is this? Because there is no money in the wallet but only some bits of paper. Later, yes, when we are at the solwara we know that this is the money of the white men but in that time before we only know money as the coins that Masta Smit gives to us.

It is Annu himself who says yes this is the money of the white man. He takes one paper from the wallet and shows us the decorations that make it the money, and the picture of Missus Kwin. Annu says we belong to the queen because she is the nambawan of all the white people.

⬚⬚⬚⬚⬚

So, we agree we are going to the solwara with Tematan. That is myself, Keramugl, and Burara and Domus and Pecto and Deni and Kot and some other men. It is not all the men who work for Masta Smit but it is plenty all the same. There are about ten of us.

Now when Annu hears that we are determined to go with Tematan, he talks to us and we listen to him because he is a big man. He says that what Tematan says about the solwara and about the white men is true. He says that it is true we will be able to work for the white men and that we will be able to buy the hanwas and the fine clothes. He says that, all the same, we will not be happy. He says this is because we are men of the mountains and that we know the mountains. Why do we want to leave our home? He says the solwara is a long way and that when we are at the solwara we will not come back. He says that here in Narangbon we know one another and there is one white man who we know also. He says Masta Smit is not a bad man because he knows all of us by name. If there is trouble we can talk to Masta Smit and he will listen to us. Masta Smit, has he ever sent a man away? No and that is because he knows us all, one by one. Annu says when we go to the solwara there are many white men and plenty of men like us. He says there are so many of us that we can die and the white man does not worry because he can find plenty more men to work for him. He says that at the solwara we are not men, we are rubbish.

While Annu is saying this, I look at Tematan. He is looking at the ground. Later I know that Tematan knows that Annu speaks the truth. I know also that Tematan's master has given him money to bring more men to the solwara to work.[16]

We listen to Annu and we know that what he says is true because it is Annu who talks. But as I hear him I know that now I know about the solwara and the beautiful white people who live there I must see it. Yes, the Highlands is ples bilong mi but if I stay, always I will want to see the solwara. I do not want die when I have not seen this other place.

🔲🔲🔲🔲🔲

All of us have the same idea. We want to see the solwara. Annu says he will come with us, so we are very happy now.

That night Grin also talks to me. He says he has seen the solwara. He says do I want him to tell me what it is like? I ask him to tell me. He says it is water, a lot of it. He says and how much water does a man need in his life? Then he spits on the floor and he looks at the floor and he says there is some more water for you Manki. He looks up at me and he says Annu talks the truth to you, it is better that you listen to him.

But I am thinking Grin is a man who has murdered his wife and he has been in the kalabus so his thoughts about everything are like our thoughts when we walk in the night where there is no moon. So I am thinking Grin is mad.

All the same, I thank Grin for teaching me to be a mechanic. When I say this he laughs at me. He says I am only a gris manki but he looks up at me again and says yes you are only a gris manki but you have it inside me to be a good mechanic. I am happy when Grin says this to me.

On the night before we leave Narangbon, Grin gives me all the money he has kept by him. I am not happy to take his money but he says I can bekim long em when I come back home. He says, until that time he will get more pay from Masta Smit. Then he looks away and will not look at me again.

Later I know that Grin talks the truth like Annu. But, it is also true that each man must learn about everything in his own time. This is how the child becomes the man.

Also, when Masta Smit hears that we are going to leave Narangbon, first he is angry but then he also tries to make us forget the idea. He says when you get to the solwara you will know it is better being here at Narangbon with me. He

---

[16] Given in Tokpisin is givim em pinis.

says the solwara will spoil you. We are thinking this is because he wants us to stay with him to do the work. We are thinking this is a lapun man and we do not listen to him. All the same, he gives us our pay and our Krismas.[17] He says suppose you come back I will give you work, don't you worry but I will never see you again and he looks sad but we are stupid and we do not listen to him.

Later we understand that what Masta Smit says is true also.

It is all true, this talk of Annu and of Grin and of Masta Smit.

On Narangbon we belong to Masta Smit. It is true. But it is our fault. It is us who have left our homes. Some men have done something wrong, like Grin. He cannot go back home. Others have done things they are running away from. Some men are loners, and some, this is my type, cannot sit down until they have seen other things.

Alright! You understand what I am saying? All of us are the kinds of men who have no wives and children. All of us are the type who has no home.

So, on Narangbon, all these types of raskalman have a place to sleep and food to eat. On Narangbon, we are men who Masta Smit knows by a name. All the men on Narangbon call me by the name Manki but also they know I am Keramugl and they know the eyes of Keramugl and they know the ways of Keramugl. Also, they know that Keramugl is a good man. If I get sick, everyone knows and they will help me. Suppose I die, everyone will be sorry and they noken lusim tinktink long mi.

This is a good thing.

But, later on the solwara, at this Van Island Palm Oil Development Company, we learn a big thing. We learn that we are rubbish men. If I die then no one knows and no one worries. Our masters throw our bodies into the sea. They will forget Keramugl. And another thing, a big thing: we can no longer go back home. It costs too much money. We are truly in the Kalabus.

[][][][][]

When we leave Narangbon the rain is falling. I have a big idea as I walk out of Narangbon. It is that this part of my life is finished. I cannot go back into it. I can go forward only. But, at the same time, I do not know to where I am going forward. I am thinking of the solwara but I cannot see it. Annu says it is like the sky but the sky is up there. I cannot imagine it being down here beside the ground.

Am I afraid? No, I am not afraid. This is because I am with Annu.

If it is only Tematan. Yes, I am thinking I would be afraid.

Also, I have the idea that we will travel for one or two days only. Then we will be at the solwara. But we travel for many days. I forget how many days and nights we travel. During the journey, I became another man. Keramugl, the boy, is left in Narangbon.

We walk from Narangbon up onto the hills that are above the valley. Our paths in the Highlands follow the ridges so it is easy to walk. Sometimes there are houses beside the path. The houses make me think of my home in the time

---

[17] Annual bonus.

before but it is nothing to me now. The men in these houses speak our language so they are our wantoks and there is no trouble and we sleep in their houses and they give us food.

All this time, Annu is one of us men. He does not make himself be the big man. He lets Tematan do the talking. In this way the men who we meet do not know Annu is different from us. But we know that Annu is different. Annu gives us our strength, it is not Tematan. All the same, some of the men we meet want to know why we are not afraid to go to the solwara. They think it is Tematan who makes us brave. Some of these wantoks want to come with us but here I see that Tematan is clever. He says nogat. Why is this?

When Tematan brings us to the white men, they give him money for us. In this way he is a rich man. You understand what I am saying? Tematan knows Keramugl and Burara and Annu. He knows that we are good men who will not cheat him. When he stays at Narangbon he watches us. These other men who we meet on the road, Tematan does not know them. He does not want to lose his money on these men if they run away.

[][][][][]

We meet a small boy when we sleep in his father's house. His name is Neki. He is only six or seven years old. Annu makes friends with Neki and Neki laikim Annu tru, tumas, tumas, so that he will not leave Annu's side. Neki follows us for one day, he sleeps with us and we think he will return to his home. But at the following night he is still with us. Annu is angry with him saying Neki you must go home to your father. But Neki looks at Annu's feet and says he will follow him even if Annu beats him. Then Annu laughs and says Neki is not a dog, he must go back to his father. Annu tells Neki that the place where we are going is a bad place where the white man eats children like him. But Neki is not stupid and he says if Annu is going to this place he is not afraid. So I am thinking this boy understands things. All the same, the boy is a problem for us. We cannot steal him from his father and Annu says the solwara is not a good place for a child. Also, Annu cannot take Neki back to his father because the boy will only become more attached to Annu. We understand this because we know Annu as the man we love also. So that night we work out a plan to get the boy home. I, Keramugl, must take the boy back.

It works in this way. In the morning I wake up Neki and I tell him I am taking him back to his father. He says no, so I tie him with a rope. He is crying out for Annu but Annu is pretending to sleep. So I carry Neki back to his place and all the time he is crying. I say if you cry out I will beat you very bad with a stick so that you will bleed. Now he is afraid of Keramugl because he does not know I am a good man who would not hurt a child. All he sees is this Keramugl who is strong and who says bad things. I say that the Annu-man is a masalai nogut.[18] I say that the Annu-man has a way to make all men love him so that they will follow him. I say that the Annu-man takes us bush-kanakas to sell to the white men. I say that the white men do not want children because they

---

[18] Spirit no good.

166

cannot work. I say that because of this, the Annu-man will kill him because he cannot get money for him. I say I feel sorry for him so I am bringing him back to his father. I can see that Neki is listening to me and thinking I speak the truth because he can hear that tok bilong mi i kamap belly hot. This is true because I am not happy to make a bad story about Annu. Olsem, baimbai, Neki listens to me so I take the rope off him and he runs home. I am sad but as I turn around to walk back Neki shouts out to me, later I will find this Annu again. And it is true, as we know.

[][][][][]

We walk for many days in the place of my wantoks. We walk along the ridge with the big mountains above us, and with the valley and big river down below us. We call the river, Orami. On the other side of the valley there are more mountains. Planti taim the sky comes down to hide the mountains.

At the time, I do not think this place, our home, is different from other places. I think then that what is called the Hailains is like all places that are not the solwara. That is why I want to see the solwara.

Now I have travelled to the solwara and to Van Island I know a lot more about things. I know that my home is different from other places. My place is a very big valley that they call the Orami Valley. All the white men and the government know the name of the Orami valley.

So in time, after many days of walking, we come to the end of the Orami Valley. All this time we are walking away from Narangbon the ren i kam daun long mipela. But we are happy with the rain because the rain is part of our home.

We walk down into the valley close to where the river i dai pinis. The ground is stony and there are many trees so that we cannot see far. Then we come to a bridge that crosses a deep, rocky ravine.[19] As we cross the bridge Annu says listen, we can hear the water. It is true, we can hear the water crying out to us but when we look down into the ravine it is dark tumas so we cannot see it. Annu says this is where the Orami River finishes. He says it falls down over the edge of a mountain and it finds its own way to the solwara. I ask Annu how is it that the water can go up onto the mountain so that it can fall down again. He laughs at me and he says Keramugl, the solwara is below the mountains, everything goes down to the sea.

Annu says to me, Keramugl you have a lot to learn but you will learn it fast because you are a good man and in time you will be very clever so that people will come to you for the answers to their problems. At first I am thinking Annu is teasing me but he comes to me and he holds my hand and he talks to me with his thumb on the palm of my hand. Then, when Annu holds my hand I feel very happy and I am thinking that this journey to the solwara is my life.

Now when we cross the bridge I think that we must be close to the solwara. All of us think the same thing and Deni, who is a clever man in many things, he

---

[19] What Keramugl actually says is wanpela kain barat i daun tumas na em i gat planti olgeta ston nabaut, nabaut. One fellow kind ditch he down too much and him he got plenty all stones about and about.

asks Tematan if we are near the solwara. Now this is where Tematan is clever because we are many, many days walking from the solwara but he says it is not far. Later, I understand why he says this, because one thing is true and that is by crossing the bridge we are leaving our home where men speak the same language. On the other side of the bridge, beyond all the trees, the people speak another language and they do not know us. If Tematan tells the truth that we still have many days to go some of us may be afraid and go back to Narangbon. At the bridge it is not a hard thing to do. But on the other side of the bridge only Tematan can take us back. So Tematan lies to us to be sure we must follow him to the solwara.

[] [] [] [] []

In the days that follow I learn many things. So many things that my brain is confused.

After we have crossed the bridge and come out of the trees the night has come. Also the rain stops falling.

A small haus is beside the path. An old woman is sitting on the ground beside the door. Tematan talks to the woman. He gives her some moni and then he tells us we will sleep in the house. He says the old woman will cook us our kaukau.

I do not like this haus. This is because although the haus is strong and tidy, it is a haus that belongs to nobody and too many men have slept in it. The masalai of the haus is confused. It is asking why people are coming into it and out of it all the time but not stopping. There is no peace in this haus. As I lie in the dark there is no sound but for the breathing of my friends. I wake up many times during the night. I am dreaming of men talking. The talking is confused and crazy. It is not single words but it is many men talking altogether and I cannot understand what they say. I remember this because this dream has not happened to me before. After, in my life in the kampani, in the life after we have crossed the bridge, this dream comes to me many times and I learn that it is part of life. But then it is new to me and I am afraid. I am thinking that the masalai of the haus knows the thoughts of Keramugl when I sleep so I am afraid to sleep. I am lying in the dark thinking. This thinking in the night is new to me olsem. Night is the time for sleeping. Then, I have a good thought. I am thinking of Annu and as I am thinking of Annu I can feel his body lying close to me in the dark. I listen to him breathing and I am happy. I am thinking another new idea and this is that if the bad masalai tries to get into the dream of Annu, then Annu will defeat it. I am thinking that the masalai knows that Annu is strong in this way and it is afraid of Annu. As I am thinking this I sleep.

[] [] [] [] []

Olsem, I am thinking it was when I cross that small bridge that I enter my new life. I am afraid I will lose my name. This is why some men, many men, take a new name when they come to the solwara. They take a name that they hear on the solwara. But I fight myself to keep my name that is Keramugl.

Masta Smit gave me the name Manki but that was my name for Narangbon. Now I am Keramugl again. When I kalapim long bris mi lusim olgeta samting pinis. That is why I hold on to my name. I do not want to lose my name. When we are in the kampani, I tell this to Burara and to Domus and to Pecto and to Deni and to Kot. I say I will keep your names for you. At first they laugh at me but later they say thank you Keramugl you have not forgotten who we are although we, ourselves, have forgotten.

All the masters can give me the name of Manki but I am Keramugl.

[][][][][]

So, it is night but Tematan is saying hurry up we must walk now before the sun is hot. I am surprised to hear this because I have not thought before that the sun can be too hot. Also, Tematan says we must carry with us the kaukau that the old woman cooked.[20] So very quickly we are walking and I am not fully awake. I am thinking it is like Narangbon this waking up too quickly in the dark, only now we are not getting money for being unhappy. It is better for the dawn to wake a man. As we are walking I say this to Tematan. He says shut up manki-man. If you don't like this you can go bek long ples bilong yu. It is then that I understand that I cannot go home. So I keep my mouth shut.

Even before the dawn comes up, I smell something that is new to me. Later I know this is the smell of the dry kunai grass.[21] When the dawn mist has gone, I see that we are in another place altogether. I cannot see big mountains on top and I cannot see a valley down below. All I can see is the ground going up a little and down a little and there is only kunai, nothing else but kunai. I can see that the sky is bigger than I have seen it before.

All of us are quiet. We walk along a narrow path with the kunai on each side. I can see that many feet have walked this path and I think so many men have walked to the solwara. I think: And have so many come back home again? Also, it is true, the sun is hotter than at home. My mind is confused because I think if the solwara i kamap long ananit long maunten, olsem long Annu i tok bipo, how is it that the sun is hotter? [22]

All this is new to me so I ask Tematan: Is this the solwara? Tematan does not answer me so I ask again: Is this the solwara?

Now Tematan stops walking and he turns to look at me. I can see he is angry but then I know that I am angry also so I am not afraid of him. It is now that I understand that I do not like this man Tematan. He says you are a stupid boy. Do you see the solwara? I say no but I look into his eyes. Then I see that Tematan is not happy but I am not sorry for him, I want to fight him because I am not happy also. I feel a pain in my belly and I know that it will stop there until after I have beaten Tematan. At this time I have forgotten Annu. I have forgotten what he said to me. Also, I have forgotten Keramugl.

---

[20] Kukim pinis.

[21] *Imperata cylindrica*, an invasive grass which covers millions of hectares of New Sudan.

[22] Ananit = Underneath. Bipo = Before.

I say to Tematan I do not know the solwara so I am asking you is this the solwara? I tell Tematan he is a bighead. I say to Tematan you don't know the solwara, you have tricked us, that's all. You are a rascal who steals things that's all and you have stolen us to sell us to the white man.

Now when I say this I can see that Tematan is very angry. He wants to kill me. And I think this is a good thing because I can kill him also. So Tematan runs at me and he shouts and he hits me on my head. This makes me mad and I want to kill this man Tematan. Yes, we are like two wild pigs that fight. There is no sense and it will stop only when one pig runs away or one pig is dead. Yes, we are mad and we can listen to no man.

But in my madness of fighting I hear a voice that stops me fighting as I hear it. I remember who I am and I remember Annu because the voice is Annu. Tematan has stopped fighting also.

Now, you must understand that this is the first time that Annu talks for himself since we left Narangbon.

And I look at Annu and as I see him I am happy. I feel that the pain in my belly is gone. I am ashamed that I want to beat my brother.

All I want to do is look at Annu and hear his voice.

I have forgotten what Annu said. It is not what he says that stops us fighting but the sound of his voice. He is a big man but it is not the strength of his arms or of his chest that makes him big. It is not the loudness of Annu's voice that makes us want him. No it is not, definitely, nogat ya. But Annu's voice is very sweet and very strong at the same time. That makes us look at him. We look at his eyes that look at us. Now we see Annu's eyes we want Annu to watch us all the time.

At that time, when I had stopped fighting Tematan, I thought that nothing in my life can be bad if I have Annu in my life. Everything else is nothing. I did not lose that idea for all the time I work for the kampani.

[][][][][]

In this kunai country, the sun is very hot and the wind is very hot and the sky is very big and white and we are hungry for water. But Annu is with us so I am not afraid even to die. I do not think of my home. I think this is my life and I am happy. I am happy to go to the solwara like the water from the mountains.

We sleep one night in the kunai country. We sleep in a cave. We have no food but there is spring water. Tematan says if we get up early and walk in the dark we will come to the end of the ples kunai before the sun is too hot. We say nothing because we do not know if Tematan speaks the truth. But Annu says it is true so that is alright.

So we walk in the dark. At dawn we see some trees on top of a hill. We are happy to see the trees and being happy like this we begin to talk again. Tematan says the trees are the end of the ples kunai. I want to ask if this is the solwara but I do not want Tematan to think I am a foolish boy again so I ask what is on the other side of the trees. Tematan says the place of the white men is inside the trees. Then he looks at me and he says it is not the solwara, Manki. Now when I hear this I am not afraid because Annu is with us. Also, as I look at this place I think it is like Narangbon because at Narangbon Masta Smit grows his coffee trees underneath the Yar trees. I think this must be the way of all white men.

Olsem I want to ask why we are going to the white man's place, so I ask Tematan what is the name of this place. Tematan says the name is Tesin.[23] He says the white men call all their places Tesin. There is Gauman Tesin, and Mison Tesin, and Pilen Tesin. I say alright why are we going to this Tesin and Tematan says because we will go in a balus.[24]

[]][][]

Now when Tematan says we will go in the balus, am I afraid? I do not remember because the idea of going in the balus is new to me. So I look at Annu. All of us are looking at Annu. But Tematan is not looking at Annu, he is looking at us. But he is thinking the same as us. We are all thinking that Annu is the man who will make us strong men in this place of the white man that is not our home.

It is true, Annu makes us strong. He says yes we will go in the balus if Tematan says so. Annu says he wants to go in the balus himself. He says he wants to know what it is like. He says all the white men go in the balus all the time. He says the white men are only men after all so that if they can go in the balus, then also we can go in the balus. So we are not afraid. I feel happy to be going in the balus.

Then Deni mekim kus liklik.[25] He says we are true bush-kanakas. He says we do not understand the white men. He says we do not know what they will do with us. He says the white men are not our friends and he says they come to our place but we do not know why they have come. He says he is not afraid but he does not know the ways of the white men. He says he is worried by his own ignorance.

Then Kot calls out I have something to say. He says that he has heard that the white men have a kind of sorcery that can make you die. He says it is a kind of stick that they can point at us. The white men can make the stick cry out at us and we will fall down dead. He says we do not have anything to stop the white men from killing us in this way. When Kot has finished talking he looks at the ground.

Before, on Narangbon, we listen to Tematan for the answer. But now we do not want to hear Tematan, we want to hear Annu. We know that Annu speaks the truth. Annu says I tell you the truth when I say you must not be afraid of the white man. The white man is the same as you and me. You must not forget that when I was a boy I was taken to live with the white men in the mison tesin. In this place I was able to know the white men and their ways.

Annu says there are good white men and there are bad white men. He says this is like all men. He says Kot says we do not know the ways of the white men, this is true. But mi tok long yu stret, the white man does not know our ways

---

[23] Station.

[24] Aeroplane.

[25] A little cough.

either. This makes the white man afraid of us also. Yes this is true, the white man is afraid of us. The white men are only men. You must not forget this. But, it is true they have kago that we do not have. They have the stick that kills. Ol givim nem long em, masket. They have the balus. Ol i gat kapa long haus bilong em.[26] Sampela man i gat tinktink that these things come to the white men because they call out to the big man who the white men say made everything and made us men. They call this big man Got. Many men think this is true because when the man mison comes to a place, the first thing he does is to make a ples balus. Then he makes a haus for this Got. They call it sios and then they sing to Got inside the sios.[27] They sing to Got and Got sends then the balus with the kago.

Then Annu says you must hear me well. Annu says this is not true. He says that when he lived in the mison tesin he learns to read the white man's books and in this way he learns that in another place there are white men who make this kago and they send it in the balus. [28] He says this making of the kago is not a big thing and in one place called Amerika there are black people just like us. He says these black people from Amerika were stolen from their place by the white men but that these black people are clever. He says these black Amerikans have learnt how to make the kago for themselves.[29]

To me what Annu says is like a dream but I know he speaks the truth.

Then Annu says, again, listen to me well.[30] He says are you listening? We say Yasa. He says sapos yu gat tinktink long ol waitman i gat hamamas with all this kago, I tell you the white man is not happy. All the white men are not happy. They are always crying out to this Got to make them happy but they are not happy. They know that other men make the kago but olsem they go down on their knees on the ground inside the sios and they cry to Got to give them kago. These men are mad. They have forgotten how to be happy by looking at the sky and looking at the mountains and being with each other and by talking to each other. I feel sorry for these men.

Annu tok, yu gat savi long tok bilong mi? We say Yesa! Annu tok, yu gat savi long mi? We say Yesa, again. Annu says alright then, you understand that with all his kago, the white man is not happy? Then, Annu is quiet.

He is waiting for us to shout Yesa!

So we singaut, Yesa!

Annu says alright, you must remember this when the white man is angry and when he acts mad and when you think he does not like you because you are a kanaka. Then you must remember that the white man does not understand our ways and that he is afraid and that all his kago has made him mad. It has made him mad because his only thought is that another man will steal his kago. He is always thinking why has this man got more kago than me? This idea makes him mad.

---

[26] Tin roof = Kapa.

[27] Church.

[28] Lived = Long taim en i stap pinis.

[29] Stolen = Stil pinis.

[30] Again = Wantaim moa yet.

Then Annu says it is better that you feel sori for the white man because he is not happy. We have no kago but we are happy many times so we know one thing that the white man does not know. We know that it is not the kago that makes a man happy. We are not worried that a man will steal our kago because we have no kago. We have nothing like this!

Then Annu says you must remember all this. You must feel sorry for the white man. If he makes you very angry and you cannot feel sorry for him then you must remember me. You must remember what I am telling you today. And another thing, you cannot fight the white man, because he has the masket. The white man can kill you isi tumas.[31]

Now, Tematan says yes Annu what you say is true but one day we kanakas will have the masket and then we can kill the white man.

At this Annu laughs. He says yes you can kill the white man but one day he will find you when you do not have the masket. Then he will take you to the kalabus and he will say he is going to kill you for Got. How will he kill you? Not with the masket. No, he will put a rope around your neck and he will hang you from a tree until you are dead. All these things will happen in the way of the white men so that plenty of men can see it happening. The name of all this is Jastes. Sapos you kill a white man you will understand that the white men will do everything he can to find you and give you this Jastes. This is because he wants everyone to know that you have been given this Jastes because you have killed a white man. This way, all the kanakas will learn that they cannot kill a white man.

Now we all feel sad because we think that when we live with the white man we will not be happy.

Then Annu says you no can forget Masta Smit. He says Masta Smit is a white man. He is not a bad man although he is mad sometimes. Sometimes he helps us and sometimes he is a funny man who makes us laugh. Is he not just a man? Annu says you all must not worry. Think of Masta Smit. We can be happy together. Also, I know that one day all of us, white men and kanakas, can be just men together.

Because Annu says this we know it is true so we are happy.

At last Annu says we are going to the solwara. He says we have come too far to go back home. He says this is our journey. He says to reach the solwara we have to go in the balus. So, it is no good that we stand here gossiping[32]. We must go to the tesin and we must go in the balus and we must go to the solwara. He says you are not afraid to be with me?

We all say Yesa!

[][][][][]

As we are walking, Tematan says the name of the tesin is Karandawa. When he says this, I am thinking Karandawa is like Narangbon. When we reach Karandawa we are tired of walking. The journey is longer than we think because

---

[31] Easy too much.

[32] Stap long hea na mekim toktok ol nabaut-nabaut.

Karandawa is bigger than we think. At Narangbon there are not many houses. There is the house of Masta Smit, there is the coffee factory, there is the store, there is the trade store. There are the small houses in which we live. And that is it. But Karandawa has more houses than I have seen together. More houses than I can count. The houses are in straight lines like Masta Smit plants the coffee. There are straight roads between the houses like the roads of Narangbon. But the roads of Karandawa are bigger. Now, I understand what is a tesin. It is a place where the white man makes things in the way he likes. That is in straight lines. It is true also that the white man likes to plant trees beside the roads.

Later, I understand that a tesin is where men and women come together to do things. But it is the white man that brings the tesin long mipela long Hailains. We have the Singsing ground where we meet but we do not live there. The white man likes to live with his brothers in the tesin.

Now, as I remember these things, I am no longer a boy who knows nothing. I have become a man because I have learnt many things. Also, I have seen many places. I have been to Port Markham. So now, I know that Karandawa is a small place. But at that time a town is a new thing to me. Everything I see is new. I am thinking this is what it must be like to be born. Then everything is new. We only know our mother and we only know things when she shows them to us. If our mother says it is good then it is good. If our mother says it is bad then it is bad. But here in Karandawa, Annu is our mother but Annu himself is like a newborn baby. What does Annu know of Karandawa?

So, we all walk close to Tematan because in this new place Tematan is our boss. If we want to eat in this place we must wait for Tematan to teach us. If we want to shit we must wait for Tematan to show us. We are like newborn babies but Tematan is not our mother. Tematan is a bighead who wants us to see that he is a big man in this Karandawa. He talks to us like we are true kanakas. I do not like the way he talks to us. It is like we belong to him. Even Annu himself is like a newborn baby. He says to us I know the mison tesin but this place is bigger. He says we must follow Tematan. Later, I understand that Annu is following Tematan, it is true, but also he is learning about the place.

Also, we are hungry so we follow Tematan because we think he will find food for us.

It is day time but there are not many people about but Tematan knows where we are going. Everywhere I look, there are buildings. I feel sick in my stomach and I am thinking that I want to eat before we go into the balus but I do not want to ask Tematan. I do not want the other men to know that I am an ignorant boy. I want to be a man in this town but it is hard to feel like a man. We are all quiet. We are walking slowly like children behind Tematan and I feel ashamed. I am thinking of Neki and I am happy he is with his father.

[][][][][]

We follow Tematan to the airfield. The ples balus is a big, empty space like a big Singsing ground. I am thinking this would be a good place for all people to meet to have a big singsing. Also, I can see the mountains and the sky so the pain in my belly is gone. I see that Annu is happy also.

We see a very big haus. I have not seen a haus like this before. I think there are many things I will see that I have not seen before. Tematan says we will go to this place to eat and to wash and to sleep. Annu says the haus is a store for the things that the balus brings. Ol givim nem long dispela haus, hauskago. Tematan says it is the store for the men that the balus takes away.

As we come near to the hauskago I look at it and I want to sit down and die. It has a very big door and Annu says sometimes the balus sleeps in the hauskago. This is why the door is big. All the time I am expecting to see a white man but a kanaka stands at the door. He is like me but wears the clothes of the white man like Tematan. Tematan tells us to sit down outside. He talks like a bighead but we obey him. We cannot do anything else. We are ignorant and we are hungry.

When Tematan has finished talking to the man he comes to us and says we must go into the hauskago. A kuskus will write our names in a book and we must put our thumb print beside the name. Tematan says when we have done this they will give us some food and they will give us a place to sleep in the hauskago and they will show us the water for washing and the hole for shitting.

Now, Deni stands up and he calls out. He says, suppose I do not want to give my name? Suppose I do not want to put my mark in the book? He grins at us because he thinks it is time for us to sit on top of Tematan.

But Tematan says alright then you cannot come into the hauskago and you will not get food.

Deni has no reply and he sits down. He is ashamed of himself. We are nothing but rubbish men in this Karandawa.

So we follow Tematan and we give our names to the man at the door. We are not happy but Annu says we gave our names to Masta Smit and we did not die. This is true but I see that the kuskus at the door is looking at Annu. I know he is asking who is this man who talks like this?

You must listen to what I am saying. I don't want you to think we are complete bush-kanakas. No, in the time before, we had lived and worked at Narangbon. So, we know many things about how white men do things. We know a little of the Tokpisin language and we know about the haus pekpek that the white man likes so much.[33] All the same, everything is much bigger than we know in the time before. It is strange to our eyes. We are confused and we need someone to show us what to do. Anyone seeing us at that time would think we have just come from our mothers but that is not true. We are confused, that is all. Because we are confused we have to do what Tematan tells us. It is like we belong to Tematan. This is a bad thing because Tematan is a bad man.

But at that time, we have Annu with us. Even if Annu is as ignorant as us, we know that in the end Annu will sit on top of Tematan. We watch Annu all the time. If Annu does a thing, it is alright. So Annu goes to the man. He gives his name to him and he gives his mark to him. We do the same.

Inside the hauskago there are many men. I have not seen so many men together in a haus in my life. So again I am confused but I follow Annu and the others follow me. Tematan shows us where we can sleep and how we can do

---

[33] Haus pekpek = Lavatory. Literally house shit.

things. Quickly we are sitting down eating kaukau and a meat that is new to us. This is the tinpis[34] that all men eat at the solwara.

[][][][][]

When we have washed and eaten again we sit down to talk a little. We talk to the other men in the hauskago and in this way we discover that there are many languages. Some of these men use Tokpisin, so in this way we can talk to them a little.

I talk to one man who says his name is Weno. He is a young man who has a red skin. He says that many men have a red skin in his place. He says his place is called Tande. He says yes, Tande is a gauman tesin like Karandawa. Also, it is a mison tesin.

Weno tells me that in the time when he is a child the white men come to his village and take him away with some other boys to live with them in the mison tesin at Tande. I am thinking to myself, this is like the life of Annu also. He says he is frightened and he is sori to leave his father and his mother but he thinks that one day he will return to them. He says he is put with many other children to learn to read and write but he says first he is ill and then he escapes. He says that he can only think of his mother and father but he does not know how to find them. He says the white men find him in Tande. Ol kalabusim em pinis.[35] In the kalabus they give him food and they are kind to him but they do not take him back home. They take him back to the mison tesin. He is made to work in the haus kuk. Later he works in the garden but he is sori he cannot read or write.

Yes, this Weno is a young man. He is the same age as me but he is a man. He is not a boy like me. He knows things and he is a bikhet liklik but he does not think he is better than me. He is arrogant because he knows things from doing them. He tells me I ask many questions but he says he is happy to tell his story. He says no man listens to him like I listen to him. He says he likes me tumas.

Also, I like this man Weno tumas. He is a funny man who can tell stories. He tells me that in his own language, Weno means puddle. He says he is his father's first born, born when his father was a young man like himself now. He says when his father saw him for the first time, em hamamas tumas, tumas. It is the time of the heavy rains. Weno's father is so excited that he runs out of the hut where Weno's mother is lying to tell his friends that he has a son. Immediately he falls down into a big puddle. He thinks: this is my little son's fault. So, I will give him the name Weno. Weno laughs when he says this and I laugh also but he is not happy to think of his father who he will not see again.

Mi laikim dispela man tumas, tumas.

I ask Weno why he is going to the solwara. He says it is because he is too much trouble in Tande. He says he does not want to stay in the mison tesin but he cannot go home because he does not know the way. Weno says this idea

---

[34] Tinpis = Tinned fish.
[35] They put him in prison.

176

makes him longlong liklik so that he is angry many times and wants to fight.[36] He says he likes to drink beer and fuck the prostitutes in Tande. He says he likes to drink the beer to forget his mother and father. He says when he has drunk the beer he is mad and he fights everyone. Weno says that plenty of times he is put in the kalabus in Tande by the polisboi because of his fighting. He says there are plenty trabelman like him in Tande.

Then, Weno says a man comes to Tande who wants to baiem boi to work at the solwara.[37] This man tokim long ol masta bilong mison na ol masta bilong gauman. They bring all of us trabelman together and the Magistrate talks to us. He says sapos yupela no laikim go long solwara wantaim long dispela man husat em I laik baiem yu mi kalabusim yupela and later I will give you very hard work that will kill you all. I am tired of you all.[38]

Weno says when he hears the magistrate talk like this he wants to fight him as well. But then he thinks he has nothing in Tande and he is only a rubbish man who will die one way or another. So he thinks beta moa yet mi go long solwara.[39] He thinks I can die at the solwara just as I can die in Tande.

Weno laughs when he has said this. He says he has no worries. He only wants to see what will happen. I am thinking to myself, this is a good way to think of things.

But then Weno says he has got one small worry. He says that when he arrived with the other men from Tande – two days earlier – a master comes with some papers.[40] He says there is one paper for each man and that each man must put his mark on this paper. Weno says he does not know what these papers are for. He says he wants to ask the white man what the papers are for but he is afraid to ask.

I say to Weno I do not know what the papers are for but I will ask Annu.

When I return to the place in the hauskago to find the men from Narangbon, I see that Annu is sleeping so I am thinking I will ask him about these papers in the morning.

I cannot sleep at first because I am worrying about the papers also.

But then I am thinking of my new friend Weno and I fall asleep.

[][][][][]

So the following day we are awake at dawn and we have washed and we have eaten. We do not know what will happen this day because Tematan is not with us. I am thinking of my friend Weno and I am thinking I will see him again. This makes me remember the paper he talks about last night and I want to ask Annu about the paper.

---

[36] Longlong = Mad/crazy.

[37] Baiem boi = Buying 'boys'. Tematan is a recruiting agent.

[38] . . . suppose you fellows no like go long saltwater one-time long (with the) man who wants to recruit you , me imprison you all.

[39] . . . better more yet I go long saltwater.

[40] Arrived = Kam pinis.

But as I am thinking of this I see that Tematan has come with a white man and also with two polisboi. I am thinking now that the white man is here, something will happen. Again I feel the pain in my belly. The white man is carrying a small suitcase. There is a small table by the door. The white man sits behind the table and Tematan stands beside him.

This white man is not like Masta Smit. He is a young man and he does not have a big belly like Masta Smit. He is tall and his hair is black so that his skin looks very white. This man is like Andrew used to be. He is a pretend master, that is all. He is afraid of us because he does not know us and because he does not know himself. But at that time I did not know these things and I am thinking so this is a white man who is a master on top of us bush-kanakas because he knows everything. Yes, I am just a stupid bush-kanaka.

Now Tematan calls out to us be quiet and to listen carefully. But it is not only us who are listening. All the other men in the hauskago are listening. Then Tematan calls our names from the book. Annu is always the first name to be called. It is the way at Narangbon and it is the way here. I am thinking that it is something that the white man knows only. That is putting the names in the same line. So Tematan calls out Annu and Annu calls back Yesa. We all call back Yesa but we are not happy. Then I am thinking of Masta Smit. Tematan says you must all say Yesa to your name olsem yu mus kamap long soldiaboi.[41] But I do not know what is a soldiaboi. It is later at Van Island that I learn what is a soldiaboi.

When Tematan has finished he gives the book to the white man. Then the white man talks to us in Tokpisin. We do not understand too good what he is saying but from time to time he stops and he lets Tematan translate his words into our language. This is the same for all the men in the hauskago and there is a lot of confused talking and I am thinking of the masalai in the house where we sleep before we leave the Highlands.

Nau, dispela waitman, em i no tok long gudpela pasin.[42] How is it that I am thinking this way? Because this white man does not know us. He talks in a way that makes mipela kamap samting nating.[43] I am thinking suppose we die inside the balus, this white man will not be sorry for us. And as I listen to his talking I am unhappy. I know the white man talks in this way because he does not have the courage to know us as men. I am thinking that the white man is hiding behind the table. He does not stand up to talk to us. Masta Smit always comes to us when he talks to us. Sometimes he touches us when he talks to us.

[][][][][]

This white man asks if we have had enough to eat. We are quiet. Then Annu shouts out Yesa and we all shout Yesa. The white man asks if we have a good place to wash. We all shout out Yesa. The white man asks if we have a good place to sleep. We all shout out Yesa. But I think this white man does not care if

---

[41] All-same yu come-up long soldier-boy: then you must come to the soldier.

[42] Now, this-fellow white man, him he no talk good-fellow fashion.

[43] . . . me-fellow come up something-nothing.

we eat or sleep or wash. His only worry is that if we are hungry we might like to fight him. This is why he brings the polisboi with him.

Then the white man takes some papers out of his suitcase. I know that these are the papers that Tematan talks about and I feel the pain in my belly again. The white man says that he has one paper for each man and we must put our mark on the paper before we can go to the solwara.

Now, mi gat wori long dispela paper because of my talk with Tematan. Mi lukim long Annu and I see that the pes bilong em i kamap strong.[44] So I ask Annu what is this paper? I am thinking sapos mipela no laik mekim mak long pepa then we will be stuck in Karandawa and we don't know how to get home. Mi no laikim dispela samting.

When I ask Tematan, he tells me to shut up and listen to the master. I am ashamed that he has shouted at me like I am a child. I am ashamed that all the men in the hauskago have heard Tematan talking to me like that. I shut my mouth.

The white man coughs. He says he will call our names, one by one, and then we must come forward to sign the paper.

I am happy that the first name is Annu.

[][][][][]

The white man calls Annu.

Annu does not move.

Annu, the white man calls again. I am sorry for the white man. I look at Tematan and Tematan is not happy because he knows Annu is not a man husat i ken sindaun antap long em.[45]

Tasol[46], Annu does not talk strong. He talks to the white man and he says something in English that I can understand a little from Narangbon. He says:

Please sir, can you tell us what the paper is for?

Now we did not know that Annu can talk Inglis. It is a big thing and I can see that Tematan is worried that Annu will sit down on top of him because he can talk English.

Also, I can see that the white man is surprised and he is a little worried. It is a new thing to him that a kanaka can talk his language.

To me, Annu talking Inglis is a good thing. I want to shout out that Annu is our man and that he is a big man. I want to shout out that we will do anything that Annu tells us to do. The others have the same idea and they begin to call out:

Annu, Annu, Annu.

This makes the other men in the hauskago come up to us to hear what is happening. It is then that I understand Annu. Annu is a strong masalai who can

---

[44] . . . face belong him he come up strong. He frowns.

[45] . . . a man who is that he can sit down on top of him.

[46] Tasol comes from 'That's all' but it is also used as English might use 'Only', 'Except that', or 'But'.

make men love him so that they will die for him. Also, because he is a strong masalai, he can make men afraid of him so that they hate him.

If Annu says to us fall down on the ground for me, we will eat the ground for him. If Annu says to us kill the white man, we will kill the white man. The white man understands this and he is afraid. He talks to one soldiaboi and this man goes out of the hauskago.

Then the white man looks at Annu. He tries to smile but the smile is dead on his face. He cannot speak so we see that Annu is so strong that he can stop the white man from talking by looking at him.

All of us bush-kanakas are quiet now and the white man cannot speak but he is looking at Annu because Annu is looking at him and Annu is smiling at him. I know that Annu is looking into the eyes of this white man like he looks into the eyes of us, his men. And I know that Annu is telling this white man not to be afraid. The white man is hearing Annu but – and this is something I understand later – he is not wanting to hear Annu because all his brothers have told him that the white man is on top of the kanaka. This is the most important law.

Alright, so Annu talks again. He talks in Tokpisin so that we understand what he is saying. He says, please sir, we must use Tokpisin so that everyone can understand our talk with each other.

So the white man says alright what do you want to know? Annu says what is this paper that you want us to sign? Then the white man talks about things we do not understand although he is using Tokpisin. He says the paper is a kontrak. He says the law of New Sudan says we cannot go to the solwara if we have not signed this kontrak.

I am confused then because I have heard about this New Sudan when I was at Narangbon. Before, Annu tells us that New Sudan is a bikpela place and that we are all inside this New Sudan. Narangbon, all the mountains we can see, our homes where we were born and the solwara. They are all inside this New Sudan. Annu says that there are other big places like New Sudan. Inglan is one and Amerika is another. Alright, I can understand this but now the white man says that this New Sudan knows how to talk like a man because it has laws like Masta Smit has laws for what we have to do at the plantation. So now I have an idea that this New Sudan is a very strong animal that rules our lives. I am thinking we live inside the belly of this animal. I am thinking this animal is so strong that we must obey it all the time.

Annu asks the white man what the kontrak says and the man looks afraid again. He looks at all of us and he says yupela no ken wori long dispela you just sign it so that I can give you some money. And Annu talks back to him: olsem, there is one law of New Sudan that says olgeta man i noken mekim mak long kontrak na sapos ol i nogat savi long kontrak.[47]

Then Annu says he wants to read the kontrak first. He says this and his voice is sweet and it is strong.

Now, as I say, Annu has told us that we must not fight the white man. And this is where the white man is stupid in the way that only the white man is

---

[47] . . . all man he no can make mark long contract now suppose all he no got understanding of the contract.

stupid. He thinks this kanaka who can speak the same as me is a bikhet tasol who wants to impress his friends. He thinks that if he makes himself to be a pretend friend of Annu then Annu will do what he wants. This is where the white man can be stupid because he does not want to know a kanaka and become a real man with him. He is like Andrew used to be. Because he has these ideas, the white man cannot hear the sweetness of Annu's voice.

So I am no longer sorry for this stupid white man. Annu has given him something good and he has thrown it away. But Annu loves the white man all the same.

The white man says to Annu you can read the kontrak when you have signed it. That is the law. Later I know that the white man is lying to us but Annu does not tell the white man that he knows he is lying. He says alright let me sign the paper and he walks to the table. The white man is smiling now. He is very happy. He gives Annu a pen and Annu signs the kontrak. When Annu has signed the white man shakes Annu's hand and he gives him the coin. Annu takes the coin. Oh yes, the white man is happy. He puts his arm around Annu but he is not looking at Annu because he is thinking he has got the better of this manki masta.[48] The white man is talking into Annu's ear but he is looking at us and he is smiling. Later, Annu tells us that the white man is saying he will give him a good job as a recruiting agent. He wants Annu to baiim boi to work at the solwara.[49]

But Annu leaves the white man and he comes back to us.

[][][][][]

The white man sits down and calls out another name in the book. He calls out Burara, who is the brother of Tematan. Now we know Burara is a man who cannot think for himself. He follows the other man, so when he sees that Annu has signed the kontrak, he is happy to sign it as well. He walks to the table but Annu calls out, stop, Burara. He calls out you cannot make your mark on the kontrak before I have looked at my kontrak.[50] He says we do not have to fear the white man, the white man can be our friend, but it is the law for everyone that we must know what the kontrak says before we can sign it. He says the white man has told us that I can read my kontrak when I have signed it. We all heard the white man say this thing, so, now is the time for me to read the kontrak before another man puts his mark on it.

So Burara is standing beside the table. The white man is looking at Annu like he hates him enough to kill him. He has forgotten the way that Annu looks at him before. He has forgotten the sweetness of Annu's voice. All he remembers is the first law of the white man. That is: ol waitman stap antap long kanaka. The white man looks at the polisboi and he looks at all of us. Then he takes the kontrak of Annu from the table and he gives it to Annu. I can see that he is thinking that Annu is a trabelman just as the magistrate thinks Weno is a

---

[48] Monkey master = A servant who literally apes his master. Generally a term of abuse.

[49] Baiim boi is to buy boys.

[50] Looked = Lukim pinis, look him finish.

trabelman in Tande. But I do not worry for Annu at this time because I am thinking this white man will be rid of Annu when we all go to the solwara.

This kontrak is only one piece of paper. Annu reads it like I see Masta Smit read bits of paper before. He looks at it for a long time and his face is strong. I am thinking this reading is hard work.

When he has finished reading, Annu says you all must hear me well. He says we have come a long way from our homes because we listened to Tematan. It is true that we wanted to work for the white man at the solwara and that we wanted to see the solwara. It is true that we have come here to Karandawa so that we can go inside the balus that will carry us to the solwara. He says, alright, this is what we want. Annu says we have left our homes behind, we cannot go back home, we have nowhere else to go. We must go forward, like the water runs down to the solwara. We will work for the white man at the solwara.

Then Annu looks at the white man and he says we will all sign the kontrak because there is nothing else we can do. We will take the coin that says we have sold ourselves to you.

I see that everyone is listening well to Annu. Me, myself, Keramugl, I understand Annu. I understand that we must go to the solwara and that we must work for the white man. In the end we must sign the kontrak.

But when Annu says we have sold ourselves to the white man, I am worried, we are all worried. I look at Tematan and I see that he is ashamed. But the white man is not ashamed. He is smiling a little because he thinks Annu does not understand what the kontrak says.

The white man stands up. He is happy now that he can show us that he is antap long Annu and that he can show us that this Annu, this man who belongs to us, is stupid. But it is the white man who is stupid because he is blind. He does not know truth and goodness when it is standing there in front of him.

The white man wants to talk but we are all looking at Annu. We know Annu talks the truth and that the white man tells nothing but lies. So Annu keeps talking and the white man sits down again.

Annu says that when we put our mark on the kontrak it is the same that we have said we will work for a kampani for three years. This kampani is like Narangbon but it is bigger so that many men must work for it. He says a big plantation is called a kampani. Annu looks at the paper again and he says the kampani is called the Van Ailan Pamwel Develoman Kampani.

Then Annu looks at the white man and he says, em i tru, yes? The kontrak says the kampani owns us for three years. Em i tru, yes? The white man nods his head. I am thinking this man is underneath Annu for all that his name is Masta. When I understand this bel bilong mi i kamap hot tumas[51].

[][][][][]

---

[51] Belly belong me he come up hot too much. 'I am filled with emotion' (which may be happiness or anger).

All the same, I do not know what is this three years. All of us do not know what is this three years. Annu says three years is the same as three times that the coffee flush comes up at Narangbon. It is three times that Masta Smit gives us the krismas and the holiday. It is the time between a baby being born and the baby becoming a little man who can run around and talk. It is the time that a strong man can become an old man and die.

Now when I hear Annu say this I am not happy. I am a young man. I work for Masta Smit for only tupela krismas and that itself seems in my thinking like a very long time. Tripela Krismas have no end. I look at the faces of my brothers and I can see that we all feel like this. I look at Weno and Weno looks at me but he makes a funny face na bel bilong mi kamap strong long em so I am happy again. I think I have Weno and Burara and Kot and Deni. They are all brothers to me and on top of all this I have Annu. So I have many things to make me happy.

Also, Annu does not want us to be unhappy so he says that three years is nothing. After three years we are still young men and the kontrak says that when these three years are finished the kampani will send us home with money. He says after the three years we can return home as big men. He says we will be able to buy pigs so that we can buy wives. He says that the work for the kampani will be like the work for Masta Smit at Narangbon. He says are we not happy at Narangbon? We will be happy just the same at the kampani because we have each other to be with.

Annu is making it easy for us. He does not tell us the bad things that we will have to learn by our suffering. He does not tell us that we will belong to the kampani for three years, like a pig belongs to a man, and that the kampani can punish us if we do not work well.

Also, Annu does not tell us the worst thing. That is that after three years we will be different men who can never return home. Why am I here at Lingalinga today? Why am I still on Van? The man Keramugl is not the boy Keramugl. Keramugl cannot go home.

So we sign the kontrak.

This New Sudan has swallowed us.

We will become men in knowledge.

We take the coin.

We bilong to the kampani.

⬜⬜⬜⬜⬜

While we are signing the kontrak more polisboi come into the hauskago. I am thinking the white man is bringing them to show us that we bilong to him now.

When we have finished signing the white man talks to Tematan who tells us we must sit down at our place inside the hauskago so that the white man can count all the men who are in the building. He says when the counting is done we will be given food. Tematan says, after you have eaten you can walk about on the ples balus but you cannot go to the town. This talk of Tematan makes me angry and I ask him are we pigs that have been bought? Tematan looks at me but he does not talk anymore and I know that it is true, we are like pigs that have been bought.

I want to talk to Annu but I see him sitting alone. I see that he is not happy. So I do not disturb him. All the same, I watch him. I feel I have lost something but I do not know what I have lost. It is the first time I have this idea in my life. I am thinking Annu has the same idea and I want to help him but I do not know how.

Yes, it is true, at this time I am thinking I want to die.

But then a hand takes mine quickly and strong. It is Weno. He is talking to me and Weno is happy. He says, I like this Annu-man of yours, he has explained to us about the kontrak. It's a good thing, that paper. You see we work for the kampani for three years, they give us plenty of money and then they send us home as rich men. You see they have already given us this coin and I tell you the coin will buy many things. I have seen them in Tande. And see the food this white man has given us. It's good and there is plenty of it. The tinpis is good. We won't be hungry at the solwara. They will give plenty of food so that we can work hard. We will be fat.

What Weno says is true. At Narangbon Masta Smit gives us plenty of kaukau and green leaves and sometimes he gives us pig meat. I see that my friend Weno is happy so I am thinking I must be happy also.

I forget about Annu and I go with Weno to walk about on the ples balus. As we go outside I see that two polisboi are standing at the door. They are carrying sticks on their shoulders that I have not seen before. I ask Weno what are these things and he says they are the masket. If the polisboi points the masket at me he can make it sing out and I will fall down dead. So I think this is what Kot talks of before. Weno says we will see plenty of these maskets when the white man is around. It is the way they like things. But he makes this a funny story and he laughs as he talks so I laugh also and it is true I am happy with this man Weno who does not think too much.

□□□□□

It is now the afternoon as we walk around the ples balus. We see another group of men going to the hauskago. Later another group comes also so that the hauskago is filling up and I am thinking how many men are there who are going to the solwara? We lie on the ground for a little time looking at the mountains and I am thinking of the Orami Valley. But it is not good to think of these things so I am thinking of Annu again because Annu is here with us. I tell Weno we will go back to Annu and Weno laughs again and says yes, Annu is our man. Then I know that Weno will stay with me. I am happy to think this.

When we get near to the hauskago I see that Annu is sitting outside. Burara and Kot and Deni and the other men are sitting with him. We sit beside them. I say this is my friend Weno. He will stay with us. Now I can see that Burara and Kot and Deni are not happy with this idea because Weno is not a wantok but Annu says yes Weno is a good man, he will help you one day. Then I see that Burara and Kot and Deni will accept Weno and that Weno will be their friend. That makes me very happy and I know that I will sleep beside Weno.

I ask them why we cannot go into the hauskago and Burara says that more men have come. They are inside the hauskago and the white man is counting them. He says that the white man has come back with the polisboi. He says that the polisboi points the masket at Annu and told him he must wait outside because the master does not want Annu in the building when the new men sign the kontrak. Annu says yes this is true.

[][][][][]

Then Annu talks to me and he says yu noken wori Keramugl, because you are a strong man. When he says this he takes me in both his hands and he pushes me to the ground and he comes close to on top of me. All I can see is his face. It fills the whole sky and I can see my face inside his eyes. I feel the strength of Annu is coming into me. He says you cannot forget me Keramugl, because I love you like my brother. He says will you remember me always Keramugl? I say Yesa, always and I will die for you. And Annu says I do not want you to die for me, I want you to live for me. I want you to remember me. If you can do this then I will never leave you. I will always be with you Keramugl. And I say Yesa and it is true I can smell Annu and kok bilong mi i sanapim strong. All I am thinking is that I want to be with Annu and mi laik kaikaim maus bilong em tumas, tumas. I think I am sleeping but Annu kisses my mouth.

[][][][][]

Then Annu pulls me up by my shoulders so that I am looking at all my friends. They are looking at me and I see that they are not happy and I do not know what is happening.

Then Annu looks at Weno. Annu is holding my hand and he is saying to Weno, are you going to look after this Keramugl for me? And Weno laughs and he says Yesa. Annu says orait I know yu tok stret, I know you are a good man, Weno.

Again, Annu looks at me and he says are you alright then with Weno? I say Yesa. He says and you will not forget me? I want to say Yesa because how can I forget Annu? But I cannot talk. I am too worried about what Annu will say next.

I know something that is not good is coming to me. So, when Annu says he is going to leave us on that night I am not surprised. Olsemit is a big thing for me to understand and I want to cry like a little baby.

So I look at Annu. And Annu says yu noken wori. He says the white man is afraid to know us. He has told me I cannot go inside the balus. A polisboi, who is a good man, says the white man says I am a trabelman who he does not want to send to the solwara. Also, this polisboi says that if I stay in Karandawa they will put me in the kalabus. So, mi noken kam wantaim long yupela.[52] But, you know me and you know you will see me again.

Annu looks at me and I say Yesa. I say Yesa again and everyone shouts Yesa.

---

[52] Me no can come one time long you fellows.

185

We shout to make ourselves brave.

I shout Annu and everyone shouts Annu.

Annu says there is one more thing I have to do. It is this. He says there is another man who will be with you until you see me again. Then he looks at Weno. He says to Weno, you know this man? He is the man who looked after you before. He is your big man.

Now Weno says Yesa, I know him.

Annu says alright, you find him and bring him to us.

Weno goes.

Then I say to Annu I am giving you my money. I am giving you the coin and I am giving the money that Grin gave me before at Narangbon. Annu says no, I do not need the money. I will find a master who will give me a job. But I say take the money because I want you to have it. So Annu says I will take the money of Grin and I will give it back to you when we meet again. But I will not take the coin of Keramugl because Keramugl must hold his coin until the day he leaves the solwara. Keramugl must bring the coin back to the Orami Valley one day. Keramugl can use the coin to buy himself back from the white man. I, also, will bring the coin back to my place, one day.

⬜⬜⬜⬜⬜

We sleep on the ples balus as I said. When I wake in the morning Annu is gone. When I open my eyes I see the morning sky. It is good but then I remember Annu and I know he has gone. Weno is not with me. I feel empty and I know the others feel the same because all of us do not move from where we are on the ples balus although it is cold in the morning. We wait for orders, that is all. Yes, we are truly the kago of the white man now.

So we sit down on the ground until the sun is up. Then I look towards the hauskago and I see Weno is coming with another man. This man is Tarlie and although he is a long way off from us, I can see he is another kind of man. It is the Tarlie we know and even then I can see it is the man Tarlie who Annu had told Weno to bring to us. Now Weno is a strong man who has good muscles. But beside this Tarlie, Weno is small and his skin is indeed red. Tarlie is a big man and a black man and his shoulders are very strong. I am thinking I would not like to fight with this Tarlie. It does not matter that he walks with a limp, I can see that he is a strong man and he has eyes that can see you.

I tell the others that Weno is bringing this man who Annu says will look after us. So we all see the big man coming.

You know what I mean. Tarlie is a good man and very soon we know his name and we know he is a good man. Also, we are happy to be with him. Tarlie tells us we must join his group because they also have signed the kontrak for the kampani.

So we join the group of Tarlie so that we make a bigger group. This is the way we Highlands men come to work at the solwara. One man comes to Karandawa with his friends. In Karandawa other men have come from other parts of the Highlands. We are different men with different languages but in Karandawa we become the same because we are all working for the kampani.

Also we have to talk the same language which is this Tokpisin. Those who do not know it must learn it fast. So we join together and when the men at the solwara see us they say we are just Highlanders. They do not see that I am from Orami and Weno is from Tande.

Annu said the truth: we are a river. Many small rivers come into the big river to make it more big. Then the big river goes down to the solwara and the river throws itself into the solwara to be part of it.

[][][][][]

Alright, now, as I tell this story, I know what is a balus and I am not afraid. When I fly to Port Markham with Missus Margaret, I am a man. I hold her hand, she does not hold mine.

But when I went on the balus the first time it was something else. I cannot be afraid if it is only me with Tarlie and Weno. This is because Weno is laughing for this new thing of going in the balus and because Tarlie is strong in his mind for all of us. This strength of Tarlie helps us.

But you must remember that many of us have not seen a balus before this time. Some of us have seen a picture and we have seen a balus high in the sky when it looks like a bird. To many men it is a bird. And who can be afraid of a little bird?

Now, when we have eaten our food and washed, the white man comes again with his polisboi. Also, there is Tematan and some other men. I can see that Tematan is looking for us and he is not happy to see we have joined with Tarlie. But when he sees Tarlie I can see that Tematan is ashamed. He looks at Tarlie. He thinks: Who is this Tarlie that they all want to be with him?

The white man talks to another man who comes to stand beside him. This man is more black than Tarlie and he is tall and he is handsome as well. I can see that this man is also a master although he is black. Now this black master calls out that there is a boss-boy for each group and we must stand up behind our boss-boy. Then he says he will call out the names. He has a good voice and I understand he is telling us what to do to make things easy. He is not talking to us as if he owns us, in the way that the white man talks to us. He says he will call out the name of the boss-boy and the boss-boy must go outside where a polisboi will go with him to his place on the ples balus. He says then he will call out the names of the line behind the boss-boy and we will join our boss-boy on the ples balus. He says we must not worry about the polisboi because the work of the polisboi is show us what to do outside.

Then this black master says my name is Simon and I come from the solwara. I was born at the solwara. My place is an island called Kuba. Later I learn that all the people from Kuba are tall and very black but that is another story. This man Simon understands how we are feeling. I can see that he will not make things hard for us.

So Simon calls the names. He calls the name of Tarlie. Tarlie goes outside and his line follow him one by one as their names are called. Then Simon calls the name of Tematan. But Tematan does not go outside. I know that this is because he is afraid that we will not follow him. He comes to stand beside us but we are not happy. Simon looks at him but he does not tell him to go outside. I know that he wants to see what will happen. Then Simon calls Burara. Now Burara is the brother of Tematan so he cannot deny his brother. So he says Yesa but he does not shout it out. So Simon calls the name again and Burara shouts out Yesa and he goes to stand behind Tematan but he is not happy.

Then Simon shouts out the name Deni. Now Deni is a bighead man. You know this. He is a man who does not have fear so he shouts out Nosa. Everyone laughs and Simon laughs also but the white man is angry, I can see that. Also, Deni does not move to stand behind Tematan.

Now the white man says something to Simon who says to Deni please go and stand behind Mister Tematan. His voice is strong but he does not shout. Also, because he calls Tematan Mister Tematan we know he understands us as men although he does not know that Tematan is a shit. All the same, Deni does not move. I can see the face of the white man is very red. It is Andrew when he is cross. He shouts yu fukinblaribasat yu sanap bihain long bossboi bilong yu kwiktaim. You want to make trouble I'll put you in prison very quickly. He is going to say some more but Simon puts his hand on the arm of the white man. Simon is frowning and we are not happy because this is no way to talk to a man. Masta Smit is angry many times but he knows us and we know he loves us like his children. Also, when he shouts he is funny a little so that we can laugh and later, sometimes he will go to a man and touch him say sori to him. This white man is just angry because he is stupid and afraid. He does not want to know us as men. I can see that the polisboi is watching Deni and I am afraid he wants to point the masket at him. This is not a good thing. I ask myself why all this trouble is coming from nothing.

Simon says something to the white man. I am thinking it is sutup because the white man is not happy now but Simon is stronger and the white man walks out of the hauskago. Then Simon says to Deni, Mister Deni why you no like stand up behind Mister Tematan? Now Deni is angry a little so he says it straight. He says we do not like this Tematan, em i gaiman tru.[53] We are not trabelman but we cannot go with Tematan. It is better you kalabusim mipela. But suppose you send us to go with this man Tarlie, it is much better.

And we all shout, Yesa!

Simon is smiling and he says who is this man Tarlie? Now Deni looks at us and he says he is our man. He is our big man. We are happy to stand in his line. We cannot stand in the line of Tematan.

Then I can see that, in his way, Deni is not going to talk again.

Now Simon is not angry. He is smiling still and he says alright you can all go with Mister Tarlie. Then he says to Tematan, are you happy with this? And Tematan says yesa but his voice is small. He has no power. But I am happy I will be with Tarlie and Weno and my friends from Narangbon. We are all happy so that it is true, we have forgotten Annu by this time.

[][][][]

---

[53] Him he lying man true.

So Simon calls our names one by one and we go outside to stand behind Tarlie. By this time there are many men on the ples balus. We are telling Deni he is a good man and we are saying we like this man Simon so we do not see the balus at first. Then Weno shouts out, look in the sky the balus is coming. So we stop talking and we look. It is true we can see the balus and we can hear the noise it makes like an angry insect before it bites you.

We watch the balus as it comes over the mountains. At first it is a small thing but it is bigger and bigger as we watch. Then it is very close and it is very big with a big noise like a very big water. Oh and then it is running so fast along the ground towards us that we do not know what to do.

Olsem dispela balus i kam klostu long mipela, mipela krai olsem tasol mipela gat bikpela sori tru i kamap. Na, mipela olgeta i pundaun long graun.[54]

I will never forget this, not until the day I die. This groan of ours is a big thing that is itself fearful. But we are not afraid. We were not afraid of the balus. We groan and we fall down to the ground because the balus is something that is so big and so new to our minds that we do not want to think about it all at once. Also, we know that this big thing that makes so much noise is made by the white man and he is the boss of it. So we understand this balus as something that is real but outside our understanding. But we understand well that we are going to a place in which we will be nothing.

The balus will eat us up and never again will we be the same as before.

This is why we groan and fall to the ground like dead men.

[][][][][]

But we are not babies so we get up and we look at the balus. It has stopped and it is quiet. I am thinking how is it that a big thing like that can fly? The wings are not moving. It is big and I don't know how it works, it is true, but I am thinking that if a stupid man like that white man can control the balus then there is nothing for me, Keramugl, to be afraid of. Also, I can see that Simon is not afraid. He is talking to another white man who has come out of the balus. The two men are standing beside the balus and it is not eating them.

Then Simon comes to us. He has a serious face but when he is near us he laughs so that we know that this laughter of his is for us kanakas only. It is not for the white man to share. We crowd around Simon. He says listen well. He says yu noken wori na tinktink long dispela balus. He says it is only a small balus for carrying men inside the place of New Sudan. He says there are many balus that are much more big. He says in Port Markham plenty of kanakas and all the white man and white woman travel in the balus. He says he himself has travelled on the balus many times. He says he likes it tumas because he can look down on the place that is called New Sudan.

Alright, what Simon says is true and we are happy to hear him say it. So we are not afraid of the balus. No, we are not afraid of anything anymore. I myself am not afraid. This is because seeing the balus come to the ground for the first

---

[54] Then this balus he come close long me fellows, me fellows groan because that is all, me fellows got big fellow sorry true he come up. And, me fellows fall down long ground.

time as the big, noisy thing that it is makes me not be afraid of anything that the white man can show me or do to me.

Also, I am thinking I am not afraid of the white man because when we see the white man here we see he is just a man like ourselves. He is a bikhet man tumas because he does not want to tell us his name. He does not want to know us as men. We see that it is easy for a kanaka like Simon to be a better man.

Only the masket it is makes me afraid. Later when we are at Van Island I know this better. Jim is a very stupid man but we are afraid of him only because he has a masket.

You understand what I am saying? In a few days mipela lainim pinis planti samting[55]. So travelling in the balus, coming to Port Markham, travelling in the boat to Van Island and being rubbish labourers, all this is a small thing to us after we have seen the balus for the first time and when we have finished groaning and falling on the ground. We do not stop on the ground do we? No, we get up again and we stand up as men in the big place that is New Sudan.

◻◻◻◻◻

Many things happen to us as we travel to Van Island. In Port Markham we are put in a kalabus until we are taken to the boat. When we see the solwara some of us throw up just at the sight of it because it has no end. When we taste it we understand why it is called the sol wara. In the boat some of us are happy and some of us are not happy because the ground is moving like a guria for one day and one night without stopping.[56] But in the night we sit together and looking at the stars, we are happy together. When we come to the kampani it is confusing but we go to a place that is like Narangbon a little but there are big oil palms, there are not the small coffee trees. The white man master is not a bad man but he does not want to know us and also there are many other men who we do not know. At first the new work is hard and the sun burns our skins but in time we are strong.

All this happened to us as you know. Many things but I do not remember. What I remember well is Tarlie being our man and the man of all the other men working with us. But I am happy that I have Weno with me. I am happy we have Tarlie to talk to the white man for us. All the same, I am empty. Mi lukim long olgeta dai bilong mi i kamap na mi lukim samting nating, I look into the future and I see nothing. That makes me afraid sometimes because I have forgotten Annu. I only remember him again when the bad things happen.

---

[55] . . . me fellows learn finish plenty something.

[56] A guria is an earth tremor.

15
Splendid Specimens

In the late afternoon the thick, billowing wads of smoke are not appreciated from the club. So thick with dust is the air that a little extra makes no difference.

"Spectacular sunset, old man, you should have seen it. Another drink? It's my round."

They discuss Jim.

"Don't go near him; the poor darling's foul. Rotten day. There was some sort of row in the office with Andrew this afternoon. Too much for Mrs L, apparently. She walked out; must've been bad. Another San Mig then, if you insist."

The western sky is throbbing with anger: beautiful in its way; like Tudak, the man who most likely started it.

No one sees it at first, focused as they are on the bar, behind which Clarence plays elderly bar-boy. He's hopeless. They chaff him as a disguise for their impatient anger. He gets the shots wrong and forgets who's next. You can't shout at him as if he's Joseph.

"Joseph knows what to do."

"Where is he? Fuck him."

"He walked out Saturday. Remember?"

"We sacked him."

"Sacked us more like."

"Get him back. For Christ's sake, Clarence."

"What?"

"I said gin and tonic thanks old man. God help me, where's he gone now?"

Couple of days later, when all the fuss has died down, Peter, doing the bar stores, will notice Clarence hasn't marked any of it down: "That was a Happy Hour and a half, I can tell you. Two hundred dollars' worth on the house." On Clarence more like, but by then he will be too ill to take the joke. It'll come out of contingencies. Or some of it will. Peter will take round the hat to make up the difference.

"What's the matter Henry? You look as if you'd seen a ghost."

"Look out there, you fool."

"Blimey!"

"The whole place must be going up."

"Anyone seen Jim?"

"Probably there already," says Henry glumly, to no one in particular, because despite all the chatter, we are waiting for Jim to do something.

"Better find Jim," says Clarence hopefully, to no one in particular. Better find him indeed to make sense of all this because I haven't the foggiest about what's happening out there. I want Jim to deliver me from the chaos that is in here, behind the bar. We'd better find Joseph and beg him to come back. Or Alloy! That's a good idea. Spare parts or drinks or men's souls: they're all the same. But Alloy's growl and his savage halo of hair. Doesn't have the servile whatever it is. Or, at any rate, can't act it like Annu, like Joseph, I mean. Too raw by half; too self-conscious. Members wouldn't stand for it. Alloy wouldn't stand for it for Christ's sake – doesn't have Joseph's ability to get out of himself. Clarence feels the pain in his chest again. Take a deep breath. It's a knife through my lungs and it's not as if I smoke. Pity about Alloy: I could ask him anyway. He could get his hair cut. Maybe it's only heartburn.

Having seen it – the plantation, apparently hopelessly ablaze, the basis of their existence going up in smoke – they stand watching, thinking, perhaps should we drive out there in our Landrovers and stand around a bit and come back smelling of smoke? So, like a flock of sheep, they . . . flock to the door. Something must be done, cries the chorus. Therefore, at the door, on cue, they are met by Jim, sweaty and begrimed with . . . grime. The sweat of his labours, his efforts, his strenuous action, plain for all to see.

He puts up his hands to stem the flood. And the flood is stemmed. Their clamour is silenced, anarchy stopped in its tracks. Wonderful, and to emphasis the point and to back Jim up, there stands Tudak behind him, large and black outside the door. The night approaching is made nearer by his presence.

"OK boys," Jim laughs, confident in his power over these wankers, "it's alright. Give me a drink."

Clarence scuttles behind the bar again to pour a large whisky-water into the Waterford glass. Pattern of thistles.

They back off into the club. As a mass they move; the chorus of some ancient Greek tragedy silenced by the omnipotence of a god here on earth. In the background the sky is bright with flames. The shadows ought to be thrown across the room but they are not. It is not that close. It is not that big.

Jim seats himself. Celestial bottom graces cushion that is flattened beneath weight of wondrous deeds. They bring chairs around but perhaps they ought to kneel. Tudak is felt, out there in the dark, waiting. No one goes out. No one dares. There stands Tudak like the very night itself. Gosh, better off here in the club with Jim than out there.

Margaret is above it all. Not by design but she is, all the same, up there.

Daphne? She has refused to return to the club since Saturday. At this point she is merely at home in ignorance. It is, indeed, a sort of bliss. She's preparing Peter's dinner.

Henry, a sort of Aaron-less Moses, approaches the god: "Jim, I think I'd better go out and see what's happening. I don't like to think of Andrew handling it on his own."

"Don't worry, it's under control."

"But Jim . . ." He gets up.

"Sit!" Jim snaps a smile.

Henry sits.

"I say, Jim?"

"Oh, Peter. You here?"

"I am."

"Well shut up." You know your place.

He does. Jim smiles.

Clarence smiles. He's happy to be guided and doesn't pretend otherwise. Decisions give him a pain these days. Right here in my chest, just below my armpits.

"Listen," says Jim.

They listen.

"I'll deal with this."

"But Jim . . ." The chorus whispers, and dies.

"I said I'll deal with it." Is this talking some sort of disease with you? Are you constitutionally unable to keep your mouths shut?

I don't want you lot out there getting in the way. A half-witted bar-boy'd do a better job than any of you. If you get near, you'll only make it worse.

Make what worse? For whom? Indeed. Better ask Margaret.

"Now listen, there's no point in us all goin' out and gettin' in the way. Andrew's got things under control. I've just left 'im. I'll go straight back. So, please," Jim indeed used the word, "please stay 'ere, stay calm and go to bed. I want you to run things, to run things smoothly for me tomorrow without a fuss. You can't do that if you 'aven't 'ad a proper night's sleep. Can you do that?"

It is supposed that they can.

"'Enry?"

"Yes Jim?"

"You act for me, please."

"Of course Jim." I am your firstest lieutenant.

"And 'Enry?"

"Yes Jim?"

"Go into town at some stage and deal with Mrs Livingston for me. Get 'er to come back. She was funny this afternoon. Time of the month, I reckon," Clarence nods, "and 'er age."

"I'll do that Jim."

"I want things normal. OK?"

"OK," indeed, indeed. They worship him.

"Good. I'll be off then."

And he's off.

They go back to the bar, relieved.

The fire rages.

□□□□□

In fact, Jim is, at this moment, like Clarence. He hasn't the foggiest. But he is, as he puts it, and unlike Clarence, thinking on the trot. He is thinking, amongst other things – as the thoughts start – that he is stuck with Andrew having said all that about him in the bar. Anyway, it wasn't a row. I was just giving him some fatherly advice and he took it the wrong way. Anyway, I'm a big man. I can laugh it off. Laugh at myself if I have to. Laugh at Mrs L, too. I'll get her a new typewriter next week. Anyway, they love me. It touches my heart and brings a tear to my eye. They love old Jim they do. Indeed I love myself.

Approaching the night's work with his usual relish, Jim climbs into the Landrover. There is a lot to be done before it is time to deal with the fire. He lets off the break so that it runs smoothly down the hill. He always does it this way, as if, as if by doing so, Margaret cannot hear.

Tudak jogs lightly behind, surprisingly light for his size. At just the right moment he jumps – bounces, more like – neatly into the back and the vehicle moves off. It is a beautifully co-ordinated movement, as it is meant to be. Tudak is beautiful to look at. Poetry in motion Andrew has been heard to remark.

He is as beautiful as Jim's love for himself.

He has been known in his life variously as Bikboi, Bikting, Manmaunten, and Diwai, which means tree. He was always tall and well built for his age. No one remembered him as a small child. In his younger days his violence was excused as adolescent growing pains. The apparent thoughtlessness made it acceptable. He hit you, or took your food, but it had nothing to do with you personally; you were merely the convenient platform upon which he expressed himself. Had it been aimed specifically at you, had he sought you out, then his violence would have been worrying. As it was, avoiding him was sufficient defence. As he grew older, it became obvious that his thoughtless violence was what he was. You could not reason with it. He was unable to absorb anything outside himself. He was feared now because his size enabled his thoughtless actions to be incidentally violent, but he was not hated. He was even pitied in the way that a man is pitied for his deformity or witlessness. They pitied him but they could not deal with him or live with him. Better to have killed him as a genetic deformity. In a civilised society he would have been chained up like a captive bear to be beaten and teased. One dark night the men overpowered him, trussed him up tightly and carried him, as they would a pig, to the government station at Mt Giluwe, forty miles distant. It was worth the effort but it took three days. They dumped him outside the District Administrator's office. He was now too far away from home to ever get back. The name he called his home was meaningless to the people who encountered him in Mt Giluwe.

He was trouble in Mt Giluwe so they exported him with a load of lesser trouble, Joseph amongst them, to Van Island as an indentured labourer. He soon found himself in the Togulo Farm Penal Colony.

[][][][][]

The Togulo Farm Penal Colony is not a bad place. All the criminals of the province, from murderers to vagrants, to those really serious types who are unable to pay their small court fines, end up in the farm. They are mostly men, who are rigidly separated from the few women who work in the cook house from where they earn substantial comfort and remission by servicing the guards. The male prisoners manage among themselves.

Early on in the colony's history it was sensibly realised that keeping the prisoners on the farm was best realised by, by not exactly making the place comfortable but at any rate by ensuring that it was not unbearably uncomfortable. You lost your freedom to roam in the outside world but the farm work was no more backbreaking than farm work generally is and the food sufficiently plentiful to enable most prisoners to leave fatter than when they arrived. Medical services, unlike in the outside world, were limited but free.

Misdemeanours were mostly punished by a flogging administered not by the guards but by fellow inmates. The penitent was stretched naked on the ground by two of his friends, the one holding his wrists, the other his ankles. A third mate (chosen by lottery from a host of volunteers) administered the chastisement while everyone else looked on and cheered. It was fun, even for the victim because his darling's caresses were focused on the buttocks and limited in their force by a pebble held in the flogger's armpit as he swung. On the rare occasions where skin was broken the game was stopped immediately by very general consent; it was in no one's interest to set a violent precedent.

So life in the penal colony was humane: most prisoners left as better men; certainly no worse. Those unsuited to the outside stayed on.

Tudak was a challenge to the system. The bugger was different and the minor indignities which could be used to tame the usual sort of antisocial behaviour did not work in his case. Cleaning the latrines he accepted as he accepted other work. In the end, he spent most of the time, when he was not immobilised, cleaning the latrines. Flogging had no effect on him at all, and, in any event, other inmates were reluctant to flog him in the erroneous assumption that he would seek retribution. But Tudak's violence had nothing to do with retribution. Regardless of what was done to him, he continued to inflict mindless violence, as an expression of his existence: I abuse those weaker than I, therefore I am. Is this not a basis for civilised societies?

Yet despite all this, they did not hate Tudak at the farm. They also pitied him. But he was, as before, a nuisance. Tying him up for most of the time upset the symmetry of the organisation. It engendered an atmosphere of unhappiness throughout the colony.

[][][][][]

Jim was interested in the penal colony. He spent many a happy afternoon there, talking to the inmates and their guards. He enjoyed watching a flogging as much as the next man and would have liked to have had a go himself. So when he heard about Tudak and understood that they wanted to get rid of the nuisance, he offered to take it. He reckoned he could use Tudak. He, Jim, could control Tudak. He never considered the alternative.

Now Jim knew what he wanted: he had a resolute belief in his own judgement. But Jim did not have the sort of mind that analysed the method and the implications of getting what he wanted. His vision was clear. It was not clouded by the usual nagging human doubts. If Jim said we invade Poland then Poland is invaded. This was his vision and questions about how it was to be done and about the human costs involved were not merely dismissed, they were a blasphemy. Be in Warsaw, the generals were informed, by the autumn or you will be shot. Therefore Poland was invaded; Warsaw obliterated.

This resolution, this getting things done without consideration of the costs, arose from a gap in Jim's thought processes. In most people it is filled with a conscience or, at any rate, with a capacity for caution, and reflection upon the consequences of action. Jim skipped all that: Ples is to be planted so it is planted regardless of the human, economic and financial costs. If pressed he might have said that planting up Ples was part of the relentless bulldozer of history and, anyway, the board in London wanted it. How could he, a mere Jim, stand up against London? But Jim, you might answer, are you not the one driving the bulldozer? Does not the board in London take its line from your action? Does not the board in London applaud your action? I don't think of things like that, replies Jim, I just got to get on with it. Don't you worry, Jim knows what he's doing, says the member of the board in London, tapping the side of his nose knowingly.

A man more educated in history than Jim – Andrew's Beaky, for instance – might have said that the planting of Ples was part of human destiny – manifest or otherwise – the destruction of Ples a price worth paying for civilization. This idea – destiny – indeed drives the expansion of civilised societies, but it needs a Jim, not a Beaky, to make it happen. Beaky – and the members of the board in London – stand on the sidelines and cheer Jim as they think of their dividends, share values, pension funds and the like.

Given all this Jim-ness then, Tudak was Jim's perfect complementary tool. Jim's evil actions could not be realised without Tudak's murderous hands and fists. Phew! And given Jim's position of leadership – brought to him to some extent by his lack of consideration – and the propensity for most people to want to be led and to be on the winning side, Jim plus Tudak equalled something pretty nasty but effective.

Jim plus Tudak plus Wilful Human Ignorance equals, to give just a few examples, the Salem Witch Trials, the Old South, the sweat shops from eighteenth-century Preston to twenty-first century Manila or Phnom Penh, the Tsarist Pogroms, the First and Second World Wars, the Holocaust, Jim Crow and all that, the Gulag, Muslims killing Christians in Acre, Hindus killing Muslims in Gujarat, Christians killing each other more often than not everywhere, the death of Nalin's daughter and so on and so on and so on and so on. The games people play.

Jim and Tudak then: a perfect master-dog relationship: Jim's mindless masterfulness perfectly manifested in Tudak's thoughtless violence. Once mastered, a Tudak can be used for anything. It is obviously better than a management team, each damn member of which tends to think for himself, and to irresistibly consider the consequences of his actions. A Jim can drive a manager only so far because a manager might – and indeed, might not – listen to his conscience, and consider his sins of commission and omission. A manager might, in a reckless moment, act upon what he hears.

Tudak was different. He quickly learnt that if he restricted his actions to those directed by Jim – get him boy – he would be fed, he would be looked after, he would be free inasmuch as he would not be bound by ropes and flogged, and he would, given the dark world in which Jim lived, have sufficient platforms upon which to express himself.

Recognising this, Jim used Tudak to do things without asking questions. Dealing with troublemakers, in the main: those antisocial types who wish, for selfish reasons, to upset the status quo. They could be beaten up behind the Mill, the screams inaudible; or they could disappear because Van was a big rough place with lots of coastline. If necessary, relatives could be intimidated: Tudak could knock down children, frighten old people or beat up women as efficiently as the next man. Oddly, rape – of either sex – was not in Tudak's book; that undoubtedly involved getting into a state of intimacy he could not face. Ugh! Beat and stick in a knife but getting in there himself was too much. When Helen came along, and the idea seemed appropriate, it was his undoing.

[][][][][]

Jim used Tudak as his tool but clearly he could not let him out on his own. Anything might, and occasionally did, happen in the earliest days of the two men's collusion. Embarrassingly, the wrong people disappeared or an innocent was beaten up. Kanakas admittedly, therefore it didn't much matter but complaints might be raised one day, which would be inconvenient. This was unlikely, as it happened, because the very arbitrariness of Tudak's nocturnal activities created an atmosphere of fear which kept people's mouths shut. Fear, ignorance and keeping your mouth shut are God's gift to a Jim.

Jim collected another couple of thugs from the Togulo Farm. These would be used as Tudak's handlers. Desperate types who had few options left in life having spent most of it as petty criminals, occasionally violent but not mindless. Their violence had generally been accidental or the result of a sudden loss of self-control. These two might be described as ordinary men; ordinary men who were ill-educated, ill-suited to the organisational structure of the plantation and who had gone wrong early enough in life for their petty crime and violence to be a way of life. In the right hands, they might have been useful, law-abiding citizens. But in Jim's hands they became as wicked as he was; on a scale of evil worse even than Tudak, because they could think about their actions and because they did not have Jim's mental gap.

These two thugs were, in fact, the most common type of despicable human being. Those who excuse their horrible actions: he made me do it; I didn't know what I was doing; I was only obeying orders. I was only obeying orders. Jesus Christ son of God fuck me rigid! I was only obeying orders. Jim and Tudak would be nothing without you fuckers. You fuckers who are forever obeying orders are the ones who cause all the trouble. We could kill Tudak but you lot keep coming in your millions.

These two, for what it's worth, were known as Rabis and Pen. Big black handsome fellows whom Jim dressed in militaristic uniforms and dark glasses. He indoctrinated them so that they believed him when he told them that the people with whom they had to deal were the scum of the earth, intent on fermenting revolution and anarchy.

Jim fed them well, he gave them a comfortable shed in which to live, they had a couple of girls to look after their needs and they were beautifully dressed, even down to their expensive underpants. What more could anyone need? In return they did what they were told. This generally meant handling Tudak. They acted – acting being the operative word – as Jim's, as Jim's intimidating acolytes-cum-bodyguards.

Jim treated all three of these, these splendid specimens of humanity with a sort of fond contempt, as a man might be proud of three racehorses. Because, of course, distinctly, they were not human in the way that white men are human. That was the accepted norm. They were kanakas, that's all.

Jim's little bag of tools, Henry called them, appreciative of their good looks. Jim's boys, Peter said. Clarence didn't think they were very nice but he didn't like to mention it.

16
The Facts of Life

Night.

Fire in the night.

The fire, like Jim himself, gives the night its darkness.

Delays the dawn.

What Alloy sees is like Joseph's view of the club members from behind the bar. Random snapshots suggesting bits and pieces of reality that must be put together to make an impression of how things are, a memory of how things were.

Andrew knows the labour compound, Joseph knows the club but I struggle to make sense of what I see now. Like I remember Angelina on that other night: I am confused. Later I will remember the bits; I will piece them together as sense.

What's this?

Fire, you idiot.

This is what happens when you start a fire.

Jim's act of commission.

Andrew's act of omission.

No less a sin if not more.

The least forgivable perhaps.

Forgiven all the same.

To Alloy's eyes the residents of the compound dart around, not in panic but aimlessly all the same. Not so in fact – in fact – if the truth be known because, aware already of the temporary and shifting nature of their lives, they quietly collect what they want – blankets and transistor radios – and move away from the fire to the interior of the plantation towards the river. Andrew sees this and merely checks each house to hasten out the occupants. They ignore him. The fire, Andrew, the company are all the same thing to them.

The fact is, Madiak has worked ahead of Andrew; he has directed the people down to the river, which, he has rightly assessed, is the safest place to be.

The fact is that a temporary flame has leapt across the road from Ples to catch the desiccated palm fronds that have been pruned and neatly laid down below the palms, waiting for disintegration. So the fire moves fast through the plantation, leaving a trail of ash, but not much damage. The oil palms themselves are hardy things; where they have lost all their leaves, standing forlornly as blackened stumps, sap continues to rise and the new leaf shoots will show within days.

The fact is, oil palms are resistant to fire. Not so wooden houses in the dry weather. Here the fire settles, finding something solid to devour. Now it roars, competing with the night itself; challenging the dawn.

The fact is, the little pairs of houses are built only so far apart. That is for the purposes of hygiene. Otherwise, obviously, they would have been long-houses of infinite length and even easier to burn.

The fact is, Andrew's labour compound is laid out in lines, waiting for the fire.

Andrew stands on main plantation road.

Usual muster spot.

Looks down grassy road between lines of quarters.

Sees all in mind's eye.

Football pitch behind him.

Alloy beside him.

Lines of labour in twilight dawn.

Cosy feel of routine morning lost in sea of oil palms, while on Club Hill they sleep. Croton hedges look neat. Tarlie trims them.

This is what it was like.

That is what I will remember.

Gone up in smoke.

You forget the reality of people.

Of Ples, one day

I will smash your English nose.

One day.

Alloy sees the reality of the moment. He watches the scene. Centre-view. The houses to the left are hopelessly aflame, red glowing skeletons of things, crashing. He thinks, he feels, this is great. This is things happening. Destruction. He cannot pull his eyes away. Wonderful to watch the intense, pulsating firelight that creates its own space in the surrounding night. As if by negotiated agreement, the night stays close. The roof of the space is the shrivelled leaves, the quivering frames of the mango tree branches dissolving into the night and heat. The floor, the suffering ground; Tarlie's cut grass a sticky, sickly strip of ground, messed up.

Alloy wants to walk into the room as if, as if to defy Andrew. A suicidal feeling that frightens him. Better to hit Andrew.

A rash of sparks flies across the space – the early morning breeze – and a piece of washing hanging on a line, some rag, tinder dry, catches, blushes as if for shame and flies away also, ashes. The buildings, the labour quarters, ignite from within.

They are transfixed pyromaniacs. The wanton, detached destruction satisfies their youthful nihilism.

This then is the truth. The thrilling view of houses burning, one by one. Watch the next go. We want to cheer. The tide destroying our childish sandcastles. Look, there's Yalu's house going. He used to sit on the veranda in the evening, his legs dangling over the edge, and shout rude remarks as we went past. Won't be able to do that anymore.

[][][][][]

"I'd better do something."

"Why? Let's watch it burn."

"No, no. I'm the manager."

"I thought Jim'd sacked you?"

"Fuck him."

"Big words."

Alloy continues to watch, as much as a challenge as because he can't tear himself away. He will consider nothing.

Or so he thinks.

Nonetheless, when Andrew moves, he follows.

This is, after all, Andrew's territory.

Andrew's Fire.

Yes, Andrew, your fire.

What will he do next this odd white man, this Englishman? This odd man with whom I've slept. Whose naked flesh I've touched and smelt and felt against mine. This stranger to whom I am, I am, I am in some way, oddly attached.

To whom I am attached as a voluntary act. Is this unnatural? This attaching to another man? But I am happy and calm about it while all around the fire burns. I can hear the fire roar as it eats the air. I hear the timbers groan, crack and crash.

Before, before this idea of Annu – he thinks so fast that the idea is lost before it is registered – I spent my life detaching. Now I am connected to this white man who cannot help himself.

Wow, thinks Alloy, what an idea. And I am allowed to, to, to make the contact. My free will enables me.

The idea is more real than the fire all around.

This is a fact.

When Andrew moves, Alloy follows.

As Alloy follows, Andrew feels ashamed.

He thinks: I am going to chuck this job.

Has he not chucked it?

Andrew walks to where the road dips a little and narrows. It crosses a stream which is confined by a culvert, just the right size for a small man to crawl through. Beyond – in Andrew's mind's eye – the road swings around the ridge upon which his house sits. There's Madiak's house, with Andrew's – lofty from here – above.

Stream? Ditch more like but it's a magic place even so because it has defeated the rigidity of the plantation. Vegetation grows thickly along the banks. There are little grassy places where people can – and do – sit. Therefore, a magic place.

Beside the road is the big old mango tree from which the muster bell – that piece of old iron – hangs. A little beyond, the generator shed. Also, under the shade of the tree, the bench upon which Tarlie sits – or used to – with Nalin's daughter in the evening.

Well, there's no flowing water in the ditch. Wouldn't expect there to be after all this dry weather. But water is there, somewhere: they pump it up every morning to the overhead tanks. Even in the driest weather there is water in the ground, which is why the houses were put here in the first place. That and the convenient elevation for Andrew's house. But the stream itself is dry.

So, Andrew is standing above the culvert looking at where the water ought to be but isn't. Water of the mind is no good.

The fact is that there isn't any.

Of course, they're not completely stupid for all Jim's characterisation of them – of Andrew and the appendage, as Jim sees it, which is Alloy – as fucking dumb, sometimes. These two who stand with their hands in their pockets.

"Andrew," says a familiar voice from somewhere.

"Bune. What're you doing here?"

Had he crawled out of the culvert? His torso glistening red in the firelight like, like something very welcome and beautiful for all his receding hairline and the lines around his eyes.

Bune might have responded: And what are you doing? Doing nothing while the compound burns? The job of a plantation manager is to do things that keep a process going to its predestined end. But he didn't say it. He didn't precisely think it either.

Nonetheless, action was required. Not the ego-maniacal action of a Jim but the obvious action to stop the fire because the Plantation Manager and the boss-boi were there to ensure that the plantation functioned. This was the job. Had not he, Bune of the river, been created, had he not evolved in this world of white men, plantation and suffering, to ensure that the universe in which they spent their days functioned? The progression of his life to where he stood now proved it.

Had Andrew said, now listen Bune, I am no longer the Plantation Manager, I am, I am, I am the agent of reform and it is my duty to destroy the plantation and free the labourers from their bondage. Will you help me? Bune would have sympathised with Andrew, thinking of the free-flowing river, of his riverside home and of his first view of the open sky. He would have agreed. But, Andrew, he would have added, then let us set about the job properly. We need to be sure that the fire efficiently destroys these damned labour quarters, the generator house, Madiak's house, and yours, there on the hill. In fact we need to be sure that the whole damn place is wiped off the face of the earth. Or words to that effect.

Indeed the right thing but for the time being Andrew was thinking of doing something about stopping the fire. Water, it seemed, was required but there was no water. And you'd need an awful lot of it. Fire engines and firemen squirting water from hose pipes and that sort of thing. He'd never seen a real live fire like this but everyone knew what happened. You called the fire station.

"I think we should stop the fire, Andrew," said Bune, since Andrew had not, after all, suggested a change of allegiances.

Andrew looked blankly ahead, towards, in his mind's eye, the comforting fact of Madiak's house. He didn't like to admit that like Jim, he hadn't the foggiest what to do. A fact he later dismissed although Alloy was equally, later, aware that Andrew had been dithering.

Bune stood respectfully by, with a look on his face that assumed Andrew to be the font of all wisdom. Yes Andrew, it seemed to say, take your time; better a successful strategy than a botched rush at things. One of the many things Bune had learnt in the world of white men doing things was how to detach himself and act the way they wanted him to be: silent, obedient and respectful.

"Yes," said Andrew, "water. We must find some water, get buckets, and things, and men. A chain-gang," I think it's called. You pass the water along it in buckets. And pass them back again, empty. To refill. "Let's find the buckets."

He searched around with his eyes as if the buckets would materialise out of, out of somewhere. Maybe Madiak had been hoarding them for years and had a secret store in his house. Do you think so? Unlikely.

Andrew had a brainwave: "The coffee drums, we'll use the coffee picking drums."

"They've got holes in the bottom, Andrew. You had us put holes in to stop people using them as buckets."

"Well, I know that Bune. Of course they've got holes in the bottom. I'm not stupid."

Did Alloy laugh? Of course not. He looked blankly ahead, into the dark. Is this how Andrew does his job?

"If we shift them fast enough they'll reach the fire before they've emptied."

Alloy laughed, but at any rate Bune kept a straight face.

"I know. We'll put banana leaves in the bottom. I've seen the men doing it. The water seeps out much more slowly. Now, there're bananas growing along the stream here. You start to cut them with the men," who were a couple of old men and a small boy mesmerised by the manifest lack of action, "while I get the buckets from the store."

"Andrew?"

"Yes Bune?"

"There isn't time."

"Isn't there?"

"And there isn't any water."

"There isn't?" Andrew looked into the ditch as if the effort of looking would produce water. It didn't.

"There isn't water, Andrew," said Alloy at last, "and there isn't any time. Let it go, for fuck's sake."

"No, no we can't do that. We must do something. Bune, have you any ideas?" Andrew did not feel in the least bit worried but he did feel he ought to do something as manager. It was his duty. If he didn't, then he would have let his own sense of himself down. Or rather, one idea of himself: the idea of an honourable Englishman, whatever that was. In time, Alloy would smash that nonsense out of him but just then he was impressed by Andrew's spontaneous request for Bune's advice. Andrew had begun to climb out of himself.

Bune said not a word but led them back to where Andrew and Alloy had been standing before. A third line of houses had caught: the one on the right side of the grass street, where the piece of washing had burned a little earlier. The breeze had died down so that the roaring fire had given way to a more settled activity.

A useful little gang of men and a couple of hardy female camp followers had gathered by now around Bune. His compact and waiting energy had done it. Bune the fisher of men.

The timing was perfect because the wind had died down. Later, with the sunrise and the day's warmth it would strengthen again. Also, Andrew was not aspiring to interfere in the practical activities of his boss-boys as he often did, messing up a good job; neither had Jim appeared to boss everyone around and engender a feeling of ill will.

Bune's plan was simple. He organised them quickly. He rightly supposed that the fire would burn itself out in the plantation which was more humid and wet in its centre and towards the river. The only severe threat was to what remained of the labour compound. They had to break the fire while it was settled and so stop it from spreading. He led them to the store, which was on the far side of the compound from the fire and told them to get tools with which they could smash the housing line in which the fire was burning and stamp out and beat down the flames.

"Have you got the keys, Andrew?"

"Um, no."

They smashed down the door and armed themselves with spades, axes and any instrument with which they could attack the burning structures. Bune let Andrew lead the way which is how Jim – from furtive night – saw things when he materialized.

[][][][][]

Jim held Tudak and co back. They watched Andrew and Bune lead the little gang steadily up the line of smouldering timber until it was a smoking straggle of ruins, exposing the unharmed houses beyond.

Only then did Jim move in with his men – Tudak and co – to stamp out the spontaneous and sporadic fires that would keep bursting out through the devastated lines.

Together, they completed the job. Together they kicked together the bigger pieces of scorched timber and damaged bits and pieces of domestic trash so that the whole thing could burn out efficiently leaving a line of clean, black ash that would later be planted with vegetable seed and watered.

Together, they worked silently. Silently, this disparate group of people, focused, actually in fact – Yes! That was The Fact – creating something valid and worthy; creating a garden, actually and This Is Another Fact, for God's sake.

Up, for various reasons, for half the night or more, they all looked exhausted. They were sweaty and dusty: the lines on their faces like those nineteenth-century photographs of English, Belgian or French coal-miners. Peasant's faces aged by the grime of the mines. Aged by the grime of reality. Battle weary, was the battle worth the fight?

Here, now, at this point in the universe, these men forget themselves. Themselves. They forget their damnable, Descartes-ian self-centeredness. They are a single thing. Not only the Alloy-Andrew thing but also the Alloy-Andrew-Bune-Jim-Tudak-Tudak-Jim-Bune-Andrew-Alloy thing.

Annu? Love? I don't know, but it was – it is for God's sake – good.

A moment that resonates forever and reaches deeper and deeper into what someone calls Deep Heaven.

Here, now – this is the fact – silent within this Alloy-Andrew-Bune-Jim-Tudak-Tudak-Jim-Bune-Andrew-Alloy thing.

The sun rises and the hard fact of the morning hits. That heat on the back which tells you Time Is Up. Jump to It. Get Moving.

Too late?

Time will tell.

Silence.

Keen sense of tragedy felt by the Alloy-Andrew-Bune-Jim-Tudak-Tudak-Jim-Bune-Andrew-Alloy thing as it breaks up. Pulls apart and separates into suffering individuals. Stupid. Yes it is. Pulled apart by the fucking facts of life. By the hard fact of the plantation, which is, for all the fire, still there. There, as a damnable fact.

Separate they are now.

The naked madman howls at the empty universe.

Screams for God.

Is his loneliness real?

Is his suffering an act of creation?

Is his blindness a reality?

Well, that's a fact: we're not used to seeing Heaven and don't recognise it when we do.

⬜⬜⬜⬜⬜

Jim lets go willingly. As, I was going to say, an act of defiance. But it is not: it is an act of creation. I'm as good as God myself – God sniggers – Jim does, sort of, say to himself. And it would not matter if Jim's acts, very definite acts, of commission did not do damage. Nearly as much damage as Andrew's acts of omission. Indeed, it does not matter, one iota, in the long run – the garden will be planted in the ashes – but it does matter in terms of Jim's own suffering. But, as Jim would be the first one to recognise, fuck Jim's suffering, Tudak is the more interesting character. There is another fact.

Tudak. Yes, he let go because he was conditioned to do it. He did not feel the tragedy – even as, fleetingly, Jim did – because his, soul, or whatever you want to call it – his Tudak-ness – was insufficiently developed to feel such things as tragedy, anguish, love. But, and this is quite an important thing – indeed, an important fact in the whole fact of creation – Tudak's letting go was not a deliberate act, of defiance or creation. It was conditioning, like a dog is conditioned. Tudak felt, just then, hunger, loneliness and things like that but without a sense of applying them to himself. His letting go was a condition of life; like rain or a hard road. You took it and you did it. That was, in fact (another fact), Tudak's great advantage: his lack of self-ness. It was just a pity that for the time being he was in Jim's grasp. Tudak was, is, innocent, the most innocent of them all perhaps for all that he would be the one who killed Tarlie. He killed Tarlie but he did not murder him. Jim did that. Tudak's beauty was real.

See the world from Tudak's eyes. His memory itself was a thing evolving. He does look up and sees – eventually he sees – the stars. Despite what he does, his time of glory will come.

I saw it with my own eyes. I saw the crowd of people. I saw the beautiful Bird of Paradise fly up. I heard its cry of love.

Father forgive me.

No trouble, my son, there's always room at the table for one such as you.

[][][][][]

"Well done, Andrew."

"Thanks Jim, but it was Bune here."

"Bune? Who's Bune?"

"The boss-boy."

"Boss-boy, eh?"

Jim looks at Bune, sees small strong man. Registers. Cute dog. Wants to pat its head. Pulls back at last minute.

"You should join us." Thumbs back to Tudak and co.

Bune looks at Tudak and co like rat looks at terrier dog.

"No Sir."

Bune looks away from Jim to Andrew and Alloy.

Jim hates Bune as he hates Andrew-Alloy but does not register it as a conscious fact just then but later, the way that fellow said Sir, I didn't like it. The way Andrew said it in the club when he went all queer. I didn't like that either. The night Margaret had rushed out like that. What the fuck were they all up to? But they can't pull the wool over my eyes: I'll get him one day. See if I don't. Fucking Annu.

Bune walks away.

Tudak watches Bune. Wants to follow. Starts out.

Hold back boy. Later.

Tudak lies on dirty ground, chin on floor. Eyes look to where Bune has disappeared.

"Cocky bugger."

"Not actually. He's my best man."

"Is he?" You fuck him, I suppose. Another of your geeks. Glimpses Alloy who disappears also.

Do you take me for a fucking idiot? Can I not trust the evidence of my own eyes? He was there I tell you. That Annu fellow. Called me Sir! I should have strangled him there and then.

Andrew and Jim.

"You better get some rest lads."

Jim walks back to his Landrover, Tudak and co follow.

Jim calls back.

"Andrew."

"Yes, Jim?"

"Get some rest." I'll get you later.

"I will."

"Henry'll be over sometime to work out what we have to do."

Business as usual.

Looks like it.

17
Daphne's Story

Look at it from another angle.

Difficult, I agree: the mind already has its preconceptions. Nonetheless, from where she sits, she cannot see, as we do, the back door into the club; the door beside the bar, that is.

But – and this is the point – the very centre of her vision is Margaret, even though she has to twist around a little in the creaking rattan chair to see Margaret who wears a red dress, high at the neck, strong shoulders exposed; shoulders round and firm but not masculine; motherly, more like. Shoulders you would want to hold in your hands if you are Joseph, or another good, loving man returning the warmth. Not Jim, of course, who is not tall enough and who, in any event, has hands not warm but sticky and not very clean. Margaret's shoulders; the faint buttery freckles which the boy from Moraine had wanted to lick off all those millions of years ago. Margaret, relaxed, leaning ever so slightly back in the chair, her legs crossed at the ankles like her mother had taught her. Without any effort at all, elegant but a sort of blousiness too in the way she wears her clothes. Once dressed, Margaret forgets her clothes. She might spill things down the front and not worry. Like another memory too.

The woman sees Margaret from behind and a little to one side so that the view is not quite a profile: vertical forehead; long nose; mouth ready to smile, always, a tiny bit open. Joseph loves Margaret's smile; he likes to cup her definite chin in his warm hand and put it in his mouth. Are Margaret's eyes vacant? She might be miles away, or nowhere, or at the very centre of things.

The room is more-or-less dark with incidental blobs of yellow light illuminating bits and pieces of the actors. But the woman can see most of Margaret and what she cannot see she imagines. She sees that Margaret's hair is blonde, old blonde which might be suddenly grey but in the hot darkness of the club night, caught in the blob of light in which Margaret sits, it is pure gold, containing all the colours of the rainbow.

The woman who watches Margaret has looked at the world. She has tried to relate herself to it but she has failed, so far, to get into it. She wants something, expects something from the world but she has no idea what it is. So, she is ready to react and to get involved if only she knew the trick. She is – as we shall see – a little bit less pre-conditioned to go along with the status quo – whatever that is – than other similar women in her position.

She likes Margaret. Or rather she likes what little she knows about her: her detachment and the fact that she does not gossip and giggle with the rest of them and yet retains, at any rate, their amused condescension. You could say she was captivated by Margaret. Younger, she would have had a crush on the older girl.

So when Margaret walked out of the club, when Andrew had seemed about to fail, she followed.

[][][][][]

I remember Joseph that night as if for the first time I recognised him. Something better than all of us brainless trash there in the club drinking like fishes and demonising everyone who wasn't like us. But he was not the critical type; he was loving. As I watched him I caught his eye and as if expecting it, he smiled. So I knew he was Annu, after all, who hadn't passed out of my life but who was still in it. I felt wonderful. I was in love. I was in love with Joseph, with Margaret, with everyone around me. Even Jim made me laugh like a bubble of joy rising up inside me. It was a split second. It couldn't last. You'd burn up. But the memory remains to this day; as real now as it was then.

[][][][][]

Andrew at the bar, facing Joseph whose face is hidden in the dark; big hands polishing tumbler with blue-and-white dish-cloth, necklace of shark's teeth on naked chest of dancing gold. Andrew leans across bar. Tumbler placed on counter. Big hand holds blue-and-white dish-cloth; other grips Andrew's wrist. There is no escape. You watch. But this drama is, all the same, in the background because it is Margaret of whom you are most aware. When Margaret gets up, you follow, thinking of her and not of Joseph and Andrew connected across the bar.

Being where you are not wanted, you hurry out the back door, where, when you come to think of it later, along with all the other momentous things, stands the other man, in the dark, whose name you cannot remember. Tall, skinny, head overloaded with hair, incomprehensible eyes. Odd he is there, you didn't think it was allowed, but it must be alright because he works for Clarence. For some reason not clear at the time you associate him with Andrew, which makes you think of Andrew back there inside, Joseph holding his wrist. You might once have thought that was odd too but it seems to be right now.

So you follow Margaret, like the junior girl following the adored prefect, and although Margaret might seem to be ignoring you, she doesn't or isn't because when you sit beside her on the veranda – Jim's house – looking over and beyond the low club buildings that are nothing under the stars and the darkness stretching out towards the Pacific Ocean, she asks if you'd like some coffee for all the world as if you've just spent the whole day with her. Yes please.

[][][][][]

Daphne is unconscious of the view from the kitchen window most of the time.

All the same, it is there. The roof of the carport cuts off most of the sky, a thin strip above the sea of oil palms. The garden shrubs block the view of the golf course below but if she stands back from the sink she sees, to one side, the bulk of the mill; chimneys dribbling thin, horizontal smoke.

At night the mill spreads its hot light to create a cocoon of space in the dark, the smoke glowing rounder and more nourished under the roof of the sky. It draws nearer. Monstrous groans and clangings; a night-time animal, out there in the garden.

The fact of there once having been the house-boy, Annu, only makes things worse. It wasn't fair.

She stands back from the sink to look at the space once filled by his compact, solid body. In his loose clothes, the tee shirt a size too large, he had looked squat and ill-formed as if he didn't fit inside the house. When he removed his tee shirt for the first time, to do some more arduous work, she had seen that he was beautiful: rounded, complete and wholesome, the light coming from within to illuminate the dreary house. It was the house and herself that didn't fit him more like. She had deliberately studied his body, trying to analyse his physical faults in order to de-deify him. His short stature, his stubby pigeon feet, his slightly bowed legs and callused knees, his receding and thinning hair, the lines around his eyes. Yet his compact, contained strength was perfect. His smile and his strong teeth were a joy in themselves. When he left a room, he left behind a scent she could only define as the scent of Annu. She would take in deep breaths of it. It was like a view of the whole beautiful world in the morning.

Stupid middle-aged woman falling in love with strong, healthy body of good, confident man. Any silly, empty-headed woman with too much time on her hands and servants can do that. But I am not that. I am not. I am more than that.

When Annu had been in the house she had not believed she was silly. Beside him she had felt better. But now he had gone she feels – looking out of the kitchen window – that she is silly and empty headed. The memory of him makes her feel nonetheless small and badly made. It was Annu who had made her kick off her high-heeled shoes. She hadn't worn them since.

It hadn't been sex. When Annu had been with them she'd loved Peter and loved him more than she'd ever done before; she'd wanted to help him and be his help-mate in life. A sort of compassion for her husband had filled Daphne when Annu had been around. An overwhelming, joyous feeling which had made her want to sing. Annu gone, she felt listless and in love with no one, least of all herself.

She makes herself sigh and pushes away from the stainless-steel sink to look at the mill glowing a little in the dusty dusk.

A view; and a woman who is Peter's wife and mother of Alison and Tommy. A woman of whom people say, when they notice her, she must have been good-looking once, she still is, a bit. She had been English plump and pink once, seeming a little on the large side because she was just a fraction taller than average. Seeming just a fraction more confident than Peter because she'd come to Australia on her own to see the place but she'd been glad to have him, to have his hand to hold in the terrifying world. They hadn't been in love or anything like it but they had given each other some mutual support and they'd discovered in a fumbling sort of way that they could make love together and rather liked it. Without her he would not have taken the mill assistant's job up in New Sudan, he would not have got away from his father who wasn't a bad old stick in the end and was fond of his grandchildren and paid their school fees so's they were near him down in Queensland in the term times and he'd put them on the plane and pick them up again you'd never catch me going up there but Peter seems to like it and I'll say this for little Daff she's made a man of him. So all in all it wasn't a bad marriage.

[][][][][]

But when I thought of Margaret I knew things were alright. When I forgot her, I felt depressed.

That night when I followed her out of the club, I barely knew her, but I followed her.

You frightened me so I rushed on to catch her up but I'd lost her. She'd disappeared.

Good thing I wasn't wearing high heels. I'd have fallen flat on my face!

[][][][][]

Peter's car fills the carport beside the family house, finally plunging the kitchen into darkness, so he can't see her standing by the window.

She watches him come into the dark house unaware of her watching.

He might have appreciated someone to welcome him, the house lights on; someone to make contact with the visible social animal that is Peter, the Mill Manager. Not the best mill manager but good enough and knows the ropes and keeps things ticking. What else can a chap do? You can rely on Peter. You can rely on Peter to say the obvious thing and do what men's men do just like his father twenty years ago only even then it was a bit old fashioned. Like that time he took them on a cruise and he turned up for dinner the first time wearing a white dinner jacket when everyone else wore open-necked Hawaiian shirts and the Greek man wore an expensive tee shirt hugging his beautiful body decorated with bits of gold. She felt over-dressed, even in her summer frock, but thank goodness she hadn't put on an evening dress like he'd wanted and Peter managed to pull off his tie when no one was looking. Almost unbearable when the old man pulled out a chair for one of the ladies who hadn't the foggiest what to do so she missed the seat and sat on the floor with a scream and everyone burst out laughing to hide their embarrassment stupid old man why doesn't he go away and die no wonder his daughter or whoever she is looks like she's sucking lemons and that dress looks like something Julie Andrews would wear on a bad day.

Peter comes through the door in his tailored shorts and long white socks, which do – it's a fact – show off very manly, brown, hairy legs of which they are both proud. Stand up straight, clench that pipe in manly jaw and prepare to meet the lady who is your wife.

"Hello Darling," he shouts in a manly way.

No answer from she who watches him.

He collapses, shrinks before her eyes, drops a heap of papers and his pipe – stupid damn thing – onto the coffee table and flops into a chair. She sees him, a dark lump in a dark room and yet she knows every detail of him as he sits; as he slumps – sit up straight, boy. You want to end up a hunchback? His mouth is stupidly open. You'll be drooling like an old woman one day if you don't watch that habit. Eyes stare into the great big frightening world. I haven't the foggiest how it works but if I stopped this routine of working and supporting my wife and two children I'm pretty sure the earth beneath my feet would dissolve and I'd be floating alone in space.

She dare not move. She does not want him to know she knows he's weak. She does not want to be the disloyal wife. She's a good actor. She can fake an orgasm like the best.

What if he turns on the light and sees her?

Oh God.

Oh God, shit. So what? I was watching you. Saw your naked soul. That's why I love you. Don't need to fake that.

He gets up, goes to the bedroom. She hears the shower.

She bangs the kitchen door, switches on the lights. Bright normality. Keep it up. Goes to the bedroom where his clothes are strewn on the bed. White underpants because real men don't wear those pansy coloured things. Therefore, endearing skid marks.

"Hello Darling," she calls. "You're early."

"I'm not. Where've you been?" Pleased to have her nonetheless.

"I was walking on the golf course. I saw your car and came up."

"It's late. You shouldn't be out when it's dark."

"My goodness is that the time? I must put on the dinner. Don't be long. Kiss-kiss."

He is so happy to hear her voice he wants to cry but he wouldn't want her to see him weak like that.

She takes his soiled clothes out into the carport, big stag beetle batting the strip light – a mass of lesser insects. Dumps clothes in cement washing sink for Martha in the morning. Turns on tap, leaves them to soak overnight, returns to kitchen, returns to carport, takes out Peter's skid-marked pants, better do those myself, watches sink fill and turns off tap.

[][][][][]

She walks, this woman, in her new flat-heeled shoes.

She walks out of the floodlit car park and onto the road. She turns left, climbing higher up the hill. Margaret ahead, she supposes, but no evidence. The dark has taken her. A substantial thing of sounds and smells. A series of dusty curtains. Her arms sweep forward to part them. She can tear through their flimsy rottenness. She knows she will find the light. She has no fear of the dark because she is separate from it. It will not hold her unless she wants it to. She knows where she's going this time. She kicks off her shoes to feel the warm, sticky bitumen under her feet. No broken glass here: Joseph sweeps the road clean every morning. Woe betide him if even so much as a tiny splinter – sliver of light – is found by Henry as he walks back home for breakfast. But how the stuff gets there in the first place is a mystery.

Jim's driveway rising suddenly more steeply than one had expected. She'd not noticed it like that before but in the dark, beneath her feet, she feels it distinctly, her calves stretching and her toes pulling a bit. Like one of those dreams but this time she gets there.

Up, up she pulls because the house is the GM's house. It must be on top.

She hadn't realised it was so, so high and above everything. The lights of the club must be down there somewhere but she can't see them for the life of her because of the hump of the garden, a little above her beyond a retaining wall.

The lights of the house are ahead now. The carport is different from theirs because it is set at a different angle so that Jim's vehicle faces the kitchen window lighting up the room with its headlights whenever he returns from wherever it is he returns. She couldn't have stood unobserved in that kitchen. Jim sees Margaret standing there, always, when he returns, but she is gone by the time he gets into the house. He never mentions it. Neither does she. Otherwise – here she is – the house is just like theirs only it looks different and she can't work out why. Is it because there is too much bright light in that big central room where life is supposed to be lived? Is it because there is more of Jim in it than Margaret, for all the light, so you can smell him? Sulphurous? Something is not right, at any rate. She switches off the lights and feels better.

She knows where she's going. Through the other dark room and out onto the little veranda where Margaret sits. A bench against the back wall sometimes used as a table; folding chairs.

Hello, dear. Sit down.

It is high up.

Is it?

[][][][][]

"Hello, dear."

High up.

Higher than she'd ever imagined.

In the darkness, the world looks as it should in this exhausting dry dusty weather we've been having. The darkness draws it all together and makes sense out of it. A great pool of darkness, in which insignificant specks of light are temporarily suspended. A faint luminescence in the distance might be the sea. A more solid blackness, the mountains. Or, perhaps not. It's what you want.

"Sit down."

The woman beside whom she sits is Margaret. Older yet not old enough to be her mother, too old to be a likely sister, Daphne nonetheless feels she has come home to her family. Here on Jim's veranda. It's ridiculous but it's Margaret who makes it home and she'd follow her to the ends of the earth, which is what she can see from up here.

"Coffee?"

"Yes, please."

"It's only instant."

"That's fine."

And it is fine to drink instant coffee beside Margaret up here way up here above everything. Well, you can see the floodlights of the car park if not the car park itself but from up here they are nothing. The club just a speck or two of yellow bits in the pool. The mill a bit more, a red burning thing diminishing the lights of the other buildings around it but, all the same, it isn't such a big thing – certainly it's not in the back garden. Here with Margaret what counts is the black space all around, below and above. Wow, there's the whole world out there and I love it and really, one has to admit, everything else is just, well it's just nothing. And I don't feel above it so much as a part of it. I could fly into it.

"How do you like it?"

"Just a drop of milk please."

"There you are."

"Thanks."

She takes the cup from Margaret and looks into her eyes. There is a light in Margaret's pale blue eyes. Could be grey. Hard to tell but it is not the colour of the eyes so much as the kindness of them. Daphne wants to cry but she does not. One is, or rather one was, English. These English girls of that type, Peter. You could do worse. A lot worse. She's not spoilt. She wouldn't be, what with rationing and austerity and all that after the war in Europe. You could do a lot worse. I'd take her if she'll have you but God knows what she sees . . .

Margaret smiles. I know all about you. You see all sorts here and there's nothing new under the sun, or the moon, when it comes to humanity.

Your father was the strangest in his way – if you want to think of people being strange – and the most beautiful. He never said a word all the time he was with me. Wasn't for lack of a tongue. He wasn't dumb but what was there to say that might put things right? Nothing. Put them wrong, more like and I'd enough to say for the both of us. I once saw him on his knees looking into the eyes of a cat. He was purring at her and she was purring back. One day he was gone. In his body anyways. You were born soon after that, Margaret.

He might have been a visiting angel.

"Biscuit?"

"Hmmm, thanks."

❏❏❏❏❏

These people.

Each one a point of emotion from which they can look out.

If the mood takes them.

Down there in the club.

Up there on the veranda of Jim's house.

Andrew walks out of the club. He is nothing until Alloy catches his hand, connects and thereby makes him significant in the universe.

Joseph behind them laughing his big laugh, his big feet in touch with the ground, the warm, smooth road propels them up the hill towards where Margaret and Daphne sit, connected also, by cups of coffee.

These People.

Each exists because of their connection with the others: I recognise you and therefore, you are. Is that it?

Connection as an act of creation.

Disconnection, therefore, an act of destruction?

Self-isolation, as was Andrew's wont until this night on the club hill, an act of . . . rejection and of suicide. I am, I am, I am turns in and in and in on itself to become an infinitely small, black, seed of . . . of what? What happens when it explodes? An Alloy, perhaps.

A brief stretch of time on the club hill in the infinite universe.

These people.

In the club, contained within fragile walls of delusion the four men turn in on each other for a moment to find nothing. Nothing in the centre because Joseph has gone.

Each has a similar idea, even so.

Fuck the man, says Jim, He is the cause of all this trouble. I got to get Him.

Who is this man whose name I keep hearing, thinks Clarence. I've got to find Him. I will ask Alloy on Monday.

How come I lost Him, thinks Henry; He seemed to have the answers. I can't remember what they were.

I barely noticed Him when he was with us, thinks Peter, but He seems to have had an effect on Daff. Should I seek Him out?

And thus, thinking of Annu, they depart, dissatisfied with something they know not. They think it is Joseph deserting them and Andrew causing a scene. Maybe it is. It is more than Margaret and Daff going off just like women, which they've forgotten in all the subsequent . . . Let's have one for the road.

Then, as a group, they cross the illuminated car park. Briefly they are frozen in an icy grey light. It fixes them for a moment. Then they disappear out into the dark, each his own way. To their empty, similar-looking houses, except for Jim who walks down the hill. If he could find that Annu fellow tonight and destroy him that would be a good bit of work.

These people.

Up on the veranda; Jim's veranda.

Sit down, sit down, you boys take up so much space but Margaret and Daphne have the only chairs. Alloy-Andrew sit on the bench. Joseph at Margaret's feet. Where else should he be? He leans against her leg. Her hand rests on his head. Where else would it be?

Daphne goes to make more coffee. It is an act of love and initiation. She brings the stuff back on a tray: hot water in a thermos, the condensed milk, a sticky tin. What else would you do? There didn't seem to be enough mugs in the kitchen I found some expensive-looking teacups wrapped up in tissue paper in a box. Delicate white things through which you can see the light, a royal blue band and gold. The lips that drink touch gold. Royal Copenhagen they say underneath but no one looks and how they got there God only knows but later someone digging the ground for the new house found one of the cups intact. He took it home. His children used it for making mud pies until it got smashed and the pieces were trodden back into the earth.

No Alloy, you stick where you are for the time being. Clarence will need you later. Then you can go.

The bloody-minded Alloy accepts this without a murmur. It saves the agony of making the decision which does not need to be made yet.

Joseph laughs silently, his big, fit body shaking. You must keep the house for me. I may need it. We may all need it. They don't need me at the club. I'll go to Tarlie tonight.

Nothing else is said, out loud, it seems to Daphne's recollection. Nothing and yet it was, in recollection, as if things were decided. Nothing earth-shattering: just an idea that they would move on and do the right things.

And maybe meet again.

Or maybe not.

[][][][][]

They'd sit formally to dinner. Not dressing up but the table set out properly in the dining room. Sometimes she'd lit candles as if they were going to be waited upon by servants, only Martha wasn't much good so Daff brought in the things herself. But they were only having a meal before doing a bit of reading and going to bed or, at weekends, watching a video – some reassuring costume drama which was not likely to challenge the idea of the universe.

It was a pattern for their lives. A setting – like the table itself – within which certain, certain things could happen but didn't have to because one could always discuss the food or the uselessness of Martha out there in the kitchen.

Annu hadn't stood for it, and the funny thing was they were not outraged by the way the house-boy changed their lives. Daphne hadn't even noticed until Peter pointed it out. Why are we eating here all of a sudden? Annu had laid the things for dinner at the bar between the kitchen and the family room. Do you mind? Not at all. I don't know why we bothered with all that dining room rigmarole.

They'd sat side by side like accomplices in something, Martha sent home and the house to themselves. Once, Annu left out a bottle of terrible wine from Chan's store but it was drinkable and they'd drunk it. Another time, Peter only had a bath towel wrapped around his waist. More wine, and after, she'd tried to take the towel off him. He'd resisted and got a bit cross. Not much though and she knew she'd get him next time.

Club nights, however, they still dressed, Daff and Peter, even if she'd stopped wearing high heels. I don't want to get varicose veins when I'm older do I?

It was after Annu had left, after that night at the club, that they began to talk. There was, after all, more to talk about. A good thing you went before things got unpleasant. Andrew going a bit too far and then walking off with Joseph like that. It was a bit much for both of them on that night but it hadn't seemed much in retrospect. So the towel came off. You practically raped me. Can a wife rape her husband? Is it statutory? That she can't? My father would say that it is statutory for a wife not to take the initiative. Well bugger your father. But of course they had drunk too much that time.

He came out of the bedroom a bit more refreshed, not merely an act.

"Want a beer?"

"Just one then."

She tossed the can at him so he had to catch it and be more like himself: "Boo!"

For a minute she thought he'd cry. He had that look in unguarded moments but he settled himself in the armchair, very Peter-like.

She wanted to know what had been happening and he wanted to tell her because it was unusual.

"I wonder if we shouldn't let the kids stay with Dad this vacation. Things seem a little uncertain."

"But I thought the fire'd been put out. It's just this dry weather. It makes everything seem tense." As if, she thought, fire might break out any moment. But she wanted to reassure him. She said: "It'd be lovely to have some rain."

"Yes, but what do you think?"

"I think you're right. Tommy and Alison are our children but they're happy with your Dad, and they're safe. That's what counts. Isn't it?" Although she didn't need reassurance.

"Yes," he swallowed, "and you can go down and join them, if you like."

Which made her laugh: "Not likely." But then she had remembered the past: Peter teaching them to ride their bikes, being mortified when Alison had fallen off going too fast down the hill when she was about nine. Blood from a scraped knee and screaming Mummy, Mummy look what he did as if it had been his fault. Tommy, too, almost embarrassed by his Dad. Whenever they came home from some expedition they'd both run to her for a cuddle. In times of trouble it was always I want Mum. Mummy called out in the night.

He watched her, and then only asked because it was the thing he had to ask: "Are you sure?"

"Yes, I am." So, that part of her life was over.

That part of his life also, she thought, had come to an end.

Later, when Peter was still not absolutely sure who he had become, he said: "There's something else I ought to tell you."

"Yes?" As if she didn't know.

"I don't want to shock you."

"Do you think you can?"

"No."

"Spit it out then."

"It's something Henry said about Andrew and that funny clerk of Clarence's."

"You mean Andrew and Alloy? I know all about that. Are you shocked?"

217

He looked at her, this new woman his wife whom he was beginning to love. It was fantastic that she, so substantial and wonderful, was really his wife. Something of which he could be sure.

She looked at him: "What do you really think? A man loving a man?"

"I . . ."

"Honestly."

"I don't think much actually if that's what they want to do. It's their lives. Good luck to them actually."

She walked over, took his head in her hands and kissed him on the mouth. She looked into his eyes as she did so and held on until his eyes opened and looked into hers, then she pulled back his head and slapped his face making him laugh like she'd never heard before. It was a big round laugh of joy.

[][][][][]

The woman walks under the sun.

We see her from the back. She is dressed like a man in trousers and in a large checked shirt that hangs over her large bum. The way she walks is a little heavy. The earth moves beneath her feet. She swings her arms through the still, humid air.

She wears a hat because the sun is high and would damage her skin. A straw hat; which is falling to pieces.

The late morning is hot, the sky an opaque whiteness of dust. The heat might shatter.

The road along which the woman walks is a straight man-made thing. Grey-white pulverised earth. When a vehicle passes – Madiak's scooter or a truck loaded with palm fruit – a choking, eye-shutting fog of dust is thrown up, settling on the vegetation on either side. From the road, the view is of a monochrome pale grey landscape. On the one side are the palms: a dust-coloured wall of fern-clad trunks and an overhanging fringe of tattered, broken fronds that give a little shade. Every so often this wall is punctuated by a dark, cool and even fragrant tunnel; an access road that might be welcoming to someone with less purpose than this woman who is walking down the middle of the empty main road.

On the other side, a messy tangle of dusty grass, shrubs and small trees that shoot up so quickly that there are, sometimes, glimpses of fresh green ahead of the dust. The forest having been destroyed, the land appears to be lying useless. But not quite as bad as that, for all that it looks bad enough.

The woman moves through a narrow version of reality. Her dusty view is checked, in the distance, by a hill, a slight uplifting of the land that takes the road up and over the horizon, around a block of oil palms. A nice touch, visually, making an attraction for the walker.

In the woman's real world, she sees over the hill. She sees through the oil palm plantation. She sees beyond the wasteland to what the land is and to what the land will be.

She walks in the forest which is not an ecological reconstruction of the forest in her mind's eye but rather the essence of the place she feels.

Nonetheless, it is the natural climax because on this coastal plain of deep alluvial soils buried by volcanic ash and then built up again by the rivers, the idea of the forest is no sentimental notion. It is reality. Given half a chance the forest of her mind will roar back. It returns when she is most relaxed, least attending to what she is doing, to where she is going. She sees it. The warm, dark-earth smell of the place. The darkness shot with bright light. The menacing liveliness. It is here she walks.

The idea is, come to think of it, like Annu Himself.

[][][][][]

Anyone not knowing the path would not notice its entry from the road. It starts before the road begins to ascend the hill – a wrinkle on the coastal plain. To the left, another road would take her up the hill and a few hundred yards into the plantation and to Andrew's house where he'd be having his breakfast. He'd offer the unexpected visitor a cup of coffee, and she might have changed his life earlier, only she is going somewhere else.

Margaret turns right.

The path runs through tall grass. Higher than her head so that the hat bobs along with a life of its own. So narrow is the path in places, she has to point her arms ahead to stop herself being whipped by the tall stems. Swimming forward now, the grass seeds falling upon her hat and shoulders like a golden shower of welcome. She is smiling.

The grass ends at a patch of ripening maize, widely spaced and growing up from a bed of groundnuts. Beyond, a ragged banana grove, sweet potato vines straggling over the ground, struggling against the heat.

The place is deserted and as silent . . . as a place that is too hot for anything. Stopping her movement she feels the heat like a furnace blast. Her clothes are too heavy. She is tired.

She comes to a group of thatched huts as the ground falls away a little. Not the best way to build in this coastal climate where the usual thing is to put your house up in the air a little to keep it dry and airy. These ground-based things make inefficient houses: hot and stuffy; damp when the rain falls so that little ditches have been dug around them to drain excess water down the slope. Useless-looking in this weather.

There is a taller, more straightforward sort of building with the cross on its roof. Shaded a little by one of the new trees that has sprung up from the battered ground. Some papaya trees – called paw-paw here – are exhausted in the heat. It makes her exhausted to look at them.

Inside, dark and cool after the blinding heat outside, the darkness is shot, like the forest before, with fine needles of light because the walls are made of split bamboo blinds. A couple of poles raised a foot or so off the ground make seats. She sits, hat in her lap. Grateful, she looks her age.

"Madam?" says the waiting Petrus.

We know the rest. Margaret did not do any teaching. She was not the type who could stand up in front of people and tell them what to do. She provided the moral centre, the heart and soul of the school. She sat at the back of the church while the children were taken through their lessons by Petrus, either, apparently, asleep, or else, wide awake and attentive, learning the simple pidgin stories herself.

At first the children were afraid of the bleached and faded-looking white woman. But they were drawn to her, silently wanting to be in her presence. Their mothers, too, would come. Often Margaret had a sleeping baby on her lap. The morning-time is the best time for teaching because the brain is fresh and the day still cool but children would, for the same reason, rather play. Thus it was Margaret who drew them. Much more than Petrus's hesitant teaching. The little faces, the wide eyes, specks of white in the shadows, would turn to Margaret, from time to time.

When Margaret was not there, her presence was felt. Not merely through the things that she brought – the paper, the pencils, the lamp and kerosene for the evenings – but through the strong knowledge that whatever happened, Margaret herself would ensure that the idea of the school would survive. It was not Margaret as a white woman who did this but the Margaret-ness of Margaret that transcended her race and sex.

In Margaret the school survived on Lingalinga plantation.

[][][][][]

Another day.

How could she know this woman when she knew not herself?

Margaret knew where she was going, but Daphne had to run to keep up with the strong woman. She watched Margaret's big woman's bum shift the shirt tail from side to side with each strong, regular step. She walked as if dancing to a happy internal rhythm that made Daphne happy to watch. She knew then and there that the pre-occupation she had about her own spreading hips was wrong. She was the right shape. From now on she'd let them spread. She felt more balanced just thinking about it and laughed out loud. Margaret turned back to smile.

As a girl, a little larger than her friends and pale, Daphne had collected things. She kept a diary and her bedroom above the front door was obsessively tidy. It doesn't look lived-in said her mother, a blousy, untidy sort of woman who had grown up with servants and expected people to do things for her. They generally did. The self-sufficiency of her daughter worried her but she loved all her children with a protective mother-love for all that they repelled her a little by their lack of dependence. Yet, she didn't want to know them intimately. They're your children she'd say to her husband as if they were a surprise to her. He'd laugh back I hope so they're not the milkman's which they might well, in fact, have been. Her father taught history at Wandsworth School. He was a good teacher for those days of kings and queens and defenestrations of Prague and Martin Luther banging things on doors in Wittenberg. His dislike for the British Empire and the fact that he let that dislike be known made him feel like an outsider, but he was happy. The adolescents who passed through his life in waves of ever-youthful caricatures of men were his children. They were unfinished and therefore good versions of vile humanity. His own children –

Daphne and her two brothers – contrarily insisted upon growing up. This made him afraid of knowing them but he drew towards them doing things for your mother who makes us all laugh sometimes because of her general uselessness when she's not driving me mad sometimes so I want to murder her or at any rate get her out of the way so I can have some peace. A matricide would have drawn them together forever. That and the love of her memory as they forgot the exasperation. It didn't come to that.

So in this loosely woven family in which she is trapped, Daphne cannot define herself. Here is my room, so here am I in it. Everything in its place and me also. She'd spend hours looking out the window across the road to a similar window from which she might as likely be looking back.

She collected postcards for a while. She stuck them in a big scrapbook, very carefully, with an explanation underneath written in her large round, careful girls, this is how we teach them, loopy, girl's handwriting, Bournemouth, July, 1953 from Uncle Wilfred and Auntie Pauline although it is Auntie Pauline writing who defines herself as the both of them, my Godmother. But Auntie Pauline or Uncle Wilfred and Auntie Pauline don't belong to her or make her feel any more substantial for all the writing of an explanation. Here Daffy, one from Kenya, but there ought to be more to me than a collection of postcards Miss Daphne Smith died today aged 101 she was well known for her famous collection of postcards the largest collection in Britain, some of which she wrote herself but we'll never know what she wrote because she glued them into the scrapbooks. The collection will be publicly burned on the common as a lesson to all those other old maids who devote their useless lives to collecting things. They take up space. Her older brother collected stamps but later developed a useful interest in taking apart radios in the breakfast room. He featured once in Meccano Magazine and later became a fuel conservation engineer in South Africa therefore, apparently, bolstering the Apartheid regime. My brother the well-known Fuel Conservation Engineer and Racist . . .

Daphne tried to keep up. If this woman is, then I am . . . not. What makes a person? What makes a person significant not merely to the world but to themselves?

[][][][][]

September 1959. So hot had it been that my younger brother – the one who became well known, a few years later, for being the first boy, young man more like, in the street to have a Beatle haircut – had rigged up a tent in the back garden. When the weather broke with those stupendous thunderstorms you remember he got drenched one night because we'd locked the French windows and he couldn't get in I think Daddy did it on purpose he had a mean streak Mummy let him in and they had cocoa in the kitchen she could understand a drenched child dripping on the kitchen floor making a mess for someone else to clear up. It gave her an excuse not to get up the next morning.

September 1959. Evening. She liked to walk across the common, overlooked by big, red-brick Victorian houses in secret, abandoned gardens. This bit had been civilised with avenues of lime trees between which ran asphalt paths. Therefore, she could walk in her new, white, high-heeled shoes. You walk putting one foot in front of the other like so, even though your legs can move as freely as they like in the wide, stiff-cotton, flower-printed skirt. Big blue flowers on a white background if I remember. I made the frock, as if, thereby, I could make myself, cutting it out on the dining room floor. Get out Mummy you'll tread on it. I'll get it and she rushes to the sideboard kneeling elegantly to get out whatever it is her mother wants. Pack of cards I think it was. She looked so sweet, I'll always remember her like that in front of the cupboard getting the biscuit tin out for me. A little frown on her young face upon which nothing had been written. I hope it never is. Not my little girl anymore but a woman. I hadn't noticed it before.

September 1959. Evening. Night almost. Premature autumn caused by dry London summer. Atlantic storm tears at desiccated leaves. Shifts the branches above my head. Glimpses of the moon which would pour silver had I wanted it.

On January the 1st 1950, leaning on the hall radiator – smell of warm brown paint – looking at her pasty, freckly face in the mirror above. The fact of moving into a new decade, of it now being 1950 something when for as long as she had known, it had been 1940 something and Mr Atlee Prime Minister; it was an exciting and even frightening prospect. The future is here and this is what it is like. She studied her face and could see nothing. There seemed such a lot of flat cheek. Did people notice it and stare at her? Ought she to cover up when she went out? Her brothers had once put a big brown paper bag over her head to frighten her. She had calmly kept it on, alone in a glowing and easily defined orangey brown world. She stuck her tongue at the inside of the bag and it began to fall apart. Too easy to get out of it and by then her brothers had left her alone sitting on the sofa in the lounge which her mother called the drawing-room making her father laugh drawing and quartering more like thinking of Merry England and the Age of Good Queen Bess. If we have a drawing-room then where's the butler?

She sticks her cheek out with her tongue to make it matter. But it doesn't.

January 1st 1960. Cold, grey Atlantic sky with seagulls. London, flat and hopeless. Like the old lady in her good-quality West End coat which is, nonetheless, pre war, who was knocked over near the railway bridge where there ought to be traffic lights there's so much traffic these days. That time. She must have died of shock she looks so peaceful but there's too much of her leg showing, marbled with blue and red veins, bruised now, and the shoes need repairing. Depressing more than sad said her mother. It surprised me she said anything. She pulled the coat down a little and we were impressed that she could touch a dead body. With love. We'll just stay here until the police come it's the least we can do. I think it's Mrs Grant. They used to have one of the big houses overlooking the common before the war but it's been turned into flats now the garden's a mess and it used to have such lovely roses. Before the war. She must have imagined once, she'd die in that house, in the cream-painted, Edwardian drawing room, with the view of the garden through French windows, not here on the road during an outing from a bed-sit.

She's beginning to collect memories now. Burdened with them before she's begun. They seem to be crushing her already because there is nothing there to stop them. Passing a bomb site once near St Paul's she wondered what they would find under all the rubble. She had a vision of herself being bombed in a house. She's in there we know. But when the rubble's cleared away they cannot find her.

They wander away for tea once the police have arrived. She plays monopoly with the children. To make them forget the old lady's leg. It's not often she takes that much interest. To make herself forget, actually. You've got to go for Park Lane if you want to win; The Old Kent Road's no good. You don't have any idea. I don't care at least I won't lose The Old Kent Road. You will in the end.

I'm going to Australia. You don't know anyone there but there hadn't been any opposition. Well in those days lots of people were going because the weather's better and you can get a house. It's safe which is more than you can say for Europe what with the atomic bomb and over-population it'll be standing room only. Daddy gave her fifty pounds and her mother kissed her for the first time in years and I'm not emigrating I'm just going for a holiday you could stay with Auntie Pauline in the South of France if you want a holiday.

I think I was doing what Mummy wished she had done. She might have if it hadn't been for the war. Then she married Daddy because it was probably one of those wartime things that got out of hand. We were all wartime children, conceived on leave, except for David who must have been born soon after. Fertility in time of war. I think it's quite unusual. I don't know. We were before the baby boomers.

April 1st, 1960. Her brothers walked her to Clapham Junction for the train. Wandsworth Common takes you forever round and round the houses. They carried her little white suitcase down the asphalt path between the naked trees and under a brilliant, clear blue Atlantic sky. She felt cold because there didn't seem any point in taking her camel coat – Christmas present, it'll be waiting for you when you come back – so she just had her white cardigan and the pale blue mac.

[][][][][]

She ended up in Brisbane where she was no longer a fraction larger but rather a fraction smaller than those strapping Queensland girls. A shorthand and typing job – studying book-keeping at night – with what seemed to be a rather rackety company mining something up north but they paid well so she could get her own room. We'll send you up there if you're a naughty girl which is what they wanted her to be but she wasn't but only because she didn't know how until she met Peter. And he didn't know much either.

So that was it: watching herself. Married to Peter and Peter's father. This is who I am? Mrs Wallacey. Made her think of Liverpool and the Mersey but we're from Cheshire originally. Everyone is. Not really sufficient but her cheeks had at last made something of themselves. Sorry we can't be with you but lots of love from Mummy, Daddy, Charlie and David. They gave her another £50. Mummy died, sorry I can't get to the funeral, so they went up to New Sudan. It was an adventure. My daughter/sister/aunt in New Sudan. Your mother left you

£1000 and all her jewellery it's worth quite a lot you'll get a share of the house one day it's worth quite a lot London property prices are booming. So she was worth quite a lot and Peter says Dad'll snuff it one day and I'm his only . . . and all that not that . . . but it's a fact. The young are heartless: impossible to think they'll be old themselves on day. Or dead first. Then Alison was born, then Tommy.

[][][][][]

Was it the children going off to boarding school?

"I was miles away!"

"You were."

She'd bumped right into Margaret so that the two women clung to each other for a second or two under the hot sun.

You could call Margaret blousy too.

Daphne clung a little longer. She subsided from clinging to holding on, as it were, for dear life. She wanted to say, to say, to say something that would express the moment. That would make it permanent in her memory. She wanted what she didn't know but she was sure she could get it out of Margaret. Margaret must have the answer. But what is the question?

Holding on, she presses her head into Margaret's neck, her vision confined for the moment to Margaret's shoulder, the contours of her back, her buttocks beneath the tail of the man's shirt and Margaret's heels resting on the dusty ground. Hold on to Margaret who does no more than support the younger woman. Take deep breaths of Margaret as if therein to find the answer.

She closes her eyes letting the strength of Margaret support her.

I remember it as if I had become separated from myself. A sense of terrific movement which was at the same time glorious and thrilling and calming. I was being stripped to my essential self. Liberated. I was falling backwards and backwards in on myself within a great overwhelming warm blackness which was nonetheless as colourful and as multi-dimensional as any human experience can be. I wasn't hearing or seeing or feeling as separate sensations, I was sensing the whole thing which is impossible to describe. Like listening to great orchestral music when you're drunk only more so. Like hearing music in your brain when you're walking through a great building or landscape only it's not music you can catch. All the broken things, the teacups and fairy cakes, the snapshots, the snatches of conversation, the postcards, the places on the monopoly board, the bits and pieces, the odds and ends of the black, senseless club nights when you feel just bashed about by everything, it all came together making obvious and delightful sense and then dissolved like a dream but without the desire to catch it only leaving a sense of . . .

Annu!

"Whoops, I'm here. Nearly lost you then."

Had she fainted? Blacked out for a second, a minute, a lifetime? She had no idea. Her mind dropped back into place somewhere behind her eyes extending down her spine to the small of her back.

She let go.

"Didn't want to lose you, dear," and such a smile of . . . well love, really. What else could you call it? There I was suddenly astonished to find myself on that road, on Van, New Sudan with this woman Margaret. I thought of the evening when we'd all sat on Jim's veranda looking out on the world together as if we had always been together like that and always would be. I had been there and now I was here with Margaret, having bumped into her as a solid fact, as a definite . . . milestone on a logical progression of activity which seemed, which was, perfectly right.

A small, black, sturdy-looking man passed them on the road. He seemed to have appeared from nowhere – "good morning Madam" – and he was gone again, so quickly that she wondered if he'd been there at all.

She was still holding Margaret's hand as if it was the most natural thing in the world.

"Do you say your prayers, Margaret?"

The older woman laughed. "What prayers do you mean?"

"Well . . . do you ask for things?"

Margaret was laughing, leading Daphne on: "What, like a new frock?"

"No . . . you know what I mean."

"Say it then." Pulling Daphne after her, off the road and down a narrow path that led through tall grass that brushed them leaving a dusting of fine seeds that they carried away with them.

"I mean do you ask for the answers?"

"No." More laughter.

"What then?"

"What then what?" It was as if Margaret was deliberately being obtuse. But she wasn't. She wasn't being clever either. Daphne wanted her to explain the secret of being Margaret. But there was no secret. There was nothing to explain. Margaret was there and that was Margaret.

"I want . . . to know, Margaret?"

"You want to know what, dear?" And Daphne half expected her to talk like some ignorant old nanny: Them who asks too many questions has their tongues cut out and served in sandwiches for tea.

"I don't know. That's the problem."

"The problem is you think too much, if you must have an answer."

"Do you think so?"

"I do. But then I dare say you had an education. They teach you to ask questions and it becomes a habit. A bad habit, sometimes." It was Nanny again.

"Why?" says the spoilt little girl.

Margaret laughs: "There you go again."

"What?"

"Asking questions. You'll make yourself ill."

They walked in silence, enjoying their progress along the easy path. Margaret stopped: "Sit down," she said emphatically, "and I'll ask you two questions, Daphne."

They sat, leaning against each other. Daphne said: "Yes?"

"Are you happy today? Now?"

"Yes, I am."

"Does it make you more happy to think why you are happy?"

"No, it doesn't. In fact . . ."

"There you are. Enjoy it as a gift and be thankful."

"But . . ."

"But nothing. Be, Daphne. Be. That is quite enough for one life. Nothing more is required."

"It's hard."

A little girl's excuse. She almost expected Margaret to say Practice makes Perfect but she didn't.

[][][][][]

When she woke up, she was standing amongst open sunny food gardens. Quiet and empty. Ground nuts and maize, sweet potato and clumps of bananas. They are standing on the top of a slight rise. A bump, no more, in the ground. They look, not at the mountains, which have retreated in that bright morning, but across a plain that leads gently down towards the river. Daphne has the idea of a whole, self-contained country before her. The land of Milk and Honey. Vast with newness and possibility. She takes a deep breath. She is astonished.

"I've been looking for this view all my life."

"Yes dear, I know."

Under the sky, the landscape is spacious but intimate at the same time. It is cut up into neat little food gardens so that the footpath goes not directly to the centre but follows an intricate and even devious route which insists on you understanding the manmade aspects of the countryside.

One goes around the edges of the gardens, you know. You cannot stride across them, like, like some invader. Certainly not if you're a woman. The Highland men don't like it. So sometimes we seemed to be going in quite the opposite direction. Suddenly we'd turn quite a sharp bend around some squared-off bit of sweet-potato ground and there we were much nearer than I'd ever imagined. One minute I was looking at the whole view and the next there was the church again and nothing more.

At first it had looked insignificant down there in the landscape although you could see all the paths, however tortuous-looking, leading towards it. Towards just another little grass house surrounded by bananas. But it was a church alright because of the little white cross on the roof. As we got nearer it disappeared amongst the bananas. If it hadn't been for Margaret just then I would have been lost. I knew we were getting nearer as the houses and the bananas crowded more together. This is where the people lived. I wasn't looking at the landscape, I was in it. I was a part of it. Someone looking from where I had stood earlier would have seen me, perhaps, as a hint of movement and clothes amongst the bananas.

As a child after the war I didn't know what a banana was. Even when they began to appear in the shops. East End barrow boys would come over and sell them on Lavender Hill from the back of a van. Mummy said they got them straight from the docks. She said they were profiteers who would not have minded if the Nazis had won the war. I didn't know what she was talking about. I liked the look of the cocky young men in their brash clothes, and shouting in their cockney accents. There was a department store near the Junction where we'd stop for tea. The waitresses were old ladies in black frocks and white lace. White tablecloths, white china teacups and heavy silver-plate cutlery. My mother would take off her coat but not her hat. I'd be allowed to choose one little cake as a treat but I never liked them. Fairy cakes or macaroons with paper stuck on the bottom. You ate them as a duty, as a ritual even though they tasted awful. The English middle class. They were funny in those days but it wasn't a joke. Clinging onto a macaroon for dear life. She laughs nonetheless.

A banana was a fruit going black in the dish on the sideboard. Mummy would eat it so's not to waste the money that didn't grow on trees. It never occurred to me that bananas grew on trees either. I was surprised to see them in Queensland. On Van, bananas grew around the rubbish in the bit of the garden down the hill. It never occurred to me either until the garden-boy told me that Annu had planted them when he was with us.

I know all about banana trees now. Did you know they walk? They aren't trees really. They're more like a vegetable. I mean our English equivalent would be rhubarb. Think about it. Except rhubarb doesn't have fruit you can eat. But it grows and moves in the same way as a banana. Fibrous too. With bananas you must look after the babies. I'm quite an expert now. That stem we call the tree produces just one bunch of bananas then it dies back. So before that happens you have to nurture just one or two of the corms – that's what they're called – which come up from the roots – rhizomes – as the babies. The next generation. So the plant walks because the new stem will have shifted along a bit. Of course if you let them go naturally they'll just become great big clumps and nothing wrong with that. They look beautiful. They're not always bananas either; just as often they're plantains you can cook.

As we got closer it all looked like one great big banana clump. I couldn't see anything else. Margaret strode on and as I looked at some bird's-eye chillies, so beautiful on a little fragile-looking bush, she disappeared into the bananas.

"Margaret!"

Daphne was alone in the morning sunshine. But, comforted by a gentle humanity, its evidence all around, she had never felt less lonely in her life. She thought of that last London morning of her life, her mother standing on the doorstep in her dressing gown. As she turned the corner of the street walking with her brothers towards the common she looked back expecting, hoping, to see the front door shut. But it wasn't. Her mother stood there still. A long way off but she could see every detail down to the coffee stain on the collar. She could smell the scent which had not been washed off the night before. She wanted to run back but it was too late. Twenty years too late. It's alright Mummy, we're still all here. Together.

"Here, dear," called Margaret.

[][][][][]

A very obvious path led through the bananas which were not a single clump at all but a sort of shrubbery on the other side of which was a group of little grass houses.

Looking at the houses, she felt ashamed. They had put one up just like this for the children in the garden. A play house. Peter had paid a few dollars for the materials which had been brought up in the back of the truck. It was when Annu was with them. He had done most of the work, letting the children help. People live like this. All the time? Yes and they sleep on the floor. He stamped on the lawn, making the earth shake with his laughter. Ally couldn't do that she's too soft. She has to have her little pink pillow and her night-light. Tommy was remorseless; Alison mortified almost to tears. I don't. You do, you liar. But Annu was laughing I have my night-light too. The children were dumb with disbelief irresistibly seeing Annu sleeping in one of their beds. It didn't fit. It's the moon, he said, and in their relief they worked all the harder for him.

Daphne blushed. What had Annu thought of her spoilt children? Of all of them? Should she have forced the children to sleep in the play house to feel what it was like? Then what? She was back in the club for a minute, sitting on one of the high stools beside the bar sipping a gin and tonic. It didn't fit. Such a great, yawning chasm between them and Annu's simple goodness. What could bridge it?

One of the houses was the little church, recognisable as such by a white cross set on top. The swept bare earth space in front would have held fifty or sixty people packed tight. More banana trees, crotons and kana lilies made it a friendly place but the young coconut palms and bread-fruit trees were too small to give any shade. Only the church could do that.

Daphne screws up her eyes against the high sun. She takes off the rucksack and drops it gratefully onto the ground. She feels the sun burn her shoulders through the thin cotton of her blouse. Little blue flowers, with hints of yellow, on a white background. Quite the wrong thing to wear in the bush. So silly.

Margaret was waving at her from the door of the church. A few dollars' worth of materials. A play house. Daphne feels so embarrassed she wants to cry.

I felt such a fool. A great big stupid galumphing girl who had stumbled into some magic place where she didn't belong. Any minute I expected them to tell me to go away. That they didn't want me in their game.

"Come on, dear. We've got work to do."

They have indeed. This is why Daphne is carrying the rucksack for the older woman. It is full of materials for the school.

It was not much work, but indeed things seemed to be happening. And with not a great deal of fuss either. The children sat obediently on the little benches under the mottled light. At the back, a few old women sat on the floor, smiling up as Margaret and Daphne entered. They gave Petrus the things and the children were shuffled around so that the two white women had room on the back bench. It wasn't comfortable because it was only a low piece of rough timber. Soon Daphne pushed herself onto the floor which was better although Margaret seemed happy enough.

Petrus began to talk.

"Mi laik tok tenkyu tumas long tupela meri husat kariem ol buk na samting long yumipela. Olsem olgeta yumipela singaut Tenkyu Missus Margaret."

The children shouted and the old women laughed. Petrus grinned.

Daphne never used the local pidgin conversationally. Her understanding did not go beyond what was required for getting the servants to do what she wanted. Again she felt ashamed. More so as she realised how little she had actually talked to Annu. So little. It was odd because from Annu so much understanding had come. An understanding of the unbridgeable chasm, she thought just then, her mind muddled and tired after the long walk in the sun.

"Wake up, dear."

She was leaning against Margaret's leg.

Such a beautiful sleep and I felt so refreshed.

"What time is it?"

"Two o'clock."

"It can't be." She thought of Peter eating his sandwiches at home on his own.

"But we haven't done anything."

"We've done enough."

"All we've done is walk all the way here and sit down."

"Isn't that enough? We've got to walk back. What else do you want to do?" Margaret smiled absent-mindedly.

She didn't know. What else could they do? They'd brought the books and things but she could as easily have sent the garden-boy. He'd have liked the time off. Daphne stood up. Her hair was sticking to her face. She felt full of energy.

"I feel I can do anything. I want to do something."

"Dig a ditch?" said Margaret, looking, actually, as if she could do just that. "We will, one day."

The children were standing around laughing and touching her clothes. Taking her hands and examining them. The engagement, the eternity, the wedding rings. Should she throw them off as her sacrifice? Should she dramatically pull them off one by one, flinging them out into the bananas? As she imagined her mother would have done, given half a chance. Was that the answer? The old women could sell them to the Chinese traders in town. But they wouldn't get a good price. And how on earth would she explain their absence to Peter? No, it would never do. Would it?

She was following Margaret out, stooping through the low door when she looked back, catching a glimpse of the crude painting above the simple little altar. She had not noticed it when she came in but now her eyes were used to the dark it stood out. It was a naïve painting of the crucifixion. There was the black Christ in his agony only he didn't seem in much pain. He was looking out at her as if to say what Margaret had said: It is enough.

She backed into the little room again, empty except for the teacher who was picking up the books. She watched his neat little figure in his big shorts and smart shirt, doing the job as if it was itself a joy. Something he must have done a hundred times before. A simple thing and yet great and, finally the word came to her, loving. Was the bridge, then, as simple as unconditional love? The way Annu had loved her and Peter and her children, for all they were spoilt and had so much that was hard to give away? Margaret was right, it was enough, but still the question as big and as looming as the mill: How to get there?

"Madam?" It was the teacher.

"Hello. I'm sorry I don't . . ."

"I'm Petrus. You are the missus of Master Peter at the mill. I know you."

"Yes. Thank you so much for . . . Do you know Annu?"

Whatever made me say that?

The man looked at me as if I had said something magic. He smiled a great big happy smile.

"Yes, I know him. You have reminded me. I will never forget him."

"Neither shall I."

And really, I don't remember if he took my hands or I took his but there we were holding hands and looking at each other as if we knew each other but hadn't met for years. There was no difference between us for all his good simplicity and my . . . complicated spoiling.

He was looking up into her eyes. She could see herself reflected in the golden brown of his. She could see the pores in his big black nose, she could smell him and she loved him.

"Petrus, I . . ." What could I have said to this man?

And holding her hands and looking at her, he laughed just like Margaret laughed.

"Em inap. Yu givim mipela pinis ol taim belong yu. Em bikpela samting. Mipela hamamas tumas bi yu sindaun pinis wantaim long mipela. Tenkyu. Em inap."

Margaret was pulling her out into the bright, boiling-hot afternoon sunshine. They walked home in silence.

She was ready for the shower when she got back and Peter had not even bothered to put his lunch plate in the sink. Just like a husband! And damn, she also thought, I forgot the camera.

That evening, Jim destroyed Ples.

18
Henry's Story

"Andrew! The boss is here."

The naked Alloy disappears; Andrew appears, looking sheepish, wrapped in a sheet.

Henry looks at him.

Andrew says: "Morning Henry. I was just catching a bit of sleep."

"I know, I know, I've spoken to Jim," Henry replies. He doesn't know where to look so he looks at his shoes − polished brown brogues. He envies Andrew and is aroused by the idea of the two young men sleeping together. Two warm bodies under that sheet. It's not fair. "This place is a mess."

Andrew ignores the remark: "You want a coffee?"

"Yes, please, but do get a move on Andrew, I'm quite busy and we've got to make some decisions today."

"Alloy," Andrew calls, "get him a coffee. I'll get dressed, Henry." He disappears and is replaced by Alloy, wearing Andrew's clothes. He ignores Henry because he does not know how to deal with him and is therefore ignored in his turn for the same reason.

▯▯▯▯▯

Apart from the charred stumps of trees nothing remains but ashes. The pressure of their clumsy boots raises the grey dust an inch or two off the ground but otherwise, they are exposed. The older man knows he is at the end of time. He is, therefore, depressed by the desolation in which he stands. The hateful sun burns his skin and makes him cross. The younger man is, by contrast, impressed by the event which has brought such sudden and total destruction, and which will undoubtedly shape a future in which he will play a part. But he is not yet exhilarated because, having forgotten the hand he has taken, he does not know what part he is supposed to play. He is, therefore, also cross.

"You'll have to get things moving, Andrew, there's nothing worse than these sorts of people not being told what to do. Time hanging on their hands. It invites trouble."

"I know," Andrew snaps back, "give me a chance. Last night was a little bit extraordinary. Don't you think?"

Henry walks away without answering. He waits for Andrew. Sulky boy. I'd like to spank him. His mouth feels dry. "You'll need to keep up with the work somehow Andrew," he shouts and is startled to find Andrew so close that he drops his voice almost to a whisper: "Are your harvesting rounds up to date?"

After a pause Andrew says, "Yes."

"How many days?"

"Twelve, or thirteen maybe."

"That's alright then, you can let it go out to twenty in this weather. That'll give you time to clear up. There's not so much damage to the palms. I've seen worse."

"I couldn't care a fuck what you've seen," Andrew murmurs.

"What?"

"I said I know what to do, Henry."

"Yes but . . ."

"And I'm going to do it."

Thus Henry warms to the boy whose skin is as thin as his own. He wants to feel its warmth.

"Andrew, I don't want to labour the point but you have been behaving a bit strangely recently and . . ."

"What d'you mean strange?"

Henry doesn't want a fight. He doesn't want to spank Andrew any more. He wants to be a friend; to them both. But it wouldn't work. "You're not your usual self," he says.

"I don't want to be my usual self, and as for acting strange . . . if you think some of the things that go on around here are not strange then I'd like to know what is." He walks away. Henry has to follow him. They move towards the centre of the plantation, where the fire has done no apparent damage and where the sun does not blind their eyes or burn their skin.

"Andrew," Henry calls, "I'm sorry. Let's just sort this out, can we? We can't do nothing."

"Can't we?"

"Not while we're drawing our salaries and living in company houses we can't."

Andrew looks at Henry. He sighs: "Yes, you're right. I'm sorry."

"That's alright. I'm sorry too." He thinks of Andrew and Alloy together again and feels his exclusion.

Andrew looks at the sky and laughs: "Look, Henry, you absolutely don't have to worry. I'll deal with everything but I would be grateful if you'd sort out the building side of things with Clarence. I'll get the site ready. I agree that there's no point hanging around. Once I've found Madiak and Bune we'll get the men together and start. Things'll be back to normal within a month. Pity about Tarlie, all the same; I could have used him."

"Can't you get him back?"

"No."

"Why not?"

"Because he's gone."

Before Henry can respond, Andrews walk away.

[][][][][]

Henry followed because he didn't know what else to do. Jim's strangeness was a familiar part of the way things worked but Andrew's strangeness was something else altogether and things weren't getting done as a result. The

232

extension for a start. Andrew hadn't done anything recently except fight Jim. This damn fire seemed to have come from all that and now here were more things not getting done and despite all the words Henry was sure that Andrew was not going to do them. And if Andrew didn't do them, then he'd have to sort things out himself. He didn't mind, he'd done it before but he'd like to know where he stood. Before, in this sort of situation, it had been a matter of mobilizing the best supervisors and doing it. Now, all the good men were disappearing, or acting strangely. Not only Andrew and Tarlie but Joseph as well who'd disappeared just when he was needed. And come to think of it, that had something to do with Andrew. Joseph had followed Andrew out of the club on Saturday night and not been seen since.

But the man he really wanted was Annu. He should have stood up to Jim that time and kept him on. And to think he'd been around only last week working for Peter and Daff. As a house-boy for God's sake. He must be around here somewhere. I'll find him. Then everything'll be alright. He'll tell me where I'm bloody going.

❏❏❏❏❏

"Let's find Annu, Andrew. That's who we need. Andrew?"

Henry looks around. He's alone. Lines of palms radiate from the point where he stands. He looks ahead down an endless avenue. He knows, if he dares turn around, he'll see the same view behind. Pull your socks up old man he says to himself and walks on.

He comes to a road. Looks left; looks right; has not the slightest idea where he is in the endless plantation. The road leads nowhere but he follows it nonetheless. In his youth it was rubber trees on either side; then the tea bushes with a view beyond; but now oil palms shut him in. He sees the endless rows of tombstones in the Somme Valley which he'd visited with his father as one of the last and one of the few things they'd done together. The old man had wanted to re-visit the scenes of his youth and to remember his dead comrades for some reason Henry did not want to understand. His father had died soon after. Henry didn't want to think of it. The vast wreck of his life.

Palm fronds rattle above. He shivers despite the heat. He is tired. He wants to go home.

"Annu!"

"Sir."

"Who are you?"

"Bune, Sir. Andrew's boss-boy."

"Where are we?"

"Near the river. I'll take you. Andrew's labourers are there."

"Have you seen Andrew?"

"He's there, Sir. He sent me to look for you."

To look for me indeed! As if I'm a child to be led by the hand.

Henry is tall, he stoops – but only a little, because he exercises and thinks about standing up straight – and he is grey. Almost a spectre here inside the cooler darkness of the afternoon plantation. His skin is damaged by years of tropical sun. His face and forearms are particularly aged and blotchy. He is a fine figure of a man even so. He commands respect amongst the labourers who are awed by his height and detachment. They give him that small thing anyway. It is not much to give.

Bune waits. Serious looking because seriousness is required.

"Lead on then," says Henry.

Bune leads. Cute he is, no doubt, wearing only a pair of old red shorts. From the back view, Henry's view, he is perfect for all the thinning hair which only serves to give him an air of wisdom. Funny how one bestows upon these fellows characteristics that they haven't got, just because they look . . . beautiful. Little muscular man, tight skin shining through the shadows. Large naked feet pad the soil as if they are making the path.

Henry trips. A hand helps him up.

"Don't fuss, don't fuss," he fusses and takes the hand.

[][][][][]

Although the oil palms have been planted almost to its edge, the river's meanderings make grassy promontories where adults rest and sandy bays where children play. The water is slow moving and incredibly clean. Also, because it breaks open the dead monotony of the rows of palms, there is more light here. One or two of the old forest trees have survived and a few youngsters have shot up so that all in all it is an enchanting place. It refreshes all but the most desolate of souls.

The first thing everyone did when they got there was have a good wash. This is why Bune is so clean, scrubbed and polished.

The homeless labourers and their various camp followers have settled amongst the palms. They have made themselves comfortable and because he was the one who had led them to the place they were willing, for once, to accept Madiak's organisation. Bune provided later stimulus when things got slack, Andrew made a senseless speech which was, nonetheless, reassuring.

Alloy and Andrew are lying on the grass, in the shade, upstream. Except for underpants, they are naked, while their clothes dry in the sun. Andrew's startling whiteness contrasts with Alloy's blackness. Beautiful youth, indeed. They do not get up as Henry approaches. Their eyes are closed.

[][][][][]

Look at them! Is that the way for a manager to behave? Half naked beside his, his, his paramour?

Henry was beside himself with anger. Everyone lying around as if, as if, as if there wasn't enough to do. Hadn't the compound just been burned to the ground? And here was Andrew asleep. He wanted to kick him. He wanted to kick them both into some sort of, sort of something.

He sighs. He'd like to lie down himself. And never get up again. Lie beside the quiet waters and sleep. Everyone else was sleeping. Or, at any rate, resting.

Naked children curled up beside their mothers, the pots from which they'd eaten unwashed. Sloppy lot.

There was the little fellow who had brought him here; who reminded him of Annu. Squatting now with other similar-looking little men. Black and shining, all of them in the hot afternoon quiet. Contented. The great, the great, the great big afternoon swallowing up everything.

He moved into the shade, leaned against a tree for a minute, and then sat down, head on his knees. How could one sleep out here? The ants would be biting any minute and really it's time we did something. Andrew, for God's sake! And you lot, you lot there, talking quietly in your little group as if you owned the place.

Nonetheless, he slept.

As big and black, and as warm and safe as the great tropical night under a thin new moon, back then when he was still young. Development manager for the company. Get the thing going they'd said in London. Give us a toe-hold. Don't worry too much about the rules. It's a lawless place anyway. All we need, to start with, is a couple of thousand acres planted and the mill. The rest'll follow. You can do it. You did it in Malaya, old man. Thousands of acres you planted for us. It's no different now.

But it was. New Sudan was not Malaya. In Malaya the whole apparatus had been set up. You pulled the right levers, and things happened. You contracted out most of the work and if you got skinned a bit, it didn't matter. Except that one time he didn't like to remember. You could do a bit of skinning yourself and get away with it if you were careful. Bought me a nice little place in Sussex. But Henry had not skinned anyone, and little good it had done him. Honour, bloody honour. What good is it if you're poor? No one cares a damn in the end.

All the same, he moved up through the ranks swiftly enough to begin with. He knew the rules. He'd been to public school, done his war service – an officer, at any rate, if not much action – then late, Cambridge, reading agricultural science. He fitted in easily enough. He played the right game. He knew, one might say, in which direction to pass the port and when not to wear brown shoes and all that . . . nonsense. Henry's alright. He's one of us. One of us. That's all he'd wanted. To be one of them, whoever they were. He seemed to have got there at one time. Phew! Now I can relax. Confirmed bachelor, Henry, but he's OK. Some of the best 'ave been like that.

Henry can do it. But he could not. Not in the rough and tumble of New Sudan. It needed someone who could paint the big canvas and splash the paint around regardless. If Henry had been a painter, it would have been neat little Victorian watercolours. It needed someone who could break the rules, and get away with it.

He had to get in Jim to help. Jim was the one who got it done.

Not one of us, but a good find. Well done old boy, they told Henry in London when they made him Senior Planter. Even asked him if he'd like to have a look at things in Sumatra for them, though it'd never been mentioned again.

Bit of an old woman, Henry, but you can't pull the wool over his eyes, although that is just what they did. You'll make the board one day knowing he never would. Push off back to New Sudan for God's sake and let us forget you.

Bit pre-war, Old Henry, forgetting what he had done for them post-war in Malaya. The shareholders had done well and, after all, Henry still had a job and his tiny little pension he doesn't need much he's got no family little flat on the south coast's all he needs. Don't rock the boat, Chappy, and all that when he raised the issue of labour quarters in the early days of New Sudan. It was a matter of honour, the company's honour, he thought but this was the nineteen-sixties, got to be more relaxed about it apparently and anyway, Jim says . . . everyone has to rough it. They don't mind living hugger-mugger. They like it. Feed 'em, give 'em beer and girls on Saturday night and you'll have 'em eating out of your hand. You're not a pinko are you, Henry? Socialist tendencies? Nothing like it: he was appalled by what was happening back home. The unions taking over the country: might as well be Russia. It was just practical management. Treat them like animals and they'll act it one day. They had: one Friday evening after Jim'd shown that film about the Zulus. Went berserk. I'd never seen anything like it. Jim had caused it and Jim had weighed in to solve it as if he enjoyed it. Leave it to me 'En', I know what's what in this God-forsaken place. He had. He dealt with it ruthlessly and brutally. It's all they understand. Animals. Look 'em in the eye and beat 'em until they know who's Boss. The few recalcitrants – commies, no doubt about it – had disappeared. Nothing was said but no one would look you in the eye for a while. Never did again, really. But a bloated, headless body had been found washed up on the beach soon after.

It was Jim's idea to break up the compound into smaller units. Divide and rule 'En', that's my motto. Trust me. He had. He was the one who made the idea work. Jim got the credit for the best labour compounds in the South Pacific. Credit to the company, old man. Surprised you didn't think of it. If he was one of us he'd get something for it. Not a gong of course, but a little recognition. It's all about honour, Henry. You shouldn't forget that.

Henry's sense of failure had been profound. It darkened his life for years but then Annu turned up. He knocked Henry for six, and as he couldn't help doing with such beautiful men, Henry put Annu up on a pedestal and fell in love with him. As he had done with a succession of servants, who, having failed to live up to his ideals, let him down. Henry's boy's run off with the radio/camera/wristwatch again. He asks for it: drools over them and then expects them to act like servants. I dare say the fellow reckoned it was a fair payment for services rendered. Seen the new one? It'll end in tears again. But it hadn't ended in the same sort of tears. The man had deserved his pedestal for all that it was the last place he'd sit. Deserved it more than Henry's puerile and needy love because he was big. Bigger than the whole thing, despite he was a small and, in certain lights, a delicately made man. Solid, all the same, with his feet firmly planted on the ground.

I stayed in love with him, even after he had gone. It wasn't the sort of crush I'd had on the others who were crushed by my infatuation and patronisation, I suppose. There never was any sex, whatever people liked to think. Might have been better if there had been. No, I loved Annu in a grown-up way. I'd never had that sort of feeling before. Well, yes, sort of, a long time ago but that's another story. But Annu was more than that. It had nothing to do with sex or carnal longing. The thought of it is almost blasphemous; like having a crush on

Jesus. The idea of Jesus, at any rate. Annu was just too big. You could never have had him in that way as if you owned him. You knew you had a personal relationship with him and you knew he had an interest in you but you couldn't have him for yourself. You could not own him because he owned the whole world. That's how it felt.

In his sleep, beneath the tree, deep breaths become lighter. Eyelids flutter; afternoon sun stimulates the senses. The idea of Annu: absorbing everything. All those layers of life stripped off one by one to the essential germ that was Henry. Yes indeed, Annu knew it, appreciated it, all the wrongs, all the evil, the burden lifted.

"Annu."

An old man calls in his sleep. The little group of men, chatting, lets it pass.

He awakes, remembering the calm times with Annu in his orchard when, together, they had cleaned the place up. Letting in the sunlight and air so that the trees bore good fruit again. Ah! Wonderful. He could hear the man's soft voice, which had seemed to vibrate in the strong breast. He was there, surely. The problems solved.

Wide awake in the hot afternoon, his body aching, his mouth dry having hung open for too long I must have looked a sight a drooling old fart. And Annu is not there. The cruelty of dreams. An almost unbearable sadness overwhelms Henry.

[][][][][]

"Henry?"

Henry looked out at the world, stirring after the afternoon hiatus. Andrew standing over him, hands on hips, tall and legs apart. Towering above, in fact, like an, an, an angel, his skin shining, his tousled hair glittering blond and all sorts of colours in a shaft of sunlight. A grin on his face as if he had . . . all the answers, damn him.

A hand extended which Henry had no option other than to accept and be pulled up again. Second time in one afternoon.

"Thanks Andrew. Gosh, I feel stiff." He brushed the seat of his pants and shook his hat. "No good falling asleep like that. We've got to get moving."

"Have we?"

A self-satisfied grin, and there behind Andrew somewhere the other chap looking at them through frowning eyes as if he was Andrew's, Andrew's whatsisname? Andrew's Svengali, for God's sake. Making Andrew into something different. Not English at all.

Henry scanned the landscape for Alloy. What he saw was the camp stirring into life: women, washing things noisily, chatting like chickens; children making an unholy row in the water; men − more quietly − busy building a variety of shelters for the night. Simple, tent-like structures roofed with freshly cut palm fronds from God knows where because there was a deuce of a lot of the stuff which meant somewhere the palms must have been virtually defoliated. It all looked rather permanent and well organised. The little man, as black, as polished and as beautiful as ever, was doing all the organising and doing it jolly

237

well, it seemed. An older fellow, all floppy jowls and big flat feet – Henry straightened himself – was following him around looking very self-important, giving little orders here and there which everyone ignored and pushing things with his feet. Henry looked at his own feet, brown boots dusty now, although they had been as shining as the little man's muscles in the morning. That little fellow, who'd pulled him up earlier was the leader all right. No doubt about it. Wonderful to see him getting things done. Quietly and solidly and, and, and there. What was his name? Might well have been Annu. Wish it was.

"Henry?"

"Sorry, Andrew. Miles away."

"You alright, Henry?"

Andrew was still shining there like an idiot. Young bugger. So sure of himself. He shouldn't let that little solid chap get so bossy. He'd have trouble with him later.

"Yes, fine thanks. I was just thinking . . ." Do stop smiling like that as if you're, you're young and have your whole life ahead of you while I'm just an old fart of the old, old school, ready for the scrapheap. "I was just thinking, oughtn't these chaps to be doing some work?"

The grin turned into a laugh. "It's nearly four o'clock, Henry."

"Well yes, I hadn't realised it was that late." He started walking towards the river. The others followed. He was the biggest boss there, after all. The place looked even less like a plantation and more like a village. Hard to believe they'd only been there for twenty-four hours. He didn't like it. Once people sat down in a place it was the devil's own job to get them moved. He remembered the string of buildings he'd discovered down by the railway line in Malaya that time when they'd been converting the rubber to oil palm. It was the Indians. They'd brought in their wives, had their children down there. There was even a Chinese trade store. Right under the nose of the company. Disgraceful. He'd had to get the police in the end. Paid them of course. You do it by Monday morning. He hadn't asked how but Monday morning muster he'd kept his distance. Didn't want to look those men in the eye. Better to be detached anyway. Doesn't do to get too close to the labour. They take advantage. That would be Andrew's problem if he wasn't careful. Look what had happened on the extension land. Jim had had to be ruthless because Andrew had been too soft. Soft: that was Andrew's problem. He wouldn't stand up to things. Didn't know the right thing to do. That was the trouble with these English boys educated in the nineteen-sixties. No sense of, of, of how to do the right thing. Jim wouldn't stand for this, this squatters' bustee. Not for one minute: don't be an old woman, 'Enry, get 'em moving fast before they know what's hit 'em.

They were walking beside the river, looking into the clear, slowly flowing water. Henry saw his reflection beside Andrew's. Tall, gawky individuals, both of them, Andrew the more so in his shorts. His legs looked huge and strong from that angle. Beautiful and young. Henry hated him. Hated him all the more because it was himself he saw, as a young man. Not even the satisfaction of being able to think, well, you'll catch me up one day or die first because Andrew had already taken a different direction. Was Andrew right? In the reflection, just behind them, between them, he saw the other half of this tall and healthy

Andrew thing, also tall and healthy, the profusion of black hair like the devil's halo and that heavy forehead that was beautifully creased whenever the, the, the handsome black bastard smiled. More so when he laughed.

And what have I got? Henry screamed at the water, his spilt agony washed away by the thoughtless stream.

□□□□□

Abus was his name. He was older than me by about ten years, he knew a lot more about planting, he could handle the labour and the contractors. I was dependent on him and yet he was my assistant. He taught me everything, this confident brown man whom my boss dismissed as a mongrel because of his mixed Malay, European and Indian blood. To me it was hybrid vigour. He was the first man – as opposed to contemporary boy – with whom I . . . well you'd have to say it, with whom I fell in love. I didn't even think in those terms then. Don't ask me why, I don't know why. I couldn't associate my ideas – of myself, I suppose – with love. Two men didn't fall in love, for all that I had no delusions by then about what I wanted. We get wise when it's too late. At any rate, I did.

The landscape we inhabited looked empty. It was raw and desolate. Hostile to humanity, at that stage of its development. It gave no shade from the sun that beat our backs every day. In that dry year, the rolling topography appeared to have been shaved clean of every living thing. The circling kites watched for anything that survived. On the distant horizon a thin black line indicated the boundary of the forest that had covered most of the country only a generation earlier.

Immediately after the First World War the area had been cleared for rubber. It was the boom time when thousands of acres were planted and Malaya became the richest of the British colonies. The crash, ten years later, put an end to further planting. The industry consolidated. Small, independent estates bought for a song by the big rubber companies. The glory years never returned but in the nineteen-thirties an ever-growing demand for car tyres ensured the economic wellbeing of the huge estates, often managed by the men who had once owned them – or bits of them. It was an efficient industry with a good system of well-maintained roads, linking plantation to factory and factory to Singapore and imperial market beyond. The very same road system that had enabled the Japanese to move down the Malay peninsula so rapidly and take the poorly defended city in 1942. I told you 'En', Jim would have said, you should 'ave watched yer back, no good pointing those big guns out to sea. These Nips are wily buggers. In those days the Henrys of the world had no time for the Jims, which is why the Henrys ended up on the scrapheap.

After the Japanese had left, oil palm was the thing. A hungry and rapidly expanding human population needed feeding. Vegetable oils of all types were in demand. Palm oil is nutritious stuff. Cheap to produce in the humid, lowland tropics where land and labour are cheap.

So the landscape over which Henry and Abus looked was being denuded for the second time in three decades. The suffering land indeed. But they were young and full of confidence. Masters of the land they felt, as indeed they were.

239

Scientifically educated, both of them, so a cut above the earlier rubber planters. They thought. The land had been cleared, burned and sterilised with herbicides. When we get a bit of wet weather we'll plant the legume ground cover. It'll all look green again, in no time. Now they were organising the setting out of the planting lines: on the contour was the thing, to reduce soil erosion. Henry had a book on the Tennessee Valley Authority project. That was his Brave New World. Man the master of nature.

Trouble was, it was an unusually dry year. They didn't dare plant the valuable legume seeds, and there were tens of thousands of seedlings in the nurseries waiting to go out. There had not been a drop of rain for months. You don't want too much to get them going – in fact too much rain retards early growth – but you need something and they'd had nothing.

The worry drew them together.

[][][][][]

"So, Andrew, what's the plan?" he burst out accusingly.

"What, Henry?" said Andrew, not as if he was miles away, far from it, but much more as if he couldn't care less.

"What are you going to do?"

Andrew looked at the encampment. He looked at the water, seeing Alloy in the background.

"I know what I'm not going to do."

"What's that?"

"I'm not going to spend the rest of my life working for this mob."

He might have said waste. Henry thought of that empty landscape years ago. He felt like tearing off his hat and throwing it in the water, smashing the image he saw but of course it would only re-form again, his hat sinking to the bottom and himself looking silly. He answered Andrew's reflection.

"I mean, Andrew, what are you going to do now? What are you going to do, to do about these people? They can't stay here."

Alloy came up close and it was he who answered, while Andrew watched through the interpretation of the water. "These people are going to stay here. Have you got any objections?"

Henry answered Andrew, or rather Andrew's reflection in the water: "That's impossible." Why should you have what I never had? "This is the plantation. Company property. They must go back to the compound, where they belong."

"Henry," said Andrew's voice of reason but to Henry it sounded like, like confounded cheek, "the compound's burned down."

Why you little, little . . . you queer, queen, homo, pansy, poofter. You bum-buddies. How dare you speak to the Senior Planter like that with my years of experience and, and useful life behind me? Not the empty desert you think it is. Oh no, I've done things, I have. Just because you have each other, you think you can sneer at me. I'll jolly well stand my ground and show you who is the boss around here. I'm not like that chap over there with the sad face and dead eyes. Oh no, I'm alive, I am. I've lived.

"Don't exaggerate, Andrew," he laughed, "there's two good lines of houses. They can squeeze into those. They must go back. Now. I insist. Tonight. If you let them stay here, well, well, they'll. . ."

Be happy?

Why was he insisting so? He seemed to be standing outside himself, watching something he didn't like. Why had he not an Alloy to put him straight? It's not how he wanted to be, and yet that is how he was.

A quiet little group had formed around them. Henry saw himself standing in the middle, surrounded. Andrew-Alloy, the little polished man – what was his name, for God's sake? – with his, his acolytes and a number of other men who seemed to be distinctly interested in the proceedings. Others also, because, no doubt, they had nothing else to do except make trouble. He felt bothered and pressed, wondering why the hell he was here at all. Isn't Andrew supposed to be running the show? He didn't seem to be but Henry couldn't put his finger on who was in charge. Who was running things? He wasn't afraid because he could see Andrew was perfectly relaxed and the little fellow made him feel things wouldn't get out of control. Something solid and central about him.

The person who made him feel uncomfortable, embarrassed almost, as if the man knew more about him than, than he knew himself, more than he cared to know, was that other half of Andrew. The fellow who had slept with Andrew, who certainly knew Andrew better than he did. There he stood frowning at me as if, as if he didn't like me, for God's sake. What had I done to him? To deserve his displeasure? What right had he to be displeased with me? I felt he disliked my very existence. Mortifying. Really, it was quite outrageous. Made me feel cross.

Yet it was Andrew who seemed to press me most. The leader of the pack, as it were. In the very presence of this new Andrew – the Andrew after he had walked out of the club, instead of facing up to Jim, the coward – who was now controlled by that other. I felt minus a layer of skin. Who had I got to run to? No one.

"Henry!" Andrew laughed as he said it: "What do you mean?"

I thought Henry had gone a little mad. Well not mad exactly, just tired and ready to go home for his bath, his meal, some reading and bed. He'd be OK in the morning. I laughed out of fondness for him. I think I did. I hope I did. I felt happy and relaxed myself and I wanted him to feel the same. I couldn't understand what all the fuss was about. He kept going off into some little place of his own but he'd always done that. Part of his charm. He'd sort of disappear when you were talking to him in the club. After a few seconds he'd blink and look at you: just listening to a bit of Mozart, old boy. He probably was. But he wasn't himself, at all. Not the Henry who was Our Henry of the club.

Andrew looked around proprietarily. He seemed to dismiss Henry entirely. The others followed his gaze as if to say yes we've done rather a good job here. You push off.

"They're comfortable."

"What?"

"I said they're comfortable."

Comfortable! Comfortable! What right have these people to be comfortable? Am I comfortable? Does anyone think about my comfort?

"Well yes, Andrew, that's all very well. . ."

"And once they've had a day's rest and sorted themselves out we'll have everyone working to clear things up."

Bune – that was his name, Bune, got it – smiled approval at the idea. Set the natural process going. That was the thing. Clarence would have said the same. No need for a fuss. Just do what has to be done and try not to upset anyone. And, in this spirit of Clarence's, the workshop ran well enough. No one had ever complained. If Clarence wants that grumpy fellow in the stores then let him have him. It works well enough.

"It'll do everyone good to be busy."

Didn't I know that? Andrew was taking me for a fool, while the other half just stared right through me, looking thunderous.

"I hope so Andrew because. . ."

Andrew finished the sentence for him: "I want everyone to feel rested and happy."

Happy! What on earth has happiness got to do with it?

"As I was saying, Andrew, that's all very well but this is a plantation."

"It is," says Bune.

"Very good. What is your name?"

"Bune, Sir."

"So it is, you told me before."

"I did."

"I'm sure Mr Bune, you, you understand what I'm talking about."

"Yes, Sir."

"So, Andrew?"

"Yes, Henry?"

Why did he grin like that while the other looked, looked ready to eat someone?

"These people may stay here tonight" – he looked at Bune, as if at an ally – "but I insist that tomorrow everyone moves back to the compound."

There was a dead silence. Or so it seems in my memory. Waiting for me to go. I wanted to go for Heaven's sake but I didn't know the way. Someone would have to show me and no one seemed inclined.

"Mr Bune. Mr Bune?" But he was nowhere to be seen just then. Disappeared from my view just when I needed him.

It was as if they were waiting for me to do something. To do something that would enable them to pounce. To tear me apart. Andrew, watching and grinning. The other, the leader of the pack now. There seemed to be more of them around. A little rag-tag gang had just arrived. It was led by a thick-set man, a young man, built like a boxer. A bruiser no doubt, but his face struck me as, as almost angelic for all that it was rather crude. Big features, the lower lip protruding a little, fresh looking and sweet. If he'd done any fighting no one had ever landed one on that mouth. He was bigger and more fair-skinned than the Bune man. More roughly made.

Better watch my step. Won't let them get the better of me. Jim'd bluster his way out of this but I'm a smooth talker, when I want to be. Educated man. I've survived this far, haven't I? But all the same I'd have thought Andrew'd be on my side. That Bune fellow's a smarmy beggar come to think of it. Where's he disappeared to? I'd rather have him in my sights. And that angelic-looking fellow: could be a problem. Probably a psychopath of some sort. Baby Face Angelino. But you're a match for these fellows, Henry. Don't let them get the better of you. Just watch your step.

But out here, in the plantation and lost, surrounded by these people whom he didn't understand, with Andrew being not Andrew, he felt vulnerable and thin-skinned. Not at all like the club where he can be friendly and genial and rather above the common herd. Where they looked up to him rather, as an educated man. Didn't matter they called him queer behind his back. He could bear that. There. But here, it was different. This was the mob. They could kill him, chuck him in the water, throw him in the ditch. Forget him. Did what I could, Jim. Forget it Andrew, these things happen. It's not a life for girls, this plantation stuff. Henry never really had it in him. He was finished anyway and what had he got to look forward to? Nothing. He's better off. Now, who wants another drink? They wouldn't even see his ghost hovering around the bar.

As if that blooming wasteland was spreading its ghastly malevolence over everything. As if it was set to go wrong.

"Yes, Andrew, you'd better get them back to the compound tomorrow morning. I insist. If you let them stay here then goodness knows they'll never move."

Alloy thought of his mother dying. The shack beside the airstrip in Port Markham. People had to sit somewhere. That was all. Somewhere half decent — Andrew'd say — would do but it had to be somewhere. Surely? He wasn't angry. He didn't hate Henry or want to kill him. He just felt sad. It was an uncomprehending child who frowned, if only Henry knew.

"No, Henry. I want people to be settled and happy, for fuck's sake. Then we'll get some work done. Tomorrow I'll put some men on the compound. Some of the women too, if necessary. They'll be glad of the money. Everyone else'll do their usual work. Keramugl here. . ." He looked around but the angelic face had been replaced by Bune's focused attention again. "Keramugl, wherever he is, says his men want to work. They've got to now since they've lost everything." Thanks to you he seemed to suggest. It all sounded reasonable enough but this was the belligerent Andrew, jaw sticking out and looking mad. Saying some of the right things but only because he wanted to fight something. He was bludgeoning Henry with the rights of the people because he wanted to fight Henry not because he believed any of the twaddle he was saying.

Andrew felt Alloy beside him, nonetheless. He could smell the clean salty sweatiness of him. He couldn't let Alloy down again. Could he? Couldn't let down the image of himself he was constructing more like. The public image with which he was beginning to box himself in. He felt he was going mad and only wanted to get out. "For Christ's sake, Henry, let's get things back to normal. That'll get us out of this fucking muddle," he says desperately, snatching at Alloy's hand which is not there.

Andrew never used to swear in public. Henry's eyebrows were raised and the others began to feel embarrassed.

[][][][][]

Out of the silence which follows it is Alloy who speaks. "Could we not forget the burden of the past and move on to the future clean?"

"Yes, Sir," says Bune just as quietly but enthusiastically so that they are all able to laugh with relief.

That is except for Henry who looks at Bune. He looks him up and down.

"I see. You've made up your mind have you?"

Bune looks at Andrew.

Andrew says: "Yes."

Henry sees Andrew-Alloy. He wants it. And he hates it because of his exclusion.

"And you'll send some people into the new section to continue the lining, I trust? Take the opportunity while it is possible, I hope. Perhaps your Kera, Keramuggle, whatever his name is, and his men, whoever they are, can do that little bit of work for us, if they'd be so kind."

Henry says this to Bune, having apparently ignored Andrew. Fact is, whenever I looked at Andrew there was that black fellow scowling at me. Most off-putting. I didn't like it and I wasn't going to have it.

So Bune answers as a man ignorant of sarcasm.

"There aren't enough men now, Sir. It's better we get things straight here first."

Henry swings his head from Bune to Andrew, slowly, widening his eyes in what is supposed to be withering scorn – or something like it.

"Am I correct in thinking you are the divisional manager, my dear Sir?" Only it is lost in good-natured laughter on the assumption that Henry is clowning for everyone's entertainment.

Bune is grinning.

Andrew is laughing.

Alloy is thinking not a bad old fool.

Keramugl – back again – sort of puffing because he tends to forget to open his mouth when he laughs, until he sneezes. He has come with the others to work. Andrew is right, they can't stay up in the mountain without Tarlie. Keramugl and co, it is now.

Even Madiak, back there, smiles his big floppy resigned smile, despite the fact that he'd rather see Bune dead at his feet.

Such a simple solution: laughter and brotherly love. OK, that's settled then. Let's get on with the work. Henry, you're a genius, breaking the tension like that. Such a simple thing. Just do it step by step, without a fuss. Just keep up the rhythm of life. The healthy beating of a healthy heart. Like Bune in his canoe in the beginning. Do the right thing, work and sleep here beside the gently flowing river. Is not the plantation the Garden of Eden? Another Ples? It could be.

[][][][][]

So why doesn't it work?

Back in the club that evening or maybe back in Jim's office, the door shut, repaired and shut but Jim's voice raised. Impossible to do anything about it because now it is an electric typewriter. Doesn't make a noise. Can't be bashed with frustration and, and this tragic illustration of men being men and therefore causing all the unnecessary trouble. So she gets up and walks out onto the veranda to escape. The noise of the mill is a comfort.

You did what, Henry?

Doesn't give time for Henry to answer. The voice of reason squashed before it speaks. Bune done in as it were.

You let those buggers settle in the plantation? Beside the river? You let Andrew do what he wants? After the way he's been acting? You can't leave a man like that in charge. That's why I sent you down. Damn you Henry.

But Henry is quite capable of damning himself.

Jesus Christ! I'll have to go down and sort it out myself. You lot are fucking useless.

He makes for the door. Henry tries to stop him but not very effectively.

Jim, Jim.

Nonetheless, there is a suspension of activity. The two men stop as if being given a chance to consider what they are about to do: dead silence. Henry stands between Jim and the door, a look of some uncertainty on his face. The Last Chance Saloon. His mouth and eyes widen a little – young again – as if he might do the right thing.

Fixed determination on that, that visage which Jim presents to the world. His lips pressed shut but the eyes search. They look around for something upon which to fix. Margaret. Where is she? If only. . . But he has rejected that idea years ago. She's there up in the house. Or sitting on the veranda watching the whole thing. All you have to do Jim is run up there and go to her. You wouldn't have to go on your knees before her – although you might feel like it once you'd taken the first step. You wouldn't have to beg – although you might feel like bursting with gratitude for all that she'd never ask for it. All you have to do, Jim, is go to her. She's waiting. And all she'd do is say, Hello, or something like it, I'll make us some tea, in that lazy drawling way in which she speaks that is so comforting.

Move forward a little, Henry, so that you intercept Jim. Stop him in his tracks. He wouldn't hit you, although he looks primed to do it, and after all it's not that physical pain of which you're afraid. Stop so's you could say, I stood up to Jim. Thinking of Margaret – or rather realising he is thinking of her – he'd listen to reason.

Why Henry, I didn't think you had it in you.

I haven't Jim, I just thought, I just thought, I just thought we'd go up and see Margaret.

See Margaret?

See Margaret.

Good idea Henry, I didn't think you had it in you.

She'll make us tea or something and it'll be alright.

Alright?

Alright.

Alright.

So hand in hand – as it were, don't ask to see miracles just yet even though one has occurred – they go up to Margaret.

What could they not do? Think of it. The possibilities, the possibilities of life are, the possibilities of life are, the possibilities of life are limitless and wonderful.

After we've had our tea we'd better go and sort out that nonsense I caused at Ples. We can climb the mountain this evening, Henry. Get to those people and sort it out. I'll apologise.

Yes, Jim, a good idea and I know they'll be only too glad to see you.

Nothing is irrecoverable.

On the way out they pass the other woman standing on the veranda.

Hello, Mrs Livingston, what are you doing out here?

Just getting a breath, Jim. I think I'll go home now. Her prayer has been answered.

Load of tosh, eh?

Indeed it is.

Suspended they are and given yet another chance – and more will come you can be sure – they dump it.

Jim moves on and pushes Henry – the pushover – away from him. Henry moves back easily. His mouth shuts.

Don't fucking Jim me you fucking stupid wanker. I should have retired you last year, year before, when you reached the age. You just take up space.

Then what? His house, his garden, everything. To lose it all. And for what? For Andrew and that fellow. Not likely!

[][][][][]

Abus was always talking about women.

When they were not working. When they were working he'd be serious. Listening to Henry sometimes as if he was talking sense, his head cocked a little to one side looking beautiful. Then they would start working again and Abus had to take charge because Henry did not really know what to do although he was learning fast.

Sometimes after work they would drive to the nearby town. An unpretentious place which had grown up beside the railway line in little more than fifty years. It was the district capital.

They would sit in a Chinese café drinking weak beer and eating little fried snacks that Abus would have bought from a stall in one of the side streets. It was pleasant, after a hot, dusty day, to sit in the cover of the arcade and to watch the dusk descend on the cricket field that was the centre of the little town. Across the field was the railway station, on the one side the residence and the government offices and on the other the inevitable club where the Europeans would congregate. Not as exclusive as it had been before the war – European invincibility having been tested and found distinctly wanting.

Wanting to relax, they deliberately avoided conversation about work. There was not much else to talk about because work was their common ground, so Henry said little while Abus would encourage him to eat the dubious-looking snacks and talk about women. It was as if he wanted to challenge Henry, to get under his skin. In fact, he had never been so near a European and he wanted to see what made Henry tick. He was fascinated because Henry encouraged him by the very fact of not discouraging him, of not keeping a distance, of just being himself in those days which was, defenceless.

Henry, in those days, was like a trusting animal who was raw to the world. In his life, up to that point, Henry had not known love. He supposed his mother had loved him until he was flung out to boarding school at the age of seven. At public school later he survived by keeping a low profile. The various gangs, sets and cliques of which he was not a member ignored him. He didn't particularly want to be a loner but he was and he wasn't particularly unhappy with that state of affairs, either. He'd much rather hang about the library on Sunday afternoons in winter or go out on his bike in the summer looking at the outsides of the famous local churches than be with the others. But, all the same, if he had to be with them, he could manage. In fact, a variety of decent people in the school had liked him and even felt affection for him but he hadn't noticed them. So, because he gave an impression of detachment, they gave up on the idea of knowing him. Some were hurt but Henry, having not made the contact, didn't notice. He had an idea about life that you were on your own. He felt he wasn't much help to others but by the same token he didn't expect any help from them. By the time he left school to do his army training he gave the false impression of an easy going-fellow who'd go along with things but you can't get to know him, he's a loner. It was about this time Henry began reading serious literature and listening to serious music when he could find it. Easier to deal with than people. These activities did, undoubtedly, enrich an otherwise arid life but they enhanced his detachment. All for art and all that rubbish.

But whilst Henry, at the time he came to know Abus, had no experience of love, platonic or otherwise, neither had he any experience of whatever is the opposite of love – platonic or otherwise. So he was and appeared to be raw and innocent. Also, in his youth, before he became what he himself described as ratty and thin-skinned in his middle-age, he had a sufficiently low opinion of himself to be quite non-judgemental about others. Thus, as a young man, quite attractive to look at and easy-going, he tended to attract the oddities just by the fact of not positively rejecting them. There's Henry stuck with Old So-and-so, the club bore. But Henry didn't find him a bore, at any rate no more boring than anyone else. His innocence and the fact that he appeared to be – he was – unspoilt and untouched, also attracted the attention of predatory women who wanted to sleep with him, not out of boredom but because they wanted his innocence and cleanliness. What must it be like with an innocent man? Most of the time he did not even notice them, not because he was innocent – which he was – but because he wasn't attracted to women. He was not, at that point either, really attracted to men because the idea of it seemed impossible. He thought it was a thing one didn't do, not knowing it was a thing one could.

Henry liked to be with Abus because he didn't have to work at it. Abus did all the talking and it was always the same. Talking about the girls he knew, he had known and whom he would know one day. Suggesting that Henry should come with him sometime but never pressing him. At least, that was how it was to start with. But working together, day after day, the two men, liking each other, began to feel relaxed in one another's company. The presence of the other reduced the tensions of life. They say that fondling a pet – a cat, or a dog – can reduce the blood pressure, calm the nerves. The working relationship between the two men was like that.

[][][][]

Surrounded by the mob, Henry feels not a bit frightened but angry and depressed. He's too old for this sort of game. He's losing his grip. He's yesterday's man alright. At night, now, he wakes up angry, a pain in his chest, re-living the injustices of the day. It is stupid, he knows that, but it doesn't stop him feeling.

He could see the sense of it, alright. It was nothing brilliant but just the obvious thing to do. He could explain it to Jim. No, Jim, I'm not going to let you do it. Measured and calm. Just let me deal with this and you'll see it'll work out. If it doesn't, I'll take full responsibility. I'll resign and you can then do what you think fit. We can't lose anything by giving them a few days. Andrew's got some good men with him and you know he's done it before, you've said it yourself. You gave him that job in the first place because you believed in him. You were right, Jim. You are a good judge of men. This place just shows you are. You're right 'En', I can judge men, it's a quality I 'ave. OK, let's see how it goes. Now let's go have a drink.

But then the laughter.

Damn them. I am not going to be laughed at. Kill me if you like but don't laugh at me. I'll show you I'm still a man. I'm the Senior Planter.

"No Andrew."

He shouted. There was silence but – had he noticed it – a near respectful silence. They still expected some sense from him.

There was that, that, that man who'd taken over Andrew, scowling at me. Who was he to scowl at me?

Indeed, Henry, who was he? Because he was only there in your mind. Alloy was no more than there beside Andrew. Where else would he be? He expected you to talk sense and was ready to accept what you said. If he did not like it he could go. Yes, that was exactly his view as well but he was ready to love you.

Bune too wanted you, to do the right thing. You would not have had a better lieutenant. And Keramugl, indeed an angel. Actually incapable of a bad action. The essence of goodness. Had he not received Annu's kiss that time at Karandawa?

"It won't do, Andrew. What I say goes. I am speaking for the company now and as your superior. If any of you, if any of you don't like it, then you can go. Do you understand me, Andrew? Andrew?"

"I understand what you say, Henry, but. . ."

"But nothing, and I am not listening to one more word. Now get these people back into the compound. Now." He explained it in simple pidgin so that everyone understood.

"If I come back tomorrow morning and find anyone here, I shall report the matter to Jim who will send in his security men."

Why am I saying this as I die inside? Henry looks at the avenue of palms continuing on the other side of the river. It leads nowhere. He sees himself walking nowhere. He blinks but he is still there.

"Henry. . ." says Andrew, who is aware of the pain, but Henry stops him.

"When I get back to the office, Andrew, I'll write my instructions on paper, if you want. If you won't carry out my orders then I'll find someone who will. I'll do it myself if necessary."

He is about to walk off when he remembers he is lost.

"Andrew, please instruct someone to show me the way out to the main road, where I left my Landrover."

"But Henry . . ." Andrew badly wants reason to prevail but Henry won't have it:

"No Andrew, I'm tired, I've had enough, I want to go home."

So Andrew gives reason one last chance: "Keramugl, please, will you . . ."

Keramugl steps forward and starts walking. Henry follows him.

It is still not too late.

[][][][][]

Henry and Abus work together preparing the land for planting. They meet each morning and together they move things forward. They separate at lunch and meet again in the office, which is a sort of shed kept cool by the shade of a few old rubber trees that have been left for just that purpose. The two men – Henry more a boy for all that he is the boss – might go out into the field again after the office to check what the contractors had been up to.

The days on the calendar are ticked off. There jolly well ought to be some rain by now but there isn't don't worry it's bound to come one day it's not the end of the world. You can't stop yourself moving forward along that piece of string that is your life. The definite beginning in the light of . . . something and the ill-defined ending in the darkness of something else being the last thing you think of when you're young and bursting with life. But the rain will come.

Nonetheless, it feels as if time has stopped, waiting for the rain. What can you do when you want to get out and do things but you can't? When you've got to make an impression? Waiting for it to happen. But waiting for what? Men have gone off to war to find out, and not come back.

Henry lived in the old plantation bungalow. Red bricks, like some Edwardian villa from Ealing with the top floor sliced off and a wooden veranda put all around. One big room with a bedroom off either side. Enormous rooms all three of them. Whitewashed and empty when I lived there. I camped, more or less. Even slept on a camp bed which I'd rigged up under a mosquito net in the middle of the living room. Spent most of the time on the veranda. I was still a child in some ways.

249

The bungalow was surrounded by an old garden, wild and full of colourful birds. An old couple looked after the young man. It did not cross his mind that they had not been there since the beginning of time. He accepted the domestic routine as a fact of life. Thank you very much, he said when the food was served. Colourful birds they were, had he thought about knowing them. He read every night by the light of a kero lamp. He read voraciously and greedily, more than he would ever do again. He read the great big Russian authors and the little English ones. These were the books which influenced the young man, in which he took refuge and to which he returned when he was older, remembering his youth. Nonetheless, the books resolved nothing.

The house and its wild garden of overhanging trees, creepers and calling birds was an island in the waste that had once been the rubber plantation. Henry had not appreciated that the house stood on a slight uplift on the undulating plain until the surrounding rubber trees had been cleared. Then, looking between the ornamental garden trees, he had a good view of the devastation beyond. Initially it had not worried him and most days it still did not because he saw, in his mind's eye, the oil palm plantation that was to be his mark upon the earth. But as the unusually long dry spell continued, the dusty, dry, colourless view would depress him and he would curse the vicious sun in the morning. Sunday mornings were the worst. You couldn't stay in bed because of the damned sun. There was nowhere to walk which was different from the weekday and to be honest, yes, I missed Abus. A whole arid day ahead of me so I'd read and read. I'd lose myself in those damn books. I read them again and again because they were all I had. I knew the characters inside out. I talked to them. I went a bit mad. I longed for the night when I wouldn't have to look at that damned view. I might have run away only . . . I'd have missed Abus. I'm not sure that I consciously thought that way but it was there in the back of my mind, not exactly buried. It's funny, when I look back on those empty Sundays now when life seems so terminally short I think why didn't I do something more constructive? Write a novel, study the local micro-fauna or something. But at that age you don't feel time in the same way. You're impatient to do things but time itself is endless. You don't think about it running out. Write a novel! What had I got to write about? Might be worth writing something now but there isn't time. The mob'll be here any minute to tear me to pieces.

Monday mornings I'd wait for Abus. I could hear his motorbike miles away. He lived somewhere in town. I had no idea where. With some woman, I assumed. It would still be dark when he arrived and I'd get up on the back of the bike without saying a word. I loved it. Sitting there behind him. He smelt warm and clean; a sort of waxy smell like good-quality furniture polish. I'd feel his body between my legs. I wanted to squeeze his buttocks. I wanted to put my arms around him. I didn't dare. If he'd said hold on Henry, I'd have held on like mad.

Don't misunderstand me, I wasn't in some sort of sexual frenzy; we'd be talking about work and thinking what we had to do in a very businesslike way. I'd suggest where we ought to start. He never contradicted me but if he thought I was wrong he'd say yes Henry and then I think we'd better do so an' so, which we did. But I was aware of him and happy to be with him.

Months passed like this. We'd done a lot. A rubber plantation when I arrived and by the time it all happened it was that bloody wasteland. Just like the fire here come to think of it, as if the scene was being set for a tragedy. Both times I got it wrong.

⬜⬜⬜⬜⬜

Yes Andrew, it was before the big strike. It was you who asked me to take Mr Henry home. It is true, he had lost his way down by the river where Bune had taken him. And it is true that his mind was confused. But Andrew, at that time, I talked to Mr Henry and I came to understand that he is a good man. It was the Company that made his mind confused so that he did some things that did not make sense. That was what Bune said later. He said that men like Mr Henry do not think properly. That is why they do the wrong thing. Andrew, in that time, you were the same as Mr Henry but Alloy made you see the right thing, and then you listened to Bune.

Andrew, you ask me to think of the time before so now I am thinking of that time. I think it is better that you shut up and let me talk. You can write down what I say. We are brothers now so I can say these things. Yes, we are brothers in the name of Annu, but also, Andrew, we are brothers because we have walked this journey together to Lingalinga Plantation.

So, Andrew, in the first place, do not forget that you asked me to take Mr Henry home. At first, Mr Henry walked a long way behind me. I understood that he did not want to be with me. He only wanted to find his way back home. I am a kanaka, that's all. I am not worried. I think: I will take him back home, then I will return to my friends beside the river.

And as I think of you all I feel happy and I laugh out loud because I am happy and I love the old white man behind me who I am leading home.

He laughed at me, the damned Angel Face. I know the type. Vicious. Half-formed human beings. You need the whip for that type. Animalistic. They don't think. Feed them, make them work and lock them up at night. Give them anything good and they shit on it. They're the barbarians at the gate. They're not like us. They don't know how to suffer.

I must keep him in my sights. If I get ahead then he'll have me at his mercy. He'll rush me and hack me to death with his panga. Nice body, even so. The way he walks is good. And natural. The animal in him I suppose. Look at the width of those shoulders and the arms definitely longer than they ought to be. Neanderthal, no doubt. Look at those hands. Huge! Made for strangling. I wouldn't stand a chance.

Henry has a fleeting image of himself lying on the ground with Angel Face above him looking down into his eyes. In the moment of death there is a connection between the victim and his tormentor.

"Hi!" It was almost a scream. "What're you laughing at? You little shit peasant."

The man stops in his tracks. He does indeed seem to be shocked. "Yes, Sir?"

I could not make out the expression on his face, but it seemed to be one of surprise.

"What're you laughing at?"

"I was thinking of my friends."

The answer, together with the look of total innocence – and beauty – on the man's face, disarms Henry. He cannot think straight. Rather, he can think straight but Jim, the club and his envy of Andrew all conspire to make his thinking wrong. The club Henry wants to smash the angelic face which had watched his humiliation and which would leave him to die in the ditch. The Henry inside himself wants to know it and look through its eyes and into the inside of its skull.

"Were you?"

The man has stopped. He waits for Henry to come to him.

There, in what appears to be an endless avenue of dark oil palms, the declining sun throwing them both into the shade, they are so far apart that they would have to shout to have a conversation of any sort. Soon, the descending darkness will cut them off from each other altogether. Yet, in their shared isolation, alone in the plantation, they are as intimate as any two men can be. The beautiful young man – which is the way Henry sees him now – beautiful beyond criticism in his youth and, although Henry does not recognise the fact yet, in his goodness, also. It is Henry's corrupted – or perhaps we should say buried – soul which has misread the angelic nature of that face. Youth and good health help. Of course they do but years later it will strike the sensitive observer in the same way. Keramugl has no sense of calculation in the way he leads his life. He does what he does, one step at a time, without worrying about the future. A more educated man in a less knowledgeable age might have called it faith. Even in his robust old age Keramugl's face shows not the lines of worry or anxiety or mere incomprehension that mark the face of Henry as we look at him now. In cruel contrast, Henry looks old, worn-out and stooped. Exhausted. He had wanted to fight but the fight has gone from him. He wants to love but he has forgotten how.

Henry shouts through the dim light. "Are you?"

Keramugl laughs again, his eyes shining like a child's. "Yes, Sir!"

Henry is suffering from a state of great inner conflict. His heart is beating like, like the rain hammering on the tin roof. Like that time before. Only this time he is older. Watch out old man, you'll have a heart attack. Well, he laughs to himself, if I stay here I'll lose him in the dark. And where will I be then? Better close the gap. Have him by my side, in any event.

The man, Keramugl, stands watching Henry walk towards him. He is smiling through the dark, his big white teeth all on show.

As Henry draws nearer, the old ticker stops racing. Henry loses the desire to fight. Himself, or anyone else. There is no fear. The hand extends out of the dark. He takes it.

[][][][][]

Everything was ready to plant. Only the rain was wanted. Day after day they had little more to do other than check that everything was ready. You could see it all out there. Hundreds of acres waiting for the rain. You could go to the nursery and see it all again: a refreshing green carpet of irrigated seedlings, the leaves neatly cut – row after row – to reduce the rate of growth.

The forest, on the distant horizon, had disappeared in the dust that hung in the air. Their world was reduced by the dust. After a morning of walking and inspecting the field, their damp bodies are sticky with the stuff, their eyes itch and their throats are dry. The sun, also lost, is defined by no more than a vague concentration of light up there in the low, white sky.

Boredom had something to do with it, no doubt. There is a lack of the sort of stimulating activity that young men need in order to prove their existence and to impress their vitality upon the world.

So, they had the opportunity. Time on their hands. The space also, because they were left alone, for all that the colourful birds in Henry's watered garden watched. The boss stayed in town or otherwise hopelessly visited the other established plantations. The prolonged drought was a problem. If that place where we've put Henry isn't planted for a while, it doesn't matter too much but, by gad, the lack of soil moisture's knocking the output of rubber and palm oil for six. Fire too could become a problem if we don't get some rain soon. Yes, of course I'm worried. He fretted because there was nothing he could do. In the end he forgot about Henry altogether. Abus never crossed his mind.

But, obviously, boredom and opportunity are not the only things. There has to be inclination. The waiting, their isolation and the slight worry – but young men do not worry that much – had drawn them closer than they might, they might otherwise have been. There was an inclination.

Henry had no doubt he admired Abus. He sensed him: he heard his warm voice; he felt the touch of his soft hands that contrasted with the hardness of his body. The feel of his back on the motorbike in the mornings. For they maintained the same routines, as if they were . . . waiting for something to happen.

Abus watched Henry and calculated. He was the calculating type. He had to calculate the risks in order to survive. He had not the security of Henry's position in the social order which gave the Europeans the upper hand in everything; gave them the benefit of the doubt if there was a scandal.

But brave also was Abus. A lot braver than Henry, it proved. Brave enough to know what he was, what he wanted and how he could get it. In the very inside of Abus there was not the shame you would have found had you stripped Henry naked to his soul. In Abus you would have found a reckless pride which carried him through all his tribulations in the end.

Given this Abus, this essential pride, you would have thought he might have rushed forward, sure of himself. But it was the knowing of Henry that held him back. At first he could only say he liked Henry, the young Englishman. After all, how could one do more than merely like that cold and reserved type? Thus Abus liked Henry, ready to use him if not to abuse him. But spending time with Henry, together, in those circumstances, he began to love Henry. To love those parts of Henry which were, in those days, loveable: the open, easy-going, innocent, giving Henry. The parts of Henry which could have given and taken love, if sufficiently awakened.

And, as reckless love can be, Abus was blind to – or rather he pushed the evidence to the back of his mind – the other less loveable parts of Henry. His theoretical bookish approach to things, his distance, his incomprehension of human needs sometimes, his self-centred cruelty. Rather like Andrew in some ways, only Alloy did not stand for it. He knocked it out of Andrew as soon as he could. Abus, in this respect, was a lot more gentle and forgiving of human nature.

[][][][]

The motorbike is still warm on the road below, making little metallic sounds through the dusty, cold morning air. They walk up the ridge, a steep bit between two planting contours. Henry is a little ahead. God, I hope it holds when the rains do come: we'll have to get the ground cover in the minute it starts. Abus is a little behind and is the shorter man. We will, don't worry, it's ready and waiting. He stumbles in the dry and fragile earth. Henry puts out hand to pull him up. Abus takes hand and holds it a little longer than he needs to do. Henry does not try to detach himself. Thus, hand in hand they reach the steady ground above. Henry reaches out hesitantly – there is still time to withdraw. Abus grabs and the two men embrace.

Henry holds tight. He cannot let go. He looks down onto black hair, a brown ear and neck, revealed because Abus's shirt is pulled down a little by Henry's own arms. He notices and remembers for ever a tiny mole on the clavicle. He takes a deep breath and he is intoxicated by the man he holds in his arms. It was like an electric shock, I had no idea the body could react in such a way.

They are alone on the dusty hillside. They are two young men and it is the age of discovery. Henry could not decide afterwards who was leading whom but he had no doubt what it was he wanted. He wanted as much of Abus's body as he could get and he wanted to sense it in every way possible. He is touched, held, caressed by knowledge and ever after he recognised that time on the hillside as the opening of the doors of the room he had been living in all his life. Yes, of course, he knew the doors were there and he had an idea of what lay beyond but it is Abus who opens the doors for him and lets the possible light flood in.

In the hours that follow, the days and for nearly a month, Henry and Abus satiate themselves with each other. You would think they would be drunk on it, delirious, glutted, but on they go. They eat each other alive. The world is themselves and beyond is nothing. They have it all. Abus's bike and Henry's bungalow. For decorum's sake Abus goes home each evening. In the morning Henry waits for him. Abus comes on his bike and off they go pretending in order to prolong the pleasant agony of waiting. A little work is done and then to Henry's bungalow for breakfast. The colourful birds watch, for all their apparently irreverent prattle, but the men below are ignorant of everything but their desire for the other's body and their own reactions.

And it's as good a basis for a life as anything. Isn't it? You had it all, Henry. The man Abus whom you knew as intimately as you would ever know any man and who knew you as naked and as shameless as you could ever be. You worked together through that early rage until you could lie quietly beside each other in that condition of mutual trust and acceptance, which is a sort of knowledge that is sometimes called love.

In the awful loneliness of retrospect, Henry saw the possibility of it. The tragedy of the loss accentuated by the reality of the years that followed, where anything could go and did . . . go. You see what I mean? Henry and Abus could have settled down in that very place. Abus could have been Henry's Alloy; Henry, Abus's Andrew. You see? The country gained its independence. The old English ways became a joke, it was the thing to laugh at them. There was plenty of work in their field as contractors and they could have made money and survived well. Accepted in time for what they were by the very fact of their success. Yes, Henry, you could have had it all, and you could have had it as a more honest and therefore better man. A braver man and therefore more respectable to yourself. Having the man Abus, who was enough; your garden, your house, your music, your collection of blue-and-white china would have been unnecessary and easy to leave as the mere frill on something much better. But you could have had it as well!

As each damned year passed by, Henry understood better the lost possibilities of his life. Lived his loss more thoroughly as the changing world threw it at him. Laughing at him. See what you lost, you pompous old fool.

Then Andrew appears on the scene. Henry reborn, as it were. The second chance? Yes. And Andrew takes, gets it, in his Alloy. You try to persuade yourself he is wrong. That he is wrong to reject the company but it won't wash. You know he is right in his stumbling, muddled way because he has taken the hand offered. The hand you refused, in the end. The pain becomes unbearable to the older, bitter man.

But Henry, you don't look at it straight. Even in your – comparative – youth you were a little set in your ways. You were already crippled. Perhaps at birth by genetic fact or maybe by some early careless trauma in the nursery, playing too much on your own and then the shock of boarding school before you knew yourself. God knows the reason, we don't, but it is a fact: you could not even then lose yourself in love. Abandon yourself to it, just as you never could completely abandon yourself to the music of dance, letting your body follow the rhythms by instinct. In the end, Abus was just another book you shut and put back up on the shelf.

Remember that, Henry, and it won't seem so bad. You would have grown tired of Abus, preferring at some stage a late Mozart piano sonata, which is a little more reliable, in any event. It's a good second best for all that you can't take it with you. Second-hand emotions and all that are often more bearable. You can put them back on the shelf when they are not wanted.

But, and this is well-fed, comfortable Henry's little pain, he does not appreciate the romance of his early experience. Neither does he appreciate that life, especially for the likes of lucky him, does give a second chance. In his stubborn, self-destructive way, Henry feels only – and more keenly with each passing year – the loss. The loss brought home to him most brutally by the evidence of Andrew and Alloy. Being Senior Planter and living in his beautiful bungalow up on the hill is indeed dust in his mouth. He would like to spit it out.

But, but, but that Mozart sonata does help. It helps a lot because it gives, it gives Henry a little glimpse of God. And later, as we shall see, Keramugl is like that little Mozart piano sonata[57]. So easy to get to know but showing an astonishing view of life when you get to know him even better.

[][][][]

What happened?

The rains came. The dust settled. The landscape expanded and filled with life as they planted the barren country. Dark, rainy skies and thunder. The smell of the earth, fantastic activity and change. The seedlings were moved from the nursery into the field as fast as they could move them before the roads became impossible mud. Night and day the tractors worked. They borrowed every bit of transport they could find. They felt a sense of power, which was exhilarating. To see, before their eyes, the landscape transformed by their own doing. It seemed to represent their relationship and yet with each day the distance between the two men widened as Henry became intoxicated this time with his power over the landscape. With the realisation of what he could do with it. Hundreds of men were working for him. He found he had a talent for organisation and that by manipulating a few key people he could manipulate a lot more to get things done. It is a dangerous game and Henry fell for it. He felt he could do anything. He was praised at the club by other Europeans. Henry gets things done. He's ambitious that man. He'll go far. The future of the company depends on people like that. They didn't give Abus a second thought even though he could have done just as much and more, on his own.

Nonetheless, Henry would have come down off his high at some stage in the game. A disaster of some sort would have dented his dangerous pride. He would have been bruised but he would have recovered a better man, realising the value of the solid Abus there beside him. He would survive a better man as the club changed its mind. Learnt his lesson that young man. I could see it coming. I could have told him, if he'd have asked for my advice. These young whippersnappers come down with a bang; it does 'em good, if you ask me.

And disaster did strike. It struck one evening at the club. Henry is basking in his silent glory having left Abus, as usual, at the café. Abus does not talk of girls these days and where he goes after they have drunk their warm beer and after they have challenged the world and triumphed, Henry does not know.

"Henry, my boy." The Boss, in those days, was a chappy who smoked a pipe, who had three daughters and a wife who was a credit to him in the way she suggested the upper-middle-class background to which he aspired although it was all the same to me old boy I worked my way up and got here by dint of hard work because I'd be the first one to admit I haven't got much furniture in the upper stories. In fact she was the daughter of a man who had ended up governor of some less important colony. She couldn't care two hoots about class and kept the secret that her husband was quite clever which was the actual reason he was where he was. He was judged a happy and successful man. That type, anyway.

---

[57] The sonata in C major, K545.

256

He didn't grind any axes but the thing is you have to go by the book otherwise you wouldn't know where you were none of us would we johnnies who aren't all that bright have to be especially careful if you get my gist.

Henry did. He agreed. The book was the thing. He certainly wasn't one to argue about that. The book had done him well so far.

"So . . . that chap of yours. Whatsisname. Mr . . ?

"You mean Abus."

"Do I? Mr Ramsey. Yes, that's the chap. English name but he's not quite, not quite one of us, if you get my gist."

"Oh no Sir, he's first rate."

Henry's a decent chap wouldn't bad-mouth anybody. The boss is looking at Henry, seems to be telling him in a decent sort of way better you don't say anything here, young fellow, none of us are perfect. "I don't want to judge a chap but better hear me out first."

Henry is bothered and looks it. Has word got out? Here in the club he really doesn't want to be seen as one of those fellows who. . . well, you know. Homos. Avoid them. Send 'em up country, or send 'em back home. Discretion's the thing. He wants to be one of them. Blimey, I've been a fool. The boss is looking at him, puts a hand on his arm, he nearly blurts it all out. Got to talk to someone. Good thing he didn't. You idiot, Henry. Why didn't you walk out then, if that's what you thought? Why didn't you run to Abus?

"Look Henry, I like to see a man stick up for his, his man. This Abus fellow is good at his job I know. Too good that's the problem."

Henry is relieved. Phew and he laughs.

"It's no laughing matter."

"No?"

"No."

"The chap's been doing us. Done you a bit but don't worry."

"What do you mean?"

"Our Mr Abus Ramsey is quite a big contractor and he's been contracting himself to do most of the work on your estate. If you'd had a bit more experience you'd have picked it up. I'm as much to blame myself. I should have given you a bit more time but what with the poor rains and all that I've been a little pre-occupied."

He'd expected Henry to look a little more crestfallen and – he'd rather hoped – a little more embarrassed and deflated. Young puppy, thinks he knows it all. But if anything, Henry looked relieved. He was. He even surprised himself by not being at all surprised at what Abus had done. It seemed to fit the man altogether: his confidence and his recklessness, his wild talk about girls. . . He blushed, the sugar seeming to drain from him. He felt nauseous and faint as if suddenly winded. He looked for a chair.

"OK, old man, it's the shock. You didn't expect it. Don't worry, don't worry, we won't say anything more about it. I feel as big a fool as you that I didn't see through him myself. I've much less excuse than you. I really ought to have known better. Sit down, sit down."

They found chairs. Henry was speechless in his agony. He really did want to cry. He felt as much a fool as anything. Had Abus been acting the whole thing then?

The older man was solicitous. My heart went out to the boy. He might have been my own son. He'd done such a good job and then this. I could see he was upset. It impressed me. He was a straight boy and it'd hit him badly. If he'd have been anywhere near I'd have thrashed that bloody man Ramsey. Not for ripping us off like that but for taking in that boy like he did.

"Pull yourself together, Henry. Be a man. Here," he called to the barman, "bring us a couple of brandies, double damn quick. Listen to me, listen to me."

"I'm listening, Sir."

"Look, you've done a bloody good job with that place. You know you have, I know you have and so does everyone else. The only thing is that Ramsey's ripped us off. And it's not that much. Prices are so good that we'll recoup it in a year. So really you mustn't take it so much to heart. It's happened to us all in our time. We've got too close to some local Johnny and he's taken advantage. That type is bound to. Lives on the edge. Neither one thing or the other. Nothing to hang on to. Not one of us."

No one to love him, like I could.

"Are you listening to me, Henry?"

"Yes, Sir." Inspecting the interior of the brandy glass and his soul. But I love him. I'd do anything for him. I can't believe he'd lie about a thing like that. I don't care if he has ripped off the company. What we've done together. You can't make that up.

"Are you listening to me, Henry?"

"Yes, Sir."

"Good. So this is what you have to do. The fellow doesn't know we're onto him. You go out, as soon as you feel better, and sack him. That'll do you good. Let him know you're onto him. Tell him he's damn lucky you're not going to make a police report. Then tell him to get the hell out of here. We don't want to see him again. We don't want that specimen of whatever it is. . ."

"Beautiful loveability?"

"What?"

"Nothing."

"Anyway, we don't want it around to distract us from the straight and whatever it is. Squash it under your boot. Can you do that? Henry?"

"Yes."

"Good. Then I don't want you to say another word about it and neither will I. We'd both look a bit silly if word got out. Alright?"

"Yes, Sir."

He soon bucked up. After all he's young and he knows his job. At that age you can take any number of knocks. Not so easy when you get here.

"Well then, Henry, you go and do that. And when you've done it we're going to have a little chat. I've got plans for you. How'd you like to go up to the McKinnon Highlands for a while?"

He looked at me as if I'd set a trap for him. I think he thought he was being got out of the way.

"Don't look so surprised. We've bought a tea estate up there and it's in one hell of a mess. I want you to put it straight."

The idea excited Henry, there was no doubt about it. It was an adventure. Something different altogether. And on top of all that the tea planters were considered the aristocrats of the planting profession. Nonetheless, he was surprised. "But I know nothing about tea!"

"So what? Neither does anyone else I can find. The thing is, I want someone who can grow things and who can get things moving and the organisation settled. You're just the man. Once you've got that under your belt there'll be no stopping you. You'll be on the board by the time you're forty."

You should have seen his face! It was a picture. I could see he wanted the job. He wanted it badly. He was like a dog who'd found the biscuits. That Ramsey fellow was nothing to him then.

"Off you go. Deal with that Ramsey fellow and I'll see you back here in an hour or so. Then we'll go back to my place for a late dinner. Alice" (his youngest) "is here for the holidays. She'll be glad to see you." He saw her as a young wife up in the McKinnons, himself motoring up for a cool weekend from time to time. Henry wouldn't make a bad son-in-law at all.

Henry rushes out. He was off like a shot to deal with that Ramsey fellow. Had the bit between the teeth, I can tell you. He was going to give him hell. He deserved it.

[][][][][]

Henry had one idea in his head. He was excited. He wanted to tell Abus the good news. To whom else would he run? He rushed across the cricket field, hoping, praying, that Abus would still be sitting in the café.

The night, large, clear after the rains. The glory of the stars that night, at that point in time, when he was between the club and the café, stayed with Henry ever after. He could not look into a night sky without thinking of that time. A mixture of all sorts of emotions churned and churned around inside him with the brandy. He stands in the middle of the field, unseen in the dark, aware of himself as never before. Here, he thinks, my journey really begins.

He wants it all. He wants the job, he wants Abus and he needs Abus's love. The doubts creep in. Not in a devastating way; he is a young man, remember, but worrying even so. Had Abus deceived him? Was it all a sham to get the contracts? To get Henry on his side. If it was, then, then he was a real fool. He had exposed himself to, to a crook and therefore to the possibility of public ridicule. Anything might happen. He could be blackmailed. My God! He hadn't thought of that. The idea that his boss, the others in the club should find out was, was unbearable. He'd be the one who'd have to go and not be seen again. His whole life gone down the drain for a moment of . . . eternity.

You idiot, Henry. If that had been all, the boss would not have mentioned it. You get men like that; they make good planters because there's no family to distract them. He wouldn't have invited you back to dinner, though. Glad I had daughters. Don't know what I'd do if I'd had one of those effeminate types for a son.

He walks towards the café. He can see the dim lights of the arcade but they are not bright enough to make out who is sitting underneath. His eyes, nonetheless, fix on the table where they usually sit. As he reaches the road, he sees that Abus is still there. Does he sit there every night? There is another man with him. One of the men he had always assumed was an independent contractor. A Malay man: small, dark and well made, his fine features pulled together by his dark moustache. He looks up as Henry approaches, smiles with a hint of gold like a handsome cat. Someone else said that. He gets up offering his chair to the master, Tuan, who takes it as his right. You can stand and wait my man while I deal with this double-dealing fellow. I am the Tuan now and don't you forget it. I know what's been going on. But what the hell? I don't care about that: I want Abus to be real to me. I want what we did to be real.

It is. One look at Abus confirms it. He wants Henry as much as Henry wants him. This is not acting and Henry does not care about anything in that moment of love, desire and possibility.

Abus is speechless. Not because Henry has found out – that is nothing and he does not know yet, although Henry thinks he does – but because for the first time ever Henry has come back from the club. He is moved and it shows in his face. He is grinning like another cat. All the more because he sees the excitement in Henry's face. He laughs when he sees Henry pull himself together and accuse him.

"Yes, of course, I've got my own contractors." He might have said, Do you take me for a fool? "Everyone here's making money. It's the tin or the logs or the plantations. There are no rules out here. Outside the club. We can be rich, Henry, together. We know what we're doing. Come with me."

"But don't you understand what I've been saying? What you've done is, is, is a crime. The police could be involved. You've defrauded the company."

Abus laughs. It is real but then he stops: "I'm doing what everyone's been doing ever since you British came here. I'm making money and I'm making the country rich. Once we get independence this is going to be a good place. Stay with me, Henry."

"But you've got to go! Didn't you hear me? The boss says if you don't disappear he'll get the police onto you. The company . . ."

"Damn the company."

Henry finds that he is shocked.

And Abus is laughing: "The company! The company's no better. How do you think it got the land we've just planted? How do you think it got anything here? By being jolly good chaps? Why do you think they came here in the first place? To make money out of gullible natives. Out of me if they could have. And then left me to rot."

Henry is shocked but attracted also by the recklessness of the man. He is stirred, there is no doubt. He wants Abus there and then. For a second or two he doesn't care. He remembers all his times with Abus. He remembers the early ideas of him. He looks at the little Malay man. Gold flashes in the shadows.

"What do I care, Henry, about the company? Do you think it cares about me? Even if I'd done a jolly proper decent job and all that rubbish, they wouldn't care if I dropped dead on the street. Come on Henry, forget them.

Come with me. I'm clearing out anyway. I'm going to Borneo. There's plenty to do there. You can tell the boss that and that you're coming with me." He meant what he was saying in the emotional heat of the moment. He did love Henry in his way. Henry had given him a trusting and easy understanding love he had not experienced before. But inside him, nonetheless, the essential Abus had an idea that Henry was one of them. He did not expect Henry to make a bolt any more than he had expected himself to buckle down and become a law-abiding plantation supervisor, with his motorbike, his little wooden house down by the railway line and his whatever else it was that went with being a good company man. He was not the type. He was nothing like it. What he offered Henry was real. If Henry had said yes, he would have stuck by him. He was loyal to his friends which is why he was a successful contractor here and would be also in Borneo.

In the end he could press Henry because he knew Henry would not do it. Henry is fascinated but he cannot step that far outside himself and abandon himself to Abus.

"Come with me, Henry."

Henry thought of the tea plantation in the McKinnon Highlands. He thought of his place in the company and his seat on the board.

"You must be mad."

"Are you more sane, Henry? Is your bloody club sanity or the lunatic asylum?"

"I'll see you later, Abus."

Henry got up, steadied himself with the back of the chair, wanted to shake hands with Abus, who was already lost. He glanced at the other man and walked back to the club.

Walking back he looked down at his shoes. They were filthy. Must get one of the birds to clean them.

Abus was off the next morning, taking his best men with him to Borneo. That was the end of Henry.

19
Smashing the China

Here they are then, hand in hand, walking a harvesting road. Dark inside the plantation; outside the evening sun is brilliantly coloured by the dust that fills the air.

Holding Keramugl's hand makes him remember holding Abus's hand. It has the same soft firmness. The same feeling of meaning about it as if, as if, as if the holding of Keramugl's hand is not an accidental thing. The young man – Henry's Angel Face – leads the older man. It is a good thing otherwise Henry would be wandering all around and all over the place thinking about his wasted life.

About to leave the plantation, they are nonetheless on the road that divides it from the extension land, from what was once, in the very distant past, Ples. Keramugl leads Henry home, having been told to do nothing to the contrary. Henry allows himself to be led, experiencing a feeling of happiness he has not experienced since, since God knows when. It is wonderful holding that hand.

Henry sees the lights of the club hill and his bungalow beyond. His collection of blue-and-white china – porcelain: one or two pieces quite valuable salvaged from the South China Sea. He loves the Chinese Ming period best and follows its influence through Europe, collecting Dutch Delft-ware and English Spode. To look at his china whilst listening to Mozart is Henry's joy. I'll just sit down and listen to some Mozart. Just be on my own. But we'll have to pass the club. What if they see me with this, with this, with this beautiful man with the spotless soul. They'll think he is one of my, of my, of my. . . as if I am a corruptor of young men? His heart-rate quickens. He feels hungry. Hasn't eaten all day, since that cup of coffee in Andrew's house in the morning when I spied the beautiful young couple, Henry and Abus. It hurts to breath. He rubs his chest. He lets out a little groan.

"Masta?" The hand tightens.

Henry feels dizzy. He wants to sit down but the hand is real and it talks to him of love.

They walk on.

"I want, I want, I want. . ." says Henry.

"Masta?"

"What shall I do?"

"Masta?"

"Tell me what to do?"

"Masta?"

Henry stops. He squeezes the hand as if he might kill it, and yet it is strong. Keramugl feels the pressure but it is nothing to him so he laughs at the inconsequential-ness of Henry's suffering in the great big scheme of things. Keramugl entwines his fingers with Henry's in order to break the tension.

□□□□□

I laugh again. This man is in pain. He says he wants the answer. But he knows the answer. So why does he ask me? I am a kanaka. I am only a labourer. He does not know my name. He would call me Boy, like he would call all the others. But I like this man and I want to help him. This is why I laugh.

So Henry returns the laughs, thinking of Abus. But this is not Abus. This is not a man whom he would embrace in that way. This is a young man who leads an old man home where he will leave him. A young man who does not calculate the risks. But the risks are severe. If Jim sees Keramugl and recognises him as one of those troublemakers . . . But that is unlikely. What Jim sees is enemy, slave, useless bugger or, in this particular case, had he been looking, one of Henry's Boys.

Jim ignores the kanaka who is left outside to wait. 'Enry! Come on in an' 'ave a drink. Tell me what's going on there in Andrew's country. Are we going to launch an invasion? Sort the place out? Flush out them commies? But they pass by the club safely enough. Soon they are in Henry's garden. Under the widely spaced fruit trees, where a low moon, yellow from the dust, gives them all the light they need.

I did not talk to him. But I held his hand for him because his house is dark. It is a big house and I would myself be afraid to go in such a place on my own. He says Thank you young man, I am now going to tell you what I am going to do. Then he laughs.

What is that? I ask. I am laughing also because I know what he is going to say.

He says I am going to do nothing. We are both laughing because this is the best thing. He looks at me and I see that his eyes are blue like the eyes of Andrew. This makes me think he is just a baby who I have to hold in my hand. He says will you tell Andrew what I have said? I say yes but he looks worried. He is thinking, this is a kanaka who will get it wrong.

"Listen to me."

"I am listening."

"What is your name?"

"My name is Keramugl. You will not forget my name."

"I will not."

They look at each other until Keramugl says:

"I have not been to school but I am not a stupid man. If you cannot trust me then write a letter so that I can take it back to Andrew."

"I trust you, Keramugl. You are a good man."

"Thank you, Masta. I will tell Andrew this thing, that you are going to do nothing. You are going to do nothing."

"Yes, and tell him to organise things in the way he wants. Tell him I trust him. I trust all of you. Tell Andrew that."

"I will do that."

263

"Thank you. And I will come to see you tomorrow."

"No Masta, tomorrow you must rest."

"Alright then, the day after."

"Yes. I will see you then."

That is what happened. Henry is happy. He likes Angel Face and he looks forward to the time when he will see him again; when he will be able to talk to the man Keramugl in calmer times. Yes, he thinks, as he switches on the lights in his living room, as he sees the blue-and-white porcelain arranged neatly on the glass shelves in an alcove he has had built especially for the purpose. Yes, I have done the right thing. He puts on his Mozart and he touches another switch beside the alcove, which is then illuminated by soft hidden lighting. A hint of blue in the white paint sets off each piece as a treasure in its own right. He turns off the main lights and settles into his armchair to listen and to look. Yes, I have done the right thing. What more can I do? Nothing. Leave well alone. I've done quite enough for one day. This is what I want. This is better than Abus. He closes his eyes and sleeps, seeing the Angel Face looking down into his, a white sky in the background.

[][][][][]

The inside of the plantation is airless. Andrew finds the noisy insect song particularly annoying. He wants to go home. The water beside which he sits moves slowly. His body is heavy, the effort of getting up too much. He sees his home millions of years away in England. A bus journey across chilled and barren hills, dusted with snow that comes out of a grey opaque sky. A mean cold. A boy in the cold, in the empty bus. He wants, he wants, he does not know what he wants. A little later, the farewell to his grandfather, in a wheelchair, the camel blanket over aged legs. The boy avoids the eyes of the dying man whom he wants to love, only he does not know the trick. How do you talk to your grandfather? How do you get him to tell you things? What was it like, Grandpa?

A sense of emptiness that comes after a period of prolonged emotional expenditure, which has, it seems, led only to a dead end. Better not to have got up this morning but one could hardly have done that what with the fire and everything. Being young, still the boy, he laughs at the possibility of staying in bed with Alloy all day. He thinks, with pleasure, of the coming night in bed with Alloy. Then they can forget about all this.

"It's funny," he says, "Henry coming round like that."

"Why?"

Alloy and reassurance. The water flows, the insects sing, the palm fronds above move in the breeze. A naked foot kicks his. Had they been lying a little closer a hand would have grabbed his wrist and twisted it to cause pain. To create reality.

"Because he must have guessed that we'd been sleeping together."

"And he'd have thought I was your house-boy. Fuck the servant. That's what they're for. It's so normal, Andrew, he wouldn't have thought about it."

"No, Alloy, you know he's not that bad. At least he has an idea of how people ought to think."

"One of your armchair liberals, is he?"

"Yes, if you like, but at least that means he'd want to think the right things. That'd start him in the right direction."

"Emotions controlled by intellect and good manners, you mean." Alloy sneers but he wants Andrew to persuade him of a better possibility.

"You know what I mean."

"I know what you mean, but he probably didn't even notice me. Just another kanaka." And he thinks, So do I want to be noticed?

"Doesn't mean he's right," says Andrew. "Do you think I wouldn't notice you? You're too ugly for a start. Do you think I wouldn't notice . . . Bune or Keramugl? And come to think of it. . ."

"What?"

"Where's he disappeared to?"

"Who?"

"Keramugl. He ought to be back by now. He was only supposed to have taken Henry back to the road."

"He's probably gone back to Tarlie. We'll have to go up ourselves at this rate."

"Why?" Andrew sits up; he knows what's coming. The breeze rattles the fronds above their heads, carrying away their voices. Keramugl is forgotten.

"Your liberal-minded Henry left us in no doubt about what he wants done. And, Andrew. . ."

"Yes, Alloy?"

"It can't be avoided."

There is no answer.

"Can it, Andrew? You have to think what you're going to do tomorrow."

"I'll get the men out to work as usual."

Last time it was merely a matter of running away with Abus who would have carried you, for as long as was necessary. This time you have Alloy, solid and there. He will die by your side if necessary. Because, what else can he do? He doesn't have the option of contracts in Borneo. But this time, Andrew, you have to do something beyond yourself to make it work. It's not that hard but you do have to make a shift away from the way your lazy mind has accustomed itself to think. What you would have called – and what Henry would have called even more emphatically – the English way. The safe little house there up on the hill from which you can look down upon the world. Think about the world's injustices but remain detached from them. Your private, privileged retreat, where you can read a book and listen to Mozart. This time you'll have to drop all that.

"So you'll get the men out working as if nothing has happened and as if nothing will happen. Just wait for the bombs to drop. Is that it?"

"What else can I do?"

"Listen Andrew, Henry will be in the club this very minute. He'll be reassuring Jim that he's Jim's man. Won't he?"

"I suppose so."

"What do you mean you suppose so? Is he suddenly going to let his emotions drive him for once?"

"I don't know."

"Of course he isn't! He's a company man. The company has his soul and it has him by the balls. I'm not even angry anymore because that's the way it is. He couldn't change anyway. He's too old. You could see he was exhausted this afternoon. He wasn't thinking straight but his instincts for survival will take him straight to Jim. Where else can he go?"

Andrew says nothing.

"You heard what he said. Didn't you? Didn't you?"

"I did."

"So if you don't get our people back into the compound, however unsuitable it is, and if you don't get going on the extension some nasty things will happen. Won't they? Won't they?"

"Yes."

"The best that'll happen is you'll lose your job because you'll stand up to them. And you'll have to because even if Henry backs down on this one Jim definitely won't. He must hate your guts by now. He's not going to give you a second chance. Is he?"

"I know, Alloy, you're right." Andrew thumping the bar again which made Alloy afraid that he would be weak.

"And that's the best thing that could happen to you, Andrew; lose your job because then. . ."

But Andrew was not listening. He was, in fact, thinking of going back home and clearing up the mess, settling down to a bit of reading and getting the men out to work the next day.

There is no Joseph to hold his wrist and he has forgotten Margaret altogether. Therefore no Annu, only Alloy who said:

"Then it'll be Tudak and co. Jim's fucking animals. They'll be here with their guns and machines to drive us out. The same thing again. And again and again until we stop running. . . Andrew?"

"Yes."

"The same thing again. But this time Andrew, you have to stay with us. You can't run away. Will you? Andrew? Andrew?"

"I fucking heard you. Do you think I'm going to run away?"

"I don't know."

"Thanks!"

Let's face it, even Alloy is indoctrinated by the company. This badly educated stores clerk assumes it is he and Andrew who will have to make the decisions. He thinks he is tough. But the time is coming when he will have to carry Andrew, and drive him and admit that he needs him. That is what will make him tough and enable him also to drive himself. The idea of Annu inspires him but, in the dark plantation, he is glad he has Andrew with him. He is afraid of the dark for all his big words.

Neither boy has the humility enough, yet, despite everything, to admit he needs the other. Alloy wants Andrew but he is too proud to say: Andrew, I need you to make me strong. He wants Andrew to come to him on his own. Yet without that sure call, Andrew is afraid.

And while they sit beside the river, the water flows.

"Andrew?"

Bune, there in the dark, a very solid and unsurprising fact.

"I have brought you some sweet potato to eat," he says.

"Thank you." The relief is terrific.

They eat. The three of them together.

Bune is patient. Each thing happens in its time. You stand by and let it happen, or you join in, or you make it happen by doing what you have to do, without, as Clarence would say, making a fuss. In this respect, Bune and Clarence are similar. In a very ancient time they may have been the same, only Clarence has lost his way amongst the Jims and Henrys of the world. This is why he feels at home with Alloy. Alloy, lost also but nearer Bune's solidness at the centre.

So Bune is apparently making a studied meal of the sweet-potato and the oily green stuff that has been put with it as a relish. It is iron. They're going to need it.

Andrew is uneasy. After all he is the boss around here. He ought to show some sort of leadership. He can hardly ask Bune's advice. At any rate, not in front of Alloy who has seen you stark naked, has tried to knock you senseless, has slept through the night with you and has heard you fart in the morning. Ah yes, but this is something different. This is me at work. This is me the Divisional Manager.

In fact, Andrew's awareness has not changed his identity but rather found it out, enabling him to be more true to himself because he knows a bit more about himself. Although, despite this awakening, his English habits – we may as well call them that – ensure that it is not so easy for him to look himself in the eye . . . and hold it. What he needs is a responsive hand. Alloy's hand. He has to grab it desperately and in desperation, win.

Is Bune keeping them in suspense? He eats in a way that suggests he is deliberately satisfied with his correctness. But he is not. Rather, his deliberation is so essentially a part of him that he does not think about it, until, that is, Andrew bursts with impatient bad temper:

"For God's sake Bune, why do you just have to sit there eating? The world has come to an end and all you can do is eat." He stands up. He sits down. Alloy laughs.

Bune continues to eat. He might have said, had he been sufficiently well educated to be sarcastic: What do you expect me to do? A man must eat, even if the world is coming to an end. But he says nothing. After all, paddling the canoe and keeping it on course comes naturally.

Andrew is about to burst out again but Alloy pulls him back.

So they calm down, they eat and the digestive juices work properly, enabling them to receive the sustenance they need both from the food and from each other.

Out of the contented silence Bune says: "I have sent Weno and Keramugl's people back to be with Tarlie. It is better we do not have too many people here."

"But Bune," says Andrew, "we've got work to do. We need as many people as we can get."

"Yes, Andrew, but how do we feed them?"

"What?"

Bune does not state the obvious twice.

"We don't usually feed them, Bune. We pay them and they buy their own things from the trade store. What are you talking about?"

"Andrew," says the solid centre of the tree, "you heard what Master Henry said."

"Yes. But. . ."

"Shut up, Andrew. Bune is right."

"I know he is."

"So shut up."

So Andrew shuts up and Bune goes on eating. You might think he was some ruthless gangster who had taken over and who was about to have Andrew – feet encased in concrete – dumped into the river, only the river at this point is no more than two or three feet deep. But Bune is merely assuming what has to be done, has to be done. There is no choice. At any rate there is only the choice between being ground down to dust by Jim or resisting Jim. "Andrew," he says.

"Yes, Bune?"

"I have talked to everyone and they are happy with what you said."

"What did I say?" He knows what he said. They all know because it has become the basis of everything; there is no need to be reminded.

"So we will stay here, like you said, beside the river, so that we have a home."

"Yes, of course."

"But, Andrew, Master Henry says we must move. He says that if we do not move he will tell Jim. Then the security men will come in to drive us away. It will be like they drove Tarlie and Petrus and their people away from Ples. That is a bad thing." Bune speaks with a different voice and Andrew responds on cue. He is furious: "Yes, Bune, I meant what I said. It's outrageous. These people must stay here. I'll make absolutely sure that there's no trouble." He starts to get up but Alloy stops him with laughter.

"Yes, Andrew, but Jim won't listen to you. He doesn't listen to anyone. When he knows where we are he'll do everything he can to drive us away. It's what he's made for. He can't help it."

"No he won't." Andrew is indignant, "we'll jolly well, we'll jolly well stop him."

"Yes, Andrew," says Alloy who is made brave by Andrew's passion, "and let ourselves be slaughtered. We need a better plan than that. What do you say, Bune?"

Bune expressed the idea that Jim cannot be ignored. He would not let you ignore him. Jim's world is not merely a world of confrontation but one of pre-emptive action. Wipe out the enemy before it gets you. It's out there. Jim needs an enemy to justify himself.

Andrew takes Bune's idea, and by talking he believes what he says and in the possibilities of glory. "OK," he says, having stood up, "only those people who have to stay on the plantation will stay here. Those who can stay elsewhere had better go. They won't be noticed scattered amongst the labour in the other compounds. Tarlie and Keramugl and co had better stay in the mountains as a reserve."

He stops, looking around for an audience which seems to consist of Alloy only, who is, nonetheless, taken in: "The rest of us will stay here, then?"

"Yes," says Andrew decisively.

"So it's a de facto strike, then."

"Yes," says Andrew less decisively, because he's only just thought about it.

"And, I tell you what," Alloy is caught up in Andrew's Boy's Own stuff because he is a romantic also.

"What?"

"We can lose ourselves in the plantation. We know our way around but no one else does. Look what happened to Henry. Keramugl had to lead him out."

"We could have killed him!"

"And no one would have known."

The sense of power is intoxicating.

"So tomorrow, when Henry comes we'll delay him at the house." And thinking of his house, Andrew is again reassured of the safe game he is playing. "By the time I take him to the river everyone will have moved."

"They'll have disappeared into the plantation. Like guerrillas."

"What do you think, Bune? Bune?"

But Bune has gone, so they walk in silence towards the house. For a short evening moment, each is sufficient for the other.

But it won't do and Bune knows it.

Is that another fire in the distance or the setting sun?

I mean, human endeavours generally progress in a muddled sort of way. When they fail it is because you didn't think it through old man, bad organisation buddy, poor lines of communication my friend, don't go for Moscow in winter, haven't you learned that one yet? Something like that. If, on the other hand, some sort of success can be gleaned from the wreckage, after we've expended as much blood and salt water as we've got and after we've cleaned up the mess, only then can we make some sense out of our heroic efforts and tremendous . . . foolhardiness. Then, we make ourselves great. You did it! Did what? You defeated the enemy. Did I? Yes, they gave up. I'm not a bit surprised, they'd just marched all the way down from the north having thrashed that other lot of . . . pirates. Indeed, but you've won and that's the thing. If we march on the capital now we'll have the country. The mob'll declare you King. They don't like change but once it's inevitable they're all for it. They'll go along with anyone who promises to feed them. But I can't. That's not the point; create a sense of security; weed out their leaders – they'll give them up to you if they think you're the man of the hour; then, later, when we're established, we can do what we like. Take over the estates, dissolve the monasteries, collectivise the farms, nationalise private enterprise, privatise national enterprise. Got to get hold of the means of production. That's the thing. We've won. God must be on our side. He doesn't have a choice, we've banned God, we've made a state religion, we're a Christian State, we're a Muslim State, we're a Hindu State, we're an Atheist State. We will – you can bet – make a window into men's souls, whichever way it goes. Blimey, you are serious, I thought this was just . . . an idea. It was but I didn't expect success. In the beginning I just dressed up for the part. I was a photographer's model. The suckers were taken in, because . . ? Because they were looking for a saviour in the right clothes. And you turned up instead. I did. The suckers. You saw what's happening in the Winter Palace? No? They've been using Catherine's Sèvres tureens as shit buckets. No! They have. The buggers. Well, that's progress. Who're we shooting today? Let me see the list.

□□□□□

Henry has forgotten Keramugl. He is listening to Mozart. The Prague Symphony. The optimistic period.

Henry's house is at the end of the road. Beyond is the cliff from which red parrots wheel out in the sunny mornings. Below the cliff, beside the river polluted by the effluent from the mill, lies the junior management compound, where Alloy has his house, in which Joseph is staying for the time being. Tarlie's head has yet to be cut off.

Keramugl might have jumped over the cliff to some sort of safety but his own safety is not his concern; what is, is his desire to get back to Andrew with the message. So while Henry is listening to the Prague Symphony, Keramugl is walking back down the hill.

Get the geography right. Geography plays an important part in the way history runs; it is not only vanity that does it. First, on the very peak of the hill, Keramugl has to pass Jim's house; Margaret there, somewhere. Nothing on the left except a steep slope. A quarry once where they dug the soft coral limestone for making roads; now it is covered with scrub into which rubbish is sometimes thrown and for which the inhabitants down below, beyond the golf-course and behind the mill, occasionally scavenge. Later someone will find a Royal Copenhagen bone-china teacup.

Above this hole in the hillside, you get a clear view over the golf course: a black void at this time of night. It might be the entrance to Hell but that is a little further on: the club car park, on the left. Opposite that, right, is the entrance to Peter and Daphne's house hidden behind shrubs.

Inside the club, as usual, is Jim. His Landrover in the car park. The only vehicle in the cold, contained cube of light, Peter having walked across to show my face, and Clarence, having toddled up to keep Jim company. Jim's men – Tudak, Rabis and Pen – hang around the car park: their sort of environment, the car park, for all that they will never own a car, unless stolen. Tudak himself likes to wander out onto the road, into the dark, or rather out of the light, to have a fag. He meets Keramugl coming down the hill.

Rules are rules. There is not actually a fence around the hill but you know the rules because if you break them you're in trouble. You get beaten up by the security. They pick you up and carry you down the hill across the golf course – emptiness in the night, your heart beating like mad – and they take you into the plantation. There they teach you a lesson. Rough justice, I know, but it's the only thing you understand. You're not like us. You don't feel the pain as much as we do so we have to give you something you'll remember. Word gets round and it discourages the others. Funny thing too I've noticed: the bruises don't show on a dark skin. Best not to break it, all the same: the sneaky fuckers just might complain to the labour officer. Coming in early on his motorcycle one dark morning, Andrew came across a body. Probably a fight over a gin; don't let it worry you. It was gone by seven o'clock. Most of the residents on the hill do not know what goes on in the night. Or, if they do, they avoid the idea. Best not to mention it, old boy, it'd only upset the ladies.

The rules are unambiguous. If you are not management, you have to have a pass with your photograph on it. Passes belong to the servants who are themselves discouraged from wandering around at night. After all, you have to be up early to get things ready for the lawful residents: all the evidence must be swept away, the rubbish chucked over the edge, before they get up.

Keramugl has no pass. Mind if I translate the conversation into English? Tudak is, after all, some sort of mongrel. Dangerous too, as Tarlie was to discover later to his cost. And to be fair, Tudak is not so much a New Sudanian – and who is? – as a projection of Jim's civilising influence.

"Oo are you?" says Tudak, just visible by the light of a yellow moon.

Keramugl assuming his brother, laughs.

Tudak looks down at Keramugl who has stopped laughing and who is filled with a sudden desire to run. Cannot do that though because not only are his legs shorter than those of Tudak but also his way is blocked by Tudak's henchmen who have wandered up to see the fun. That is, Rabis and Pen.

"See yer pass?" grunts one of them.

Keramugl does not know what they are talking about.

They look at him. He is naked except for his lap-lap. The pass ought, therefore, to be hanging from his neck. It is not. It is, therefore, stuffed down his underpants. That is where the slaves generally put their passes and their money. Jim would rather tattoo the marks on their foreheads so you can see who the buggers are. Scratch the skin and pour in battery acid. Careful though, you don't want to blind the fuckers: they'd be useless for work then.

They make a grab at Keramugl, tearing off his lap-lap. No underpants. No pass either so he must be one of them commies Jim's always telling us about. The only good commie's a dead one cos they want to take everything you have for themselves and because they're godless. Kill 'em and show no mercy before they overrun us. Tudak, Rabis and Pen have never seen a commie, assuming from Jim's references that they are some sort of animal. Keramugl, in his nakedness, under the dirty moon, looks remarkably human. An especially good specimen if anything. Beautiful and new looking, which enrages them all the more. It is not right that a commie should be so, so human, and afraid and beautiful.

The fear they see in Keramugl's eyes drives them. They will take him down to the plantation and deal with him good and proper. Keramugl will fight not like the Devil but like the angel he is. That will only make it worse. His cries will be heard along with the other night noises of pain and anguish. They're noisy those buggers. In the morning the sun shines on the colourful hibiscus hedges and the watered lawns. Another body on the road. One this time that Andrew will recognise. They move in like wolves.

"Give him to me."

Fuck off, they might have said, we'll deal with you later, we can only kill one man at a time. But the voice does indeed stop them.

I have forgotten what Annu said. But it was not what he said that stopped us fighting. It was the sound of his voice. He is a big man but it is not the strength of his arms or of his chest that makes him big. It is not the loudness of Annu's voice that makes us want him. No it is not, definitely. But Annu's voice is very sweet and very strong at the same time. That makes us look at him. We look at his eyes that look at us. Now we see Annu's eyes we want Annu to watch us all the time.

Keramugl remembers the time on the sun baked plains of Karandawa. Despite his nakedness and despite the real likelihood of his being strangled to death there and then by Tudak, he is filled with joy. If this is death, let me have it. His mind is fixed upon the idea of Annu. Annu was what he wanted more than anything else.

Tudak also heard the voice.

□□□□□

In less unusual times Andrew's house on fire would have inspired no less than an absorbed interest. If anything could be done – throwing on convenient water, for instance, or chucking the contents out the windows – it would have been done joyfully and without complaint. Afterwards condolences would have been offered. Madiak in his house below would have waited just long enough – say, until bits of ash began to alight upon his wife's washing in the back garden – before wading in to ensure minimal salvation, while Tarlie or Bune would have organised an efficient and willing fire brigade inevitably saving the day just before it was too late.

But these were the days of Annu, the times of the troubles, so the house burned with not a soul, apparently, to appreciate a good fire and the not insubstantial evening fireworks display as the wood split and curled in agony, as the glass cracked and as the zinc roof buckled and groaned in the heat. An impressive sight as Andrew and Alloy approached, running up the hill and out of breath to see one of the huge water tanks at the back collapse with a sigh allowing the water to spill impressively in the wrong direction.

Andrew rushes for his car parked under the house but Alloy pulls him back: "Idiot."

"Fuck!" replies Andrew but such is the apparent devastation that he is beyond devastation himself. The irrevocable loss leaves him free to do nothing. Had it been a small fire there would have been the bore of clearing up the mess and repairing things. He hangs on to Alloy nonetheless. Alloy is impressed. Had Andrew exhibited symptoms of excitable distress he would have laughed.

They watch, fascinated, as they had watched the labour quarters burn earlier but without the restless feeling that they ought to do something. This is something that must burn itself out and the more complete the process the better.

Andrew is on a youthful adrenaline high again not insignificantly influenced by a sudden realisation of Alloy's dependability. He is so excited that he wants to laugh. The loss of the house is nothing but he is already composing a letter about it to somebody. Maybe to Alloy. He thinks he might dictate it into the little tape-recorder thing he has, remembering at the same time that it is in the house with all the other stuff. He slips off the high so that laughter comes: "Wow!"

And Alloy wants to hold him tight: "You've got me, anyway."

"Small consolation!"

They watch the fire burn itself out, the ruins collapsing with a pathetic gesture of sparks and hot air to become a heap of glowing rubbish in the dark.

There is however, on one side of the garden, under the palms that have grown big over it, a sort of gazebo, a summerhouse which they call a house-wind in that part of the world, where Andrew's predecessor used to sit and drink himself to stupefaction in the evenings. Having nowhere else to go, the boys go to it and beneath the rotting thatch discover most of the contents of Andrew's bedroom: his clothes, his spare boots and some of his books including the one that holds Alloy's letter. Even the mattress. It is like coming upon the store of some devious little rodent.

Andrew stares at the remnants of his past life accepting that, under a roof of some sort, it is all he wants. He is flooded with a feeling of release. "Blimey," he says, "I wonder who did that?"

They sit in the dark looking out.

A small compact figure appears, burning red.

"Bune?"

"Master?"

"What are you doing here?"

[][][][][]

Henry had always allowed servants to do things for him; took it as his birthright. First it was Nanny and then, through his schooldays, someone had always made his bed and emptied the pot beneath. He had known his fag as a human being but it was not done to treat it as such. Later, in the army, he had made a small effort to know the specimen of the lower orders who had been his batman. It had a nice body, at any rate. At university, after the war, he had got used to the mysterious and unquestioned bed-making and potty-emptying again, and continued the habit as a planter.

But the one thing he did for himself was the dusting and the cleaning of his collection of blue-and-white porcelain. Not only because he did not want unfeeling hands to touch it but also because it was one of his great pleasures. The dusting he would do whenever he felt the need to commune with his china, when he felt the need to pull himself up out of his increasingly grubby and necessary life with Jim. By the time Keramugl had deposited him, alone, at his house after the confusing day in the plantation with Andrew who was not Andrew, this happened about once a fortnight. He would do a shelf at a time, because dusting the piece itself and putting it back on a dusty glass surface was counterproductive: the sort of pointless activity which annoyed Henry. The pieces were removed, one by one, and carefully placed onto the seat of an armchair, drawn up for the purpose. He liked to look at the gorgeous things lying there, higgledy-piggledy and priceless on the plain, raw Thai-silk covers, the colours of which changed according to his seasonal moods: hot primaries for the wet season, cooler pastels for the dry. He would stand back to admire his treasures; shock himself with the wantonness of his possessiveness; once, even, getting on his knees as an act of worship. He would have liked, really, to strip himself naked and abase himself in front of it all. The idea seemed a little ridiculous when he thought of it – like looking at your bum in the mirror – but it would come back.

The cleared glass shelf was lightly polished with a chamois clothe, used for no other purpose. Each piece then taken up, carefully, and ever so lightly flicked with a special sort of duster made of Egyptian cotton he had found in the old market in Kuala Lumpur years ago. He had bought a great quantity. You mustn't rub – naughty – because you might scratch the surface if there's some especially gritty bit of dust inside. Blow and flick is my motto.

The twice-yearly washing took a whole sacred weekend. No one was allowed near when he was doing it. Every piece was put onto the sofa, which was then moved well away from the shelves. The shelves were washed on the Friday night – Where's Henry? Not often he misses a club night – and polished with absorbent paper the following Saturday when he would get up early, like a kid at Christmas. The entire day was devoted to carefully washing and drying the sixty-odd pieces and most of Sunday arranging them back on the shelves. Wonderful and the house-boy was given the day off: I can just see him sitting on something without thinking, the great galumphing idiot.

Only Annu had been allowed to touch, to dust and wash, but Henry had, in fact, lost interest in his collection when Annu had been around. The man's indifference to its value beyond the fact of its potential usefulness in the kitchen or dining room had embarrassed Henry. Damned nuisance when you come to think of it. Same with the Mozart: wonderful stuff but it's a substitute; a real view of the sky's as good, he had said in the club one time. What?

Annu gone, the stuff assumed some of its old value. The Annu effect had not made a deep enough impression on Henry for all the thinness of his skin. Me and my Ming. Doting on Delft. Mad about the Spode, he would sing as he tripped around the house with his duster, delighting in his possessions, oblivious, briefly, of Jim.

The dealing with his china was a thing Henry did as a positive thing. He had to be in a galvanized, sunny sort of mood in order to get up, fetch out the dusters and start the job. If you're going to dust you've got to do it properly; nothing shoddy. Mozart was another matter. He put it on as a habit, even if he was not in the mood. The new house-boy – some odd fellow called Tematan whom Henry had picked up about the time that girl was killed in Andrew's labour compound – would put on the record player just as he would put on the lights or draw the curtains, in the evening. Mozart because that was the record Henry generally left in place.

⬜⬜⬜⬜⬜

A week after Keramugl's deposition of Henry in his empty house. Still not a drop of rain and Henry has not the faintest idea whether Keramugl is dead or alive. Remembers the man, forgets the angel.

The blue-and-white porcelain gathers dust.

Evenings, Henry eats his badly cooked dinner alone. Rice or sweet potato and a relish of some sort that the other men's wives have made up for him and stored in the freezer in little plastic bags and boxes. Fruit from his fruit trees keeps Henry alive.

Another piece of Mozart plays, night after night. A later piano concerto, K491. The famous one; doom-laden, filled with regret, memories and a portent of change and farewell. Henry hears it but does not listen. He would like to get out, have a meal in the Thai restaurant in town but it's no longer safe to go out at night, not at all. A lot has happened in the past week. His message has not got through to Andrew: I shouldn't have trusted that fellow: bad or stupid; most likely both. Why the hell didn't I take it myself? Well, I didn't and it's too late now. Andrew and that black fellow with the scowl, who's definitely led him astray, seem to have encouraged the strike on the plantation. I can't believe Andrew'd be such a traitor to his, his, his race, for God's sake. No point in being romantic and sentimental, we Europeans have got to keep the upper hand or else everything'll fall apart and it'll be the dark ages all over again. Look at the mess the Americans've made of Indochina. The British did a much better job in Malaya, just by being cool and methodical.

Henry wanted to be cool and methodical, dealing with the issues as they arose, one by one, like the pieces of blue-and-white china, placid and detached on glass shelves, making sense and fitting together. But the new idea of Andrew, the Andrew-Alloy thing, made Henry restless and wild; the pieces of his life no longer fitted together.

There's always been something unstable and odd about Andrew. He's shown his true colours at last, anyway. In this, Henry found himself agreeing with Jim. Got to keep the savage hordes away from, from whatever it is, and Jim's the man to do it. Good ol' Jim; he'll see us through. Just let him get on with it and don't ask any questions. Let us listen to our Mozart in peace. That's what civilisation's all about. Has been for a few thousand years and you can't have it without Jim. Let Andrew stew in his own juice. I hear his house has been burned down. Serves him right and if it was Jim who did it, I'm glad.

⬜⬜⬜⬜⬜

There'd been a riot too down at Chan's store. But Jim'd sorted that out. Said it was Annu, for God's sake. But it wasn't: the ringleader had a limp, apparently. Tematan said he knew him and he was a bad lot. He'd got some gang or other up in the mountains. That's bad: it'll be like Port Markham next with gangs coming down at the weekends to thieve and kill and then retreat back into the hills out of reach of the law. Jim should've been more thorough; should've kept that fellow and . . . brought him to justice. Pity it hadn't been Annu. Things'd settle down then. None of this, of this disorder and . . . unnaturalness – fancy Andrew of all people getting mixed up in it. And even Annu's name being dragged in too. Something wrong. The Mozart plays.

Then that other fellow'd been killed. Nothing new about that; they were always killing each other but it was particularly gruesome: decapitated and just below the house here if you don't mind. Joseph, beautiful Joseph, accused, of all people. Not even denying it either, just keeping mum and Jim assuring everyone he'd got the evidence for all that the head was missing. Upsetting to say the least. We've had strikes before but they'd been contained with the usual carrot-and-stick stuff. Jim did his bit and then I'd go in and make it up: 'Offer them something 'Enry so's they know we're not that bad and we'll have 'em eating out of our 'ands and wagging their tails before you can say 'scuse me.' But it had not worked this time. Nothing like it. Things were getting out of hand. They had downed tools at the mill and more or less chased Peter out of his office at lunch time. He'd gone back but he said the place was empty with fruit coming in and no one to deal with it but there was nothing coming out of Andrew's place. Peter'd mentioned it in the club sending Jim right off the deep end even for Jim. Said he'd get Andrew arrested and deported. I'll send mi boys out to git 'im and that fucking bum-buddy of 'is I wouldn't like to be in their shoes. The Waterford whisky glass smashed against the back of the bar, knocking a couple of bottles off a shelf. Nalin had ducked down, quick.

[][][][][]

Silence inside the club. But beyond, beyond the roar of the night, a discernible agitation. Humanity on the move.

With Tudak and his men out searching for Andrew and Alloy, they all feel vulnerable. Jim is breathing heavily.

"Jim, Jim, they're just boys." Clarence laughs nervously, his cosy world in tatters.

"What you say?"

"Boys."

"Your boys, eh Clarence? That smarmy fucker of yours. 'E took you in good and proper. You sucker. Better go through the books. I bet 'e's skinned you alive. Skinned us and you let it happen. Just oo's side you on I'd like to know."

Clarence looks as if he is about to cry.

"Jim, Jim." This is Peter.

"Fuck you too. Not much help in the mill were you? First sign of trouble and you were off like a frightened rabbit."

"That's not very fair, Jim. Fact is . . ."

"Oh shut up. Shut up the lot of you. I'm thinking."

Yes, but we got to talk, make a noise and laugh, slap each other's backs and call each other mate. We got to buy drinks all round and keep our spirits up. If we don't, we'll hear the world outside. We'll see our own mortality and we don't want that.

You bet!

But Jim has been in worse scraps before and lived to tell the tale: "Nalin, get up and give us a round." He beams. They relax. A little. The world outside threatens but here Jim is King. He'll save the day. They'll follow him to Hell if necessary.

"Listen you lot, don't worry."

So they don't.

"It's these commie bastards. They're on their way and we got to stand firm. Got me?"

They get him; cannot resist his reassurance.

"I got enough men to settle this thing once and for all. See?"

They see.

"They'll do as I want cos they're my men. Don't ask me why."

They don't.

He looks at them one by one. Catches each one until they look elsewhere. Except for Clarence, that is, who grins straight into Jim's face feeling happier than he has for weeks. 'E's a buffoon that one, Jim might have said to Margaret only he did not see much of 'er these days what with one thing and the fucking other I don't know what she's up to. Some Jesus freak business I shouldn't wonder they get like that these women oo can't have kiddies an' are past it. Poor bitch.

"I dealt with a few of 'em already." He winks at Henry.

"They've been arrested, have they Jim?" James, old boy. Brought them before the magistrate within twenty-four hours, have you? Habeas Corpus and all that. Kept in police custody or released on bail. Is that how you did it?

"Don't be an old woman. We got to deal with this now. I wasn't born 'ere for nothing."

Indeed not.

"An' I don't want you lot interfering. You 'ear me?"

They hear him. They will turn a blind eye, a deaf ear and whatever else he tells them to turn. Anyway, I was only carrying out orders.

They all drink a bit too much and Henry feels distinctly that he's had too many. Join us for dinner, Peter says. No thanks, I'll go and puke up back home if you don't mind and he has done just that to the sound of the K491.

[][][][][]

He sits down and drinks a whole bottle of Cabernet Sauvignon he has saved from some dinner party or other. Vin de Pays D'oc it says on the label. Nice fruity taste: he appreciates it until the K491 sinks in. The sad slow movement. He thinks, he thinks, he thinks of all his life. He thinks of Abus as he throws the empty bottle at the glass shelves of blue-and-white china watching the beautiful, delicate, shattered fragments drift to the floor and over the back of the sofa. In a split second he thinks: I've done a lot of damage, I wonder what I can salvage. A whole life seeking out and buying the rubbish. I'm an expert only no one's ever asked for my opinion. Tears of self-pity fall down ruined face of old drunk.

The crash of breaking glass has awoken Tematan in the little shed he inhabits out the back. There must be a break-in. He doesn't care for Henry's

277

things but he'd be blamed if anything's stolen. They'd cart him off and deal with him. He knows about the headless body. They all did and he's no less on edge. He rushes to the kitchen door which is locked. He doesn't know what he's doing any more than does Henry. He hammers on the door.

At the same moment some of the more foolhardy strikers from the mill – Alloy types from the Junior Management Quarters – a little drunk themselves, are marching along the road and chanting in front of the empty main office. Ho Chi Minh, Ho Chi Minh, Ho Chi Minh. The noise drifts up through the dusty night air to Henry's bungalow.

To his befuddled brain the revolution has started. The mob is come for him. It hammers at the door, the Mozart plays. It's not fair, it's not fair, he cries to himself. I don't want to meet humanity and die. I don't want to meet myself.

Is he afraid? He is. But not of the mob. He can deal with the mob. At any rate meet it and defy it. Rant at it and ridicule it until it tears him to pieces or else, laughing, lifts his easy body and places it lovingly on the warm wooden bench of the guillotine. His head off and it's not fair. Put his head on a pike and carry it high for Ho Chi Minh. Here, look at Henry as you've never looked up to him before.

Henry has an instinct for survival. He is up and flies to his French windows. In the end it is fuck them and I'll live to fight another day. Across the back lawn and under his fruit trees Henry's long legs carry him. He is young again, flying. On, on, on and over the cliff from where red parrots wheel out on sunny mornings. Henry's flying too. And falling now.

Does Henry fall splat on the hard ground below?

Not quite. The cliff is not so high. A little short of twenty-five metres or so and by no means sheer. He gives himself a good shove and he leaps but it is not enough. He hangs in the trees – in what is called gallery forest – falls, rolls, hits some of the jagged rocks and lands bloodied but still breathing at about the same place where Tarlie had his head hacked off behind Alloy's house, recently vacated by Joseph following his arrest for the murder.

He lies there. Dazed, looking up at the stars that are so beautiful he smiles out of pure joy. The same feeling I'd had when I held Abus for the first time. Free at last.

There is someone in the tacky little house behind which he has fallen with a thump. Ever heard a body hit the ground like that? You cannot avoid shivering all over. A man comes out. He kneels beside the body.

"Masta?"

"Keramugl." Of course he had not forgotten the name because the man had told him not to.

There is Angel Face above him looking down into his eyes. The glorious stars behind, sparkling like the frost of his youth.

The soft hand holds his firmly and the last thing Henry sees before the blood fills his eyes is the face of Abus.

PART II

. . . poor boy! I never knew you. Walt Whitman, The Wound Dresser

20
The 5% Man

The Van Island Palm Oil Development Company, of which Jim was General Manager, was an outlier of an illustrious and profitable global commercial empire known as Barbary and Northgate which traced its origins back to the early days of the industrial revolution. B&N clippers had been amongst the first to bring Indian tea to London after the mutiny.

The head office of Barbary and Northgate could be sighted in a side street of the illustrious and profitable City of London, the building as good a representation of Barbary and Northgate as anything could be. Crowded around by functional post-war office blocks, it held its own as something superior. A pupil of Sir Edwin Landseer Lutyens had designed it: steel frame and American elevator disguised by costly English stone. The coal soot had been removed not long before Jim's one and only visit to the place, a year or two before the troubles on Van Island began. Possibly the grand old man himself – Lutyens that is, not Jim – had taken a hand in the matter, for the building was a chaste and beautifully proportioned imitation of a late Roman palazzo, impressively solid but with hints of decay, decadence and Art Deco. The directors' dining room – also used for the annual board meeting – was on the top floor. Its large windows looked down upon the world below beyond the range of the stones flung up, from time to time, by the outraged mob.

A pair of massive steel and brass doors were set in the windowless, rusticated stone of the ground-floor wall of this palace-cum-fortress. Depicted on the doors – in the style of Jacob Epstein – were the essentials of the creation of wealth. Two panels on each door: top left, a landscape of forested plain, mountains, river and sea shore set below a rising – or, conceivably, setting – sun; top right, Egyptian slaves (apparently) constructing a pyramid upon a plain not forested but set out with a rigid pattern of fields; and bottom right, piles of coins before a factory of smoking chimneys, the mountains quarried and the river dammed or, conceivably, damned. The fourth panel, bottom left, had defeated the artist's imagination. It was a blank. Henry – on his first visit, when the building was surrounded by sunlit bomb sites filled with colourful rosebay willow herb – imagined a cornucopia spilling out mock-Tudor houses beside golf courses, bypass roads, fish-fingers – a novelty at the time – and, like the sun in the panel above, the atomic mushroom cloud rising above it all.

Above the doors stretched a massive fanlight in which the Invisible Hand was very visible as the steel-and-brass opposition to the entry of anything but a very small amount of yellow-tinted light. Jim, on that one and only visit, was impressed and even more impressed in the dining room by the selection of cutlery: fuck me, he said afterwards, I 'ung on to the biggest and sharpest and didn't let go. He hadn't, using the same large soup spoon for steak and kidney pie, pudding and the cheese that followed. Rough diamond that fellow: just the man we need. Next time we'll take him down to the pub on the corner for a beer and a dog biscuit.

Nonetheless, despite its restrained luxury, the B&N building was modest by City standards. At the beginning of the 1930s, when it was built, everything else was losing money but the collapse of commodity prices and capital value enabled the illustrious company to buy up, cheap, the bankrupt plantations in India and Malaya which had once been the proud and independent foundations of its trading wealth.

Barbary and Northgate became the biggest producer of rubber in Malaya and by 1940 it was the rubber plantations of Malaya which made it such an essential ingredient of the British imperial war effort. The fall of Singapore to the Japanese in 1942 was the critical blow from which the British Empire never recovered. Terminal decline thereafter. Not so B&N. In the comfortable dining room of its modest City palazzo – spared the bombs as if by divine consideration – the directors plotted and thrived in the post-war boom; empire or no empire. Its critics, with a view of the externals only, saw a pompous remnant of the past and laughed at its apparently old-fashioned ways. But anyone who got hold of shares – and it was not easy – in the 1960s, did well. The shareholders made a good deal of money out of the sale of the Van Island Palm Oil Development Company and the subsequent shift of emphasis towards chemicals.

[][][][][]

Thornley, English, he said it himself, to the soles of my boots, held 5% of the B&N shares.

He'd inherited them from a spinster aunt when still quite a young man. He was already working for the company – there was some family connection about that too – but it was the shares marked him out.

Intelligent, well-educated and self-motivated, Thornley would have done well in B&N under any circumstances but the 5% assured him a place on the board and gave him an edge over his contemporaries. You had to listen to Thornley and as he got older you called him Sir. He was an easy man to hate but there were those of a sycophantic tendency who said he was sensitive to one's feelings and a good friend. Thornley'll look after you, old boy, he's a decent chap. But he wasn't and he didn't. He was sensitive alright but only insomuch as he would be sounding you out and deciding how you fitted into his scheme of things. Didn't matter if you were the scoundrel MacDonald (Jim) or the homo Parfait-Wilson (Henry), Thornley worked out precisely how you could be used in the Van Island Palm Oil Development Company. He knew Jim despised him and that Henry pretended to, but he didn't care. They were mere factors in the equation that equalled VIPOD that, in turn, equalled himself.

By the time Thornley was fifty – when London swung and he ignored it – he would have said only three things mattered to him. Wide-eyed with incredulity, all the same, that you should ask such an impertinent question. He would have said that the thing that most matters is B&N and inseparable from it the Van Island Palm Oil Development Company; the second-most-important thing is the little property in Somerset I've bought for my retirement, and where August of every year is spent; and the third-most-important thing is my son because he is an extension of myself into the future and because he will inherit the first two things. His name is not significant although I do recognise that his physical and mental attributes pass muster. I would have expected no less.

There were two or three other things in Thornley's life which were as essential but which he did not consider objectively because they were his birthright. There was his well-bred and well-dressed wife, Agnes, who had done him the honour – and to give him credit, he saw it as an honour – to decorate his life, to manage his domestic affairs in Eaton Square and in Somerset, and, it occurred to him one memorable evening while he was shaving his fat face, without whom there would have been no son. Then there was his golf, which he played at Sunningdale, taking the train out every Saturday morning for as many years as Agnes could remember; that is, when they were not in Somerset or when he was not making his annual visit out East in February. At Sunningdale, Thornley relaxed, becoming, to his golfing partners, what he had been as a young man. That is, Larry. Old Larry later, who, although a punctilious golfer, gave a glimpse of the humane man that the Thornley of B&N and in Eaton Square had all but eclipsed. On the golf course, losing did not worry Larry. He barely noticed he was no good and therefore he was popular. But Thornley was there, all the same: the golf kept him fit for B&N and for the Van Island Palm Oil Development Company in February. It enabled him to meet useful people at the club house where he had lunch before his afternoon nine holes and the train back to town.

Lastly, there was his son's boarding school, which was important because it provided the education for he who would continue Thornley's holy dedication to the 5%. The school was not, as it might have been, Eton, Harrow or Winchester, but a less-well-known place near the country house in Somerset, chosen by Agnes who had set her mind on it as the most tenacious thing Thornley had ever known her do. At the time he had been staggered that anyone should question his decision. But he gave in: I had to, he said in the club-house. I think, if pressed, she would have left me. For some reason I couldn't fathom, she set her mind against the other places. But that's a woman for you, no rational thought processes. To her he had said I didn't know you felt so strongly, my dear (this was in 1957, the year Daphne gave up collecting postcards and Ghana gained its independence). Then he turned his back on her and locked himself in his study until dinner time.

But the son's school – an ancient foundation with a Board of Governors that viewed the reforms of the English public school system a hundred years previously with deep suspicion – nonetheless became another interest to Thornley. After all, he had to be sure it was doing a proper job. Apart from other considerations – his son's education for instance, wellbeing not a part of that particular equation – having bestowed upon the school the honour of . . . his consideration, Thornley could not allow it to be seen as in any way sloppy. It must come up to the mark. The Headmaster hated Thornley who invaded his study a couple of times a year, not when other parents did it, at the beginning or end of terms, but unannounced, mid-week, mid-term, often about tea time. Most annoying but a necessary annoyance because with Thornley came money and the promise of more. The eventual manifestation of this interest was the Van Island Palm Oil Development Biology Lab. An embarrassing name after all the publicity but people have short memories and we've got the lab now the old bugger's dead we'll change the name.

[][][][][]

Those people who knew Thornley sufficiently well – in a business or a social sense, that is – to have met Agnes, or at any rate to have come across her, said she was a credit to her husband. He was a lucky man – even a lucky devil – despite his own view that luck had nothing to do with it. A man who went around with a woman like that – who'd got her, as it were, in marriage – must have something special. Indeed, the 5% claim to that surplus value of the sweat of men. But to do Agnes herself some credit the 5% was not the reason she married him. Having learned a thing or two later she might have said, but never did, I married the man because I was young, I was spoilt and I thought one had to marry someone. He had, she might have said, the superficial good manners and the ability to dominate social situations that impressed a girl of my class. I thought, I imagined, ever since I had noticed men, that this was the way a husband, my husband, would act. What Agnes did say later, able, at a distance, to feel some compassion, was: I was not sufficiently experienced to appreciate that the way he acted was indeed no more than an act. Such a good act that not only did it take in me but also it took in my husband himself. I married a monster; a short monster. She blushes and laughs a little, turning the ring on her finger, this woman grey but elegant and ready for life still, now she has got rid of him: I was young and silly and shallow and witless. So silly that I wanted my picture taken for the Country Life magazine. Of course I realise it was a stupid thing to do but at the time it seemed perfectly natural. It's what one did, God help us.

In his consideration of all the things in his life, in his valuation of them, Agnes was a creditable decoration, wearing her Chanel suits and small bits of Bond Street jewellery. She made Thornley feel he was a worthy and valuable man in himself. It was for this reason, mostly, that Thornley had bought Agnes. Also, for two practical purposes for which a wife – my wife – is useful: first, because Agnes knew how to decorate and furnish the houses – set the stage, as it were – in Eaton Square and Somerset in just the right way. And second because Agnes would be able to produce the heir. This she achieved perfectly the first time round (phew, she might have said but didn't, phew, got that out of the way). The resultant son was indeed a credit, to them both. He was not much but he was more creditable than all the other things for which Thornley took the credit, including the Van Island etc, etc, etc.

And the interesting thing about Thornley's son, or at any rate about his credit-worthiness, was that his father often disliked him despite the fact that he was his only son and that he was as good as a son could be in all aspects of filial duty. Remarkable also because upon knowing the son and the father you would have said that two men sharing fifty percent of the same genes could not have been more different. In the final judgement, when all things are being argued out, Thornley will argue convincingly, if hopelessly, for his deeds in life, for his life as a worthy life and for himself. His son will argue for his father. Remember the onion?

[][][][][]

It is an ironic fact about the way Thornley felt about his life and about the things in it, that he did not consider the idea of his son as a comfort. Rather – forgetting his own immortality – he thought of his son as a nuisance in the smooth running of his life that included his wife, Agnes, who would – it was a nuisance – sometimes make demands for her son. Her stubbornness over the school thing was something he would always remember against his son. Outrageous, indeed, because his son was, in the end, the only thing that had weight enough to be a real comfort. Ironic also, because his creature and psychological comforts were central to the fact of the man who was Thornley.

So central was this idea of comfort to Thornley that it was not something he thought about or about which others commented. Thornley's need for comfort was an essential part of Thornley. Therefore, his thoughtlessness about others was so thorough that it could not be separated from his general arrogance and from his power in the company. It was more than a right, it was what the world was all about. He got the best of everything and the most preferential treatment: travelling Out East, as he still called it, he was treated with deference even in places out of which the British had only recently been kicked; in a hotel with his wife, he had the first bath and got the best bed; in restaurants he did not notice other people being moved to give him the best table, at which he took the best seat. He had not always been like this. Not as an adolescent, the Young Larry time. He had been likable then. It was the 5% did it. Woke up something nasty in him.

But, and another irony if you like, Thornley was not, like Jim, a bad man, or like Henry, a man embittered by regret. Nonetheless, he was, and there is no better word, a silly man. Silly in his arrogance and in the absolute confidence he had in his judgement and in the result of his endeavours. The fact that he had thought something or done something, made it perfect and right. He was made silly by the 5%, which had, as he would come to understand later, been the curse of his life rather than the comfort. As an adolescent, Larry had wanted to paint pictures, to catch the light of the dying sun and the whispering of the leaves of an Aspen tree in his parents' suburban garden; he had enjoyed gardening with his father on Sundays. It was that stupid doting aunt who had spoilt all that; she had got him the job in Malaya in the first place and then capped it with the bloody shares a bit later. The disastrous road to his silliness. But most of all, Thornley was silly in the fact that he did not recognise his own son.

When he thought of the Van Island Palm Oil Development Company – actually VIPOD, stated as such on the top of its stationery in green and framed by a couple of deferential oil palms – Thornley felt that it was the apotheosis of his life. In Thornley's mind, everything that was Thornley (including the 5%) and for which Thornley was created, was divinely intended to be for the establishment of VIPOD. Everything thereafter was the new world of VIPOD, arising radiant, after the inundation. Thornley himself, thereafter – he recognised the fact and explained it to an astonished Agnes one night as she sat on the edge of her bed in an expensive nightdress – was as a man new-made and blessed with immortality by the fact of, the achievement of, VIPOD, manifested by the facts and figures of, the Annual General Report of, B&N. The idea brought tears to his eyes. He forgot, in his love of himself manifested as VIPOD, his son.

Thornley's Last Will and Testament, sitting in a safe-deposit box somewhere in Gray's Inn, did not mention his son, his human issue. Everything, the 5%, the houses in Eaton Square and in Somerset, the other financial assets, was his estate to be administered by a board of trustees for the benefit of his heirs. Who these heirs were, was not specified but in order to have the benefits of the estate, the heirs must perform certain duties that included the maintenance of the 5% and the house in Somerset. The house, or rather the lease of the house, in Eaton Square, could be sold once his wife, should she survive him – unthinkable that anyone should survive him – had spent out her time in it.

[]||[][]

The Van Island Palm Oil Development Company was the centre of the world, a fact illustrated by a map which Thornley had put together himself with scissors and paste in his study in Somerset one August. This put Van Island in the middle; to the right spread the great Pacific Ocean, the Americas an incidental boundary; to the left sat Asia with Europe an insignificant protrusion up near the Arctic Circle. The Atlantic flowed off the left-hand edge of the map. Thornley's world was flat.

But for Thornley, the Van Island Palm Oil Development Company and Van Island were not only the centre of the world physically, but also the centre of world affairs and a central factor in the consideration of those affairs by men. He related the great events of his time to the Van Island Palm Oil Development Company: the decline of the British Empire, the rise of the new Japan, men walking on the moon, the wars in Indochina. In the first place, he had always seen the success of B&N in Malaya as the prime factor in the British resistance to the Communists; and indeed he was right in his judgement that B&N played a significant role in the economic success of independent Malaysia. Furthermore, he interpreted the Vietnam war of the 1960s as a devious plot by the Chinese to get control of B&N interests in the region. The Van Island Palm Oil Development Company is strategically important, was Thornley's line, not only in the provision of essential vegetable oils that would, if required, be put at the disposal of the American war machine, but also as a model of how the post-war Indochina would be developed: there will be no Communist nonsense in Vietnam, Cambodia and Laos if they are developed along the lines of Van Island. Thornley's knowledge of history ended in 1914 but – ironically – subsequent events bore him out and global warming – created by the farts of men like himself – became the thing, not communism, but Thornley was dead and forgotten by then.

After all, was not the Van Island Palm Oil Development Company something? Something not small or irrelevant in the world? Indeed not and Thornley – English to the soles of my boots – believed he could as easily create a country along the same lines. Johor and Singapore, he used to say quite seriously at the golf club, would be ideal: Johor a sort of giant plantation and Singapore its processing plant and port. He saw himself as President for Life or even King. Queen Agnes would look superb at state occasions organised by Henry. Jim as Prime Minister, probably, God help us.

But if Johor and Singapore was a dream, Van was not beyond the realms of possibility. Idiocy, more like. Silliness, at any rate. Because, because the Van Island Palm Oil Development Company was a model that worked; no doubt about it. A model for the post-colonial world where England and Englishmen maintained critical influence. By virtue, surely, of having got hold of the centre of the world: Van Island.

If things had not gone so publicly wrong on Van Island, Thornley would have got a knighthood. He had already got an OBE. He might have ended up as Lord Thornley of a village in Somerset, over which he had bought the worthless manorial rights. Not of Eaton Square because the house was leasehold, albeit a long one. I pay my rent to the Duke of Westminster, he would tell people at Sunningdale. Just like some whore in Pimlico.

Yes indeed, the Van Island Palm Oil Development Company was something: a feather in my cap. More than its own plantations and processing mill, it was the focus of the Van Island Provincial Development Programme. The company ran the show because no one else was much interested. It paid its taxes – about ten percent of all government revenue before the troubles – and thus was left to its own devices. Blimey, if Thornley was not the monarch of Van, then who was? And that indeed did make Jim the Prime Minister and Henry the chief eunuch.

□□□□□

Thornley's first job, in Malaya, had been to convert a rubber plantation to oil-palm. Just as the young Henry was to do after the war. Thornley had just completed the job when the Japanese occupation scuppered the project.

In the concentration camps and during the forced march to Thailand, many died but Thornley, a weedy little fellow in those days, was spared. He's a water rat, damn him, a fellow prisoner commented during a particularly terrible wet season when prisoners were dying by the dozens every day of dysentery. Survival convinced Thornley that he was meant to survive and he concluded that he was one of the chosen. The fact changed him from being the dreamy suburban schoolboy, Larry, into the arrogant little shit who later became the Holy Roman Emperor Charles V, or whoever it was he imagined himself to be. Thornley, at any rate. He felt he had a special relationship with a god who had especially considered him. This made him proud.

After the war, he had six months' leave with his parents. He still enjoyed the gardening with his father but he had lost his interest in painting. Then he went back to continue where he had left off, leaving Larry behind. By the time the palm oil boom hit, he was the Thornley we all know: he was on the local board; he was recognised as the king of palm oil; he was married to Agnes; the boy had been produced; and, he had got his 5%. He wasn't fat; in fact he was a fit man, able to walk for miles in the tropical sun during plantation inspections followed by a fawning entourage. But because he was short he looked tubby, particularly because he wore short trousers and long white socks, showing off his strong and hairy little legs. Agnes always wore flat-heeled shoes when she was with him in public. But no one called him Tubby. He was generally known as Thornley or That Bastard.

If ever there was a man in the right place at the right time, Thornley was he. The world's post-war human population was exploding and needed to be fed: rice and vegetable oils were the solution. Moreover, newly independent countries – many in the humid tropics – were expected to develop export-orientated economies. (Primary products only, please, we don't want you competing with our manufacturing industries.) There was plenty of undeveloped land, mostly rainforest. Oil palm was the perfect solution. Pre-war Malaya became part of independent Malaysia in the 1960s. On the back of palm oil production it prospered and could tell the British to go to hell. Some local politicians suggested that B&N might go to the same place but others had interests in the company. Enough to ensure that they did not want to kill the golden goose and all that. Thornley had engineered the situation. Also, he had set up the New Sudan deal in such a way that only when VIPOD was up and profitably running did nationalisation of Malaysian B&N occur. Bright Future Holdings came into being. A clever scheme by which not only did B&N get well compensated but also it retained a profitable interest in Bright Future Holdings which in turn owned a stake in VIPOD. No one understood this complex web of ownership, interest and control better than Thornley himself. He was brilliant; he was the coming man, etc, etc. His future was made. He basked in the glory.

This was not all: in New Sudan, Thornley got to know the right government people, desperate to get something established there before the country also got its independence. In the end B&N got free land and a cheap development bank loan. All it had to do was set up a local company, in which it would hold 49% of the shares, and run the thing, dividing and ruling the other 51% in good old British fashion. It was like taking sweets from a baby but to give a number of people, including Henry, credit, a good job was done and the Van Island Palm Oil Development Company became a model for what were called nucleus estate plantation projects. The bank got its money back in record time and usefully faded out of the picture; B&N shares doubled in value; Thornley got his OBE.

Breaking the bush of Van was an exciting job for young men but Thornley was now on the London board and too important to be intimately involved. He settled into the routine of the annual February tour of inspection, trusting the likes of Henry, Peter and a few others to do the right thing according to proven B&N ways. When it was obvious that a stronger hand was needed, Jim was brought in. Thornley had heard about him on his second annual visit; something to do with quelling labour unrest on a neighbouring island where something was being mined. He liked what he heard about the rough-and-ready nature of the man. He sought him out and learning that Jim had been born on Van, offered him the job of Development Manager – Henry Parfait-Wilson'll explain the finer details – suggesting that if he could find himself a wife once things really got going he could expect to be General Manager. He promised the same thing to Henry, well aware that Henry would never marry.

Thornley liked Jim but it worried him that he did; not because of Jim's ill-educated vulgarity or thuggery, which were the man's sterling qualities, but because Thornley envied Jim's upbringing on Van compared with his own suburban background. Also, he envied Jim's nihilism. The idea that Jim had no moral standards made him think about his own. It was a disturbing idea.

Fair to say, though, that Thornley didn't really like anyone; he merely appreciated their useful qualities or otherwise dismissed them. He appreciated Jim for what he was and he appreciated Henry because Henry was educated, polite and, in his presence, not merely deferential but suggesting that others too should bow down before the great man. At the same time, however, Thornley did not want people to associate him with the effeteness of Henry; rather, he wanted to be associated with the rough, tough diamond, the man of action, who was Jim. He was proud of his idea of Jim and Larry Thornley and would regale other members of the golf club with stories of his friend Jim of Van Island: that's how I'd like to have lived my life.

21
A Lamb

About the time Van Island things were beginning to fall apart, Thornley was a little over sixty and up to his neck in other B&N things: expansion of plantations in Indonesia no nonsense about human rights there; agro-chemicals selling like wild fire Silent Spring still considered subversive; and timber from the Philippines no questions asked Marcos is a man you can do business with. They'd even got involved in the down-streaming side of the UK DIY business – we're not as stuffy as we look but not for Eaton Square thank you.

Busy then, was Thornley. Someone else had better go to Van for me this year. There seems to be a bit of trouble down there. Nothing Jim can't deal with all the same someone ought to show support from the London end. The more troublesome sort of shareholder – the type who goes in for DIY – might ask questions. We'd better have something to say. We could have hushed things up if it hadn't been for Henry dying off that way. Off his head too by all accounts. I'm not surprised. Those hysterical types. Agnes'll be upset. She liked him for some reason. Thoughtless thing to do. You're supposed to go away and retire so we can forget you. The wholesale clearance of settlements, strikes, decapitations and so forth are part of the game. Play a straight bat, no hitting below the belt and football is for sissies, but Henry drawing attention to himself like that is a bad show if you ask me.

The someone who went out was Thornley's son. Let's call him, let's call him Dick. Dick Thornley. Nice chap. Not going skiing this year? Gets so busy just after Christmas. Everyone seems to be doing it now. Age of the Common Man, damn him.

Dick left school and did the right thing. He might have gone to Cambridge, thanks to his father's money. He didn't because, what with his father's money, what was the point? He'd inherit the 5% – and the house in Somerset – so the right thing to do was to go straight into Barbary and Northgate. Learn it from the bottom. Start in the Estates Department; which is what he did. Would have been better had he gone straight out to Van to learn what it was really like: Plantation Assistant like Andrew. Then. . . But he didn't, so he never did understand about the wholesale clearance of settlements, strikes, decapitations and so forth. Better to understand things from the London end where we're doing our little bit to resist the red menace out there in South East Asia. And not doing too badly out of it ourselves because, I'm telling you old boy do you want to try the '59 or shall we leave it for later, I'm telling you, I'm telling you, what was I telling you? Oh yes, capitalism works it's the only, it's the only, it's the only way we'll deal with those commie bastards is bomb them back to the stone age. Surplus value is ours by right of investment.

The Estates Department in London was where Dick started: a sort of administrative clearing house between our possessions out in the East and the gods up there in the dining room. Dick worked for a chap whose name Thornley himself always got wrong the '54's altogether a better vintage but I think we're a little too far gone to appreciate it although it may have been Butler or Bouncer or something like that. Funny chap something in the war we took him in afterwards.

This chap lived in Wandsworth or Wimbledon or somewhere like that in a terraced Edwardian house with a garden that, in summer, was glorious with roses, honey-suckle and bees. He ought to have retired years ago but he's been with B&N twenty-five years man and what else could I have done after I was shot down in 1940 and not quite right in the head afterwards your father saved me from the bin and I am eternally grateful. Thornley did not deserve that either but he got it. Those types get everything: drink the best wine and do not appreciate it for all they know the year. Butler, Bootle, Bombardier, whatever his damn name is, does a good job and he's cheap hahaha the longer we keep him the less pension we have to pay him hahaha his wife I suppose he has one can bury him when the time comes Dick can take over but I'm not going to make it easy for him he ought to do the right thing by his father.

Dick did do the right thing by his father. He went into the Estates Department of B&N in the London office. It was located in a couple of back rooms with a view of the windows of another office block where bored-looking and badly dressed girls did things with coffee cups and scraps of paper serving unhealthy-looking young men wearing white shirts with the sleeves rolled up who did . . . something else. For a while there had been a view of the river, over a bomb site. Dick did it for his father. That is what a son of mine should do. Chip off the old block he said at Sunningdale once although he had not much idea what the block was and he had not the faintest idea about the chip. Disappointing he didn't get into the first eleven. Or was it the first fifteen? Either way, I was disappointed. Felt he'd let me down. If Dick was a chip off anyone's block it was Agnes's. Dick loved his father. If anyone let anyone down, Thornley let Dick down.

Dick did do the right thing by his father. If he'd done the right thing by himself he would not have gone into B&N or anything like it. He would have been an architect. Not the best architect at first but better than most because he understood that architecture was not primarily about buildings but about the spaces that buildings create. The spaces in which people live their lives. Growing up in Somerset but detached from the rural Somerset of those days and alone in the holidays he got to know the churches and villages and small towns in that part of Somerset that was a world apart and in decline in those days. Did him good. If he had been an architect he would have been better than most by the 1990s and beyond because he appreciated people despite being unable to get close and he had an adventurous streak in him. Agnes did not worry about him because she recognised that also he was a chip off her block alright. Agnes was interested in Tudor gardens down in Somerset and she helped at the local old people's home on Tuesdays and Thursdays when she was in Town. Her husband did not know this.

[][][][][]

Loveable: that was the essence of Dick as a boy and young man, which was all there was going to be of Dick. Not an overtly expressive, or rather receptive, over-the-top, calculating, feed-me-cute-puppy-dog, loving chap but a decent, generous and apparently easy-going, modest, take-it-or-leave-it fellow. Nice chap, that son of Thornley's, whatever his name was, I've forgotten. Loveable and therefore usable too. In the end, some over-the-top, calculating but undeniably loving, loving older woman – decent and generous too but not easy-going, not by any means, more given to histrionics, jealousy and fits of depression and self-doubt when she would be silent and question her motives but loving Dick all the more for it – older woman, at any rate, would have got hold of him.

But she didn't get the chance, and so Dick hung on to his soul, which had something to do with the Perpendicular church towers of that part of Somerset and his interest in the music of Gustav Mahler. Or Anton Bruckner, but he was mad about that sort of architectural music for a while. Everyone was, about the time Dick left school. After his loveability – clean boyish limbs well into middle age, had he got there – after his loveability, the tenacity with which he hung on to his soul was the other remarkable thing about Dick. In this respect, therefore, no one knew Dick well enough, not even Agnes who did not ask him, or try to. She was, after all, his mother, so she might have had a go, but having a go in that respect would have exposed her own . . . inner Agnes too early. A thing her generation did not go in for damn them and George V and all his type. She would have watched Dick's marriage to the older woman, and kept her distance. Said nothing. His father would have said what had to be said after a glass too many and a sort of bloated feeling down there. Let me down that boy, don't like that woman who's only after our money, blah, blah, fucking blah, you thoughtless silly old shit. But he didn't get the chance.

Dick then: loveable and unknowable and entirely unknown. Better than anyone knew but not so much better than the rest of us after all was said and done and likely to be as corrupted by the 5% and antique shops and a house in Tuscany as the rest of us would be. It was, in fact, the best thing he was ever likely to do. Although it looked like a monumental lack of tact it was, in fact, a monumental lack of knowledge compounded by Jim who of course, of course, knew it all.

[][][][][]

No big thing in itself. Normally, such an event would pass without comment or, at any rate, no more than what those fuckers been up to or that's what they're like when they get drunk only they weren't in this case they must have been stands to reason. Problem was, Thornley's son, whatsisname, went and got himself killed, silly bugger. Shouldn't have happened of course it shouldn't but it did and that makes things awkward. Son of the MD, Englishman and all that you can't keep it out of the papers someone'll smell a rat even from that far away. It becomes an incident, the Van Incident in the good old days a gun boat would have been sent in and Van scooped up into the empire no more nonsense about treaties we'll do what we like and they'll benefit from religion, trade and the civilising influence of, of providing us with the surplus value.

This is not Nalin's daughter: gang rape and murder of a gin. This is something serious: the mob at the gate, disturbing our lunch and making us fear for, for our wives and daughters and our other property. If it had been only a couple of local children trampled to death in the panic after the guns were let off, the papers wouldn't have been on our backs then, the vultures. But a couple of children were indeed killed after those stupid frightened boys let off their guns in every which direction. Two little girls, apparently, and some woman. Well, those people have plenty of children, they won't miss a couple and I can tell you, I know what I'm talking about, they don't feel it like we do. And after all's said and done he was Thornley's son a white man. There'll be an inquiry. There'll have to be. It won't be easy but we have to do these things properly but don't worry, I'll have a chat with the Prime Minister and things'll be smoothed over. Henry'd have been the man for that job.

It was almost funny. Not even the dignity of a calculated murder. A mistake really and with a bit of forethought it would never have happened. No one was to blame. Everyone was to blame. The crowd got out of control and he was killed as the, as the scapegoat. You could call it that. I'd call it a sacrifice. Sacrificial goat. Lamb to the slaughter: I reckon he hadn't the foggiest what was going on. If he had he could have saved his arse. By rights it should have been Jim or any one of those bastards who keep the show on the road. And isn't Dick as much to blame and as worthy of being torn to death by the enraged mob as Jim, or Thornley himself or Henry who might well have been? As worthy of it as Peter had he not walked out of the management meeting the day before? As worthy as Daphne had she not got wise and, as has been suggested before, cut and run to Margaret? No Dick, your charm, your easy-going nature and your ignorance are no excuse. Who paid for those Perpendicular church towers in Somerset and for your school fees? You chump, for all that you loved your father who was not aware of you, as Dick, until it was too late, you were as much to blame as anyone. In this respect, Jim was right.

[][][][][]

It may have been, it must have been, a big thing for Dick at the time, but it was nothing and everything to, to anybody who considered it in some way or another, because he was Thornley's son. An unknown and usable quantity that was Thornley's son. He might have been a blithering idiot but he was the King's son and as the King's son, who else would deal with him but the Prime Minister? He did, and no Henry around to smooth over the rough bits. Neither Margaret, the Prime Minister's consort and damn the bitch I'll get her see if I don't, to bring out the Dick-ness of Dick and to organise a dinner for him to which she would have invited Henry, had he been living, and Peter and Daphne. Daphne would have remembered Dick as Dick rather than as, as no one.

Dick might have spent a day or two with Andrew. Same type really only Dick is a little younger. They would have got on well those two and Andrew would have shown him the ropes and given Dick a good idea that the Van Island Palm Oil Development Company was not a bad show in fact my father hasn't done a bad job at all I could live in one of these labour quarters myself mind if I take a few photographs good chap that Andrew he showed me how to harvest the fruit it's quite easy when you know how but I wouldn't like to have to do it for a living. Yes Dad, nothing to worry about Parfait-Wilson's death was an accident apparently he'd been drinking a bit too much. Yes Dad, nothing to bother yourself about he wouldn't have enjoyed his retirement. He was the type who'd have wanted to have died in harness that's what everyone said. He probably had cancer or something and that's why he was drinking. It was an accident. No, there was no hint of impropriety I reckon he was one of those fellows who preferred his own company not a family man at all Jim spoke very highly of him said he could not have managed without him all those years of making your dream come true. Jim is devastated. Lost his right-hand man blah, blah, blah and all that baloney just to put his father at ease and reassure him everything is going well. Was Dick too easy-going by half? Telling lies for a quiet life does not help anybody in that sort of situation. Or maybe it does.

But Andrew was on the run so Dick did not spend a couple of days with him. Instead he spent most of the time with Jim.

Dick went out to New Sudan and on to Van an innocent. His father briefed him only inasmuch as he ensured that his son would appreciate the splendid thing his father had caused to be built out there amongst the stone-age savages who were the – well, you couldn't call them citizens – inhabitants then, of that chunk of wilderness known as New Sudan. Development, Dick, we're at the forefront. Cutting-edge stuff, we're leading the pack. A bulwark against the red menace, the vanguard of civilisation and the standard-bearer of, of British values. Like Australia, Dad? Yes, like Australia, only Van is not quite an entire continent we can fuck up. Dick looked at his father waiting for the pearls to drop. What you have to appreciate, Dick, is that everything about Van Island Province is the creation of B&N. We did it all and I'm proud. You'll find Jim a rough diamond but he's a good fellow and he's done the company proud. He'll look after you and you're bound to learn a thing or two from him. I don't want you to criticise, you don't know enough, you're representing me.

[][][][][]

If you had said to Thornley, afterwards, you knew Jim would hide anything unpleasant, the broken Thornley would have mumbled yes he knew exactly what Jim would do. Jim his firstest and bestest lieutenant. Jim did what Thornley knew Jim would do and, in the process, he got Dick killed. Or, maybe, even, he killed him.

But at the time of Dick's departure, Thornley would have denied anything of the sort and he would have believed what he was saying to himself, pulling the wool over his eyes and his nose but not over his silly mouth. Jim'll look after Dick alright, Belcher, Booby, Butler, whatever your name is and I'll thank you not to question my assessment of the situation for all that you are the only one who reads the reports thoroughly and has a better idea of what is going on than do the shareholders, the Board and even my exalted self but you are a brain-damaged cripple and if you value your job. . . Butler, shot down in 1940 and never quite the same since, was the only one who was fond of Dick for his own sake. Fond of the child he'd never had. You talk of that spoilt boy as if he was your own, his wife said, one summer evening in the fragrant back garden of roses, honey-suckle and grass freshly mown with the old push mower because there was so little lawn it wasn't worth getting a motor and we like to see the daisies and the dandelions don't we in Wimbledon/Wandsworth. Hambledon Road, where they bought the house in 1947 after he had got out of the nursing home with some money his mother had lent them. A long way from Eaton Square where there was only a tiny paved yard that didn't get any sun to warm the lonely clipped bay tree in a wooden box tub like the ones you see in the Orangery at Versailles or at Hampton Court you can wheel them around. There is a bit of green mould growing where the white paint is cracked. Watch out!

□□□□□

You could be whoever's fucking son you wanted to be but you had to take account of yourself and Dick didn't, although his death was a sort of accounting, one could have said but no one did.

Towards Jim, Dick was deferential and polite: he did not pull rank, could not have done had he wanted, he was not that calculating type. Hasn't got the spunk to play that kind of game. To act the part like his father had done until the part took over the man and all that it's been said before. Jim was stuck with him for three days and he cursed Margaret, Henry and Andrew in equal measure for not being available.

He didn't want Peter and Daphne. That fucker Pete's going funny too he said to anyone who'd listen at the club. They listened – Clarence, Polly and her husband the accountant – but they were not sure what he was talking about. Fact is, I don't trust 'im no more. Told 'im to get out but he's still around. He didn't want Dick to hear what Peter might have to say. Although he didn't credit Peter with any independent thinking his instinct told him something was going on and he had half an idea that Pete the fucker might 'ave an idea where Margaret's gone an' 'idden 'erself. But that sort of trouble, Jim did not want just now, if she's down there, then I know where I can find 'er.

Nonetheless, Dick did spend a morning with Clarence who also took him to one of the smaller plantations where work was still going on. They went past the mill where Dick did not see the fruit piling up and going rotten because he had not seen an oil mill in his life. Bit of trouble but nothing unusual was Clarence's comment, Jim'll sort that out in a day or two. He believed it too.

Therefore, Dick ate at Clarence's, and they both went over to the club after. Jim joined them later, leaving Tudak and co in the car park. Jim was in high spirits having, as it happened, sorted out the problem at the mill. It was easy in the Jim fashion. He had gone to the mill office – broken the door since Peter had the key – and sat at Peter's desk. Tudak and co had been sent to the mill supervisor's house in the Junior Management Compound. Bring 'im here. They had brought him. You going back to work tomorrow or are you not? It was a simple threat backed up with Tarlie's recent demise and the fact of Rabis, Pen and a few similar types sitting on the mill supervisor's veranda imprisoning his wife and children inside. Because if you aren't I'd like you to tell me now so's I can do something about it, quick. Thank you and if you'd be so kind as to go tell your lord and master, Mr Peter, that Mr Jim has sorted out the little problem, I'd be grateful.

So that was that little problem sorted. Man of Action I am let's move on to the next. It worked, as it had worked before. Jim had no notions of a critical mass beyond his own.

Seeing Dick at the bar with Clarence, Jim was in an expansive mood. He almost liked the little shit. There was another little problem that needed solving. Dick could help him do it. It'd make him feel like a man, take some account of himself, do 'im good. The idea that it might be dangerous given the current climate of restlessness did in fact cross Jim's consciousness. It crossed Jim's confused consciousness and met, at some sort of spaghetti junction of his, his festering and fermenting resentment for Margaret, for Andrew and even for Henry, all of whom had, in one way or another, escaped his grasp. These were people that Jim's muddy state of consciousness, his Jim-ness, desired with a sort of maddening passion so that they might distinguish him from the lower beasts. The dubious loyalty of Pete would be tested by his return to the mill tomorrow, but Jim did not think much of it. Clarence's dog-like devotion was a pretty second-rate prize, and that of Polly's husband not even worth his consideration. Thornley did not count because in his own way he used Jim and not so very deep down, Jim understood this: Jim was – he barely dared contemplate the idea – he was Thornley's Tudak. None of these relationships was worth the having, control only being truly satisfactory when it covered the more valuable specimens: Margaret, Andrew and to a lesser extent the defunct Henry. And here was his newest, his newest whatever you want to call it, acolyte, Dick. The worthless nonentity Dick, who was quite emphatically in his loveable essence a waste of time and of space. His hanging on to his soul was of no consequence to Jim whatsoever. Therefore, Jim hated Dick very much at that point in time of the disintegration of the Van Island Palm Oil Development Company. And funny that, because it was not as if Jim was completely blind to what was going on. He did have a sort of instinctive understanding that things were falling apart. He resisted understanding it in an objective way but the little bits and pieces of evidence were beginning to add up to something substantial. Not that I can't 'andle it. That's what I'm 'ere for. Man of Action, I am.

But all the same, on top of everything else, to have this Dick shit, this useless son of a something he did not know Agnes but in his mind's eye he saw Margaret, was poor compensation for the others, and a nuisance to boot. The puppy nuzzles you and gets kicked for its pains. Jim wanted the sort of loyalty he did not entirely despise. He needed it to maintain his own status. In this respect he much preferred a Joseph behind the bar than a handful of Dicks.

However, at this point in the loss of Jim's control over the more worthy, the more worthy indications of humanity, his response to Dick was more emotional than intellectually calculating. It manifested as the utmost affability. Henry would have noted it and remarked upon it: at that point in time, Dick's loveability was perfectly balanced by, and as if the inspiration for it, Jim's affability.

"Got the very thing for you tomorrow, Dick mi boy."

"Have you, Sir?" It was in Dick's nature to please men such as Jim by calling them Sir. The tree surgeon who dealt with the trees in the little park that surrounded the house in Somerset had once been called Sir by Dick in error. He would have made a good tree surgeon's assistant would Dick. He was the type to be an assistant. Come to think of it, he was more likely to have been the architect's assistant than the architect himself: I'll do the general outline Dick and you can fill in the details for me, check out the engineering and all that but I'll get the knighthood and blame you if the bridge falls down.

□□□□□

"I 'ave."

"What's that, Sir?"

"Something I'd 'ave asked 'enry to do." Here Jim touches his chest, Napoleon-like, for some reason, and looks at the ceiling fan, dimly revolving above the bar.

Dick looks into his glass.

"We got a bit of trouble in one of the settlements. They're 'olding out against us. Against your father. We got to do something." Jim looks at Dick. His grubby, bloodshot eyeballs reflected for a moment in the vague blueness of Dick's.

"Are they?"

"Yes. They are," you little faggot, thinking of Andrew for a moment.

Dick looks back into his glass, as if expecting therein to find the answer. Jim wonders, for a moment, if the little prick has taken in what he's said. He has an irrepressible desire to impress himself upon the company at large.

"Oo wants a drink?" It's an order to all and sundry – with an emphasis on the sundry – to gather round and listen to the Man of Action . . . in action. My words are my deeds. At any rate around the bar. Come, warm me with your adoration. Drink from the cup I offer. Does the chorus sing the drinking song, early-Wagner style or Carl Maria von Weber? Stamping its feet because it knows where it stands and will not be moved. No, it shuffles forward like a gaggle of hesitant school children. It bunches behind Jim as Jim's only support there in the dark, the ceiling fan working its way through the turbid night.

It is a movement of free-thinking, educated men and women. Educated in good schools in England, Scotland, Australia and even New Zealand. They gather round. Wonderful, is it not, that Peter has got away? Publicly dumped Jim at the management meeting that afternoon.

Minus Peter, then, it gathers, this expensively educated chorus of men and women. There is Clarence, forever optimistic that the fight can be avoided and things will turn out alright on the day. He has a puzzled expression on his face and winces from time to time because of a pain in his chest that woke him the other night with such vigour that he cried out: Mummy! Awake, sitting in the yellow night light, he tries to calm himself: Thinks of Joseph, no longer there behind the bar. Thinks of Alloy, absent these last few days, who has impressed himself upon my soul, by his absence. I need him about to scowl at the world and to be cross, to do his efficient, honest job as if he hates it and to call me Mr Clarence as if he'd strangle me given half the chance. I love him. He's a good boy, Alloy. I need him to take away my pain.

It gathers, this chorus of men and women. The flotsam and jetsam beached here on Van, as if for a purpose, for God's sake: Polly – we've fixed her name now but it's about all we have fixed – and the other Pollies who have not the faintest idea. Look, there's the bloated, headless carcass that was Tarlie, the flies as close as anything living'll get now. Oh, I don't like that but they can look because they feel nothing for it. You would have to make them carry the carcasses, the cadavers, themselves, the stench of putrefying meat stinging their nostrils; then perhaps they might think: this was by our sin of omission.

Their hubbies, their darlings, their men, follow thoughtfully behind, clutching their drinking cups – fill 'em up mine host before we march boldly into battle singing our hymn to victory. They clutch their glasses for want of anything else to hold on to. If it were not for the beer glasses, the whisky glasses, the rum and coke glasses, they would clutch their crotches, play with themselves and straighten their dressage for the want of something to do with their hands. But these cups are filled with the dregs of whatever it was they had ordered in their hopeful youth. Hold on, hold on to whatever it is. That is my wife, the missus, the madam, the Madame, the definition of who I am as a married man who also owns a motorcar and aspires to two children and who is, therefore, someone of account in this world of men drinking in bars, driving motorcars and talking about motorcars, watching sport and talking about sport because I can't do it and because I'm stuck with this person whom I do not know.

It gathers, this chorus of expensively educated men and women, around Jim who makes it feel safe and whom, later, it can blame. He made me do it, I was following orders, I was afraid. The little shits. And Joseph is no longer behind the bar to watch you playing at this thing called . . . life. Only Nalin: the sad little man, the creep, the wasted creature behind the bar who, for all his faults, does not get things in a muddle like Clarence did that time to the tune of two hundred dollars. Nalin thinks of nothing – he daren't – other than serving the drinks: SP, San Mig, G&T, whisky-water, whisky-ice, whisky-soda, coke, coke and rum. That's it. That's humanity. That's it. No brandy these days with Henry gone. Nothing interesting for me? Joseph Darling, now Joseph's gone. Joseph could have urinated into the glasses and they would have drunk it. Will-o'-the-wisp I think he called it, Henry helped him: tequila and cheap sherry in equal measures, dash of brown sugar, nutmeg, lemon juice from a whole lemon and something sort of solid I can't put my finger on. I love it. I'm sure it does me good.

"You give 'em what they want," says Jim, though they are nothing to him except perhaps Clarence whose head he would pat or have shot as an act of something or other.

They get what they want.

"Now listen, Dick."

Dick listens. The chorus listens with varying expressions of interest, adoration and incomprehension written upon its faces. Clarence gets another pain. Wow, impressive, is it not, this scar tissue building up?

"Them f... them settlers 'ave 'ad everything from us. Too much if you ask me but that's what we 'ad to do. All they 'ave to do is sell us the stuff. We give a fair price." It was true. He gives the audience a wounded look, then challenges Polly's hubby to deny the fact. Polly's hubby does not. "All they got to do is plant the bits of land we give 'em. 'Enry used to sort that out. Now, they want to discuss matters." Jim gazes at the ceiling fan once more as if to catch a sympathetic expression upon the face of God. You and me, God, we can sort things out. We can put these fuckers straight.

Jim continues: "Discuss what, I'd like to know? I can't change the prices they get and they 'ave to plant the land. It's the system an' they 'ave to do it. There's an agreement." There was. "They signed up." They had done. "We give 'em everything." Except the sweat of their labour which we expect to get at a substantial discount. "And now this." Jim sighs, the chorus sighs with him. The dregs indeed.

[]·[]·[]·[]·[]

Fact was, the settlers were part of the wider provincial development project to make Van Island Province the palm oil centre of the country. The aim had been, still was, to get as many oil palms planted as quickly as possible. There were three types of organisation. One was the nucleus estates – like the plantation Andrew ran – that in the long run would produce about forty percent of the total of what is called in the industry Fresh Fruit Bunches – FFB. Presently these estates produced over sixty percent of total FFB, which is what the company liked because it meant tighter control over production and not having to mess around with the nuisance which was the small farmers and all the humanity that went with them. The nucleus estates were supposed to ensure that there was always enough FFB to keep the mill going and cover overheads.

Then there were the village growers, the company supplying the seedlings and guaranteeing a market for the FFB produced.

The settler projects were the third type of organisation, halfway between the estates and the free village growers. The settlers themselves, likewise, were somewhere between the free villagers and the indentured labourers of the estates. Ordinary men and women as enslaved to the Van Island Palm Oil Development Company as ever their forebears had been to Akaranda Plantation before the First World War, and as ever English villeins had been to their Norman lords.

The settlers then. The idea was to bring people from the densely populated valleys of the New Sudan Highlands and the Optic Lowlands on the North

Coast, and settle them on the comparatively sparsely populated coastal plains of the mainland and the islands, where, heretofore, malaria had limited human activity. Here the potential for intensive production of export crops was substantial, based on virgin soils. Oil-palms were indeed perfect for the coastal soils of Van. The new population would also supply the essential cheap labour for a rapidly expanding plantation industry. The settlements varied in size from a few hundred to just over a thousand hectares. The forest was cleared, dirt roads put in and community centres established with markets and primary schools. It was assumed that a fast-growing local economy and community pressure would provide other self-sufficient services. A good idea, post Second World War, and as the subsequent ideological wars raged in nearby Southeast Asia, it was indeed a good idea by the lights of the age. Each settler family was given a clearly defined six hectares, title subject to the correct planting of three hectares with seedlings supplied by the company. The remaining three hectares would be used for subsistence farming until an income flow was established by the supply of FFB from the first three hectares. This income was expected to start flowing about three years after planting. By the time Andrew arrived on Van, the first settlers were producing substantial quantities of FFB. By the time the unofficial settlers were cleared from Ples, the company was thinking about getting the earliest settlers to plant their second three hectares. It was, as Jim knew well, in the agreement. This planting programme would not be done immediately but within the coming two or three years. Significant forward planning and investment was required, because the total land area was nearly a thousand hectares involving the establishment of nurseries – it takes about twelve months to produce a good seedling from seed – and a second processing mill.

Payment for the settlers' FFB was based on world prices and, by a complicated method, on the quantity and quality of the palm oil produced. Harvest a bunch too early and the quantity of oil was reduced; harvest it too late and the fruit began to go rancid, reducing the quality of the oil. The price was reviewed every week. Method of payment subject to a binding agreement. Payment made into the settlers' bank accounts, less a small deduction for a stabilisation fund in which, although few understood it, the settlers were shareholders. A slightly larger deduction for what each settler owed the company for the cost of the seedlings. Debt payment spread over five years including interest which equalled the preferential interest the company paid the bank.

On the assumption that the international banking system is a fair system, the company's financial arrangement with the settlers was all above board. There was, at this stage, no discontent and no reason for it. Moreover, since the beginning of the project there had been an upward trend in the prices of vegetable oils. At the time of Dick's visit prices were at record highs thanks to the failures of the sunflower crop in the USSR and of the soya bean crop in the USA. The settlers had experienced a steadily rising income. Good for the B&N trading arm that imported motor-cars, generators, hi-fi equipment and suchlike into Akaranda town. Boom-boom time. The settlers were generally happy. They were good farmers: their yields of FFB and the quality of their palm oil outdoing the company estates. Bound to be the case because the settlers took an intense interest in every bunch of fruit and every palm that belonged to them. As they were supposed to do, they maximised their income and discounted the nominal cost of family labour.

Yeomen, rich peasants, kulaks, these farmers had listened to Henry and were happy with the way Jim ran things. They were not stupid and they knew what went on in the process of maintaining the order required to ensure their income flow. When fleeing relatives arrived talking of the rout at Ples, the fire on Andrew's plantation, the strike, Annu, they were politely heard and then advised not to rock the boat. Things would settle down. There had been problems before and plantation labourers were, in any event, the lowest scum of the earth. Nonetheless, the decapitation of Tarlie was unsettling. Jim had gone too far. This was why he was not welcome on the settlement. He knew he was not. Cutting off a chap's head like that was, let's face it, bad form, despite the fact that it was not the first time.

No, the problem the settlers wanted to discuss arose from their wealth. They were doing well from their three hectares of oil palms. On the other three they grew their staple foods and a good deal else for sale at the local markets. Some, against the agreement, had planted fruit trees that in the future would provide mangoes, custard apples and avocados. Not a few had rented out the odd hectare – also against the agreement – to relatives and to plantation labourers who had settled their families and planned to retire on a little farm. Everyone was comfortably avoiding the idea that they were more–or–less owned by the company. The idea of having to plant more oil palms and give up their comfortable freedom was unsettling but confrontation with Jim even less attractive. Everyone knew that whatever the outcome, Jim'd get what he wanted and they might lose everything. It was not to be contemplated. Pull down the wool, pull down the wool.

[][][][][]

Assuming him to be the more reasonable, Henry had always been the man to whom the settlers had appealed; assuming, also, that he had some influence over Jim. A fantasy: those small things they got from Jim through Henry, they would have got anyway. Nothing else had ever been achieved. Whenever Henry remonstrated with Jim the reply was the same: you don't understand a thing about it 'En. They got too much to lose. They won't make any trouble. Jim was right, so far.

But Henry's dead.

"'Enry used to sort these things out but 'e's gone." Hand on chest, gaze up at ceiling fan, the face of God, etc, etc.

General one minute's silence. Look down into dregs.

"Anyways, what I think is all these wankers, sorry Dick I was thinking of the shareholders, all these settlers want, is for someone to take notice of 'em. You know: love 'em. I know I love 'em but they don't appreciate that, so's it's better I don't go along. 'Enry could get 'em eating out of 'is 'and. 'E was good at that. 'E'd be saying well old chappies I'll see what I can do for you, I'll have a word with Mr Jim. All that crap. So I want you to go along for me."

"Me?"

"Yes, you." Or, Jim suggested, are you afraid?

Dick was not afraid. He had not the experience to be afraid. He had an image in his mind's eye of a group of Somerset farm labourers, a Perpendicular church tower rising in the background and his bike leaning against a stone wall somewhere. He was flattered.

All the same, Jim wanted him to be afraid, then he could say there's nothing to be afraid of, all in a day's work, what we have to put up with all the time so's your father can live in the house in Somerset and you can go round looking at churches.

"I'd love to do that for you, Sir. Just tell me what to do."

Jim stared at the gormless buffoon. The chorus gazed in the same way, then looked back at the dregs, ashamed of something.

"You don't 'ave to do anything much." Jim frowned: "Just listen to what they 'ave to say. Agree with 'em and then say you'll see what you can do. Say you'll have a word with good ol' Jim an' see if you can't persuade 'im to see it from their point of view. Then say what 'Enry'd say. Just say if you'd just keep quiet for a while, I'd be ever so grateful." He mimicked Dick without seeming to realise he was doing it. "Got it? Dick?"

"I have, Jim. But I was just wondering. . ."

"What's that Dick?"

"I was wondering if I should say who I am. Might help. Should I?"

Jim looked at Dick. He looked at him as a new type of human animal whom he had not come across before. The chorus, also, following Jim's lead, inspected Dick as a new piece of machinery, recently arrived.

Jim was not sure what to make of Dick, just then. Was the little shit trying to get one over him? In which case, in which case perhaps the fellow was making some account of himself after all. That would be interesting. Or – and a lot more likely in Jim's experience – was this son of Thornley's really the mentally deficient he took him to be? He suspected the latter but he was not sure.

Jim looked at Dick, out of the general gloom of the club night. Screwing up his eyes and staring at this specimen of. . . monumental stupidity or what? As if by looking at Dick hard he might be able to understand him. The chorus, struck dumb, studied Dick in a similar way.

Thing was, if Dick went around saying he was the son of Thornley, son of the Managing Director, son of one of them in London, if he gave that impression, then God only knows what they might say to the cunt about me. Can't risk it.

"No Dick, I really don't think you should do that."

"No?"

No you little fucker and if you go on like this I might just decide to do something about it. "No, Dick, because these people don't like that sort of thing. Throwin' your weight around. They might think you was showin' off, pullin' rank and they won't like it. In fact I'd avoid the issue altogether." If you know what's good for you.

"Alright Jim, but then what should I say?"

"You don't 'ave to say anything Dick but if you do, just say you're my representative. They'll assume you've taken over from 'Enry. You got that?" You twerp.

"Yes, Jim, perfectly," and Dick beamed at the chorus which beamed back at him, relaxed and started to sing Drink, drink, drink to the . . . whatever it is, and then stopped to respect Jim's further pontifications: "I wonder if 'e ought to go with you?" He thumbed back at the husband of Dolly, looked at the expression of naked white fear on the boy's face and decided against the idea. "P'raps not." Looked back at Dick. Decided what he'd do. One lamb was enough. Save the other.

"Good, that's settled. But don't worry, my security men will be with you. They'll drive you out tomorrow."

The chorus watched Dick leave the club with Jim.

Can't remember the fellow's name.

Thornley's son apparently.

So it appears.

Hope he knows what he's doing.

22
To the Slaughter

It was the heat everyone remembers. But apparently it was not that hot. Although it was exposure to the midday sun that did it.

Not one of those flame-brilliant tropical days of colour and light, when all the senses are forced to be on duty. Not like the bright afternoon after the rain when Andrew put the body of Nalin's daughter into the back of his truck. The time Tarlie rebuked him and he felt ashamed of himself beside Petrus. Not like that beautiful rain-washed afternoon at all. Nonetheless, Dick himself saw it bathed in gold.

It was, in fact, another of that intolerable succession of dry breathless days where the sunlight is interpreted through the medium of dust.

One might say the dust of Dick's life, as an associated metaphor of some sort, but that would be untrue. Dick's life had been happy or at any rate he looked back on it as having been happy, which is the same thing. He welcomed the sun that morning, unaware – blissfully – of what the dust above contained. The blood of Nalin's daughter for a start.

Blast the sun. It is a sly but determined light that hits you awake like a night before of too much drinking cheap wine and beer with formaldehyde in it. Diffused, fragmented, ricocheting and confusing light that is noisy, for Christ's sake. Damn its insistence. Damn the spontaneity of the day.

There is, actually, no sun, as such, to be seen. Only something felt that is unwelcome. Only a sort of concentration of light in that part of the sky where, one assumes, the sun ought to be. Well yes, it's pretty obvious the morning end of the day but getting towards midday, when the sky is bleached white yellow; then, it's not so obvious. Up there somewhere. You feel it at any rate. Like a painful slap on your back, your shoulders and your head. Flayed you are, the heat on exposed skinless flesh burning. They don't feel it like we do. Who? Those whom we would flog skinless given half a chance. They can sit out there in the midday sun and not feel a thing. So why all the trouble then?

Apparently the ambient temperature was not so high. The dust itself kept off the direct rays of the sun. That makes a difference. Direct sun can push the temperature of the skin up to forty degrees and above, the whole body system working like mad to keep itself cool. Can kill you. That is why the Egyptian slaves you see in pictures wear those sort of tea-cloths on their heads. No, the temperature on the unread thermometer on Henry's veranda was well below the highs reached on the early days of the drought when there was not so much dust. Oppressive all the same, which is why everyone remembers it as hot. It was the heat, old boy. Mass hysteria and all that. There's nothing you can do against that. Have to let these things work themselves out. Margaret would have agreed.

Dick assumes Jim to be an early riser. The house empty, he scavenges for breakfast, finds coffee and some biscuits, a can of beer in the otherwise empty refrigerator. Jim lives on what? Dick wonders. Neighbourly charity, no doubt. Or perhaps human flesh?

Thus, Dick is on a caffeine high. There was no milk but he has found white sugar. In this state he meets Tudak waiting outside beside the Landrover. Little Sammy, the driver, inside: black and inscrutable, he does what he is told, no more and no less, immune by now to the world around him and apparently dumb. Blind also, possibly, to what he sees. His job to do or die and keep the Landrover going. No Landrover equals no Sammy. The two are indivisible. Might as well remove the carburettor as Sammy, it's the same thing.

Dick has not met Tudak before. He knows nothing about him. Tudak is the man to whom Dick has been handed by Jim. Tudak, Jim's instrument, the one who hacked off Tarlie's head.

What does Dick see?

He sees something remarkably beautiful as in the beauty of his dreams as in the beauty of his daydreams. The more so because he expected to see Jim whose Jim-ness does not run to physical beauty despite having had that raw, chunky, indifferent, muscular beauty as a youth.

Tudak then. Or rather Tudak in Dick's loveable, gullible, non-judgemental and innocent eyes. Dick, the marked man.

"Hello!" You're a sight for sore eyes.

"Sah!" Tudak clicks his heels together as he has been taught – Jim showed him a video film of it once, from some American film about violence in the name of duty and loyalty to your fellow officers. Tudak manages to stick out his chest, stick up his chin and at the same time look down at Dick who is standing close, an inch or two shorter. So close in fact that he can smell Tudak who ought to smell rotten but who, to Dick's dreamy nostrils, smells pleasantly of soap as if recently scrubbed and his clothes freshly ironed, which is, indeed, the case. There is something about Tudak, this morning, of being brand-new. Straight out of the box, the tissue paper still clinging. This perfection of body and its presentation is not unlike Bune, as Andrew thought of him, the devil himself presenting his offering in no less an attractive wrapping than the other chap.

There is a well-known Finnish artist who specialises in titillating pictures of butch young men of the Marlon Brando On the Waterfront type. Grossly exaggerated, muscular, broad at the shoulder, narrow at the hip, with washboard, or is it six-pack, tummies. Tight-trousered and tee-shirted there is an insistent suggestion of sexual prowess and hunger. Also, boots, leather and metal. Men's men, their chiselled good looks expressing understanding cruelty or bruised innocence but never kindness. Men's men, with a suggestion of sadomasochism. That is how Dick saw Tudak. Polished black beauty indeed in his tight navy-blue, short-sleeved uniform, that did not so much look too small for him as look as if the frail fabric was about to be burst by Tudak's muscular, disciplined body. That is what Dick saw. His eyes could not resist the bulging crotch. Dick recognised his type. On the last day of his life as it happened. He recognised his angel.

[][][][][]

Dick had jumped out of bed like a tiresome Jack Russell terrier. The nature of the morning light, or rather the lack of it, had no impact on him, on the light-receptor cells of his eyes. It was the mill muster bell, in fact, that woke him. Sounded romantic to the auditory function of his ears. What went on that morning went on inside Dick's head. He was not preparing himself to die. Does anyone? Best not to know. This is the life, this is the doing of things and of being here where they happen. What are they doing in London at this very precise moment of my getting up to this new life of adventure? I'm going to tell Dad I want to stay out here and be his man on the spot. He thought of those other young or youngish men, just past their wasted prime, in their suits and raincoats, walking over London Bridge carrying their briefcases. Dick did not feel superior because he was not that type. Or, walking up the steps of the Monument Tube Station because actually Dick had a flat in South Kensington – he did not live in Eaton Square with his parents at that age a youngish man just past his prime, hair thinning before it has been ruffled or tugged by loving, or at any rate, hungry hands – wearing overcoats and scarves because it would be cold in London. He did not feel superior because a part of him liked doing that very routine, reassuring thing, but here was life and this beautiful man. Actually, he was wrong because Van was about ten hours ahead of London so that at this precise moment those youngish men in their charcoal-grey or navy-blue, sometimes pin-striped, suits wearing raincoats or overcoats and scarves but not hats because in those days people had stopped doing it, were arriving at cold, night-time Greenwich or Woolwich or West Wickham or, if they were older, down Wimbledon/Wandsworth way and thinking about something to eat and what might be on the television. In South Kensington, the Rogers or Peters or Carolines or Dianas were playing at being grown-up and wondering if marriage would be any different only with children of course and then we'd have to live in Fulham where you can get a house quite cheap but it's still north of the river and up and coming.

What does Dick see?

He had expected Jim. Jim was a character in Dick's eyes, in his head. He also had this other idea of being Jim's right-hand man and of getting to know the diamond embedded in the shit. He saw himself being sent out – and about – by Jim to sort out problems like this one. He saw, fleetingly – a premonition perhaps or something like it, linking the ideas that flew around the inside of his head – Jim dead and people saying poor ol' Dick, he'll miss him. Those two were like that. But Jim the morose, chivvying, irreverent and chummy Jim was not there to meet him in the dim, dusty, hot and oppressive morning. It was Tudak. The ideas of Jim flew out of Dick's head and in flew others about Tudak. Jim was right, perhaps, to despise him but the one thing you could say about Dick was that he lived for the moment.

Oppressive the morning might have been in everyone else's mind but not so in Dick's. He was on a high – caffeine and white sugar – enjoying every minute of it, jammed as he was now between Sammy and the gorgeous, grinning and affable Tudak, for all that he was a prisoner being taken to his execution. Marie Antoinette with friends.

The landscape through which they passed, depressing under hot yellow sky, was unremarkable or at any rate was to the few of us who remember that day. The day was like Dick himself: unremarkable and unmemorable. We remember only the consequences of his death which had nothing, nothing whatsoever, to do with him. Whatsisname he was soon to become. Bloody nuisance going and doing a thing like that he was about to become: the forgettable you, Dick.

Down the hill, Sammy cruising as was his silent habit under Jim's tutelage, so that they pulled up suddenly as he let his foot off the clutch and the engine jumped to a start, Dick thrown against the iron indifference of Tudak which Dick interpreted as holding him. Let's have some more of that he thinks. Nice to fall asleep leaning against this chap but he is too excited for that, full of caffeine and not breakfast. Visions of the slave market: I'll buy some of that. Meat, I'll pay for that don't blame Dick it was the economic class into which he was born you could buy what you wanted like a flat in South Kensington or a piece of physical beauty. Like Tudak. The parched golf course on the one side: on the other, beyond the wide verge burnt black to the earth as a fire precaution, a wall of oil palms, their fronds on the unprotected edge of the plantation as brittle, as useless and as finished as Dick himself. Then it is the same on both sides under the flat, low sky that presses the heat down upon them directing them to where they must go. A wide junction, power lines, turn left – or right, it does not matter at this point – then the same again. Off the main road the walls close in on them a little as they get near their destination. The settlement palms are a bit neater but as parched and hopeless looking as the rest. Gaps from time to time show neat little houses – thatch or tin or cement blocks – and neat little farms of raggedy bananas and other things dying for rain.

To Dick's eyes, from out of Dick's head, this dull and defeated-looking landscape is fascinating and beautiful, like Tudak himself. And Dick sees colour where there is none, feels movement that is not there, the smells the odour of . . . Tudak big and strong and safe beside him. Cycling the Somerset lanes from one church tower to the next. That is how he used to do it, sighting them. Wonderful but never as wonderful as this, he thinks, living for the moment. As was South Kensington when he first went to live there: the smell of damp and rotting brick, the peeling stucco, exotic. Fuck me, if the human mind does not have an amazing capacity for foolish romance. Had Dick lived he would have remembered this dull, commonplace morning with Tudak as one of the most wonderful of his life. A turning point. Well, in a sense it was: up a blind alley.

[][][][][]

The sun shone and – it is as true and as real as anything can be – in Dick's eyes Tudak glowed with beauty.

"I love you."

"Yes Sah."

One wonders what Tudak's reaction would have been had he caught the meaning of those words. We'll see about that later.

A straight road running between the oil palms, the distance lost in the dust stirred-up by a truck gone ahead. Looking, therefore, across the hot, flat landscape, the sky is brilliant blue for Dick, above the dust. He is enchanted, sitting here next to Tudak his protector.

"I love you."

"Yes Sah."

Does Tudak hear the loosening of Dick's soul?

A space so large that the oil palms around are nothing and the dust-filled sky everything. It is actually a football pitch upon which not a blade of grass is to be seen the boys play in a whirl of dust and laughter. On the one side the covered market, an over-bearing barn of a place; on the other the grey concrete-block primary school, as cheap as you can make a building within which children can be educated just sufficiently to be used as the next generation of labourers. At least that was the idea. The crowd, hanging around and waiting for something to happen, is substantial in its body but counts for nothing – it seems – in the space. It will show its mettle, later. The sky is all and, as remembered, the heat is oppressive in a way that makes you cross.

Dick smiles his idiot smile looking up at that Perpendicular church tower he is amazed at what flawed humanity can do with stone, arrogance and love: Bruton, Evercreech, Wyke Champflower.

"I love you."

"Yes Sah."

What does Tudak see at this point of taking Dick out of the vehicle? Sammy drives off to the shade at the edge of the palms: he will be needed later to take the body to the morgue in Akaranda. Tudak sees a white man. Like all white men but not so old as Henry because the skin is not yet ravaged by the sun or so young as Andrew who has more hair and who, even Tudak catches it, just has the bloom of life left in him. Dick is, nonetheless, bar the detailed details, got out of the vehicle by Tudak. Having been got out he straightens himself up in his clothes and makes an effort to react. All the same, this is one who does not know what to do. So Tudak himself has to react in the way he has been taught by Jim. He does not expect to be spoken to as if he is human so he does not hear:

"I love you."

"Yes Sah."

One assumes he does not hear.

So, Dick, directed, marched to the place of whatever it is. That is inside the covered market, which is like some huge uncompleted building of some sort. It has a roof but no walls and the floor is dirt. Might be an early Christian basilica built for the burning of martyrs. From where we were standing, Dick appeared to have taken Tudak by the hand but, I confess, my memory may be deceiving me. He is nonetheless, and because of all the ideas and memories mixed together in his head, happy. There is no doubt about that fact whatsoever: he is radiantly happy. This could be my life, he thinks, being with this wonderful handsome man who is beautiful as well and who gives me so much love and security. I feel it as my flesh touches his: as his flesh touches mine. He thinks, also, of his father in his study in Somerset pasting the bits of the map of the world together with Van at the very dead centre. He is absorbed in the job. Dick is on Van Island. He laughs out loud from pure happiness.

"I love you."

"Yes Sah."

"Sit here Sah."

"There will be refreshments Sah."

"Wait for me Sah."

Tudak goes to deal with the crowd. There are his men, his guns and his whips with which he can whip it into place, into shape, the unruly white-man-seeking crowd which crowds in on Dick. It is the usual thing. Dick sits on a chair around which a space is cleared. Nearest to him, the old men squat on the ground doing all the usual things in settling themselves down to watch. Their eyes never leave Dick's face which is going to have all the answers, for once.

Tudak and co with their instruments; and the authority of the company; and Tarlie's recently severed head; and the dried blood of Nalin's daughter in the dust which is moved around and around by the hustle and bustle and sat on and even breathed in because one can't avoid breathing for all that it is dusty and seems to be getting more so by the minute. I feel I am choking. Tudak and co, and their instruments and the authority of the company represented, for God's sake, by Dick there in the centre of it all, are moving in ever-widening circles quelling the crowd and making it sit down and be respectful to Dick as if he is the young Pharaoh and they the slaves. Settling it down. Or agitating it?

It's so damn hot and who wants to sit down out here in the sun apart from anything else it's so undignified. So as Tudak and co and their instruments move around the outer rim of this, this manifestation of the manifest destiny of mankind, the crowd, shuffling on bums or creeping on flat feet and haunches pushes itself closer to the young Pharaoh – Ramses II maybe, the architect king – and into the shade of the covered market, where it is no cooler, in fact maybe a degree or two hotter but the thing is to be sitting inside the edifice itself. Not outside.

There are some boys on the edge of the crowd who are making a noise and laughing as boys do in order to impose their presence upon the world and upon any girls present who nonetheless look away with disdain. With one eye, at any rate. Shut up, sit down and behave or words to that effect. Out in the sun. They try to move inside. Whipped back into place. And it is hardly a whip in the real sense of the word more an improvised nylon sjambok thing for beating crowds into place. Able to draw blood if required but that is not always necessary. Symbol of authority more than anything. But symbol of the company and therefore terrifying. Undignified, also, to be hit with it in public. Causes a spurt of anger like when you are punched in the face for no reason or for all sorts of reasons. Angry boy squatting on ground with others sullen and resenting the fellow in the uniform who, isolated from his mates – Tudak and co – feels . . . isolated and vulnerable. Cocks his gun; one of those rapid repeater things that tend to get out of control. Gets out of control for some reason. Spurt of bullets like stones on the tin roof and maybe just that thinks half the crowd an old woman spits out betel juice indifferent. Surge nonetheless from that side pushing the crowd in on where Dick sits who is just fascinated by the whole thing being apparently enacted for his entertainment. Another crackle of stones on the roof and a scream. Panic and anger. Part of the crowd rushes to the edge of the space for a better view of the action. A few are downed for no reason at all as they flee, it is the usual thing: Kent State, May 1970; Sharpeville, March 1960; St Petersburg, January 1905. Panic all round. These kids fire their silly guns off in any which way as has been said before because they are frightened.

The other, angrier, part of the crowd surges forward towards where Dick sits. Whether by desire or because there was nowhere else to go, no one is sure. Perhaps some saw Dick as a sanctuary against the bullets. Anyway, Dick felt no fear, only. . . barely even. . . surprise, it was all new to him. Perhaps this is what always happens. This is the life and Dad'll be proud of me Jim's right-hand man and slave-owner of Tudak. He actually grinned at the man – as one does, as a sort of welcome Hello who are you? – who raised the panga knife that blacked out his life so quickly he was dead with the grin still on his face. Like being hit by a car, I imagine.

An odd wound, all the same, as if some animal had climbed up his chest and, and gone for the throat. I mean how else would you have got a wound like that in at that angle? Anyway, he's dead and he was definitely bashed on the head with a panga. No doubt about that and it's the usual way of killing people around here. I'll put that in the report. If I suggest anything else there'll be a fuss. He's dead, poor sod. Get him buried. He can go in the old European cemetery. Nice view of the sea up there. Let's go for a drink. I need one.

◻◻◻◻◻

The bright, hot light makes the inside of the covered market a black box. The crowd has scattered to the edges of the space, except the dead and wounded few who lie under the sky. There is an atmosphere of waiting; expectation that something will happen. Tudak appears as if, as if our own imagination has conjured him up from nowhere. That is how I remember it. He is a giant, walking casually across the space, his gun over his shoulder, he swaggers as if he owns the place. He does own it. He disappears into the black box. We hear the Landrover moving slowly in the same direction as if it does not want to raise the dust that it nonetheless does, a little. We watch it. A small thing out there in the blinding light so that the ground around shimmers as if it is water and the wheels are under the water so that the vehicle floats out there in the distance. The young king's death bier. Tudak appears again carrying Dick's body, small like a child's, happy to be in Tudak's arms. Tudak feels the dead weight of Thornley's son. It is surprisingly light; but tested, it is found worthy.

23
London End

Oddly, what I remember most about that day was the sky. It was so beautiful I thought my heart would break. I wanted to look and look and look at it. It had been such a cold, grey March. The leaves on the plane trees in the square so reluctant to come out that year and London so dead and flat. I thought, well what's the point? By the end of August they'll be burnt up and dead anyway.

I'd been shopping in Harrods all day. To get away from the weather, I suppose. They got me a taxi at the door but we were so snarled up in the traffic on Knightsbridge I couldn't bear it any longer. I gave the man the money and got out. I left the shopping behind. I thought of walking across the park, I wanted the earth beneath my feet but it would have been impossible in the shoes I had on. So I walked the streets back home feeling sorry for myself, taking the long way round down Sloane Street and back to Eaton Square that way. I remember wondering why on earth we lived in such a place, with all the stinking traffic. We'd spent thousands converting it back into a house. A little mews house was all we needed, or a flat. I was thinking of a flat, high up somewhere, with a view, so I looked at the sky.

There was a farewell glow in it, the low sun reflecting on the upper window panes of the buildings, a thousand pieces of gold. It was the London I remembered as a girl before the war. I remembered going out into the square – Berkeley Square – to look at our house for the last time before we moved out. It was just such an evening. I had felt the same sudden heartbreaking sadness because I thought the beauty was a portent of something awful about to happen. They pulled down our house, and all the others on that side of the square, to build a block of American offices. We went down to the country and more or less missed the war.

I was looking and looking at the sky, wanting to hold it. People were bumping into me. Rushing for the train back home. But I wanted to stop them and tell them to look. Look at the sky. It's beautiful. I thought of Dick and I thought of Larry and I thought why are we not looking at this sky together? It's something we've never done together. I would have liked to cry but then I didn't know how. One is not supposed to show emotion. You hold it in, and crumble from the inside. We have a key to the gardens in Eaton Square. I had it with the house keys, so I let myself in. I looked at the sky through the bare branches of the trees. I didn't hear the traffic and I didn't feel the cold. I watched the sky until it was dark. Then I went home. Alice told me that Larry had phoned from the office to say that Dick was dead.

[][][][][]

It had got into the evening paper before he'd been notified officially. Officially, he wasn't notified. The evening paper on his desk every afternoon, about four-thirty. Final edition. There it had been put every afternoon like clockwork except for that printing strike a few years back. Doreen puts it there quick-like when she's checking for anything he's signed for the last mail.

Good thing Jim kept quiet about the name mum's the word the first thing that goes through his mind. They'll have dealt with the body and everything out there. Pity Henry's no longer around to see the thing's done properly but at least there won't be a body landing on the doorstep. She'll want a memorial service of some sort. I suppose. Better in Somerset than up here. I can sort the vicar. Bombardier, Butcher, Belper, whatever his name is can deal with it. He knew Dick. Wonder if I ought to send him out there like I sent. . .

People like that don't crumble because there is nothing left to crumble. Something goes on, all the same.

An old man – tubby you might say in his clothes – who smells of an expensive cigar and brandy, gets up from his desk and turns towards the window. Puts his hands in his pockets and looks out into the afternoon. You can't see much of the sky but there is, no doubt about it, a sort of glow. What does one do? Would you be so good as to put me through to Eaton Square. Thank you so much. Alice? Would you be so good as, so good as, so good as to tell Mrs Thornley that Dick is dead. Yes indeed, terrible news. If you would be so good as to buy the evening paper it will explain. Thank you. He puts down the phone and picks it up again. Mr B. . . ? He's gone home has he? Thank you. He puts down the phone again. He sits at the desk with his hands together wondering what he ought to do. What does one do when one's son is dead? He gets up and walks across the expensive Turkey carpet to the oak coat stand with its brass hooks that was designed for the room along with the rest of the furniture in the room by a pupil of Sir Edwin who later went on to become quite well known for designing the interiors of London tube stations for another famous architect.

Thornley, disregarding the old man, takes up the coat and slaps a little dandruff off the shoulders. He looks at the coat. It is a good coat but not actually his town coat. It is a comfortable tweed coat that he usually wears when he is going down to Somerset. Harris Tweed it is but it does not smell of the peat fires of the Isle of Harris so much as of London, which can be depressing. Nonetheless, the coat is a comfort for which he is thankful. He does not take the lift but walks down the stairs knowing no one else does it. Except that is, for Dick, when he was alive, only his father did not know this having never once walked down the stairs with his son. He walks home. Not that far for a man who is fit and who enjoys walking for all that he is an old man now. It's not so far once you're at St Paul's. Fleet Street, the Strand and Trafalgar Square, St James's Park, Buck House and you're almost home. The park is the hardest part in the dying light because of an idea of a small boy feeding the ducks but he is not sure.

Inside, the house is lit up for the evening. Discreetly because one doesn't waste electricity, however much money one's got. Alice turns on the lights as she has been shown; Carlos turns them off – except for the stairways – when everyone has gone to bed because Alice lives in Pimlico. Carlos has quite a nice room with a television set at the front of the basement so there is a whole floor between him and the drawing room. They could be screaming blue murder at each other for all he knows. He came after Dick. His girls can come down into the area without bothering anyone and why shouldn't they he thinks he owns the world but he doesn't own me.

You cannot see the staircase from the front door. A passageway: expensive, dark green, polished brass and bevelled glass. Looks more like a club, leads to a real hallway with a large circular table upon which there are fresh flowers and the latest magazines. Do take one to your room if you're staying but please put it back the lower type of guest stuffs one into his suitcase. The place is like a posh hotel. There is also an early Victorian sofa, which the antique shops on the Kings Road call Regency, beside the dining room door where you can sit and wait in the suspension of this space in the centre of the house that is only vaguely lit by a skylight way up above. A curving staircase goes on and up into a similar setting for your life beneath which is a passage that goes to a modern kitchen in what must have been the morning room or the library or something like that before. A cloakroom where you can hang your coat and have a wash and brush up because they don't really like you using the family bathroom. What family?

She is sitting on the sofa so that she can look down the passage to the front door.

⬚⬚⬚⬚⬚

If you live out that way, there are various ways of getting home. The District line, hoping for a Wimbledon train straight through or otherwise changing at Earls Court. Or a mainline from Waterloo. Walking home from Putney, Wandsworth Town, Earlsfield or even the slog from Clapham Junction, if he is in the mood. If it is Waterloo, and it more often is than not, he takes the tube to Embankment, walking across the river on Hungerford Bridge, the crowded, narrow footway beside the crashing Charing Cross trains, until the open concrete spaces around the Royal Festival Hall. Sometimes he will get out at Temple and walk the embankment under the plane trees beside the river. It can be quite beautiful and he thinks of Monet up there in his hotel room. The air is cleaner today but he remembers the pea-soupers when he was a boy they lived at Charlton. You could get lost up there on the heath in the fog.

He is walking across Hungerford bridge. Glances, as he does, down the cold river towards St Paul's. The clear, clean beauty of the late afternoon sky registers for later consideration. He has been up there in it. Detached above the world of patchwork fields and woods, of clear downs, flat-looking from up there, incidental villages and dense towns straggling a little along the main roads which nonetheless look irrelevant in the landscape below. I'd like to have stayed up there and never returned. Lost in the fog on the heath. Better that way but he had been forced back into a life that had to be endured. Sterility and no kiddies, as his wife would have said but words like that were not to be spoken, to make the lounge untidy and spill toys through the French windows out into the garden.

The garden was their child. Not a bad substitute and it meant they had something in common and an excuse to be busy and occupied and to avoid one another when it was required. But the garden was their love. They thought about each other in terms of the garden. It was a tolerable endurance, after all.

The boy Dick, in the office, was his son. He was their son because – and it started in the garden, Saturday afternoon in early June, getting the roses ready so that they could go mad – they talked about him as if he were. It might as well have been they who had sent him to boarding school and looked forward to him coming home in the holidays. They each had their thoughts of what it would have been like in the holidays. Up to town for the museums, flying a kite on the common on Saturdays in the First World War that was an airfield Dick, it looks small Dad, now we fly our kites on it. It's jam Dick I'll teach you how to make it. He had been over for tea and they each pretended it was their son on a visit. A private game each played but they wished it as much for the other as for themselves. It was a good bond in what you would call a marriage. Three or four in the morning was the best time, touching, holding hands before the best, deep, sleep of the night.

He had been hurt when Thornley's son first came into the office. It had made him confront his own mental deficiency. Good of Barbary and Northgate to take me in after the war. But after all, he was the real hero. But that first morning was a wonder to him always. The boy, the young man had been so full of, of love, I'd have to call it. Acting like an apprentice and calling him Sir. A little later, knowing Dick, he learned it was real. Taking him around the office and introducing him as if already My Son Dick. This is My Son, Dick, Miss Chandler. What a nice boy Mr B, you must be proud. I am. So Dick, bring any typing you have to Miss Chandler. She's in charge of the typing pool. You see? Yes Sir. But he was, after all, Mr Thornley's son, so it was Doreen who came up every afternoon to see if there was anything and Dick got his stuff back quick because he was, of course, Mr Thornley's son. They worked together and had their lunches together and sometimes took the tube home together I get out at Gloucester Road and Dick came round for supper a couple of times easy to get back to Gloucester Road on the District Line and Saturday tea one glorious afternoon when the garden was at its best and the roses triumphant climbing everywhere and its simply heavenly for such a tiny space I wish you could come down to Somerset. He came to love his work and the journey to work was a journey of love: pure, undiluted joy. It's good for you to go out there and you'll be back in three weeks. He counted off the days.

The street had a sort of curve in it because that must have been the old field line or something. Anyway, you couldn't see one end from the other which made it a little claustrophobic sometimes because the houses are close together and have no front gardens to speak of. Also, cut off from the world a little and private. Nothing like the publicity of Eaton Square. But at the back their garden opened out a little because they lived on the outside of the curve. There was an old brick wall at the back which would have had a lean-to greenhouse on it once when this land was part of the grand old house he used to call it yes and my grandmother probably did for them. So that made the garden more private, which is another reason why they bought the house and having been built just before the First World War it was quite roomy and solid you wouldn't get a staircase like this in anything built after 1918.

He was early so I knew something was wrong. I was at the back getting things ready for supper when I heard his key in the door. There were no lights on because it was early. The house was cold. I had my slippers on and an old red cardie. Normally I'd smarten up for him. Have the place looking cosy. But he was early. I rushed to him because I knew something must be wrong because he was early. He was standing in the hall and I couldn't see him clearly until I got up close. He looked at me and said Dick's dead and his face sort of crumpled up.

He had been the one who kept the name out of the papers. Last thing he did. Then he put on his scarf and his black winter coat. He was just getting into the lift when Doreen had called him to say Mr Thornley was on the phone and he said fuck Mr Thornley.

[][][][][]

People used to say she was taller than him. But she was not and when you saw them together, you realised it. With her high-heeled London shoes and her hair up, yes she looked taller but standing together in their riding things down in Somerset you could see they were about the same height. You wouldn't say she was beautiful but she had fine features and in her expensive clothes she looked striking. Rich-looking so that it was the women more than the men who looked at her. A credit to him, no doubt. Not cold but I can't think of her ever talking beyond what is necessary to facilitate the effort of living. She must have but I can't say I ever had a conversation with her. I'm told she was a different person down in Somerset.

Thank you Alice, you can go home. Don't bother coming in tomorrow. No, please, I'd rather be on my own and if I need anything I can ring for Carlos. Beautiful Carlos down there in the basement with his girls. It was the wiry hairs on the back of his brown hands she'd noticed first. Strong hands doing things around the house.

Sitting in the hall, you could just hear the noise of the television set. He didn't come on duty until six. She enjoyed the expectant interregnum between Alice going home and Carlos coming on duty at six. If she went into the kitchen he'd ignore her. She could watch him a little doing things at the sink, his narrow hips and his neat bum in the black slacks and the good-quality, white cotton shirts she's given him as his uniform. Just for me please Carlos, Mr Thornley'll be late. Yes, he's eating out. Why didn't she eat down there in the kitchen with him instead of in the dining room on her own? It had been his idea for her to have a tray in the drawing room.

Now she is waiting. What does one do when one's son is dead? Carlos probably would have the answer. But it has to be gone through. Her husband will go up to his room without saying a word, she knows that, so she waits in the hall for him. What else is there to do? The passageway lights were put on by Alice as she went out. The hall itself is in darkness but for an illumination from the passage, a narrow band of reflected light striking a bowl of large white hothouse flowers on the polished circular table. The flowers were past their best, brown at the edges – wrap 'em in newspaper and throw 'em out – but the bowl was expensive and looks it. Ming and it wouldn't be fake either, knowing her. Blue and white. Henry would have been the only man to appreciate it. She liked Henry, the one time she met him but she is a credit to her husband and looks it.

She sits in the dark. Incidentally, also, wearing a short red velvet jacket, Chanel style, that she puts on in the evening without thinking. Because one must wear something. It is rather inappropriate given that her son is dead and she knows it.

□□□□□

The houses all look the same from the outside. In this respect, similar to the other street, Wandsworth/Wimbledon way. But the architectural detailing and scale is expensive here. Classical you'd call it rather than suburban picturesque. Big and expensive to heat with high ceilings and tall windows. Oil-painted stucco, black-painted railings and an apparently endless repetition of pillared porticos that look rather silly, presenting front doors up a substantial flight of steps from the York stone pavement. In the good old days before the war, before the conversion to flats, if you had a party, you'd run a red carpet from the foot of the steps to the edge of the road, as if you owned the pavement. Which in a sense you did because it ran over the top of your cellars, the coal-hole there in the pavement to prove it.

A straight terrace of houses that looks across the service road to the trees locked inside the railings of the gardens. It's the same way on the other side. A busy main road runs between the two. Quite right too because secluded behind the locked-up trees, the service road, the wide pavement of York stone, the black-painted railings and the flight of steps up to a front door that is very solid and about ten feet high, we are on show. On show but untouchable. What are we worth if you can't see us?

There is no sense of claustrophobia here, one might as well be on the sea-front at Brighton. All the same, the man who walks past the repetitive architecture is alone. We might watch him from a little vantage point in our mind's eye, up a little so that we can look down on him a little ahead of us, in that spacious passage between the empty trees on the one side and the tall, quiet and may-as-well-be-empty houses on the other. The traffic roars beyond the trees, the city throbs all around, the night sky aglow with it but all this only emphasises the silent loneliness of the man who is Thornley.

One might say the man who was, at some other point in it all, Thornley. The Thornley of the 5%, decorated by this house in Eaton Square and by another in Somerset and by Agnes who is a credit to him, who is given additional substance by the fact of a son who is also immortality of a sort, and whose crowning achievement, this damned man's whole reason for being, is the Van Island Palm Oil Development Company. Thus and therefore a man of substance within Barbary and Northgate who is unloved, who is feared and who is, after all is said and done, a little, puffed-up, tubby and well, rather silly man. But they don't say that at Sunningdale because he is, if they think about it, a reflection of themselves, in some ways.

This spacious passage of reality through which Thornley walks appears empty despite the man who is, or rather who was, Thornley. As he walks between the pools of light given out by the street lamps he ceases to exist. Illuminated, he is not much more relevant in the great scheme of things.

Only we, the jury, as it were, see him take a flight of steps up to one of the front doors that looks like all the others in its quiet, strong good taste. That a man so rich must laboriously climb the steps – and later that rich curving staircase, also – is odd. Alice, in Pimlico, takes a high-speed lift to her flat that looks out over the bright city. Good thing, since she's been on her legs all day.

While he watches the television, Carlos is getting dressed to go on duty. He knows she watches him. He is aware of his charms as an asset he can use but like Thornley, who pays him, he takes his assets for granted inasmuch as they are a given factor in his life. He does not thank God for them but he does maintain them at a gymnasium near Victoria Station twice a week. Therefore, the white cotton shirt is not one of those body-hugging things but loose and generous. To be able to appreciate Carlos' torso the shirt would have to be removed. Nonetheless, the breadth of his shoulders and the slimness of his waist cannot be hidden any more than the narrowness of his hips or the neatness of his buttocks when he is bending over the sink in the black slacks for which Thornley has paid. She would like to clasp him gently with her hands, just above the hips.

As Thornley moves through the front door and along the grand entrance passageway to the house, it is interesting and maybe significant that Carlos moves through a narrow corridor in the basement, past a storeroom at the back and towards the narrow back stairs that lead up to the kitchen. On different levels, planes one might say, Thornley and Carlos move in perfect unison, unaware of each other.

But each is as equally aware of Agnes as she is of them. The one catches sight of her as he enters the hallway; the other knows she will watch him as he bends over the sink for her.

[][][][][]

She holds his shuddering body tight. As one would hold a hysterical baby. She takes each heaving eruption until she has got the rhythm of it. Now they are adhered as one in the reality of what marriage is supposed to be. She utters the familiar endearments as one might talk to an animal, coaxing it, not because there is anything that needs to be said but because there is a need for the sounds of reassurance in the quiet house. She might have hummed a tune and the one that came to her was the old Harry Lauder thing her father used to sing when he had a bit to drink but not that much. Roamin' in the gloamin' on the bonnie banks o' Clyde, for all that they were not a Scottish family but you met those rowdy Glaswegians at Whitley Bay in the summer.

She got him to the settee in the lounge and settled him. Got his scarf off but what did it matter if he was still in his coat and outdoor shoes? I'll put on the gas and he watched her kneel to do it, missing it and wasting matches because it was his job until with a plop it was on and the room glowed a little with the pinkish-blue warm light. He watches her big broad bottom as she kneels there on the hearth rug they'd made together soon after they were married. Picture of a Spanish galleon. Not his precise taste but he likes it because she'd wanted it. He knows she'll say ooh my knees as she gets up and she does. He opens his arms for her and she comes into them and they lie on the settee – his black coat and her red cardie with the zip – for hours until they are calm and resigned to the fact like all the others.

He was a nice boy.

He was.

It'll kill his parents.

It will.

[][][][][]

He stood at the end of the passage looking at her. He couldn't ignore her and it would look odd to bolt, like a frightened rat, either left into the dining room or right into the little sitting room they used for guests whom they didn't want upstairs. He noticed immediately that she wore no make-up although she had dressed for dinner. Her face was flayed to the bone, almost. Tiny red veins over the cheekbones, the lips thin, the eyes vacant and her hair, he saw, as if he'd never seen it before, streaked with grey. She was facing him but as if she saw him not. The thought flashed through his mind that she was mad. The idea was a relief.

They had no habit of communication so that at this moment of, of, of, of what? Of emotional stress? The thought that one ought to react? Ought one to fall to the ground and howl? He smiled at the thought of it. She might have thought he'd smiled at her; he hadn't but she also had an idea of going onto her knees and inspecting the carpet for failings. She wondered what one would do afterwards. Pick oneself up and straighten the magazines on the table? Really, these flowers have gone, I can't think what Alice was thinking letting them stay like this. But one needs a bowl of something living otherwise the wood dries out and the marquetry will spoil. Modern central heating ruins good furniture if one isn't careful. The bowl is Ming and will go on while it is valued and not smashed but the flowers are past their best.

He'd hoped she'd be thinking about organising a memorial service or something. She's good at those sorts of things. She knows what to do. Come to think of it, London would be better than Somerset because people could just come without having to go all the way down there. Thornley's son: of course it's tragic for them but I didn't know the boy. It's a trek, all the way down there and it is rather wearing your heart on your sleeve. Yes, London is much better. I'll be out for an hour or two. Memorial service for Thornley's son better show my face. Yes, much better. Bessemer, Biggles, whatever his name is can do the donkey work. Then you can go straight down to the country. On your own with all the memories of your son Dick. But what ought one to do?

I . . . um . . . I'll go and change. I'm not very hungry.

Yes do. I'll tell Carlos to do toast and a little pâté. Perhaps a bottle of something.

317

Yes, that Beaujolais since no one's here.

Well, we got through that alright. Reminds me of when Dick was born. It's one of those things you have to get through.

He walks past her up the stairs.

She gets up and goes through to the kitchen. Carlos is bending over the sink for her. Yes Madam. What she needs is a good . . . Maybe, but in fact Carlos is better than that. A lot. He is a good man when it comes down to it. Better than her husband. But afterwards what he always said was that although we did everything intimate you can think of she never said much and I never felt I knew her as a person if you know what I mean.

[][][][][]

The tidying up of Dick, it might have been. Heartless? No different from Margaret's attitude to Henry. Daphne saw the joke and did think it would have been better had Henry's body stayed in the house and been burnt along with it. His funeral pyre, as it were. Dick's body could have been disposed of in the same way, come to think of it. Two fairly useless Englishmen, having done their little bit, off on their way to eternity together. Better than the cemetery on that blasted hill in Akaranda.

Anyway, let the dead bury the dead. Agnes and Battledun, his name turned out to be, sat together and worked it out in the sitting room, to the right of the passageway, on the ground floor of the house in Eaton Square. The guest list, the music I don't really know what he liked but I think Handel at a time like this don't you? Yes he was interested in churches as a boy I think perhaps Somerset would have been better but it's too late now. Afterwards tea and something here don't you think? It's only a short walk from the church. Yes, we'll have caterers in to do a light buffet in the dining room. People can sit in here if they want a bit of quiet. So kind of you to think of it.

By the time they could get the church it was June. The Battleduns were not invited. Why on earth should they be? He was only doing his job but one or two of Dick's South Kensington friends turned up. A well-behaved tear shed by one Sophie. Late and a glorious day, the trees at their best don't you think and quite warm. I wouldn't have worn a coat only it is a funeral. Well yes, you're right, a memorial service perhaps black isn't *de rigueur*. I don't know.

The Battleduns sat in the garden that glorious June day. The scents, the sounds, the light of an old-fashioned English garden in summer. This is what Dick would have wanted. Let's just think of him. Later in the year they went for a holiday to Somerset. Those church towers are a wonder. I'd never thought about them before. Let's just take a peek up the drive. It's a beautiful house well you'd expect it. He was a nice boy I expect he had a happy childhood down here.

Agnes goes to Somerset about the same time. She takes Carlos with her because he can go. He's a free agent. Alice has to stay in town because her Mum lives in Pimlico and I'm a town girl really. It's another story but you can't expect Carlos to stay forever and he didn't. Not a bad man, not at all but at his age you wouldn't expect him to stay down there for the rest of his life with a woman twenty years older. Her life, helping out with the old people in the village. It was something to go on doing. Money wasn't a problem. She started to write a book on Tudor gardening. Then she met and married a local farmer about her age with grown-up children and got back into the swing of things, and the book was forgotten. There were the three scholarships in Dick's name at the school to administer, which she had to do because Thornley never came down again, he couldn't after the divorce and anyway he was hardly in a state to make the journey even in the car that can you believe it Alice drives now she does everything for him. They emptied his study and sent the things up to town. It'll make a guest room for your children what with the view of the garden. The little ones can use Dick's room it has a marvellous view of the church tower fifteenth century.

You could say that those flowers, apparently past their best, shot out roots down there in Somerset. No longer being a credit to ol' Larry and a good thing too.

[][][][][]

So to end with there is Thornley. What little bit of Larry was left − gone perhaps for good the moment he saw her anguished face there in the hallway and knew not what to say. Not the foggiest idea. Wrap up the feelings in convention because how else do you express them? Not the foggiest idea. Beyond those sorts of feelings he was by now, way beyond them. Because what use are they?

The idea of a son, a son and heir, his immortality. Known as Dick to his friends and to the world in general as Thornley's son and to some as that fellow whatsisname who got himself killed down there. Take away that idea and Thornley is less. Less than he had imagined possible.

Take away the decorative wife and the house in Somerset and there is less still. The house in Eaton Square is less, also, without the wife, well dressed and well bred who manages it. No more flowers in bowls or the latest magazines there for the guests to steal or potpourri in those little Chelsea and Bow bone-china bowls − teacups, before handles had been thought of − she collected for a while she was quite an expert. Gathering dust. Soon the bright glittering colours, the warmth, the subtle lighting and freshness he had taken for granted are gone.

Gone also, the smell of clean things and good food down in the kitchen where that Carlos would bend over the sink, for the benefit of my wife, Agnes. Gone, so that the cold house smells of the black London dust that covers and corrodes everything to a matt monochrome of corruption and decline. Alice does her best but I can't do it all. Before, I understand it now, I did it for Mrs Thornley. And there was Carlos to help and actually, when you come to think of it, Mrs Thornley did quite a bit of the work herself. She wasn't above making a bed or changing the sheets or doing a bit of hoovering. We'll have to get someone in to do the windows Mr Thornley, it's too much. No I don't mind doing the driving when it's required. He pays me well, I can say that, but he's not a man you can know, if you know what I mean. He wants me to move in. I can't leave Mum. She'd have to come with me but the room down there's a bit depressing for the day all you can see is the area and a bit of the pavement above. Mum's been used to a view of the sky. So have I, for that matter. I love to see the city spread out below for me.

Thornley learns, a little too late, what it is to be uncomfortable. He realises that comfort has to be arranged and can involve quite a bit of hard work. Sheets don't change themselves as Alice has implied. What goes on under the bed is another factor. It is a shock to his system

Therefore, there is less of Thornley but there remains the 5% and the crowning glory of his life, the Van Island Palm Oil Development Company. There's no need to tell him it's going up the spout for the time being he must read the papers but I don't know these days if it wasn't that he owns those shares I reckon they'd give him his marching orders he's not all there sometimes when I put the paper on his desk he looked at me he's never done that before it gave me quite a turn.

Battledun keeps things going. He reports directly to the Chairman because he has come to accept I don't care a fuck for Mr Thornley. I can't stand his fat face. Battledun, another good man who maintains the memory of Dick without going to pieces because he has done that and been put back together by his wife, that good woman, for the second time. Having achieved this together and knowing that they can do it makes them a good team.

Mr Thornley's ill don't bother him Battledun. You and I can do whatever's necessary but we have to get rid of that palm oil venture in New Sudan. It'll pull us down if we're not careful. Now's a good time to sell because palm oil prices are good. It's saleable because of the assets and whoever takes it will think they've got a bargain because things can hardly get worse. Fact is, Battledun, I don't like what's going on. We ought to do something more but I have my duty to the other shareholders. Now is the time to sell before B&N gets the blame and the share value is hit. There's the Malaysian outfit interested, I've heard. It'll give them a foothold for the logging later. I can work out something in the city but mum's the word. That fellow McDonald will have to carry the can and from what I hear, he deserves it. No, there won't be a crash because everything else is sound. Shareholders don't generally think about these things so long as the value is maintained and they get their dividends from time to time.

[][][][][]

For Christ's sake, Thornley is no fool and would not want to be thought of as one. He is not entirely a devastated man but having lost those other parts of himself he looks more to the Van Island Palm Oil Development Company only to discover that it too is shattering day by day if what the papers say is true although you do have to be careful about what you read. Mind you, being stripped to one's essential self leaves one feeling very naked and vulnerable. Also, aware of the fact that . . . there is very little there at all. Humbling some would say but not Thornley.

He continues to trust – with an instinct for which Thornley is famous, the old fox – that B fellow knows what's going on and that between B and the people out there, things are being dealt with. You can sometimes depend on other people's sense of loyalty – duty at any rate – even if your own is a bit wobbly. I'll wait for B's report and I'll deal with the issues as they arise, from there on. The lines of communication between down there at the back and up here at the front do seem to have broken down somewhat. But he does not want to repair them and anyway it is not his job to do something like that. He trusts B will do whatever is necessary. He could send a memo requesting, demanding to know what the hell's going on. But that would initiate a reply; he doesn't want that. Avoids reading the papers. They will insist on bringing me the evening paper that will remain unread upon the edge of my West African mahogany desk or is it English oak like the coat stand which came from a tree that was felled for some road-widening scheme in the 1930s when there was nothing to stop you chopping down a tree if you wanted to or a whole line in a hedgerow come to that which had been there since the time of Alfred the Great. Might be some awful mixture of the two but the thing is that planting a tree or felling it is beside the point so long as it was done for my benefit. Fuck him as he waits for the inevitable report. No doubt someone ought to go out and sort out the mess. He catches her looking at him and doesn't like it. Who's she to look at me and my 5% like that? Henry P-W and Dick both dead and other ghastly things going by all accounts. I'm not that stupid. Perhaps I ought to go out.

I'm not that stupid, he thinks to himself looking out the window to the narrow street. Cold out there he thinks for all that it's July and there'll be no Henley or Ascot this year because Agnes used to organise all that sort of thing and what with all this I don't want to see anyone let alone talk to them. He's been on an upswing all his life. He has little idea about how to deal with a down. He is, as it happens, resigned to the fact that the Van Island Palm Oil Development Company is in a mess. If it crashes then what is left? Stripped naked, nothing much at all. He goes on through some indecisive days trusting B to do what has to be done and, like the 5% did, years ago, trusting something'll turn up. Problem is, I can't feel much. The loss of it all leaves me empty, I can feel that but I don't want to cry or shout. I couldn't even if I wanted. I want the same routines and the same respect. My seat on the board is because of the 5%. I know that but look what I've achieved: the wonder of the Van Island Palm Oil Development Company. But there's the other 95% I haven't got. That has to be taken into account, at last.

He is, at this stage, quite rational about the whole thing but afraid of what will be left after the crash which is beyond his control.

So there is Thornley, intelligent, well-educated and selfish, with that 5% sitting between him and the rest of humanity. And, as has been said, even without those shares, he would have tended towards arrogance because he knew he was a little bit cleverer than the average man. But with the shares – wow! They had seemed enough for most of his life. The houses, the wife, the son and heir, truly decorations. The Van Island Palm Oil Development Company a vanity. But one has to do something to justify one's existence before God, he supposed. Especially since he was, was he not, one of the chosen? And it was, in the end, only himself and God, because he had no friends. Barely acquaintances, those other men around the table in the board room, the chaps down at Sunningdale. He had no one, he thought, hands in his pockets, as he looked down at the narrow street, empty and enhanced only by the building in which he was a manifest part.

[][][][][]

The old man watches and watches the empty street. A girl, a young girl who walks well and fast, her arrogant little feet going clack, clack, clack on the pavement. Can't wait to get away in her light summer dress and her strong little legs. The same flibbertigibbet who puts the paper he doesn't want each day on his desk. Next time she does it he'll ask her what she thinks. If he did, she'd run a mile. The manifestations of humanity come too late.

He watches and watches for another healthy young person to come out of the door of the B&N building into the deserted street. He watches and watches and watches as if his watching will produce Dick. His boy whom he now recognises as his son and the overwhelming credit to him. The little thing that gave him that unconditional, unquestioning non-judgemental love. He is not a fool, this Thornley, for all that his mind is turning in the moment of realisation. The memories flood in helter-skelter: the baby in his arms who looks up into his eyes and smiles; the little boy who runs into his study in Somerset to show him things yes I'm busy later the bruises inflicted and forgiven; gosh Dad thanks for the first bike with gears; over-careful and all-seeing pencil sketches of church towers stuffed into a drawer somewhere down there in Somerset and I want to see, I want to see, I want to see them now there ought to have been one up there on the wall it could have gone in a good Hogarth frame there beside the coat-stand thing I could see it from my desk; at school and knowing he was there and once running into him and seeing a look of delight on the spotty face why didn't you get in the second fifteen; coming to work in this building in the same building as me for a number of years. I must have known he was here and it warmed me. Now he has gone. I sent him away. He died. That one piece of me who was my one acquaintance, my one friend, my one beloved.

But he could feel nothing but emptiness within. His face would not crumble into tears and even if it did there was no one who would put it together again for it could only have been Dick. He wanted Dick to help him now and there was no Dick.

[][][][][]

Thornley began to walk back to Eaton Square every day. Wanted to avoid the house during the daylight. As the summer matured and drooped he would stop for a drink on the way. Pubs on Fleet Street, on the Strand, on the lanes leading off and a couple of places near Victoria Station in one of which the tarts would try to pick him up. He didn't notice. Past all that. No warmth left. Larry's gone. He would drink alone watching the chatting, laughing crowd around him with a small inclination to dislike it but nothing more. Buoyed up a little by the drink he would think what he could do to make some sense of his life and, for that matter, the 5%. He began to have the idea that he himself would go out to New Sudan and sort out the mess there. In one pub on a Friday evening, on the south side of Whitehall, the Trafalgar Square end, he had an idea that especially buoyed him up. He thought he would go out to New Sudan and sort out the mess in order to justify Dick's death. The buoyancy lasted all the way to Eaton Square where the trees looked gorgeous. As Agnes had noted in March, in the polluted London air, the leaves would be dying by the end of August. But for now they were wonderful and optimistic in the evening. The house depressing by contrast. He forgot the idea as he climbed the steps but he'd paid Alice to be there. She would have his supper waiting on a tray and his bedroom would be neat and tidy, overlooking the tops of the trees. Once it was dark and he'd had his bath and the radio was on with the ten o'clock news, it was not so bad. Until the empty morning that is, the traffic roar of London only emphasising the emptiness of the house.

He would go to Sunningdale Saturdays as usual but coming back was hard and he would have to be sure Alice was there. Pay her double or triple or more to make sure she was there. Missed Carlos' television when he went up to the front door. Only noticed it now it was gone. There was nothing to fall back on. So he went to Sunningdale Saturdays. Ignored the sympathy. Thornley's lost it but they keep their mouths shut he is after all a sort of reflection of themselves. Got the train once to where he had lived as a kid, Dulwich way. A block of flats where the house used to be but he recognised the gate posts. The neighbourhood had gone downhill, the front gardens mostly gravelled over for parking cars that nonetheless spilled onto the road, dustbins everywhere and most of the trees gone so it looked naked and the architecture bad no definition of space. Dirty and unloved. He might have ended up in one of those rooms, sharing a lavatory if it had not been for the 5%.

Tended to walk down the stairs now and out through the door beneath the invisible hand. Saw Dick's ghost sometimes. Willed it, in order to see what his response was. None. I'll go out there. I'll do it for Dick. I want to do it with Dick. I need Dick. No Dick. No feeling. Odd.

August in London. The leaves dying and a sky that you saw as blue but was not when you looked at it properly. A wondrous possibility of life that high summer. London, warm and green, full of activity and affluent tourists. It affected everyone, B&N and Thornley no less than the population at large, for all that they assumed they were above it all. Summer light flooded through the tall windows of the dining room on the top floor. Sherry was being drunk in small sips, comfortable lightweight suits were being worn and these days one doesn't have to go in for all that heavy stuff with waistcoats in the summer. That trouble in New Sudan was going to be sorted out later after a good but light lunch because we want to be up to the mark after but not so much up to it that it'll go on after four o'clock.

We've sorted it out with the city boys. That Malaysian outfit in which, in any event, we have an interest, definitely wants to get its hands on the Van Island Palm Oil Development Company. No embarrassing public inquiries out there. Let them do what they want. They can take over Jim as well if they want or . . . wipe him off the face of the earth for all we care.

The minutes will make it sound right, proper and above board. Careful what you say. Company secretary's on holiday. Battledun's acting. Taking the minutes. I'll have a look over them afterwards. We can trust him. It's going well, the Chairman rubs his hands as though it might be cold outside. He is a happy man. The wife's seen an old farmhouse to buy in Tuscany of all places. Flying out tonight to have a look. He wears a nice, cream-coloured linen suit, dull red tie makes him look like a bit of a lad and he feels it. Panama hat in his bag. Brown shoes can you believe it and I'll get a taxi to Victoria at four o'clock to miss the crowds. I'll be in Turin by dinner time. We're driving down on Saturday. It'll be fun. Thornley, old boy, you're looking pukka.

Thornley had made up his mind. He would sell his 5% and use the cash to buy the Van Island Palm Oil Development Company. Then I'll go down there with Dick and sort out the mess. We'll do it together. He was a happy man. I feel it, old man.

After lunch and good coffee which was one of their own imports, the board meeting started at two o'clock sharp. The mob hammering on the doors down below was ignored.

The usual business. The last minutes and matters arising. Not even three but I think we can have tea now we're a little bit ahead of schedule Battledun if you'd be so good thank you Doreen just leave it there. Sale of the Van Island Palm Oil Development Company. I think we've all read the report. The offer from Bright Future Holdings then is one we can recommend to the shareholders my plane is at six-thirty which means I must be at Gatwick by five meeting my wife in Turin this evening I travel business on these short trips. Unanimous? Battledun please record . . .

Consternation. You pompous little windbag; you've had us for years with your 5%. Put that number of shares on the market all at once and the price'll crash. In any case, it'd have to be put to the shareholders. You'd have to outbid and – this is off the record, Battledun, thank you – I'd like to remind you that we have an interest in Bright Future Holdings. We don't want to queer their pitch. On the record, thank you Battledun, this is the very best deal we can offer our shareholders. Off the record, it's impossible for you to flood the market just now. You might even make a killing which is even worse because you know what others don't. Insider trading and all that. I'm not an expert in fraud but we'll have to take the advice of our lawyers, meanwhile – off the record, if you don't mind – we might take you to court to stop you selling your shares against the interest of the other shareholders but you are not an ordinary shareholder you are a member of the board and as such. . . In that case you should resign your position you cannot have your cake and eat it, I might remind you, and meanwhile I fully intend to close the meeting at four o'clock my taxi is waiting. If, that is, it has not been overturned by the outraged mob to whom, I am inclined to feel, I would feed you, given half a chance. Yes, that is off the record.

The fact is that the superior indifference in which Thornley has held his colleagues and fellow shareholders over the years is thrown back at him. He is not such a fool that he does not realise this. It is, in Sunningdale parlance, par for the course. One would expect nothing less from the board of directors of a company that has gained its position in the world, its position above the mob down there below, through superior indifference to the wellbeing of mankind in general. That is not our job. Our job is to maximise profits, consider the interests of our shareholders and allow ourselves to be guided by the invisible hand and all that crap. Quite.

I'll bide my time. I'll sell my shares little by little so that no one suspects. I'll go out East as usual and offer them, through some convoluted process, to the Malaysian directors of Bright Future Holdings if necessary. That'll cook their goose here in London. There's life in the old dog yet. Dick and I'll go to Van where together we'll sort out the mess.

〔〕〔〕〔〕

The summer weather in London has no less of an impact on Thornley than it does on the other members of the board who are looking forward to weekends in Turin and on to Tuscany on Saturday, in Norfolk, somewhere near Southwold and we may go over the border to Snape there's something on, in a garden on St George's Hill in Weybridge and perhaps some golf, stuck in Town but we'll do the theatre and lunch on Sunday at that new place on the Fulham Road. So indeed, fuck off, and it is unanimous and it's a pity about his son and his wife leaving him and all that but are you a bit surprised?

Neither did he feel sorry for himself. He walked out looking a bit silly in that old-fashioned suit. But what can you expect? He walked back to his office humming. The idea crossed his mind that he felt as light as a feather. He knew what he was going to do. He was going out to New Sudan with Dick. I'll go straight back home now and talk it over with Agnes. They'd talk about the boy and his being born and his school days and his drawings and his first bicycle and how wonderful it was to have him in the office. Ring him up now, Agnes, and get him over. Ask him to bring those people with whom he shares his flat in Cornwall Gardens I really must go and see how he's getting on there he won't mind his old Dad popping in on a Friday evening we could go have a jar together in that pub on the Gloucester Road. Walk across Kensington Gardens in the evening scented with the blossom of the lime trees and watch the moon come up. Do you remember me taking you to see the Peter Pan statue when you were a little boy? Yes Dad.

He hums as he goes down the stairs.

Goodnight Mr Thornley.

Goodnight Foster. See you Monday.

Yes Sir.

Ahead of him the other chap is climbing into his taxi – the mob keeps back, impressed by his indifference – and he is off. A little flustered because I'm late thanks to that old fool who's never been easy and the sooner we get him off the board the better.

The invisible hand fells Thornley just as he passes through the brass door. The one with the top panel depicting the Egyptian slaves building a pyramid and the bottom one blank where Henry imagined a cornucopia spilling out mock-Tudor houses beside golf courses, bypass roads, fish fingers and the atomic mushroom cloud rising above it all. On this same panel, Thornley had wanted to see the Van Island Palm Oil Development Company, possibly with his own name inscribed below Lord Thornley of Dulwich or the village in Somerset, the first of a line but it was already past the hereditary stage.

The mob, having trodden him underfoot, perhaps, has fled. The street is silent and it is Friday afternoon in the summer. He lies there, half crippled, for half an hour before he is found. Foster, the porter, said it was just after the taxi had left with the Chairman. Might have seen him fall if he had looked back out of the window. Might have done and done nothing. Thornley's not going to make me miss my plane and Foster'll catch him. What can I do? Have to sort out something with those dubious types in Turin or else it'll be the devil's own job buying the farmhouse she wants and getting the papers sorted out properly. I'd rather pay one big fat bribe at the beginning and have done with it.

Men of that age and class who have suffered bereavement and taken to drinking a little too much and whose wives have been sent down to the country tend to have heart attacks. A stroke. Walking is not enough if you are under that much stress and you are eating the sort of food Alice feeds you.

Battledun does what has to be done because it's his job. He is good because he is a compassionate man but he will not visit the private hospital at the weekend. Alice does that because she is paid to. I'll have to move in now but I've made it quite clear I'll not live in the basement and Mum comes too. Houses like that are silly these days. Who wants a place like that except for show? They ought to be made into flats.

24
Visit to Cornwall Gardens

Battledun sits at his desk in the back room. The desk is small. The room is small and, because it has insufficient shelves, some of his files are neatly lined up against the wall. Others are inside the filing cabinet in the corridor.

He has neatly laid out his papers on the other small desk. The one at which Dick used to sit.

The lights are on because the late-afternoon sun barely enters the room. From time to time the man squints up to look at the bruised London sunset. A little later he will get up and walk to the window, watching and watching the sky before he turns back into the room.

He will look at the papers on the other desk: less than a dozen say it all. It is so little and yet he would die to have it undone.

Remarkable, eh Dick? He smiles as if his heart would break. Remarkable that the press should make so much of so little.

It is what they want to read, Johnny-boy. You know that. Beer with Bob at the bar. His clothes smell of beer because he had spilt the stuff down his trousers in the crush of the lunchtime bar. Beer, blood, sex and guts spread out for you to see only you turn away because in the end you do not want to see the truth. Your heart breaking because that is what it feels like: a knife in the guts.

The news had come in a rush, landing like an unexpected punch in the guts, winding you and making you want to cry from self-pity and lack of blood sugar. Things had fallen apart so quickly there was nothing on paper recording the fact. No report you could get your teeth into. Not enough to go over and hang on to. To go over and over and over.

A memory of the man telling him on a bad line that Dick was dead. A tight, apologetic Australian accent of the man he knew only as a name in the records for the mill manager, Peter, who kept saying his father, his father. Not answering the desperate questions: Peter, Peter, Peter. Tell me, Peter, Peter, Peter: they were cut off and he was talking to the air.

A small note of confirmation from the British High Commission. Very small in the diplomatic bag. We confirm your employee . . . Thus, the end of Dick. His body buried on the island . . . His body buried but what about Dick?

Best thing is . . . to list the dates we know. Put in the press cuttings. Best . . . to forget. The press whip up the public imagination but they get the basic facts right. And the dates: you can't write about something before it happens. Best . . . to look at the headlines only. Distil it all down to a list of dates, plus bald facts.

At the end of the list Dick is dead. But this fact is the one he cannot get his head around: Dick is dead. They buried his body but what about Dick himself? The essential thing that was Dick? The living Dick who experienced his death alone out there? They tell you what happened at the Battle of Bosworth Field but what was it like to die there? Apparently the local stream not only flowed with blood but also eventually blocked up with the mass of dead bodies. The dead bodies of the boys. Ten thousand of them not to mention the horses. Lives smashed so some fucker could sit on top of the shit heap. He imagined the wide Midland fields: the hawthorn and ash trees, an old oak, the crows hanging around, waiting to pick up the bits, peck out the eyes. Dick's eyes. While a few fields away life went on: people have to eat, repair the roof, think their lustful thoughts. As the wild boys kill each other. Are they carried away by their own enthusiasm like a football crowd? Filled with the idea of living as they die? Or is it a grim determination to do the deed and go down with it?

Did Dick die frightened? What had his life been about? Had he lived it? Had it been happy? There in the South Ken flat? Did they love him? His flat mates? Did he wake up in the morning and stare at the ceiling with blank incomprehension into the day? Alone? Or did he leap up to join it? His life? Can I hold it? See it? Feel it?

". . . poor boy! I never knew you,
Yet I think I could not refuse this moment to die for you . . .
If that would save you."[58]

Walt's lines made sense at last. He sensed his loneliness in Dick, his heart was breaking for something.

Better not to think the bruised London sky disappears into oblivion as the city lights thrust themselves up into it.

He turns back into the room: to the papers on the desk. Dick's papers but the shareholders won't see it that way.

He wants to make something solid of Dick that will survive the memorandum. Forgetting he had been up there and had not wanted to come down. Forgetting he wanted to see London bombed to a wasteland: wanted to come down if only he could live amongst the ruins.

Battledun draws down the blinds. The room is a block of light containing papers. He opens the door and switches off the lights. Passing into the corridor he locks the door behind him. The coat stand is in the corridor. From it he takes the maroon-coloured scarf his wife has lovingly knitted for him, from the wool left over from her cardie, which is why he wears it. The demonstration of his love, as it were, which she deserves. He puts on his heavy black coat that hangs from his broad shoulders, beginning to stoop with the weight of memories best forgotten.

"Goodnight Mr B."

"Goodnight Doreen."

Do him good to get off early for a change. He is a detached sort of man but I could deal with that. I'd like to see him in his pyjamas.

He stood all the way to Gloucester Road despite there being seats at this hour before the rush.

Of course there would be no one in because it was early but I'd like to have a look at Cornwall Gardens where he lived. Wistful they look, holding on to a little of the winter dark in the bright London night. The flat is the top two floors

---

[58] Walt Whitman, The Wound Dresser.

of the house that had once been . . . something else, a little grander, so that the stairs end abruptly at the front door. Better . . . knock. Dick might answer but a dishevelled girl with fair hair across her sleepy face opens it.

Hello! Posh, bossy accent. She could deal with this man in his big coat: his face tragic as if he was the entire lonely city. The ladies of easy virtue lived downstairs. It had happened before. She didn't mind. It was a story she liked to tell against herself. Her mother pretended to be shocked, wishing her own virtue had been more easy.

His embarrassed silence seemed to confirm the mistake. He had expected no one. She liked him for it, surprised, a little, by the idea that she'd like to creep naked inside the big coat in order to explore the big bony man beneath. One couldn't, of course, but the idea . . . was there, all the same.

So, she was glad when he said he had worked with Dick and she asked him in old enough to be my father.

Sorry about the state . . . I'm in. The daily's done the flat but not me I've taken the day off. Monthly I told them, you know I'm a fraud but I've read a whole good book about a gangster in Brighton who is a boy have some tea. Won't you?

She wanted to be the right type for him.

She was the type. Just the type with whom Dick would live. He was glad this girl had bossed Dick around a bit and given the flat what a woman gives a place. You can tell they have money, he told his wife later. All good things but you could put your feet up on the sofa. Of course I didn't.

The tea was in mugs and the sugar in a jam jar but the spoons, beautiful silver things. Georgian, early and lemon sliced into a bowl that might have been Ming but cracked. Ginger biscuits in a tin with Lord Kitchener on the lid.

She had put on a frock and a sweater that might have been Dick's: navy blue. But her hair was a mess. She smelt warm.

The others'll be back soon as if she wanted to warn him. I'm Sophie.

John Battledun.

Oh, she screamed, his boss. The Boss. He likes you so much. Visited you in . . . in Clapham.

Wandsworth.

Wandsworth, that time.

Yes.

He loved the garden. Roses. Typical Dick to see that.

Another woman might have cried. This one nibbled at a biscuit and was silent.

Yes. He glanced around the room to catch Dick.

I wasn't his girlfriend. Nothing like that. But . . .

I loved him too. I used to pretend he was my son.

I used to pretend he was my son, despite our being the same age. Do you want to see his room?

Yes please.

It was on the next floor. A tiny cell at the back. Cold with a view over rooftops. It would have been a servant's room: mean with a black cast-iron fireplace that would not hold a handful of coal. All white paint and a sloping ceiling. A pen-and-ink drawing of a Perpendicular church tower Bruton, Evercreech, Wyke Champflower.

She steps back. She has seen it all, seen it all, seen it all. Lain on the bed, watching the towelling dressing gown that hangs on the door.

I had no right to him. If he had been my son I would have wanted him to go. He didn't have an unhappy life. Twenty-seven years isn't bad. Let him go. Those boys at Bosworth Field were younger: a gang of naughty boys. I was twenty-one up there. I wanted to stay. I wanted to miss my life.

He had his. I am twenty-five. I want to have a baby who will live.

And die at twenty-seven?

It would be enough.

You should have had Dick's baby.

The idea was a new one. Watching him, in the room, thinking of Dick, she thought she would like to have this man's baby. They could do it there on the bed. She was naked under the frock, she could lift up the skirt but she wanted to be naked beneath his weight so that he would close his coat over them both. Then the baby would be Dick's or it would be Dick himself but it didn't always happen. She knew that much at twenty-five.

Watching him this way the girl at last became a woman because she realised that if she could not have a baby from this man now, she would not want a baby from anyone. She did not want to cry because she did not want his pity to embarrass them both.

Seeing him from the back and to one side a little, she saw the thick, iron hair brushed back to reveal his forehead that bore down upon a cave where an eye might be watching the room, an eagle nose and mouth that could snarl or sneer. She held him tight, pressing her face between his shoulders, drawing his warmth into her through the thickness of his coat that smelt of pubs and the tube train. She screwed up her eyes against the tears. Her body heaved against him with the effort. Afterwards she was happy. The room will be perfect for the baby but I'll brighten it up a bit. She wanted it now. Dick's baby, despite the iron hair. No one questioned the idea and her mother thought well that's alright then.

Thank you. I feel much better now.

So do I.

She showed him to the door. He walked up Gloucester Road to Kensington Gardens. Around the pond, getting the train home from Kensington High Street.

About a year later, at the office, he got a note: You're a grandfather. I've named the little girl after my mother who dotes. Please – underlined – be happy. I am. More than I ever imagined. Thank you so much. Three kisses, Sophie.

PART III

And immediately there fell from his eyes as if it had been scales: and he received sight forthwith, and arose, and was baptized. Acts, 9, 18

25
Keramungl is Taken in Hand

Joseph, having scrambled up the steep side of the hill, came out opposite the entrance to the club where he met Keramugl, stark naked and therefore, visually, in a vulnerable position vis-à-vis the well-known and despicable Tudak and his henchmen. Joseph was on his way to find Margaret. He knew the rules appertaining to the hill, hence his entrance by the back, unguarded door. Finding Keramugl in a fairly desperate predicament he says the obvious:

"Stop."

Said, it has to be emphasised, with a certain amount of passion, seeing the way things were.

Had Joseph been, say, Andrew, even taking into account the trouble Andrew had got himself into, he would have given them all a thorough ticking off. He would have sent them about their business. It would have been an act but it would have worked. Jim, your men are beginning to act like thugs. Fuck off then Andrew. How do you think your three square meals – or, at any rate, two – get put on the table every day? Clean sheets on your bed? Clean water on tap when you want it and light when you push that little switch there? See? Have another drink. This is how the world works. Better up here on the hill than down there in the swamp of humanity.

Something like that.

But Joseph had not the authority of the company or Andrew's white skin. All he had was himself, with not even a pair of shoes on his feet. But it worked. It worked by the same magic which made the Pollies and Dollies around the pool need his presence in order to feel that they approached anything like being alive. No longer behind the bar, he is missed, profoundly.

Therefore, when Joseph says stop, they stop.

Rabis and Pen scoot back into the car park from the safety of which they will ineffectively bark and make faces or, as likely, find some interesting carrion to smell because they are more likely to sniff the shit at their feet than stare up at the stars above, blocked out for them, in any event, by the lights of the car park. Not so for Tudak on the road: he has the full tropic firmament above him. Not as glorious as it might otherwise be, because of the dust, but impressive all the same.

Therefore, Tudak does not do what he was about to do to Keramugl.

[][][][][]

Now, in terms of the whole Annu thing, this point in time – just beyond the point where Joseph says Stop – is significant. Einstein said it, I think: the speed of light is constant but time is not. Nothing and everything might happen within a period of time we think of as constant – four seconds, four months – but which is, according to one of the laws – or is it hypotheses? – of quantum physics, as infinitely flexible as the emotional dynamics it contains. A love affair might be started, be ended, be entirely played out within what is marked by the prosaic definition we give it, 4.35 to 4.38pm, say. And what happens, happens and cannot be wiped out for all we would like to wipe it out. Cut out your tongue indeed the words have been said and cannot be unsaid. Time the great healer? Don't believe it.

See it? This bubble of time? The three men in it? Tudak in his uniform, with all its bits of boots, leather and metal, having some sort of hold over the naked Keramugl who is in some sort of ecstatic trance. Joseph – we are looking over his naked shoulder, for he wears only a lap-lap and he stands on his naked feet on the warm, smooth road surface – is in command. What he says goes. It goes for Tudak and all. Jim would be mortified.

There they all hang, in the night, entranced, for the moment; therefore, forever. Not only Keramugl. Then, moving to another point in time, Keramugl is handed over to Joseph who takes him, by the hand.

In command is Joseph but not in a cocky, self-assured, bossy way. As if he might be wearing Tudak's uniform. Nothing like that. He is not buoyed up with a splendid, youthful, I can do anything and I'll never be old, adrenaline-flushed sort of thing. He is indeed young and ought to have most of his life ahead but he is not sure that everything is funny and everyone is loveable, like he felt on the day he collected the coffee things from the girls around the pool, the day he pushed the knot of his laplap down just a fraction of an inch so that a couple of pubic hairs showed, when he was confident enough to show Andrew how he should act on the night they both walked out of the club, confounding everything that Jim stood for. Nothing like any of that because now, after the destruction of Ples, he is more like the old Joseph being the hard-working Joseph behind the bar in the old days, doing the right thing. And because he is doing the right thing, and not making a fuss about it, he is even more solid. A right-minded person must now say Yes, Joseph, alright, I'll do what you want.

All the same, Joseph is not a simple idiot; he is not foolishly hoping he is doing the right thing, keeping his fingers crossed. He knows about Tudak. He is aware that something unpleasant could happen. He is – and it shows if you look closely – a bit frightened: at first he avoids Tudak's eyes. Joseph, the man, does not want to challenge the unknown quantity that is the unsavoury reputation of Tudak. Like the now star-struck, or rather Annu-struck, Keramugl, a little earlier, his instinctive feeling is to run, grab Keramugl and run like hell to the top of the hill to Margaret: Phew, I feel better now we've put a bit of distance between us and him. A lot better. Yes dear, do you want a cup of tea?

[][][][]

The action slows down. Tudak watches the distance between himself and Joseph-Keramugl grow larger. A feeling of loss and worthlessness invades the void that was Tudak's place in Jim's world. Tudak does not recognise the feeling. This makes him uneasy. He blames it on the man there, irresistibly commanding him. His hands itch to do something. Joseph and Keramugl are moving away from him but they are still close. He might whisper in that particular, slightly grubby night and they would hear him:

"Annu."

A name he has heard somewhere. Has Jim not thrown it out as an expletive? A name, a thing associated with, the manifestation of, them, them commies, them Viet Minh, them Viet Cong, them Khmer Rouge, them Pathet Lao. A thing that must be stopped at all costs, at all costs. Is that not it? Is that not how it is supposed to be? This Annu thing? So get it. Get it. Take it, hold it, shake it, kill it and you will feel better like, like after the orgasm. Tudak wants his body – not yet his soul – to do what it wants with this thing Annu. And there it is, within his sight, his call, his touch.

"Annu."

Tudak whispers again.

This Annu who is moving away from him. Deserting him. Abandoning him to. . . to what? Tudak cannot answer the question. He barely knows how to ask it so he lunges forward with the instinct to take and to destroy the idea that threatens to disrupt the automatic responses that carry Tudak from one day, one meal, one change of underwear, one act of bestiality to the next. But he is, nonetheless, a worried and a confused dog because the voice of Joseph – assured, steady, big-chested – has had some impact, pushing him towards the feeling he would later be able to describe as emptiness. A feeling that did indeed stop him in his tracks, momentarily, enabling Joseph to take the star-struck Keramugl – at that moment, willing to die for communion with the Annu whom he so wholeheartedly desires and therefore experiences – away to safety.

Tudak wants. . . He does not know what it is he wants beyond the fact that he had better hang on to this fellow who has created the feeling of emptiness, anguish, it might be called. Hang on to him and destroy him so that the pain will go away.

Tudak lunges forward. As he does so, Joseph looks at him.

Tudak, the man who inspires fear because he is the instrument of Jim's wickedness, Tudak is on his knees. He is prostrate. He sees the entire universe as an apparently endless stretch of black, smooth road from which rises him whose name is Annu. I want, I want, I want to worship You is the simple message Tudak gets from his own germ of a soul. Look at me, take account of me, make me of some account by your recognition of me in the great . . . emptiness I feel.

Look at me forever.

This is how he feels and yet still he does not get it. Tudak is not sufficiently formed to understand these things. He is not yet human enough for that, at this point in Einstein's time.

□□□□□

Time moves forward again. Joseph and Keramugl disappear into the night.

Out of sight. But Tudak hangs on to the Idea. The Idea, which is everything, worries Tudak like a fly worries a dog. Or, one might say, worries him like a rat he has cornered. He will have to kill it soon. He will do that but the act will involve love.

Tudak prostrate on the smooth, black road, felled, it seems. Rabis and Pen watch in astonished incomprehension. Joseph and Keramugl, hand in hand, gone from his sight, walking up the hill towards Margaret. He won't lie on the road like this for ever; it's a ridiculous position for a start; he'll get up, and as he is conditioned to do, have a fag, and bounce elegantly into the back of Jim's Landrover as it cruises silently down the hill. But in the end, it'll take Annu to raise him up to realise his full stature, as intended.

Be this, Tudak. Soon you will be more. Like the seed in the dry ravine, an nth of moisture has had its impact.

But the time of suffering is yet to come, and so it is easy.

I was only following orders.

[][][][][]

But things do move forward with the end result – or rather, a result – that John the Baptist does indeed lose his head, which ends up on a large plate, upsetting a lot of people in Munich some years later when Salome appears to make love to it set to the music of Richard Strauss who merely considered it an outrageous something or other that would make a lot of money and get people talking about the decadence of near-atonal music, which it was not but only rather a little over the top. John loses his head and He ends up hanging from the same old tree from which all the others were hung for our entertainment. Entertainment conceivably, in a Ken Russell sort of way, backed by the music, this time, of Richard Strauss's Ein Heldenleben, perhaps. An ignominious, ridiculous or glorious outcome, depending on the way you want to look at it.

[][][][][]

So, Joseph takes the naked Keramugl to Margaret. She is, as expected, sitting on the veranda watching the night below in which hang the usual insignificant bits and pieces of whatever it is: Human Endeavour if you like.

Margaret looks at Keramugl, naked in the night. She knows what has happened and she can read in Keramugl's face what he is feeling as he holds on to Joseph's hand. Keramugl is dumb at this point. He is beyond speech. It is part of the making of Keramugl: this being picked up by Annu – Narangburn Plantation, Karandawa, Van etc, etc – and being presented, as it were, to this woman who is pretty old in the eyes of the youthful Keramugl but he remembers what Grin told him all those centuries ago on Narangburn Plantation. The idea of being stark naked in front of Margaret does not strike Keramugl as embarrassing. The only one of them who did not appreciate Keramugl's physical beauty at the time was Keramugl himself. Why should his soul be afraid in the face of God? It was not.

[][][][][]

Translated for Andrew by Daphne.

I am walking and I am thinking of the message Mr Henry has given me for Andrew and I am seeing the white light that is like a hole in the night. It is a bad thing because the night is a time for the dark but this light is too big for the night and I am confused.

I am looking at the light and suddenly some men come out of the night and they surround me. I recognise one of the men as the man we call Tudak because he is very big and handsome. I am afraid. I am afraid because I have heard about this man. He wants to fight me and I know he will kill me without thinking. I want to run away but there are too many men around me. Then Joseph comes. I do not know where he came from but I know it is Annu come for me. This is something I cannot forget all my life because I am happy then to find Annu again. If I am to die, just then, I am happy. This is how I feel at the time. Joseph speaks and I hear the voice of Annu. I have not forgotten Annu talking to me when I wanted to kill Tematan that time before near Karandawa. At the sound of Annu's voice, all the bad men run into the car park because they are afraid. The man Tudak falls on the ground as if he is dead. Then Joseph takes me away and it is true I hear the Tudak-man call out the name Annu so I know Joseph is Annu. Yes, this is strange, because I have known Joseph before and I do not think he is Annu. But now, as he holds my hand I know it is Annu. This makes me think of Tarlie. I think of Tarlie talking to me with his thumb in my hand. Joseph talks to me the same way so that I feel very good. He says you are my friend. You do not have to be afraid of anything. I feel strong. I think: am I also Annu? Yes, this is stupid but at the time that is how I think. Joseph takes me to Missus Margaret. I know about this woman because she has worked with Petrus at the school at Ples. I know she is a good woman. Joseph does not tell me that she is good, I know it. So I love this woman, Margaret, before I meet her in Jim's house. When I see Margaret, I see that she is beautiful although she is not a young woman. I see that she loves Joseph and I see that Joseph loves her. I know at once she is my friend. I know I will help her one day. I know that this is why I have come here to Van.

Margaret gives me food to eat and clothes because Tudak has taken my lap-lap. She gives me one of Jim's shirts. We sit on the veranda in the night and we talk. She tells me she knows that Jim has destroyed Ples. She says she is sorry but I must not worry because good things will come. She says we are on a journey that we cannot avoid and sometimes the road is difficult. I say yes and I tell her about my journey from my ples in the Highlands to Van. I tell her about Annu. She does not answer me but I know she is listening to Keramugl. I want to talk to this woman; I want to tell her everything about myself. Her listening to my story makes me learn that I am Keramugl. When I have finished talking I eat the food that she gives me. When I have finished eating she says yes, Keramugl has been brought to Van by Annu. She says yes, the road is hard but the walking of it is not so difficult because the putting of one foot in front of the other is not difficult. She says yes, it is easy to do the right thing. She says, well Manki is a good gris manki, so Manki is a good man. This makes me laugh because I can see the boy Manki at Narangburn Plantation and I can see he is a good boy. Margaret laughs and she says there are good people who will do the right things when the time comes. She talks the truth. She is my mother whom I did not know.

I look out into the night and I see that the light of the car park below is nothing and I know that Jim is nothing also and I know that one day Jim will die but Annu will live. But when I have this idea, also I think that I will kill Jim. This makes me laugh. We are all laughing, thinking of Annu. I see that the world looks bigger than I have seen it before. It is bigger than the Orami Valley, it is bigger than all the kunai grasslands near Karandawa.

I say to Margaret that I have talked to Mr Henry and that I know he is a good man. I tell Margaret that I have a good message from Mr Henry to take to Andrew. Margaret says, yes, Mr Henry is a good man but it is dangerous for you to walk back to the plantation tonight. She says I must go back to Alloy's house with Joseph. She says she, herself, will take the message back to Andrew. So I give her the message. Yes, I know she will do a good thing.

Margaret is very strong in the way she is talking to me. She does not talk loud, she is sitting in her chair but she looks at me when she is saying these things. I listen to Margaret and I know what she says is right. I do not answer her and when she is finished talking she looks away. I think she is sleeping.

Margaret is strong in the way she tells things. You know this, Andrew. Also, Andrew, you understand I did not bring that message to you. I gave the message to Margaret.

So, I went to Alloy's house with Joseph.

That is why I find the body of Tarlie the next morning and I know that Margaret speaks the truth. Yes, Andrew, at first I am unhappy that Tarlie is dead but Joseph says I am not to worry. He says this is the purpose of Tarlie. He says Tarlie is the first Annu but that still Annu lives. I know that this is true because was it not Annu himself who told Tarlie to guide us to the saltwater? Tarlie had done that and now Joseph himself is taking the power of Annu from Tarlie. Joseph said to me I must trust what he says and understand what he does. Because Joseph says this, I trust him and I know that it is Jim who has killed Tarlie.

Joseph says he will go to Margaret and that he will not come back. He says I must wait in the house until they take the body away. He says I must wait for some days. Then, he says, I must go back to Margaret and she will tell me what to do. This is what I do and this is why I find the body of Mr Henry in the same place where I found the body of Tarlie. But Mr Henry is not dead at first. His eyes look at me and he smiles at me. I want to help him as he dies, so I kneel beside him and I put my hand beneath his head. With my other hand I stroke his hair away from his eyes. He looks at my face, he smiles again and he calls me Abus. Then he dies. I do not know who is this man Abus but I think he means Annu, so I am happy.

And yes, Andrew, I do not know if I wanted to kill Jim because of Joseph or because of Margaret.

Now you must let me rest.

26
Dealing with the Body

Born in the confusion of men's hungry minds it may have been that the decapitated body discovered behind Alloy's house that morning was indeed the body of Annu. Also, arising from the same confusion and hunger, it was Annu it was who carried the bloody knife up to Missus Margaret and Annu it was who was known to have been at the Togulo Farm about that time. All this being the case then the fact of Annu cutting off his own head as a way of escaping Jim, Annu taking his head up to Missus Margaret who must have, therefore, restored it to its rightful place, was the truth by act of faith. No more proof was required.

☐☐☐☐☐

The young man, Keramugl, sleeps peacefully on Alloy's sofa. The same cheap timber frame and loose foam-rubber cushions upon which Andrew had lain the night Alloy found him exhausted in front of the house.

In the same way, one of the back cushions has been removed to make a head-rest over one of the arms, but because Keramugl is shorter than Andrew his feet do not rest upon the opposite arm. Neither is Keramugl in the same state of agitation as Andrew had been, Alloy sitting beside him removing his boots and gently laying the warm palm of his hand upon Andrew's stomach.

Alloy, of course, is not in the house, he is with Andrew, somewhere.

The young man, Keramugl, has slept through the decapitation of Tarlie. He did not hear the wordless struggle behind the house, the loving embrace a sort of choking gurgle and a wasted, cut-off intake of breath as the throat is cut and thereafter a silent determined butchering that is no more than that: an animal thing born out of pain and need, therefore exonerated, the head taken away as another fumbling, misunderstood act of love, and as a sort of prize.

The young man, Keramugl, was looked upon and touched by Joseph who left him sleeping in the certain knowledge he would do the right thing when the time came. Had he not touched his lips with love in Karandawa? And there was, after all, Margaret above and the incriminating knife taken away. Keramugl is clean.

Joseph picks up the panga knife and takes it up to Margaret. He does this, not as a slave to his destiny but because upon seeing his friend lying headless upon the ground he wants her.

They sit, together, again, on the veranda, overlooking the world below, hand in hand. In the face of what appears to be a catastrophe, their inactivity and calmness would seem inappropriate to those who do not know them. And not the least aspect of this apparent catastrophe is the possibility of Joseph being blamed for the murder. He is, after all, out of favour – to say the least – with Jim and he holds a piece of incriminating and – from Jim's point of view – convenient evidence.

Margaret and Joseph do not indulge in a panic-stricken elimination of the evidence. Such thoughts do not even begin to form in their joint consciousness. Rather, they are calmly aware of the certainty of a progression of events that have been set in motion and in which they are to be involved.

If pressed, Margaret might express the idea that the fact of them being here together on the veranda, at this specific point in time, is enough. They have no sense, like Jim has, of moving history along – for all that they do – or, like the self-centred Andrew has, of being, however unwillingly, at the centre of things – for all that they are. Margaret and Joseph – hand in hand – are outside that sort of considered egocentricity.

So they sit holding hands. They might have kissed, mouth touching mouth, but it would not have been an erotic kiss. It would have been a kiss that said remember me and be with me; as Joseph had kissed Keramugl upon leaving him. They might have kissed had such an emphatic action been required, but it was not.

[][][][][]

For the duration of their marriage and of their sojourn in the house upon the hill, Margaret and Jim would eat breakfast together at a small table on the veranda. Jim was sure this hadn't been his habit before the marriage but he accepted it as one of the things she's done and she's welcome to it. And he might have added – across the bar – if it makes 'er 'appy, because he'd heard people say that sort of thing about their wives. But he went along with it, not in order to make her happy but because it was another of those performances he had to go through in order to be the General Manager. In this respect he didn't question it, any more than he questioned the dinner parties that had to be given for certain guests when they passed through – Thornley, for instance – or, for that matter, the little rituals that Mrs Livingston made him undertake in the office as part of the fucking GM business. Dogs through 'oops he might have said.

Margaret's cooking was plain and necessary: a touch heavy on the carbohydrates if you sat too long in an air-conditioned office or on the seat of a moving vehicle; colourful vegetables, apparently rather undercooked for the delicate Anglo-Australian palate; and meat more-often-than-not, missing altogether for some reason she forgets things sometimes, like 'er mother. At the beginning she had, obviously, cooked things with the raw, unbleached palm oil that Clarence had brought her one time but Jim put his foot down. I 'ad to. It was 'er mother in 'er and I 'ad to stamp it out. We can't eat that shit, girl, I told her and she took it straight. Never said a word but he couldn't shift her on other things and dinner he generally avoided preferring a beer or whisky down the club as a prelude to his nocturnal activities. A charred steak when Joseph did a barbecue was more his line.

"No egg then?" Jim stares intently at the pile of lightly fried rice and vegetables – stuff, he calls it – on his plate, suspecting palm oil. He stares and pokes with his fork as if this action might provoke an egg to appear. On those two or three mornings a week when an egg does appear he can still aim at her by wondering out loud – of the plate of food rather than of Margaret directly – how it was that sometimes there was an egg and sometimes there was not and by what unaccountable law the egg was sometimes fried and sometimes boiled.

Depending on his mood the world that produced Jim's breakfast was either funny, stark-raving mad or fucking stupid. Margaret's response was always one of open amusement. Amusement that ever offers love to a child. Only, of course, Jim was not especially beloved of Margaret who had said, as a girl and therefore not as the completely formed Margaret, you want your Mummy, you silly boy, or words to that effect which having been said once could not therefore be said again although Jim heard them still and it was something else he held against her.

Mrs Livingston, down in the office, found in herself, when he didn't drive her mad, the same amusement aroused by Jim's silly, self-centred and bad-tempered response to some necessary office routine which made life easier for him as well as for everyone else. But unlike Margaret, Mrs Livingston still worried about the amusement that Jim aroused, sometimes even to the extent of allowing it to upset her, desiring, therefore, as a refuge, her Ted back home. In this respect Mrs Livingston sometimes drew a cloak of clouds around her sunshine, in the process, therefore, she restricted its warming influence on her Ted, on Andrew, on the girls in the office and even on Alloy, who even in his blackest moods noticed its absence. Only after things had happened worse than Jim's self-centred silliness did she understand that she did not have to ration out her sunshine as something that might otherwise be used up.

This morning, on the morning after the night within which Tarlie has been decapitated, there is an egg. A fried egg, token, maybe, of a job well done. Jim stares at the egg, at the very yellow centre of the egg. For once he is tongue-tied. There is nothing he can say to justify himself to himself today. There is no shit he can throw at her. So, girl, what was Joseph, our erstwhile bar-boy doing? Why was he sitting beside you with that bloody bush-knife lying across his lap? He might have asked such questions had the night not existed. He could rearrange the facts as well as the next man – or woman – and thereby avoid the personal consequences of his actions. But he could not wriggle out of his involvement in this one. That would take a bit of explaining. And if he asks too many questions, she might just answer him. He might then have to ask her if she is not somehow implicated herself. Then she might laugh in his face or, more likely, walk out on him again, challenging his very existence. Because he has an idea – a vague Jim-like idea – that without Margaret, there is no Jim. He dare not test it.

Did you kill him, then?

Did you cut off 'is 'ead?

Did you chuck 'is head into the river for it to be carried out to the ocean?

Did you call up Joseph from wherever it is inside you, you, you conjure him up to get you out of trouble?

Did you do all that? Jim?

Did you do all that? Margaret? Girl?

Are your hands sticky with the blood of Annu?

Tell me you did it. Tell me you did it. Tell me you did it, girl, then I can sort it out for you. And make you my slave in the process.

Jim stares at the centre of the egg, imagining she watches him.

Why you lookin' at me like that? He thinks, looking up suddenly so's he can catch her but of course she's turned away as quick as he can look, the sly bitch, as if butter wouldn't melt in 'er mouth. Looking at something out there don't ask me what.

He stabs the egg. Well if you don't want to talk that's your lookout but you better stop looking at me like that. You can't pin it on me. I never touched 'im and you know I didn't.

But she did know and that was the thing that got at him. She, whoever she was, knew him for the baby he was who still wanted his Mummy.

P'raps it'd be better I cut your 'ead off. Eh, girl?

Perhaps it would be.

He didn't touch the egg again. He had sandwiches sent down to the office for lunch. She didn't see him for dinner either.

[][][][][]

He'd laughed when he saw Joseph there with the knife in his hand. What could be more bloody perfect? And natural. Joseph and Margaret holding hands was something he did not see. A kanaka and a white woman don't hold hands: it's a fact.

Joseph was detained at – it's a fact – Jim's pleasure. Take 'im and 'old 'im 'til I tell you what to do. They did, such was Jim's authority in those last few days. No legal niceties were required: if I'd wanted your opinion 'Enry I'd 'ave asked for it. If you want to be useful, sort out Andrew and if you want my opinion, don't worry about legal niceties.

"Sammy," he said, "you can take him. 'E won't cause any trouble." That's the beauty of it. Better not drag Tudak into it at this stage of the game. Do you think I'm bloody stupid? Not me! I keep ahead of the game. She might well know what's going on, that one, but a wife can't shop 'er 'usband, I'm telling you. The law won't let 'er. An' even if it did they can't pin anything on me. Was I there? I was not but I'll tell you one thing about 'er and she's as queer as they come but I know 'er if anyone does: she won't say a word.

"Take 'im up the Togulo Farm and tell 'em to keep 'im for me."

[][][][][]

They chatted on the way, as friends do. Most likely they chatted about Jim. Joseph most likely told Sammy what he'd done and thinking back on that night when Tarlie had so publicly stood up against Jim outside Chan's store and before the wide and knowing eyes of Tati, they would most certainly have concluded that Jim had something to do with all this, in which case it was most certain he hadn't done it himself – decapitation required a certain amount of strength. This being the case, Joseph would have said something like you better watch yourself Sammy and Sammy would have laughed and said something along the lines of you bet I will I don't want to lose my head as well. You can see Joseph laughing his big laugh at that and Sammy – small, compact and able to make himself very inconspicuous when required along the lines of Bune in that respect only a little bit older and a lot less certain about himself in fact existing on a lower and much less complete human plane altogether but not a bad man for all that and likely to end in the right place one day – suggesting, without thought but from the very depths of his being all the same, look, get out, run away, get on a boat to Port Markham and forget about all this. I'll tell them you put the knife to my throat and you made me do it. Joseph laughs and says: "Why not come with me?" Sammy says: "I might, one day."

Just beyond this space then, that would one day become what is known as a public open space – an incident of grass and trees where litter will be deposited, where public dignitaries will erect objects of civic beauty and where people will hang around for a variety of reasons, some of them known as illicit, either objectively appreciating or being indifferent to the dynamic interaction of whatever it is all around them – and at a point where the track to the Togulo Farm had been washed out resulting in a gully that was sufficiently deep and difficult for Sammy to negotiate that he had to stop the vehicle altogether and say to Joseph:

"Get out, get out and run."

Joseph, in response to the urgent advice, laughs again and says: "Do this for me Sammy."

"I'll do anything," Sammy replies.

"When you pick up the body of Tarlie as you are bound to do, call to Keramugl who is in the house of Alloy."

"I'll do that."

"He'll help you do the right things. You'll do that Sammy?"

"I will," says Sammy, I'll do it because by asking me to do it you have made my life significant and I will serve you and the idea of you to the end of my days.

"And you will tell Keramugl what has happened to me and you will tell him to do what Missus Margaret asks him to do."

"I will do that."

"Thank you," and Joseph gets out of the vehicle at that point on the road, mostly hidden from public view by a tangle of bush and, as it happens, barely recognisable as a road at all. "Go now Sammy, I'll walk to the Togulo Farm. It's a good place to hide."

They start their separate journeys without looking back.

So sure of Sammy's goodwill is Joseph that he no more considers it than he considers the oxygen in the air. He might think of Sammy later with some pleasure in the same way as he might appreciate the early warmth of the sun on a cold morning but at this particular moment he is filled with a more abstract sort of joy. The joy of being alive and of feeling himself walking the incline of the track up into the hills. See him as he rises in the landscape, the sea behind him becoming wider, the sky above him bigger and the wilder hills around him the reality of the earth beyond the populous activity of the coastal plain and the temporary dynamic interaction of human futility that is the town. He throws back his head, stretching his strong neck – ribbed like the trunk of the old Casuarina tree – and he laughs his big laugh, calling the name of Tarlie so that the hills take it and carry it higher into the sky and above the sea.

[][][][][]

"You know that fellow Master Andrew fucks? The one works for Master Clarence? Skinny bugger?"

"Yesa."

"You know 'is 'ouse?"

"Yesa."

"There's a body at the back."

"Yesa."

Jim had let the statement fall upon the assumption of an expression of surprise from Sammy, who, sometimes, momentarily, registered a human response to Jim's outrageous instructions before snapping back to the automated mode expected of the General Manager's driver.

Thus was Jim, momentarily, disconcerted. Sufficiently so, and in an instinctive sort of way, to want to scrutinise Sammy and wonder if the fucker wasn't up to something you can't trust these kanakas further than you can see them. But Jim held back, coming to the satisfying conclusion that Sammy was incapable of independent thought and would not be other than Sammy, which meant, after all these years of having got used to him, that if I told 'im to stick 'is 'ed in a bucket of water 'e'd do it and drown if I didn't tell 'im to take it out.

Nonetheless, although Jim did not think out the idea in a way that might have occurred to someone else as amusing, or at any rate odd, a sensation did manifest itself to him as something akin to a hard and inhuman smell – such as burning plastic, for instance – suggesting that there was something unreal about Sammy's matter-of-fact response to an instruction to dispose of a body. Jim actually sensed this to the extent of shaking himself as a dog would shake the water out of its ear. And as Jim shook so again he experienced fear of the unknown and along with the fear he had an idea of Margaret – a barely perceived idea – of Margaret looking at him and he hated her for it. Fuck her.

"Yesa."

All this happened – this massive, millions of years' worth of, degrading journey that Jim took – in a moment so small that Sammy saw nothing that was other than the Jim he'd got used to over the years also. They were standing as usual beside the vehicle outside the office to which Sammy had driven Jim after breakfast.

"Take the vehicle and deal with it. I've sent the boys ahead so there won't be any trouble."

"Yesa."

There wasn't; the mere suggestion of Tudak in the breeze kept the mob away and was enough to engender a ripple of fear that went through the community around Alloy's house and beyond. Along with it also the unspoken but palpable intelligence that Tarlie had been done to death by the machinations

343

of Jim and that Joseph had taken the rap. This is what had happened and despite the fear he provoked Tudak was not blamed and Sammy only doing his job as they knew they also would continue to do. Better to forget the whole thing, keep your heads down and be glad it's not you. How else to survive? Jim was Jim is the reality of our foul existence. Challenge him and look what happens. Horrible things.

None of these ideas were spoken out but they were muttered and thought about and the shameful consequences of our existence understood only too well. And for this reason there were those who exalted Tarlie and Joseph and there were those who hated them for exposing their own nakedness and there were those who got on with whatever they had to do and tried to pretend it was nothing to do with them. But the ideas would not go away and as they rippled ever outwards so there was an exponential multiplication of understanding and of incomprehension and of subsequent justification, explanation and jumping to the right conclusions although they didn't realise it and to the wrong conclusions even though they were sure they were the right ones even to the extent of being prepared to kill for them. In the plantation, in the boys' quarters up on the hill, even in the club mostly for the wrong reasons, the name and thence the idea of Annu was caught up in all the cross-currents of ideas and dynamic conversational or even argumentative interactions amongst the friendly, incidental or pugnacious relationships between and amongst men. Thus the idea became real and indeed it was real as much for Jim as it was for Keramugl, for Daphne, for Henry, in the few days he had left to live, and as it had been for the late and sometimes lamented Tarlie.

□□□□□

Tudak returns, alone. The sleeper sleeps on. Tudak might be waiting to have a go at Keramugl but he is unaware that his angel of the night is inside the house. So, he sits alone beside the decapitated body that he has created. It is now meat, already beginning to swell and to lose its similarity to human form in the morning heat. The insects roar. The body is of interest only, it seems, to the body of flies, an irreverent thing that nonetheless plays its necessary part. The same trio of vultures circle above: small things that make the sky big.

There had been a connection, no doubt about it. Tudak had embraced Annu, briefly, as Rabis and Pen brought him to the ground, on his face, holding him, while Tudak did the job, straddling the oddly compliant body of Tarlie who had, Tudak was able to reflect later, made the job easy for him. He had been able to raise the head gently, cupping the forehead in the warm palm of his hand. He had felt its weight and understood its worth. He had held it so for millions of years and beyond, forever, even though he stretched the throat sufficiently to cut through it easily. The compliant body had made it easy because of the warm hand on his forehead. He had killed Tarlie as his first act of love.

So it was that in the moment of knowledge, Tarlie suffered no pain, the quiet choking noise he had made was not complaint or resistance or a desperate hanging on to life but laughter. After all, Tarlie was the one most likely to suffer in the moment and then only in the process of transition, the giddy hanging on to the onion above the rapidly shrinking world. Tarlie laughed at the idea and at the idea that this was indeed the Annu whom he had been seeking. Tudak's suffering lasted longer, but not for ever.

So Tudak had foolishly taken the head away with him and he had foolishly left the knife behind, for which he might yet get a flogging, which he would take. But the foolishness made a hairline crack in the remarkably thick and hard shell around the seed that was inside what was called Tudak and through which, a tiny sliver of light barely a single vibrating ray of light barely even the most minute hint of energy suggesting light had nonetheless been able to touch the seed promising the possibility of germination.

But having detached Tarlie's head, Tudak cherished it for its own sake. He took it away and hid it. The idea of eating Tarlie's body would return but as a different idea.

Now Tudak sat beside Tarlie's body outside Alloy's house while Keramugl, the Brave, slept peacefully inside. The idea that Tudak was guarding Keramugl, protecting him, is not entirely inappropriate. In a parallel world, Keramugl, considering the events of the night before, walks out onto the little flimsy veranda, rubbing his eyes, to be confronted by Rabis and Pen slavering on the lawn. Tudak, seeing him and recognising the angel of the night, calls off the dogs. Keramugl sits on the veranda, unaware, in his sleepiness, of what it is beside which Tudak sits. The two men – a black devil, as it were, and the angel – look at each other waiting for the revelation, the transformation, the realisation of the wondrous beauty that is a man's clean soul. In a parallel world, but in the one we inhabit Keramugl sleeps on while Tudak waits beside the decapitated body outside.

🞎🞎🞎🞎🞎

Late morning. The heat is exhausting, as usual. The vegetation around the house and the cliff rising above, upon which Henry's house sits, are claustrophobic. The men who are entitled to live in the Junior Management Quarters have not yet returned for the lunches being cooked by women and small boys; of more necessary and immediate interest than the real smell of the decapitated body, headless and rotting out there, somewhere. Nonetheless, they all hear Jim's vehicle as it bumps and bangs over the tired ruts of the track that runs between the crowded gardens, eventually ending up outside Alloy's house in which reside people who are no longer Alloy. The same route Andrew had taken and Tarlie had taken some days later, leading them both to portentous events on their particular journeys. Remarkable, come to think of it, who has ended up at this cheap bungalow beside the river and below the cliff upon which Henry's house sits. People hear the noise, subconsciously or consciously – perhaps frozen in motion, holding a spoon or taking a pinch of salt – conditioned to know what it means. Jim himself will not be in the vehicle but it is an instrument of his devious activities all the same. No one holds it against Sammy; or against Tudak personally. Only doing their jobs.

Sammy halts the vehicle in front of Alloy's house. The ground is dry enough to take its weight. Tudak stands up a colossus in his smart uniform, stretched

345

over his body in a way the loveable Dick will later appreciate. His muscular, meaty body nonetheless no more essentially alive than the other which he has already, in fact, dragged to the front of the house. It is not recognisable as something that was once Tarlie, this headless, swollen piece of meat; evidence to be got rid of.

As Sammy gets out of the vehicle, so Keramugl, the young man, having been woken up by the noise and surprised into full wakefulness by the brightness of the miday sun, comes out. He recognises Sammy as Jim's driver but as no more than that, and he recognises Tudak as the terrifying vision of the night before, shrunken a little, nonetheless, by the daylight and, it must be said, by Keramugl's own new certainty and calm acceptance of things as they are. Remarkable, in fact, given his state of terror only twelve hours previously, how calmly Keramugl accepts the situation. For all he knows, at that moment, Sammy is the sort of mean little shit whom one would expect to work as a stooge for Jim. He might be another Tudak, as Keramugl has understood Tudak so far, black wickedness beyond reason or reasoning. He might, at any moment, have his lap-lap ripped off, be brutalised, tossed into the back of the vehicle and fed to the crocodiles along with whatever else it is that lies at Tudak's feet. A reasonable conclusion given the circumstances. But Keramugl is as calm as Margaret herself might be. He feels the irresistible Keramugl urge to laugh. It shows on his face.

The body lying at Tudak's feet is not recognised by Keramugl, the odd body or two, lying around, decapitated precisely so as to avoid recognition, not an unusual event in those dire days of distress and despair. Keramugl did not give it a second glance; the possibility of an attack from Sammy and Tudak was of more immediate concern, although a smile lingered on his face.

Sammy returns the smile, a rare radiant Sammy smile so that Keramugl is reassured. Tudak is another matter. What is Tudak's response to the sudden and unexpected appearance of that angelic apparition of the night before? The thing that had been taken away from him? The thing, maybe, that had helped to make that fracture into a crack or even an element of the light itself that had entered his dark being? This dumb, albeit beautiful-looking, animal who is not known to utter more than grunts and Yesa when it is spoken to, and who when response, other than immediate action that is, is required, has nothing to say. Obviously. Whatever transformation was to occur, it was not going to be a miraculous verbal articulation of Tudak. But it might be progress in the right direction.

Tudak watched – struck no dumber than usual – his mouth open a little so that his neat, regular facial features did not look as handsome as they used to do. It was, someone noted later, from about that time that Tudak began to look his age; the lines began to appear on his face, his skin lost its gloss; his shoulders looked as if they did indeed carry a burden. Margaret caught his eye and smiled.

Sammy smiles at Keramugl spilling out all that Joseph has told him to say so that Keramugl is reassured not only of Joseph's safety but also of Sammy's friendship. Jim ceases to exist and therefore the fear of Tudak is gone. The body lying at Tudak's feet is also explained and the death of Tarlie accepted as a real thing which will be considered over time, but which is not a thing that can, or should, induce rantings and ravings of self-centred grief. Keramugl thinks of

Tarlie as he knows him so he laughs. The idea of Tarlie is much more real than the lump of meat at Tudak's feet. Tarlie lives, indeed. Long live Annu.

Sammy's smile radiates still more as Keramugl laughs at his words and Tudak watches. He watches the interaction between the known Sammy whom he has, heretofore, understood as a kindly, albeit indifferent, dog-handler, and the other, understood as a thing vulnerable and fragile, the young man, thick-set and built like a boxer, although he is a short man. Henry's baby-faced, pathological killer, appears to Tudak – with a vision of the naked Keramugl, the night before – as a thing so vulnerable and fragile that he wants to take it back home with him in order to keep it safe and intact. Drag it back to his hole, to his sleeping place, to pet and to hold – the way he has treated Tarlie's head, as it happens. Perhaps to kill it in the end either from jealousy of it or from indifference even, forgetting to feed it or locking it up in a place of safety and leaving it there too long. This is how Tudak's dim and uncomprehending brain responds to Keramugl at that suspended mid-day moment. He wants Keramugl for himself.

"I've come to collect the body." Or words to that effect from Sammy.

An instruction received: Tudak responds. He drags the body by the ankles towards the vehicle and drops it. He is a big, strong man and could easily have flung it over his shoulder and dumped it into the tray of the vehicle.

But he is aware – in the sense of an almost-but-not-quite incomprehensible pressure around him – of the interest in the process of the other two. He feels – as much as he can feel that sort of thing – he is being watched. And why should they not watch the beast doing its work? His bestiality has proved him so to be; Tudak the man, of no account. Get the job done and let's get on but Tudak responds to this perceived interest. He wants – not as a thought-out idea – he wants to make a connection with these two who watch him.

He drops the legs of the body he is holding by the ankles as if exhausted. He is exhausted, as it happens: dog tired of being Tudak he is – not an idea but a general feeling which he is incapable of analysing.

"Ugh," or something like that. He points to the inert weight of the body upon the ground.

Sammy and Keramugl move forward. All together they lift the body. Sammy and Keramugl take a leg each while Tudak carries the shoulders, the end with which he is already well acquainted.

They put it into the vehicle and as they do, one of the arms is left hanging over the edge. Being on that side, Keramugl takes it by the hand and thus remembers the hand of Tarlie holding his. He remembers the pressure of Tarlie's thumb telling him to be calm in the face of adversity and to resist his violent inclinations. Thinking of this, Keramugl remembers Nalin's daughter, her head held by Tarlie's large hands, one of which he holds now. Thus he looks at the body of Tarlie lying in the back of Jim's truck with no head that he can hold. Anger fills up Keramugl as these ideas flood his consciousness together with more ideas about the journey from Narangburn Plantation to Karandawa. He remembers the duplicitous Tematan, he remembers his friend the tragic but happy Weno and he remembers the white man who fed them into the belly of New Sudan. Then he remembers the kiss that Annu gave him and he remembers the fear of seeing the balus for the first time thinking that nothing can be so bad as travelling in the balus for the first time and yet here is Tarlie, his friend, lying dead in the back of Jim's vehicle. Anger fills up Keramugl until there is nothing but the anger and the world around is a red fire he wants to fight with his bare hands and tear it apart to the death and in doing so he may bow down and worship the god of violence who is the master of the world. Then he may truly become Keramugl the Terrible whose vengeance is known to all men who will therefore fear him and no more will he be subject to his own fear. Would he not, in his youthful vigour, have scaled the cliff there and then, rushing at Henry, just coming in for his lunch, his Mozart and a little siesta, and have torn the surprised Henry apart limb from limb? He would, and the baby-faced killer would have done a good job of it. For it is true that the whole world around was silent in the midday dead heat as Keramugl thought these things.

Keramugl holds the cold hand of the body that emphatically does not belong, any more, to Tarlie, and he looks at the grisly stump that once held Tarlie's grinning face. Even the body of flies has fallen silent, moving noiselessly about its business as the vultures watch, a little nearer now, perching on a tree that hangs from the cliff. The decision alone is Keramugl's; the struggle is plain to see. He cannot let go of the hand but his other hangs loosely at his side, clenching and unclenching in the heat of his anguish.

Sammy steps forward. Tudak steps back so that he may watch the action in which he is not allowed to partake. He watches.

Sammy, smiling his Sammy smile, takes Keramugl's free hand. But as he takes it, it clenches in a spasm of resistance so he must fight with it a little. Force his fingers, his older fingers, into that clenched, crunched-up bunch of fingers that is all that is left, at this awful moment in time, of beautiful, youthful Keramugl with his wondrous clean soul.

Sammy wrestles with Keramugl. He is not going to let go. He will hold on forever if that is what is required of him. He is filled with joy is Sammy, who is, in fact, created for this very purpose of wrestling with Keramugl's dark Keramugl at this very eternal point of time within the whole of creation, Alpha and Omega and all that, and for all time, within what we call God, those two held on to each other in this moment.

Keramugl's breathing calms down to normality, he opens his hand, he holds on to Sammy in a proper, grown-up way and he smiles his angelic Keramugl smile, the lower lip large and protruding somewhat. His Keramugl laugh bursts forth as such an explosion of heat in the hot day that Tudak feels a searing pain.

Does some rat come forward to screw it up?

No, not this time. This time it is not a small thing. Margaret is up there, above even Henry's house with its Mozart and Ming china about which she cares nothing. This is something that will happen in a right way. The only rat around is Jim and in respect of Keramugl, Sammy and Tudak at this moment, which will last forever, Jim does not exist.

And, Keramugl holds on to the hand of the body that was once that of Tarlie, because the stage directions have not specified how he should let go and because there is, as a little part of Keramugl's consciousness, an idea that it would be irreverent to let the hand drop against the side of Jim's vehicle with a thud.

So, fed up with watching, Tudak steps forward and takes the hand, detaches it from the other and holds on to Keramugl – hand in living hand. Has he done it in imitation of Sammy? Has he done it as a dog instinctively licks a hand that might feed it? Who knows but, and this is the great thing, he does it. Not only does he do it but also he holds on to Keramugl as if he might hold on forever. So Tudak holding Keramugl's hand who is holding Sammy's hand. And, therefore, it holds; there is no conscious decision by Tudak to let go as there was by Jim that day after the fire.

Tumbling through Tudak's Tudak-ness, which is beginning to take shape, are a cascade of ideas; less conscious and specific, more muddled and more difficult to hang on to than those that had troubled Keramugl only seconds before but ideas all the same: of being flogged in the Togulo Farm; of being both spoiled and mistreated by Jim; of lying on the burnt ground and watching Andrew-Alloy walk away; of being nothing to them and equally irrelevant to the likes of Bune and those others getting away from him and whom he nonetheless wanted to hold for reasons that were obscure to him; of watching Annu walk away, in the night; of watching Annu take this one away from him making him aware for the first time in his existence of a limitless space within him which he had, until that moment, assumed was filled with himself; an emptiness that had, through habit, driven him to a childish anger which had made him want to smash what he could not have, and which had made him destroy Annu and want him at the same time. And now the emptiness inside him was filling up with a pain that expanded from his stomach into his chest like a memory of something dear to him which had been lost. And the pain moved up into Tudak's chest as a real thing that threatened to burst into his head and overwhelm him as an emotion. This was a new thing to Tudak and he thought he was dying; only, in fact, he was crying for the first time so that he hung on to Keramugl's hand all the more because the hand, like the onion, would save him. It would, as was also predestined, save him for the time when he would pick up the body of the other boy and find it also worthy.

[][][][][]

They worked together to dispose of Tarlie's body. The idea of some kind of burial was a non-starter without the head. Tudak admitted to having it but expressed in mono-syllables a desire to hang on to it that could not be reasoned against. Eating the body was a distinct consideration because had this been done the head itself would have been saved as a sentimental memory, something to be preserved and placed on the metaphorical mantelpiece. The idea of ingesting Tarlie, using his nutrients and maintaining actual parts of him in their own tissues and shitting out the waste to fertilise the trees was attractive. Time counted against this however: apart from the eating itself, that must not be rushed and that should be part of a reverential meal followed by a riotous party, there was the work of butchering and cooking. It was a twenty-four hour job at best, not counting sending out the invitations.

Feeding to the crocs was, therefore, the best thing. In this way the body would be respectfully returned to the earth.

The decision having been made, therefore, Jim's vehicle is understood to be driving through Akaranda – although no one wanted to know what it was doing. It drove past the tank farm and out along the old coast road towards Lingalinga Plantation. Wanei, the caretaker, is well known to Sammy. He will cooperate, Sammy knows that.

Lingalinga is on the other side of Akaranda. A long way, almost as far as Cape Hereford, where the soil is not much good because of the raised coral reefs upon which the land is formed and because the volcanic dust rarely drifts in that direction. So there is not much interest from the agro-industrial . . . interests. Pockets of good alluvial stuff, all the same, for those who are interested in farming. A coconut palm and cattle sort of place, Andrew said later. He was right for once in his life.

The plantation is owned by Chan who bought it in the days when he was Jim's employer. Although, like Jim, Chan has moved up in the world – the company trade store, his store in town and his property investments down South – he hangs on to the place because at one time he thought he'd use it at weekends but he never does. Fact is, and with good reason, he's afraid: better to stay in his house in Akaranda secured by his own Togulo boys. One of the rooms in the dilapidated plantation house – a two-roomed wooden bungalow with wide sagging verandas and views of the sea – is occupied by the aforementioned Wanei.

With Chan's blessing, although she has nothing to be afraid of, Helen, the volunteer school teacher who will become significant later, visits Lingalinga every month or two, on a Saturday or if there is a public holiday. She travels out on her little motor-scooter which is very slow and which takes about three hours to arrive but that's part of the fun. She swims and walks, spends the night and returns the following morning after another swim. For a while she studied the bird-life but gave it up as a waste of time. I'd rather watch the sea and the sky. The sea fascinates her. Wanei fascinates her also. He has one eye and a wicked smile. He catches fish and cooks them for her and he sits at her feet ready to take advantage of the smallest sign; but she's a sensible girl and he is a good man for all that he sometimes eats people.

At the back of Lingalinga Plantation low limestone cliffs guard a plain which was once part of the sea-bed, exposed by a seismic shift not long ago. At their foot runs another lazy river, but shorter than the other one. It issues into a swamp more or less brackish and frequented by crocodiles famed for their gargantuan size even though no one has seen them since the seismic shift. Lingalinga is at the more sparsely populated end of Van Island thanks to the thinness of the soil, through which protrude the coral limestone rocks. Fishermen inclined to fish in the swamp are warned off by Wanei's stories of the gargantuan, man-eating crocodiles.

Wanei had taken Helen into the swamp a couple of times in his canoe so that she could see the birds. She had laughed at his stories about the crocodiles so he had laughed as well and he had been happy to catch her a fish which they'd cooked on the beach over a driftwood fire under the stars. He didn't ask her to pay, the pleasure of her company being sufficient for his needs. There was something about Helen that tamed Wanei and made him want to serve her. He'd watch her with his one eye and wonder, under the stars, why.

As a result of Wanei's magic, the swamp was sacred. A body dropped here is taken in minutes, he says, so long as you don't stop to watch.

Thus the men, now including Wanei – the grinning, white-teeth flashing, one-eyed, silent, knowing, humorous little bastard who could act the servile lackey in the days past when Chan'd bring his friends for drinking and gambling parties, and the charming, bossy servant to Helen in the days present when she comes to make him thoughtful – carry the body down a track through long grass and past pandanus palms. They reach a sort of beach that is more mud than sand but drier in this dry weather than it usually is. They deposit the body – even less human-looking now than it was and looking nothing like Tarlie. It is no more Tarlie for Keramugl than it is any old lump of meat for the crocs – and depart without ceremony in single file, Sammy leading and Wanei bringing up the rear. Wanei looks back, squinting his one eye. He grins and snaps his teeth. He'll be back later to check that the deed has been done, he tells them.

Thank you very much, Wanei, says Sammy. They wave goodbye and return to Akaranda. Keramugl is oppressed by the wide straight road between the oil palms, the mill chimneys dribbling smoke into a flat, heavy sky. He would rather have stayed at Lingalinga with Wanei and wonders why he didn't. Weno is one of the answers he gets and thinking of Weno he thinks of Margaret and he is happy. Sammy drops Keramugl off before he reports back to Jim that the dirty job has been done. He thinks of the day when he will have saved enough money to settle on a little farm somewhere. Then he'll walk out on Jim without warning even if it means losing a month's wages. He'll leave the keys in the vehicle and he'll walk down the road whistling on what will be the happiest day of his life. He thinks he might go back to Lingalinga and do something with Wanei.

Tudak jumps out of the back of the vehicle as lightly as usual landing on the ground as if it is sprung. The moment he is on the ground, Rabis and Pen join him. Thus he feels once more the burden he cannot shake off and does not understand. He feels for a cigarette and immediately, on cue, the despicable Rabis, or possibly the odious Pen, supplies one as the other lights it. But Tudak is watching Keramugl walk into the distance. He wants to follow. It is remarkable; he'd serve the young man, Keramugl, given the chance. He starts off but as he does so a familiar command stops him: "Oi, boys, I got a job for you."

27
Neki's Story

The hills above Akaranda Town have shown the impact of agricultural activity since the time of the Akaranda coconut plantation which was established during the copra boom at the end of the nineteenth century by a Russian who arrived on Van Island via Siberia, China and the Philippine Islands.

Wanei claims descent from the Russian, along with all the others who claim part of the rent paid for the land upon which the government has built the new town, but Wanei is lying. He has descent, through three or four generations, from an English missionary who did substantial, albeit well-meant, damage to the people of Van Island about the same time as the Russian was planting other alien ideas. Wanei explains his family history to Helen as they sit on the beach beneath the stars eating a fish he has caught and cooked. His one-sixteenth of European blood, he says, explains his special understanding of the white man's devious ways. His one eye winks.

The labourers were, in the days of Wanei's great-grandfather, brought in from neighbouring islands. These lost souls indentured themselves for a period effectively forever, and when they had finished with or were finished off by the plantation below, they settled in the hills above.

The aboriginal forest was pushed back up and into the higher mountains hanging on to the steeper slopes and within the deeper ravines. It was replaced by a patchwork of fields, small plantations and fruit trees around the simple houses. A pleasant human landscape to look at and in which to walk, although it had, within its process of coming into being, enabled an increased amount of soil to be washed out to sea during the wet season. Some of this washed-out soil enriched the Lingalinga swamp.

The establishment of the Togulo Farm Penal Colony pushed the forest further back but otherwise it settled well into the landscape. The colony's rules were rigid but not excessive. It was a self-sufficient farm, the inmates its units of production as well as its beneficiaries. The only income it received from the government was the salaries of a supervisor and his staff of three, a clerk and two guards, one of whom was the supervisor's father-in-law. The odds and sods who were the colonists worked hard but willingly because the work balanced lives otherwise unbalanced; in the process they developed a sense of self-worth. There was no overriding wish to escape and in any event there were only two directions in which to go: up into the mountains to live or to die like an animal or down into the town where their red lap-lap ensured immediate arrest, a return to the farm and an affectionate flogging.

No need, therefore, for man-proof wire, only a traditional ditch and a low palisade to stop the local pigs from damaging the crops. One could enter or leave the farm at any point but there was, nonetheless, a symbolic gate: a primitive boom-gate affair operated by a prisoner who sat in a little thatched shelter beside it and who could have walked out at any time. From his vantage he had a view of the sea and the sky above trees. Akaranda town did not exist.

[][][][][]

Robert, the guard, was a half-decent bloke who had, all the same and quite early on in his life, got into the habit of being drunk and, in that state, beating his wife. One day he drank too much and beat her to death. He turned himself in immediately, at his trial he pleaded guilty and such was his good behaviour that he was allowed to stay on Van rather than being sent to Port Markham as a capital offender. For eight years he had been an exemplary prisoner. He did not miss his drinking and he went to church regularly. He would die in the colony; he was about the same age as Joseph when he saw him for the first time, walking up the hill towards the gate.

Can I come in?

Why?

Because Jim has sent me here.

Sufficient reason? Who, in any event, is this Jim?

The boss of the Van Island Palm Oil Development Company.

In that case you had better come in and get in fast. You can explain things to the boss yourself.

Thus Robert opens the boom-gate and allows Joseph to perform the formality of entering the Togulo Farm Penal Colony. Vagrants, lost souls and others who are not so well established in the world have similarly requested entry, which has sometimes been given: those without a bona fide criminal record and who do not, therefore, come up to scratch, can give a place like this a bad name. Robert watches Joseph walk up the track. He scratches his head: this man does not look like the usual type.

[][][][][]

Joseph walks up the hill, finally waking up the boss, known as The Supervisor, who sits in another grass shelter masquerading as an office, beside a flag-pole. The Supervisor is an easy-going fellow who runs the place through trusted inmates. So long as the rules are followed he does not make a fuss. Lassitude can be a virtue but his ignorance is so wilful that he barely exists beyond his symbolic authority for which, if tested, he would, nonetheless, kill or at any rate get a trusted inmate to kill on his behalf. This type of soft man is inevitably eclipsed by a large, interfering sort of wife who is so sure of her deserts in this life that she is bound to be disappointed, mortified even, by those she will receive in the next.

The Supervisor shifts himself no further than he needs to shift. He listens to Joseph's story from under hooded eyes and understands the situation well enough although the thought of the strapping Joseph swinging for something he didn't do amuses him. Amuses him a little, but he fears Jim. Did he not hand

353

over Tudak to Jim upon demand? Glad to have got rid of him but the prime reason was that he can refuse Jim nothing.

In the end he is indifferent to Joseph whom he happily hands over to the appropriate trusty for registration – name written in book against date of entry Joseph's mark made beside it – and for assignment to a work gang, which defines a patch of earth floor upon which to sleep. Joseph's own lap-lap is removed: he'll never see that again. In return he is given the regulation red replacement in order to mark him out as one of the scum of the earth. In addition he is given an aluminium spoon – wonderfully manufactured on site from scrap – and a small plastic bowl. These three things are all he will own for the duration of his stay and for some of the inmates are all they ever have owned and all they ever will own in their entire lives.

Inevitably, and quickly, Joseph is adored by everyone. He is soon in charge of the best-fed and the most efficiently working gang of men. The gang to which all aspire to belong. Jim leaves him alone. Out of sight out of mind? Not so: the troubles continuing, Jim assumes Annu is at large. 'E must 'ave escaped, but I'll get 'im in my own time. Of The Supervisor he says I'll deal with that fucker later–.

□□□□□

From his father's house, Neki watched the regular passage of men following their impossible dreams and determined to follow his own. He dreamed, however, not of the saltwater and of the possession of cargo; he dreamed of Annu. He would recognise Annu when he found him again.

He was, in any event, the type who intensely wanted to follow the track to see where it led. So it was that one day he followed a group of men going down to the coast. The recruiting agent taking this particular group had only a small amount compassion. He signed Neki on, despite his youth, thinking only of the money he would get.

Thus was Neki swept up into the world of men. He would have to sink or swim. He was not the best swimmer but he was the type whom it would be difficult to drown.

That boy's gone!

I knew he would.

One day.

There's no point in stopping him.

But he's a good boy. I'll miss him.

Therefore, Neki travelled to Karandawa and thence to the coast. He was swept up in the mass of what is called humanity. He has learned, as quickly as did Keramugl, that to be a man in the world is to be nothing.

Even less a man of the world than Keramugl was Neki at this stage of the journey: no apprenticeship on the benign Narangburn Plantation. He was a child-boy and looked it, but no allowances were made for that. His journey was to be started without a hand to hold and without an Annu. Neki's only-ness and his requirement for self-sufficiency was the significant fact of the journey. It toughened him into a little fellow who had the capacity to survive, who could scrap and fight if necessary and who would not be put down as rubbish. Bruised and bleeding, the essential Neki would not be beaten to death. But he was a child to start with, having no practice of devious calculation. Therefore, despite everything that happened he lost not the capacity to take the hand; the desire for Annu survived intact for all that it was covered in grime.

⬜⬜⬜⬜⬜

At Port Markham they were loaded onto the ship that would take them to Van Island. A two-day journey across a stormy sea. Many had been sick at the very sight and smell of the salt water. Not so Neki. He was tough by now, surprised, shocked, astonished at nothing. Not bravado but because this was, after all, the world. Life was a weary journey through an incomprehensible deluge of people, commands, visions of things that could not be explained, pushed here, shoved there and somehow getting fed from time to time, finding a place in which to shit, falling asleep with others and waiting around for something to happen.

So this was the sea was it? Well it was like the sky inasmuch as it was a limitless thing that was there but at the same time defying any definition and holding of it. Despite being water, it could not be drunk, and, unlike the water that cascaded down the mountain behind his home back there, it was hard, threatening stuff.

In the sea, coming out of and undoubtedly part of it, were the ships. Small out there and interesting but bigger than any object could be up close. Not big like the mountain is big, part of the limitless bigness of the earth, of which Neki is also a part so that he cannot separate the mountain from himself but big, as something separate from himself, seeming to have the possibility of falling down and crushing him.

Neki might have been frightened but there was no point. He had nightmares, all the same: he dreamed of a ship growing bigger and bigger, way beyond his ever being able to understand its bigness. He woke with a scream or a whimper: shut up and sometimes he received a cuff. So this is what life is like amongst men. He didn't complain.

⬜⬜⬜⬜⬜

By not being scrapped years ago, the ship that carries them breaks all regulations. Anyone who might care doesn't know what to do about it and, in any event, wouldn't want to . . . rock the boat. The sort of tub into which cattle have been herded, a good number failing to survive the experience. We won't do that again it has been said time without reckoning. Sheep next time, they don't break their legs when they fall over. Men are best because they can look after themselves and sometimes manage to puke overboard rather than onboard. It is one of those ships which could have been a car ferry in one of those places which has cars and people rich enough – and apparently stupid enough – to want to take them from one side of a body of water to another. It is a rusty old can having a few cabins and some public rooms taken up by the few paying passengers, one or two of whom, a couple of nuns perhaps, wonder about that lump of male humanity down there below: it doesn't do to think too much but we'll remember them in our prayers for ourselves. They forget.

The lump of male humanity, unwashed, smelling bad, is herded into the part which used to take the cars: the hold. It is not packed so tight that there isn't an air of spaciousness in the heaving, gloomy cavern. An area is roped off for eating and there are very basic ablution facilities that will do if the trip does not last for more than forty-eight hours although it has to be said that some of these men, some of the best of them, have not used those sorts of shit buckets ever before.

No children or women allowed but they ignore the boys. What would we do with them if we stopped them? They've got this far and we don't want them stuck here in Port Markham, so Neki gets on board.

He goes along with the herd and hangs on to the little gang of other hopeful suckers to which he attached himself back home. The recruiting agent won't lose sight of him because he's worth money. That is, until he remembers the boy has no hair under his arms. He might catch it. Better to forget him, so Neki is forgotten.

The men who do the cooking and who more or less keep order have done this sort of thing before and know what they are about. Their boss is a man who might be Chinese. He might not be but he has that air of being ancient although his years are not so advanced. He has seen it all and done a lot of it by going along with the others; he has detached himself from what might have been his better nature; and he has corrupted himself in the process. No one ever offered him a hand so he has managed without. He wouldn't know what to do if it was offered, and certainly has no more idea about putting out his own hand. He has lost himself. Not totally beyond redemption as it happens but he'd need some help and his attitude is not welcoming. He's waiting for the last bus you could say, and has, very likely, missed it. You'd think he was indifferent to everyone around him but he sees Neki.

You can help me.

Neki does not understand the words but he is aware of the indication. Thus, and as had become his habit since he was taken up by the now studiously indifferent recruiting agent, he goes along with it. The intention, the command, after all, proves his existence, and it ensures he will be fed – a significant consideration.

Neki follows the man who already, by his intention to have Neki, has attracted the boy, who wants an interest of some sort to stand between him and the incomprehensible world beyond. This man is it and already, in a matter of moments, the two have formed a relationship where the man will whistle and the dog will come.

The man needs a name. We can call him, we can call him, we can call him Glory. Believe it or not, that is his name and how he came by it is a mystery to the story of Neki. Glory, in his larger sense, having dimensions beyond the immediate facts of their relationship during the voyage, will remain a mystery to Neki for all his life. Older and a lot wiser Neki understands Glory as the instrument that brought him to Annu. Hence the memory of the name. A man must have a name in order to be, thus in his compassionate memory, Neki remembers Glory. An immortality of sorts.

Incidentally, with no philanthropic motive, Glory, in his turn, adds to the Neki-ness of Neki. Needing help, he teaches Neki to cook for the lump of humanity, if you can call it that, out there beyond the portion of the hold where food is cooked. He is a rough teacher. There is no time for niceties: it's this is what you do and if you don't get it I'll tell you once more and after that I'll thrash you 'til you get it and if you still don't get it I'll throw you overboard. Neki believed what Glory told him and learned fast.

Neki became the cook-boy in an environment of indifference and necessity. Glory thought no more of him, at the beginning, than as a boy who helped him do the work. There was not an ounce of affection or concern for Neki. Glory got no pleasure in having the boy around him as, for instance, a Grin would get from a Gris Manki. Glory had not lived his life: he had survived it and if he held anything dear to himself it was the fact of his survival against the odds in a world that would, given half a chance, exterminate him without a second thought. Neki was part of that world. Thus a hand-in-hand connection was an impossibility. Had Glory thought it out – which he didn't – he would have said I need this boy to help me survive and I resent the fact that he should get anything out of it. He envied the help he might give the boy and therefore he disliked him and wanted him and wanted to maintain control over him all at the same time. An unhealthy relationship which Neki took to be the norm.

Feeding the lump of humanity was the same as Glory's need for Neki. It was something that had to be done, or rather, that could not be avoided. There were various minimum essential tasks that had to be performed in order to convert the basic raw materials into edible stuff. Jim would have said, if they had asked him for food, or for more food: Why do you want it? You only turn it into shit. At the bar he would have explained to Andrew that you feed the labourers in order to keep 'em quiet and in order to supply the necessary energy required to do the desired work. A nice turn of phrase, Jim would have thought, smirking and turning to receive the applause from his acolytes he's a character that Jim, our Beloved Boss. For what am I, if he is nothing? Perish the thought. And it does.

But Jim, says Henry, eating is a communion; it brings men together and makes the community. The relish is as important as the substance to a man's soul. But that was years ago when Henry saw himself as the upholder of, of something finer. I am, at any rate, above the cockroach. Don't be too sure.

The shipping company had the same idea as Jim only the focus was on keeping the lump quiet and keeping the costs down. In forty-eight hours on the sea – sixty if there's bad weather – you don't need to waste money on vitamins and essential nutrients and all that nonsense. Fill their bellies so's they sleep is the rule. Thus, boiled sweet potato with salt, sweetened tea with powdered milk and, for variety, once a day, rice boiled to a porridge and made tasty with monosodium glutamate. Many of the men, most of them, had known neither tea nor rice until their arrival in Karandawa. Monosodium glutamate is addictive. You feed it to puppies in pet shops to make them sleep.

Neki got the hang of it quickly. Within twenty-four hours he was as good a cook-boy as Glory expected him to be. He was well fed himself and he was too tired to appreciate the night-time attention he got from Glory who understood Neki in this respect as he understood his blanket; something that passed your way, through the workings of the world, and which, therefore, you used as you wanted. It was, after all, yours and your ownership of it proved your existence.

[][][][][]

The idea of fucking Neki did not occur to Glory but only because within the forty-eight hours' travelling time the easy opportunity would not arise and he was too tired by the time he got to bed, falling asleep with Neki in his arms – as a sort of bolster – before he got around to doing anything. They slept – and here Neki already considered himself to be fortunate in the world he was learning to know – in a cabin approached by a short flight of stairs running from the area of the hold designated the kitchen. It was a space that had grown, as an internal cancerous growth, out of the decrepit rustiness of the ship. It contained a pair of bunks and a foul foam-rubber mattress upon the floor. The staff of the hold – rough cattlemen – slept here. One man to a bed was a waste of useful space so that Neki slept beside Glory as a matter of form. A couple or three skinny forms with naked, dirty legs, shared the mattress most nights. This was the world, so that if the right convenient circumstances prevailed, Neki would be used as desired.

What went on inside that cabin sometimes was what Matron, Miss J, had recoiled against, at any rate boys being boys in times of stress, and distress. Andrew and Nwufoh at some point earlier in history. Nothing wrong amongst boys playing or amongst consenting adults. Neki was neither consenting nor adult. Glory was no boyish playmate.

It would not have happened had the voyage to Van Island been for the usual forty-eight hours. However, rough weather ensured that anchor was dropped for another twenty-four hours beside a small island, not much more than a rock, used for just that purpose since the days of Wanei's great-grandfather.

Thus time on their hands. No one allowed on shore but open the hatches to let in some air and fortunately it's cloudy so it won't be like an oven in there some of them are already sick but there's nothing we can do until we reach Akaranda.

Thus time on their hands because only enough food for one extra meal but plenty of tea to keep them happy. So that night in the little cabin they are not so tired. There's four or five of them, plus Neki, squatting on the floor around the kero lamp against which insects bat. Shadows are thrown grotesquely up into the larger shadows above. The light is sickly as if it will not do but for that night it does.

Glory has a bottle of grog, cheap stuff of which nightmares are made and the morning after like hell. There is a snug, contentment of sorts in that space filled with unsatisfactory light and the shadows of the four or five men plus Neki. From where Joseph or Robert might be looking the ship is barely a pin-prick of light in the roaring universe. Remarkably insignificant. The rough weather has passed, as it happens, but the ship cannot approach Akaranda port until daylight.

"Have some."

358

Neki takes a sip, splutters and chokes, as they knew he would so ready for it they laugh at the boy who smirks back. Neki is not some downcast little chap, pressed down by the world, as the child Andrew would have been in the circumstances. He is not a sulking, scowling little monster, turned away from the world he hates and wanting to fight it at the same time, like Alloy. Neki presents a tough face to the world learned from the men around him. He'll join in to survive. If the prevailing company expects love and affection he'll give it, if it expects bestiality, he'll go along with the best of them because he wants, as Henry always did, and at this stage of his ignorance of the better things, to be one of them. The child Neki, that is: the man who will emerge, given a chance, has an idea of Annu to whom in the end he will run. Thank God for that innocent instinct, for despite Glory, Neki is incorruptible.

"Have some."

They feed him with the drink and he acts it up for them. The choking is an act now as the bottle is passed around. The four or five of them, plus Neki, drink more and are affected by the rough alcohol, Glory no less than the others for all that he has been through it a thousand times before and buys the stuff himself, shares it because, because he cannot drink on his own. The creation of the brotherhood of drinkers is the thing. In the club, around the bar, around the café table, it's all the same illusion of love and friendship when boys will be boys and it's forgotten in the morning. Best forgotten too, those acts of bestiality, brutal and fatal like the knife stuck in the girl that time. One could say that she merely got in the way of boys being boys.

One of the men, the one with the skinny dirty legs, is screaming with laughter at the sight of Neki's drunkenness which has become real. The boy is lost to himself. The skinny man wants to push it to the end to see what will happen. He can't stop himself he's the type'd hold a kitten under the water for the sake of it but it's himself he's holding, he'll push himself over the edge one day – the liver can only take so much. He smells of rotten meat and when he laughs his breath is foul, the gums around the loose teeth brilliantly red. Go on, go on is his motto.

They go on. Neki is their pet. Glory watches with pride: the boy belongs to me. If anyone is going to have him I am going to have him. When I've finished I'll throw him to you.

They drink to the dregs. The skinny one has gone out to look for something else. He comes back defeated and sulky. They are sleepy now but ready, all the same, for something else to prove their existence in the universe. They need to relieve themselves. Most men will shout at the world, grinning back at their mates over their shoulders, boys being boys. Some men will fight, some will shit where it will offend, others like to piss and show off their dicks in the same way. These querulous men, small within themselves, so small that it hurts them, must do something to prove they exist and are of significance in the roaring universe. Fighting's the best thing, fighting as sex. Stab a man or fuck him, it's all the same. My power and possession of you is the thing. Glory feels proud that he owns Neki. The skinny man has no desire in that way – fact is he can't do it and would indeed have to resort to the knife or the gun to prove his power. But he'll push the others and smirk and giggle as he watches.

Not enough light to fill the room. Shadows squeeze it into odd and unfamiliar shapes. Nothing is defined. Only bits and pieces of things, felt and wondered at and repulsive inside a dirty old sack. You bump into things, hearing only the filthy sounds of water contaminated by its contact with the side of the filthy rust bucket of a ship; the grunts and groans of men, belches and farts, the scratching of dry, flaky skin, flea-infested clothing and lice-afflicted hair. Apparently, human flesh may become so filthy that the body rejects it: the skin drops off and with it the dirt, whole patches of hair but pimples, boils and ulcers encrust so that the puss beneath must find a way out elsewhere, hence, perhaps, the dead-meat smell.

Neki is asleep, drugged by the unfamiliar alcohol. He is slumped on the floor. The ship heaves, an empty bottle rolls across the floor hitting metal, rocking to and fro. A smell of something rotten fills the dark air. Someone had pissed into the empty bottle and the stuff has spilt across the metal floor: a pleasant smell compared to the smell of rotten meat. Glory, possessive, picks up Neki – so light this weighty boy, you'd think there was nothing inside the ragged clothes – and places him on the lower bunk. Lovingly it seems but it is only that he doesn't want to wake the child. The skinny man is sitting in his own urine, too drunk to know what's going on but he wants it to go on all the same. The others watch with apparent indifference but they are also interested and will take whatever opportunities arise. They will pick over the rags. So there is a conspiracy of shared will to do something to this boy if Glory starts it and therefore makes it OK. Drink makes them forget their stomachs.

The boy is fresh meat. In the shadows some of his clothes are removed. Good thing he is drugged if you want to call any of this good. A nice clean murder would be better. The decapitation of Tarlie by the hands of Tudak is better than this. This degradation expressed as grunts and violence. Glory feels but he feels only the power of possession while the others watch waiting their turn or masturbating. This is how you survive Neki and get your free meal. There is no pity in the world for those who cannot afford it. There is only hatred for you who have caused the shame that will come when they persuade themselves you asked for it as they slit your throat or merely toss your drugged body over the side for the sharks. These things happen. Neki will not be missed, down here. He does not exist beyond his village where they say he was a good boy, assuming he is at large somewhere out there in the world. He was a good boy.

Neki has been put onto the bed – the filthy mattress – with gentle hands, the first apparent affection he has experienced for a while and surely better than no attention at all. He is handled as if he exists, too sleepy to resist the removal of his shorts. But the pain is searing. He screams a childish scream and as he does so they rush him. Beat him, smother him, work fast to get what they want. Hate him, think it better that he is out of the way, think he asked for it. It's a fight to the death. One flies out of the room in fear of that scream: the boy awoke in his sleep. A nightmare he says and he cowers in the corner afraid for himself and beyond shame.

The bits and pieces mean nothing in the night: merely fragments of bodies and sounds and ideas. Put together they remain meaningless; in the daylight they are gone altogether, these actions of the night: Nalin's daughter, Tarlie, Keramugl who missed it by a whisker and now Neki. A sigh of relief in the morning. No one knows except Margaret who says nothing, judges not, condemns not, saves not. But her knowledge is a terrible thing that shakes the universe.

[][][][][]

But Neki has savvy. The savvy that made the little boy follow Annu in the first place. The savvy that made him leave his village and go into the world. The savvy that carried him onto the balus and onto this ship towards Van Island. It's going to get him out of this too. The lower bunk is only just above the floor. The bottle rolls towards the bunk and taps at the metal. The arm of the half-conscious Neki hangs over the edge of the bed. It meets the bottle, one of those tough bottles in which soft drinks are sold and that can be returned for money. It is made to last and it'll crack open a skull, which is what it does.

Blood oozes from Glory's head. Darkness and a deathly silence.

What is left of the others creeps away, the skinny man scuttles back into his rusty crevice, Glory lies in blood and Neki lies in his own pain manifested by his anal blood that mixes with Glory's blood on the filthy mat in the odious room into which a grey daylight enters. The captain, a half-decent last-chance fellow is appalled. He throws up and assumes the foulest of murders. In the end it is Glory who gets tossed overboard.

[][][][][]

Neki was brought to the Togulo Farm in the late afternoon, a mess, filthy, wounded, limping and lost. He moved as if – we see it in captured soldiers, refugees, bereaved wives, criminals stunned by the fact of the crime they never thought they would commit – as if detached not only from the world in which he once lived but also from himself. The blank expression, the stumbling gait. Shoved around by others: that way, that way, go in there, sit there, there, stand up, stand up while we take the mug shot. A zombie was the once lively Neki who had followed Annu in the bright optimistic morning of his life, no longer the innocent child but a vicious animal better to snuff it out now. Put it in a sack and drown it, shoot it and put it in the back of Jim's truck with the others, bash out its brains and throw it into the rubbish pit with all the other thousands of Nekis so we can forget about them.

The Supervisor takes one look at Neki and decides he can't be bothered. If he had to take account of every bit of rubbish then I'd never get anything done.

Thus, as the incidental right thing, Neki is given over to Joseph's gang. Along with Neki come the aluminium spoon, the plastic bowl and a neatly folded piece of red cloth. The latter is not to be worn as a lap-lap until the boy is washed. He is naked now but it is not a bad start for one who has been stigmatised.

The inside of the little hut in which Joseph's gang sleep is as snug and as pleasant as men who have nothing can make it. For a start, under Joseph's

361

direction, a low sleeping platform has been built that allows the men to sleep up off the earth floor. It is made out of the same grass mats as are the walls of the house itself. A strong grass, not unlike bamboo, that is flattened and then woven. The roof has been newly thatched, a primitive door has been made and the place is swept clean each morning. Colourful crotons have been planted around the house to stop the dogs pissing on the walls and define the footpath to the door. It is home to the homeless men and to this place the wounded Neki is brought. It is night and the men are sitting inside the house in a circle around a little fire against the night chill up there in the hills.

Neki is taken in without comment by men who are themselves outcasts. Little to give, they give, all the same. They will make room for him on the sleeping platform, they will share their food with him and they will take him out to work with them and teach him, silently, what it is they do. No pity or judgement, merely acceptance. Neki is their fate as much as they are his.

Neki watches them eat. They chat amongst themselves, offering bits of food to him but not pressing him, tempting him until the right bit comes along and is taken.

Joseph does not detach himself from the group at first. He it is, however, who goes to Neki as they think of sleeping. He has been watching Neki as he watched Andrew that night, as he polished another glass. He takes Neki out to wash him, he does not make a fuss and such is his gentle assurance, his firm but disinterested affection that Neki responds, allowing himself to be washed and, in a little time, he helps with the process. When Joseph understands the wound he merely gets on with the job holding Neki a little more strongly and it is in that moment of strength that Neki finds his Annu, his spirit returns as a soft transition from dislocation and separateness to oneness with himself. The transition is, as it happens, enough to shake the universe but it is a quiet thing of which only Joseph and Neki are aware. Neki's wonderful knowledge of Annu cancels out Joseph's painful knowledge of Neki's wound so that the universe is brought back into balance once more. It does indeed shake for those who can feel such things.

Neki sleeps beside Joseph and is comforted by his breathing.

[][][][][]

Neki is accepted for what he is and he is, now, a mute. The fact is an accepted part of his Neki-ness. From here on, communication with Neki is by all the ways of communication other than speech. He becomes known for his soundless laugh.

A fact of life on the Togulo Farm is that if you get on with your work, keep your nose clean and mind your own business, things generally do not catch up with you. No one adds up to very much beyond a name in the register, which is as likely not to be your name as it is. You are no one and one of the new people at the same time. Joseph was no exception to the rule but there nonetheless developed in the consciousness of those who lived and worked with him, including The Supervisor, a barely considered and certainly not articulated consensus that for whatever the reason Joseph was up there it was not because he went around cutting off people's heads. It stood to reason. It even crossed The Supervisor's mind that Joseph was being got out of the way for some reason but what could he do about it? Nothing. Justice, or whatever it was, was nothing to do with him. Anyway, another idea that was getting around – an unsettling idea that did not quite make sense – was that Joseph was the fellow Annu, the one who was supposed to have had his head cut off not the one who'd done it. This idea was articulated albeit not hotly debated, least of all amongst the men who made up Joseph's work gang although after he'd gone they missed him as a pain not dissimilar to that which Tudak was experiencing about the same time. A little later, time having done its healing work, they not only articulated the idea but also hotly debated it, insisting that they had known all along that Joseph was Annu and that it stood to reason he'd cut off his own head and resurrected himself especially for them. A year or two later when some of them had got to Lingalinga, the idea was confirmed in the most astonishing and . . . reasonable way. As for Neki being a murderer it also stood to reason he could tell you a thing or two if only he could speak but he chose not to and that was his decision and we respect him for it. The idea was beyond the realms of any sort of reason. If you suggested it even The Supervisor would laugh in your face along the lines of that dim-witted kid with the limp wouldn't have it in him and why they dumped him here I don't know but if he keeps his nose clean I'm not complaining and if he ups and runs I wouldn't stop him either. The idea even crossed his mind, at one stage, that if no one made any objections he could get Neki a job in Chan's store but in the end he didn't do anything about it. In the event Neki clung to Joseph as a sort of servant as if it had been the purpose for which he was born. It was in the nature of Joseph not to mind the boy sticking to him like a limpet but he did not encourage Neki with too much affection because the time was coming when he would not be there. It was likely to come before Neki could learn, as Keramugl had done, that the Annu he sought was within himself.

[][][][][]

In time, with Joseph being Joseph up there on the Togulo Farm, the shit, one could say, piling up down there below, began to obscure the view. The unrest down there was such that The Supervisor thought that he might have to get off his fat arse and do something. Had he thought about it . . . thoughtfully . . . he need not have worried but he did worry and the worry made his heart beat a little faster and made him feel hot so that he wanted to remove his shirt and sit in his vest only the idea of himself as The Supervisor of the Togulo Farm, Penal Colony, Van Island, did not allow him to do it. He worried that the colonists, taking heart from what was happening down there, might want to stage a mass break-out up here. He could not stop them downing tools and walking off if they wanted. The small police force in town could do nothing because it was, by and large, out of town dealing with, or rather failing to deal with, the so-called troubles elsewhere. He would therefore be left supervising a penal colony with no colonists, an idea which caused little bubbles of sweat to form on his shiny forehead. He would be left alone with his large wife, his ancient uniformed

363

father-in-law and the other two who could stand to attention, shout Yesa with the best of them and go through all the motions that one would expect of smart prison officers except doing what was required to maintain the incarceration of its inmates.

The ground beneath The Supervisor shook. The bubbles of sweat grew larger.

He called Joseph to his office, the grass hut: "Um . . . Joseph," he said.

"Yes, Sir?" replied Joseph to whom was attached Neki.

Oh God help me, I am lost. I don't know what to do. If the men up here run away then not only shall I look a fool but also my reason for being will be shattered. Without the prisoners inside the Togulo Farm, I shall be nothing.

The idea of nothingness overwhelms The Supervisor, the bubbles burst as little threads of sweat running into his eyes and down the sides of his nose. You'd think he was crying only he isn't. He wipes his mouth: "Um . . . Joseph," he repeats.

"Won't you sit down?" But there is only one chair so Joseph sits on the ground. The Supervisor would like to join him but thinks better of it. Awkward, all the same, to have to look down onto the top of the head of the one whom, as it happens, you are inclined to regard as your saviour and before whom you would like to prostrate yourself and beg for, beg for, beg for something only you don't know what it is for which you want to beg.

"Um . . . Joseph?" The man is in an agony of wanting to maintain his idea of himself and simultaneously realising it does not add up to very much so that there is nothing much worth maintaining.

"Yes Sir," says Joseph at last, "what is it you want?" He pulls Neki to sit down beside him and pushes him away a little.

The Supervisor is disconcerted by the presence of the dumb boy but then mollified by the way Joseph handles him. He sees that Joseph handles people in a good way. I want you to save me. "I want you to talk to the men," he says, "they'll listen to you." They won't listen to me more likely laugh in my face.

"I cannot do your work," says Joseph. "Only you can do that."

The Supervisor is not used to being thrown back upon his own resources. He looks back at Joseph open-mouthed. He is desperate.

Joseph smiles at him: "But you have nothing to worry about." You know you don't, if only you'd think about it.

"I don't?" The Supervisor cannot work it out but he is, nonetheless, relieved that Joseph has an answer which, as he considers it later, must be the right one.

"Do you think," Joseph continues, "that with all the trouble down there the people up here will want to join it?"

"I don't know. Tell me what I should do."

"Do nothing."

"Nothing?"

"It is enough. You'll see. It's been enough so far." Joseph laughs and nudges Neki.

So The Supervisor is profoundly grateful: "Thank you," he says as he watches Joseph leave with Neki. Phew, that was a close one. I was nearly done for. I don't know if it was Annu or not but he saved me that day.

􏰀􏰀􏰀􏰀􏰀

The Supervisor watches Joseph and Neki walk down the track towards the boom-gate, operated, as if by some prior ordination, by Robert who releases the rope, allowing the boom to rise. Ceremoniously, therefore, Joseph and Neki walk out into the world.

"Goodbye Robert."

"Goodbye." He watches them out of sight amongst the trees that crowd the road. Only after he has lost sight of them does he think he might have done the wrong thing. Who am I to do such things he thinks, worried a little because he does not want to get flogged although later, when the danger has passed, he has an idea of himself being flogged for Annu. I would have gone through hell for him – and tested, he might have. "I saw Annu, I tell you," he told me later.

28
Tudak Sees

Tudak: Jim's Man. Tudak the man indeed he became. Love made him that.

[][][][][]

I love You.
Who are You?
He whispers. To the dead body in his arms? To the empty space in which he is stranded?
Who are You?
And receiving no reply, comes the idea: Who am I?
Tudak becomes aware of himself and therefore aware of his loneliness.
The small idea drifts around, as ripples of dust on the dry floor of the market place.
Awareness is painful. His body responds with exhaustion and his head hurts. Before, pain had been something separate from him. He could, as it were, step back and look at it, detached and contemptuous of it. Easy, therefore, to inflict pain upon others. Now that his pain is an essential part of himself, he understands it. Tudak-ness has begun, creating, to start with, anguish.
I love you. Thus, Tudak holds the body, still warm, as if there might yet be life in it. I love you. But he knows, with pain, that he is alone.
Tudak looks into the sky bright with a blinding brightness, the light reflected and reflected through the dust that obscures the sun. The light stabs his eyes suddenly and painfully. He smells the burning of corrupted flesh, tastes the foul ash on his tongue. He hears the drifting of dust upon the boundless space in which he is lost.
Tudak is blind.
Testing again the weight in his arms, it is as light as a feather. The sense of loss makes him afraid. Fear of darkness and of the unknown is another new thing. His body is taken from him and shaken.
Light as a feather nonetheless the body is a burden. His back and shoulders ache. He sinks to his knees in the dust that drifts around him, in the dark, holding the body of the beloved.
He stretches back his neck and he opens his eyes wide but the density of the blackness he sees is terrifying in its reality. The warm hands of darkness caress Tudak finding every vulnerable spot until he is known intimately. These hands might strangle a better man but Tudak must suffer first. Not a glimmer of hope.
Thus Tudak holds the body as the only comfort he has. He might cry out but to whom would he cry? No one would hear Tudak the Horrible held down on the dry dusty floor of his life by a weight that is as light as a feather.

Tudak remembers.

[][][][][]

Annu, held by the crowd in its hand: its champion against Jim. Annu holding back the young man. Annu and the young man, hand in hand. The young man is a man in the making by his significance to Annu who holds his hand thereby speaking to him and the young man hears. The young man who is more crude and unfinished-looking in his earthy inelegance than is Tudak himself. The young man who would, were it not for the gentle restraint of Annu, leap forward in his youthful foolhardiness and kill Jim. Easy it would be in that time of madness, Jim too drunk to stand up and no love lost for him despite the bought loyalty of his bodyguards. His body. Worth guarding? Annu saved it by his gentleness. Made Tudak gentle also, who would otherwise have had to kill the young man. Reactive violence rather than intrinsic evil but an unnecessary waste of our Keramugl, all the same.

Tudak remembers.

[][][][][]

The same young man whom he had found on top of the hill as an incidental nuisance to be dealt with. But having stripped him naked, recognised him as the foolish innocent whose hand had been held by Annu. Only this time a little more finished by his nakedness. Tudak is, therefore, filled with the idea that he must get down on his knees and worship what he sees. But his trained response to overpower and to inflict pain as a proof of his own existence, confronts his desire to submit so that a hint of a frown appears on the otherwise perfectly flawless visage that had, heretofore, been Tudak's face.

At this time also, Tudak remembers, he had been momentarily blinded until he heard the voice of Annu: Stop. And, upon hearing the voice and upon feeling the eyes of Annu upon him, so had the conflict within him been temporarily subdued. Thus, he submits, laying his cheek upon the warm and smooth surface of the road, watching the giant figure of Annu lead the young man away, by the hand making the young man significant by the handling. Beautiful is the sight of Annu and Keramugl hand in hand. But painful also because I am left behind.

Tudak remembers and understanding the memory better, re-lives the pain of that time when he had wanted and wanted and wanted. Look upon me and make me significant, let me hear Your voice. And because he is yours, I want that young man whom you have made significant. For is he not a part of you in his significance?

But at that time, upon the hill, Tudak remained separate from himself. He knew not love or even the desire for love. His desire translated into an impulse to hold for himself that which he wanted and, therefore, to be sure of his ownership he must beat it, strangle it, stab it, better than lose it. Thus losing sight of Annu, Tudak is up again, ready for the fight.

[][][][][]

Now, crouching on the dusty floor in pain and darkness, Tudak begins to understand. His body shudders uncontrollably as the reasoning man, Tudak, begins to unite with the emotional animal, Tudak. Only let me hear Your voice, only let me feel Your eyes upon me. Take me by the hand so that I shall be with you forever. Be my light. Make me one.

Tudak remembers.

⬜⬜⬜⬜⬜

Embracing Annu in the night, on the ground that is warm and moist and giving and fragrant in its rotten way. Annu pliant in his arms, the body yet throbbing with life. And loving because Tarlie had not expected Annu to jump him like this, silently, powerfully holding him firmly and with such ardent love. Held so, Tarlie's surprise, his little fear, his beating, fluttering heart settles into the arms of Annu, happy beyond his imagining. Bliss, his last earthly thought: For this, my life was made: to serve Annu who is returned as promised.

Blind also was Tudak then, holding Annu whom he would hold for ever, calming the fretful animal in his arms. Had they not taught him how to do it up at the Togulo Farm? He was good at killing the big semi-wild cattle, settling them for the slaughter, his large hands caressing their flanks, his body leaning against their heaving sides until they were still, their eyes drooping with the pleasure of him. Then, quick as a flash, the sharp panga knife did its work, slicing through the great artery, and with each beat of the heart the life drained away towards a satisfying sleep. And yet still Tudak wants. He wants Annu. He hugs the body with his arms and legs, squeezing the life out of it drop by drop. To possess Annu this way must be the thing. But still it is not enough and blind in the night Tudak rearranges the body, laying it on its front and kneeling astride its back, clasping it tightly with his legs, riding it. He feels about the face, understanding its contours and the large mouth that would have once split it with Tarlie's ferocious grin. He pulls back the head and with the already-bloody panga knife hacks at the stretched neck until he has severed the spinal column and cut through the tough sinews. Aah! He is triumphant, tossing the knife over his shoulder and holding the head aloft with the one hand while with the other, bloody with the pure blood of Annu, pulling at his beautiful cock – pure polished ebony, curved – to ejaculate high into the night, the warm blood of Annu is mixed with the warm spunk of Tudak down on the grass, catching the moonlight for a second until it is lost in the night. For an ecstatic moment Tudak blacks out, coming to, to see only the dusty old yellow moon between the clouds. But he has the head of Annu. He will boil it and eat its parts. But still it is not enough. His proud cock deflates.

Again Tudak remembers.

⬜⬜⬜⬜⬜

The young man, sleeping peacefully inside the house behind which lies the decapitated body, now, in daylight, decomposing meat swelling in the heat around which the flies buzz. He has him now. Is this it? Will the young man's head be enough? My spunk mixed with his blood? Perhaps, but meanwhile I will watch over him to keep him from Jim, the idea of whom, I find, interferes with my thoughts and begins to make me angry. His head I do not want.

Tudak watches the sleeper. He is confounded by conflicting ideas again. His body reacts in ways hitherto unknown to him making him angry with something that might be Jim or else that might be himself. Action is required? It is supplied by the matter-of-fact arrival of Sammy driving Jim's vehicle.

Sammy, a fresh morning Sammy, is a relief as is also the waking up of the young man who is beautiful in his innocent awakening and who, upon seeing me watching him, expresses fear that is dissolved into relief by the matter-of-fact presence of Sammy and by the matter-of-fact message from Annu that Sammy imparts as if it is a piece of insignificant gossip tossed up by the wind rather than the momentous statement of fact: I am or, rather, He is.

The message is no less a relief to Tudak. It makes the events of the previous night indeed only a dream that is neither unforgivably bad nor, determinably good. Tudak is content to work, in a matter-of-fact way, with Sammy and with the young man to dispose of the black buzzing thing that is very ordinary have I not dealt with such things before but this is different this Annu which I thought I had killed but which I have, it seems, brought back to life is a mighty endless place that absorbs and absolves all my actions into itself.

They work together by joining hands. Tudak knows that as they deal with the body of Annu, it is the body of Annu no more because of Sammy's wonderful message that joins them together. His contentment grows as the work progresses. He is content with the way things are on that morning with Sammy and with the young man whose name he has yet to learn. He is content in the knowledge that Annu is alive. He has not felt this way before. Thus he does not need the head of Annu in order to have him or, indeed, the head of the young man who is brave in a matter-of-fact way so that he is willing to work with me, his brother. Brother! The joining together does it. Moving together as a solid, organic, real and, nonetheless, matter-of-fact thing not unlike the black buzzing itself. Wonderful and the heart of Tudak swells as his hand clasps the hand of Sammy who is also hand-in-hand with the young man whom Tudak no longer wants in a possessive way but whom he rather wishes to protect from the predations of one such as Jim.

Yes, and through Sammy, Tudak understands the struggle between the young man and himself that the young man innocently wins so that, in the end, they are together as willing partners hand-in-hand.

Therefore, Tudak hugs the other lump of meat that is also beginning to attract the buzzing. He regrets it is not able to respond to the pressure of his arms I love you.

⬜⬜⬜⬜⬜

I love you in the darkness that presses in on him. He fumbles for the lifeless hand. The unresponsive fingers will not take his intertwining own, warm with life. The contrasting cold lifelessness touches him with an unbearable pressure as a part of the hard darkness all around. Thus he is pressed around the lifeless thing in his arms that he might squeeze life into it and together with it begin again beyond the painful memories I love you.

But there is no response and the memories do indeed press down, all the more painful for his understanding of them. Watch me my Lord and make me significant in this terrifying universe in which I am no more than a speck of dust, if that, hold my hand as You held it before. Otherwise I am alone in the dark. I am less than a speck of dust in the dark that will take me into its dark self. I am, yet it is not enough. I am alone. I want You. I want You to talk to me, to watch me, to hold my hand, to make me not alone. I love you.

I love you he hears the memory of the words in the darkness that is thick with shame, with loneliness, with anguish and therefore with awareness. The awareness that has the potential to destroy the earthly Tudak, his elegance and his robust, polished beauty which, in any event, is worthless. But awareness cannot destroy the essential man. Broken down in the dust, less than a speck of dust, he is a pathetic sight in the dark. Jim would kick the man who is down, Keramugl would take his hand.

Thus there remains the essential man which becomes a palpable thing that is beautiful. Tudak's soul, one might say, is beginning to be written upon the blank space that was the old Tudak, Jim's Tudak. All the nonsense about his physical black beauty and his arrogant stopping of people up on the hill, and his cutting off of people's heads and feeding their bodies to the crocodiles and so on and so on, is just that: nonsense.

And fever takes over the body of Tudak who screws up his eyes like a child who hopes, therefore, it will stop. He hugs more tightly what is in his arms, the I love you. He presses himself so hard against the ground that he feels it pressing back hard against himself, knowing only the fear that has become a habit during all the million years or so he has been down on it. His body shivers, his eyes shut tight, his heart pumps as it has never pumped before as the old Tudak hopelessly resists the awareness of himself the essential Tudak. The strain on his heart is terrific as he shuts himself tighter and tighter against the fear that is new to him and thus overwhelming because, being a part of him of which he is more acutely aware by the second he cannot shut it out.

He is afraid.

Of what, for God's sake? Of nothing more than a perception of nothingness that is his old unaware self realised by his new Tudak self. Actually, wonderful. The cosmic seeming thing – too big for him – is, in reality, a purely physical thing: the straining of the body against itself. A big thing it seems to Tudak but from the outside he looks insignificant on the floor of the big expanse of the market place less expansive and wasted, nonetheless, than it was as night takes over. Rabis and Pen watch from inside the Landrover, not unduly perturbed by the antics of this animal they call Tudak and whom, in the past, they have had to sometimes restrain. He has, after all, done stranger things and will, no doubt, do so again. They do not laugh: they are not the type, these only doing my job, Sir, only obeying orders, not my fault types who sit there and watch in their millions.

[][][][][]

But to any more-thoughtful creature, Tudak looks strange there on the ground, inviting investigation. Thus do Joseph and Neki come across him as they walk through the market place, positively cosy now in the early evening. They see Tudak and laugh. Joseph laughs his big, strong laugh, squeezing, as he does, the hand of Neki, talking to the apparently deaf and effectively mute boy by massaging the inside of his wrist with his thumb. The boy laughs his silent laugh with him.

[][][][][]

From inside, Tudak hears the voice:
"Get up."
Tudak opens his eyes. He sees Annu towering above him, his head amongst the stars and holding a youth by the hand.
Tudak rises to his knees, the body of Dick lying between himself and Joseph/Neki. Joseph laughs:
"Get up," he says more gently this time. He looks fondly at Tudak, stretching out his hand which Tudak takes.
Neki looks at the body, then he looks at Tudak who stretches out his hand which the boy takes. Thus they stand truly connected in a circle around Dick's old body, making both the idea of Dick and the reality of Tudak significant in the universe.
Tudak squeezes the hand of Neki, thinking, simultaneously, of the young man we know as Keramugl. The hand responds. The joy is terrific.

[][][][][]

They stand in a circle around Dick's old body. They know not his earthly name but Tudak remembers him as I love you. So Tudak says it, explaining the phrase to Joseph as he heard it from the dead boy. "Only," he says, "it meant nothing to me at the time. Later I remembered it as an echo that seemed to buzz around and around my head. Now I understand what it means."
"So you have heard the voice of Annu," Joseph replies, laughing.
"I hear it now."
"And will you do one thing for me?"
"Yes, I will do anything for you."
"Then remember me. That is all I ask."
"Master, I will do that."
Joseph laughs again and looks at Neki: watch this one for me he seems to say. What he says out loud is: "And I promise it will rain again, soon."
Night falls and a small breeze shifts the dusty clouds a little.
Joseph assures them that whoever the boy is who once owned the body, he was brave. "He came to see us in order to express his love."
"I felt it," says Tudak.
He gave it you, replies Joseph, and hear this: "She also told me that you would be the one whom this boy would love and what is more, you would be

371

worthy of that love. You are. You are because of what you will do for me. Others will love you and follow you."

"And I will follow in the ways of Annu," replies Tudak in the warm star-filled night, holding the hand of Joseph on one side and of Neki on the other. Later, he was able to say I knew what happiness was.

Joseph laughs again: "Let us remember the boy who loved Tudak and who thus made him significant before his belief in Annu. We remember the boy who brought his unconditional love all the way from London, the place that makes Jim do what he does."

Thus Joseph squeezes the hand of Neki who thereby, because it is time, speaks:

"Yes Sir."

Then Joseph takes the hands of Tudak and of Neki and throws them away from himself so that only Tudak and Neki are holding hands. "It is done," he says.

So Neki speaks for Dick: "I love you." And he will remember all this and write about it later. He is the witness.

Then Tudak takes up the body and carries it to the vehicle where Rabbis and Pen wait. They will take it to Wanei and the crocs. They do not notice that Tudak looks his age at last and is therefore truly beautiful. They still believe he is a dog.

The Landrover leaves the market place, while Joseph and Neki continue their journey to Alloy's house and Margaret.

The palm fronds rustle. Two black, beady eyes watch from the undergrowth.

29
Petrus and the Child

In the debacle on the mountain, where the insurgent guerrillas had been captured by Jim, or rather where the lost children had given up the struggle, hopeless in the face of the odds against them, Petrus had been left behind. Also, a few others including the injured child whom Tarlie had carried and the old woman, Nakini, who had been their guide. She sat down one day, beneath the Nulu tree, and in her last breath remembered her life without regrets. This place, at least, was as she had known it as a girl, foraging the forest with her father. The rest of the island, the coastal plain below with the white men and their peculiar madness, was but a fleeting dream that Nakini now escaped leaving behind only her worn-out body.

The child, a tough specimen, survived with a limp that twisted its body as it walked.

"Who are you?" asked Petrus soon after Nakini's death when he was alone with the child.

"I am the one whom Annu carried across the river," replied the child, "because I was hurt."

Petrus looked at the child until the child continued:

"He healed me."

"But you walk with a limp."

"So what?" The childish face smiles. "He gave me life. Therefore I will be like him."

Petrus looked at the child and decided that it was like Tarlie.

The child followed Petrus, sometimes smiling and sometimes frowning. Petrus was not sure if the child's moods reflected his own or if they determined them. Nonetheless, he was glad to have the little servant around and together they wandered the wooded slopes.

But Petrus was not happy: he was afraid: his fear depressed him and made him distasteful to himself. He had wanted to join Andrew and Alloy but he was afraid that Jim would seek them out. If Andrew had only stood firm in the first place, none of this would have happened. Andrew had broken his promise. It was all Andrew's fault. Also, Petrus knew that as a good teacher he ought to be suffering with Keramugl and the others, so he dared not look at the child, not wishing to see the reproach in its eyes. Out of the blue, the child said:

"Be brave."

"Why should I?" Petrus was resentful. "I am no worse than anyone else. People live their lives and are not tested like this. It's your fault, Andrew. Where were you when Jim came to Ples and caused me to acknowledge my fear? I've lost the school, I've lost Missus Margaret, I've lost everything and it's all your fault."

The child said nothing more and became sullen and even a little sick but it hung around all the same.

Petrus' dreams became full of hatred and of fighting those whom he had once loved. He would wake up in the dark, crying. He was eaten up by his hatred but somehow the company of the child kept him going. Otherwise, he would have sat under the Nulu tree with Nakini – her body was still there – and let himself die. If the child stopped looking at him he would ask a question to keep him there. One day he said:

"Why am I?"

The child looked at him, then looked away with disdain, so Petrus asked another question, one he had been wanting to ask for a long time:

"For what purpose was I made?" He looked up into the dusty sky towards its blinding centre and then added, bravely: "What am I to do?"

"Be brave," said the child.

Then what?

"Do what is your heart's desire."

"I want to find Missus Margaret."

"Then go find her," replied the child pointing to the world below.

Recognising the obvious Petrus was immediately pacified. He slept the sleep of the exhausted dreaming the same dream of hatred for Andrew but seeing beyond Andrew to the face of Alloy as part of the same animal. Waking, he focused his mind on that better picture. He said to the child, who was sitting beside him:

"We must find Missus Margaret, today."

"Yes." The child smiled again.

The idea of Margaret filled Petrus' heart to bursting. He thought of nothing else as they walked through the devastation that was once Ples.

PART IV

For now we see through a glass darkly . . . 1 Corinthians, 13, 12

30
This is What Happened

And in the great clamour of human activity, in that great swelling wave of human endeavour destined to dash itself against the cliffs again and again, what happened was . . . nothing. A crystal of salt upon God's tongue. Thus what happened on Van Island in those days was nothing much. An insignificant incident that became a book or two of high adventure or philosophy or self-opinionated history because some men saw it that way. It was a tale told in letters home, in bars, in airport lounges. It was an idea to be remembered in lighted London buses, passing through the dirty night up Tottenham Court Road to Newington Green. An idea that grows, a myth that glows until God belches and either extinguishes it altogether or else allows the fire to burn down the house.

ⵔⵔⵔⵔⵔ

Extract From: A History of Van Island by Andrew Owens-Montague – New Sudan Press, 2010.

The Thornley Affair, 198...

The social upheaval in Van Island Province in the early 1980s arose from the injustices of the plantation system that have been described in the preceding chapters.

In summary, as we have already seen, plantations began to be established in the region at the turn of the nineteenth century. The reason for this was the insatiable demand for soap and candles by the rapidly growing industrial populations of North America and Western Europe. A demand that could not be met from traditional sources, such as whale blubber. The high-quality oil extracted from copra, the dried kernel of the coconut, was a perfect substitute. There was, therefore, a scramble for tropical territories in the Pacific where coconut palms grew. Extensive plantations were established. Although migrants were drawn in from such places as the Indian sub-continent and China, the labour supply was limited. This resulted in draconian methods of recruiting, maintaining and managing labour. Plantation workers were often appallingly treated even by nineteenth-century standards. The isolation of the islands upon which many plantations were established allowed plantation managers to flout what few laws existed to protect the workers. Moreover, prior to 1914, the prevailing assumption amongst white Europeans was that their darker-skinned labourers were a lower human order that neither appreciated nor was entitled to the same human rights as they had. Chinese manager-owners tended towards the same attitude.

Van was no exception to the economic development of the region by Europeans. A large coconut palm plantation was established on the Island in 1908, the ground having been prepared, as it were, by the Anglican mission. The plantation was a commercial success and Van Island became part of the British Empire: indentured labour was brought in from neighbouring islands, the lowland forests were cleared, indigenous cultural, social, economic and administrative structures were undermined, and by the introduction of cash wages that could be spent on trade goods, the Island and its people became a part of the capitalist, industrial, twentieth-century world. Van's experience was the experience of a large part of humanity between about 1890 and 1975.

During the depression years of the 1930s, the plantation industry stagnated. After the Second World War, demand for vegetable oils, with which to feed a rapidly expanding human population, prompted a second plantation boom in the humid tropics. Oil palm was the preferred crop. However, this time around, the Pacific was less well favoured for a wide variety of reasons already described, not the least being the comparative shortage of labour (see Chapter. . .). Large tracts of land, more conveniently located, could be obtained elsewhere. Particularly in South East Asia and South America. Nonetheless, newly independent Pacific nations were eager to obtain the economic benefits that were perceived to arise from the establishment of industrialised plantations. These benefits included employment, tax revenues and associated capital infrastructure such as roads, ports and electricity. New Sudan was no exception and Van Island once again experienced rapid economic development and an influx of migrants from other parts of the country. The catalyst was a large international company working in partnership with the government and funded by the World Development Bank (WDB). The aim was to establish a palm oil industry as one of a number of engines for national economic development (Chapter. . .). International economic conditions were good and initially the project was such a success that it became a model for other WDB projects.

Although legislation was enacted to protect workers' rights and ensure basic social services, and while housing and sanitation conditions were good, discontent amongst the general population was such that in the early 1980s Van Island experienced violent social upheaval. As a result of these problems, for more than a year, central government authority over the Island was ineffective and to this day, Van Island Province maintains only a tenuous link with the rest of New Sudan.

As discussed in Chapter . . ., the problems arose from two root causes that acted upon each other in dynamic fashion to create a political climate in which the law and the norms required to maintain civil society collapsed. The first cause was the dysfunctional nature of the Island society before the establishment of the palm-oil industry. In common with numerous other communities that had, until this time, easily identified themselves with a geographical location, contact with the global industrial economies of nineteenth century Europe and North America had resulted in a social trauma that was still a warm memory of contemporary experience at the beginning of the Second World War. Van Island was occupied by the Japanese until the famous Battle of the Cannibal Seas in 1945. Barely had the Van Islanders recovered from this further trauma than they were subjected to the disruption of the oil palm project that was viewed as yet another unwelcome imposition from the outside world from which they had little to gain.

The second root cause of the Troubles was an influx, generated by the project, of thousands of migrants from other parts of the country. Not only did the migrants, by weight of numbers alone, have a significant impact upon the already-dysfunctional society of Van Island, but also the migrants themselves had their own psychological problems associated with their relocation. Although some later arrivals joined established family groups and were also attracted by what was known, for a short while, as Van the Last Frontier, the bulk of the migrants were indentured labourers who had been drawn to the Island by a variety of dubious methods that had changed little from the infamous recruiting methods of the nineteenth century (see description of Blackbirding in Chapter...). The migrants came from a variety of cultural traditions but had in common a Highlands background where life, up until the 1960s, had hardly changed for hundreds of years (not since the introduction of sweet potato cultivation, see Chapter ...). The plantation labourers suffered the most for a range of reasons: they were overwhelmingly male; they were lumped together as 'Highlanders', regardless of actual origin; they had been transplanted to a climate and to physical living conditions entirely different from their original homes (see The Human Ecosystem and Migration by Helen Keramugl, New Sudan Press, 2005); and they were subjected to an incomprehensible and novel work ethos, to an apparently unreasonable style of discipline, and to the prevailing moral code that placed them as barely human in the order of things.

Thus, two traumatised and dysfunctional communities were brought together, living side by side and increasingly amongst each other. A tendency for conflict between the two was tempered by mutual frustration and resentment of the company that controlled their lives and that manifested all that was wrong in their lives.

The general perception held by people living on Van Island at the beginning of the 1980s was that they had received no benefits from the dramatic changes they had witnessed. They were frustrated daily by the lack of control that they had over their lives, by their own ignorance about what the oil palm project was all about and by the obvious fact that their hard work mostly benefited someone else. The future held as little promise as the present.

The limited exception was the Settlers who had title to land and who were experiencing a rising standard of living. They had the least to complain about. It was surprising, therefore, that the general social discontent and malaise was shifted towards violence and anarchy by the Thornley Incident, which occurred in one of the Settlement communities.

However, the facts of the case suggest a population pushed to its limits. The action of the despicable Richard Thornley was the spark that ignited a tinder-dry bonfire built by years of injustice and repression.

Richard Thornley was the representative of his father, the Managing Director of Barbary and Northgate, the company responsible for establishing the palm oil industry on Van Island. He was the successful head of the company Estates Department that had, in the 1970s and 80s, established a number of plantation projects in South East Asia in partnership with governments and with the benefit of cheap WDB loans. It was a lucrative business by the 1980s when world food shortages and harvest failures elsewhere had pushed vegetable oil prices to record highs. Barbary and Northgate shareholders made money on the back of subsidised WDB rates of interest, free land, the inexperience of the governments of newly independent states and the prevailing world political climate of development at any cost. Barbary and Northgate methods were aimed at maximising returns on capital on the basis, widely held up until almost the end of the twentieth century, that they had no responsibility for external costs.

Richard Thornley was an experienced and successful trouble-shooter for Barbary and Northgate. He spent his life inspecting its projects and enforcing the solutions to the problems he encountered. The management of the Barbary and Northgate interests on Van Island was known to be weak. One of his first actions on arriving on Van had been to sack the senior agronomist, a loyal and long-time employee of the company, who subsequently committed suicide. Then, in collusion with the general manager, the infamous Jim MacDonald[59], he visited one of the Settler communities in order to enforce a WDB agreement whereby the Settlers had to plant up vacant land with oil palms. Thornley's collusion with MacDonald would have predisposed the Settlers against him in any event but his own arrogance and thoughtlessness, and his outdated racism were what caused his death. The day of Thornley's visit to the settlement was exceptionally hot. Having arrived with an entourage that included MacDonald's heavily armed and infamously murderous security guards, Thornley set himself up inside the local covered market to meet with the Settlers' leaders, who had been forewarned of the visit. A large and essentially friendly crowd gathered. However, there were too many to all take shelter out of the sun in the market. Those who were inside heard Thornley berate the Settlers' leaders. Typically he was arrogant and rude, demeaning them all publicly. There was a minor disturbance arising from those at the back of the crowd pushing both to hear what was being said and to get out of the blistering sun. The security guards dealt with it, subduing the crowd with the sight of their guns. A number of young men were held, handcuffed and made to sit down in the sun but in view of Thornley. Then, lunch was brought to Thornley: bottled water and food from an insulated cooler box. Thornley ate his lunch in full view of the handcuffed men who were not only suffering from the heat of the sun but who were also thirsty and hungry. The onlooking crowd became restless and then furious. Some of them set upon Thornley and the security men. The security men fought back, killing a number of people in the process. Thornley was also killed in the fracas and his body mutilated. There was an attempt to cut off his head that failed. The crowd then marched to Akaranda, the Provincial capital, shouting for the right to be allowed to do what they liked with their land. But meeting no opposition and an indifferent administration, their energy dissipated and they dispersed back to their homes.

---

[59] See Beast of Van – Racism and the Plantation Industry in Twentieth-Century New Sudan by Helen Keramugl, The Cooperative Press, Sheffield, 2007.

No one was ever charged with the murder of Thornley. He was buried in the cemetery in Akaranda. At the time of writing, the site of his grave has been lost.

Local public opinion was indifferent to Thornley's murder. On the other hand, the international press was outraged, laying the blame on a mythical figure known as Annu, who was supposed to have planned and organised the troubles of which Thornley's murder was a part. Annu was either a communist terrorist or a liberator, depending upon the political leanings of the commentator concerned. Intercession by the former colonial power was suggested. However, in the end, the good sense of the New Sudanian Government prevailed: if there had indeed ever been such a man as Annu, evidence was presented to prove that he had been killed during the troubles. Troops remained on standby in the capital although the Island was effectively cut off from the rest of the country until the unrest had worked itself out, which it did. Nonetheless, as I will explain in the next chapter, the Thornley Affair ignited a series of disturbances that were to radically change the plantation economy of Van forever.

[][][][][]

Extract from Fire in Paradise, a Novel by Cheryl Arty, EasyRead Paperbacks, Brisbane and Chipping Camden, 1993.

Sir Richard Thornley, The Bastard, was a colonial of the old school. We know that. On that fateful day, the 14th April 1984, he drove to the Settlement in his Landrover. In the back were his gang of desperate soldiers. The vehicle bristled with guns. They sped along at breakneck speed throwing up dust and stones at the onlookers who stood at the roadside well aware that "something" was going to happen. A vicious sun blasted them out of a steel-blue sky. It was as hot as hell down there on Van Island that day!

The market place was packed with a colourful and happy crowd when the vehicle hit the place scattering the people in all directions as it skidded to a halt. An ominous silence prevailed. You could have heard the proverbial pin drop.

The crowd cowered under the gun-toting soldiers, vicious and impersonal in their dark glasses which flashed with anger under the high midday sun. A circle of submission surrounded the Landrover in its wide dusty space. A youth tried to speak but was felled by the back-hand of the biggest and strongest of the soldiers. The giant man whom we know as Tudak the Horrible. They hated him with all their might. The women held him secretly in their hearts. His loins fascinated them and made them shy.

Sir Richard Thornley was nothing without the soldiers, the beasts, but with them he thought he was The King.

"I'll take no more nonsense from these slaves," he thought as he got out of the car, in his perfectly pressed safari suit of cream linen and his freshly brushed desert boots. On his head he wore a broad-brimmed hat made of the skin of some animal he had shot in Africa. The Last Tiger. He slowly took off his dark glasses and swept the crowd of cowered people with his steel-blue eyes. "Slaves, ha, ha, ha! Your lives are to serve my purpose and then die."

"Die!"

The crowd looked uneasy. Thornley was a bastard of the highest order. He would have been good-looking had it not been for his weak chin and his long neck that made his head wobble like the wobbly-man toys people put on the back shelves of their cars in the 1980s for good luck.

There was no doubt that Thornley was the biggest bastard of a bunch of bastards. These white masters who thought they ruled the world but who were soon to meet their doom. Thornley in the forefront. He'd be the one to "die"!

Thornley climbed onto the top of the Landrover.

"Listen to me, you lot . . ."

He stopped, horrified, for a little child, an innocent little child, naked, was crawling across the space between the People and himself. The mother hovered on the edge of the crowd, her hand across her mouth. She was frozen with fear.

"Do these subs breed?" Thornley asked Tudak the Horrible.

Tudak the Horrible smiled back with his evil smile: "Not if I can help it, Sir."

With that, Tudak the Horrible with a swift move kicked the baby into the air like a football. The mother screamed and rushed forward. She was grabbed by Tudak the Horrible as a hostage.

Tudak the Horrible looked at the crowd: "Anyone move and she gets it," he laughed.

The crowd was silenced and cowered under the broiling sun. You could have heard the proverbial pin drop but it was only the baby hitting the ground with an awful plop. The mother wanted to move forward to pick it up but she couldn't because she was held in the vicious grip of Tudak the Horrible.

Silence.

Then: "Oi!"

All eyes moved to a brave and handsome young man who had moved forward out of the crowd towards Tudak the Horrible. We recognise him as Keramugl, his strong brown muscles rippling and glistening in the sunshine. He held his head up nobly for all to see. He was not afraid of Tudak the Horrible.

The crowd cheered: "Our Hero, Keramugl the Brave!"

Tudak the Horrible was feared no longer. He trembled and his mouth drooled. His glasses slipped down his sweaty nose to reveal unsteady eyes. He let the woman go and she rushed towards her baby who she picked up and held to her breast.

Tudak the Horrible, now merely Tudak the Defeated, fell upon his knees at the feet of Keramugl the Brave.

"Oh Lord and Master," he said, "I will serve you faithfully to the end of my days, if only you will spare my life."

Keramugl the Brave took the hand of Tudak the Defeated and lifted him up onto his feet.

"From now on you are Tudak the Faithful and you will marry my daughter, when I have one."

Saying this he scanned the crowd until his eyes rested upon Helen the Fair, his school-mistress girlfriend who had, as we know, stood by him through thick and thin.

"Come forward, Helen the Fair, and be my wife."

Helen the Fair moved forward and took the hand of Keramugl the Brave. The crowd cheered.

"Hurrah for Keramugl the Brave. He shall be our King. Hail the King. Hail, also, Queen Helen."

Sir Richard Thornley, The Bastard, stood on the roof of the Landrover. He was struck dumb, his face a mask of fear. But his arrogance reigned.

"I will not bow down to you Keramugl," he shouted, "I would rather die."

With the one word "Die", the crowd moved forward to pull Thornley down.

Keramugl the Brave put up his hand: "Stop," he cried. "Richard Thornley, will you give up your evil ways and come with us?"

"Never," returned Thornley, throwing out his arm in a Nazi-style salute. "Never will I serve one such as you who is not a pure Whitey."

"Then you have sealed your fate," Keramugl the Brave replied and to the crowd: "Do what you have to do."

Thornley's cowardly screams were short-lived as he was torn apart by the indignant crowd.

[][][][][]

London Daily Wire … … December 201…

If you want a good read over Christmas you could do a lot worse than buy Andrew Owens-Montague's fascinating book, Pacific Mischief (New London Press). It is a true story of thirty years ago which is as compelling and violent as a thriller. A number of murders, some of them rather grisly, build up as evidence against one villain who is run to ground himself to meet the same sort of rough justice he has been handing out himself. It is also an intriguing insight into the exploitation of a small Pacific island by outside interests which eventually leads to social disintegration and violent reaction. A cautionary tale, the lessons of which we here in Europe have still to learn, I fear.

At a deeper level, Mr Owens-Montague tries to analyse the human psychological background to what are still known, locally, as the Troubles. He is clearly of the school of historians who understands history in terms of the emotional reactions to events. He links his analysis to the cult of Annu which has subsequently arisen on the island. Not entirely successful but food for thought. Nevertheless, I can recommend it as a good Christmas present for any of your nearest and dearest who worry about the Why of history. At £50, it's a bargain.

Cheryl Arty.

[][][][][]

We are nothing but the dust that is blown around for a while before it is swept away. I wanted to know why myself once. But Margaret taught me not to worry, so I didn't. There was a woman once, Mrs Grant, who'd lived in a big house beside the common before the war. She was knocked down by a car near the railway bridge where my mother said they ought to have had traffic lights. Her old, naked leg, mottled blue with old veins, old blood and old memories.

My mother covered the leg and when the police came we went home to play monopoly. Then, my mother's turn: now mine.

31

A Way of the World

Tuscany, I call him. You know the chap. Flamboyant, egotistical type. The one who will come to the board meeting in the cream-coloured suit and who put his Panama hat on the table. Ready for the off, he'd said, got to sort out that little deal in Tuscany for the wife, he'd laughed, as if I'd ever be the hen-pecked husband. Pecks her more like. He's the type who's not interested in women – or anyone for that matter – despite the fact that he plays the old flirt who values a woman for her mind, who's done it all, only he hasn't. He's the one who wants the old farmhouse on the hillside with the cypress trees. She'd rather stay in London – Chepstow Villas to be precise – living another sort of life. He thinks he's the coming man in B&N. He's the type; the new type.

Tuscany prefers to work in the board room; high up and sunny. Above the gloom of the street. Makes him feel good in the mornings. Feels he can do things. And it's about time I did something about this Van Island business. We have legitimate interests. World Development Bank loan, duty to shareholders. Pretty savage bunch out there all the same. One death's unfortunate but two's not what we want. We've put a lot of eggs into what I trust is not going to turn out to be a rotten basket. New Sudan's the next big thing, according to Thornley, and there're my own investments not to mention all the money I'm spending on the house in Tuscany. Thing is – he's no fool this aging ladykiller, dressed, today, in sharp pinstripes a little over-tailored to flatter sagging figure – Thornley knows the field better than any of us or, at any rate, knew it, got to give him his due, he got the show going, losing a son like that's no joke. Daughters myself, in the flush of youth and all that can't think how we did it never much interested in that department if I'm honest.

Thornley's lost his marbles. I'd better get up Barlborough – whatever his name is. He might know what's going on.

Yes Sir?

Up in a jiffy. The type. Not much in the brains department but a useful cog in the machine. Faithful servant of the company. Man and boy, I imagine. No idea where he sprang from. Lower-middle-class type. Rough accent; the aitches come out properly although don't is nearer dun but not quite. The hint of the thug about him. Might be a gangster. Big hands. Smells of shaving soap.

Tuscany fancies himself a patrician and the likes of Battledun, plebs. Public school gave him that odour of superiority. Battledun's grammar school gave him a better education. If he had not been knocked about up there, likely to die for his country, for Tuscany and co, Battledun would have gone a long way. The lion to Tuscany's donkey. He would have been a post-war New Man with a good engineering degree from Leeds, Manchester or University College Wales. But what had happened up there in the clouds had done for him. He liked classical music: Mozart piano concertos and late Brahms. Tuscany attended the opera. The depraved type.

What're we going to do about this Van Island thingy? Storm in a teacup if you ask me but we must do something. Magnanimity to a fag he bullies because he wants him to do something outrageous. Got any ideas Battledun? Because I'm damned if I have. He laughs at his own generous depreciation of himself. The outside picture of himself, that is.

Battledun stays inside. Won't come out for the likes of Tuscany. He has seen more than Tuscany can imagine − the world of patchwork fields and woods, of clear downs, flat-looking from up there, incidental villages and dense towns straggling a little along the main roads which nonetheless look irrelevant. I wanted to stay but you have to come down sometime. Hence his love for Dick which, like Tudak's, had not only made Dick significant but himself also. It has made him a better man and a better husband but like Alloy, whom he will never know, he has X-ray eyes. He sees the hollow, lonely pomposity of Thornley and the shallow, empty suaveness of Tuscany. But the difference is, having been up there, he makes no big deal about it: not the type to beat his chest and rage at heaven. Upon meeting God he will laugh in a good-natured way and then apologise, knowing himself to be the human fool he is.

You know more of the details than I do, old chap. B, B, B. . .

Battledun.

Battledun: you must have seen every bit of paper. Tuscany is playing genial, leaning back in chair, tips of fingers joining hands above which he gazes at Battledun, who sits on the edge of the expensive chair because instinctively he does not want to dirty his trousers. Tuscany swings forward to press elbows on desk in over-acted aggressive way, expecting the other to be taken aback only he is not. Tuscany is, more like, who therefore decides he does not like the bloody fellow, damned oik. Fact is, old man, your job, you ought to know it.

I do.

You do?

Why, otherwise, have I been sitting in that back room all these years? Every bit of paper, both ways, has been through my hands. You only want the big picture and that is what you get. I'm the one who knows the details. I'm the one who placates the financial press over a beer in the pub round the corner. I'm the one who issues the press releases. He smiles, he is not bragging, merely stating the facts. And you know what?

Tuscany makes a smile: What?

I couldn't care a fig if VIPOD sinks to the bottom of the sea. I know what's going on out there and it's a disgrace.

Tuscany does not know the meaning of the word but, it is true, he avoids the details; leaves them to the back-room boys. They know what they're doing; this chappy apparently does, the silly bugger.

So our man out there, um. . .

MacDonald.

Yes. He's managing. Is he?

As always.

You used to call me Sir.

I did.

Not now?

Not now.

I see. Good man, MacDonald.

Depends on how you define good.

Good enough for our purposes.

He is that.

I remember him, in the dining room, drinking his soup the wrong way. Rather a rough. . .

Diamond?

Indeed.

Battledun watches Tuscany's unease. He does not want to make the man uneasy but how can he describe the moral pit into which B&N has descended to a man who has no morals and who is not interested in the details beyond a man's table manners? How can he describe Dick's death to such a man? Thus he swallows and, sitting on the edge of the despicable chair, it seems as if Tuscany's penetrating gaze, man of steel and all that, knows what's what and can see through all the shit act, as if Tuscany's eyes upon him make him uneasy. But they don't. The watery, dissipated eyes are irrelevant.

I think you, no, we, because I am a party to this, can let Jim MacDonald continue with. . .

Yes, yes, Tuscany grabbed at the fact: Jim, Jim, that's his name. Capital fellow, empire builder, rough diamond and all that. Tuscany knows where he is at last. Doing a fine job for us. Needs encouraging.

He does a very fine job, of it.

Can you draft something?

I can.

I'll sign it Monday.

Yes.

Sir? For me?

No.

Alright then. Time for lunch. Join me? For a pint and a sandwich? I wouldn't take the likes of you to my club. Too embarrassing in that big, black, heavy coat. I bet he keeps it on. I'll go there after and make a short day of it. Friday and no point in pushing yourself.

No thanks.

Tuscany is relieved.

I wouldn't want to eat with your kind. The food'd stick in my throat. You'd embarrass me in those silly clothes.

[][][][][]

Therefore, it is essential that processed palm oil continues to be exported from Van Island.

The Prime Minister read through the memorandum that had been prepared for him. He always liked to make a few alterations to show he had taken it in. I'm not a complete fool. He knew his expatriate advisors called him a savage in a skirt but he despised trousers as hot and unhygienic. He it was who had set the trend for wearing the more traditional lap-lap in parliament, together with leather sandals on naked feet and a lightweight, short-sleeved jacket. Still a travesty, the lap-lap itself a colonial introduction to cover native nakedness, but he needed to strike some note of independence. Prove to himself, God help me, that I am an independent man who can lead my people through a threatening world. And what is tradition anyway? Something we invent to make ourselves proud of being. . . what? New Sudanians? What are we? What do we have in common? We share half an island, we wear lap-laps and we speak Pidgin English. That's about it and I suppose there's not much more to being a country, apart from our seat in the UN.

Of all the assortment of things that were New Sudan, the PM was most proud of the language. He had not an ounce of jingoism in him but he believed that New Sudan Pidgin represented a uniquely innocent and naïve attempt to come to terms with an unwelcome but unavoidable, complex world. In the process, a language had been created that was poetic and subtle with meaning. He loved its diversity, its versatility, its eclecticism and its infinite range of expression. He was proud that its grammar was precise and effective. His mastery of what he called the Queen's English was superb, and he was the first New Sudanian writer to be published internationally, but he preferred the vernacular pidgin.

He crossed out '*essential*' and inserted '*vital*'. The tax and export revenues from VIPOD were indeed vital to the electricity and telecommunications programmes he had promised as his election campaign. He needed the VIPOD money, at least until the Mt Frederick copper mine came on stream. Needed it for the quasi-modern, dressed-up state that was New Sudan with its currency, its flag and its overseas missions in Washington, London and Singapore, its growing national debt.

. . . Be assured that additional police units can be drafted to Akaranda at 48 hours' notice. . .

They could, but what they would do was the issue. If there was any raping, pillaging and arson, they'd be the ones to do it. They'd round up anyone they could get hold of, beat them up and then ransom them back to their relatives. The police did not enforce or uphold the law to protect New Sudanian citizens but rather threatened an unruly population with their own special brand of unruliness.

The PM sighed, there had been numerous parliamentary enquiries about it but nothing happened. The parliamentarians were no better. Worse, because they broke bigger laws, looted more valuable things and got away with it as a perk of the job.

I can assure you of my personal support . . .

But what was his support worth? He was powerless beyond the special relationship he had with the few big companies who were the law where they operated. For them New Sudan was a place to be logged, mined and planted, having the added advantage that international standards could be flouted and cheap labour abused without the chattering objections of a middle-class electorate. They paid their corporate taxes and not-so-subtle bribes thereby buying the right to treat the place with contempt, raping, pillaging and setting fire to it. The expatriate staff made their money then returned down South to live in the dream homes they had built with their tax-free salaries, spending their retirement complaining about the kanakas in New Sudan. He had been there – owned a couple of houses himself – and could not understand the mentality of these white, yellow and brown people who will rape a whole country for a suburban house.

Beware the white man and his ways, his father had said, born early enough to remember the first impact on the coastal area that had become Port Markham. Invincible and magical these white men had seemed, with power irresistible in its force and in its seductive materialism. The white men had created New Sudan. The indigenous people, on the coast, had no more idea of the interior than they had of themselves, fearing what lay inside. Not so the white men who had barely arrived when they were trekking up the valleys into the mountains, their aeroplanes following. It was they who had opened up the country, discovering the masses of people in the wide highland valleys. They had created New Sudan, fought the Japanese over it and then abdicated government, despising the natives for not being like them while continuing to take whatever they liked.

And am I any better? Sitting here in my luxurious office complaining about them? Should I not be in the hills fighting them? I might have done once but I had a political agenda, I organised campus protests, I got them out, or so I thought and where did it get me? Here, to this state of impotent collaboration. I am corrupted by the trappings of power but I don't have the power to do what I ought to do. He shook his head, dismissing the impossible idea and returned to the old I'll do what I can, the best man in a bad situation rubbish.

. . . I commend your actions. . .

Do I? I barely know the man but he's a rare breed. Born on Van, with no loyalties outside the country. He's travelled a little but we know he has no foreign assets. If anyone can claim to be New Sudanian, he can. How can I judge him from Port Markham? Someone has to do the dirty work and this Jim does it. He keeps the income flowing. It's dirty money alright but I can do good things with it. Another old excuse that would not do. The PM knew it.

. . .Your tenacity in the face of adversity is admirable. . .

Not his sentence but he was too tired to change it despite the fact that he knew Jim was a flawed man. The idea had always worried him. He had met Jim a number of times. Twice as an official guest on Van, taking in a round of golf. Shifty, uncertain eyes and sudden changes of mood was what he remembered. Sulky and rude one minute, apologetic and bullying the next. The man would commit a murder one day: he was the type. New Sudan gave him too much freedom and he'd cause mayhem if he was given too much rope . . . If I had any spunk I'd go over there myself.

. . .and I am confident you will act within the law and take the advice of the relevant authorities.

But there was no relevant authority on Van. Nothing effective. I can't get involved even if I want to. What can a few armed policemen do except make things worse? I'm not going to train guns on my own people, even if it does keep the income flowing. Damn the income for once. I can blame the damned company, neo-colonial bastards, if things go wrong. Another old excuse.

The Prime Minister's signature was unsteady. He pressed the buzzer on his desk and yawned, avoiding his reflection in the dark window. He prayed for sleep. Just a few hours would help.

[][][][][]

The London Intellectual, ... March, 198...

British Company Tried to Buy Berettas Assault Rifles, Restraint Equipment, for New Sudan Police

A document seen by this paper details a plantation giant's request for $100,000 of 'upgraded weapons', 'restraint equipment' and 'crowd control items' to arm the New Sudanian police.

Barbary and Northgate, which owns and operates the Van Island Palm Oil Development Company in New Sudan, has been negotiating to buy more than a hundred thousand dollars' worth of upgraded weapons and restraint equipment to arm the New Sudanian police, a confidential document passed to the Intellectual reveals.

The document shows that Barbary and Northgate sought tenders last year from arms and combat-equipment suppliers in Britain to provide semi-automatic rifles, double-action Beretta pistols, pump-action shotguns, handcuffs, legcuffs, waist-chains, neck knives, sjamboks and rattan canes. Earlier negotiations included 50 Beretta submachine guns and 100 Kalashnikov light machine guns.

The request was issued at the height of the troubles on Van Island last year when a strike by employees of the Van Island Palm Oil Development Company developed into an island-wide campaign of civil disobedience and a revolt against Barbary and Northgate's interests. Local anger had been aroused against the company's brutal suppression of the strike, which allegedly involved summary imprisonment, torture and execution. A company spokesman has denied the reports.

... March 198...

Press Statement: Barbary and Northgate plc.: London Press

Following the advice of lawyers, the Directors of Barbary and Northgate wish to state that recent reports concerning negotiations for arms and restraint equipment are inaccurate. The negotiations were made by one member of the board who has since resigned and who is currently residing in Italy. British and Italian police are investigating.

Intellectual Business, ... March, 198...

Barbary and Northgate Shares Stand Firm

Blue chip shares Barbary and Northgate wobbled yesterday in what was otherwise a dull new-year market. At the opening of trading the shares fell by nearly 17% on news of problems at the company's plantations in New Sudan. However, prices recovered somewhat to end the day 8p down at 182p. Analysts say that despite public perceptions, the company's investments in New Sudan

389

represent only a small part of its income. For some years now the City has recommended that B&N offload what plantations remain in its portfolio and concentrate on its other activities. These include chemicals, timber and food processing.

The London Intellectual, ... March, 198...
New Sudan Prime Minister's UN Statement Says Conditions Returning to Normal on Paradise Isle
Unrest on Van Island, New Sudan, is subsiding, according to the country's Prime Minister, Isaac Waninara. In order to contain serious unrest arising from a strike at the plantation subsidiary of the British company Barbary and Northgate last year (see Intellectual of November 18th), the New Sudan government isolated the island in November. Access has remained difficult since then.
The Prime Minster made his statement to the press yesterday, following discussions with the Secretary General of the United Nations, Javier Como de Pasco. This followed his inspection of conditions on the island after which he flew to New York, having first briefed his Australian counterpart, Wally O'Hara. Mr Waninara asked the international community not to interfere in what was an internal matter for New Sudan. However, he appreciated advice he had received from a number of world leaders including Britain's Prime Minster, Margaret Thornton. He said conditions on the island were returning to near normal despite the fact that the Van Island Palm Oil Development Company was inoperative and likely to remain so, adding that it was opposition to the company's activities which had sparked the unrest. He further stated that the New Sudan government was confident it was in control. Answering questions, he said it was his strong personal view that the people were better off than they had been when the company was operating. Violence is inexcusable, he added, in an emotional outburst, but the high-handed and neo-colonial attitude of the company towards its labour-force and towards the community at large had pushed local people to the limits. He confirmed that journalists would be allowed to travel to Van within weeks.
A Commonwealth investigation mission will visit the island later in the year.

The London Intellectual, ... March, 198...
New Sudan Currency Collapses
Port Markham: the New Sudan currency, the Kulu, has gone into a tailspin, falling by almost 200% against the US dollar in the past week. Confidence in the economy has been shaken by unrest on the palm oil producing Van Island. Export of palm oil, the major foreign exchange earner, has all but ceased.
Officials from the International Monetary Facility are visiting Port Markham to discuss debt rescheduling and additional loans.

Intellectual Business, ... March, 198...
Barbary and Northgate Shares Crash
Blue chip shares Barbary and Northgate crashed yesterday in what was otherwise a dull market. At the opening of trading the shares fell by 15% on the

back of news of an IMF visit to New Sudan, where problems at the company's oil palm project on Van Island have shaken the otherwise stable economy.

Intellectual Business, ... March, 198...
Barbary and Northgate Shares Climb
Blue chip shares Barbary and Northgate rebounded yesterday in an excited market. Analysts have long said that despite public perceptions the company's investments in New Sudan represent only a small part of the company's assets. Investors seem at last to have grasped this fact, rushing in to mop up the undervalued equities.

For The Commentator, April 198..., Life in the Slow Lane
Domestic Bliss, Gun-Running and the Value of Other People's Shares (Un-edited)
Far be it from me to cast the first stone. My own life has not been blameless. Twenty years ago – gawd blimey, is it that long? – I was no stranger to sex, drugs and rock 'n' roll, albeit a little past my prime. The King's Road set, free once you got inside. I particularly remember a house in Paultons Square. But that is another story. I too have frequented the odd Soho massage parlour or three, receiving, for a small additional fee, extra services. Drunk and disorderly I have been many a time, for which I have paid my debt.

Disorderly, you might say, describes a life I do not regret, despite swapping my salubrious Kensington abode for this tenth-floor flat overlooking the glories of Southwest London. My wife, my understandably ex-wife, is welcome to Holland Park, God bless her. We are still friends. Did she not put up the curtains here, and pay for them? She did, and our children give us their love and tolerance without favour, despite – perhaps because of – my precipitous descent. They do not judge, God bless them. I would not blame them if they did. Gawd lummy, a sentimental tear escapes my eye.

But to the matter in hand and another drink: let us consider the foolish crassness of the British upper crust. Let us consider their propensity to want the best of everything regardless of the cost to society at large and, I would venture to add, having been through the mill myself, their own emotional wellbeing.

Let us consider one particular member of the British upper crust. You, the well-read readers of the Commentator, will know about whom I am talking. This fool of an erstwhile director of an illustrious and highly respectable icon of the British way of doing things, the head office of which is situated in one of the finest small buildings in the City. I wish I had some of its shares.

Common knowledge: all London is talking about it. Nonetheless, no names, Nigel, no names. Do not worry your editorial head about it.

This miserable man has brought himself down. He is entitled to do that. But, in the process, he has smeared that illustrious and highly respectable City institution with enough dirt to sink it.

Or so one would assume.

At any rate, enough dirt has been smeared around to diminish the share value of the illustrious and highly respectable City institution by a sufficient number of percentage points to send congenitally apoplectic retired colonels in

Tunbridge Wells and pathologically nervous spinsters in Leamington Spa into a tizzy. It is a DISGRACE! Is it not? That members of our rentier class should lose a little of their capital and, in the process, be made aware of the threatening mob upon whose labours the value of that capital rests.

Of course, you, the well-read readers of the Commentator, know that it is not a disgrace that our rentier class should be brought to an understanding of the conditions of the world in this way. If the mob in the street below was to break down the doors, storm the grand stairway and carry those same rentiers off to the guillotine, it would be the least they deserve.

No, what is a disgrace is that the value of these shares, no less blue chip despite the howling mob – I wish I could lay my hands on a few – should fall in value, not because of the disgraceful troubles the company has brought upon itself by the inhumane treatment of its labourers in New Sudan but because of the silly shenanigans of one of its directors.

The boys in blue, with the help of their Italian counterparts, are investigating, so it is said, and a good thing too.

You all know the story by now. The fool, wishing to buy some damned farmhouse with its associated peasant holding in that part of Italy fashionable amongst the same English upper-middle-class which knows no better and which would not recognise the smell of rotten fish if one was stuck right up its nose, ran foul of local regulations and of Italian laws relating to the expatriate ownership of property. He also, no doubt by acting the superior English milord, aroused the animosity of the local criminal fraternity which runs the place and to which he ought to have acted in a more deferential manner.

British, old chap, and I know better. Only he didn't. If he must have a place in the country, why not Norfolk for God's sake or Ireland if he wants something exotic?

So the next thing is that this congenital idiot has agreed to source small arms and pay for them as part of the deal in which his return is a run-down old farmhouse on the side of a hill with views he won't die for but is likely to live to regret. His business, you might say, only it happens to be illegal to export arms without a licence.

And, I would like to add, as one who has succumbed to the heavy sales techniques of liquor and cigarette vendors, if shits like this fool didn't want to make quick deals, quick money out of arms dealing, we might, we just might, not have some of the problems we do have in this benighted world of ours. He deserves to get what he's getting for being one of the most stupidly ignorant, selfish and bad buggers of the year.

It's illegal too, so I am told, to have anything to do with overweight Italian men in dark glasses and sharp suits who forget to shave in the morning.

Well, indeed, good to see a man of that type get his comeuppance, readers of the Daily Mail and the Daily Express, will feel, but there is more to it: Sun, Mirror and Daily Telegraph stuff. To start with, this fool of a director, instead of doing the job shareholders have a right to expect him to do, is gun-running, or whatever it is called. That's bad enough, but the bad man decides he must take it further. Cannot help himself, I suppose: he decides to add one or two items to the list of 'equipment' for which he is seeking quotations to be delivered to his house in that quarter of London between Kensington High Street and Cromwell Road. The sort of place he would live in because there he gets the best at a low price. Belgravia, and he'd have to make do with a horizontal sliver in Eaton Square.

His wife, another ignoramus but, more likely, trusting and blameless, living the life but not asking any questions, opens the boxes. She draws the right conclusions but rather than letting sleeping dogs lie, she has the father of her children followed to the massage parlour he frequents and at which the equipment is to be used. She then kicks him out of the house − not being so foolish as to run back to mother − leaving her in possession (nine tenths of the law and all that) of the ancestral domain. He, naturally, runs off to the farmhouse in Italy where he assumes he can lie low. He has, after all, kept his part of the other bargain, which, he soon discovers, did not include protection.

The rest, we know.

He is a despicable fool, and shows it all the more because having been caught, he begins to spin the yarn that he was doing it all for his company (might as well have been queen and country − those types will do anything for that myth), with the agreement of his fellow board members. The arms, restraint equipment and all were to be shipped to New Sudan in order to deal with the little problem they had out there. Has a ring of truth but it's a pack of lies and here is what is really disgraceful:

Despite the fact that this upright and proper company did have trouble in New Sudan and might well have been illegally importing arms (I can make this aspersion because what has recently come to light is worse), it was not this that caused the shares to slide, wobble, crash. It was a sex scandal, trouble between a man and his wife, and the fall of one of our high and mighty causing the great British rentier class and the various City institutions to get their knickers twisted.

Our great British left-wing press takes a holier-than-thou attitude which generally infuriates me, but for once − and without the usual errors − the Intellectual has made a valid point. This great company, which shall for ever remain nameless on these pages, has trading and plantation interests all over the world and a history going back to the days of the Cutty Sark. One of the first companies to bring us that beverage, and, the Intellectual informs me, other items essential to our well being including sugar, coffee, rubber and, increasingly since the Second World War, I am told, a commodity of which I had not heretofore heard: palm oil. Apparently we eat great quantities of the greasy stuff under the assumption that it is ice-cream.

But the point is, we want all this stuff, brought to us by companies such as the one which Nigel will not allow me to name, and have come to depend on it. So much so that − rich as we are, and even richer as are other Europeans, Americans and even, these days, Japanese − a large and valuable industry has developed. Upon this industry, a sizeable chunk of the wealth and subsequent power of nations depends.

The Intellectual explained all this to me last week, with the result that I am a much wiser and chastened man. Much chastened: as the sixteenth- and seventeen-century Spanish wiped out entire nations and cultures for the love of gold, creating a subsidiary slave trade in the process, so has our addiction to tea, coffee and now it seems palm oil, enslaved and is still enslaving millions of people and trapping entire economies in a poverty cycle which is hard to break. Look, I am no expert, and I can't quite add it all up but if you read the Intellectual you'll understand what I mean. They explain it so much better on the rough, tough Theobalds Road than we do here in the rarefied atmosphere of Bedford Square. It seems that the people who work on the plantations which produce palm oil not only earn a pittance but, if companies such as – damn it, I'll name and be hanged – Barbary and Northgate are anything to go by, treated rather worse than animals.

About the time the B and N shares were wobbling and sliding as a result of the gun running and sexual antics of one of its directors in – let us not forget – his private capacity, what was happening on B and N plantations in New Sudan would have made the Nazis proud. It is common knowledge now, and I suggest you read our more salacious press if you want the gruesome details. When all this became known, as the Intellectual has rightly pointed out, the heat came off the scandal and the shares recovered! In other words, Dear Readers, a sex-and-gun-running scandal caused the shares to crash, but the revealed fact that human beings were being oppressed by a British company in a most disgraceful way only reassured the City that things were going on as usual: the shares recovered. As I say, I wish I had some.

Need I say more about the moral values of our rentier class of our rentier society?

I do: I have been a part of it. I need a drink.

Indeed Angus, enough said. The points are: one, the shares of Barbary and Northgate wobbled because of a sex scandal, not because of human rights abuses; and two, most of the natural commodities we consume come at a ghastly human price. Also, Angus, three, our rentier class is despicable. I know that. But are not most of our readers of that class? It's an old story which no longer raises eyebrows. But your own inimitable style charms. Can you get it down to eight hundred words by Thursday? No names and no libels please. We are the Commentator. Nigel.

For The Commentator, April 198…, 2006, Life in the Fast Lane
(Un-edited).
A Good Cause

Is, in her own words, what drives Lady Annabel Halesowen's annual fancy dress balls. This year her ball was held in favour of some charity for children about which I have never heard in the war zone of a country about which I never think. All of it too near my own origins for comfort. Fortunately, the ball, held in The Dorchester, made no reference to children or to the country in which they suffer. I suffered, all the same. The idea was to attend as a married couple, the female party to the union as the chief suspect. I therefore attended as Potiphar, à la Rembrandt, the mother of my children attended as the wife, à la Gentileschi, hair ruffled and clothes in a state of disarray. She takes these things literally, this woman with whom I share my offspring, and when she spotted her Joseph – a dusky Darnley-or-other who had lost his Queen of Scots – I lost sight of her. I consoled myself and the suffering Potiphar at the bar. Better to be Joseph, Lady Annabel explained. She was right. I told her not to sell her Barbary and Northgate shares. The way they treat their people out in the colonies shows they are a sensible, no-nonsense lot. The lower orders appreciate a strong hand. That silly fellow should not have let himself get caught. Next week to St Moritz to spend time with my old friends the Bernadottes and then with the Onassises on the Aegean. Do I want to recall my roots? I do not.

Pad this out a bit, Leo. 600 words? It won't work unless you make the Intellectual readers really cross. Nigel.

The London Intellectual, ... April, 198...
New Sudan Issues Arrest Warrant for Missing General Manager
From our correspondent in New Sudan: following the findings of the Commonwealth mission to Van Island (see Intellectual of the 18th March) and evidence uncovered by this paper, an arrest warrant has been issued for the General Manager of the defunct Van Island Palm Oil Development Company, a New Sudan national, Jam MacDougal. Substantial evidence, including statements by senior staff, points to murder and serious human rights abuses. . . MacDingle's whereabouts are unknown.

32
Variations on a Theme of Reality

Dear Mum,

I hope this gets to you quickly because you mustn't believe all the things you read in the papers. It's not true at all about us being abducted – we're quite safe.

The man who was killed – which is in all the papers – was the son of the managing director of the company which set up the oil palm project here which I told you about before. I don't know his name. But it must be awful for his family. No one is quite sure what happened but he was at a meeting here with the settlers near where the school is. There was a disturbance, a sort of riot and at the end of it he was dead and some of the people had been hurt. School is cancelled for the time being.

What I didn't say was that all this happened near the school. And Mum, you won't believe it but at first I didn't notice. I just thought people were being a bit noisy like they are. Real life isn't at all like you read about it in the papers. It's funny!

Anyway, Mum, I'm okay. Anything else you read is NOT true. Alistair and his girlfriend, Cheryl, were staying with me, as you know, and because of everything going on this funny little man came to help us get away. He took us to a village in the mountains. Alistair and Cheryl were a bit frightened but I couldn't understand what all the fuss was about. We didn't know anyone had been killed just then so I quite enjoyed it. I met another man, really nice, called Keramoogle – I think it was. He told me a lot about himself and wanted to know all about me and England. He came to the village later with some other men, one of them had a sort of fight with Alistair but it was Alistair's fault. You know what he's like. He can be a bit touchy at times. Oh and Mum, you mustn't worry about me and Alistair. Don't blame him because we weren't suited at all and to be honest, I don't know what I saw in him.

Anyway, Mum, I must stop here because one of the journalists is going to post this as soon as he gets to Narangburn. I'll write again soon. So much is happening. I met this really nice woman called Margaret.

I hope James likes his new school and you are managing without Dad. Give my love to Gran.

With lots of love from,
Helen. XXXXXXXXXXXXXX

[][][][][]

Narangburn Morning Courier, 24th March, 1984

Port Markham: A British visitor has been killed during a riot in Van Island Province, New Sudan. The disturbance has been linked to a strike of plantation workers at the World Development Bank-funded Van Island Palm Oil Development Project. Reuters.

Narangburn Morning Courier, 28th March, 1984

Port Markham: Following the murder of a Briton during a plantation strike on Van Island, a British volunteer teacher and two tourists, one of whom is said to be Australian, have been abducted by striking workers. The Australian High Commissioner has requested the New Sudan Government to secure their immediate release. Reuters.

Narangburn Morning Courier, 30th March, 1984

Australia Offers Help to New Sudan Government

In view of the deteriorating labour situation in Van Island Province, the Australian government has offered to help the New Sudan Prime Minister, Isaac Waninara, to pacify the situation. "We have offered to advise the PM," said Australia's High Commissioner, Des Matterson, on Tuesday. "Where Australian citizens are concerned, the situation warrants our serious attention," he told our correspondent over the telephone. "We have always stood by the government of New Sudan in times of need," he said, "and will continue to do so."

Rumours that an Australian tourist has been abducted by rebels are unconfirmed.

New Sudan gained independence from Australia in 1974.

Port Markham Messenger, 1st July, 1984

Editorial – New Sudan and Australian Influence

The problems presently being encountered on Van Island are a symptom of New Sudan's rapid economic development since independence from Australia in 1974. Labour disturbances are a fact of life of all free societies. The current acrimonious strike at the Sunderland steel mill in New South Yorkshire shows that Australia itself is no stranger to violent labour reaction. Yet the Australian government has the temerity to offer advice to the New Sudan Prime Minister. Why? Because of a false report that an Australian citizen has been abducted and raped by striking New Sudanian workers. This false accusation, which certain Australians are all too ready to believe, is a convenient excuse for Australia to pursue its neo-colonialist and racist policies in order to dominate the region.

This newspaper strongly urges our Government to resist the interference of Australia in the internal affairs of New Sudan. Ed.

London Daily Wire, 1st April, 1984

New Sudan: Unconfirmed reports suggest that a number of Britons have been caught up in labour unrest associated with a World Development Bank-funded plantation project on the paradise island of Van. A spokesperson at the British High Commission in the capital, Port Markham, said that the situation was being investigated.

London Daily Wire, 3rd April, 1984

New Sudan: The British High Commission in Port Markham has confirmed that a Briton has been killed during labour unrest in the New Sudan island of Van. The man, whose name has not been released, was the representative of the London-based plantations, timber and commodity-trading company, Barbary and Northgate, which has commercial interests on the island.

Two other Britons and an Australian tourist are missing.

Narangburn Daily Courier, ... March, 1984

Australia Demands Action in Van Island

The Australian Prime Minister yesterday sent a strongly worded statement to his New Sudan counterpart demanding that immediate action be taken to secure the release of an Australian citizen, Cheryl Arty, who is being held by rebels on Van Island.

Miss Arty was recently abducted along with two Britons. They are being held hostage by supporters of the rebel leader known only as Annu. A British citizen, whose name has been withheld, was killed during disturbances on the same day as the abduction took place.

Mr James MacDonald, General Manager of the Van Island Palm Oil Development Company was contacted by telephone yesterday. He made an exclusive statement to this paper, saying that Annu was well known to him as a Communist sympathiser who was suspected of being funded by the Vietnamese government. He went on to explain that Annu and his supporters have terrorised the island for a number of years, culminating in a series of murders and arson attacks on villages and plantations in recent weeks. He said he had put the resources of the company, which is the main employer on the island, at the disposal of the New Sudan Government.

Australia annually provides 350 million Australian Dollars to the New Sudan government in budget support.

□□□□□

February 1982

Dear Helen,

I can't stay with you on this basis. We are incompatible. You are enslaved by your bourgeois morals, imprisoned like a battery chicken. I can see you in 4 or 5 years' time with a husband in your mortgaged house in the suburbs. You will have a yelling baby and another on the way. Good luck to you Helen, I hope you'll be happy. I don't know what you want but you'll get what you deserve.

Me, I need the fresh air of freedom and I refuse to be trammelled by the chains of your hypocritical petty-bourgeois morality. The middle-class attitudes and gross materialism of this country sicken my soul. I shall leave little England to the Little Englanders and go to Australia where I can express my solidarity with the sons of the convicts who people like you sent to Laboratory Bay.

I want to be free!

Alistair Sallow.

February 1984
Dear Helen,
How yer doing?

When I didn't hear from you I wrote your Mum. She said you'd gone out to New Sudan! Wouldn't give the address at first but I telephoned her and used my irresistible charm!!! Got it out of her in the end. I'm not surprised you wanted to get away. That middle-class British repression makes me sick too.

I'm here in Narangburn having a great time. We practically live on the beach and it's parties all weekend. Mondays are a bit grim and my boss is a bastard but I can ride that. As soon as I've got the money saved, I'll chuck the job, get a car and we'll drive to Aberdeen. It's supposed to be a great place.

Helen, I'm coming up to New Sudan with my girlfriend, Cheryl. At the beginning of the year. Can we come to stay with you? Should be a buzz, eh? Remembering old times. What's the beer like up there? It's like piss here. The Australians have no idea. You'll like Cheryl. She's not your usual tight-assed Australian. She can get pissed like a man! But seriously she's an artist so just your type. She studies indigenous art here and she does abstract things with different coloured muds but of course the art establishment down here doesn't understand it. They're stuck in the stone-age, I can tell you.

Looking forward to seeing you. We'll turn up March time.
Thanks and lots of love and kisses from your old beau,
Alistair.

... March 1984
To Eric McBin,
Pacific News Services
Narangburn

Dear Mr McBin,

The Troubles in New Sudan

Thank you for talking to me on the telephone just now. As agreed, I will come into your office on the 1st April 10 am with a draft of my in-depth story on the troubles in New Sudan. As I said, I am in a unique position to give you the truth, because I was one of the people who was abducted. In the process, I met Annu.

I am looking forward to working with you on this story to our mutual benefit.

I am very keen that the truth is told and thank you for the offer of an advance.

Yours sincerely,
Alistair Sallow.

Narangburn Sunday Courier, ... April, 1984
Abducted Tourists: What Happened?

Since its independence from Australia in 1974, reports of a deteriorating civil situation in New Sudan are so common that we no longer take notice. Some are undoubtedly exaggerated by the press for the sake of a good story. It is difficult to corroborate the truth in an undeveloped country: rumour soon becomes fact. The country has again been in the headlines. This time, because of disturbances on the palm-oil-producing island of Van in which a number of Australians have been caught up. The Sunday Courier has a reputation for factual and objective reporting. We want you to know the truth. It is your right.

Meanwhile, our doughty Eric McBin has obtained an exclusive interview with the brave young Englishman, Alistair Sallow. Alistair, you may recall, was abducted by the messianic terrorist known as Annu. With his Australian girlfriend, Cheryl Arty, and a British volunteer, Helen Holmes, Alistair was taken to Annu's mountain hideout where, so Eric explains on page 24, remarkable things happened.

McBin: Alistair, how do you feel towards the people of New Sudan after your ordeal?

Sallow: I have no personal bitterness. They are letting themselves be led astray by a false ideology.

McBin: And that is?

Sallow: Communism.

McBin: An unusual point of view for someone of your age. Is it not?

Sallow: I'm an independent man, Eric. Now I've seen what sort of people these Communists are, I realise that they are no better than mindless terrorists who want to destroy normal, civilised society without having anything better to put in its place. They are no better than common thieves and rapists.

McBin: Interesting, Alistair.

Sallow: Yes.

McBin: You met the man they call Annu. What did you make of him?

Sallow: He's demonic. (Glares at McBin defiantly)

McBin: What do you mean?

Sallow: It's as if he puts a spell on people. They do just as he says. It's weird.

McBin: What sort of things?

Sallow: It's well known that he led people to burn a village, to set fire to the plantation and to riot in the market place and kill people.

McBin: Yes, so it's been said. It's a pity your camera wasn't working. But your personal experience of the man? Why do you call him demonic?

Sallow: He makes . . . (Hesitates, reluctant to continue)

McBin: Alistair, I understand your reticence, you've been traumatised, but it's important you speak out. You've met this man Annu, and you spent time, let us put it, as his guest. What you have to say now will influence how our readers think about him: you can help draw the picture of the man, so to speak. This is history in the making. It's important we have the facts. Before they're distorted. You have a duty to posterity, Alistair. You have a duty to this paper. You've strung us along, we've paid you a substantial advance and my reputation, as a tough man who digs down deep, is on the line. I'm not going to let a little shit like you get the better of me. Do you understand? (Sits back, looks at Sallow, wanting to understand why he dislikes him.)

Sallow: (Opens mouth, closes it, blinks twice, smiles) I understand.

McBin: Good. Because, you see, we need to create an idea of this man, Annu, which we can build up over the coming months, and years, if necessary, to steadily increase our circulation. Annu will be the manifestation of this thing we call communism, this thing we cannot nail here in Australia but which we feel is a threat, out there, threatening our idea of ourselves, in here. Fact is, they, who have nothing, want our things – or so we believe – and we don't like to think that all we care about is our things – we who have so much. Better, you see, to set up a personification of all we fear that we can conveniently label as demonic. Something more than bad, something positively evil against which we can set ourselves as positively opposite and, therefore, positively good. A wicked character upon which the government can hang the public face of its foreign policy because the public has become a little fed up with the yellow peril thing and Annu up there in New Sudan is something we can deal with, go in and get. Doesn't matter if we don't find him because we can control New Sudan in the process and feel safer here having New Sudan between them and us. (Looks Sallow in the eye)

Sallow: (Opens his mouth, closes it, blinks twice) I see.

McBin: New Sudan's our backyard. See? It's easier to think about than the great big frightening world full of real things. We're paying you to tell us about it. So Alistair, tell us about Annu. Give us some of the salacious details our readers are waiting for.

Sallow: (Opens his mouth, closes it) The thing is, I don't mind for myself. I don't mind talking about myself but other people're involved. My friends. I'm a loyal man, loyal to my friends, to my ideas and to myself.

McBin: (Incredulous) Are you? Do you mean the two young ladies, Helen Holmes and Cheryl Arty?

Sallow: Yes, I do.

McBin: We've asked Miss Holmes and Miss Arty to make statements for us but they've declined. Miss Holmes told us you knew everything there was to know. She implied we could go to hell so that she could get on with her life. A determined little girl, that one. The other one, Miss Arty, has disappeared into some sort of religious retreat in Charlotte. I don't think either of them will mind you speaking out. Speaking the truth on their behalf. If they subsequently feel they've been misrepresented by the Sunday Courier then they have the right of reply. But if they seriously want to challenge the line that will be taken by this newspaper then it will squash 'em like flies. I deplore this way of doing things myself but I'm a powerless pawn or rather no more than a wounded butterfly irresistibly swept along by the tide of History. You will feel like this yourself when you get to be my age, my middle-age just before precipitous decline. But as I was saying: will you please get on with what you've been paid to do. (Looks at the ceiling)

Sallow: I can tell you that Annu has a special attraction for the women whom he uses. It is as if he hypnotises them. They fall for him.

McBin: Do they? A sort of Rasputin figure? Would you say?

Sallow: (Becoming excited) Yes, exactly.

McBin: There's something sexual about the attraction?

Sallow: Yes. Definitely. (Eyes open wide)

McBin: What makes you say that?

Sallow: Helen, Miss Holmes, fell in love with Annu. I've known her for a long time. I could tell. She was willing to be taken in by him. She's that type. Weak and easy to manipulate.

McBin: Interesting, Alistair. But you'll agree, will you not, that it's not unusual for impressionable and perhaps even romantic-minded young women with an idealistic streak, to be taken in like that? There's the Patty Hearst case in America, for instance. The abducted one sympathises with her captors and joins them. Even after she was released I seem to remember she married her bodyguard. A woman attracted perhaps to a strong man. One who is able to protect her? (He looks at Alistair as if trying to see more of him)

Sallow: Yes. (Again becoming excited) No! I don't know. Those two, Helen and Cheryl, they go along with it. Hook, line and sinker. That's why Annu's dangerous. He has to be stopped. Only strong people like me, who are willing to speak out, can resist. I am strong.

McBin: But not strong enough to hold Miss Holmes and Miss Arty, it seems. (Tries not to laugh) Did Miss Arty show a similar . . . shall we call it a similar disposition? Or, if you like, infatuation?

Sallow: Yes, she did. (He is slumped in the chair) She went with another man. They went off together. I know something happened because when we returned to. . . I can't call it civilisation. This place where we stayed. When we returned, she was very quiet. I couldn't speak to her. She would only speak to the old hag who looked after us. On the way back to Akaranda she did the same thing with another man who stopped us on the road. She's that type. Leads a man on and then screams rape.

McBin: Indeed. We'll come to that later. But returning to Annu. You suggest there was no coercion? The women went to him willingly. Did they?

Sallow: (Thinks a little and then comes to a decision) No. It was as if they were hypnotised. He's demonic. I told you.

McBin: But you were not . . . um, hypnotised, as you put it, Alistair?

Sallow: No. (Laughs in a forced way) I'm a strong man. I can resist things like that.

McBin: Like what?

Sallow: (Looks uncomfortable and hesitates before answering. He is working out an answer again) I wasn't going to be pushed around.

McBin: Did they, did Annu, try to push you around?

Sallow: No. He didn't. No one pushes me.

McBin: You push yourself, eh? But seriously, what was your personal reaction to this Annu.

Sallow: (Opens his mouth but says nothing)

McBin: What did he look like, then?

Sallow: Small and muscular, like a boxer. About thirty, maybe younger. One of those baby faces that hide evil. He smiled a lot but he had a very efficient way about him and he was always calm. I'm sure he'd be ruthlessly violent if he wanted to be. The men with him were half afraid of him.

McBin: Half? What about the other half?

Sallow: (Hesitates) The other half? I think they were also sort of hypnotised by him too. When they looked at him, it was as if. . . (He's lost for words)

McBin: They love him also?

Sallow: Um, sort of. I don't know.

McBin: Like the women?

Sallow: (Laughs) I don't know.

McBin: Did you feel an attraction, yourself?

Sallow: (Laughs nervously and crosses his legs, trapping one of his hands that he pulls away as if burnt) No.

McBin: Nothing?

Sallow: Nothing. (He is outraged by the suggestion. He blushes but pulls himself together)

McBin: So nothing violent happened to you?

Sallow: Annu tried to do something to me but I fought him off.

McBin: Do what?

Sallow: Nothing.

McBin: He touched you? Intimately?

Sallow: Yes. No.

McBin: Raped you? Committed sodomy on you? Took away your women to humiliate you?

Sallow: Yes, yes. That's it. That's why I hate communists. They're sodomites and rapists. They take our women and they try to rape us to prove their power over us and to unman us. Helen and Cheryl were prepared to go along with it. I hate them.

McBin: Whom do you hate? Annu? The communists? Your ex-girlfriends?

Sallow: I hate them all and I'll get my own back. I'm a free spirit and I demand my rights. Helen wouldn't sleep with me but she'll sleep with that black bastard. Cheryl slept with me but some black bugger clicks his fingers and she's off. All the women there are the same. That old hag, we stayed with after. Even she was having it off with one of them. I tell you . . .

McBin: Thank you, Alistair, you've had your advance. You've had it under false pretences. What we're interested in is the psychological truth about this Annu phenomenon. If you want to peddle this nonsense about your own insecurity, then you should go to the Record. They'll pay you the sort of money you want. They'll be only too ready to take that sort of filth. You have just the sort of imagination they like. I only wish I could match you. Now fuck off. But before you go, tell me, what did he look like? Annu?

Sallow: (He is not put out because he has heard little of what McBin has said) Tall and slim but muscular, about thirty-five with a strong neck; red skin. He laughs a lot but he has a very efficient way about him and he is always calm. But I think he could be ruthlessly violent if he wanted to be. I think the men with him were half afraid of him.

McBin: You've said that. But before you go, tell me, what did he look like? Annu?

Sallow: Dark with burning eyes, which I never wanted to leave me, short and stocky, thirty-five or perhaps forty years old. Always grinning. Gentle but tough with it. I want to see him again.

□□□□□

Narangburn Record, ... April 1984
Tourists Abused, Raped by Communist Rebels in New Sudan
While our government stands by, Australian tourists in New Sudan are abducted and raped. A witness tells his story on page 3. Horror in the Jungle by Alistair Sallow.

Narangburn Record, ... April 1984
Your Hard-Earned Cash Supports Corrupt Government
While our government stands by, New Sudan squanders millions of dollars' worth of Australian taxpayers' money.

Narangburn Record, ... May 1984
Teach Them a Lesson They Won't Forget
While our government stands by . . . .

Narangburn Record, ... June 1984
New Sudan Takes Australian Jobs
While our government stands by . . . .

Sunday Record, ... 2004
The Book They Tried to Ban
The New Sudan Government has failed to get an injunction to ban the publication of Alistair Sallow's sensational new book about sexual practices in New Sudan (Sex and the Savage, published by the Popular Press, $19.99). The book will be serialised in the Sunday Record throughout March. Read about Warrior Homosexuality, The Right to Rape, Child Abuse as Cultural Heritage, I Beat My Wife Because I Love Her and Prostitution is Beautiful. These extracts will open your eyes and broaden your mind.

Alistair Sallow has been the Record's roving anthropologist for two decades now. His particular brand of down-to-earth reporting has got the paper into hot water from time to time. Alistair has been banned from entering a number of countries but, as our readers know, we have stood by his research over the years. We have always won the day and increased our circulation.

Narangburn Daily Messenger, ... 2012
Writer Found Dead: Well-known writer Alistair Sallow was found dead in his luxury apartment in the Narangburn suburb of Windy Bluff. Police say he had been dead for a number of days when discovered by his New Sudanian maid, on Friday morning. Police say that the condition of the body suggests that Mr Sallow was severely beaten. Neighbours say they heard nothing suspicious

and know very little about Mr Sallow except that he was reclusive in his habits. Inquiries are continuing.

Sunday Record, ... 2012
Soft Porn Writer Murdered by Boyfriend?
King of the soft porn novelette Alistair "Alice" Sallow was found dead in his penthouse apartment on Narangburn's posh Windy Bluff on Friday. He had been dead for some days when discovered by his maid, Bruno. Sallow was well known amongst the Narangburn gay community for his taste for the rough trade. Interviewed by our reporters, neighbours said that there was a non-stop procession of tough-looking young men visiting his apartment. Shouting and arguments were common.

London Daily Wire, ... April 1984
New Sudan: three young tourists, who disappeared during the disturbances on Van Island have re-appeared unharmed. However, because of continuing unrest on the island, the Foreign Office is advising tourists not to travel to the island. In recent weeks two Britons have been killed.

〔〕〔〕〔〕

Dear Mum,

Another quick note to say everything really is alright but I wouldn't say normal. And Mum, I am going to STAY HERE, so don't try and persuade me to come home. I can't come all this way and run away because of a little bit of trouble. We knew New Sudan might not be easy so . . . Mum! I miss you all a lot.

I told you that we'd been taken up to a village in the mountains for safety. Actually is was a bit of a muddle because it turned out that we needn't have gone up there after all. It WAS funny because the little man who took us – Bune is his name – frightened me just a little bit. All the same, Alistair and Cheryl were acting so oddly and being afraid – well Alistair really, I don't think Cheryl knew what was going on. I thought I'd better get them away. Then this Bune turned up on the doorstep and I found myself just asking him to help us. I don't know why. Actually, I wasn't frightened of him but he seemed so confident and sure of himself I thought well if he wanted to kill us he would. He'd do it very efficiently and think no more about it. I mean that's how I felt. And honestly, Mum, I don't see why they don't kill us sometimes because we are just a nuisance here. But they're nice people. There was a little man called Petrus who was just so sweet and helped us settle into the village, which wasn't really a village but a sort of camp of people who'd had to leave their village because they'd been chased out. I'm not sure who chased them out because some people say it was the man they call Annu, and some say it is the company because it owns the land. I wouldn't be surprised if it's the latter because Keramugl (I spelt the name wrong last time) has been telling me all sorts of things. He says the company is really bad and that he knows this Annu man who is so wonderful he'd die for him.

Anyway Mum, it was Keramugl who came to the mountain to find us. He said we needn't have gone up there at all because we should go to this Australian lady called Margaret. He seemed to think it was very funny that we'd trekked all that way for nothing. But actually I'm glad we did because it WAS interesting and the forest IS beautiful. When Keramugl was telling us Alistair got really angry with him saying he was fed up with being messed around. You know Alistair! Well Keramugl just looked at him, made a funny face and then looked back at me raising his eyebrows as if to say is this dog with you because I don't like it very much. It made me laugh and Alistair looked like thunder but he didn't say anything. I felt a bit sorry for him then but honestly Mum I can't think what I saw in him and I think his girlfriend, Cheryl, is beginning to have doubts too. She's quite nice actually but very quiet and timid. I think this whole episode has shocked her. She's never been outside Australia before and she just wants to go home. I think Alistair dragged her up here because he has to have a girl with him for some reason. But I mustn't be mean.

So we went down the mountain again. I said goodbye to Petrus but he said we would definitely meet again and that he wanted me to help him. In what, I don't know! Bune left us at the bottom of the mountain and he gave me such a big broad smile that I really liked him. I don't think he'd kill me but he might have killed Alistair. And, I couldn't help thinking, eaten him. He's like a little wild animal who does things by instinct but makes a good pet as well. Just like the ferret James had for a while.

Keramugl then took us to this Margaret. He kept talking about how wonderful she was all the way there and also about the Annu man as well so that I was almost sure they were the same person. You'd like Keramugl, Mum. He's very open and honest. He just says what he feels and although he's very sure of himself he's sort of modest with it. He'll say something quite wise and then look as if he's just remembered he can't possibly know anything and be quiet for a while. I like him. He must be the same age as me but of course he's had a hard life, working on plantations since he was a boy, so he has a face that looks as if it has seen a lot. Not wrinkles but the flesh sort of exaggerates his expressions. No, it's not exaggeration it's more like enhancement. It's beautiful. Sometimes when Alistair says something particularly silly, Keramugl looks at him in mock anger and it's like those masks in an ancient Greek play. He talks with his expression. Well I don't know if you'd call him good-looking but he's very strong and I'm sure he'd be a boxer in England. He walks as if he is determined to get somewhere and he is stamping the ground to make sure it knows what he is doing. Only just a little bit taller than me but stocky. Not a bit like Alistair at all.

Oh I've written a lot of rubbish and now I have to let one of the company women here who is going to Port Markham take it for me to post.

We're staying with Margaret whom Keramugl thinks is so wonderful. And she is. I'll tell you about her next time. If you see Mrs Sallow tell her that Alistair's alright. He said he couldn't be bothered to write.

Lots and lots of love to you and James,
Helen. XXXXXXXXXXXXXXXXXXXXXXXXXXXX

Yes, Andrew, at that time I am living in Alloy's house with Missus Margaret because she has run away from Jim because it is true that Jim is a man whom people run away from. Jim does not know where Margaret is hiding. Margaret says to me, Keramugl, those children will be afraid, it is better that they are with me. Go to the mountain and bring them here.

I go up the mountain, Andrew, and this is when I see Helen for the first time. I see that she is calm and she is brave. Yes, it is true Andrew, I think this is the woman to be my wife but I cannot say anything to her because a woman like that would not think of a man like me. It is true, I am just a kanaka. That is what I think at the time. But I am happy to be with this woman. When Bune tells me I must take her as my wife that is when I think it is a good thing that this white woman should marry a kanaka.

Also, I am happy to find my friend Weno. It is Weno who tells me about the other two white people, the girl and the boy. He is laughing in the way Weno does and so I am laughing too. He says he goes to the white boy to help him, he touches his leg and he tries to take the rucksack away from him so that he can sleep. Now, Weno does not speak the language of the white boy and the white boy does not speak our language so there is confusion. The boy tries to run away into the forest so that Bune and Weno have to fight him a little and tie him up so that he cannot run away and be lost. As Weno talks to me, he is pointing to the white boy who is quiet now but he holds on to his rucksack and I can see he is unhappy. He sees us laughing so he is angry again and he shouts at Weno. So I go to him and I sit close to him. I do not sit so close that he thinks I am his friend or his enemy but I sit as if I do not know him and I just want to sit down because I have climbed up the mountain and I am tired. You understand me Andrew, this is the way we do things. I sit near the boy but I do not look at him. I can sit there all night and I am happy because I know Helen is looking at me and she is looking at the boy as well. She is thinking Keramugl is a good man. Andrew, I am proud but then I think of my poor clothes and I am ashamed because I think Helen who is a white woman does not like this kanaka in his laplap. I try to cover my chest with my arms but it is no good. I feel naked.

I sit like this a long time, thinking of Helen and of myself and I want to be a man for this Helen. I want Annu to be with us because I know Annu would put us together and Helen would like to be with me because of Annu. Yes, Andrew, that is how I feel at the time because I did not know Helen then.

I am thinking of the boy so when he talks to me I do not hear him. This is a good thing because he thinks I do not want to talk to him and he is lonely. He is defeated by his loneliness. But I hear what he is saying because by this time, Andrew, I understand some of the ways you talk. It is not so different from our Tokpisin. He talks quietly, this boy, but he is frightened. He wants to know who I am so I tell him I have come to take him down the mountain to a white woman. I do not say anything more because I know that is enough for him. But I know he wants to talk and when he understands that I will not hurt him he says please get us away from here, I will pay you money. This makes me laugh. I do not want his money and I tell him this. Then he is angry again but he does not shout. He whispers to me. He says these men are wicked men, they are trying to take my things and they are trying to rape me. Andrew, I laugh when he says this. I think if you want a wicked man I will take you to Jim. That is easy. So I look at this boy and I am stern. I pretend I am angry, like the time I was angry with Neki when I take him back to his father. So I say to the boy you keep your mouth shut and you behave because if you make a problem for us we will fuck you. I say it is our fashion to fuck the arse of white boys like you. When I say this he is very quiet but Andrew, although he is afraid I see also that he wants to be my friend. Helen is not looking. She has gone, I walk away.

Then I see my friend Weno and I say to Weno if you want to fuck the arse of that white boy I think he will let you. Weno laughs and he says, no Keramugl, it is only your arse I will fuck because you are my true friend.

That night I take the three white people down the mountain to Margaret. We walk in the night because I do not want anyone to see us going to Alloy's house where Margaret is staying. But Jim finds out where Margaret is staying because of these white people. It is true, Andrew, they did make trouble. But Margaret said it has to be like that so I do not blame Helen and the others. I think, yes, Margaret is right, it has to be like this. Keramugl has to meet Helen.

I did not talk to the white boy again but I talked to Helen so that we became friends.

□□□□□

Dear Andrew,
As I said to you last week, I do keep all my old shorthand notebooks. I don't know why. When we leave Van I will throw them into the sea. It was easy to find the memorandum you asked me about because it is the last in that particular notebook. Mr MacDonald (and I am ashamed he should have a Scottish name) had been behaving very strangely for a while as you well know! Throwing the typewriter through the door that time was only the half of it. So I typed that last memorandum for him, wrote out my resignation and I never went back. I didn't get my final month's pay but it was a small price to pay for my peace of mind. Ted (Mr Livingston) was much happier having me at home, anyway, when things got out of hand. It is kind of you to suggest that the main office would have gone to pot without me but it was not that. The whole place went to pot. Not only the main office!

Anyway Andrew, what I have done is translate the shorthand for you. That is, exactly as I wrote it at the time. My mind was not focussed when Mr Macdonald started dictating so I did record some of the dreadful things he said. As soon as I realised, I stopped and I did not begin again until he had calmed down. He knew it was no use trying to get around me. I am not surprised his wife ran away from him. I used to think she was a dull soul under her husband's boot but I was wrong. She has spirit, that woman. I admire her. Please tell her to call next time she is in town.

The dots show where Mr MacDonald went off into another childish tirade. I just stopped until he began to make sense again. But when one is taking down shorthand fast one tends to fly on before you are aware of what you have written. I ought to have walked out of the room there and then, but to be honest Andrew, I did want to know what Mr MacDonald was going to say. It meant I was able to warn Peter and Daphne Wallasey. He was either suffering from some sort of delusion or else he was under a misapprehension about his own powers.

Here goes then, verbatim:-

VIPOD Memorandum as dictated to Mrs Livingston by Mr MacDonald and written in shorthand, ... March 1984

Fuck the bitch! Yes, Mrs Livingston, I am referring to my wife. And when I get hold of her. . . Memo to Mill Manager, from General Manager.

It has come to my attention, you little. . . That you and that stupid wife of yours . . . have been visited by that . . . Who has, until heretofore, called herself my wife. I heard this in the club from the Workshop Manager. He told me that she . . . had brought those tourists whoever they are who went and got themselves kidnapped and raped by all accounts by Annu and his chums. Serves them right. How they got away, God only knows. But I'd like to know and if you've got any information you'd better let me have it quick. Clarence said that she, the . . . asked you to take them in for the night and then take them into Akaranda the next morning. Is this true? You had better tell me exactly what happened or else I can tell you, you . . . you won't know what's hit you. That goes for your wife too. . .

It has also come to my notice, that, that, that woman who I am going to . . . has taken refuge in a house in the junior management compound. What do you know about that? I had better warn you that I am in the process of obtaining special emergency powers from the New Sudan government which will enable me to detain, for deportation, anyone who may be said to be a danger to the stability of this . . . island.

I don't know whose side you're on you . . . but if you want to get back into my good books you had better get on with your job quietly. Also, I want to see you coming up to the club again. You're beginning to think you're too good for us are you? You . . . That is not a suggestion, it is an order you little . . . I'm warning you.

But this is how I typed it out. I told Jim I'd signed it for him and such was his frantic state at the time, he didn't seem to mind:-

VIPOD Memorandum as typed by Mrs Livingston
... March 1984
To: Mill Manager, Peter Wallasey
From: General Manager.
File: ...
Reference: JM/PL

It has come to my attention that you and your wife have been visited by Mrs MacDonald. I was told this by the Workshop Manager, in the club. I understand that Mrs MacDonald brought up to you the three tourists who had been abducted by Annu and his men. It would be interesting to know how they escaped. If you have any information, I'd be grateful to have it.

Mr Smith, the Workshop Manager, tells me you took the tourists in for the night and that, at the request of my wife, you took them into Akaranda the following morning. Please can you confirm this. I would like to know precisely what happened.

Furthermore, I understand that my wife is presently living in the Junior Management Compound. Can you tell me if this is indeed the case?

Also, I am taking this opportunity to inform you that I am obtaining special emergency powers from the New Sudan government which will enable me to detain, for deportation, anyone who may be said to be a danger to the stability of Van Island.

I trust I can count on your support and that your work is going well. I look forward to seeing you in the club again very soon so that we can discuss these issues further.

Etc., etc.

Yes, Andrew, we will come down to Lingalinga as soon as it is safe. God Bless You <u>All</u>,
Prudence Livingston.

Note from Dolly, at home, to her husband, the accountant, in his office.

Darling Crosspatch,
Why are you working late? Please come <u>now</u>. I am very frightened. I don't want anything to happen to the baby. I have just come back from swimming at the club. Jim came into the bar with Clarence at about four o'clock – drinking even more than usual – he threw his glass out to the swimming pool area and started to shout. He saw me and said f . . . . women. I was terrified. Darling. Please come up now. I want to get out as soon as possible.
XXX Dolly.

Letter, dated ... March 198...
From: Ben Otuwaka, Director, Department of Migration, Ministry of Foreign Affairs, Port Markham.
To: Jim MacDonald, General Manager, Van Island Palm Oil Development Co. Ltd, c/o P.O. Akaranda, Van Island Province.
Dear Jim,
Thank you for your telephone call last night. It was good to hear from you and we must meet up for a drink next time you are in Port Markham.

As you requested, I am responding to your questions immediately and I will be sure this letter gets onto the afternoon plane to Van.

First, then: The status of your expatriate staff is that their residence in New Sudan is conditional upon having a work permit. Immediate family members are also entitled to residence status. These people have long-stay visas of one year, renewable as required. Short-term visas of up to three months are given to tourists and other people wishing to enter New Sudan for bona fide purposes.

These latter are generally businessmen and a variety of people wanting to do research of some sort. Anyone who has legally stayed in New Sudan for longer than a year may request a three-year visa and through a variety of processes may be able to request permanent residence. However, citizenship can only be granted to those people who have lived in the country for ten years or more and who can prove a commitment to the nation. A number of Australians have emigrated in this way.

Second: You are right to say that anyone in New Sudan on a visa is not only subject to the laws of the country but must also not participate in any activity that may be considered injurious to the stability of the state. As you pointed out, we expelled a number of communist agitators recently. Although the press indicated that this was at the request of the Australian Government, the immigration department was already investigating the situation. We do like to feel that we are a little more liberal in our approach to political dissent than is Australia, but that is beside the point. You are correct in assuming that the New Sudan government does not want any political activity that is likely to upset the development process or scare away foreign investors.

Third: I appreciate that you were born on Van Island. For that reason, you have all the rights of a New Sudan citizen. I appreciate also that, at the time of independence, you chose to be New Sudanian rather than Australian because you felt yourself to be a New Sudan citizen and because you had faith in its future. We are proud of the fact that in New Sudan, the colour of someone's skin is irrelevant to their rights of nationality. Your white skin makes you as much a New Sudanian as does my black skin.

Fourth: Yes, indeed, the New Sudan government fully supports the Van Island Palm Oil Development Company project. It is a cornerstone of our economic policy. Any activity that may lead to a disruption of the project will be taken very seriously by the government, which reserves the right to intervene according to the constitution and our international commitments. Your position as the General Manager and as a New Sudan citizen puts a special onus upon you to maintain law and order. As a Justice of the Peace, you do, you are right, have a certain amount of authority at your disposal. I know you will use this authority judiciously.

Finally, Jim, I would like to take this opportunity in saying that the Minister is very supportive of you and appreciates the problems you are facing. Furthermore, as your friend, I would advise you to take the problems you are facing one at a time. Do not let them get on top of you. You seemed to be a little agitated when we spoke yesterday.

With best wishes,

Yours sincerely,

. . . .

[][][][][]

Dear Mum,

I am just writing a quick note to keep you in the picture and to reassure you I'm well. I want to say I am happy. But it seems to be a bit selfish to say so what with all that's going on here. Anyway, the wife of the accountant of the oil palm project is leaving for Narangburn today to have a baby. She's going to post this for me. She says you can't fly too near the date so she's got to go now. Apparently it's impossible (her word, not mine) to have a baby in New Sudan. Thousands of New Sudanian women do it! I would have said, but of course it's not me having the baby. Anyway, I'm sure she's wise to leave but it can't be much fun being away from your husband when you're having your first baby. I shall never do that.

I can't remember what I told you last time Mum. So much is happening I can't keep track of it all . I said I wanted an adventure but I wasn't thinking of all this but as I say I just feel enormously happy. It's funny.

When Keramugl brought us down the mountain he took us to this amazing woman Margaret. I can't begin to describe her properly but we seem to have become friends so I'll tell you more about her as time goes on. But the big thing about her is that she is so quiet and calm and yet she radiates enormous strength so that everyone around her feels right. You have this feeling when you are with her that whatever happens is right. Keramugl adores her. He is like a little boy when he is with her in a way but he's not because he is also strong but he does not seem to realise it. I love him. No I don't. Yes I do. You know what I mean. I mean I don't mean love in that way. Don't worry. I don't know what I mean.

Anyway, Mum, it was night when Keramugl took us to Margaret. It had to be night because Margaret is the wife of the general manager of the oil palm project who is an awful man so she has left him. She was living with Keramugl in the house of another man whose name I have forgotten who is the boyfriend of the Englishman I told you about before. Well that is why he was so odd and didn't contact me again I suppose but he seemed nice. But don't go getting the wrong idea Mum. Margaret is really a very extraordinary woman. She is about your age and she seems quite tall because the New Sudanians are generally quite small. You can't call her beautiful but she walks in a beautiful way and she has a very relaxed expression. Funny old baggy clothes, big bones I suppose you'd say, fair skin, no make-up, her hair blonde going grey just tied in a sort of loose bun and she hardly says anything apart from what is necessary and very re-assuring. She sounds a bit boring but she's not. You just want to be with her. When she walked out the door we all just trooped after her without thinking of anything else. I always think that is what it would be like if Jesus came into the room. If he said follow me, you'd just do it wouldn't you and all your problems'd be solved.

I've got to finish. Keramugl is waiting for me. And I have to get the letter to Mrs Accountant! Margaret fed us and calmed us down, then, very early in the morning, she took us up to some other nice people Daphne and Peter who is the manager of the palm oil mill. We had breakfast with them and then the idea was that Peter would take us all to Akaranda so that we could fly back to Port Markham as soon as possible. We were supposed to have been traumatized but if we were Margaret had de-traumatized us. Alistair was very quiet, almost rude but at least not a problem and Cheryl seemed radiant and confident. I was impressed. Apparently, on the way to Akaranda in Peter's car there was a bit of trouble on the road but Peter said that it was Cheryl who handled it. Alistair was just frightened.

Rushing! Anyway, I said I definitely wasn't going to Port Markham. I was going to continue my job at the school. At first Peter said things were getting too hot. I ought to get out while the going was good and Daphne was nodding agreement. I did think for a moment he might be right because I didn't want to be a nuisance. Then, Mum, I looked at Keramugl. He was looking straight at me. He didn't shift his gaze and he looked very serious. Oh Mum, it gave me such an odd feeling in my stomach. For an awful moment I thought I was going to cry. I don't know why. He said, in a very low voice, I will look after Miss Helen. Margaret was sitting down saying nothing and when I looked at her she seemed to be miles away. I didn't know what to say so I asked her what she thought. She just said you make up your own mind dear, you'll do the right thing. So I said I'm definitely staying and I was so happy and I didn't dare look at Keramugl. Mum, you don't mind do you? You know I wouldn't do anything stupid and I can look after myself.

Lots of kisses, Mum and to James,
Helen.

□ □ □ □ □

Dear Helen,

Thank you for your letter. It's so long since I've heard from you but I'm glad we've managed to keep in touch over the years.

In answer to your first question, yes I am quite happy to tell you what happened on Van. It's interesting that Andrew Owens-Montague is writing his history of the island, and good that he wants to write it from the human angle. I will certainly get my friends in the publishing world here in London to look at the manuscript when he's finished.

In answer to your second question I am not upset thinking about it all again. Not in the least. Really, in my whole life, it was a very small thing and it was quite out of my head until you mentioned it. All the same, having begun to think about it all again, I can say that it did have a significant impact on my life. Oddly, what happened to me on Van that time changed me into the person who can say, years later: It was a small thing. Do you see what I mean?

When I came up from Australia with Alistair I was a very typical child of my time and place. Very spoilt, well educated in formal schooling but nothing else, and very, very self-centred. Not specifically selfish, which I was because of all those things, but self-centred: I felt I was the centre of the whole world and everything that existed or that happened only had any worth insomuch as it related to me. I could not see myself as an observer but always I was observed. If I walked into a room, I assumed everyone must look at me and I hated them or loved them according to my mood. That is youth, I suppose, to some extent, but also I was a taker rather than a giver. I don't think, up to the time on Van Island, I had willingly given anything in my life. I had given nothing naturally and I had never even given anything as a calculated gift.

What a horrible person I must have been and thank God that thing did happen. I'm still rather selfish, I'm afraid, but I fight it Helen, I promise you.

I'd like to say I don't know why I went up to New Sudan with Alistair that time but I do know. He was very attractive in those days – you know that – tall and lean with those sharp and well-defined features and that mass of curly blond hair. His skin was beautifully smooth and honey coloured. Do you remember? So charming and bossy getting his own way all the time and everyone willing to let him have it. I was flattered by his attentions and I wanted people to see me as the person he had chosen. What a chump I was! I loved to hear all the horrible things he said about you – just because you wouldn't sleep with him and of course it's the first thing I'd done. But, obviously, once we arrived even I, in my self-centred way, could see that you were nothing like he'd described and the way he made up to you, flirting with you, after what he'd done, just to get free lodging was awful. I think, also, although I'm not sure he realised it himself, he rather admired you taking that leap to New Sudan. He was drawn back to you and I felt rather left out and lonely and I began to hate you both very much. Also, I was so unused to the basic way you lived. I'd always had hot water and electric light. I hadn't any idea how to get on without them and there was you dealing with it all as a matter of fact. Made me feel even more inadequate and hate you all the more. I hated the entire English nation in those days!

So when that man came along, who you must admit looked a little, not threatening, but so confident and sure of himself that he might well have been ordering us to go with him, I looked at it all from the very worst of angles. This silly girl from the Narangburn suburbs dragged up a mountain in New Sudan like a prisoner. I was a prisoner when you think about it because I had no control over myself or over events at all. I just had to do as I was told and I didn't like it. I wanted to go home to things I knew so that I could complain about the world in comfort. What a monster I was! But I was frightened. I was terrified. I was sure we were going to be killed. I mean why not kill us? And that man would have killed us without a second thought, I'm quite sure. We were just a nuisance. Then Alistair being so silly and scared and unreasonable himself made things all the worse. For the first time I saw him for what he was: two dimensional and having only an idea of acting life rather than living it. It didn't make me feel any better about myself, having gone to bed with him at the first snap of his silly fingers. Then he seemed to deliberately make those men angry with him, begging them to fight him and kill him as it were. If they killed him then I was sure they'd kill me. If Alistair was worthless then I was absolutely nothing.

And even when I stopped being frightened, Helen, when your darling Keramugl came up and when you talked to me so nicely, I still had that feeling of worthlessness. It wouldn't go away. I wasn't being my old uncommunicative self, I really couldn't say one word. I had nothing to say and the words wouldn't have come even if I had.

Helen, in my life that has followed, my good life here in England with Ned, all that really was a very small thing but it was the thing that set me on the road to where I am today. Writing to you like this is bringing it back vividly. And do you know Helen? It is as if now, looking back, it is as the man said: all is bathed in glory, or beauty, or sunshine or whatever it was. It is true! I cannot see anything bad or wrong about it.

So, feeling very, very sorry for myself, we arrived at that funny little house where Margaret was staying. That woman, Helen! She was an angel. I have never met a person like that. She isn't even a woman in my memory so much as some wonderful heavenly being manifested to us as that middle-aged, motherly, warm woman. Yet she didn't do much at all, did she? She let Alistair prattle on until he had said all there was to say and she let me cry until I'd cried out all I had to cry. All she did was be there and give us all that food and, wonder of wonders, organise hot water for me to have a bath. Do you know Helen, my period started that night? Until that time they'd always been very irregular and painful and made me feel even more hateful of the world than usual. That evening it felt just right and ever afterwards, up to this day, they have been as regular as clockwork – except when I was having Margaret and Benjamin and Dagmar, of course. It's as if she just put me all together and plonked me in the world and said there you are. I felt fine and I remember already realising that nothing bad had happened up on the mountain and I saw you clearly as such a nice warm person and Keramugl as being so sweet and Alistair as being so absolutely silly I just could not work out what I'd seen in him. Amazing, as I think back on it. It was as if I – all of us – had been taken up that mountain to find what we really wanted in our lives or even to find out what we didn't want. Although I wonder what it was Alistair found out about himself.

And, come to think of it, didn't they keep talking about the man Annu who was in all the papers when I got back? I really cannot remember because they were saying awful things about him and Alistair had sold that ridiculous story about him which was quite untrue although he may have believed it himself for all I know.

Annu! People would ask me about him and I would just say he was wonderful and that it was Annu who saved us. And that is how I thought about it. I was saying Annu but in my mind's eye I was seeing the funny little man, so sure of himself, who'd taken us up into the mountain in the first place, I was seeing your sweet and loveable Keramugl and I was thinking of Margaret as a sort of Annu-ness radiating, well, love is the best word for it, all over the place.

Helen, this is a therapy for me. It's all coming back and I'm feeling quite hot with pleasure! I am a happy woman. I must have caught the happy bug up there on Van and I'm still infected.

Back to Earth, Cheryl!

That's it isn't it? No it isn't. How can I have forgotten but it only goes to prove that I really was changed because what happened to us on the way to Akaranda was really quite horrid and the old Cheryl would have had hysterics. The new Cheryl took it so much in her stride that I don't think of it as anything and even when it happened I didn't think it much either.

I think Andrew may want to know about it all the same. As you know, Peter, Birkenhead was it? The man who drove Alistair and me into town the following day. It was quite early, wasn't it? About seven o'clock, if I remember. Margaret had said we ought to get away from the company territory as soon as we could. The idea was we'd stay in the hotel in Akaranda and get a flight to Port Markham as soon as possible. I was quite calm and content as we left and Alistair seemed to have calmed down as well. Peter was chatting away nineteen to the dozen and I wasn't really listening. I was looking out of the window when the car stopped. It was a road block. I wasn't worried at all because I thought it was the normal thing until I heard Peter say in quite a loud voice: What's all this about? I realised something was wrong then but still I didn't feel afraid as I would have done before. Peter was trying to control the situation and failing and Alistair was palpably frightened. At least I think he was, I remember him as being frightened although he said nothing. I have this image of him in my memory of being unable to control himself for fear. He is shaking. And for myself, I remember vividly, it was as if I was not actually there but watching it all as if it was on the TV screen. Perfectly calm and knowing that it was just something happening that I had to go through in order to get to the other side, as it were. A sort of test. There were big oil drums on the road and a rope and men standing there in uniforms with guns. I don't remember any of them as individuals just autonomous things. But one man stood out. He had walked to Peter's side window and he seemed to be the one in charge. He was huge – in my mind's eye, at any rate – very black and in his uniform, no doubt, very, very handsome. Beautiful in a totally detached way. Alistair could not take his eyes off him. Neither could I. I had always been susceptible to superficial beauty, that's why I'd fallen for Alistair but this man didn't just leave me cold, I saw him as something un-human in his physical beauty. Do you know those toy soldiers? Action Man, they're called, Benjamin went through a phase of wanting one. They're a sort of caricature of human male beauty. A Greek statue thing. But imagine if one of those things came alive and was over six foot tall. It would be a horrible, monstrous thing. Terrifying if you were inclined to be terrified. But I wasn't. I wasn't even amazed at not being frightened, although perhaps I ought to have been. I felt very strong.

Well, he told us to get out of the car and we didn't argue. Too many threatening men and guns to do that. Peter was just impatient but Alistair was shaking and sort of fell to the ground when he got out of the car so that the big giant of the man moved him with his foot – you couldn't call it a serious kick – and nudged him with the point of his gun as if he was nothing. Alistair actually screamed. It was like a chicken and I felt terrible shame and embarrassment. That was all I felt and I was thinking – Helen I'm just writing this down as it comes to me – I was thinking about that more than anything when the big man comes to me. He sort of pushes me aside with his gun so that I am standing opposite him at the side of the road. I think well this has to be got through and I'll catch his eye but I can't. He refuses to look me in the eye. Don't make human contact and all that. Someone must have taught him. I can hear Peter shouting but as I look at him another man hits him right in the face which is away from me and when it looks back it is just covered in blood and silence. It is Peter's bloody face I'm thinking of as this giant man edges me into the jungle at the side of the road.

Honestly I can't remember what happened but I absolutely knew he wanted to rape me and I was thinking, keep your head because I'd quite like to live now, whatever I thought before. I really was not afraid of dying and I was thinking how silly I had been in my life and it almost made me laugh to think of that silly Cheryl who thought so much of herself being killed so pathetically here beside the road on Van Island, New Sudan. It was funny. I wonder that I didn't laugh out loud.

Inside the bush we stopped. He said nothing, he did nothing as if he was waiting for me to do something. I looked into his man's eyes and this time I caught them. Golden brown and deep. Sad actually. I saw my upturned face reflected in them. Two of me. Odd.

Standing there, hopeless, he was human. Just another man, as silly as Alistair himself. He seemed to expect me to make the next move. I was tempted to ask him to put down his gun. I thought, well if I just give in it will be alright. But then men are so odd sometimes after and that is when he might have killed me or something. So I did nothing. I just stood there like an idiot. Then he put the gun down, very gently and I looked onto the top of his head and there right in the middle, his hair was beginning to thin. When I saw that I had this huge feeling of love for him. Not sexual love but a sort of Christian love. Like a revelation. I loved him as all humanity and I loved Alistair in the same way. It was a relief. Even if he had killed me I would have loved him.

Helen, it is wonderful to make that sort of human contact when you've never made it before.

He stood up and began to undo his trousers. Then he looked at me again and I held his gaze determined to look very angry. Not afraid because I wasn't afraid. He said something I couldn't understand. Something like Madam sorry too much. I thought he was going to cry. He put his hand out. I took it. It was soft and pathetic and I just led him out to the road like a child. And I was comforting him! It's alright, it's alright, I was saying.

When we got to the road, Peter was being held by the other men and looking fairly beaten up. He'd tried to get to me but failed. Alistair was just a heap on the road. My man – I think of him as my man, even today – ordered the others to let them go and motioned us back into the car. Peter wanted to remonstrate with them but I just said I'm okay, let's get moving. We did and that was that.

When Peter asked what had happened, I said 'nothing at all, I'm fine'. Whatever he thought he didn't press the point except to say we ought to get out as soon as possible, nothing like that had ever happened before. He left us at the hotel assuming Alistair would look after me. Alistair did nothing of the sort but of course I didn't need looking after. All the same I think he thought I had been raped and because I hadn't put up a fight I had been complicit. He wouldn't talk to me again although it was me who organised everything for our flight. He was aware that I had given him up for good. We didn't have a proper conversation again and I don't think he looked properly at me once. I didn't try to catch his eye.

And that's it Helen. Nothing more. Alistair had his own interpretation and had his stupid life getting himself murdered in the end as you know.

But really it was all that which led me to where I am today. Because Alistair wanted to sell the story of my "rape" I had to go to that Eric McBin to tell him it was not true. I told Eric what had happened just before he interviewed Alistair. He said, don't worry, I'll cook his goose, which he did in a way although Alistair got $1000 out of the paper. Quite a lot in those days. I saw Eric a few times afterwards because we liked each other but nothing serious because he was a lot older than me and divorced with children and all sorts of muddle in his life. But he gave me a chance to write and then got me the job in London. I was so fed up with all the stupid press reports in the Australian papers that I wanted to get away. It was quite easy because my father was born in Liverpool. I met Ned and here I've stayed all my life. Funny, I never expected to end up English of all things. But it's been good to me, hasn't it? I wrote that silly novel but it made me a useful sum of money. We bought the house. Now I get to write my own column. What more could a human being want for a job. I can't imagine! Paid to pontificate. And you, Helen, a New Sudanian with New Sudanian children.

Dear me, I have gone on but it's done me good and I'll let you have it all, Helen. Andrew can decide what he wants. Please write and tell me more about yourself.

With best wishes and love from,
Cheryl Arty-Newman.

□□□□□

Dear Mum,
I'm going to be honest with you. I've had James' letter saying you are ill. Don't be angry with him because he's agonised over his decision. I was bound to find out at some stage and then how would I have felt? I would have been pretty angry with James, for a start. So that's it, I'm coming over as soon as I've sorted everything out here, which will mean I'm back in Sheffield within three weeks. K is happy about it, after all we've been married long enough to stand a few weeks apart. The children are old enough to manage without their Mum for a while. In fact it will do them good. They can concentrate on their schooling which is going very well under their Uncles Andrew and Alloy. But I tell you, Alloy is by far the best teacher. He will stand absolutely no nonsense. I'm so glad it's working out because honestly, down here on Lingalinga, the only option would have been to send them away. I could have managed that in my hard English way but it would have broken K's heart for all that he would never have admitted it.

Oh, Mum, my dream, to have had you here with us. But you were right. England was your place and James and Eli and your English grandchildren, your family need you. Little M (not so little now, sixteen any day, I can't believe how time's flown), K2, DD and PP all know about their Grandma in England but they have masses of uncles and aunties here. And of course Margaret and Daphne have been their stand-in Grandmas for you. When

Margaret died they were, I was going to say devastated, in the way Daphne says it but they weren't. They were just thoughtful and quiet for a while. Margaret was always there and a world where she could not be safely seen around the place was something very strange indeed. Strange because in a sense we feel her here with us still: Annu. And, Mum, don't think I am quite mad because I've talked this over with the others, it seems almost the right balance in things now that Annu is as alive here at Lingalinga as ever. I think now that Margaret has gone in a bodily sense the children are quite happy because she hasn't gone and we are always talking about Margaret as if she is still with us, which she still is. All the same, Mum, I miss her, she stood in for you in many ways, although it has always been Daphne who did the mother's practical things for me when required. When Little M was born I was quite frightened, I can tell you, here at Lingalinga and not a medic in sight. I had this book Where There's No Doctor, that's all. But there was a local midwife and it all went fine. Daphne organised everything down to a T and just having Margaret there beside me, watching me, quiet and unruffled was a wonder. I felt completely relaxed and no problems as I told you at the time. I just wanted more children after that and I would have gone on but it was K who drew the line at four. That's enough he said and that was that. He was right, of course, he always is. I am lucky to have such a good man.

I wish you could have met Margaret. Well I've told you enough about her over the years. In your last letter you asked how old she was. I don't know because she was ageless but not so old. One day she looked fifty, another eighty. But she can't have been seventy when she died. Andrew and I worked it out. And she didn't die of anything. She just stopped, I think, because she had done what she had to do. Got us all focused on Lingalinga as if there wasn't any alternative. There isn't! She left just after PP was born. Maybe he took over her soul, I like to think that.

Oh Mum, I am rambling on as usual but I wanted to give you a good long letter for once because I've got the time. Sitting here on the veranda looking out to sea at the table Petrus made us when we first moved here. K is away with Andrew dealing with some cattle which got themselves into a neighbour's farm and destroyed a whole grove of papaya trees. That'll cost us but I've told them if they pay anything to get the fruit for the pigs. We never seem to have any money but we survive! I'm putting Daphne in charge of the children while I'm away. She's still painting like mad and her paintings all look a bit mad! But there's something in them which catches you. Very free and full of sky. I'm to bring one back for you. Also, some of the children's. See if you can spot the difference! Nothing else because what can I bring? Thank goodness it's summer. I haven't anything warm except the raincoat I brought out here. That big yellow one we bought at Selby that time. Do you remember?

I'm so excited to be seeing you. Nearly eighteen years since I've been in England and I'm quite nervous. What will you think? I'm forty! But not fat like you always said.

Everyone sends their love. Look after yourself. I'll soon be with you. We'll soon have you better and perhaps I can persuade you to come back with me.

Lots and lots of love from your loving daughter, Helen.

PART V

. . . Lord, remember me – Luke 23, 42

33
Club at the End of the World

The last Saturday night.

Inside the club, which is, now, indisputably, after Annu.

Jim alone: no Margaret up there, no sycophantic chorus.

I don't need it: I, alone, will take them all on, and win, taking my triumph to the cheering crowd I despise.

The reason for his being is himself, and himself, therefore, the whole world.

Jim on one side of the bar, Nalin on the other. A glob of stale yellow light holds them tightly together. Dark emptiness beyond.

Jim is the last drinker in the club at the end of the world, where the drinks are free. Drink until there's nothing left but you won't feel any better. Jim doesn't care. He knows what he's doing or thinks he does. The idea of Annu, fuck the bastard, keeps him going. See girl? See what I'm doing. Fuck you.

Jim drinks and Nalin books nil.

They alone take advantage of this end of the world. Clarence might have kept Jim company as an act of charity, the embodiment of which he might have been. But his heart is broken by the defection of Alloy to the queer Andrew English boys never used to be like that don't put money on it ogling the meat on Bondi Beach in the 1950s five pounds a go all the way from Southampton. Daphne has taken him in, mothering him it is almost worth dying for the attention. Must get him away says Peter, Dolly whatsername's mad to go and that husband of hers next to useless. I'll organise the helicopter from Markham you go too. Not without you Darling now I've got you I'll keep you. Never a truer word spoken in jest or, rather, in love. They keep away from:

The club at the end of the world. Opening the fridge throws a pitiless light on the deserted, ill-lit, ill-kept, filthy ghastliness of the place. And that not for much longer: the fuel to run the generator will soon run out.

⬜⬜⬜⬜⬜

Jim and Nalin. Shit.

"What's this I 'ear then?"

"Sah?"

"Them fuckers."

"Sah?"

"Them fuckers I 'eard about. Got stuck up the mountains."

"Sah?"

"Them tourists."

"Sah?"

"Those white fuckers, for God's sake."

"Yes Sah. Annu Sah."

The word is electrifying for all that it is dribbled out in the foul yellow patch within which they, they converse. Fridge door effect. Jim, unnoticed by Nalin, a study of alertness for a moment before he subsides better bide my time get it right. Jim's your man for a job like this: cool and as hard as steel. Jim's our man they say in London saved the day: got the bastard. Licks his lips pushes the tumbler forward. Nalin does his duty with water not boiled but Jim is beyond such, such niceties.

You see girl, I'm the one to sort it out. I'll go up there with my men, my men, my men. I got 'em. Indeed he has if you can call them men. Rabis and Pen and those obeying-orders types who can't think for themselves. He has enough weapons too, and instruments of torture. Would not have needed help from Tuscany. Fuck those wankers in London. I can manage. He laughs a Jim laugh. Nalin looks at his feet only he can't see them in the dark at the end of the world.

Sammy would have told Jim his tourists were by now safely with Margaret but Jim needed them up in the mountains so he could get Annu. Fuck Sammy too. Do I need 'im? I'll get 'im. The other one will be there. His job to watch, to guide Jim, if necessary, to where he has to go.

Sammy. Fuck you. He glares at Nalin, daring him and almost, as another reaction, reaches into his pocket for coins but no need for that in the club at the end of the world.

Outside, the Landrover is waiting in the bright, unnatural light. I can manage. He does and Tudak steps back. Get the others I got a job to do.

⬚⬚⬚⬚⬚

Confused in the darkness, they know not where they are.

Weno has told them they are somewhere up on the white man's hill: I was here with Margaret, he brags, I remember the sudden uplift. He had been the one who started the laughter as they were tumbled against each other in the sealed black of the Landrover. Packed tight; ankles shackled but free enough to be thrown around and hurt. They hold on to one another. Free, Jim was well aware, and despite the guns, they would have hopped it out the back. Scattered like rats into the night disorientated until, sensing familiar ground beneath their feet, they would have run home to Andrew or Margaret, fuck 'em. Run home to Annu. Run home to Keramugl, only Keramugl is here with them, so, thus, no need to run. Home here, as it were, coming up the hill to the club at the end of the world.

Booted and pushed with the butt of a gun out onto the sharp gravel. Beaten and kicked into the cold concrete of a small room, empty, smelling of beer and cardboard. They are in the dark. A consignment of animals they might be, waiting for slaughter only they do not know it and this fact keeps them calm. Jim knows how you do it from Lingalinga days: see the trust in their eyes first and then let 'em 'ave it. The blood drains easy then and the meat is tender. Ignorance . . . is . . . bliss. They got to die, Jim used to say, laughing, it's their job.

Keramugl and co: Burara, Domus, Pecto, Deni, Kot plus those they picked up on the way: Weno and the other lost ones. Thousands of them, millions, uprooted from their homes. Bought by Tematan for Jim to use and mis-use. Useless if they will not work, useless, more so, if they will not buy from Chan's store. A waste of space, the plebs, them, they, the fucking-bloody-bastards, kanakas, the wogs, the nigs, the chinks, the serfs, the slaves, the cannon fodder, the labour, the below stairs, the public, the consumers. A rotten, lumpen[60], loutish, hopeful mess packed into a cell waiting to be dealt with.

They are, at any rate, in the club at the end of the world. It makes a good camp. The fence put up to keep them out keeps them in. Now we are all members connected by the chains, the handcuffs, the leg-irons, the waist-chains that bind us together in a sort of brotherhood.

Who makes the best sort of jailor? Nalin? Not the best. Once they've caught his eye he might show signs of humanity. Remorse for what he did to his daughter. Selling her like that. He might ask for forgiveness and consideration. And then where would we be? Because, for God's sake, they'd give it. This rabble at the end of the world.

Rabis and Pen, then? No: too much the only-obeying-orders type. They'd get bored and do something stupid. Take off the leg-irons because, please Sir, can I have a pee, have a shit, take a bath? Be human? And the idiots'd do it. No imagination you see. Food and water likely to be withheld because it is forgotten. It takes a bit of imagination and remembrance to be a good jailor. To remember some hurt or slight you want to get back at. To take revenge. Take it out on these prisoners over whom you have power. Here, food and water are withheld because it is within my power to withhold them. I shall use food and water and all the comforts as tools: give a little here, withhold a little there. Remarkable what people, desperate people, will do for a little comfort, a piece of bread, a piece of corrugated cardboard upon which to lie at night, between your aching backside and the cold floor. Sell their grandmas and their most cherished ideals in the club at the end of the world where we are all our animal selves.

No, not Nalin or Rabis and Pen. They do not have the intelligence to manipulate this sort of situation. They do not have the warped humanity to torture their fellows intelligently. Beat 'em, Jim says, and they'd get beaten. But Jim does not want that. It's more you know what you got to do, so Tematan's the man for this job and Tematan it is. He's got an agenda, we know that. And since Henry died, he's been looking for a job.

[][][][][]

Industrialised to a most efficient degree in the 1940s, the idea, nonetheless, was not new. Any more than was, than is, Guantanamo Bay. Captors and captives brainwashed. Members, all of them, in any event, of some silly club or other. Now, ironically, brought together in the club at the end of the world. Concentrated and I can tell you, it is not the physical discomfort, the pain of the beatings, the beatings themselves, not even the hunger and humiliation – we can all learn to shit in public in time – no, what hurts the most is, one, not knowing

---

[60] Shortened form of lumpenproletariat, generally used as a term of abuse.

what is going to happen, and, two, being locked up, being a non-person the world has forgotten.

Forgetting is what makes the suffering. We all do it: the great, weekending on a ranch in Texas or on a country estate in Buckinghamshire, the less great, watching the telly or shopping or writing. We excuse ourselves as it happens. How can we be constantly outraged? So the thing, that thing, which is happening, becomes yet another institution, the inhabitants of which are comprehensively dehumanised by our forgetting of them. Behind that wall lies the ghetto we no longer see as we do the shopping or hurry to work, those closed cattle trucks carry a human cargo, that smoke coming up from the pine woods over there is the smoke of the incinerator. It all happens in another country now, as you read, as I write. Our forgetfulness maintains it.

[][][][][]

Three nights have been spent in Joseph's storeroom behind the bar. Empty, now, except for the incarcerated men, the as good as dead, the forgotten. They have counted the days because light is visible through the cracks of the blocked-up window. Also, the heat: like an oven in the middle of the day. The smell, they no longer notice, is of human waste. Conversation pointless, they wait to die. The body does it well, I can tell you, not because it is itself defeated but because the mind has accepted that there is no chance of better things to come. The mind leads the body.

The end of Keramugl and co, the hopeful gang from Narangburn Plantation now viewed through the mythical past as a paradise. And as he dozes through the hours, Keramugl is tortured most by a dream wherein he sees Mr Smith and Grin doing the work he cannot join in with because he is shackled still. They barely notice him. He is a brief memory best forgotten.

Keramugl groans in his sleep, waking himself and Weno to whom he is chained. His hand is grasped and he squeezes it in reply. The relief is terrific. I have not forgotten. I will do Your work. Keramugl presses and plays with Weno's hand which returns his warmth. Like puppies rolling on the grass they are again. Keramugl gains strength from the strength he incidentally gives.

Keramugl is the Man. The man they follow regardless of his reluctance to be, to be followed. Why? Because having taken Helen and her friends to Margaret he returned to the mountain thereby confounding the conviction that they had again been deserted despite Weno's conviction that Keramugl would return.

Keramugl will not leave me, he had said.

He will leave you for that white woman, they had replied. The one who has bewitched him. She has taken him.

No, it is he who has taken her. Did you not see it in her eyes? She is in love but she is strong and would send him back to do his duty if he did not come by himself.

They had not been convinced, their faith, weak: we are afraid.

Is she not like the other? Our White Missus?

So the idea of Margaret, whom they trusted as a mother, calmed their fears and they waited for Keramugl who did indeed return so precisely when he was supposed to return that they greeted him with familiar laughter, ashamed they had ever doubted. And, that he was with them again – greater for the love of that young woman who was like Margaret – was enough. The eyes of the young man – doubtful, still, of himself, unsure and hesitant but nonetheless moving forward – the eyes of the young man were sought, the voice, a joy to hear. Blessed are those who believe.

Keramugl's presence was enough. It had to be. What could the young man have done against Jim with his bad men – the obeying-orders men – who had the guns, who bound them in chains and who packed them inside the back of the Landrover? He could do nothing it seemed and yet the violence was checked by the gentle hand of Annu which held him back, which spoke to him of love. This was the big thing up there on the mountain. Had they fought Jim and co, the guns would have been used – in self defence, we 'ad no choice, I tell you – and they would now all be dead, Keramugl and his gang, like the boys of Bosworth Field. As it was, love prevailed up there and they left with hope in their hearts.

But hope died in Tematan's dark cell. What is three days when you are free? It flies past. But three days incarcerated is forever and Tematan understood this well. He wanted them almost dead. He wanted them to know their failure; he wanted them to understand where their journey had brought them. He wanted them to lose faith in Annu. He wanted them to feel as he felt.

[][][][][]

The third day. On the western horizon, a thin line of light.

Tematan sleeps inside Jim's house. Rabis and Pen guard the gate. Together, they feel safe, these partners in an unholy endeavour. Justifying it to each other – he made me do it – but you cannot shake the universe in the way they do without upsetting your own equilibrium. Hand in hand? No. Side by side in sin? Yes. But neither can look into the face of the other. It is a sin, no doubt. Not the forgetting, but the conscious act.

I will do it.

They hand him the keys.

Go.

They react to the irresistible instruction rather than to the speaker from whom orders have not been heard before. There was a time when they had controlled him. Controlled him inasmuch as they had held the leash, releasing him to do Jim's dirty work. Only obeying orders your honour. You told me to do it. My commanding officer first and foremost. For God's sake! Would you hang Him on the cross for your commanding officer? Indeed, Sir, we would.

The man, Tudak, has come out of the night. A small part of him remains a part of the night. One moment was the night and the next, there he stands. Remarkable, had they been the types to remark. Remarkable, also, that he commands. Not so, that they obey: obedience in this way is their habit and thus relieved, they are gone into the night as is also their habit. The sunlight it is that robs them of their substance. They are ghosts in the day, insubstantial wraiths, afraid of the sun that might warm them.

Tudak has been here all along, his blackness catching the moonlight, making more of it. You could see in the night by him, Daphne was to say later. In the daylight he positively shines. Catch him forgetting? Not likely, for it is by his constancy that their suffering is made worthy. He will watch over Keramugl or die in the process.

He stands guard now, watching the declining night. Breathing in the dusty air, remembering the dust beneath Annu's feet. Before, before Annu, he would have had a fag. Not now, the early morning air is better; the dust, after all, contains the blood of Nalin's daughter.

Tudak opens his hand.

In the bushes on the other side of the road – perhaps in the garden of the house where Peter and Daphne stay, nursing Clarence – there is a rustling, a scratching and then, silence. A pair of eyes examine the night. It is safe: the coast is clear.

Tudak closes his hand over the hand of Bune, whom he remembers from the day of the fire, when he had wanted to stay behind with them. The joy of recognition is terrific. This time he will not let go. He thinks of Keramugl, sleeping on the veranda.

Bune asks: You have the key?

I have.

Then will you give me the key and go inside? Bune tightens his grip.

Tudak considers the idea of giving himself up: Yes, I will. What then?

Stay inside.

Tudak is excited, betraying his vanity, thank God, his humanity: I will bring them out? He sees himself the hero, the man of the hour. Has he not been with Jim for years? But his hand is squeezed. He hears Bune laughing and laughing himself, the preposterous idea passes.

No. I will lock you in. Do you understand?

I understand.

So will you do it?

Of course I will.

Good. The time is coming but it is not time yet. Quick, the day is here and I must go.

□□□□□

Light but the sun remains hidden. A grey light, a sort of silent fog of hopelessness within the club compound, surrounded by the fence put up to keep them out.

Locked inside with them, Tudak walks across the car park to the back of the clubhouse. A place where once he kept guard as a terrifying presence. He is a big man. Like a tree. Easy for him to break down the door of Joseph's little storeroom. It splinters with barely a shove. The poor light floods in, nonetheless a blinding revelation to those within who upon seeing Tudak between them and the outside are not terrified – they are beyond that – but rather finally convinced of the hopelessness of their situation. The time to die has come.

This is real: it happens.

But looking towards Keramugl for support they are surprised by the smile of pleasure upon his face. Instead of the rough gesture expected of Tudak a helpful hand is offered to Keramugl. He takes it.

There is not, in any event, energy enough for words. The little action required for thinking these things out is itself exhausting.

Tudak wants to carry Keramugl in his arms. Like the other one. But he cannot because Keramugl is shackled to his friend Weno, whose hand he also holds. Tudak must help them up together and thus he does. Leading them out into the poor, foggy light which is nonetheless pretty marvellous to those lucky boys who have not died on Bosworth Field. Or perhaps they have, and are here resurrected as Keramugl and his gang taken into the loving arms of, of him who takes them.

Thus the boys follow Keramugl. They go around to the front of the clubhouse to the deep veranda overlooking the little swimming pool. The veranda across which Joseph had once archly tripped, carrying the tray of coffee things, including the sticky tin of condensed milk. Beyond, lost at this moment of morning fog, is the view. The view of Van Island, albeit not quite as good as the view from the mountaintop. In the distance, across the great bay, is the silent volcano. When they see the view later, they will not be surprised because they come from high places, these Highland men. They will, however, discuss it with each other, for it is a new angle from which they now view the world.

You would think they have been lying down long enough but they are starving and desperately thirsty. There is no drinking water because the water tanks are empty. No rain for ten weeks. Not a drop since the death of Nalin's daughter.

Before, a tanker would fill the club water tanks once or twice a week. Peter keeps it going for his own house and for Jim the bugger who doesn't deserve it. The houses down below, alongside the golf course and in the Junior Management Compound, being more in the world that is becoming Van Island, have a more secure water supply based on an artesian facility. Living on the posh top of the hill has its cost unless you are prepared to carry up buckets. That would be the boy's job, anyway, if you live on top of the hill.

All the same, these boys are thirsty, lying out in the fresh air on the wooden floor of the veranda with an expensive view in front of them. Better to die here than in the little hole but a bit of water would be welcome and Tudak sees that they get it. Easy for him to break through the back door of the clubhouse with another shove. Inside, the smell is of what he will, henceforth, associate with those who had been members, including, for it is a fact that she was once a staunch member, leading the ladies' reading group for a while with such books as Mansfield Park by Jane Austen and North and South by Elizabeth Gaskell, although Middlemarch by Mary Anne Evans proved too big a project, Daff who became Daphne. The warm and airless place smells of sickly sweet alcohol overwhelmed, almost, by a brittle odour of decay. Those of us who know it – and Tudak did not – would recognise an Anglican church in the 1960s, which, having been messed about a bit, or quite substantially rebuilt, or even raised from nothing in respectable suburb or rough slum district, by academic Victorian architect working within strict budget and thus preferring grim, debased Early English style is, fundamentally is, soul-destroying. Once the rains come, the smell will change, a more healthy, wet rottenness will break in as the wildness takes over. But for now, Tudak is repelled, in a hurry to get out with Joseph's cleaning bucket and some of the remaining beer tankards that the English members had got in to remind them of, of Early English-style Victorian churches. Nothing alcoholic to drink – everything having been cleared out on Jim's orders, the bottles, mostly, now lined up on the work surface of what used to be Margaret's kitchen everyone helping themselves Jim taking something to his bedroom most nights fuck 'er why shouldn't I. Someone straightens the bedclothes but the place stinks. Of Jim and of the hard smell of cockroaches.

Tudak straightens the Bosworth boys out a bit, shakes them up, cleans them up and gets them as comfortable as he can despite the chains and things. He leaves Keramugl alone and then sets about watering them. That is what the job is for Tudak who has not yet quite got the art, or rather, artlessness of falling in love beyond his obsession for Keramugl, of whose name he remains in ignorance. Gently, nonetheless, thinking of the other, he brings water from the swimming pool, helping each one of them to drink, doing it all for the other whom he will leave until the end.

Saving the best til last? Not quite because Tudak the Terrible, Jim's primary tool, had, heretofore, performed his tasks as jobs to be done without thought beyond himself, without expression beyond the technically efficient. That is, until the vision of Annu, naked, then abandoned. That is, until the possession of Annu, dead, then the delusion realised. That is, until the communion with Annu, after the fire, then deserted. Heartbreak after heartbreak, unrecognised because how could Tudak the Terrible understand heartbreak? An animal out of whom humanity had been beaten since God knows when. Thus he still performed his tasks in the old way: he did not save the best 'til last because such ideas as savouring the best had not entered his head. He had done the terrible things as Jim's instrument, thoughtlessly, his humanity suppressed until, that is, his eyes were opened in the market place. Now, the light floods his consciousness like it had flooded the boys' cell.

Tudak works towards Keramugl. He wants Keramugl only. The others are in the way, not least the fellow who shares Keramugl's chains, the red-skinned fellow who keeps them all smiling, playing with the hand of Keramugl who smiles broadly with pleasure. Tudak the Terrible would have torn the chains apart – he is strong enough and he would have torn flesh in the process – strangling the one and carrying away the other. Instead, he humbly brings the water bucket watching the adored one drink. But the new ideas clash in his head, hurting him. He slumps down beside Keramugl, no less exhausted himself and sleeps.

[][][][][]

He dreams of the night. He is standing on a path that runs up the side of a hill between trees. The stars are brilliant, a small point of light at the foot of the hill only one amongst many.

That is, to start with. But the point of light grows brighter. It moves towards him. Joy unimaginable. The other stars are extinguished by it, one by one, bowing down to the inextinguishable. The brilliance hurts his eyes but he sees, nonetheless, that it is a naked young man who glows with a golden beauty. The eyes of the young man are fixed on the top of the hill.

He dreams that he opens his arms to receive the light but as he does so, so does his heart beat fast with fear. The light is too bright. He cannot face it. He is afraid of its honesty.

Afraid, he steps back into the trees. Stopping beside where he hides, the young man looks sad, covering his nakedness with his hand. As he does so his radiance fails a little.

Tudak has a desire for the young man that is not his old terrible possessiveness but rather a desire to protect him from the night. He takes a step forward and in doing so re-ignites the young man's radiance which is like a burning fire, so hot that Tudak falls back, again afraid of being burned. And as he steps back so does the light fail totally.

Darkness is total. The night roars back in triumph. More happily in his element, Tudak steps forward again, feeling for the young man's hand, anxious to hold it, to drag him into the forest, to save him from the night. But he grabs at nothing and looking up sees the stars once more and the path leading up the hill.

Ahead, the young man glows, and Tudak sees that it is Annu now who is leading the young man by the hand. Who illuminates whom, Tudak cannot tell. He expects to feel the loss of the young man, he expects that his heart will break but rather, seeing the young man thus saved, in Annu's hands, relief surges through him. Happily he sets off to join them. He will follow, happy enough to hang behind a little but in his dream state he cannot move fast enough even to catch their leisurely pace. With despair, he understands what he has lost through his fear of the light. Pain now grips his stomach. It rises to his throat as a groan that wakes him up to the dreadful normality of the day and an overwhelming sense of loss.

Annu!

His hand is taken.

Relief fills him as food to the starving. Here, beside the chained man whose name he does not know but whom he knows intimately, and with whom he has willingly incarcerated himself he is happy beyond his experience of his whole life. What he now has in his hand, he has for keeps. Wow! Remember your first love? The one you should have held on to at all costs.

I am Tudak.

I know that. I am Keramugl.

Keramugl: a beautiful sound, perfectly fitting the crudely beautiful face he has looked at so often, the beautiful strong body like the mountain itself and which he has watched and watched move with sure, solid confidence, the big feet set firmly on the ground that nonetheless has no right to hold them and does not. He is sure Keramugl can fly. Keramugl's hand in his. A hand that securely holds his own big black hand. Gripping the hand he grips Keramugl.

Thank you very much, says Keramugl, remembering the time with Sammy when they carried the body of Tarlie together.

For what?

For. . . He hesitates, thinking of Helen, thinking of being the man he wants to be in her eyes. So he says: For helping us. He knows it is not what he means.

Tudak knows it too and the idea of Keramugl justifying himself to himself and to the little world inside the fence makes him laugh. And laughing, he is confident. He looks into the brown eyes of Keramugl seeing himself reflected there again, only this time he has the hand in his for keeps so he laughs again. In his hand he has the man who is safe with him.

Keramugl smiles at Tudak. He thinks of Tudak the Terrible who is not this man in his hand who is another new Tudak to whom he can talk as easily as to Weno, the man in his other hand. Watching Tudak thus, he thinks of the time when he was naked up on the hill, when Joseph took him to see Margaret who was not at all surprised by his nakedness, any more than he was embarrassed by it. This leads him on to thinking of Helen and he is surprised that the idea of Helen seeing him naked is not such a simple idea. In fact, he is confused by it and blushes, there and then, deciding that, for the time being, it is easier to think of Weno and this new man Tudak, than to think of Helen.

And remembering again that Tudak knows him naked, he understands that there is nothing he need hide from him. So he laughs again, in the mood to tease: You were following me?

Yes, indeed, I was following you.

Then I am happy you found me because I would feel alone without you.

But you have your friends?

I do but they expect things of me and I am afraid I might let them down.

You make me laugh when you say that.

Why?

Because how can you let us down by being you? Being Keramugl is enough for us all. You cannot be more than Keramugl? I will follow you even when you make a mistake. More so, when you make a mistake for it is easier to love weakness than strength.

Someone else said that to me.

Was he not right?

She was. And thinking of her, he wants her to see him naked again. She is.

She is the wife of Jim?

She is Missus Margaret. She has left Jim behind.

I am glad to know that. But. . .

What?

Where is she?

I left her in the house of Joseph. She sent me back to the mountain and then she sent Weno, my friend on the left here, to tell me that Joseph had been taken by Jim to the Togulo Farm.

Keramugl thought of Margaret and Helen together, with no one to protect them from Jim. He loosened his grip on Tudak in his concern but he was pulled back.

You must not worry because I met Annu in the market place with the boy who follows him. He told me he was going to Margaret.

So Annu is here?

He is here.

And he is with Margaret?

Have I not told you so? Do you not believe?

I believe. But. . .

What?

It is hard . . . to know what will happen, when I am here shackled and powerless. I am not afraid with you beside me but. . . where is Annu?

Keramugl begins to let go but Tudak holds him tight, the memory of Annu in the market place holding out his hand so strong that he does indeed stretch out his free hand, reaching into the air. He remembers what Annu asked him, so he asks Keramugl: Have you forgotten Him? What did he ask you?

Keramugl remembers Annu. He remembers what Annu told him on the airfield at Karandawa: I want you to live for me and I want you to remember me. If you can do this then I will never leave you. I will always be with you, Keramugl. He remembers the kiss and he remembers his reaction to it: I remember Him.

So you do believe?

I do. I believe and saying so he sees the new morning view, over the golf course, away over the flat plantation, somewhere in which are Andrew and Alloy and the others. He sees the hanging layer of dust and he sees the volcano beyond the bay. I believe.

Tudak replies, surprised even by his own confidence: And He is with Margaret and Margaret is right about Keramugl: to be yourself is enough.

Yes, I can be myself and I am not ashamed of being naked. Annu taught me that. I want him to see me naked. But he did not add that Helen seeing him naked was another idea. An idea that surprised him: that he wanted to own her as her master and yet at the same time he was ashamed of the idea and would ask her forgiveness, burying his face in her lap. But only as her master could she see him naked. The idea stuck. Then, they would be naked together which was something different altogether that he did not understand but which he knew was a good thing. This thinking about Helen and wanting her made Keramugl feel happy and anxious for her at the same time. So, despite Tudak here beside him, he felt angry with Tematan, angry with himself for being taken and particularly angry with the chains so that he shook them, waking up Weno.

[][][][][]

A delicate flower, the small song of a bird, struggling in a field of abominable filth, in Bosworth Field, in the Flanders Fields, alone and fragile in the dead silence after the battle. The inevitable triumph of good over evil, which in the end, must go down. The hand of pure love grasped in the abomination of the concentration camp. The triumph of humanity over the only-obeying-orders, the honour of the regiment, the queen and country, the jolly good chaps whining they made me do it, the me first I got my rights.

But it is hard, all the same, to maintain the right view, in the circumstances. Hunger, the need to wash, to shit in some comfort, the overwhelming sense of having been abandoned and forgotten, the desire to kick the fucker to whom you are chained. For God's sake talk to me, give me some peace. Keramugl's quiet anger, shaking his chains and waking Weno who blinks and looks around at the unexpected world in which he finds himself. Then the relief at finding the beloved Keramugl beside him. At any rate if you've got to be chained, he begins but seeing Keramugl's thunder he tries to disappear.

You deal with them fuckers, Jim had told Tematan and Tematan had done just that, excited by the idea of official power. But not much he could do, to start with, except keep them locked up, and Rabis and Pen and co on guard. Better get a list of the names he thought, a little later. We can start a roll call. Make it normal only I ain't got no food to give 'em. The feeding, the watering, the sleeping, the washing had, after all, been an issue during the journey to Karandawa. Tematan knew about these things.

'Ere, you better buy them something, came a couple of days later from Jim with a wad of dirty paper. In one corner of his mind they were comfortable in the club compound which we let 'em 'ave. I 'ad to do something with 'em, couldn't let 'em run around wild causing trouble could I? I was doing my duty. In another corner, they made me do it. I'm the one who does their dirty work. See girl, I carry the 'ole thing on mi shoulders. Feels like some weight, anyways. Then he forgot: time flies by when you're free. I got better things to do than wipe their arses. Indeed you have Jim.

So Tematan was left in charge. And, no doubt, he could have done a good job. Done it well and cooperated with them and got things sorted out like good men do. Made them comfortable for all their captivity. After all, was not Burara his brother?

34
Some Men Would Have Wept

The Landrover cruised down the hill, easing up beside the locked gate. Jim, elbow sticking out the window, saw all was quiet. "Over to you Sergeant Major," he sneered at Tematan, who jumped out the back.

The small, muscular man, with sharp, darting eyes, who had appeared from nowhere, helped unload the bags of sweet potato. Tematan had bought them with a small proportion of the money Jim had given him – I got to get some stuff for myself, he had justified, keeping most of it, I'm only doing what he tells me.

As the Landrover rolled down the hill, Jim called back: "An' if you see the other one, tell 'im to fuck off."

Tematan hoped he would not see him. He was afraid of Tudak. He had assumed he would be Jim's bestest lieutenant, his right-hand man. He had imagined himself sitting in the front beside Jim, Tudak in the back. But now Tudak was gone, a little man had replaced him who was as tough, as solid and as silent as a stout piece of wood. As silent as Tudak but not dumb silence, rather, a wily and sleek silence, all watching and deviousness. Tematan did not trust the black-eyed little monster who smiled at him but said nothing. Who had given him the keys with a knowing smile but without a word.

Alone outside the gate, the silence worried Tematan, forcing him to think about the times before, when he was the cocky fellow in fine clothes, recruiting labourers in the Highlands. He had been proud of himself then. Not now, and remembering how the limping, screw-loose Annu had humiliated him in Karandawa, taking his men away, he hated them all, especially Annu, whom he wanted dead at his feet. He relished the idea of seeing their suffering in the storeroom and of him being the one to let them out like dogs who would lick his feet, and if they didn't he'd make 'em.

He lugged the bags just inside the gate. They can get 'em from 'ere an' do what they like, he thought. Eat 'em raw for all I care.

His first reaction upon finding the door broken and the room empty was of disappointment mixed with anger. He wanted a whip with which to whip them back. Fear gripped him for a moment. But he laughed at his fear, remembering how he had got them: they'll be crawling around in their chains, despicable creatures, eating grass and shitting in full view of each other. All the easier to kick. His cock stiffened a little at the idea and he went to search them out, exaltation in his heart.

〔〕〔〕〔〕

Tematan was allowed to do what he liked. And he was surprised, following his initial fear, how easily he could subdue Tudak, who indeed acted like a

433

whipped dog. Moreover, Rabis and Pen did exactly what they were told, proving particularly good at the whipping and beating.

At first, he had wondered what was the point of keeping Keramugl and the others alive but Jim told him to keep them in good condition because the nosey parkers and the do-gooders, whoever they were, would, apparently, want it that way. Sometimes, when Tematan raised the subject, Jim would get suddenly angry, ranting at them in London wherever that was, saying they made him do their dirty work because he was the only one could do it. The only one, he told Tematan, arm around his shoulder and apparently crying, oo'as the guts to do what no one else dares do. An' why? – looking straight over Tematan's shoulder – Because I'm Jim, I am, an'. . .

At which point the little man with the all-seeing beady eyes would appear and lead him away. In the mornings the same little man would be waiting by the Landrover, perfectly in order, to carry Jim through the day. Tematan going down to the club had to pass him every morning coming up to the house. The man would catch his eye however much he tried to avoid it, smile, and say something trite that always struck Tematan as insolent: a good day for it, or have a good time or good day, eh? Tematan would ignore him but having passed by the little rat he always felt he was about to be bitten. Once only did he look back. The man had disappeared but there was a distinct animal scratching amongst the dry vegetation that made his flesh creep. The little man spoilt his days; he resented him.

Bad things happened in the club compound, which I will not describe. If you want gratuitous violence, there are plenty of books on the subject. Look in any big book shop. There will be a section on war, and whole shelves about the Third Reich, the Nazis and the Final Solution. Also, one or two books about more recent events in places like Rwanda and the former Yugoslavia. If you really want to hear the truth read the Russian books: The House of the Dead or, better, The Gulag Archipelago, the third volume of which I have put off reading for forty years. Jim and Tematan are not the only ones: we are all to blame.

And Tematan was not entirely unreasonable: he considered what Jim had said, in the spirit of keeping them alive, he did not force them back into the storeroom. Rather, he allowed them the veranda and the freedom of the grounds, which were, however, limited within the fence, the only serious bit of open space the gravelled car park, useful for the useless and interminable roll calls and big enough to kick or throw a ball around, had they been able to do so. Chained, they were not. They could not entertain themselves in such a way but they entertained Tematan. It fascinated him to contemplate a couple of men chained together, forced to live as a single animal. He got a kick out of watching their sub-human, shuffling antics.

No longer human but an animal this thing, this pair of shackled humanoid bodies, was to Tematan, who had no respect for animals either. He found it easier to abuse an animal, even more an animal that had lost its dignity. The cowering or hurt-looking eyes only made him angry. He found himself mumbling or else louder, shouting for Rabis or Pen, in a parody of Jim: "eh, come 'ere an' whip this animal, I don't like the way it looks at me". I don't like it! He did not. Once, when he caught himself feeling more ashamed than usual, he took the whip from Rabis and whipped the thing himself.

Made me feel like a man, he told Jim later, wanting to massage his cock.

That's mi boy, Jim had replied but there were times when he wanted to whip Tematan himself, an' I will one day just you see, you monster. He wanted Margaret's resistance. He wanted someone to stop him, not egg him on: he could egg himself on well enough.

Tudak, free of chains, cooked the sweet potatoes in pots he found inside the club, using, as firewood, bits of the furniture that he pulled apart. The curtains he took down for their bedding. Also, he managed what little water was left in the swimming pool and repaired the roof gutters and pipes that fed the water tanks. Rain was on its way. Annu had promised it and with Annu in mind, Tudak found it easy to discipline himself and to thereby maintain the morale of the others. Day by day, he pressed on with doing what had to be done, like he was still the old automatic Tudak. Had Jim's do-gooders stuck in their noses, the almost-bearable living conditions they would have found – the scars on the prisoners' backs, buttocks and legs etc notwithstanding – would have been entirely due to Tudak.

The Bosworth boys, with reason enough to distrust the world of men, felt Tudak's kindness and concern growing daily and thus began to trust him. But Rabis and Pen suspected no subversion. Tematan also, at first, assumed the dumb animal of old, who had wandered in by chance, content to stay behind the security of the fence.

"Boss?"

"Yes?"

"He's with them."

"Oo?"

"Tudak."

"That fucker?"

"Yes Sir. You want him back?"

"What did I tell you? You deaf or something?"

Apparently deaf.

"What did I tell you?"

"You told me. . ."

"'E can fuck off. 'An 'e can. You told 'im?"

"What?"

"God 'elp me. To fuck off."

Apparently deaf.

"'Ave you?"

"No Sir."

"You tell 'im then. I got the other fellow now. Popped up out of the blue, 'e did. Right as rain, 'e is. An' if you see Sammy. . ."

"Yes Sir?"

"You can tell 'im to fuck off, too. Got it?"

"Yes Sir."

"Do it then."

But Tematan did not do it. Sammy had disappeared off the face of the earth, apparently, and he was afraid of Tudak.

[][][][][]

Intellectual Business, 22nd January, 1985
Barbary and Northgate Pull Out of Plantations. Share Price Goes Through the Roof
For some years now the City has recommended that B&N offload what plantations stocks remain in its portfolio. Yesterday, the Chairman, Lord Burton-upon-Trent, until recently the Anglican Bishop of Burton-upon-Trent, announced that the company had done just that. It will now concentrate on its trading and industrial activities. The former includes commodities: the latter, chemicals, paints and food processing. In response to a recent Amnesty International report that severely criticises the company's activities in New Sudan, Lord Burton-upon-Trent admitted that it had faced problems in New Sudan.

Intellectual Business, 5th May, 1985
Shareholders Endorse Barbary and Northgate Directors at AGM
Presenting the Barbary and Northgate Annual Report at yesterday's AGM, held in the Dorchester Hotel, the Chairman, Lord Burton-upon-Trent, said he was proud of what the company had achieved during the past twelve months. He stressed that Barbary and Northgate was a good example of what Britain stood for. Shareholders' representative, Lady Iveneverdoneadecentdaysworkinmylife, said that the board had the fullest support of shareholders. She led a round of applause. Share prices reached an all-time record on the London Stock Exchange.

[][][][][]

Wow for the day! And yet there are times when the opposite is the case. When the signals to the day are a prelude to the day I do not want to face: the dismal end of blissful night's oblivion. Thus was it for Jim, these days. These days, not only in which he had lost his comfortable certainty but also in which he had the ever-present, nagging idea – fuck 'er – that he no longer held the centre. He was alone, Bune his only comfort.
"Morning Sir."
"'Ello."
Enough said: the small black man stood economically by suggesting respect. An efficient presence indeed a comfort. Compact and solid. Also, elemental, essential and inescapable.
Impossible, in any event, to escape: Bune was, no doubt about it, a comfort during those last few days, and Jim, for all his denial, hung on to it. In the swirling, whirling, down-dragging turbulence of those days Bune was the piece of solid black wood upon which Jim hung like the very devil.

The Landrover hums, ready: Jim takes the driving seat. Bune is ignored.
Apparently, but the man in the back, whose eager eyes see all, is acknowledged.
There so surely that leaving the dreary house filling with unwelcome morning
light, Jim's spirits revive. He takes control of the vehicle – the solid black
presence behind – and passing the club, looks straight ahead, cruising down to
the foot of the hill. How easily he could have taken the rougher road to
Andrew's plantation: the road Margaret had taken to Ples with, one time,
Daphne following behind. Instead, he takes the other way, skirting the golf
course with Andrew's oil palms, again on the other side, a threat now rather than
the integral part of Jim's world they had once been. This way leads to the office,
empty of Mrs Livingston. Behind the office rises the mill, wrongly silent, and
beyond, the workshop where Clarence is not but where Pete tinkers and wanks
away – fuck 'im, fuck 'im to 'ell, fuck 'em all – doing the necessary jobs that
just about keep things going. Pete the nonentity for God's sake. Jim slumps and
shrinks within himself. Impossible that things have come to this but they have,
Jim. An' 'ow does the fucker do it, I'd like to know? With the help of a few
kanakas oo must love 'im or else 'e's got 'em by the balls cos there's no money
to pay 'em with. An idea that makes Jim chuckle and feel a little more his old
self: for Christ's sake, I'll sack 'im an' do it miself. Do it better. His hands
release their grip on the log that keeps him afloat? Sack 'im, an' – he glances at
the oil palms with distaste – come to think of it, that fucking poofter, Andrew.
He sticks a finger up his nose: 'aven't I dun it already? He is not sure what he
has done but the idea puffs him up a little. He grips the steering wheel and lets
go of the log so that the little unnecessary effort is like a knife in his chest. Ooh:
he deflates, his flesh hangs in green folds, bags beneath his eyes, baggy knees
and his dick, even, shrinks. He's had enough. What's the point of it?

The Landrover lurches to a halt. It stalls. Jim gets out and stands upon the
ground. He is supported by the open door. Surveying the world around, the
silence presses upon him. A Sunday sort of silence only worse because no grace
or pleasant diversion from the weekly round attends. Habitually, noisy activity is
what buoys up Jim, proving his drive, his pull, his force, his face. The man who
gets things done. But nothing is getting done and he will not recognise that . . . it
is Bune that buoys him up now. Drifts not the man of action but a man alone in
the desolation he can no more recognise than he can recognise Bune. He cannot
deal with it – without a drink. Needs to do something to banish it.

"What?"

"Sir?"

"I thought you called me?"

"No Sir."

I wish you had. I wish you had called out: Jim, come with me and I'll show
you how it's done hand-in-hand. Fuck that. Fuck that hand-in-hand, poofter
nonsense. It'll be Andrew and that other one next: the kanaka with all the hair
and the angry eyes.

Nonetheless, Bune jumps down, stands firm upon the ground beside Jim and
points towards Andrew's division: "I'll take you there?"

Jim must be offered the choice but he shakes his head. Desolation rains down. Anyway, he might have thought, only he did not: What if Andrew is in one of his surly moods and the other aggressively defensive? He dare not risk the snub. Thus Andrew lies well within the fuck 'im category.

Jim allows himself to be taken to the office, weary of the whole fucking charade damned if I can be bothered. But he can for a little longer, damning himself all the more.

□□□□□

Jim is deposited at the dusty, litter-strewn, desolate office where a few staff hang around as a matter of form, chatting, reading old newspapers, writing novels. Mrs Livingston's absence is palpable.

In his little room, Dolly's Dickie puts the financial records in order and waits for any task that Jim may invite him to do. Thus, inevitably: "Oi, whatsyername," Jim calls, inspiring nervousness rather than fear which is no longer excused by respect such as gosh the man's got guts but rather by an unnerving and creeping realisation that the man is stark raving and might, even more so than before, do anything. A realisation, in fact, that this is a grown-up situation where grown-up forethought and subsequent grown-up action are required. More so and much more so than the whole palaver of getting married, getting this job, getting over here, settling into the house, dispensing with the condoms and getting Dolly pregnant in order to give her something to do. That was easy, the rules written and everyone around pitching in because what else do you do and they're such a sweet couple who don't seem to know what's what sometimes but he got her pregnant I suppose it was him. But this is different:

"What can I do?"

He would like to turn tail and run. The Dickie part of him, but there's Dolly and in her condition I got to do what a man's got to do and oh for the daily safety of a little room above, or even behind, a suburban bank where I can put the figures in order and where a little girl, smart, deferential, not too bright but without pretensions and perhaps working hard on her aitches brings me cups of tea and a nice chocolate biscuit and in the evenings I go home to a tidy flat and after a plain supper I watch the telly or read a novel. In peace for ever.

I call him Dickie because there is something of Dick about him only less. He has not the intellectual curiosity about why men do what they do. Build those church towers. For instance. Has not the grand compassion either. Dick is a real man in the end by his willingness to love – and thus save – Tudak. Dickie is on a smaller scale altogether.

Jim, the old Jim who thought he was the centre of certain significant things, would have laughed, even a little good naturedly once: that boy might do something yet. He would have called him Rich or Rick as an appropriately manly name thinking of him as another obedient dog: ' e can do tricks.

"'Ere . . . um, you, er. . . What's yer name, for fuck's sake?"

"Yes Sss. . ." The word dies and the man's man he wants to be forces out "Jim".

Old Jim laughs at this: "Come 'ere. Can you?" Please, he might have added, had he not seen the joke. And is this another mincing poofter, Andrew style? Talks like one but surely he's 'itched to that one oo fancies me. P'raps that's why. I 'adn't thought of that. He preens himself, green skin and all.

Dickie comes, sits where Andrew had sat only tries to act relaxed. Cannot, not without a fag or a glass in his hand. Andrew, at any rate, did not have to act his bad-tempered, sulky awkwardness, it came naturally, overwhelmed him beyond any acting, even good manners.

"What's yer name? Dunno what's come over me. Forget mi 'ed next." Jim, the GM, still, acts his good manners, overwhelmed, himself, all of a sudden by a little self-interest that he needs, or thinks he needs, this, this, this man, of sorts, if he is going to survive the coming few days, just as, let's face it, I need the Pete, fuck 'im, fuck 'er, fuck 'em all. Anger. Blank. What was I thinking? Panic, blinks, pain in chest, got to grasp something solid like the fellow, the other fellow, out there, in the car. The thought makes Jim feel better like a swig of whisky in the old days.

The boy – which is all he is, having had time to get over his disappointment with the grown-up world – looks at Jim. He sees an old man who is a little disgusting for lack of any characteristic that might elicit sympathy. Later he will remember that Jim seemed to be rotting from within, collapsing in upon himself. This sense of disgust, of wanting to throw something at Jim and run away, childlike, banishes the offence he might have felt at Jim's, the GM, forgetting his name.

"Richard," says Dickie, rolling the R pleasantly as if he knows what he is doing. He does not but it was one of the things which attracted Dolly in the first place. That, and his large, loosely structured frame which might do anything and sometimes did.

"Ah, yes," replies the old Jim. "Richard." He beams a ghastly smile, having indeed found something to hang on to. "Well Rich, you see. . ." Little things add up inside Jim's head. He changes tactics. He cannot help himself: "'Ere, Rich?"

Dickie, Dolly's Dickie, sees Jim slumped in the office armchair he used to fill so comfortably. Fill as if he would burst it apart with one energetic intake of breath. Indeed, it would creak and groan as he placed his ripe bum upon it, when he pushed down upon the arms to roar at some Henry, Pete or Rich in the old days. Now he is shrunken fruit, a dusty, bitter-smelling fungus spreading across its skin. Dickie conquers his disgust: "Yes Jim," he says but his mouth is dry.

"Your wife, er. . ."

"Dolores." The R rolls a little.

"Of course, Dolly."

"She's going to have a baby," for this fact made her more real and worthy. He was proud of the worthiness bestowed on both of them by the accomplished fact.

"Is she? 'An' you got something to do with it? You not a poofter then?"

"What?"

"You not a poofter like Andrew?" Jim insists the point, hoping to make an issue out of it. Hoping to enjoy the boy's discomfort. He wants to sit on someone and this one is all he has left.

But Dickie is only made uneasy. He wants to run, not from fear but in order to find fresh air to check his nausea. Run, also, he finds, to Dolly to whom his thoughts fly. He wants to help her in her time of trouble, ashamed that he has brought her to this mad place and made her pregnant in it. Through mists of youthful innocence, ardour and idealism he sees the foolish woman as a sort of failed Madonna. All his life he will see her as such, making her a little less silly by his adoration. She does not deserve it but he has caught an atom of what is Dolly: her naiveté and her pathetic desire to be of consequence in a worthless world.

And loving Dolly, suddenly, in this way, with a swelling, courageous heart, Dickie feels ashamed, also, for having once admired the disgusting Jim. He thus hates Jim and wants to get himself and Dolly away as soon as he can. He almost hates himself but finds that the Van Island Palm Oil Development Company will do as a substitute.

He stares at Jim, reluctantly: "Andrew?" What on earth is Jim talking about? He barely knows Andrew who being one of the rough outdoor types who deal with the men and who are undoubtedly men's men to boot are respected for that but despised also for being just that and not very bright as a result. Dickie had imagined himself at one time employing men like Andrew one day, giving orders to Andrew while Andrew stood respectfully by, receiving them. "Andrew?" he says again.

"Yes, yes, Andrew, Andrew, for God's sake. You know 'im?"

A stink comes out of Jim's mouth hitting Dickie full in the face he wants to hit. He turns away. He hates Jim and therefore he hates Andrew also: "No I don't know him. Why should I?"

Jim is nonplussed, sinking back further into his big chair. His feet, like Clarence's, no longer touch the floor. But he holds his ground, grasping the hard woodenness of the arms for comfort. He presses on. He badly wants this man onside, wants this Rich, this boy, this baby to know Andrew, to bring Andrew into focus for him so that Andrew, for God's sake, is not indisputably associated with her, but rather with this, this, this wet specimen of a, a, a wet rag, so that he can finally squash Andrew together with that other bastard forever lurking in the background like, like, like. . . Jim has no word for what he feels. Reproach would have done. But also, perversely, like something pleasantly remembered and painfully regretted, he wants his old idea of Andrew as not a bad sort of pommie I'll make something out of 'im 'e can be useful to me. 'E ought to be one of us, 'e isn't, God help me. I want 'im to be. I don't want 'im to be this new Andrew with the other one scowling over 'is shoulder at me. "It frightens me."

"What?"

Jim's hands clasp and unclasp the chair arms. He feels as helpless as he's ever felt in his life but he presses on: "I said you must know 'im. 'E isn't much old'n you. You lads ought to play together and not get involved with these kanakas. Tennis, golf, go fishing. Don't you?"

"No."

"Why not? You should 'ave." Jim is defeated. He sighs, deflates a little more, his shirt at least one size too big, if not two by now, collar stained with sweat. Needs a shave, pink patches on skull where bits of thick mop of dull, colourless hair have dropped out.

Dickie wants to fly, pushes back his chair and stares at Jim, turns a little to one side, more like the position in which Andrew had sat. He wants to see the car park through the window, normality, but the blind is down, the strip light glaring down unflatteringly upon the folds of Jim's face. He thinks of Andrew and decides he does not like him either: part of the whole Van thing he does not like. This Andrew, he remembers bits of him, the wrong bits as it happens: arrogant and self-opinionated, ignoring him at the club. Ignoring Dolly also, with whom he did not safely flirt as was the club custom – even Henry had flattered some silly woman from time to time and given her a decent turn on the dance floor.

Dickie blushes at the memory of Andrew's slights. Andrew talking down to him when he brought in his returns, insisting he should have a copy of the completed accounts and, moreover, claiming he understood them. Newly arrived, Dickie had hoped to know this man who was nearest to his age and who would explain how things worked. The idea of the healthy, good-looking man becoming his established friend, his matey mate, popping in on each other and being seen together and greeting each other at the club – Hi Dickie, wotcha mate, how yer doing – had been a daydream of no small potency so that the apparent indifference, the sulky-seeming rejection of Dickie's overture – want a drink? – had hurt. The fresh boy had been awkwardly embarrassed. Now, here with the disgusting Jim, he remembers his humiliation. He hates Andrew intensely.

Jim watches carefully and in doing so pulls himself together, pleased with his manipulation. He sits up and wipes away the saliva that has dribbled down his chin. He has forgotten Bune: "Rich, my boy." Confidence temporarily restored. The pretence of normality steadies, a little, the vertigo one feels upon staring into the void.

"Yes?" says Dickie feeling he is being cornered.

"Well, you see . . ." Jim waves his arm at the disordered office, patched-up door, cracked glass on expensive desktop, and the noisy air-conditioner Alloy – sly fucker – no longer repairs. "You see, things 'ave slipped a little, lately. 'Aven't they?"

"Yes."

"Yes," agrees Jim, "our dear – dearest darling fuck 'er – Mrs L ain't 'ere for a start."

"No," says Dickie, adding more confidently but without any sense, "she isn't."

"No," agrees Jim. He looks at Dickie expecting an answer but none comes. He continues: "So would you mind doin' a few little things for me?"

"Not at all." But no tail wags. Let's get it over and I'll be back to Dolly and out of here so fast.

Jim notices. Little prick. I got to hold 'im a bit longer all the same: "Andrew. . ."

"Again?"

"We bin talking about 'im."

Dick leans back. He yawns because he is tired.

Jim is astonished. Not another Pete for God's sake but he is not sure so he presses on: "'E's the one's caused all the trouble round 'ere. 'E's a troublemaker."

"Is he?" I'm pleased to hear it now you've planted the idea in my head I hate him. And you, for that matter.

"'E is. 'Is division's on strike, you may 'ave noticed."

Dickie's mouth opens but Jim pushes on: "'E's told 'em to strike cos 'e's a commie."

Dickie's mouth stays open.

"Don't worry, we'll get 'im but fer now no fruit's comin' in an' 'is division's the biggest. So, 'e's fucking us. An' anyhows, if 'e's not a bolshie – an' all these bum-pokers are – 'e's lost control an' they got 'im by the balls down there. An'" – old Jim jogs his old laugh – "I bet 'e likes 'em 'oldin' 'is balls like that."

Dolly had once held his balls, Dickie remembers, as if she was weighing them. Then she had dropped them, slapping them so hard that the idea of his sudden dismissal had hurt him for days. "What?"

"I said . . . we got 'im both ways an' 'e's got to go. See?"

"I see."

"An' the other one."

"Who?"

"Never mind 'im. So look" – Jim pulls out of the rubble of his desk a piece of dirty paper scrawled over with pencil – "I've drafted a note to London sackin' 'im proper this time. Can you type it out an' make it sound official? Mrs L, fuck 'er, used to make a good job of it. I'll sign it an' you can get it out on the next mail." Jim looks helplessly at Dickie, a flat grin on his face.

"Can do."

"What?"

"I can do it."

"Do it then."

And soon enough, Dickie is typing quietly away on the new electric typewriter. But having got Andrew, he's not so sure it's what he wants.

[][][][][]

Now, the old Jim would have stirred himself, if only – and there were other Jim reasons – to prove his own idea of himself to himself, man of action. Thus Pete wheedled into apparent tail-wagging obedience and within twenty-four hours the mill steaming away. Thus even Andrew, in spite of the Alloy factor, maybe with it, in the same vein. Daff encouraged to work miracles with Clarence, thus giving him a new lease of life. Jim could do these things with people: had done, for Christ's sake, time and again. How otherwise the Van Island Palm Oil Development Company at all? Jim could have done it. He could have found out Margaret – she waited until the last minute – and with her help, and no doubt about it, with the help of all the others, all of them, he could have sorted out the muddle on top of the hill. Would he not have been forgiven?

Imagine Weno or Burara withholding the hand of friendship? Impossible. Tematan and Nalin even, their bitterness sweetened with affection, were not beyond restoration to the family. Had not Tudak achieved it? Rabis and Pen even need not have feared the warmth of the family hearth: creeping towards it they would not have been driven away. Jim had it in him to inspire all this because these things can happen and do, just as much as the other. Jim the centre of something good. But Jim is a cynic. He has been spoiled and he must move the wrong way. He must move towards his own destruction and if there's going to be a crash it might as well be a big one.

[][][][][]

Jim, beyond constructive thought, falls back in his chair fuck me if I can think of a single thing to do. Odd, disjointed ideas nonetheless flash across his brain: jagged remnants of light caught as the shattered reflection of his self-image collapses. Tiny, sparkling things, good things. Margaret's kind eyes looking down at him once, he knew not when, telling him he was a baby. Chan carrying him to bed years ago in surprisingly loving arms he was too drunk to resist. Undressing him tenderly: I'll put you straight James M and we'll stay here together. But Jim was not going to hang around some Chink. Not likely: he was going to take on the world: something he could bash and beat. The affectionate young Chinese man therefore also went another way. They both abandoned Lingalinga.

Lingalinga! Wow, I'll go there now with that fellow waiting for me outside.

The idea soothes Jim. He sleeps, dreaming of his boyhood, running wild on Lingalinga. Waking, darkness has crept in around him. He is alone in the desolate office. Some men would have wept. Jim doesn't know how.

35
The Day Market

The Day Market served the people who lived and worked in the centre of things. Here also, on off-Saturdays, the people from the outlying compounds – Andrew's amongst them – would gather to savour a taste of the greater world of ideas beyond the plantation and to which they could add their own observations. Therefore, and significantly – for the mob – the Day Market was the exchange for daily gossip, reportage and fantastic invention. It was the place in which the behaviour of the animal that was the Van Island Palm Oil Development Company was analysed. This analysis, arising from the interaction of the views of individuals, fairly rational in the organisation of their individual lives, resulted in the mob. The mob added two and two and came to an answer anything between five and infinity, acting accordingly within a range from indifference, through hysterical outrage and murderous hysteria to exhausted resignation. Political movements, riots, strikes, demonstrations and insurrections started in the Day Market. From here the mob left for Versailles to drag Marie Antoinette back to Paris, stormed the Winter Palace and sacked Chan's store chanting Ho Chi Minh on its return the night Henry died.

Jim loved the Day Market. In the old days. It was the seed-bed of disorder, the energetic control of which had given him so much satisfaction over the years, proving, by decisive and ruthless activity, his hold on the centre. Jim could see the market from the back window of his office. He could hear it if he turned off the air-conditioner. Music to his ears and whilst he often had the place cleared, not unusually wielding a baton himself, he could not be persuaded by Henry to have it moved altogether: stands to reason, he'd say, if we couldn't see it every day we wouldn't know what they was up to an' we don't want that. Do we? 'Ave another drink.

In any event it was the convenient location of the Day Market that gave it its reason for being because, as was emphatically pointed out in the September 1985 report of the findings of the investigation into the disturbances on Van Island, this location was a significant factor in the nature of the disturbances.

〔〕〔〕〔〕

In colonial Malaya, when the British established an administrative centre, they laid out a rectangular open space called a Maidan, around which the most important administrative buildings were erected. Upon this space, polo and cricket were played and other demonstrations of imperial superiority enacted. The Maidan survives even in Kuala Lumpur and Singapore today. The company centre on Van was no different except that the space was laid out as a nine-hole golf course. The Day Market occupied a strategic position at the southeast corner. A road ran around the golf course providing access to all the other important places and linking the various roads which converged on the centre. The road linking the company with the rest of the island came in beside the market.

This centre of things, the golf course, looked harmless enough, attractive even. On two sides were pleasant-looking oil palms, their drooping fronds waving a little in the breeze. The Day Market, an extensive, high-roofed affair, had been set amongst the palms which, as they grew up, shaded it and kept it a little out of mind. On another side stretched a line of pleasant-looking bungalows, half hidden by garden foliage. Only one short side expressed the very reason for the place: the office and rising, massive, behind it, the oil mill. The workshop compound straggled up the road to Chan's store, its mess of standing equipment, stores, temporary-looking buildings and oil-stained ground not immediately evident to anyone coming into the centre. What was evident, day and night, was the mill, threatening in action and made ominous by its silence. Anyone looking out from the office, of course, saw only the spacious, park-like, sweep of the golf course.

[][][][][]

Under the iron roof and surrounded by the palms, the Day Market was full of shadows on the sunniest of days and pitch black at night even under the fullest of moons. The market women gave the place its light and life. Fat and generous, loud and chatty, laughter was their nature. But these days they were sullen, the wind taken out of their sails. They flagged and drooped, pale, collapsed remnants of what they used to be.

There was a lot less money around. The little heaps of kaukau, creamy white, pink and purple were not worth what they used to be. Neither were the green-and-orange pawpaws, the great scaly taros, the tiny pyramids of shiny red tomatoes, four by four, the cigarettes, one by one, the neat cellophane packets of salt, sugar, tea leaves and washing powder. All these things, usually swept up by the crowd, little worried by the cost, lay rejected or else moved for niggardly prices that demeaned their excellence. Super abundance had depressed prices in the past but the market women had worked together to withhold supply and generally times had never been other than good. This check in an apparently limitless growth of prosperity was unbearable, particularly with its portent of total collapse. The invisible hand indeed that could not be resisted by holding back supply. The money was not there. Where had it gone?

The women sulked and were listless, their energy contained needing only an idea to release it.

The small man sits a little in the shadow. A muscular leg shows and a broad, almost webbed foot protrudes into the consciousness of the fat woman. Big girl more like, with the innocent love she has, or rather had, for life.

The solid there-ness and confidence of that leg is so reassuring and obvious that had the man attached been stark naked she would only have wondered at the inappropriateness of clothes.

Thus are her emotions buoyed up a little by Bune.

He takes one of the stubby, yellow, slightly bitter cucumbers and bites off the crunchy end. White teeth flash as he passes across the coin without looking.

She pushes a couple more cucumbers at him. Then, adds a fourth as a favour to him whom she would bite herself in order to savour the neat bundle of contained energy that is presented. The first sale of the day, after all, and he must have his breakfast. He might bring luck. Had he got up just then and walked away she would have followed him.

Now she watches him eat.

"Sister?"

She shifts her position, wanting to get closer. She wants this man to understand her unhappiness. But she does not answer him, only watches him with large doleful eyes.

"What's worrying you?"

No reply. Self-consciously she wants him to cajole her out of herself. She wants Bune's affection.

He finishes the first cucumber by tossing away the small end he has held, and picks up another. Very self-contained is the little man, and patient.

"They're not buying my things," she sobs, "I don't understand it."

"They have no money."

"Why? There was plenty before."

But he only laughs, his eyes sparkling, his teeth flashing in the dim light.

She could eat him and his round laughter is contagious. In spite of herself she laughs too: but it is not funny. You're my first customer today and you might be my last. "I shall die of it."

"Yes, you might," he answers seriously. She looks at him with a spasm of fear. What secrets does he know?

"Why have they no money?" she demands again, no longer looking at him.

"Because the white men no longer give it."

"Why?"

"Because they are angry."

"Why?"

"Because, because of. . ." Bune looks up into the darkness of the roof. He picks up the third cucumber and plays with it in his strong round hand, the thumb surprisingly large and bent back a little. "Because of this Annu-man I suppose."

The idea ignites the anger she has been containing for days. "Annu!" She spits it out. "Annu, Annu, Annu is all I hear. What is he?"

Bune looks at the cucumber in his hand, showing it to himself, caressing it. He might be loving it, pitying it because he is about to eat it. "I am not sure." He shrinks a little inside himself becoming old for a while, a wandering outcast, ready to disappear. His nose twitches. "I am not sure." He is himself once more. "What have you heard?"

But her anger makes her spiteful. She has swallowed the laughter he gave her and turned it into bile. She closes her mouth dramatically and looks away.

Bune watches her through narrow eyes as he squeezes the cucumber. "Tell me," he says kindly.

So she tells him, almost ashamed of what she has heard: "The Annu-man is come to lead the Highlands men. He is a trouble-man. He breaks Mr Chan's store, he eats that girl. Then he fights Master Jim. He is very strong, this Annu-man. He has magic so that he cannot die." She glares at Bune, daring him to contradict her.

Bune scrapes off the yellow skin of the cucumber with his teeth, more concentrated on this job than interested in Annu: "Are you sure there is magic? Is not the white man stronger?"

She is indignant: "I am telling you. They cut off his head, these white men, everybody knows they carried away his body in a truck but he came back again with a child of his own." This idea, her own words, frightens her so that she looks around for Annu who might be listening, ready to pounce.

Bune looks at her, completely himself now. He moves out of the dark, sits down beside her and neatly bites off the end of the cucumber: "They cut off his head, you say?"

"I do. You think I am lying? Ask anyone." She shakes with her anger.

"I hear you. You are not lying."

She is mollified. She sits back, vindicated, hands primly in her lap.

"Yet he lives."

She remembers the reality beyond herself, looking at him out of the side of her eyes, her mouth open again. The idea of Annu's invincibility is frightening, after all. She would rather that this man could convince her she was wrong. "He lives?"

"You know he does. And . . . he is causing the trouble."

"Why?" she begs him.

"You understand. You know he has told the plantation men they cannot work."

"Yes?"

"You know he has told the factory men they cannot work."

"Yes?"

"So?"

"What has that got to do with me?"

"So the workmen have no money, so everyone has no money to buy things in the market. You understand?"

"I understand." She faces what she has always understood, not bothering, until now, to make the connection that this attractive man has forced her to make. Some of the joy of her life is forever banished by this stark understanding of the truth.

"But why does the Annu-man make this trouble?"

"Because he wants to break the company."

"But why?" I am comfortable with the way things work for me, I am afraid of change, I do not want it.

"So that he can become the Big Man over us." And he might well have told her the truth: So that we can be free. But Bune, of all people, as the hard truth at the centre of all things, knows that she will have to experience freedom before she understands what it is.

And, because deep down inside herself she knows this, she laughs, but she understands her own laugh as something that ought to depreciate the Annu-man: "Ah," as if she would stamp him out, "he cannot do that. The white men will not let him. They are stronger than his magic, you said so."

"Then why are the white men dying?"

Her mouth hangs open.

"Is not Master Henry dead?"

"True."

"Where is Master Clarence? He has disappeared."

"True." The world is falling down around her.

"The tall white woman who used to work for Master Jim, she has gone."

She can barely mouth the reply. "Annu?" She whispers.

"It is."

"It is very bad."

"It is and he will do more bad things yet. He will kill the Big Man of the company himself, Master Jim, and then. . ."

She looks at Bune who is fully within her sight now as another comfortable market trader.

". . .everything will fall apart. There will be no market and these Highlands men will take everything. If they do not kill you, they will take you for their own wife and make you their slave."

She hugs herself with horror: "You are sure?"

Bune smiles and begins to pick his teeth. "I am not sure but I see that Annu has magic which is killing Master Jim who is going down more each day."

Now, the public opinion of Jim was just a little on the positive side of neutral. As a personality he was neither liked nor particularly well known. As a public figure his bad manners, his crude treatment of the local people as a lumpy mass, his drunkenness and his brutality were all what was expected from a white man protecting his cargo. Moreover, the atmosphere of fear and intimidation which was the manifestation of Jim's system of management was not associated with him personally, but rather accepted as the way in which companies worked, just as those who became employees accepted that they were dehumanised in some way not clearly understood. And despite Jim being the obvious centre of the monstrous system, despite his self-centred, bullying nature, his cruel way of doing things, he was almost revered – loved would have been taking it too far – as a father figure. A tyrannical, an exacting and often a senseless father but the father nonetheless without whom the whole gigantic structure that kept them alive would come tumbling down.

The market women, amongst other dependants, needed Jim for their survival. Had they not, time and time again, seen Jim save the day? His decisive action and ruthless energy defeating the mob, which was, in the minds of the indigenous islanders, the Highlands migrants, for all that any disturbance was common ground for everyone's discontent.

"Annu's magic is stronger," added Bune, as if the idea had only just occurred to him. "They cut off his head but he's still causing trouble. Big trouble."

"But where is he?" She imagines a headless man wandering around, which makes her feel more angry than frightened. If she had this little man beside her she wouldn't be frightened of anything.

"They say Master Jim's got him prisoner."

"So why is Master Jim going down?" And us, she thinks, with him.

Bune meditates on this, or seems to: "How do I know? His magic is stronger. It must be."

"Then why can't he escape? I heard he escaped from the Togulo Farm." She is pleased to have checked him.

Bune scowls at her as if he would bite.

She draws back, searches her wares, sighs, frowns, sulks and rises up again. She is not a stupid woman. "This Annu is a problem. You say Jim has got him prisoner?"

"Yes."

"Where?"

"On the hill." Bune nods his head in that direction.

"Ah! That is why Jim is going down."

"Why?" Bune is one of those men who haunt the market living off the scraps. He is Fafi, the lunatic, for a moment. "Why?" His mouth hangs open.

Now she has the ascendancy. She preens herself and swells up: because – you blithering idiot – while Annu is held, his magic works bad things on Master Jim. "If we can get Annu, then Master Jim will get better." It stand to reason.

At any rate, this is the idea that sweeps through the market and beyond.

"So what will you do with Annu when you have him?"

She laughs: "Keep him."

"How?"

"Feed him. What does he look like?"

Bune describes Keramugl and then slips away becoming one of the few buyers. He talks to one or two others in the same way.

Thus the gossip sweeps and swirls around the Day Market irritating the discontent until it has become inflamed hatred and an irresistible desire for revenge.

Bune returns to Jim's Landrover, the silent, respectful driver Yes Sir.

[][][][][]

The staff have gone leaving behind their litter and turning off the lights. There is a smell, the air-conditioner switched off, of human bodies having been around but not much. If they had thought of him at all it was the thought of getting away from him.

Jim feels his abandonment as suspension in an infinite space, empty except for himself, and within which he is destined to float, helpless, forever. He cannot move his body and grasping at the air, his hands like the convulsions of a dying man, finds the chair arms on either side of him. The solidity of those chair arms – good New Sudanian mahogany – reassures him. He remembers the man outside, his comfort. His feet touch the ground.

He looks out into the black night that fills the room. A dense and heavy unpleasant substance that smells of himself.

A little bit of the old Jim – the instinct to survive another day – lifts Jim to his feet. He pushes himself up using the chair arms. At first he does not want to let go, afraid of the endless space but then shift yerself Jim and he stumbles across the room, fumbles with the door and negotiates the familiar outer office.

Outside, the night receives him. He breathes in the fresh air gasping but the silence and then the smell like burning plastic unnerves him. "Jesus fuck me." He wants to fight the fear. But how? He sinks as his knees, inside the sagging flesh, give way. He holds the back of the Landrover to support himself.

"Sir?"

A hand, warm, alive and strong, holds his arm. The relief is terrific. Jim stands up as straight as a Jim can stand, the collapsed bulk of a man who was once a boy.

But Bune stands firm: "Sir?"

The choice remains, as always, Jim's.

'Op it, might once have been the reply these kanakas creep everywhere, Holy Jesus, the thought. Now, a very small grunt: "The 'ouse." Where Jim is taken. He is sat in the kitchen – smell of rotting food, of old beer and of Jim himself – lights dim. Is it mi eyes thinks Jim, or 'ave those fuckers fucked the genny? For seconds at a time he sits in darkness. Fuck me. Indeed Jim, fuck you, the choice is yours. "Get me a beer."

It is got. By Tematan with whom Jim would like to speak but the eyes will not meet.

"Where's the other one?"

What other one? Tematan wants to run. He wants his brother Burara at last.

Thus Tematan runs and it is Bune who prepares for Jim the boiled kaukau and a little salt. Also another beer laced with whisky.

Seeing Bune move in the dim light of a flickering candle, Jim thinks he is the bar-boy, Joseph, returned to him. His heart races. It is not. It is altogether something else more compact and dangerous likely to explode any minute. He fails: Fuck me, what do I do now? He is imprisoned with a wild animal.

Outside, the Landrover has been washed. It is in peak condition, the key in the ignition.

36
Insubordination and Sodomy

Madiak, having efficiently settled them in the heart of the plantation, and set up the routines which Andrew could manage, steps back. He watches as he has always watched. The progression of things. He does not judge, he does not regret. For Madiak has no god. We might call him a fatalist. But if we called him that to his face, he would wearily lift his collapsed eyebrows implying – as an obvious fact – we were fools to call him meaningless names. What will be will be. He looks at us blankly, waiting for the next inane comment. Smile Madiak, and he would do that little thing for us but don't ask me to stand on my head. I am too old for those games.

Madiak did not think Andrew was a fool and indeed knew his worth. But Andrew believed the opposite and acted accordingly. Am I not in charge? The weary eyes watch for a moment and turn away.

Madiak watched the progression of things inevitable, using them to his advantage as required. Why not? The river runs down to the sea. Where else? We cannot stop it but we can divert a little of it to water our crops. Had Alloy murdered Andrew, Madiak would not have shed a tear, only regretted, mildly, that Andrew was not around to be of some limited use to them for a little longer.

Madiak alone, so it seemed, showed any sense at the time. True enough, he ought to have had some: he was older and therefore more corrupted by contact with the plantation. He had been born in the labour quarters of the old Akaranda Plantation son of an indentured labourer and a girl from one of the coastal settlements debased by the knowledge of cargo. Hence her desire to marry a wage earner. A Van man was Madiak through and through. He understood things were falling apart because he had always expected them to do so. He pictured his subsequent inheritance: himself in the same spot ten years hence, in the centre of his own little farm, sitting, in the evenings, under Tarlie's mango tree.

But the progression of events towards the inevitable had come to a halt. Andrew was not enough and Madiak found himself – to his annoyance – wondering what had happened to Bune. The man whom he had once imagined dead at his feet, was, apparently, a necessity.

[][][][][]

In retrospect, those moonless nights were the best. Sitting by the fire: the world drawn tight around us by the darkness beyond. We relaxed, unperturbed about what we ought to be doing, the over-bright reality of the afternoon no longer challenging us for action impossible.

A mood of resigned stupor following dinner. Tomorrow does not exist. Andrew is stretched out, hands behind his head, the mosquitoes not as troublesome as they have been. He has bathed, he is wearing clean clothes and he has Alloy beside him. The day has not gone badly, his authority apparently unchallenged. A few lines harvested and generally tidied up, the fruit bunches neatly stacked beside the road for collection. Even though they will sit there until they rot.

"When I was about fifteen we called ourselves communists just to annoy the grown-ups. We read Mao's Little Red Book and then from the safety of our privileged life we'd despise the poor people in the town." Andrew is mumbling to himself but Alloy answers:

"What town?"

"Where I was at boarding school."

"Poor people? In England?"

"Plenty. There were two prostitutes. At least we assumed they were. We used to bait them. They lived in an old cottage opening onto the street opposite the church. We'd bang on the door as we passed and they would shout back obscenities. They were called Molly and Lil. At least that's what we called them."

"Were they beautiful?"

"Oh no. Bloated things with fat legs and dyed hair. I suppose they were pretty girls once. They hated us. Everyone in the town hated us."

"Why?"

"Because it was a poor place. Empty crumbling houses in the high street but overwhelmed by a mob of badly behaved posh boys from Bournemouth or the comfortable suburbs of London. We thought we were better because we were richer. We could terrorise the local tradesmen."

"I don't know what you're talking about. What is England?"

"It doesn't exist. It's all in my head."

Andrew hits himself dramatically which makes Alloy laugh.

The night draws closer.

They look at each other.

Faces in the firelight.

Watch him as he watches me.

I might look over my shoulder.

At what?

At the night.

At the night beyond.

The night is wonderful in its massive way.

And terrifying.

The Bosworth Boys tremble.

Quivering leaves upon a fragile tree.

A storm is coming.

With a sudden collapse of sparks, the fire subsides and is smaller. No one attempts to mend it. Better they are hidden by the dark. Madiak no longer watches but Andrew feels he must say something: "For God's sake we can't go on like this." He wants to kick Alloy.

"Like what?"

"Like pretending we're doing the right thing and not knowing what's going on outside."

"No we can't Andrew, and I was wondering when you'd come to that conclusion. But this has been a good time to rest."

"Has it? I don't feel rested when I start to think about things." He raises his voice a little. "Do you? I feel restless." He raises his voice so that they can all hear him.

The Bosworth Boys hear the swinging rhythm of the two voices similar in tenor. Not strong voices but insistent and self-absorbed.

"A time of adjustment then."

"For you and me perhaps. But what about them? What about you lot?" He shouts out: "Are you there?"

"Yes Sir!" You bet we are but we may go mad in this time of uncertainty. Something will have to happen if only, if only, if only we bash you up.

"It's the waiting that does it."

"Does what?"

"Makes us restless."

"And what are we waiting for?"

"For Jim."

"Jim?"

"Yes." He's got us surrounded. He'll pounce and have us in no time. Before we know it, we'll be his captives paraded naked before the crowd.

Jim's coming!

The Bosworth Boys tremble.

Madiak waits. He will step back and he will watch what happens.

Jim's out there coming to get you. He'll squash you flat.

He'll come in the night and have your head off before you know what's hit you.

Andrew thinks, of nothing.

Alloy watches him.

Madiak waits.

The Bosworth Boys shift themselves restlessly. Those who have not fallen asleep.

The night has a solidity that holds them tight. No moon. No breeze, to shift the palm fronds above. They ought to feel stifled but, oddly, they do not. The night air is pure and clean.

[][][][][]

"There're no rations left."

Andrew woke up to a view of flat feet and skinny, veined calves. He smelt cheap soap. The rest of Madiak was disembodied in the dark. Madiak's flat feet upon the ground suggested a response required. He had been dreaming of Molly and Lil, sitting with them in perfectly clean and decent surroundings drinking tea and discussing some ecclesiastical matter of great significance. But he knew the time was coming when he would have to say goodbye.

453

"What rations?" Andrew's ignorance was momentarily real because the company did not officially provide rations. Cash was the thing, to be exchanged for cargo at Chan's store. But Andrew, like all the divisional managers, was entitled to a small social fund. It was – or rather used to be – an official item on the budget which he might use for a football or for the Christmas party. Andrew used it to buy in a stock of dry foods to be doled out as a reward for especially good work, to feed labourers newly arrived or to help someone unable, for some financially embarrassing reason, to feed himself. The stock had conveniently accumulated and it was what they had been eating.

He looked at Alloy sleeping peacefully by his side. "Yes I know," he lied, "I've been thinking about it."

Madiak said nothing.

"I'll do something in the morning."

❏❏❏❏❏

Andrew wakes up to a morning barren with worry. Alloy by his side maybe but snoring like a pig. Andrew kicks him.

"Leave him alone."

Says Bune, the night having distilled itself into this small, dense, sure black thing. Andrew breathes in deeply and smells the smoke from a fire upon which the billy-can boils. Wonderful indeed is the morning now with beauty all around. Andrew's body is adjusted, Molly and Lil happily wave him goodbye, and he is ready for anything: "Am I glad to see you," he says beaming up at Bune the god.

Bright smile, kingfisher flash, and in his little bag he has brought for Andrew coffee from Chan's store. The comfort of that thing is terrific. Tea, sugar and tinned milk as well there will be no mutiny today. At any rate not before lunch.

The early morning is cool.

"So Andrew?"

"Yes Bune?"

Alloy opens an eye and listens.

"Today you will feed the men on something good."

"I will?" Thinks Andrew: human meat perhaps. A sacrifice and a worthy one. An honour, surely, to be subsumed by Bune and the men around.

"We will eat the heart. I've brought salt."

"Whose heart?" The idea ought to be shocking but coming from Bune it seems perfectly right. Tarlie's heart would have been the thing. A strong heart to give them strength. Andrew looks at Bune. Yes, one could eat a good man. You would eat his parts in reverence and excrete his nutrients into the soil to nourish the trees. Then eat the fruit, his parts also. It makes sense.

Andrew looks at Bune again, at the strong hands and at the sharp, white teeth. "It's a good idea. I agree." He is solemn. It is no joking matter. "Who are we going to eat?"

Bune looks at the ground, between his squatting legs, muscles bulging. He could crack Andrew's head between his knees. "You Andrew, you."

Andrew is not shocked. He had seen this coming: "But I'd taste awful. I am bitter meat."

"No Andrew," says Alloy, making a sudden grab at his ankle, "you would taste sweet." He sinks his teeth gently into Andrew's calf. "I will not hurt you, I promise."

The inclination to resist is resisted. The idea solves a lot of problems and Andrew has no fear. So this is what I was made for, he thinks, also thinking how he would write about it. "But, Alloy." He looks at him seriously.

"Yes?"

Are the eyes a little wild? Or laughing?

"Can I make one condition?"

"Depends what it is."

"I want you to kill me."

"I'll do that."

"With your hands."

"A pleasure."

Bune looks at them: "This is good. Let us start."

"Now?"

"Now. We must eat. A sacrifice must be made. Before we do anything else."

Andrew is surprised, absolutely, but nonetheless he shows remarkable calm in the face of the definite change in his status: "Give the men their tea and let's get started then." He looks at the men, the Bosworth Boys, innocent in their sleep and waking. Hard to believe they would soon be working away with their bush knives and licking their lips. Patting their hollow bellies. He is not keen on the public process and looks at Alloy: "Let's go off quietly and you can do what you like." He imagines the beloved hands around his neck. "I insist."

Thinks Alloy: Is this what England means? Andrew insisting on his selfish rights at this time of significant sacrifice. "No Andrew, Bune is right, we must all be part of this. You and I cannot separate ourselves at this time."

Bune nods assent.

A drop of fear enters Andrew's blood: "No, not that way. I don't agree."

"Andrew, it has to be done. The men are hungry and after all it is the company we will be attacking. Why are you supporting it all of a sudden?"

"I'm not. You know I've left all that behind. But surely I have some say in it? I'm not asking much of you Alloy and I'd have thought you'd be with me. In fact I won't do it on any other condition. I'll fight you!"

"For a few rotten palm tree hearts?"

"Eh?"

"You're mad!" He laughs, bites Andrew's leg and jumps up. "He's mad this man called England. Isn't he, Bune?"

Bune is laughing too. He rolls on his back and kicks his legs in the air. The Bosworth Boys laugh with him. With this Bune they would have killed Andrew while Madiak watched. Cooked and eaten him without hesitation. Had not white men been eating them for long enough?

Andrew drinks his coffee, ashamed, but only a little, of his thoughts while Alloy teases him: "I'll strangle you if you really want it." And gently he puts his hands around Andrew's neck.

"Promise?"

"Promise."

"OK, so long as I don't taste too bitter for you."

[][][][][]

When they put out the fire, Andrew appears to be directing operations, accompanied by Alloy who is again impressed by Andrew's assumed superiority and by the deference given to him. Was this England then? If so then I despise Andrew's acceptance of the deference which he doesn't deserve. He takes it, nonetheless, and I'd like to hit him for that.

He watches Andrew getting things done. Not by doing anything himself but by telling Madiak and Bune what to do. And the remarkable thing is that they do it. Or rather appear to do what he tells them. Studying the situation more closely, Alloy sees that they are doing things regardless of Andrew and yet, and yet, there is Andrew at the centre. Is he holding things together?

"You make me laugh."

"Why?"

"Because you are arrogant. You assume the centre. . ."

"I am given." Andrew is firm: "I am a juju doll set up, around which . . ."

"The savages dance?" Alloy watches Bune and Madiak, who are actually the ones directing affairs.

"Yes, and I will be sacrificed like some failed god if things fall apart."

"Is that England? You are made the master, made the boss? By a couple of prostitutes who will eat you in the end?"

"What are you talking about?" Andrew is surprised.

"I said I love you."

Andrew laughs: "Why?"

"Because I watch you work with Bune who is actually directing you and you are willing to be subjected to him. Why would a damned white man do that? I watch you with Bune and it makes you . . . loveable, Andrew."

"Thanks for that," Andrew says with warmth, "because when I'm with Bune I do forget I'm the damned white man, the damned plantation manager of whom things are expected which I can't deliver."

"But you do deliver them!"

"Only because of Bune and. . . even fucking Madiak."

Who watches. And approves, seeing the point of Andrew, and of Bune. They will give him what he wants and what he wants is not a bad thing. Andrew will approve of it and Bune will see it as highly appropriate.

And when he sees the oil palms hit the ground with a thud, Madiak feels a thrill of exaltation he has never in his life felt before. That very evening, left on his own – he cannot help himself – where the palms have been cleared he plants kaukau, some maize and groundnuts. He scatters pumpkin seeds around the holes where the palms had once stood. Later, paw-paws will grow and tomato vines will scramble around.

So, the Bosworth Boys eat. We feel better but we cannot go on doing this. We must do something. We must prove ourselves. Let us face that unknown fear beyond.

"Where did that beer appear from?"

"Bune brought it."

"On his head?"

"Seems like it!"

Well Andrew, what do you think? Will you take them to Chan's store? They expect it of you, Alloy, now, by your side. It is an easy thing. All you have to do is go. Put one foot in front of the other and all that.

OK, let's do it.

Hurrah for Andrew and England, the Bosworth Boys shout. And by that shout they have him, they have caught his vanity and will melt away from him to be hanged when the time comes.

So off they go, that raggle-taggle band, pushing Andrew before them.

Suitim lek,

Taitim bun,

Na hariap kwiktaim.

[][][][][]

Remarkable how things get through in times of war. Battledun gets a formally typed memorandum – official looking with a stamp and a signature of sorts which might be Jim's – all the way from Van Island informing him of the termination of Andrew Owens-Montague's contract for. . . a great list of sins including Sodomising His Labour and Gross Insubordination. Is Labour a collective noun referring to people or a descriptive noun referring to work? Has insubordination got subtle shades of degree through gross to, to what? To light, perhaps, as in sticking out your tongue and making faces at your boss behind his back? In which case what is gross? Perhaps sodomy? Sodomising not the labour but rather, as another collective noun, the board. Perhaps the sodomy is metaphoric and the whole memo a coded message from Jim suggesting that Andrew – Battledun hears Jim's voice – that Andrew was fucking the company. In which case. . . Battledun warms to Andrew and finds the idea of insubordination attractive. He thinks of Thornley, mad as a hatter, in his grubby Eaton Square house. Indeed, fuck him. He thinks of Tuscany and all his elegance, elegant now in his elegant overalls in an open prison somewhere in the Home Counties. Well, fuck him too. Insubordination is a great thing, is a great and glorious thing. Why have I been so gratefully subordinate all my life to shits like Thornley and Tuscany who are the ones who've been sodomising the labour all their lives if anyone has? Sod them for once.

Battledun leans back in his chair and tilts back his head so that his neck is strong and sinewy with a pronounced Adam's apple not unlike Joseph's strong neck. He is not one of your pasty white, flabby Englishmen, this man, Battledun. He is tougher than that; he is one of those men who walks, despises the motor car. His skin quickly turns brown in the sun, his hair thick and black because his bones are strong like his teeth, ought to shave twice a day. He is not a young man. He thinks of his wife in her red cardie, with her wide hips, he thinks of Dick's girlfriend in South Kensington, he thinks of the baby she will have one and of its blessed grandparents. The ideas stir him. He thinks of them all with an equal love and he is not sure any longer that he does want to be up there looking down on it all like a map through the clouds. Better to be here being insubordinate like Andrew out there and not stuck up above it all with the maddening sound of thunder in his ears and trying to make sense of the infinite and only sometimes succeeding like old Beethoven not in the symphonic anger of the Ninth but more like the quiet solitude of those amazing string quartets wherein he has come to terms with himself.

So Battledun thinks of Dick and thus he remembers Andrew who he has only met twice. Once at the interview as a hairy student amongst others, wanting the job so much and so nice not having the foggiest what an oil palm was having read up about cocoa in an old edition of the Encyclopaedia Britannica that he got the job. Better to know nothing and know it than pretend to know it all, Tuscany had said, amused to be feeding the boy to the wolves or at any rate to Jim.

Eighteen months later, Andrew had called in, no longer hairy, on his first leave. Before the glorious Dick days. Just thought I'd um . . . pop in and um . . . thank you for the job. Battledun had forgotten that pleasure, eclipsed, later, by the worthy Dick, another Andrew without the New Sudan hardening. Pity really it came too late to Dick. Who was Dick? Was he Andrew? Same thing if you like. Andrew, that time, visiting might have been Dick visiting – thank you Sir. We went for a drink round the corner. Could have been my son, Dick, sunburned, blond and clean shaven, tall and healthy-looking, awkward in a suit. White shirt brilliant. Dick glows in his mind's eye.

"Such a nice boy he came to see me."

"Who?"

"Dick."

"Dick? But Dick's. . ."

"Alright."

I know, dear. He is and it's her turn to cry first for the boys, all of them. She's their mother, especially to this big one burnt out of the sky. The damaged boy who will always be so but she has terrific love for him that will burn to the end and he knows it.

So Jim's memo is tossed into the waste paper basket which Doreen empties a little later. It ends up in one of those barges which takes out London's rubbish and dumps it into the North Sea.

[][][][][]

Come on then, for God's sake. He is desperate they should follow him and make a good show. Where's Bune when he's wanted? Disappeared as usual and only the hopeless Madiak flapping around and watching me. Am I an idiot? He's talking to some of the boys, the young men, wild to be men but afraid all the same.

Andrew strides off ahead; alone in a bad mood. I'll find Jim, give myself up, do some work and forget all this nonsense.

The temptation is terrific. The road rises up around the foot of the hill, his house, he imagines, still there on top where he may drop off, have a cup of coffee, read a book, forget all this nonsense. He presses on nonetheless: the road bends around, dips into a sort of green gully thick with ferns, the palms overhanging, cool and quiet. A little further, and it will turn into the long straight dusty road that will take him to the centre of things, where, he assumes, something will be required of him. I can't scramble up the side of the hill to my house because someone burnt it down. He feels the pressure behind: the Bosworth Boys are coming.

So the gully sweeps around and sweeps him like last night's party litter into the road that will take him out of the plantation. Straight, dusty and depressing. Gone is the exciting freshness of the morning, the sun suddenly hot on his back and no option other than to go forward between the palms drooping on one side and the dusty bush on the other. A dusty sky above does not help.

Come on you buggers. I can't go on my own. Bune's fucked off as usual. Alloy too, by the looks of it. Everyone, damn them and I have to do it. And why? Because I'm stuck and Jim will laugh at me. Where else can I go?

Then behind him he hears the roar of the crowd, a dusty stampede in his mind's eye, and seeming to cheer him on. Above the noise the clear voice of Alloy: Annu, Annu, Annu. The roar distilling itself into three, clear syllables again and again like a mighty fist that thumps and thumps a celestial table. A wave that lifts Andrew and carries him forward.

At the same time, far away but clear in his imagination, he sees a man who holds, by the hand, a child. The vision draws him forward just as the roar of the crowd drives him from behind. And so the question is answered: I can go to Margaret. Why did I forget? He laughs out loud. The vision dissolves but the fact remains and Andrew no longer doubts himself. In a minute he is joined by Alloy and the Bosworth Boys. You rushed ahead as usual. We lost you. You were dawdling, as usual, dragging your feet. I thought I'd lost you. Come on then, let's get going. Am I not with you? I heard you shouting for Annu. Did you? Yes. I had to get them moving somehow. They wanted you. I don't believe that. Madiak told them you'd lead them out of the plantation and here you are doing it. I thought you were running away. I was afraid.

Andrew thought: Do I want this dependant? And as he wondered he was ashamed that such a thought should have occurred to him, simultaneously feeling excited that he had someone who would stick to him without conditions. He had a grotesque image of Alloy flailing around half mad, his deep-set eyes sightless. "I love you," he said. But no one heard him.

37
"Women in Love"

I see the three women standing; their faces turned up to the sky. Hand in hand. Elemental faces they are, skin tight over jaws and necks. Beautiful their smiles and their eyes radiant.

Decisions made and triumphant, one might say, in the face of uncertainty. They have defined the future themselves with their determination to be. Beautifully will they handle the Bosworth Boys who return, and beautifully will they cherish the memories of those who fall.

Peter fell first, doing his duty. His body lay beside the main road to Akaranda, a bloated caricature of Peter, his face grinning, ready to split, like Tarlie used to grin only this is the mask of death. His body only, that is, the spirit is free and his dad would be proud: Daphne is.

The hand holds her tight with understanding, not with words. She is glorious, this Daphne, in her triumph over an adversity that in retrospect is small. She has stepped beyond herself and is with Margaret now, her mother, her daughter, her sister. The mother becomes the child in her grubby dressing gown smeared with old make-up no longer needed.

And do I remember the man my husband whom I love? Because I loved him with a love more than he could understand. Too big for a man. No man is worthy of the love a woman gives to the flesh torn from her body. The flesh he has torn. I did not understand it myself. I think it started before I knew him, when I saw my mother decently cover the veined legs of Mrs Grant who died where they should have put up traffic lights beside the common. It grew from the last time I saw my mother's face grow smaller and smaller as I left her, and even now I want to rush back and tell her it is alright, because it is. He caught me, accidentally almost, when I needed him the most he caught my hand but I could not understand it then and would ask questions until I met Margaret who told me not to worry but to take what came with joy. So I did and now my husband is dead and I love him now with a joy that surpasses all the joy that has been before.

The three women stand together on the dry open space that the men had insisted was a golf course. This centre of things. They watch the helicopter ascend, its furious impatience to get away blasting their faces, which look alight with joy, throwing back their hair, pressing their flimsy cotton frocks against their bodies exposing the elemental women that they are.

[]|[]|[]|[]|[]

Peter got the helicopter, driving into Akaranda to arrange things. Get it there fast, in and out within minutes, please, or else there'll be a riot. They'll be waiting. On his way back from Akaranda he had been stopped by another road block. This time not so lucky, Tudak is not in attendance. Law and order has broken down, the Togulo Farm a place of safety, Akaranda Town defends itself under the instruction of Mrs Livingston who does no more than ensure that the administration runs like a well-oiled machine. Someone else, with a weaker spine, wears the crown.

The helicopter departs with Dickie and Dolly, a few others who should never have been here in the first place and Clarence past recovery: Darling Clarence you have to go I can't look after you any longer and we may have to run at any minute, Daphne had told him. Had we been a Neolithic tribe, dear, dearest Clarence, we would have lain you gently by the wayside and let you die of cold. It's a good way to die, the body numbed and the brain following. Sleep is welcome and deep. The heart beats ever so slow until it stops.

Clarence looks down. He had never seen Van like this and had never meant to. Never meant to be carried off a cripple either. He had arrived by boat: an old coastal steamer from Port Markham coming to pick up copra. The villages strung out along the beach, the thick forest of the low hills behind, gently steaming under the morning sun. Beyond, misty mountains reaching into the sky and a part of it. Not his first youth but his second well enough and he knew how to cut a road through the bush if anyone did, and get something going. The camp site, the genny, some willing boys whom he loved like a father and spoilt rotten. They'll rob you blind Jim had said but Clarence loved them. Bought them beer and meat on Saturdays, happy to be robbed and taken for a ride by these Bosworth Boys, Alloy, one of the best. His rudeness and raw moods had touched Clarence who responded with pure love.

By the time the helicopter reached Port Markham, Clarence was dead, Dolly awfully upset.

[][][][][]

Daphne feels she must ask the question: Do you want to go with them? They'll say you ought to go. The people in Markham will say it's not safe. For a girl.

Who is talking? Sounds more like old Daff than Daphne.

What would your mother say?

What would you say?

I told you: they'll say why did she stay behind when she could have got away. There's nothing for her there.

What would you say to your daughter?

Daphne is stuck. If it was Alison, what would I say? I'd say, I'd say, I'd say, I'd probably say follow your heart but don't lose your good sense. I suppose, she adds lamely because it is not what she means, or rather, she means more.

So, Daphne pulls herself together and disposes of Daff. What would Margaret say? No, that will not do either, although Margaret is part of the answer. What would Daphne say, is the point now. The Daphne whose Peter — and with a jolt she realises she has forgotten him or, really, totally accepted the fact of him not being physically with her — whose Peter is gone from her but

Margaret is holding her hand now just as she is holding Helen's. Somehow she has got herself in the middle of the other two. They are walking back to Alloy's house. She will not go back up the hill now that Clarence and Peter have gone. Strange that up to this morning she had lived there with Peter. A big chunk of her life had happened in that house and now, without any notice, she had left it with a couple of bags.

So they are walking together, the three of them and Daphne wants to tell Helen the truth, conscious that Margaret is listening. Or, that Margaret knows everything, which is a comfort.

Helen does not give a definitive answer. Rather academic anyway, she thinks, since the helicopter has gone, the excitement it caused dissipated and the morning becoming warm mocking their earlier activity and chatter even Margaret chatty for once, fussing a little around the pregnant Dolly who therefore had felt important despite that great big lump of a useless husband. I want a useful husband, Helen thinks and thus a picture of Keramugl comes into her mind just as Daphne takes a deep breath and begins to talk again.

I mean, not follow your heart but be honest with yourself. Don't do what you think you ought to do for anyone else. She comes to a halt.

Helen pictures his head turned away but his eyes searching for her beneath his low protruding brow. She wants to trace the fresh eyebrows with her finger and watch his smile grow towards her. He breathes, she remembers, almost imperceptibly through his mouth in a slightly adenoidal way and she imagines his breathing in sleep will be heavy. She is going to have a husband who will snore one day. It is what she had always thought about.

Don't do it for those who say you should be a sensible girl and definitely don't do it for those who expect you to do something wonderful. Don't do it for me or Margaret. Don't act Helen, be Helen and do what you really want for yourself. You won't be any good for anyone else if you don't do that.

I won't and as the idea of Keramugl again fills her head, she thinks: I don't remember what he smells like. It made her feel sad.

That's what I'll tell my daughter. If she ever asks.

Thanks, Daphne. So I'm here and I'm staying. There's nowhere else I want to be.

Daphne thinks: Good. She says: I may never see my daughter again.

Don't say that.

Why not? I might be knocked down at a road block like Peter and be killed by a man in uniform. And I don't care a hoot.

She drops the hands on either side of her and walks ahead with the distinct feeling she'd like to kick off her shoes for Margaret to pick up.

[][][][][]

Helen, that English girl from where there is comfort and money never a real problem or if it had been she had never noticed there were grandparents ready to cough up. Leafy suburbs in 1970s England, Surrey or Berkshire or the Peak side of Sheffield although inflation is hitting records and the unions are holding us to ransom it's outrageous. Helen untouched by the troubles of the time like the

Yom Kippur war. Its impact on Woking was minimal and you couldn't imagine a girl like that coming from Moss Side, the Gorbals or Tower Hamlets. She had an idea she was blessed when she was fourteen but she did not like to brag, hence, eventually, the New Sudan adventure which would be twenty years or more of her life. Was it a dream? She would wonder if it was. Had she succumbed to a romantic temptation? Keramugl looked good enough to eat, she built castles in the air, she had once thought of being a nun.

They walked back to the house, which they had quickly made their own as women do. Margaret had taken Alloy's room. The others did not dare for all they had packed up his things: yes, said Margaret, with a rare bit of verbal determination, he will be back to pick them up. Then. . .

Yes? Says Helen because she will pick at things she shouldn't.

Then we'll all move on. Together.

Where? She is excited.

You know where. Don't ask. Pointless questions. Have you prepared that kaukau? There'll be people to feed. I'm going to take my bath. She keeps them busy, stops them thinking about their men.

When she sees him step up onto the veranda, the sun especially shining on him, Helen is struck dumb by his beauty. He is not a young man and yet the inward curve of his belly is a marvel. There is nothing wasted about his body and yet nothing superfluous. The feint grunt of a hungry man as he lifts himself up onto the veranda makes her adore his humanity. More so when the boy follows. A small boy but not so young. Wisdom written on his face, his eyes laughing.

She has been sewing, miles away and thinking about Keramugl. A sensible girl from the English suburbs. She won't lose her head in times of danger. Had not Wanei cooked for her and sat at her feet ready to take advantage of the smallest sign? Had she not appreciated the lithe grace of his the blackest of black bodies that shone in the moonlight of Lingalinga? She had, as she patted his head like that of a black Labrador puppy in Woking, so that he had fallen asleep beside her, protecting her from the naughtiness within him until morning.

She remembers Keramugl folding his arms that time, as if he is cold. He looks away and yet sees her out of the corner of his eye and all in his mind's eye. His shoulders relaxing to open his strong arms which will take her gently into them. Will she come? She's a sensible girl from a leafy English suburb. And what do I know about these kanakas from wildest New Sudan? The expression of love may be no more than the set of the face in a certain light. Wonderful what the mind can do, seeing things the way it wants. That swamp is an English lawn on a wet, Wednesday afternoon. But it sucks you in and devours you.

And the other one. Here, now, with the beautiful curve and the small boy in his hand. She knows what she wants but whether she is going to get it or not is another matter.

Helen had not met Joseph before. Hello, she smiles.

He throws a grin, pulling the boy after him. He squats lightly, his lap-lap tight over his thighs, the curve a fold of efficient flesh that glistens with a little sweat. Here, in the shade of the veranda, his skin is lighter while darker is that of the boy who watches her like a silent black cat.

You be the one Keramugl has taken, he laughs, unsteady with a form of English that is unusual to him. He does not ask questions.

I be, she laughs back at him, thus, at last, declaring herself.

And you be Joseph, she adds, suddenly recognising him. I'll bring you something to eat. Margaret, she calls, he is here.

[][][][][]

They have eaten together, sitting on the floor of the veranda. It is the coolest place to be, the house airless behind. Beyond, the desiccated garden is flayed by the noontime sun, the sky yellow with dust. Margaret had served them: the kaukau boiled in a thin, salty English soup – so like Andrew, Daphne had thought – fish from cans and something the boy had brought, dried but tasty. Also, a mass of dark green vegetables, a variety of leaves lightly boiled and then fried with onions. A good meal directed in silence by Margaret who makes sure they have eaten enough. You never know when you're going to eat again in a place like this.

Finished, the boy, Neki, clears away. He is Margaret's now, the final gift from Joseph.

Is he Nubian?

Who?

Your slave?

Of sorts. He'll do.

Very well.

The four, the famous four, perhaps, because they are children, true innocents in their honesty with themselves and with each other. Innocent for all Joseph's sexual innuendo at the poolside; Daphne's seduction of her husband; Helen's thoughts of Keramugl; Margaret's knowledge of everything. Margaret. She is remarkable: quiet and passive, and strong, as is forged iron, as is the rock of ages, as is the tree of man. She it was who blessed the meal while Joseph watched. She confirmed their communion.

They have slept a little, thinking their own thoughts for a while. Drowsy, but awake they look around at each other.

Helen, the eager, wants to ask questions. She catches Joseph's eye: Have you seen. . .

Keramugl?

Yes. Hearing his name, she glows like someone . . . in love.

I have not.

She is disappointed but only a little. It has not occurred to her that Keramugl might be in danger. He is out playing with the boys, he is with that Andrew, I think. She is sure he will return to Margaret.

He is not. Joseph is ruthless.

No? Her heart sinks. A dream, a childish girl's romance of a dream. She blushes for her foolishness in front of Daphne who might be feeling for her. She does not want to be felt for. Little girl's foot stamps the ground. She wants to cry.

It is Margaret who watches, and she will not say a word.

Daphne, as it happens, is watching Margaret. She plays with her wedding ring as she does so. She wonders if she should pull it off, fling it away because it is the past that might never have happened. Only the now is real. She looks at Helen, sees her blushing. Why?

Helen wants to die of shame. She feels alone and thinks of the security of her parents' garden back home. Joseph smiles, reaches across and touches her lightly but with such warm understanding that she is immediately reassured. She looks up at Margaret who also seems to smile or maybe she has always looked like that. They both tell her she is a big girl in the real world. She looks back at Joseph who speaks to her: Jim has imprisoned some of the Orami men. He says they are troublemakers. Keramugl is with them.

Behind the house rises the wooded cliff on top of which sits Henry's vacant house. Helen glances back at it: Where is he imprisoned?

Margaret laughs. She reads Helen's thoughts. Not an entirely kind laugh. Daphne is shocked for a moment. Is it Margaret who laughs? She is reminded of Jim and a chill runs through her body.

Joseph also grins a little and thumbs crudely over his shoulder: Yes, up there.

Daphne rises to get closer to Helen. She feels protective but Margaret's surprisingly strong hand stops her. It is, nonetheless, kind and she too feels reassured.

Margaret smiles at Joseph: You had better go and fetch him. You know what to do.

And the bar-boy jumps to his feet: Yes Sah!

Margaret is sitting on the edge of the veranda, her legs dangling over the side, not quite reaching the ground upon which her shoes have dropped. As Joseph passes behind her, he hides her from view and seems to linger for a few seconds. Helen remembers that last picture of him for the rest of her life, rising from the floor, behind Margaret, like a massive tree. Somehow he is always lingering there and not quite gone. It is a picture of eternity.

[][][][][]

There is the girl and the boy, the man and the woman, the two people who know each other so well and who are so intimate that all words between them are superfluous. They move as one, freely in the world and at last have no ties except to each other. They can do what they like. I will take you on a boat to an island I know. We can go to Lingalinga at last and live happily ever after. The greatest temptation the devil can offer us: happiness and contented peace with a beloved. It is that for which we sell our souls.

He caresses the top of her head, looking down upon the washed-out blonde hair that he only wants to watch turn white. She feels the generous warmth of his hand. Oh my Lord, I would ask for no more than that. She can smell him and she shivers with adoration as she dismisses him.

He jumps down from the veranda and trots off in an elegant Tudak-ian way. He does not turn back or utter a farewell but in the quiet afternoon they call to each other like two doves. I love you. I love you my darling. I love you. I love you forever. More and more distant until their cries are only the breeze that disturbs the dusty leaves.

38
Bird of Paradise

Keramugl is happy. The certainty of his life behind the wire, the dependable protection of Tudak, his friendship with Weno, Burara and the others, erases anxiety. He sits, this young man, watching the glorious sun finally shaking off the dust to become a clear burning disc, and thinks: I want to die like this, with a view of the whole sun. Wise he is becoming because he has understood the futility of men. He thinks of Helen, whom he would like to know. Thus his thoughts of the great sun and of death pass. He smiles at whatever his eyes fall upon: an ant toiling through the dust or his friend Weno, smiling in his sleep.

Keramugl also smiles when he hears the tumult of the crowd and sees it roar up the hill like the great night. Wow, he thinks, this is life. I was kissed by Annu then I slept and I dreamed the rest: the odd white man, Andrew, who listened to me; the good white woman, Margaret, who looked at my naked body with a mother's love; the bad white man, Jim, who I wanted to kill and who made me laugh; the beautiful white woman who might have been my wife. These white people are the dream world. They are not real. My blackness is real: a labourer I am: a kanaka who will die. Even my shackles are but a dream. He opens his hands seeing that he is free, his friend beside him nonetheless.

⬚⬚⬚⬚⬚

"I don't want to be part of this nonsense." He is angry and pulls himself away from Alloy. "I'm going to find Margaret." He feels that someone has again grabbed his wrist but this time he is held back, watching Alloy disappear with the crowd. I hope he'll be OK.

The noise above recedes. The flames from Henry's old house do not make much of a splash in the dead afternoon. They cannot see the glorious sun from down here.

"Phew!" He crashes onto the sofa where he had once lain for Alloy, wanting to unfold his tale of adventure. He is proud of himself.

"Coffee, Andrew?" says Daphne.

"Yes, please." Then he rattles on but they do not listen to him.

My goodness, you have been busy, destroying the world and killing people. She might have said that Peter was dead. But for now Andrew's self-importance reigns. It's a man's life. This charging around and doing things.

Andrew must do something. This sitting around is bad for him. He will start thinking. He had better be the driver. She looks at Margaret who smiles at Andrew: "Andrew, Clarence's ute is out the back. Go to the workshop, fill it up and get as much fuel as you can, we are going to need it." They had used it in the morning to ferry the evacuees to the helicopter, Bune driving and then handing the keys over to Margaret.

"Where's Peter?"

"Gone. Now, go."

He goes.

The place is a desert in the afternoon. Not a soul around. They're up there. He looks towards the hill, notes the sun defining itself in a sky yet colourless and wonders again how he got separated from Alloy. He swears he can smell rain but he is not sure. Anything could happen and he wonders where Alloy has got to: Why'd he rush off like that? Typical. He wants to be part of the mob, I suppose. Andrew whistles to himself, happy with the idea of Alloy in his head.

◻◻◻◻◻

It did not happen as he had imagined. Life is not a story book of brave deeds done, hardships nobly borne. It is more a tale of things not done, history re-written afterwards.

At the top of the hill, the citadel taken, as it were, Alloy feels only nausea. Home left behind, limitless eternity confronts him. He is lonely in the crowd that does not know him. He grasps the hand that is not there – where's he gone to, the prick? – he wants to cry: Ma! Andrew! Annu, Annu, Annu. The crowd takes up the chant. Is it joyful? Is it angry? Neither: it is pathetic in its hunger: I want, I want, I want. You. To save me, to die for me, to ease my pain.

And this is it? The end of the journey? The ugly fence, the locked gates of a car park without cars? This is the goal towards which I have fought and struggled? This is our just reward for silent suffering? For whining, for doing our duty, for paying our taxes, for obeying orders, for doing as we were told, for doing what we were made to do? Is this it? Then come out and save us and make our lives glorious. Where are you, Annu, whom we have sought?

◻◻◻◻◻

Here comes the mob to free us. Not bright, carrying garlands with which to decorate us but rather, it seems, the scum of the earth bringing clubs. The two masses of humanity stand silently eyeing each other, on either side of the wire.

The poor generally look wretched. This lot all the more so for being the poorest of the poor. Less than dropouts, they are rubbish. Who can fall lower than he who hangs around the market because he has nowhere else to go? Sleeps there too. Seeking work in the plantation, there is nothing lower to seek. Selling your body as another man's slave. Keramugl, homeless, jobless and parentless in a place that is not his own dreams of marrying the white girl. The barefaced cheek of the man. It is right that he should be the sacrifice to folly. Jim's brick shit house, the squat man with the muscles that bulge because of his shortness, with a chest like an iron door and a smile that shows no fear because he is too stupid to know what is going on. He faces the mob grinning.

◻◻◻◻◻

There was, first, the joy of walking in the morning with the happy boys. The moment was the thing and all men brothers. Andrew in his hand and he, himself, roused to chant Annu, Annu, Annu. Nothing like it and once the crowd had it he relinquished the lead. He took on the subsequent rhythm of the little mass of single-minded humanity which wanted to believe that it, in particular, would be there at that moment in history when Annu would appear to save it from the tedious plantation and a life of anxiety.

Meeting the larger crowd on the golf course he had been momentarily disconcerted but then he had allowed himself to be swept forward. He lost Andrew, struggled a little and became part of the mob. I felt its pulse, its desperate thirst for a solution. My morning joy had turned to afternoon anger. Let this thing come. Let it be done. All my habitual resentment, my sense of being an outsider, my paranoia, came upon me that hot heavy afternoon dark with the gathering storm. We, the animal, the monster, toiled up the hill as in a nightmare where the end will not come quickly enough. A bubbling cauldron of hatred, desiring only vengeance and nothing less than death. I wanted it as badly as the monster itself. Death lust was upon me. Here was the dramatic culmination of my life: a lunatic plunge into an orgy of violent destruction, destroying, foremost, myself.

I had the picture – I think I had – of Jim in my mind. I wanted him in my hands, grasping his throat, hammering his head, kicking his body. I was a mad man at my maddest. Any idea of Annu as he should have been was lost.

I cannot remember the details. If I try too hard they drift away. I make up things that did not happen but coming up the steepest bit of the hill we came to the damnable club, surrounded by the fence, put up to keep us out. The gates into the car park were shut but pressed against the wire were the other lost boys waiting for us to release them. I suppose, but I have in my mind only a picture of Keramugl, or rather, just his face. Just his smile: that innocent-seeming smile he has which is also so strong and full of confidence. It was the calm trust of that smile that did it for me. It came at me like a douse of cold water, a slap in the face, a terrific flash of lightening in the thrashing night storm. I saw everything as it was, frozen for only a moment but impressed upon my memory for ever.

They were going to take Keramugl. He was to be the sacrificial lamb. His beautiful innocence, the flower just beginning to open, was to be crushed in the brutal hand of the mob.

I took a step back out of myself, so definite a feeling of disembodiment that I can feel it now. I don't think, from that moment, I ever quite joined up with my body again. It was like that moment when you are drinking. You are just about to take the drink that will take you one step beyond control. You know it. You watch yourself and the madness all around, of which you are still, blessedly, separate. You totter on the brink and then you plunge in, you take it and you are lost.

Only I did not take it. I saw the madness all around and I did not want to be part of it. I was ashamed of myself. I felt that Margaret was watching me through Keramugl's eyes. I was bitterly ashamed. Was this what the love of Annu had brought us to? Brought me to? I had allowed my wrong emotions to take me beyond reason, beyond the quiet voice of Annu that I had always wanted to hear. I had allowed my hatred for Jim and all that he represented to take me beyond – I can say it now – beyond the humanity of which I was capable, beyond the better, the best, Alloy.

I wanted the still, quiet voice of love. And I got it. The clamour became something distant, down there, a long way off, in the street, on the other side of the river. I saw, I heard, I felt only myself. And I was amazed. My whole life had brought me to this point – storming the Bastille, or whatever – in time and place. All my anger, all my love. All my desire for Annu, whom I wanted and wanted and wanted with my whole spirit which cried out with anguish. Only Annu could fill the void.

What could I do? I saw down, down, down there, as something small and helpless, through the wrong end of your binoculars, Keramugl being man handled to his death. The gates had been torn open, the mob had rushed in. His expression was not one of fear but of blank incomprehension. Annu where are you? Had I not felt that before, watching Ples being destroyed? Blaming you Andrew – my wide-awake other self – for not being Annu. And yet again, now. Where was He? He in whom I had no doubt and He who was not here, it seemed, when wanted?

Did I faint? Or what? Andrew? I don't know but I had a vision that changed my life. I saw Margaret up there in Jim's bloody house above us. She was watching. She was watching me. As serene and as beautiful as ever, waiting. She was my life, our life, beyond the madness of our existence. I was drawn to her and I wanted to go to her. She was all there was that was real and through her I knew I could escape. It seemed that she spoke: "Give him to me."

It came to me like in a dream, disembodied and all around. To this day I do not know if it was real or if I was in some sort of trance. I heard the voice but I kept my eyes upon Keramugl whose expression was now one of undiluted joy. He was in a state of rapture that looked almost sexual.

I don't know! I'm confused. I'm trying to make sense of my emotions at the time. The memory plays games, I admit, but these things did happen. We know that. We know that Keramugl was taken by the crowd. And I was there. I saw it. And don't I know my own mind? Did I not at that time understand the futility of my anger? Did I not recognise Annu at last? I did, I tell you, and it was the voice that did it. The voice of Joseph, which I had heard a hundred times and yet, not until that moment did I hear it properly. Oh, it was so beautiful. I wanted to get down on my knees, I wanted the eyes of that voice to look at me, to see me, to recognise me because if they did not then I know I did not exist beyond my shadow. Please look at me My Lord. He did and he smiled his Joseph smile at me for the last time as he turned towards Keramugl and – I promise you it happened – he kissed him on the lips.

The crowd was mesmerised, like me. Joseph indeed had it in his huge hands and with it he could have done anything he wanted. He could have taken over the world.

"Give him to me."

The crowd handed Keramugl over to him.

He took Keramugl by the hand, held him and looked around, searching for someone who was not me. And then, out stepped Tudak, who until that moment I had known only as Jim's instrument, the manifestation of Jim's dark mind. And here was Joseph handing over the innocent to him. I felt giddy, I understood nothing.

Tudak took Keramugl by the hand. Phew, Joseph seems to say, that's alright then and the crowd might have applauded. At any rate, if he had said fall down and worship Me, it would have fallen down and worshipped Him. I know it to this day.

But Joseph said: "Take me."

And again, Andrew, like the time at Ples, when you were not there, I was alone. Terribly alone. I rushed forward to take him for myself. To save him. I was disarmed by his gentleness. He looked at me with his kind eyes, which I never wanted to leave me:

"Let me go . . . Alloy."

[][][][][]

Alloy lets him go. He watches them take him away. But then with a cry of pain he rushes forward. "Joseph," he cries, "you cannot have this." He would save him for his own sake. He swipes at the hands holding Joseph. They swipe back, brutally. No match for the mob, Alloy is beaten, broken, overcome by tearful self-pity. Mongrel, someone says, with a parting kick.

He lies beside the road, turned in on himself, listening to the noise of the crowd die away. Distant thunder grumbles, the afternoon grows dark. He does not know what to do until the idea occurs that he can do anything. I have a new life, he grins, stretching himself out to his full height.

Only one thing is certain: things will never be the same again. Except, that is, he thinks with a sigh, Andrew, who is absolutely reliable: it is up to me to have him or to reject him. Alloy smiles, wipes his bloody nose and sets off to find Margaret.

[][][][][]

Tudak takes Keramugl up past Jim's house, through Henry's abandoned garden and around Henry's burnt-out house. They climb down the cliff face, through the tangle of trees and end up at the place at the back of Alloy's house where Keramugl had discovered Tarlie's decapitated body. Keramugl is taken into the house through the back door and pushed straight out again through the front, onto the veranda. Tudak, himself, stays inside unseen, watching. He does not want to frighten anyone.

The three women sit on the floor, beside a pile of boxes, bundles, rucksacks, holdalls, and one very dilapidated suitcase. Also, a couple of kerosene lamps and some tools. They appear to be waiting for something, which might have been Keramugl, or not. Nevertheless he dumps himself on the only chair, looks at Margaret, ignoring the others, and immediately begins to tell her his story which he spills out like a child but it is heard as the story of a man who not long

471

afterwards accompanies Margaret to the Highlands where he impresses himself upon Father Hermann, and a man who teaches Helen how to be a woman.

Yes, I keep telling you, that time, I talk to Missus Margaret as my mother. I did not have the idea at the time. Only another time, later, I think, yes, that is the way a child talks to its mother. It is not ashamed. It knows that its mother will have the answer. And, also, I think: Why is she not in a hurry to tell me what to do? But, as I have this thought I know what I must do. As I am thinking this, Andrew comes with the truck.

[][][][][]

Helen had felt like a small girl all day. Margaret and Daphne were the older girls who knew the ropes but were too busy to show her what to do. She followed them around and was not, in the end, even allowed to do the menial tasks because whenever she started something, Neki, with gentle, smiling insistence which she had no power to resist, would take over. At first she thought he was Sweet, describing him as such in the letter she was composing to her mother in her head. But she soon learned that Sweet did not describe this tough-as-old-boots boy-man. Gentle and loving he was but in a wounded sort of way. He would look at the ground in front of her and then look up at her with the most knowing of smiles: it will take more than that to soften me, he seemed to say but didn't. No one will ever hold this boy was the thought that came to her, but Margaret held him and he became an extension of her gentle, irresistible will.

I was shocked when I heard Keramugl's voice. In the first place, because I was surprised by someone coming out of the house like that. We were all a bit tense. I thought there was only Neki inside. Then, of course, I didn't expect to hear his voice at all. I'd been willing myself not to think of him and I hadn't really noticed this man who dropped himself onto the chair so that it groaned. But what most shocked me was the thrill I felt as a girl hearing the voice of the man whom she knew would be her husband. A purely sexual thrill and definitely not something I would write about to my mother. I had no doubt about its reality. It was nothing like Alistair's voice which was one of those upper-middle-class voices, all accent and affectation with no substance in it. Keramugl's voice vibrates in his chest. It is low and quiet so that you must listen to what he says. But all the same, the voice was not quite as I remembered it. It was harder, less thick and it had an edge to it. Almost mean. Certainly urgent.

He was more emphatic, sitting on the chair as his by right. He sat there, with us around him on the floor, and he dominated us. I loved him for that; even more when I looked at him properly, although he ignored me – more important things were happening. It was not that he had changed but rather that the change stressed his essential characteristics: he was leaner, the muscles of his arms were more sinewy and more definitely moulded; his face was haggard, older and sticky-looking with the heat and dust; his hair was ragged with bits of things in it; a tiny tuft of a beard sprouted from his chin. The passiveness of his eyes had completely gone; now they blazed as in a fever and he leaned forward in his chair, impatient of it despite his obvious claim. He smelt hot and human and I

472

loved him for that too. I loved the terrific energy in him and above it all the very essence of what is him: his four-square, grounded solidity, the great strength of him that gives him his gentleness. I was madly in love.

His speech to Margaret was a rush of pidgin I could barely follow but its urgency was evident. He was going to do something and he began to rise from the chair but she moved forward, kneeling in front of him. She touched his knee. She might have touched it with her cheek, so loving was the action. His naked knee, which was rough and scarred. I had not looked at him like that before and seeing that knee of his I realised the life he had led. His naked feet, bruised and battered, told the same story. They were not young man's feet but the feet of an aged man who had suffered many things. I wanted to cry for him, I wanted also to kneel in front of him and acknowledge his life. So much more worthy than my own. I wanted to kiss that knee and wash his feet.

At Margaret's touch, Keramugl sat back and relaxed. He stopped talking but still he did not look at me. His mind, as I came to learn later, would focus its energy on only one thing at a time and at this time it was Joseph.

[][][][][]

They sat motionless as the darkness became thicker until lightening broke the sky like the final word. The afternoon weighed down upon them and they felt such anguish that they were sure their hearts would break. All their lives before, everything that had happened up to that dreadful moment, when the world might well have come to an end, was picked up by the mighty hand, weighed and found wanting. A clod of drought-stricken soil that is crumbled to dust and allowed to trickle back to the earth from whence it had come.

Keramugl, the strong and the brave, ready for anything, slips off the chair, onto his knees to join the women. He cannot help himself as he again remembers Annu. Remembers Annu kissing him in Karandawa, up there in the Highlands, and Annu asking him to do one thing for him: do not forget me. Never, my Lord. The pain is terrific. He puts his forehead onto the floor.

Helen thinks of England, her childhood, Mum and Dad, the comfortable house in the garden with the swing at the bottom between the potting shed and the compost heap. How she had cried when they wouldn't let her have a pony, you don't understand she had screamed and her mother had laughed saying she didn't want her daughter turning into one of those awful fat-bottomed, horse-riding girls and silly gymkhanas. She hated her mother then and slammed the door it was never mentioned again. Thanks Mum, for everything, because here I am now altogether another sort of girl loving this man but how is it I feel so dreadfully sad? She lets out a tiny moan and feels better wanting to touch Keramugl whom she sees is in real pain so that his body is hunched on the floor shaking with sobs. She wants to hold him like a baby but she cannot get near. Nothing exists beyond his pain.

I was thinking of Peter and all that life before. Was this the end of it then? It must be. I thought I felt sad because I couldn't see the point of it and because I couldn't feel sad about Peter or about never seeing the children again. Was I such an empty, hopeless thing? Someone without emotion? I tried to feel more than this empty sadness and I tried to think of what it was which was making me think this way. Nothing made sense. It was silly thinking about Mrs Grant's leg or of the last view of Mummy, as I walked away from her. Smaller, more pathetic, more childlike each time I turned around to look back. I had not waved. Why does cruel youth hang on to the connection that is being deliberately broken? I hadn't felt sad then, so why should I feel sad now? In fact, after all these years, I wasn't sure it had even happened like that. Perhaps Mummy had turned back into the house the minute I left it, slamming the door and going back to bed to read until mid-morning. It would have been more like her. Had I created my own myth about my mother? About myself? I thought very hard about her and I felt nothing. The empty sadness was for something else. What was it?

I looked towards Margaret for an answer and saw that she too was struggling. She had remained in the kneeling posture in a sort of trance, staring out beyond us. I had never seen her quite like it. She seemed to be struggling to hold on to the calm self-possession which was the very essence of her. I was impressed, and frightened because I had come to rely on her strength. Oddly satisfied also, to realise that she too had conflicting emotions raging inside her.

Oh Lord, must this be?

Of course.

And Margaret smiles at the simple obviousness of the truth.

I watched Keramugl return her smile. Not as mine was, a brief smile of gratitude but rather a conspiratorial smile. Those two understood each other perfectly and watching them, I felt a surge of reassurance and optimism. A feeling that reminded me, for some reason, of our house-boy, Annu. Immediately all the fuzzy, blurred memories I had tried to recapture swung into the single, clear idea of Annu. I did not have to try and picture him because the idea of him was enough. The same warm, safe sensation of that time when he was with me, with Peter and with the children, with us altogether, when we were with him under his strong protection. That time of our lives, I realised, as I sat on Alloy's veranda, waiting, had been the defining time, enabling us all to go on and live our lives better, bathing, as it were, in his radiance. It was fantastic but true: the children went back to Australia to live with Peter's dad. I never saw them again but letters came regularly and they did indeed go on to live good lives sweetening the last years for their grandfather whose forceful love had made Peter's childhood such a miserable affair. Oh and then I felt so happy that Peter had known Annu and had lived such a rich life before he died, that our love for each other had flowered so richly and beautifully. All thanks to Annu and thinking of him, my sadness rose like a bubble inside me, got to my head and made me cry so that I felt a lot better.

[][][][][]

Tudak, unseen, watches Keramugl as a proud father might watch his son go out and deal with the world. Only this father – and perhaps it is a good thing – has no advice to offer. Rather he wishes to learn from his son. To learn how he might become a part of that sunnier world. For it is true that although the afternoon is dark, from inside the shadows of the house, where he stands, and certainly from the viewpoint of his own dark past, the outside looks bright enough for Tudak.

He recognises Margaret as Jim's wife. But he sees her as Keramugl's mother. This is odd. How can a white woman be the mother of Keramugl who is black? Especially this white woman whose paleness is transparent like a ghost. Tudak wrestles with the idea, frowning, until watching her the answer comes that she is their ancestor, their common ancestor so that she is also his mother. He feels good about this idea and looks out beyond, up to the sky from which the dust is clearing. Purple clouds gather in the distance. Lightening cracks and he sees Keramugl crouching on the floor. He wants to rush forward and comfort him also but as he moves a small hand clutches his. Neki, again: the one who had helped lift him up off the dusty floor. He looks down into tearful eyes and grasps the hand that seeks his, sensing the pain. Now it is his turn. He smiles glancing back at Margaret seeing that she is indeed his mother and Keramugl his brother.

Thus Tudak also remembers Annu. He wants to look and look at these people who are part of Annu of whom he wants to be a part also. He wants to breathe them in like a great gulp of fresh air. He does not want to look at them in a general way but he wants to look at each of them exclusively so that he can see what is inside them and what it is that makes them who they are. Why, he wants to ask, are they not me?

He looks at the other woman whom he recognises as the wife of the man who had once run the mill. He can see that she is now alone. He wants to look at her because she is beautiful but in a different way from his mother. She is shining, glowing and sunny. She is not young but she is, she is ripe, like a fruit ready to pick. And as he thinks this his prick moves as he has not known it move before. Not like a hunger as a prelude to aggression but more like, more like a regret because he wants not to violate her but to protect her. He knows he will have to wait for this woman to invite him and he is astonished to feel this. His mouth hangs open a little, but he knows it will happen one day.

He looks at the woman who is such a young girl that he wants to laugh. She has thick, black hair and her skin is blotchy red but she is strong. He sees that she is adoring Keramugl and he knows Keramugl will love her and watch over her for that alone. She will give him his children and he is glad to know that it is settled.

He breathes in and thus again watches Keramugl whom he feels is particularly his own. He knows that Keramugl will take care of all these women, and will do more. The man! He laughs again, enjoying the new sensation of laughter. He looks down at Neki who laughs also.

Then Tudak thinks: It is good to be alive with these people. But the thunder rumbles again which makes him think of Jim. The smile falls from his face and he drops Neki's hand. The sunny people on the veranda withdraw and are obscured by the darkness. He imagines them all blind with only Jim, a grotesque figure, able to see in the element that is truly his own. Tudak shivers and remembers his lonely anguish. He wants these people safe. The old primitive urge takes him. He must bring Jim down here. He will lay Jim dead at the feet of his mother. He growls and Neki clings so that together they set off back up the cliff to find Jim.

[][][][][]

Keramugl has returned to his chair, more concerned now about his hunger. In fact, Keramugl's stomach is the centre of attention. He has not eaten all day and the rumbles of his stomach are more restless than the distant thunder. Helen remembered this many years later: the man had to be fed.

Keramugl also remembered, but in a more profound way: Yes, Andrew, it is true, I am not thinking of Annu, I am thinking of my stomach, which is talking to me. It is telling me that in the same way that it is at the centre of me, so (olsem) I am at the centre of my life. I look at everything and see the three white women sitting round me. I do not think it is strange. I think: this thing, these women, are my life. One is my mother, one is my sister and one is my wife. My life has brought me here to a place (wanpela hap) where I am a thing like my stomach is big inside me sometimes. I want to laugh because the idea is something new to me. I have my whole life behind me and it is a big thing but here, at this time, it is me sitting on a chair. That is all. I think of all the things I have eaten and I think of all the people I know eating these things with me. It is a good thing. But (olsem) now, all this eating is only (tasol) a noise like water running over rocks in my stomach. So, I know it is time to look at Helen. I look at her, I smile and I pat my stomach. Now, suppose she does not understand me (na suppose em i no savi tingting belong mi) or suppose she asks someone else (arapela) to make the food. Then I will not be happy. But she looks at me and she smiles (em i lap) and she gets up to make my food. So I think, yes, she wants to be my wife.

That was the best thing. When he looked at me and patted his stomach, grinning like a bad boy. It was the first time he had recognised me since he had come back. And, more so, since he was recognising me as the one who should get his food, I was very happy. Not thrilled, Andrew, in a sexual way. Don't put this down wrong. But just happy to be the one who got his food. The one who would define how he was to be fed. At the time I had not realised how little experience he had had of a woman, in a family, in his family, getting food ready for him. He had not had a proper family in his village which was why he left it in the first place. He had no idea who his father was and his mother died while he was still on her breast. It's astonishing how he survived. His first idea of a family was with the men on the plantation. The thing is, I didn't have to battle any cultural preconceptions he might have had, he merely accepted the food I prepared for him as right.

Helen was determined to not let Neki overrule her this time. She would get Keramugl something to eat if she had to fight the self-possessed little boy. But she need not have worried: "Has anyone seen Neki? He's disappeared."

"Tudak em i stab?" Where's Tudak?

"Tudak? Who's he?"

Keramugl explained shortly. "Tasol, kisim kaikai bilong mi. Mi klostu long dai pinis." Bring me food before I die.

Margaret told her not to worry. Tudak and Neki had things to do: "Helen, you must cook something quickly because we will be moving soon. I'll make a fire. We'll just boil some kaukau with salt. Find a can of fish, Daphne, please. I dare say Andrew will want something when he gets back. We must fill these men's stomachs. It's always the best thing to do."

So they are kept busy as the thunder takes over from Keramugl's stomach. Then the thunder becomes a vehicle bumping over the dry, rutted road. Andrew arrives, proud of himself: Right, I've got it am I not a hero? He is blissfully pleased with himself and grins like a schoolboy when he sees Keramugl: "Am I pleased to see you!" He looks at Keramugl and tries to hug him but does not know how, so that they love him, for a moment, for his clumsiness and forgive his self-centred Englishness. Keramugl knows how it is done and hugs Andrew as, as a Roman captain might hug one of his soldiers. Duty before affection and all that it looks like but Andrew feels the warmth. "Phew, Keramugl, you need a bath."

"Yes Andrew, you are brave," says Margaret, "but if you want to eat, eat now because we must get moving."

They look at her, for a moment, astonished but the flash of urgency has gone. She sits on the chair because Keramugl is squatting on the floor, eating, quickly. Andrew has joined him. When they have finished, she gets up, climbs into the back of the vehicle and sits waiting for the others. She is very calm.

Of course I remember what happened then, Andrew. It is something else I will never forget. No one else noticed. Not even you, which is why I decided to like you. Yes, that and the way you were so pleased to see Keramugl. Alistair would have been outraged but you took it as perfectly natural that Keramugl should take charge just then. He stood up, brushed the bits of kaukau from himself and wiped his mouth: "Andrew, did you see any disturbance?" Yu luklukim sampela pait na ol man wokim kranki?

"No, I came the back way. But I thought I heard some sort of commotion coming from near the market."

"Please drive us there, now."

And you obeyed him, Andrew, just like that.

Daphne and I were left behind.

[][][][][]

Yes, it is Petrus here. Keramugl says he cannot talk anymore because he is tired. He says he will rest and we can do some more writing tomorrow. He says it is time to get up the generator.

But I know why he is tired of telling his story. It is because he remembers the laughter of Annu. We all remember this because when Annu laughs he throws his head back so we see his strong neck and his big mouth open with the laugher coming out like a thing that we can see. His neck is like the strong Yar tree. His laugh is like a great Bird of Paradise that comes out of him. We hear the wings beating and then we see it come from his mouth in all its colours and fly into the air. We can watch this bird for a long time and hear it sing. When we can no longer see the bird, all the same, we know that it is there, somewhere.

This memory reminds us of that time. We remember the time when we thought we would not hear the voice of Joseph again and we would not see the laughter of Joseph again. Then also, we remember our thoughts at the time and we remember the pain in our belly. At that time the pain is so real and great in our belly that we want to kill the white man who makes it. We feel an anger that we have never felt before. The fire of anger is burning us.

We have talked about this many times.

I myself, Petrus, feel this pain very strongly at the time. I feel this pain so strongly, that I think all my life before that time has been burnt up. I cannot forget it. The others feel this way also at the time of Joseph being hanged from the tree.

I feel there is nothing anywhere and I feel that God is laughing at me because he is not God but the very devil.

My belly is on fire and I want to find Andrew to kill him because he is a white man. It is not Jim I want to kill, it is Andrew because I know that the killing of Andrew will take away the pain and it will make me happy. Yes, at that time, the devil has got hold of me and that is how I feel. The killing of Jim cannot be the same as the killing of Andrew because Jim is like a cockroach. Where is the pleasure in killing a cockroach? But Andrew! Ah! I sat beside Andrew in his car on that day when Nalin's daughter died. When Andrew was acting the master. When Andrew was the stupid Andrew and Tarlie had to teach Andrew to be outside himself. That made Andrew a better man. I was happy to see Andrew listen to Tarlie. I was happy that Andrew could love Tarlie and I was happy the white man in Andrew was not angry at himself for the shame of loving Tarlie. I sat beside Andrew in the church in Ples when Andrew said that Ples was safe. This was Andrew again hiding inside himself. He thought he was separate from us so that he could say that thing that was a lie as he said it. I knew it was a lie when he said it. Andrew thought he was stronger than me. He thought he was stronger than all of us so he could make that false promise. What could he do? He was a boy then and I felt sorry for him then because I knew it would be better for him to say he would be with us when Ples was destroyed. It was after Tarlie had been killed that Andrew became a proper man. Because then Andrew had no power and he learned that he had no power. Then Andrew was the same as us and when he was the same as us he was with us. Then Andrew needed Annu just as we needed Annu. And the big thing was that Andrew knew that he needed Annu. This is why Bune did not kill Andrew. It was not because Bune knew Andrew and it was not because Andrew was the friend of Alloy. It was because Andrew suffered with us and had no power to help us.

You see what I am saying? I loved Andrew because he had become a man. He did not pretend strength. He knew his weakness as a man.

So, at that moment of Joseph's death when it was blood that came out of his mouth, it was the white man Andrew I wanted to kill. I wanted to kill this thing Andrew that I loved.

That is me, Petrus, who you know as a quiet man, I had these feelings.

At that moment of Joseph's death I know for sure I have been wrong in the past. I know for sure that God is the God that Annu described to Keramugl and to the other men when they were travelling to the Solwara. That God is the white man's God. The God that the white man uses to kill kanakas. At that moment of Joseph's death, I am thinking, all this talk in the Bible is just the white man's bad shit and vomit and I have been eating it. And as I am thinking this, it is true, in the crowd of angry people who have seen Joseph hanging from the tree, with the noises of the white man's guns all around us, I throw up.

Yes, I throw up everything that is inside me so that the fire is in my mouth and I can smell my vomit. It is a bad smell and I am thinking I am going to die. I am going to die in all the noise and movement that is around me.

You must understand well what I am going to write now.

When I have thrown up, the pain in my belly is gone but I have a feeling of emptiness.

There are many people all around. There is much noise and confusion. There is the sound of the gun and people screaming and crying out. There is anger and fear all around me. I see clearly all this happening. I see the blood from Joseph's mouth and it is red as blood is but it is a new red colour that I have not seen before. The blood has a light inside it that comes out. All the colours are like this.

And I can see everything I want to see, I can see the lines below a woman's eye and a coin that is dropped on the ground and is trodden into the dirt. I see the white man, Jim. I see the fear in his eyes very clearly. I am so close to him, I can smell him.

So all this is very real but at the same time I feel that I am in another place so that already it is a memory. But I am there. Do you understand what I am saying? I feel I am watching myself in all this angry crowd. I am flying like a little bird above all the sadness and all the anger and all the pain.

I am flying as a little bird above Petrus. I see Petrus as clearly as I see the fear on the face of Jim and the pleasure on the face of Tudak. I see the ugly Petrus who is in pain. The Petrus who is shouting and screaming with the crowd. The Petrus who wants to kill Andrew. I see all this but as I fly higher and higher I feel nothing of Petrus. I have lost Petrus but I know Petrus is a part of the crowd that is the animal with no sense.

The little bird is seeing but it is dying inside itself. Its small life will soon end.

The little bird is very small. It is not a big bird like the Bird of Paradise that is Joseph's laugh but it is like the birds that drink from the hibiscus flowers. If you can catch this bird in your hand you can squeeze it dead.

Where the crowd has been, the place is empty. The ground is trampled and muddy, there is rubbish all around. The crowd animal has run after Jim who is the white man they want.

The little bird flies aimlessly for a while because it is lost. It has lost Joseph and it has lost Petrus. The place in which the bird flies is empty. It feels sadness for the loss.

So the little bird flies higher and higher until he sees Andrew's truck. And in the back of Andrew's truck there is Missis Margaret holding the body of Joseph and she is bending over it and she is looking at the body of Joseph so that she sees the wounds from the beating that the people gave to Joseph before they hanged him. She is touching the scars with her fingers and she is wiping the blood from Joseph's face with her dress that is a dress the colour of the inside of the cooked kaukau that is now coloured with the blood of Joseph. And because the little bird sees everything he sees that Missis Margaret is crying but that it is her tears that are washing Joseph and she is smiling also because she remembers the Bird of Paradise. And as she remembers the Bird of Paradise the beautiful bird itself is flying above the body of Joseph.

The little bird remembers how Tarlie held the head of Nalin's daughter before and it sees how Margaret is holding the body of Joseph and loving us all just the same. So the little bird is happy and he thinks he is not going to kill Andrew. He wants to be with Andrew and with the other people who love Annu.

39
Journey to Lingalinga

Margaret would have been a good potter. The dull clay, in her hands, would have been formed into things of exquisite beauty. In her hands, washed with her tears, the body of Joseph was as beautiful as it had ever been in life. How can we forget that? His death as experienced for us by Margaret was undiluted joy, Jim utterly confounded.

Stripped naked, the neck broken, yet in Margaret's hands, the embodiment of human beauty. The indignities of his last moments made noble by her. How could her love do otherwise? Margaret, no less than Tarlie, no less than Nwufoh, come to think of it, had the wonderful ability to absorb evil and convert it into something good. She could swallow evil and not know it; it was no more to her than a crystal of salt upon her tongue.

[][][][][]

Jim sits on the veranda where he had once sat and breakfasted with Margaret. He cannot avoid seeing her in his mind's eye: "fuck off can't you?" But she will not go away.

He has been tidied up a little, even shaved. His clothes are clean but they hang loosely on his body. Bune has done all this having seen off Tematan with the suggestion he join his friends, they may take you back, they did. Jim has eaten the meal provided. There is a litter of fag ends on the table. He feels he would like a beer. One appears, open. He swigs it leering at the vision: "'ere's to you an' do yer worst, yer bitch." Another bottle appears.

He drinks, listening to the hullabaloo below with an amused grin. These kanakas are like children. He hears the racket swell up the hill and knows not a drop of fear. They may be coming for me for all I care but I can deal with them and I'll fight to the end. See if I don't and indeed he might have dealt with it successfully, like the old days, and invigorated, gone on to fight another day. His supporters would indeed have come out of the rotting woodwork

They must be in the car park, the fuckers. He strolls across the lawn, trips up on something and rights himself with a grunt. He looks back over his shoulder expecting to see her on the veranda but it is only Bune clearing up. He is more efficient than either Nalin or Tematan: the place is as clean and sweet-smelling as if Margaret was still there, damn the b. . . .

At the edge of the lawn, laterite soil and thin grass, Jim looks down into the car park. And it is a fact that as he appeared, the day became darker and palpably thicker. Thunder rolled in from the distance. Bune disappears.

Jim sees Joseph with annoyance: "An' 'ow did 'e get out, I'd like to know." For a while, and even more annoying, it is clear that Joseph can do anything he wants with the crowd. But the atmosphere changes and Jim is gratified to see Joseph grabbed by the mob. "An' they'll tear him limb from limb, don't I know them like the back of mi 'and." He laughs his Jim laugh, his body jogging as he grunts with amusement. He cannot tear himself away. Greedily he watches, egging on the mob. "Go on, get 'im." The mob obeys as it would have obeyed him to do the opposite. His last chance.

He watches them take Joseph away and then returns to his seat on the veranda, profoundly satisfied: "I've got 'em both and 'e'll git what's comin' to 'im. She'll miss 'er pet." But the thing is, he misses Joseph too and the desire to go down to the club and be served a drink by ol' Joseph is almost irresistible. He begins to think that if he could just get that back he'd do things differently. I'd 'ave got Andrew on side some'ow. And so the ideas go round and round inside his head until he's not sure what he is or where he is. He watches the afternoon grow darker, until the idea comes around again: time for a drink. He can see the club warm and welcoming down below. It's just what he needs and with any luck there'll be Peter and Clarence there for him to gently bully. I'd better talk to Henry about that planting in Andrew's division. We got to get it started. He feels quite bucked up despite feeling a little stiff as he pushes himself up. Blimey, he belches, I bin sitting around too long. He walks round the house to the carport where the Landrover waits, as brightly clean as ever, well oiled, full of fuel and humming, Bune in the driving seat: "Time to go now, Sir."

"Yes you fucker and you can drive me."

"I will."

The devil take Jim. He did. Tudak and Neki were in the back.

⬜⬜⬜⬜⬜

The mob, having expressed itself by hanging the man, has moved on. You'd expect its members, you and me, to be marked, perhaps by a lack of noses, but each one looks as normal as we usually do, our faces containing all the right bits and pieces, our expressions . . . fixed somehow, now we've grown up, lost our childhood innocence, become men of the world. We might as well be blind for all. . . there's no need to say that again.

The storm was indeed in a bone-china teacup.

⬜⬜⬜⬜⬜

As two drunkards they bump into each other and stick.

Alloy and Petrus.

Petrus! What's happened?

Petrus told him.

It's alright Petrus, follow me. Petrus followed, and stuck.

They find Andrew, apparently as Andrew ought to be, at the wheel of the truck which was standing beside a great tree, older, it seemed, than anything else around. It stood between the market and the road in the space where vehicles generally parked, now filled with people milling around aimlessly, Andrew's elbow sticking out of the car window. He was chatting to someone, negotiating the price of lemons, probably.

They were looking at the body hanging loosely from the tree which was no less benign-looking than it had always looked. Was this for what it had been created? The particular branch just right for the purpose? The idea of hanging the man the process of creation?

What?

Look what has been done.

I see it illuminated by the last light of the day that blasts through the broken, purple clouds like the melodious vibrations of a thousand golden trumpets. Look at the beautiful bird. You see it?

I do not, says Andrew. Up close he is a ruin. More than the familiar uncertainty of his pleasant face, struggling with some practical problem such as, such as, such as the salvation of his soul or the boiling of an egg. Rather, he is devastated by the realisation that what had seemed to be the state of things was not . . . the state of things. Nothing like it: the earth is indeed flat, the sun is undoubtedly rolled around by a dung-beetle which is quite likely to be trodden flat at any moment by a supremely careless god I am the Emperor of China and China is an idea far too big for any mind, let alone the floundering fish of a thing which is mine, to grasp and to cap it all John Lennon is dead and will not appear as the Messiah of the North Circular Road in London which the archaeologists assure us is not . . . something divine but they are not sure of the connection between Kew Bridge and the Hanger Lane roundabout. It was undoubtedly created for a religious purpose the excited man on the TV screen assures us.

Alloy laughs, realising, as he does, that he has not brushed his teeth for days. Come on, Andrew.

Come on what? Don't you see what's happened?

Yes, I do, and that's why you can't sit here feeling sorry for yourself.

Why not? It's dreadful. The world has ended.

Your world, Andrew. He grabs Andrew's wrist. Get out of it then. Petrus will look after you just like any slave will look after a white man who cannot look after himself and who has no ideas beyond his superior feelings. You can fuck off then. He twists Andrew's wrist brutally. Andrew is stung for the third time, surprised by Alloy's sudden passion. Thank God for you, Alloy, he says.

Fuck God, Alloy replies, seeing Margaret sitting in the back of the truck for the first time. Patiently she sits like an ordinary market woman. She is watching the three of them – Petrus, Alloy and Andrew – with a patient smile, tears falling down her face.

Something, God knows what, pushed, pushed me downwards like a heavenly weight upon my shoulders. I wanted to lay my cheek upon the ground. I wanted to see the colossus rising above me. I wanted to abase myself as the only way I could think of, of expressing, of expressing, not my inferiority, but her superiority over all of us. My desire was overwhelming but at the same time I hated to go down on my knees like that publicly. Even to Her. I am blushing now as I think of it. Would she laugh at me? No, not her: she knew my feelings down to the last crumb.

What?

My desire? No, you idiot. Don't you know me? My desire was for Him. It was His eyes I wanted to rest on my humiliation. It was His voice I wanted to hear. Even rebuking me. It was His sweet breath I wanted to feel upon my face and the smell of his body I wanted in the air I breathed. But He was gone, His body hanging there a lifeless, dangling, distorted thing. And only through Her could I reach Him. She was, she still is, the heavenly gate. And there she was, Andrew, in the back of the ute, alone and the tears streaming down her face. I tell you, fuck you, I was ashamed. I was ashamed of myself, I was ashamed of you being so useless in this time of, of terrible times. I was ashamed of Her, even, for sitting there silently crying. I was ashamed of the whole human race, damn us. What had we done to Joseph? Joseph, the man who laughed. Sweet Joseph, let me see you once more, for one minute, with one eye, even, if I am allowed. A passing glimpse of your departing heel. And often have I woken in the dead of night or in the early morning, a cock crowing, or after drowsy afternoon sleep, hot and lazy, the flies buzzing, to know I missed you by a fraction of a second. You were there, watching me, the loving smile upon your lips, the tenderness of your eyes. Your hand ready to take mine.

I left you, Andrew. Remember?

He had forgotten.

Yes, I told you to fuck off and I went straight to Her and She gave me Her hand. At any rate, I held it for a while, feeling it small in my own clumsy hands. I wanted to take the anguish out of Her and tell Her She was as strong and as certain as the mountain. Then I dropped it and returned to you, Andrew, as I am always bound to do, damn you, the anger welling up inside me so that all I wanted to do was to hit your silly uncertain face.

For Christ's sake, Andrew, help me. You too, Petrus. Aren't you supposed to be the practical one? The carpenter? The one who made the cross. Yes, Andrew, move: drive the car under the tree.

Andrew moved. Then he got into the back of the truck with Alloy and Petrus, and, none too gently, for there were other things going on around them, they cut down the body, as if it was nothing to do with them, and let it drop down to Margaret. She caught it and she held it.

[][][][]

As they messed around with His body, a shiny, brand-new-looking vehicle appeared nearby. A fantastic looking thing, dripping with water from the rain which had fallen. It gleamed in the pure, rain-washed air, catching the golden light of the setting sun. The little crowd which had surrounded Andrew's truck to watch the body of whatsisname, being cut down, had forgotten what it had done. It melted away, reforming as a single animal again around the astonishing vision of metallic beauty that had appeared, apparently, from nowhere.

I was as much astonished as was the crowd.

So they told me.

Word went around until everyone swore that is what they had seen.

I suppose I must have seen something.

Margaret does not deny it, or else she says she can't remember. Anyway, what does it matter?

Alloy is the only one to state emphatically that all he saw was the burnt-out rusty hulk of the thing. Rusty was the word he always used whenever I asked him: rusty hulk, rusty wreck, nothing but the rusty remains. He insisted upon rustiness. I didn't challenge him. I never really listened. Now, when I think of it, when I try to remember, I can see the rusty piece of scrap lying in the yellow kunai grass, smelling of rust in the hot dusty air. But that must have been years later, not on the very day, despite the heavy rain that fell later. Things don't rust that quickly.

I look at the thing with my mind's eye. As it would have appeared at the time they cut down His body.

Am I not right, Petrus? Was it not a wonderful sight? Everyone says so. What did you see?

Yes Andrew, it was a fine thing. They had made it well. Not with nails but the joints fitting together so you could not see them unless you looked very close. Dovetail they call it like they taught me at Markham when I was an apprentice in the Mission. The wood was so fine, I wanted to touch it. They had cut it with the grain and planed it smooth.

It was a marvel of creation.

Petrus, you long-long man! It wasn't made of wood, it was metal. Everyone says so. I can see it now. Something like, something like a shiny new toy I got at Christmas so long ago it must be the first I remember. The cosy, bright room dark outside. A wonderful, gleaming thing catching all the light. I want to feel and feel and feel the hard polished surfaces. Feel it in my hands, smell it and touch it with my tongue. I would eat it if I could. It has colourful, new pictures on its surface that are as alive as anything else breathing in the room and the smell of the Christmas tree goes with it. Was it magic? I cannot remember the thing on any day other than that day. It was snatched away darling that was not meant for you and I got something meaningless instead.

I would say, all the same, that it was not beautiful in its shape, which was angular. Not the sweeping curves of Art Nouveau, the Rolls Royce lady. Neither the bulbous streamlining of the American 40s and 50s, which for some reason reached its, its apotheosis in the design of radio sets. No, the beauty of the thing was in the quality of its construction. Something Edwardian about it: designed as if it was a horse-drawn coach only it was a motor car apparently in the 1890s the horse-drawn traffic of the richest city on earth moved in a stately procession, without end and wonderful to see, along the main thoroughfares Piccadilly, Park Lane, Pall Mall, the Bayswater Road, chaotic only at the crossroads Hyde Park Corner, say, or Ludgate Circus where the skill and good manners of the coachmen kept things going but always the clatter of hooves and the pungent, healthy smell of horse and leather. Gone by 1905 and men made rude by the machine. Lacquered coach-work, electroplated details and thick rainbow glass bevelled can you believe it.

Come and look, come and look. The young man calls. He is undersized: the unkind call him a runt but he is healthy and confident don't mind what they call him. They cannot keep him down, now he's up. Cockney accent or New South

Wales? Could be both around 1905 and he is minded by the biggest brute of a black man you've ever seen. A silent giant, a muscular pillar of polished ebony. Wouldn't like to meet him on a dark night it's been said before but all you can see are the whites of his eyes and the gentle golden light that reflects off his gentle skin.

Behold the wonderful thing.

The crowd edges forward. It looks at the thing described as wonderful: undoubtedly a piece of cargo dreamt up by the white man. It wants to touch but dare not. The young man is encouraging – he would take their money – but the other, for all his human beauty and potential gentleness suggests hands off I'm warning you. His one-ness with the night un-nerves the crowd a little, makes it cautious and silently excited.

The young man laughs. You would think, and so you remember, he would be constantly looking over his shoulder at his . . . lover you might call him because he is so constantly and happily aware of him for all that he does not look over his shoulder even once you might swear he did but in fact, he did not.

Yes well, looking at a thing is all very well but you cannot go on looking and looking, however fine it is. Something has to happen it did.

The young man stands beside the passenger door, the other lounges behind. Neki steps forward towards the crowd, huge now, filling the night with its chatter and fidgeting. He is a little less certain: watch out my dear. The crowd moves back: I will. Tudak moves between Neki and the beautiful vehicle. The crowd is reassured: gosh, we are going to see Something tonight. You'd have thought they'd seen enough a man hanged don't happen every day in your backyard.

Behold the monster.

Tudak opens the door and out steps Jim.

Beyond the crowd, which might be millions, a few dozens, or one or two ghouls, Margaret has just taken the body of Joseph onto her lap. It lies, as I have already described, a little awkwardly. If she wanted, she could see Jim, see the sweat on his forehead, his dry lips, his bloodshot eyes looking around uneasily, hear his uncertain breathing. Like a shining light she is visible to Jim. He could have walked through the crowd which would have opened out before him. He could have gone to her and stayed with her as easily as the others had done.

Jim looks around. Fuck me, 'ow did I get 'ere? Must be a reason. He pieces together a little memory for himself. Of course, the kanakas are revolting – his body jogs merrily at his own stale joke – an' I was in the club she'd fucked off somewhere an' I said listen you useless buggers you stay 'ere I'll sort it out Jim's your man for a tough job I am. Sammy! An' this cocky young bugger might as well be Sammy or near enough like him what does it matter they're all the same. Get the lads an' 'ere's the fucker I got from the penal colony 'e'll strangle a man for me puts the fear of whateveritis in 'em all. And so forth on and so forth etc, etc. Jim's on a roll. Is it? On a high, at any rate.

He looks above the crowd, sees Andrew and some other buggers messing around in the back of a ute. Oi, you fuckwit, I sacked you. Piss off, arsehole. I'm the man of action 'ere, don't you forget it, shithead. Andrew hears him not. 'E's with the other cunt too, I'd like to strangle 'em both poofters.

The crowd laughs at the funny man. It does not hear Jim's bomb, bomb, bombast either but it sees his mouth opening and closing and it sees his face screwing itself up into amazing contortions. It sees him stamp his foot on the ground to no avail: things Do Not happen. Is this little chap the Jim we once feared? The terror of our life? The thing we dared not think about yet knew? There ought to be more than this to a monster. Two heads? No. One only and that nothing special I seen a more in'eresting 'ead on a dog.

Jim steps forward. The crowd holds its ground, and holds its breath. I'll fight you then. And live to fight another day. Neki does now look at Tudak, over his shoulder, grinning at him like the fellow conspirator he is. Then he is serious but Tudak winks leave it let them have him if that's what he wants. Neki smiles: slyly he moves towards Tudak feels Annu's hands upon him again. They walk to Lingalinga ahead of the others, together. At some stage they will be overtaken on the road but they will refuse a lift: we'll see you later, we'd rather walk into our new life.

Jim is finally on his own. Pathetic? No: he is in a fighting mood and will go down fighting. Inside himself he is certain. No more detachment. I'll get 'em. Biff, bang, bong. I ain't Jim for nuffink. Face to face now with a heavy man about his own height who sweats a little and smells sweetly of distilled alcohol. Jim would have said gin but these fuckers drink some awful concoction which makes them do things for which they are abjectly sorry the following day. Do things like what they did to Nalin's daughter and to Neki. Hanging him up on a tree like that was a daft thing I did but it hasn't worked its way through yet. Not half! The heavy man does not recognise Jim, sees rather . . . rather something that is in his way and which makes him inexpressively, inhumanly angry. He recognises the feeling like an old friend. It's me mate, the other me and in this respect he is different from Jim. Jim is one lump of shit, this one is two.

Out of my way. The heavy man is astonished and inclined to laugh. Instead he does what comes naturally and hits Jim on the side of the head, just beside the left eye, with the flat of his mighty hand and with all his weight behind him. Eighty solid kilos, I should say, against Jim's seventy of much less solid, bloated flesh they are both short men, mean when set against the others.

Jim was brain-dead before he hit the ground. At first, it seemed he was carefully getting down to pick something up: bending his knees and keeping his back straight. About half way, however, he stopped a moment, swayed a little as if testing his muscles and keeled over hitting the ground with a thump in one distinctly inelegant gesture that was, that was just plain bad manners really and typical of the man. A minute trickle of blood ran from the corner of his mouth and his yellow eyes stared into nowhere. Margaret, in the back of the ute with Joseph on her lap was the only one who regretted the man who might have been, the muscular, chunky lad who had run wild at Lingalinga with a pain in his stomach he couldn't understand. Jim, she knew, did not get what he deserved. He had, at the beginning, deserved what we all deserve as a kicking, yelling, angry baby with the miraculously new soles of its feet: he deserved a life. He missed it or most of it, living it only in the split second between being hit and being brain-dead on the ground. He saw stars alright, lots of them, which were the broken fragments of his life bumping over the rocky soil of Lingalinga and being put to bed by Chan that one wonderful time, and opening his one eye and seeing Margaret looking down at him and laughing at Henry and hearing Joseph's generous laugh, the light flashing off the big teeth which was the last thing he saw before his brain died. Funny, Joseph's teeth being so . . . geographically near at the time.

End of Jim.

Almost.

The crowd moves forward, hesitantly, to take its prize. The show has failed. The crowd is not yet breathless. It takes the body of Jim and bundles it into the back of the wonderful vehicle. A half-hearted sort of cheer as the thing is half pushed, half pulled in the direction of Chan's store, past the project office, past the workshop, out of sight to the sports field, the playground, where Jim's burnt-out Landrover is later found by, by someone at any rate who has better things to do. Of Jim's body, of the crowd, not a sign. Same old story Guv, nothing to do with me and even if it was, it wasn't my fault, I was only obeying orders. Jim is, always has been, an idea only, as much alive in your mind, or not, as you want him to be. A lesson that must be learnt or else our hearts would forever be breaking. Margaret knows this and smiles at the memory of a blond, sunburned and chunky young man who had seen her with one eye, distinctly not yellow or looking nowhere. One eye would have done had it stayed open. Life does not have to be tragedy and is not if it is remembered in the right way.

❏❏❏❏❏

Yes Andrew, I can tell you how I felt that day. How can I ever forget it? First there was a great, clean brightness all around as the sun broke through the boiling purple clouds. Then we smelt the rain. I breathed in as much as I could: a lovely wet earthy smell. Helen said look and we saw a great black wall of rain roaring towards us from the plantation side. Wonderful! And I remember rushing to get the things inside the house just as the first big black spots were hitting the veranda floor. Then it was on us. Not a storm. There was no wind only the pressure of all that water which felt like, like, oh like some great thing rushing past and sucking in all the air behind it and the lighting coming from inside the rain. Helen ran straight into it, kicking off her shoes and looking up into the rain laughing so that water fell full on her from head to toe as if some great pair of celestial hands were smoothing and caressing her young body, measuring and taking note of all the curves. She looked so beautiful and young and new, I could not take my eyes off her. She was being washed as clean as the day she was born, ready for anything.

Come on, she called, bring some soap. I brought it, kicking off my own shoes to join her. The rain was coming down in buckets, cold and clean, taking my breath away. We washed and giggled and helped each other to wash, washing our clothes at the same time and watching the soap suds run away with all the dirt and bad things of the last few horrible weeks. Helen got right out of her knickers to wash them and then, finished, pulled her frock right up over her head and stood naked for a moment before standing on one leg to get dressed again. Trying not to fall over and giggling. She didn't care a hoot. I was happy for her. I wanted her to be as happy in her life as anyone could be. We held hands and danced in a circle pulling each other around as hard as we could. I slipped down, Helen tried to pick me up and I pulled her on top of me so that we rolled in the mud. And we lay there for a while letting the rain pound on us. I thought of everything I had done in my life, I took a deep breath and threw it out. I was going to start my life again, washed clean by this marvellous rain. I'll never forget that feeling.

The old woman smiles.

Then, as if I had shifted a little in time, I remember pulling myself up on the edge of the veranda. Helen did the same. I was shivering a little. So was she. We looked at each other and we began to laugh. We laughed and laughed and laughed. We laughed like children laugh sometimes Andrew. They don't know what they're laughing at. It's an attack of hysterics. Suddenly they are crying and so were we. I was crying beyond all control because in the end Andrew, life is nothing but inevitable death and the moment is the thing, the great thing. If you don't live for the moment, you are damned. If you look ahead you see only tragedy. You look at your beautiful baby and you see the unhappiness he will suffer and you see that he will have to grow old and useless and die. I looked at Helen as if she was my daughter, my Alison, and seeing her little girl's heart breaking as if it never would be put back together again, I cried for her. I wasn't crying for Mrs Grant or for my mother or for the fact that I would never see my children again, I was crying for Helen, there and then, in the rain. I was crying because she would have to watch her children grow up and leave her and watch the husband whom she loved grow old and die.

I held her tight and she held on to me. I might have been the last person in the world. I remembered holding Margaret in the same way. I understood then I was crying for Annu because out of the rain there appeared from another time, without warning, something slow and momentous and awful. Something I didn't want. It was something I couldn't bear to see. It was you Andrew, driving the truck, with Alloy sitting beside you looking awful, like the bringer of the end of the world. There was nothing to him except those great hollow empty eyes. I knew what you were carrying and I walked over immediately because I had to get it done; Helen came with me. We walked hand in hand so that together we saw Margaret in the back kneeling and holding his broken body from which all the blood and dirt was being washed by the rain, so that we wanted him to be just sleeping but we knew he was hopelessly dead because he was as still as, as death in the rain and so beautiful; all the beauty of the world was distilled in that lovely face, whose understanding eyes I would never see again, whose lips I would never see part in a smile again, whose warm voice I would never hear again. Andrew you must remember the awful pain of that terrible time when there was nothing but endless, empty pointlessness. I thought my heart could not bear the anguish of it and that I must drop dead myself. There seemed nothing left but my own pain.

I had to cry Andrew, then. Nothing could stop me. Were we not all crying there in the rain, heaven itself weeping? It was like being sick. I wanted to cry and cry and cry all the crying out of me. I screamed up at the rain and it was over. Thank God for that rain. It washed all my tears away. Margaret was smiling at me. I felt so much better.

Later, Margaret did tell us, Helen and I, what had happened. Yes, unlike her, but she wanted us to share the moment. She wanted us to know and, I think, by expressing her thoughts, she was able to come to terms with what she had to live with for the rest of her life. She said that after you and Alloy had cut down the body – How did you do that, Andrew? – and given it to her, in the back of the truck, she didn't know what to do. She, our Margaret, did not know what to do because Joseph had been the only love of her life. He had been her lover in the very deepest sense of what is love because he had entered her soul and adored her. He had planted himself inside her as his chosen woman. She said she wanted to wash his body, to make it decent but she hadn't known how she was ever going to do it because here he was with the death agony on his face. How could she ever wash that fact away? She said she was blinded by her own tears, which she could not control even though, she said, she had known this would happen. She said that in the rain she felt totally alone but she was not worried by the loneliness. She was afraid of what would happen when the rain stopped. She didn't think she could face us or her life again. For the first time in her life she was at her wits' end. But then, just as she was sure she was about to lose her sanity, Keramugl came to her out of the rain, looking, she could say later, like a drowned rat. He sat beside her and stroked the darling face of Annu, closing the eyes and putting it back together. He put the tongue back inside Annu's mouth, straightened the broken neck and settled the limbs so that the body lay beautifully for Margaret to hold and for us to see. Keramugl took Annu's head, cupping the face in his hands, determined to remember it like that forever. Then he bent down and kissed Annu on the lips. Tenkyu, Master, mi no lusim tingting long yu. And with supreme control he had looked at Margaret with a smile: yu noken wori, missus, em i stap long yumipela, long olgeta taim. Em i no die pinis but we will take his body to Lingalinga.

□□□□□

All that has to be done has been done. The things have been tidied up and put back into the toy box. In other words, later on the same day over which turmoil has rained down upon the market place, the golf course and the club hill, when Annu had been hanged and Margaret had doubted, for a terrible moment, the rightness of it all, and when Jim had been taken by Tudak and Neki to be finally and irrevocably dealt with, Sammy and Wanei have come to the end of a peaceful and delicious day's fishing at Lingalinga.

Sammy, Jim's erstwhile driver, is the one who told Joseph to run and who had watched Annu walk into the Togulo Farm. The same Sammy who had helped Tudak and Keramugl to lug Tarlie's headless body into the back of the truck. The one who had given Jim up as a bad job to join Wanei here at Lingalinga. The same Wanei who had eyed Helen with his one eye while she ate the fish he had caught her. A naughty boy was Wanei in this respect but a good man also who would go on catching fish and cooking them for as long as he was needed. He fed the hungry mob – it might well have been the five thousand –

whenever required and would feed them, one by one, to the crocs when their time came. As elemental a man as Bune, in this respect.

And talking of the devil, here he is also. Has he brought tidings of joy? Tidings, at any rate, of something or other, of the momentous, tumultuous events which have been happening a few miles up the coast, including tales of a great, red, long-tailed, Bird of Paradise seen ascending into somewhere or other? Earth, or rather, mind-shattering thingummy-jigs going on? No, he has nothing to say. He passes with a smile and they smile back. They are told nothing, these two, who want to know nothing more and care even less. They swing their legs out over the edge of the veranda looking out at the bountiful sea. The evening is as cool and clean as their own rain-washed bodies. The setting sun, across the sea, appears beneath retreating clouds, laying a cloth of gold upon the motionless waters.

They watch the small man walk towards the water's edge. The dying sun catches him. For a moment, there is something gold about him too. But a transitory goldness: he is more enduring than soft metal: he will move forward until the end of time, this Bune, and beyond. The endless ocean awaits him, the broad sky is his roof, this small, elemental, naked man who does his duty to Her and moves on.

[]IIII[]

The litter on the beach contains a log, pickled in the saltwater and seasoned by the sun. It is Bune's canoe, provided. He has the paddle, balanced on his shoulder. He found it where he had hidden it in that time before. Before Annu had been made, with his help, in the minds of men. This man, Bune, from the beginning of time. This Adam, or else, Her Darling.

Andrew will remember Bune whom he assumes to have been his own Boy rather than the reverse. Tarlie was right. He still is: Andrew is not that bright and never will he catch Bune for all his pontificating.

They watch Bune drag the canoe through the near dark that is moonless yet, but nonetheless accessible. In the silence they hear it scrape the soft sand and meet the water's edge with something like a sigh, a small grunt of satisfaction I am where I want to be at last I am ever so ever so ever so happy, and my familiar burden rides me, legs astride.

Sammy peers through the dark. To make sense of the idea he waves to Bune, who – for there is a connection – undoubtedly waves back and is gone into the eternity of the starry night. Wanei sees it all, as clear as day, with the super-sensitivity of that blessed space where an eye might once have been: the perfect depth Helen had wanted to touch with the super-sensitive tip of her left-hand forefinger having eaten with him the fish he had prepared for her to eat. Wanei is a good man good as only true poverty and wandering can bring elemental in its own way also the one-eyed man but earth-bound. Thus, he sees that Bune is gone. The sense of loss is for a moment – the life of one of those stars – unbearable like a needle through the centre of his fisherman's stomach that contracts with pain as hard as Bune himself. So Wanei grasps the hand of Sammy who grasps Wanei's in return so that the pain is gone.

☐☐☐☐☐

Time, says Wanei, to cook the food. By morning they will come to Lingalinga as exhausted children for whom the dawn is but a grey prelude to the future which is unknown and therefore terrifying. They will be inclined to be querulous. But she will say there is no mystery, feed them and let them sleep: the bright day will come because Annu lives. Can you not see Him, Sammy? I do.

THE END